Children's Classic Tales

CHARLES AND MARY LAMB
Tales from Shakespeare

EDITED BY ANDREW LANG
Tales from the Arabian Nights

EDITED BY ANDREW LANG
Tales from King Arthur

ANDREW LANG
Tales of Troy and Greece

Wordsworth Editions

Readers who are interested in other titles from
Wordsworth Editions are invited to visit our website at
www.wordsworth-editions.com

For our latest list and a full mail-order service contact
Bibliophile Books, 5 Thomas Road, London E14 7BN
Tel: +44 0207 515 9222   Fax: +44 0207 538 4115
e-mail: orders@bibliophilebooks.com

This edition published 2005 by Wordsworth Editions Limited
8B East Street, Ware, Hertfordshire SG12 9HJ

ISBN 1 84022 063 5

Typeset by Antony Gray
Printed in Great Britain by
Mackays of Chatham, Chatham, Kent

CONTENTS

TALES FROM SHAKESPEARE

Tales from Shakespeare

Charles and Mary Lamb

with illustrations by
ARTHUR RACKHAM

CONTENTS

Preface

The following tales are meant to be submitted to the young reader as an introduction to the study of Shakespeare, for which purpose his words are used whenever it seemed possible to bring them in; and in whatever has been added to give them the regular form of a connected story, diligent care has been taken to select such words as might least interrupt the effect of the beautiful English tongue in which he wrote: therefore, words introduced into our language since his time have been as far as possible avoided.

In those tales which have been taken from the Tragedies, the young readers will perceive, when they come to see the source from which these stories are derived, that Shakespeare's own words, with little alteration, recur very frequently in the narrative as well as in the dialogue; but in those made from the Comedies the writers found themselves scarcely ever able to turn his words into the narrative form: therefore it is feared that, in them, dialogue has been made use of too frequently for young people not accustomed to the dramatic form of writing. But this fault, if it be a fault, has been caused by an earnest wish to give as much of Shakespeare's own words as possible: and if the '*He said*', and '*She said*', the question and the reply, should sometimes seem tedious to their young ears, they must pardon it, because it was the only way in which could be given to them a few hints and little foretastes of the great pleasure which awaits them in their elder years, when they come to the rich treasures from which these small and valueless coins are extracted; pretending to no other merit than as faint and imperfect stamps of Shakespeare's matchless image. Faint and imperfect images they must be called, because the beauty of his language is too frequently destroyed by the necessity of changing many of his excellent words into words far less expressive of his true sense, to make it read something like prose; and even in some few places, where his blank verse is given unaltered, as hoping from its simple plainness to cheat the young readers into the belief that they are reading prose, yet still his language being transplanted from its own natural soil and wild poetic garden, it must want much of its native beauty.

It has been wished to make these tales easy reading for very young children. To the utmost of their ability the writers have constantly kept this in mind; but the subjects of most of them made this a very difficult task. It was no easy matter to give the histories of men and women in terms familiar to the apprehension of a very young mind. For young ladies too, it has been the intention chiefly to write; because boys being generally permitted the use of their fathers' libraries at a much earlier age than girls are, they frequently have the best scenes of Shakespeare by heart, before their sisters are permitted to look into this manly book; and, therefore, instead of recommending these tales to the perusal of young gentlemen who can read them so much better in the originals, their kind assistance is rather requested in explaining to their sisters such parts as are hardest for them to understand: and when they have helped them to get over the difficulties, then perhaps they will read to them (carefully selecting what is proper for a young sister's ear) some passage which has pleased them in one of these stories, in the very words of the scene from which it is taken; and it is hoped they will find that the beautiful extracts, the select passages, they may choose to give their sisters in this way will be much better relished and understood from their having some notion of the general story from one of these imperfect abridgements; which if they be fortunately so done as to prove delightful to any of the young readers, it is hoped that no worse effect will result than to make them wish themselves a little older, that they may be allowed to read the Plays at full length (such a wish will be neither peevish nor irrational). When time and leave of judicious friends shall put them into their hands, they will discover in such of them as are here abridged (not to mention almost as many more, which are left untouched) many surprising events and turns of fortune, which for their infinite variety could not be contained in this little book, besides a world of sprightly and cheerful characters, both men and women, the humour of which it was feared would be lost if it were attempted to reduce the length of them.

What these Tales shall have been to the *young* readers, that and much more it is the writers' wish that the true Plays of Shakespeare may prove to them in older years – enrichers of the fancy, strengtheners of virtue, a withdrawing from all selfish and mercenary thoughts, a lesson of all sweet and honourable thoughts and actions, to teach courtesy, benignity, generosity, humanity: for of examples, teaching these virtues, his pages are full.

The Tempest

There was a certain island in the sea, the only inhabitants of which were an old man, whose name was Prospero, and his daughter Miranda, a very beautiful young lady. She came to this island so young that she had no memory of having seen any other human face than her father's.

They lived in a cave or cell, made out of a rock; it was divided into several apartments, one of which Prospero called his study; there he kept his books, which chiefly treated of magic, a study at that time much affected by all learned men: and the knowledge of this art he found very useful to him; for being thrown by a strange chance upon this island, which had been enchanted by a witch called Sycorax, who died there a short time before his arrival, Prospero, by virtue of his art, released many good spirits that Sycorax had imprisoned in the bodies of large trees, because they had refused to execute her wicked commands. These gentle spirits were ever after obedient to the will of Prospero. Of these Ariel was the chief.

The lively little sprite Ariel had nothing mischievous in his nature, except that he took rather too much pleasure in tormenting an ugly monster called Caliban, for he owed him a grudge because he was the son of his old enemy Sycorax. This Caliban, Prospero found in the woods, a strange misshapen thing, far less human in form than an ape: he took him home to his cell, and taught him to speak; and Prospero would have been very kind to him, but the bad nature which Caliban inherited from his mother, Sycorax, would not let him learn anything good or useful: therefore he was employed like a slave, to fetch wood and do the most laborious offices; and Ariel had the charge of compelling him to these services.

When Caliban was lazy and neglected his work, Ariel (who was invisible to all eyes but Prospero's) would come slyly and pinch him, and sometimes tumble him down in the mire; and then Ariel, in the likeness of an ape, would make mouths at him. Then swiftly changing his shape, in the likeness of a hedgehog, he would lie tumbling in Caliban's way, who feared the hedgehog's sharp quills would prick his bare feet. With a variety of such-like vexatious tricks Ariel would often torment him, whenever Caliban neglected the work which Prospero commanded him to do.

Having these powerful spirits obedient to his will, Prospero could by their means command the winds, and the waves of the sea. By his orders they raised a violent storm, in the midst of which, and struggling with the wild sea-waves that every moment threatened to swallow it up, he showed his daughter a fine large ship, which he told her was full of living beings like themselves. 'O my dear father,' said she, 'if by your art you have raised this dreadful storm, have pity on their sad distress. See! the vessel will be dashed to pieces. Poor souls! they will all perish. If I had power I would sink the sea beneath the earth, rather than the good ship should be destroyed, with all the precious souls within her.'

'Be not amazed, daughter Miranda,' said Prospero; 'there is no harm done. I have so ordered it, that no person in the ship shall receive any hurt. What I have done has been in care of you, my dear child. You are ignorant who you are, or where you came from, and you know no more of me, but that I am your father and live in this poor cave. Can you remember a time before you came to this cell? I think you cannot, for you were not then three years of age.'

'Certainly I can, sir,' replied Miranda.

'By what?' asked Prospero; 'by any other house or person? Tell me what you can remember, my child.'

Miranda said: 'It seems to me like the recollection of a dream. But had I not once four or five women who attended upon me?'

Prospero answered: 'You had, and more. How is it that this still lives in your mind? Do you remember how you came here?'

'No, sir,' said Miranda, 'I remember nothing more.'

'Twelve years ago, Miranda,' continued Prospero, 'I was Duke of Milan, and you were a princess, and my only heir. I had a younger brother, whose name was Antonio, to whom I trusted everything; and as I was fond of retirement and deep study I commonly left the management of my state affairs to your uncle, my false brother (for so indeed he proved). I, neglecting all worldly ends, buried among my books, did dedicate my whole time to the bettering of my mind. My brother Antonio, being thus in possession of my power, began to think himself the duke indeed. The opportunity I gave him of making himself popular among my subjects awakened in his bad nature a proud ambition to deprive me of my dukedom; this he soon effected with the aid of the King of Naples, a powerful prince, who was my enemy.'

'Wherefore,' said Miranda, 'did they not that hour destroy us?'

'My child,' answered her father, 'they durst not, so dear was the love that my people bore me. Antonio carried us on board a ship, and when we were some leagues out at sea, he forced us into a small boat, without either tackle, sail, or mast; there he left us, as he thought, to perish. But a kind lord of my court, one Gonzalo, who loved me, had privately placed in the boat water, provisions, apparel, and some books which I prize above my dukedom.'

'O my father,' said Miranda, 'what a trouble must I have been to you then!'

'No, my love,' said Prospero, 'you were a little cherub that did preserve me. Your innocent smiles made me bear up against my misfortunes. Our food lasted till we landed on this desert island, since when my chief delight has been in teaching you, Miranda, and well have you profited by my instructions.'

'Heaven thank you, my dear father,' said Miranda. 'Now pray tell me, sir, your reason for raising this sea-storm?'

'Know then,' said her father, 'that by means of this storm, my enemies, the King of Naples and my cruel brother, are cast ashore upon this island.'

Having so said, Prospero gently touched his daughter with his magic wand, and she fell fast asleep; for the spirit Ariel just then presented himself before his master, to give an account of the tempest, and how he had disposed of the ship's company, and though the spirits were always invisible to Miranda, Prospero did not choose she should hear him holding converse (as would seem to her) with the empty air.

'Well, my brave spirit,' said Prospero to Ariel, 'how have you performed your task?'

Ariel gave a lively description of the storm, and of the terrors of the mariners, and how the king's son, Ferdinand, was the first who leaped into the sea; and his father thought he saw his dear son swallowed up by the waves and lost. 'But he is safe,' said Ariel, 'in a corner of the isle, sitting with his arms folded, sadly lamenting the loss of the king, his father, whom he concludes drowned. Not a hair of his head is injured, and his princely garments, though drenched in the sea-waves, look fresher than before.'

'That's my delicate Ariel,' said Prospero. 'Bring him hither: my daughter must see this young prince. Where is the king, and my brother?'

'I left them,' answered Ariel, 'searching for Ferdinand, whom they have little hope of finding, thinking they saw him perish. Of the ship's crew not one is missing; though each one thinks himself the only one saved; and the ship, though invisible to them, is safe in the harbour.'

'Ariel,' said Prospero, 'thy charge is faithfully performed; but there is more work yet.'

'Is there more work?' said Ariel. 'Let me remind you, master, you have promised me my liberty. I pray, remember, I have done you worthy service, told you no lies, made no mistakes, served you without grudge or grumbling.'

'How now!' said Prospero. 'You do not recollect what a torment I freed you from. Have you forgot the wicked witch Sycorax, who with age and envy was almost bent double? Where was she born? Speak; tell me.'

'Sir, in Algiers,' said Ariel.

'Oh, was she so?' said Prospero. 'I must recount what you have been, which I find you do not remember. This bad witch, Sycorax, for her witchcrafts, too terrible to enter human hearing, was banished from Algiers, and here left by the sailors; and because you were a spirit too delicate to execute her wicked commands, she shut you up in a tree, where I found you howling. This torment, remember, I did free you from.'

'Pardon me, dear master,' said Ariel, ashamed to seem ungrateful; 'I will obey your commands.'

'Do so,' said Prospero, 'and I will set you free.' He then gave orders what further he would have him do; and away went Ariel, first to where he had left Ferdinand, and found him still sitting on the grass in the same melancholy posture.

'O, my young gentleman,' said Ariel, when he saw him, 'I will soon move you. You must be brought, I find, for the Lady Miranda to have a sight of your pretty person. Come, sir, follow me.' He then began singing: 'Full fathom five thy father lies; Of his bones are coral made; Those are pearls that were his eyes: Nothing of him that doth fade, But doth suffer a sea-change, Into something rich and strange. Sea-nymphs hourly ring his knell: Hark! now I hear them – Ding-dong, bell.'

This strange news of his lost father soon roused the prince from the stupid fit into which he had fallen. He followed in amazement the sound of Ariel's voice, till it led him to Prospero and Miranda, who were sitting under the shade of a large tree. Now Miranda had never seen a man before, except her own father.

'Miranda,' said Prospero, 'tell me what you are looking at yonder.'

'Oh, father,' said Miranda, in a strange surprise, 'surely that is a spirit. Lord! how it looks about! Believe me, sir, it is a beautiful creature. Is it not a spirit?'

'No, girl,' answered her father; 'it eats, and sleeps, and has senses such as we have. This young man you see was in the ship. He is somewhat altered by grief, or you might call him a handsome person. He has lost his companions, and is wandering about to find them.'

Miranda, who thought all men had grave faces and grey beards like her father, was delighted with the appearance of this beautiful young prince; and Ferdinand, seeing such a lovely lady in this desert place, and from the strange sounds he had heard, expecting nothing but wonders, thought he was upon an enchanted island, and that Miranda was the goddess of the place, and as such he began to address her.

She timidly answered, she was no goddess, but a simple maid, and was going to give him an account of herself, when Prospero interrupted her. He was well pleased to find they admired each other, for he plainly perceived they had (as we say) fallen in love at first sight: but to try Ferdinand's constancy, he resolved to throw some difficulties in their way: therefore, advancing forward, he addressed the prince with a stern air, telling him, he came to the island as a spy, to take it from him who was the lord of it. 'Follow me,' said he. 'I will tie your neck and feet together. You shall drink sea-water; shellfish, withered roots, and husks of acorns shall be your food.'

'No,' said Ferdinand, 'I will resist such entertainment till I see a more powerful enemy,' and drew his sword; but Prospero, waving his magic wand, fixed him to the spot where he stood, so that he had no power to move.

Miranda hung upon her father, saying: 'Why are you so ungentle? Have pity, I will be his surety. This is the second man I ever saw, and to me he seems a true one.'

'Silence!' said the father. 'One word more will make me chide you, girl! What! an advocate for an impostor! You think there are no more such fine men, having seen only him and Caliban. I tell you, foolish girl, most men as far excel this as he does Caliban.' This he said to prove his daughter's constancy; and she replied: 'My affections are most humble. I have no wish to see a goodlier man.'

'Come on, young man,' said Prospero to the prince; 'you have no power to disobey me.'

'I have not indeed,' answered Ferdinand; and not knowing that it was by magic he was deprived of all power of resistance, he was astonished to find himself so strangely compelled to follow Prospero: looking back on Miranda as long as he could see her, he said, as he went after Prospero into the cave, 'My spirits are all bound up, as if I were in a dream; but this man's threats, and the weakness which I feel, would seem light to me if from my prison I might once a day behold this fair maid.'

Prospero kept Ferdinand not long confined within the cell: he soon brought out his prisoner, and set him a severe task to perform, taking care to let his daughter know the Laid labour he had imposed on him, and then pretending to go into his study, he secretly watched them both.

Prospero had commanded Ferdinand to pile up some heavy logs of wood. Kings' sons not being much used to laborious work, Miranda soon after found her lover almost dying with fatigue. 'Alas!' said she, 'do not work so hard; my father is at his studies, lie is safe for these three hours; pray rest yourself.'

'o my dear lady,' said Ferdinand, 'I dare not. I must finish my task before I take my rest.'

'If you will sit down,' said Miranda, 'I will carry your logs the while.' But this Ferdinand would by no means agree to.   Instead of a help Miranda became a hindrance, for they began a long conversation, so that the business of log-carrying went on very slowly.

Prospero, who had enjoined Ferdinand this task merely as a, trial of his love, was not at his books, as his daughter supposed, but was standing by them invisible, to overhear what they said.

Ferdinand inquired her name, which she told, saying it was against her father's express command she did so.

Prospero only smiled at this first instance of his daughter's disobedience, for having by his magic art caused his daughter to fall in love so suddenly, he was not angry that she showed her love by forgetting to obey his commands. And he listened well pleased to a long speech of Ferdinand's, in which he professed to love her above all the ladies lie ever saw.

In answer to his praises of her beauty, which he said exceeded all the women in the world, she replied, 'I do not remember the face of any woman, nor have I seen any more men than you, my good friend, and my dear father. How features are abroad, I know not;

but, believe me, sir, I would not wish any companion in the world but you, nor can my imagination form any shape but yours that I could like. But, sir, I fear I talk to you too freely, and my father's precepts I forget.'

At this Prospero smiled, and nodded his head, as much as to say, 'This goes on exactly as I could wish; my girl will be Queen of Naples.'

And then Ferdinand, in another fine long speech (for young princes speak in courtly phrases), told the innocent Miranda he was heir to the crown of Naples, and that she should be his queen.

'Ah! sir,' said she, 'I am a fool to weep at what I am glad of. I will answer you in plain and holy innocence. I am your wife if you will marry me.'

Prospero prevented Ferdinand's thanks by appearing visible before them.

'Fear nothing, my child,' said he; 'I have overheard, and approve of all you have said. And, Ferdinand, if I have too severely used you, I will make you rich amends, by giving you my daughter. All your vexations were but trials of your love, and you have nobly stood the test. Then as my gift, which your true love has worthily purchased, take my daughter, and do not smile that I boast she is above all praise.' He then, telling them that he had business which required his presence, desired they would sit down and talk together till he returned; and this command Miranda seemed not at all disposed to disobey.

When Prospero left them, he called his spirit Ariel, who quickly appeared before him, eager to relate what he had done with Prospero's brother and the King of Naples. Ariel said he had left them almost out of their senses with fear, at the strange things he had caused them to see and hear, When fatigued with wandering about, and famished for want of food, he had suddenly set before them a delicious banquet, and then, just as they were going to eat, he appeared visible before them in the shape of a harpy, a voracious monster with wings, and the feast vanished away. Then, to their utter amazement, this seeming harpy spoke to them, reminding them of their cruelty in driving Prospero from his dukedom, and leaving him and his infant daughter to perish in the sea, saying, that for this cause these terrors were suffered to afflict them.

The King of Naples, and Antonio the false brother, repented the injustice they had done to Prospero; and Ariel told his master he was certain their penitence was sincere, and that he, though a spirit, could not but pity them.

'Then bring them hither, Ariel,' said Prospero: 'if you, who are but a spirit, feel for their distress, shall not I, who am a human being like themselves, have compassion on them? Bring them quickly, my dainty Ariel.'

Ariel soon returned with the king, Antonio, and old Gonzalo in their train, who had followed him, wondering at the wild music he played in the air to draw them on to his master's presence. This Gonzalo was the same who had so kindly provided Prospero formerly with books and provisions, when his wicked brother left him, as he thought, to perish in an open boat in the sea.

Grief and terror had so stupefied their senses that they did not know Prospero. He first discovered himself to the good old Gonzalo, calling him the preserver of his life; and then his brother and the king knew that he was the injured Prospero.

Antonio, with tears and sad words of sorrow and true repentance, implored his brother's forgiveness, and the king expressed his sincere remorse for having assisted Antonio to depose his brother: and Prospero forgave them; and, upon their engaging to restore his dukedom, he said to the King of Naples, 'I have a gift in store for you, too'; and, opening a door, showed him his son Ferdinand playing at chess with Miranda.

Nothing could exceed the joy of the father and the son at this unexpected meeting, for they each thought the other drowned in the storm.

'O wonder!' said Miranda, 'what noble creatures these are! It must surely be a brave world that has such people in it.'

The King of Naples was almost as much astonished at the beauty and excellent graces of the young Miranda as his son had been. 'Who is this maid?' said he; 'she seems the goddess that has parted us, and brought us thus together.'

'No, sir,' answered Ferdinand, smiling to find his father had fallen into the same mistake that he had done when he first saw Miranda, 'she is a mortal, but by immortal Providence she is mine; I chose her when I could not ask you, my father, for your consent, not thinking you were alive. She is the daughter to this Prospero, who is the famous Duke of Milan, of whose renown I have heard so much, but never saw him till now: of him I have received a new life: he has made himself to me a second father, giving me this dear lady.'

'Then I must be her father,' said the king; 'but, oh, how oddly will it sound, that I must ask my child forgiveness.'

'No more of that,' said Prospero: 'let us not remember our troubles past, since they so happily have ended.' And then Prospero embraced his brother, and again assured him of his forgiveness; and said that a wise overruling Providence had permitted that he should be driven from his poor dukedom of Milan, that his daughter might inherit the crown of Naples, for that by their meeting in this desert island it had happened that the king's son had loved Miranda.

These kind words which Prospero spoke, meaning to comfort his brother, so filled Antonio with shame and remorse that he wept and was unable to speak; and the kind old Gonzalo wept to see this joyful reconciliation, and prayed for blessings on the young couple.

Prospero now told them that their ship was safe in the harbour, and the sailors all on board her, and that he and his daughter would accompany them home the next morning. 'In the meantime,' says he, 'partake of such refreshments as my poor cave affords; and for your evening's entertainment I will relate the history of my life from my first landing in this desert island.' He then called for Caliban to prepare some food, and set the cave in order; and the company were astonished at the uncouth form and savage appearance of this ugly monster, who (Prospero said) was the only attendant he had to wait upon him.

Before Prospero left the island he dismissed Ariel from service, to the great joy of that lively little spirit, who, though he had been a faithful servant to his master, was always longing to enjoy his free liberty, to wander uncontrolled in the air, like a wild bird, under green trees, among pleasant fruits, and sweet-smelling flowers.

'My quaint Ariel,' said Prospero to the little sprite when he made him free, 'I shall miss you; yet you shall have your freedom.'

'Thank you, my dear master,' said Ariel; 'but give me leave to attend your ship home with prosperous gales, before you bid fare-well to the assistance of your faithful spirit; and then, master, when I am free, how merrily I shall live!' Here Ariel sang this pretty song:

> 'Where the bee sucks, there suck I;
> In a cowslip's bell I lie:
> There I crouch when owls do cry.
> On the bat's back I do fly
> After summer merrily.
> Merrily, merrily shall I live now
> Under the blossom that hangs on the bough.'

Prospero then buried deep in the earth his magical books and wand, for he was resolved never more to make use of the magic art. And having thus overcome his enemies, and being reconciled to his brother and the King of Naples, nothing now remained to complete his happiness but to revisit his native land, to take possession of his dukedom, and to witness the happy nuptials of his daughter and Prince Ferdinand, which the king said should be instantly celebrated with great splendour on their return to Naples. At which place, under the safe convoy of the spirit Ariel they, after a pleasant voyage, soon arrived.

A Midsummer Night's Dream

There was a law in the city of Athens which gave to its citizens the power of compelling their daughters to marry whomsoever they pleased; for upon a daughter's refusing to marry the man her father had chosen to be her husband, the father was empowered by this law to cause her to be put to death; but as fathers do not often desire the death of their own daughters, even though they do happen to prove a little refractory, this law was seldom or never put in execution, though perhaps the young ladies of that city were not unfrequently threatened by their parents with the terrors of it.

There was one instance, however, of an old man, whose name was Egeus, who actually did come before Theseus (at that time the reigning Duke of Athens), to complain that his daughter Hermia whom he had commanded to marry Demetrius, a young man of a noble Athenian family, refused to obey him, because she loved another young Athenian, named Lysander. Egeus demanded justice of Theseus, and desired that this cruel law might be put in force against his daughter.

Hermia pleaded in excuse for her disobedience that Demetrius had formerly professed love for her dear friend Helena, and that Helena loved Demetrius to distraction; but this honourable reason, which Hermia gave for not obeying her father's command, moved not the stern Egeus.

Theseus, though a great and merciful prince, had no power to alter the laws of his country; therefore he could only give Hermia four days to consider of it: and at the end of that time, if she still refused to marry Demetrius, she was to be put to death.

When Hermia was dismissed from the presence of the duke, she went to her lover Lysander and told him the peril she was in, and that she must either give him up and marry Demetrius or lose her life in four days.

Lysander was in great affliction at hearing these evil tidings; but, recollecting that he had an aunt who lived at some distance from Athens, and that at the place where she lived the cruel law could not be put in force against Hermia (this law not extending beyond the boundaries of the city), he proposed to Hermia that she should steal out of her father's house that night, and go with him to his aunt's house, where he would marry her. 'I will meet you,' said Lysander, 'in the wood a few miles without the city; in that delightful wood where we have so often walked with Helena in the pleasant month of May.'

To this proposal Hermia joyfully agreed; and she told no one of her intended flight but her friend Helena. Helena (as maidens will do foolish things for love) very ungenerously resolved to go and tell this to Demetrius, though she could hope no benefit from betraying her friend's secret but the poor pleasure of following her faithless lover to the wood; for she well knew that Demetrius would go thither in pursuit of Hermia.

The wood in which Lysander and Hermia proposed to meet was the favourite haunt of those little beings known by the name of 'fairies'.

Oberon the king, and Titania the queen of the fairies, with all their tiny train of followers, in this wood held their midnight revels.

Between this little king and queen of sprites there happened, at this time, a sad disagreement; they never met by moonlight in the shady walk of this pleasant wood but they were quarrelling, till all their fairy elves would creep into acorn-cups and hide themselves for fear.

The cause of this unhappy disagreement was Titania's refusing to give Oberon a little changeling boy, whose mother had been Titania's friend; and upon her death the fairy queen stole the child from its nurse and brought him up in the woods.

The night on which the lovers were to meet in this wood, as Titania was walking with some of her maids of honour, she met Oberon attended by his train of fairy courtiers.

'Ill met by moonlight, proud Titania,' said the fairy king.

The queen replied: 'What, jealous Oberon, is it you? Fairies, skip hence; I have forsworn his company.'

'Tarry, rash fairy,' said Oberon. 'Am I not thy lord? Why does Titania cross her Oberon? Give me your little changeling boy to be my page.'

'Set your heart at rest,' answered the queen; 'your whole fairy kingdom buys not the boy of me.' She then left her lord in great anger.

'Well, go your way,' said Oberon; 'before the morning dawns I will torment you for this injury.'

Oberon then sent for Puck, his chief favourite and privy counsellor.

Puck (or, as he was sometimes called, Robin Goodfellow) was a shrewd and knavish sprite, that used to play comical pranks in the neighbouring villages; sometimes getting into the dairies and skimming the milk, sometimes plunging his light and airy form into the butter-churn, and while he was dancing his fantastic shape in the churn, in vain the dairymaid would labour to change her cream into butter. Nor had the village swains any better success; whenever Puck chose to play his freaks in the brewing copper, the ale was sure to be spoiled. When a few good neighbours were met to drink some comfortable ale together, Puck would jump into the bowl of ale in the likeness of a roasted crab, and when some old goody was going to drink he would bob against her lips, and spill the ale over her withered chin; and presently after, when the same old dame was gravely seating herself to tell her neighbours a sad and melancholy story, Puck would slip her three-legged stool from under her, and down toppled the poor old woman, and then the old gossips would hold their sides and laugh at her, and swear they never wasted a merrier hour.

'Come hither, Puck,' said Oberon to this little merry wanderer of the night; 'fetch me the flower which maids call "Love in Idleness"; the juice of that little purple flower laid on the eyelids of those who sleep will make them, when they awake, dote on the first thing they see. Some of the juice of that flower I will drop on the eyelids of my Titania when she is asleep; and the first thing she looks upon when she opens her eyes she will fall in love with, even though it be a lion or a bear, a meddling monkey or a busy ape; and before I will take this charm from off her sight, which I can do with another charm I know of, I will make her give me that boy to be my page.'

Puck, who loved mischief to his heart, was highly diverted with this intended frolic of his master, and ran to seek the flower; and while Oberon was waiting the return of Puck he observed Demetrius and Helena enter the wood: he overheard Demetrius reproaching Helena for following him, and after many unkind words on his part, and gentle expostulations from Helena, reminding him of his former love and professions of true faith to her, he left her (as he said) to the mercy of the wild beasts, and she ran after him as swiftly as she could.

The fairy king, who was always friendly to true lovers, felt great compassion for Helena; and perhaps, as Lysander said they used to walk by moonlight in this pleasant wood, Oberon might have seen Helena in those happy times when she was beloved by Demetrius. However that might be, when Puck returned with the little purple flower, Oberon said to his favourite: 'Take a part of this flower; there has been a sweet Athenian lady here, who is in love with a disdainful youth; if you find him sleeping, drop some of the love-juice in his eyes, but contrive to do it when she is near him, that the first thing he sees when he awakes may be this despised lady. You will know the man by the Athenian garments which he wears.'

Puck promised to manage this matter very dexterously: and then Oberon went, unperceived by Titania, to her bower, where she was preparing to go to rest. Her fairy bower was a bank, where grew wild thyme, cowslips, and sweet violets, under a canopy of woodbine, musk-roses, and eglantine. There Titania always slept some part of the night; her coverlet the enamelled skin of a snake, which, though a small mantle, was wide enough to wrap a fairy in.

He found Titania giving orders to her fairies, how they were to employ themselves while she slept. 'Some of you,' said her majesty, 'must kill cankers in the musk-rose buds, and some wage war with the bats for their leathern wings, to make my small elves coats; and some of you keep watch that the clamorous owl, that nightly hoots, come not near me: but first sing me to sleep.' Then they began to sing this song:

> 'You spotted snakes, with double tongue,
> Thorny hedgehogs, be not seen;
> Newts and blind-worms do no wrong;
> Come not near our fairy queen:
> Philomel, with melody,
> Sing in our sweet lullaby;
> Lulla, lulla, lullaby; lulla, lulla, lullaby;
> Never harm, nor spell, nor charm,
> Come our lovely lady nigh;
> So, good-night, with lullaby.'

When the fairies had sung their queen asleep with this pretty lullaby, they left her to perform the important services she had enjoined them. Oberon then softly drew near his Titania and dropped some of the love-juice on her eyelids, saying:

> 'What thou seest when thou dost wake,
> Do it for thy true-love take.'

But to return to Hermia, who made her escape out of her father's house that night, to avoid the death she was doomed to for refusing to marry Demetrius. When she entered the wood, she found her dear Lysander waiting for her, to conduct her to his aunt's house;

but before they had passed half through the wood Hermia was so much fatigued that Lysander, who was very careful of this dear lady, who had proved her affection for him even by hazarding her life for his sake, persuaded her to rest till morning on a bank of soft moss, and, lying down himself on the ground at some little distance, they soon fell fast asleep. Here they were found by Puck, who, seeing a handsome young man asleep, and perceiving that his clothes were made in the Athenian fashion, and that a pretty lady was sleeping near him, concluded that this must be the Athenian maid and her disdainful lover whom Oberon had sent him to seek; and he naturally enough conjectured that, as they were alone together, she must be the first thing he would see when he awoke; so, without more ado, he proceeded to pour some of the juice of the little purple flower into his eyes. But it so fell out that Helena came that way, and, instead of Hermia, was the first object Lysander beheld when he opened his eyes; and strange to relate, so powerful was the love-charm, all his love for Hermia vanished away and Lysander fell in love with Helena.

Had he first seen Hermia when he awoke, the blunder Puck committed would have been of no consequence, for he could not love that faithful lady too well; but for poor Lysander to be forced by a fairy love-charm to forget his own true Hermia, and to run after another lady, and leave Hermia asleep quite alone in a wood at midnight, was a sad chance indeed.

Thus this misfortune happened. Helena, as has been before related, endeavoured to keep pace with Demetrius when he ran away so rudely from her; but she could not continue this unequal race long, men being always better runners in a long race than ladies. Helena soon lost sight of Demetrius; and as she was wandering about, dejected and forlorn, she arrived at the place where Lysander was sleeping. 'Ah!' said she, 'this is Lysander lying on the ground. Is he dead or asleep?' Then, gently touching him, she said, 'Good sir, if you are alive, awake.' Upon this Lysander opened his eyes, and, the love-charm beginning to work, immediately addressed her in terms of extravagant love and admiration, telling her she as much excelled Hermia in beauty as a dove does a raven, and that he would run through fire for her sweet sake; and many more such lover-like speeches. Helena, knowing Lysander was her friend Hermia's lover, and that he was solemnly engaged to marry her, was in the utmost rage when she heard herself addressed in this manner; for she thought (as well she might) that Lysander was making a jest of her. 'Oh!' said she, 'why was I born to be mocked and scorned by everyone? Is it not enough, is it not enough, young man, that I can never get a sweet look or a kind word from Demetrius; but you, sir, must pretend in this disdainful manner to court me? I thought, Lysander, you were a lord of more true gentleness.' Saying these words in great anger, she ran away; and Lysander followed her, quite forgetful of his own Hermia, who was still asleep.

When Hermia awoke she was in a sad fright at finding herself alone. She wandered about the wood, not knowing what was become of Lysander, or which way to go to seek for him. In the meantime Demetrius, not being able to find Hermia and his rival Lysander, and fatigued with his fruitless search, was observed by Oberon fast asleep. Oberon had learned by some questions he had asked of Puck that he had applied the love-charm to the wrong person's eyes; and now, having found the person first intended, he touched the eyelids of the sleeping Demetrius with the love-juice, and he instantly awoke; and the first thing he saw being Helena, he, as Lysander had done before, began to address love-speeches to her; and just at that moment Lysander, followed by Hermia (for through Puck's unlucky mistake it was now become Hermia's turn to run after her lover), made his appearance; and then Lysander and Demetrius, both speaking together, made love to Helena, they being each one under the influence of the same potent charm.

The astonished Helena thought that Demetrius, Lysander, and her once dear friend Hermia were all in a plot together to make a jest of her. Hermia was as much surprised as Helena; she knew not why Lysander and Demetrius, who both before loved her, were now become the lovers of Helena, and to Hermia the matter seemed to be no jest.

The ladies, who before had always been the dearest of friends, now fell to high words together.

'Unkind Hermia,' said Helena, 'it is you have set Lysander on to vex me with mock praises; and your other lover, Demetrius, who used almost to spurn me with his foot, have you not bid him call me goddess, nymph, rare, precious, and celestial? He would not speak thus to me, whom he hates, if you did not set him on to make a jest of me. Unkind Hermia, to join with men in scorning your poor friend. Have you forgot our schoolday friendship? How often, Hermia, have we two, sitting on one cushion, both singing one song, with our needles working the same flower, both on the same sampler wrought; growing up together in fashion of a double cherry, scarcely seeming parted! Hermia, it is not friendly in you, it is not maidenly to join with men in scorning your poor friend.'

'I am amazed at your passionate words,' said Hermia: 'I scorn you not; it seems you scorn me.'

'Aye, do,' returned Helena, 'persevere, counterfeit serious looks, and make mouths at me when I turn my back; then wink at each other, and hold the sweet jest up. If you had any pity, grace, or manners, you would not use me thus.'

While Helena and Hermia were speaking these angry words to each other, Demetrius and Lysander left them, to fight together in the wood for the love of Helena.

When they found the gentlemen had left them, they departed, and once more wandered weary in the wood in search of their lovers.

As soon as they were gone the fairy king, who with little Puck had been listening to their quarrels, said to him, 'This is your negligence, Puck; or did you do this wilfully?'

'Believe me, king of shadows,' answered Puck, 'it was a mistake. Did not you tell me I should know the man by his Athenian garments? However, I am not sorry this has happened, for I think their jangling makes excellent sport.'

'You heard,' said Oberon, 'that Demetrius and Lysander are gone to seek a convenient place to fight in. I command you to overhang the night with a thick fog, and lead these quarrelsome lovers so astray in the dark that they shall not be able to find each other. Counterfeit each of their voices to the other, and with bitter taunts provoke them to follow you, while they think it is their rival's tongue they hear. See you do this, till they are so weary they can go no farther; and when you find they are asleep, drop the juice of this other flower into Lysander's eyes, and when he awakes he will forget his new love for Helena, and return to his old passion for Hermia; and then the two fair ladies may each one be happy with the man she loves and they will think all that has passed a vexatious dream. About this quickly, Puck, and I will go and see what sweet love my Titania has found.'

Titania was still sleeping, and Oberon, seeing a clown near her who had lost his way in the wood and was likewise asleep, 'This fellow,' said he, 'shall be my Titania's true love'; and clapping an ass's head over the clown's, it seemed to fit him as well as if it had grown upon his own shoulders. Though Oberon fixed the ass's head on very gently, it awakened him, and, rising up, unconscious of what Oberon had done to him, he went towards the bower where the fairy queen slept.

'Ah! what angel is that I see?' said Titania, opening her eyes, and the juice of the little purple flower beginning to take effect. 'Are you as wise as you are beautiful?'

'Why, mistress,' said the foolish clown, 'if I have wit enough to find the way out of this wood, I have enough to serve my turn.'

'Out of the wood do not desire to go,' said the enamoured queen. 'I am a spirit of no common rate. I love you. Go with me, and I will give you fairies to attend upon you.'

She then called four of her fairies. Their names were Pease-blossom, Cobweb, Moth, and Mustard-seed.

'Attend,' said the queen, 'upon this sweet gentleman. Hop in his walks and gambol in his sight; feed him with grapes and apricots, and steal for him the honey-bags from the bees. Come, sit with me,' said she to the clown, 'and let me play with your amiable hairy cheeks, my beautiful ass! and kiss your fair large ears, my gentle joy.'

'Where is Pease-blossom?' said the ass-headed clown, not much regarding the fairy queen's courtship, but very proud of his new attendants.

'Here, sir,' said little Pease-blossom.

'Scratch my head,' said the clown. 'Where is Cobweb?'

'Here, sir,' said Cobweb.

'Good Mr Cobweb,' said the foolish clown, 'kill me the red humblebee on the top of that thistle yonder; and, good Mr Cobweb, bring me the honey-bag. Do not fret yourself too much in the action, Mr Cobweb, and take care the honey-bag break not; I should be sorry to have you overflown with a honey-bag. Where is Mustard-seed?'

'Here, sir,' said Mustard-seed. 'What is your will?'

'Nothing,' said the clown, 'good Mr Mustard-seed, but to help Mr Pease-blossom to scratch; I must go to a barber's, Mr Mustard-seed, for methinks I am marvellous hairy about the face.'

'My sweet love,' said the queen, 'what will you have to eat? I have a venturous fairy shall seek the squirrel's hoard, and fetch you some new nuts.'

'I had rather have a handful of dried peas,' said the clown, who with his ass's head had got an ass's appetite. 'But, I pray, let none of your people disturb me, for I have a mind to sleep.'

'Sleep, then,' said the queen, 'and I will wind you in my arms. Oh, how I love you! how I dote upon you!'

When the fairy king saw the clown sleeping in the arms of his queen, he advanced within her sight, and reproached her with having lavished her favours upon an ass.

This she could not deny, as the clown was then sleeping within her arms, with his ass's head crowned by her with flowers.

When Oberon had teased her for some time, he again demanded the changeling boy; which she, ashamed of being discovered by her lord with her new favourite, did not dare to refuse him.

Oberon, having thus obtained the little boy he had so long wished for to be his page, took pity on the disgraceful situation into which, by his merry contrivance, he had brought his Titania, and threw some of the juice of the other flower into her eyes; and the fairy queen immediately recovered her senses, and wondered at her late dotage, saying how she now loathed the sight of the strange monster.

Oberon likewise took the ass's head from off the clown, and left him to finish his nap with his own fool's head upon his shoulders.

Oberon and his Titania being now perfectly reconciled, he related to her the history of the lovers and their midnight quarrels, and she agreed to go with him and see the end of their adventures.

The fairy king and queen found the lovers and their fair ladies, at no great distance from one another, sleeping on a grass-plot; for Puck, to make amends for his former mistake, had contrived with the utmost diligence to bring them all to the same spot, unknown to one another; and he had carefully removed the charm from off the eyes of Lysander with the antidote the fairy king gave to him.

Hermia first awoke, and, finding her lost Lysander asleep so near her, was looking at him and wondering at his strange inconstancy. Lysander presently opening his eyes, and seeing his dear Hermia, recovered his reason which the fairy charm had before clouded, and with his reason his love for Hermia; and they began to talk over the adventures of the night, doubting if these things had really happened, or if they had both been dreaming the same bewildering dream.

Helena and Demetrius were by this time awake; and a sweet sleep having quieted Helena's disturbed and angry spirits, she listened with delight to the professions of love which Demetrius still made to her, and which, to her surprise as well as pleasure, she began to perceive were sincere.

These fair night-wandering ladies, now no longer rivals, became once more true friends; all the unkind words which had passed were forgiven, and they calmly consulted together what was best to be done in their present situation. It was soon agreed that, as Demetrius had given up his pretensions to Hermia, he should endeavour to prevail upon her father to revoke the cruel sentence of death which had been passed against her. Demetrius was preparing to return to Athens for this friendly purpose, when they were surprised with the sight of Egeus, Hermia's father, who came to the wood in pursuit of his runaway daughter.

When Egeus understood that Demetrius would not now marry his daughter, he no longer opposed her marriage with Lysander, but gave his consent that they should be wedded on the fourth day from that time, being the same day on which Hermia had been condemned to lose her life; and on that same day Helena joyfully agreed to marry her beloved and now faithful Demetrius.

The fairy king and queen, who were invisible spectators of this reconciliation, and now saw the happy ending of the lovers' history, brought about through the good offices of Oberon, received so much pleasure that these kind spirits resolved to celebrate the approaching nuptials with sports and revels throughout their fairy kingdom.

And now, if any are offended with this story of fairies and their pranks, as judging it incredible and strange, they have only to think that they have been asleep and dreaming, and that all these adventures were visions which they saw in their sleep. And I hope none of my readers will be so unreasonable as to be offended with a pretty, harmless Midsummer Night's Dream.

The Winter's Tale

Leontes, King of Sicily, and his queen, the beautiful and virtuous Hermione, once lived in the greatest harmony together. So happy was Leontes in the love of this excellent lady that he had no wish ungratified, except that he sometimes desired to see again and to present to his queen his old companion and schoolfellow, Polixenes, King of Bohemia. Leontes and Polixenes were brought up together from their infancy, but being, by the death of their fathers, called to reign over their respective kingdoms, they had not met for many years, though they frequently interchanged gifts, letters, and loving embassies.

At length, after repeated invitations, Polixenes came from Bohemia to the Sicilian court, to make his friend Leontes a visit.

At first this visit gave nothing but pleasure to Leontes. He recommended the friend of his youth to the queen's particular attention, and seemed in the presence of his dear friend and old companion to have his felicity quite completed. They talked over old times; their schooldays and their youthful pranks were remembered, and recounted to Hermione, who always took a cheerful part in these conversations.

When, after a long stay, Polixenes was preparing to depart, Hermione, at the desire of her husband, joined her entreaties to his that Polixenes would prolong his visit.

And now began this good queen's sorrow; for Polixenes, refusing to stay at the request of Leontes, was won over by Hermione's gentle and persuasive words to put off his departure for some weeks longer. Upon this, although Leontes had so long known the integrity and honourable principles of his friend Polixenes, as well as the excellent disposition of his virtuous queen, he was seized with an ungovernable jealousy. Every attention Hermione showed to Polixenes, though by her husband's particular desire and merely to please him, increased the unfortunate king's jealousy; and from being a loving and a true friend, and the best and fondest of husbands, Leontes became suddenly a savage and inhuman monster. Sending for Camillo, one of the lords of his court, and telling him of the suspicion he entertained, he commanded him to poison Polixenes.

Camillo was a good man, and he, well knowing that the jealousy of Leontes had not the slightest foundation in truth, instead of poisoning Polixenes, acquainted him with the king his master's orders, and agreed to escape with him out of the Sicilian dominions; and Polixenes, with the assistance of Camillo, arrived safe in his own kingdom of Bohemia, where Camillo lived from that time in the king's court and became the chief friend and favourite of Polixenes.

The flight of Polixenes enraged the jealous Leontes still more; he went to the queen's apartment, where the good lady was sitting with her little son Mamillius, who was just beginning to tell one of his best stories to amuse his mother, when the king entered and, taking the child away, sent Hermione to prison.

Mamillius, though but a very young child, loved his mother tenderly; and when he saw her so dishonoured, and found she was taken from him to be put into a prison, he took it deeply to heart and drooped and pined away by slow degrees, losing his appetite and his sleep, till it was thought his grief would kill him.

The king, when he had sent his queen to prison, commanded Cleomenes and Dion, two Sicilian lords, to go to Delphos, there to enquire of the oracle at the temple of Apollo if his queen had been unfaithful to him.

When Hermione had been a short time in prison she was brought to bed of a daughter; and the poor lady received much comfort from the sight of her pretty baby, and she said to it, 'My poor little prisoner, I am as innocent as you are.'

Hermione had a kind friend in the noble-spirited Paulina, who was the wife of Antigonus, a Sicilian lord; and when the lady Paulina heard her royal mistress was brought to bed she went to the prison where Hermione was confined; and she said to Emilia, a lady who attended upon Hermione, 'I pray you, Emilia, tell the good queen, if her majesty dare trust me with her little babe, I will carry it to the king, its father: we do not know how he may soften at the sight of his innocent child.'

'Most worthy madam,' replied Emilia, 'I will acquaint the queen with your noble offer. She was wishing today that she had any friend who would venture to present the child to the king.'

'And tell her,' said Paulina, 'that I will speak boldly to Leontes in her defence.'

'May you be forever blessed,' said Emilia, 'for your kindness to our gracious queen!'

Emilia then went to Hermione, who joyfully gave up her baby to the care of Paulina, for she had feared that no one would dare venture to present the child to its father.

Paulina took the newborn infant and, forcing herself into the king's presence, notwithstanding her husband, fearing the king's anger, endeavoured to prevent her, she laid the babe at its father's feet; and Paulina made a noble speech to the king in defence of Hermione, and she reproached him severely for his inhumanity and implored him to have mercy on his innocent wife and child. But Paulina's spirited remonstrances only aggravated Leontes's displeasure, and he ordered her husband Antigonus to take her from his presence.

When Paulina went away she left the little baby at its father's feet, thinking when he was alone with it he would look upon it and have pity on its helpless innocence.

The good Paulina was mistaken, for no sooner was she gone than the merciless father ordered Antigonus, Paulina's husband, to take the child and carry it out to sea and leave it upon some desert shore to perish.

Antigonus, unlike the good Camillo, too well obeyed the orders of Leontes; for he immediately carried the child on shipboard, and put out to sea, intending to leave it on the first desert coast he could find.

So firmly was the king persuaded of the guilt of Hermione that he would not wait for the return of Cleomenes and Dion, whom he had sent to consult the oracle of Apollo at Delphos, but before the queen was recovered from her lying-in, and from the grief for the loss of her precious baby, he had her brought to a public trial before all the lords and nobles of his court. And when all the great lords, the judges, and all the nobility of the land were assembled together to try Hermione, and that unhappy queen was standing as a prisoner before her subjects to receive their judgment, Cleomenes and Dion entered the assembly and presented to the king the answer of the oracle, sealed up; and Leontes commanded the seal to be broken, and the words of the oracle to be read aloud, and these were the words: 'Hermione is innocent, Polixenes blameless, Camillo a true subject, Leontes a jealous tyrant, and the king shall live without an heir if that which is lost be not found.'

The king would give no credit to the words of the oracle. He said it was a falsehood invented by the queen's friends, and he desired the judge to proceed in the trial of the queen; but while Leontes was speaking a man entered and told him that the Prince Mamillius, hearing his mother was to be tried for her life, struck with grief and shame, had suddenly died.

Hermione, upon hearing of the death of this dear, affectionate child, who had lost his life in sorrowing for her misfortune, fainted; and Leontes, pierced to the heart by the news, began to feel pity for his unhappy queen, and he ordered Paulina, and the ladies who were her attendants, to take her away and use means for her recovery. Paulina soon returned and told the king that Hermione was dead.

When Leontes heard that the queen was dead he repented of his cruelty to her; and now that he thought his ill-usage had broken

Hermione's heart, he believed her innocent; and now he thought the words of the oracle were true, as he knew 'if that which was lost was not found', which he concluded was his young daughter, he should be without an heir, the young Prince Mamillius being dead; and he would give his kingdom now to recover his lost daughter. And Leontes gave himself up to remorse and passed many years in mournful thoughts and repentant grief.

The ship in which Antigonus carried the infant princess out to sea was driven by a storm upon the coast of Bohemia, the very kingdom of the good King Polixenes. Here Antigonus landed and here he left the little baby.

Antigonus never returned to Sicily to tell Leontes where he had left his daughter, for, as he was going back to the ship, a bear came out of the woods and tore him to pieces; a just punishment on him for obeying the wicked order of Leontes.

The child was dressed in rich clothes and jewels; for Hermione had made it very fine when she sent it to Leontes, and Antigonus had pinned a paper to its mantle, and the name of 'Perdita' written thereon, and words obscurely intimating its high birth and untoward fate.

This poor, deserted baby was found by a shepherd. He was a humane man, and so he carried the little Perdita home to his wife, who nursed it tenderly. But poverty tempted the shepherd to conceal the rich prize he had found; therefore he left that part of the country, that no one might know where he got his riches, and with part of Perdita's jewels he bought herds of sheep and became a wealthy shepherd. He brought up Perdita as his own child, and she knew not she was any other than a shepherd's daughter.

The little Perdita grew up a lovely maiden; and though she had no better education than that of a shepherd's daughter, yet so did the natural graces she inherited from her royal mother shine forth in her untutored mind that no one, from her behaviour, would have known she had not been brought up in her father's court.

Polixenes, the King of Bohemia, had an only son, whose name was Florizel. As this young prince was hunting near the shepherd's dwelling he saw the old man's supposed daughter; and the beauty, modesty, and queenlike deportment of Perdita caused him instantly to fall in love with her. He soon, under the name of Doricles, and in the disguise of a private gentleman, became a constant visitor at the old shepherd's house. Florizel's frequent absences from court alarmed Polixenes; and setting people to watch his son, he discovered his love for the shepherd's fair daughter.

Polixenes then called for Camillo, the faithful Camillo, who had preserved his life from the fury of Leontes, and desired that he would accompany him to the house of the shepherd, the supposed father of Perdita. Polixenes and Camillo, both in disguise, arrived at the old shepherd's dwelling while they were celebrating the feast of sheepshearing; and though they were strangers, yet at the sheepshearing, every guest being made welcome, they were invited to walk in and join in the general festivity.

Nothing but mirth and jollity was going forward. Tables were spread and great preparations were making for the rustic feast. Some lads and lasses were dancing on the green before the house, while others of the young men were buying ribands, gloves, and such toys of a pedlar at the door.

While this busy scene was going forward Florizel and Perdita sat quietly in a retired corner, seemingly more pleased with the conversation of each other than desirous of engaging in the sports and silly amusements of those around them.

The king was so disguised that it was impossible his son could know him. He therefore advanced near enough to hear the conversation. The simple yet elegant manner in which Perdita conversed with his son did not a little surprise Polixenes. He said to Camillo: 'This is the prettiest low-born lass I ever saw; nothing she does or says but looks like something greater than herself, too noble for this place.'

Camillo replied, 'Indeed she is the very queen of curds and cream.'

'Pray, my good friend,' said the king to the old shepherd, 'what fair swain is that talking with your daughter?'

'They call him Doricles,' replied the shepherd. 'He says he loves my daughter; and, to speak truth, there is not a kiss to choose which loves the other best. If young Doricles can get her, she shall bring him that he little dreams of,' meaning the remainder of Perdita's jewels; which, after he had bought herds of sheep with part of them, he had carefully hoarded up for her marriage portion.

Polixenes then addressed his son. 'How now, young man!' said he. 'Your heart seems full of something that takes off your mind from feasting. When I was young I used to load my love with presents; but you have let the pedlar go and have bought your lass no toy.'

The young prince, who little thought he was talking to the king his father, replied, 'Old sir, she prizes not such trifles; the gifts which Perdita expects from me are locked up in my heart.' Then turning to Perdita, he said to her, 'Oh, hear me, Perdita, before this ancient gentleman, who it seems was once himself a lover; he shall hear what I profess.' Florizel then called upon the old stranger to be a witness to a solemn promise of marriage which he made to Perdita, saying to Polixenes, 'I pray you, mark our contract.'

'Mark your divorce, young sir,' said the king, discovering himself. Polixenes then reproached his son for daring to contract himself to this low-born maiden, calling Perdita 'shepherd's brat, sheep-hook', and other disrespectful names, and threatening if ever she suffered his son to see her again, he would put her, and the old shepherd her father, to a cruel death.

The king then left them in great wrath, and ordered Camillo to follow him with Prince Florizel.

When the king had departed, Perdita, whose royal nature was roused by Polixenes's reproaches, said, 'Though we are all undone, I was not much afraid; and once or twice I was about to speak and tell him plainly that the selfsame sun which shines upon his palace hides not his face from our cottage, but looks on both alike.' Then sorrowfully she said, 'But now I am awakened from this dream, I will queen it no further. Leave me, sir. I will go milk my ewes and weep.'

The kind-hearted Camillo was charmed with the spirit and propriety of Perdita's behaviour; and, perceiving that the young prince was too deeply in love to give up his mistress at the command of his royal father, he thought of a way to befriend the lovers and at the same time to execute a favourite scheme he had in his mind.

Camillo had long known that Leontes, the King of Sicily, was become a true penitent; and though Camillo was now the favoured friend of King Polixenes, he could not help wishing once more to see his late royal master and his native home. He therefore proposed to Florizel and Perdita that they should accompany him to the Sicilian court, where he would engage Leontes should protect them till, through his mediation, they could obtain pardon from Polixenes and his consent to their marriage.

To this proposal they joyfully agreed; and Camillo, who conducted everything relative to their flight, allowed the old shepherd to go along with them.

The shepherd took with him the remainder of Perdita's jewels, her baby clothes, and the paper which he had found pinned to her mantle.

After a prosperous voyage, Florizel and Perdita, Camillo and the old shepherd, arrived in safety at the court of Leontes. Leontes, who still mourned his dead Hermione and his lost child, received Camillo with great kindness and gave a cordial welcome to Prince Florizel. But Perdita, whom Florizel introduced as his princess, seemed to engross all Leontes's attention. Perceiving a resemblance between her and his dead queen Hermione, his grief broke out afresh, and he said such a lovely creature might his own daughter have been if he had not so cruelly destroyed her.

'And then, too,' said he to Florizel, 'I lost the society and friendship of your brave father, whom I now desire more than my life once again to look upon.'

When the old shepherd heard how much notice the king had taken of Perdita, and that he had lost a daughter who was exposed in infancy, he fell to comparing the time when he found the little Perdita with the manner of its exposure, the jewels and other tokens of its high birth; from all which it was impossible for him not to conclude that Perdita and the king's lost daughter were the same.

Florizel and Perdita, Camillo and the faithful Paulina, were present when the old shepherd related to the king the manner in which he had found the child, and also the circumstance of Antigonus's death, he having seen the bear seize upon him. He showed the rich mantle in which Paulina remembered Hermione had wrapped the child; and he produced a jewel which she remembered Hermione had tied about Perdita's neck; and he gave up the paper which Paulina knew to be the writing of her husband. It could not be doubted that Perdita was Leontes's own daughter. But, oh, the noble struggles of Paulina, between sorrow for her husband's death and joy that the oracle was fulfilled, in the king's heir, his long-lost daughter being found! When Leontes heard that Perdita was his daughter, the great sorrow that he felt that Hermione was not living to behold her child made him that he could say nothing for a long time but 'Oh, thy mother, thy mother!'

Paulina interrupted this joyful yet distressful scene with saying to Leontes that she had a statue newly finished by that rare Italian master, Julio Romano, which was such a perfect resemblance of the queen that would his majesty be pleased to go to her house and look upon it, he would be almost ready to think it was Hermione herself. Thither then they all went; the king, anxious to see the semblance of his Hermione, and Perdita longing to behold what the mother she never saw did look like.

When Paulina drew back the curtain which concealed this famous statue, so perfectly did it resemble Hermione that all the king's sorrow was renewed at the sight; for a long time he had no power to speak or move.

'I like your silence, my liege,' said Paulina; 'it the more shows your wonder. Is not this statue very like your queen?'

At length the king said: 'Oh, thus she stood, even with such majesty, when I first wooed her. But yet, Paulina, Hermione was not so aged as this statue looks.'

Paulina replied: 'So much the more the carver's excellence, who has made the statue as Hermione would have looked had she been living now. But let me draw the curtain, sire, lest presently you think it moves.'

The king then said: 'Do not draw the curtain. Would I were

dead! See, Camillo, would you not think it breathed? Her eye seems to have motion in it.'

'I must draw the curtain, my liege,' said Paulina. 'You are so transported, you will persuade yourself the statue lives.'

'Oh, sweet Paulina,' said Leontes, 'make me think so twenty years together! Still methinks there is an air comes from her. What fine chisel could ever yet cut breath? Let no man mock me, for I will kiss her.'

'Good my lord, forbear!' said Paulina. 'The ruddiness upon her lip is wet; you will stain your own with oily painting. Shall I draw the curtain?'

'No, not these twenty years,' said Leontes.

Perdita, who all this time had been kneeling and beholding in silent admiration the statue of her matchless mother, said now, 'And so long could I stay here, looking upon my dear mother.'

'Either forbear this transport,' said Paulina to Leontes, 'and let me draw the curtain or prepare yourself for more amazement. I can make the statue move indeed; aye, and descend from off the pedestal and take you by the hand. But then you will think, which I protest I am not, that I am assisted by some wicked powers.'

'What you can make her do,' said the astonished king, 'I am content to look upon. What you can make her speak I am content to hear; for it is as easy to make her speak as move.'

Paulina then ordered some slow and solemn music, which she had prepared for the purpose, to strike up; and, to the amazement of all the beholders, the statue came down from off the pedestal and threw its arms around Leontes's neck. The statue then began to speak, praying for blessings on her husband and on her child, the newly found Perdita.

No wonder that the statue hung upon Leontes's neck and blessed her husband and her child. No wonder; for the statue was indeed Hermione herself, the real, the living queen.

Paulina had falsely reported to the king the death of Hermione, thinking that the only means to preserve her royal mistress's life; and with the good Paulina Hermione had lived ever since, never choosing Leontes should know she was living till she heard Perdita was found; for though she had long forgiven the injuries which Leontes had done to herself, she could not pardon his cruelty to his infant daughter.

His dead queen thus restored to life, his lost daughter found, the long-sorrowing Leontes could scarcely support the excess of his own happiness.

Nothing but congratulations and affectionate speeches were heard on all sides. Now the delighted parents thanked Prince Florizel for loving their lowly-seeming daughter; and now they blessed the good old shepherd for preserving their child. Greatly did Camillo and Paulina rejoice that they had lived to see so good an end of all their faithful services.

And as if nothing should be wanting to complete this strange and unlooked-for joy, King Polixenes himself now entered the palace.

When Polixenes first missed his son and Camillo, knowing that Camillo had long wished to return to Sicily, he conjectured he should find the fugitives here; and, following them with all speed, he happened to just arrive at this the happiest moment of Leontes's life.

Polixenes took a part in the general joy; he forgave his friend Leontes the unjust jealousy he had conceived against him, and they once more loved each other with all the warmth of their first boyish friendship. And there was no fear that Polixenes would now oppose his son's marriage with Perdita. She was no 'sheep-hook' now, but the heiress of the crown of Sicily.

Thus have we seen the patient virtues of the long-suffering Hermione rewarded. That excellent lady lived many years with her Leontes and her Perdita, the happiest of mothers and of queens.

Much Ado about Nothing

There lived in the palace at Messina two ladies, whose names were Hero and Beatrice. Hero was the daughter, and Beatrice the niece, of Leonato, the governor of Messina.

Beatrice was of a lively temper and loved to divert her cousin Hero, who was of a more serious disposition, with her sprightly sallies. Whatever was going forward was sure to make matter of mirth for the light-hearted Beatrice.

At the time the history of these ladies commences some young men of high rank in the army, as they were passing through Messina on their return from a war that was just ended, in which they had distinguished themselves by their great bravery, came to visit Leonato. Among these were Don Pedro, the Prince of Arragon, and his friend Claudio, who was a lord of Florence; and with them came the wild and witty Benedick, and he was a lord of Padua.

These strangers had been at Messina before, and the hospitable governor introduced them to his daughter and his niece as their old friends and acquaintance.

Benedick, the moment he entered the room, began a lively conversation with Leonato and the prince. Beatrice, who liked not to be left out of any discourse, interrupted Benedick with saying: 'I wonder that you will still be talking, Signor Benedick. Nobody marks you.'

Benedick was just such another rattlebrain as Beatrice, yet he was not pleased at this free salutation; he thought it did not become a well-bred lady to be so flippant with her tongue; and he remembered, when he was last at Messina, that Beatrice used to select him to make her merry jests upon. And as there is no one who so little likes to be made a jest of as those who are apt to take the same liberty themselves, so it was with Benedick and Beatrice; these two sharp wits never met in former times but a perfect war of raillery was kept up between them, and they always parted mutually displeased with each other. Therefore, when Beatrice stopped him in the middle of his discourse with telling him nobody marked what he was saying, Benedick, affecting not to have observed before that she was present, said: 'What, my dear Lady Disdain, are you yet living?' And now war broke out afresh between them, and a long jangling argument ensued, during which Beatrice, although she knew he had so well approved his valour in the late war, said that she would eat all he had killed there; and observing the prince take delight in Benedick's conversation, she called him 'the prince's jester'. This sarcasm sank deeper into the mind of Benedick than all Beatrice had said before. The hint she gave him that he was a coward, by saying she would eat all he had killed, he did not regard, knowing himself to be a brave man; but there is nothing that great wits so much dread as the imputation of buffoonery, because the charge comes sometimes a little too near the truth; therefore Benedick perfectly hated Beatrice when she called him 'the prince's jester'.

The modest lady Hero was silent before the noble guests; and while Claudio was attentively observing the improvement which time had made in her beauty, and was contemplating the exquisite graces of her fine figure (for she was an admirable young lady), the prince was highly amused with listening to the humorous dialogue between Benedick and Beatrice; and he said in a whisper to Leonato: 'This is a pleasant-spirited young lady. She were an excellent wife for Benedick.'

Leonato replied to this suggestion, 'O my lord, my lord, if they were but a week married, they would talk themselves mad!'

But though Leonato thought they would make a discordant pair, the prince did not give up the idea of matching these two keen wits together.

When the prince returned with Claudio from the palace he found that the marriage he had devised between Benedick and Beatrice was not the only one projected in that good company, for Claudio spoke in such terms of Hero as made the prince guess at what was passing in his heart; and he liked it well, and he said to Claudio: 'Do you affect Hero?'

To this question Claudio replied, 'O my lord, when I was last at Messina I looked upon her with a soldier's eye, that liked, but had no leisure for loving; but now, in this happy time of peace, thoughts of war have left their places vacant in my mind, and in their room come thronging soft and delicate thoughts, all prompting me how fair young Hero is, reminding me that I liked her before I went to the wars.'

Claudio's confession of his love for Hero so wrought upon the prince that he lost no time in soliciting the consent of Leonato to accept of Claudio for a son-in-law. Leonato agreed to this proposal, and the prince found no great difficulty in persuading the gentle Hero herself to listen to the suit of the noble Claudio, who was a lord of rare endowments and highly accomplished, and Claudio, assisted by his kind prince, soon prevailed upon Leonato to fix an early day for the celebration of his marriage with Hero.

Claudio was to wait but a few days before he was to be married to his fair lady; yet he complained of the interval being tedious, as indeed most young men are impatient when they are waiting for the accomplishment of any event they have set their hearts upon. The prince, therefore, to make the time seem short to him, proposed as a kind of merry pastime that they should invent some artful scheme to make Benedick and Beatrice fall in love with each other. Claudio entered with great satisfaction into this whim of the prince, and Leonato promised them his assistance, and even Hero said she would do any modest office to help her cousin to a good husband.

The device the prince invented was that the gentlemen should make Benedick believe that Beatrice was in love with him, and that Hero should make Beatrice believe that Benedick was in love with her.

The prince, Leonato, and Claudio began their operations first; and watching upon an opportunity when Benedick was quietly seated reading in an arbour, the prince and his assistants took their station among the trees behind the arbour, so near that Benedick could not choose but hear all they said; and after some careless talk the prince said: 'Come hither, Leonato. What was it you told me the other day – that your niece Beatrice was in love with Signor Benedick? I did never think that lady would have loved any man.'

'No, nor I neither, my lord,' answered Leonato. 'It is most wonderful that she should so dote on Benedick, whom she in all outward behaviour seemed ever to dislike.'

Claudio confirmed all this with saying that Hero had told him Beatrice was so in love with Benedick that she would certainly die of grief if he could not be brought to love her; which Leonato and Claudio seemed to agree was impossible, he having always been such a railer against all fair ladies, and in particular against Beatrice.

The prince affected to harken to all this with great compassion for Beatrice, and he said, 'It were good that Benedick were told of this.'

'To what end?' said Claudio. 'He would but make sport of it, and torment the poor lady worse.'

'And if he should,' said the prince, 'it were a good deed to hang him; for Beatrice is an excellent sweet lady, and exceeding wise in everything but in loving Benedick.'

Then the prince motioned to his companions that they should walk on and leave Benedick to meditate upon what he had over-heard.

Benedick had been listening with great eagerness to this con-versation; and he said to himself, when he heard Beatrice loved him: 'Is it possible? Sits the wind in that corner?' And when they were gone, he began to reason in this manner with himself: 'This can be no trick! They were very serious, and they have the truth from Hero, and seem to pity the lady. Love me! Why, it must be

requited! I did never think to marry. But when I said I should die a
bachelor, I did not think I should live to be married. They say the
lady is virtuous and fair. She is so. And wise in everything but
loving me. Why, that is no great argument of her folly! But here
comes Beatrice. By this day, she is a fair lady. I do spy some marks
of love in her.'

Beatrice now approached him and said, with her usual tartness,
'Against my will I am sent to bid you come in to dinner.'

Benedick, who never felt himself disposed to speak so politely to
her before, replied, 'Fair Beatrice, I thank you for your pains.' And
when Beatrice, after two or three more rude speeches, left him,
Benedick thought he observed a concealed meaning of kindness
under the uncivil words she uttered, and he said aloud: 'If I do not
take pity on her, I am a villain. If I do not love her, I am a Jew. I will
go get her picture.'

The gentleman being thus caught in the net they had spread for
him, it was now Hero's turn to play her part with Beatrice; and for
this purpose she sent for Ursula and Margaret, two gentlewomen
who attended upon her, and she said to Margaret: 'Good Margaret,
run to the parlour; there you will find my cousin Beatrice talking
with the prince and Claudio. Whisper in her ear that I and Ursula
are walking in the orchard and that our discourse is all of her. Bid
her steal into that pleasant arbour, where honeysuckles, ripened by
the sun, like ungrateful minions, forbid the sun to enter.'

This arbour into which Hero desired Margaret to entice Beatrice
was the very same pleasant arbour where Benedick had so lately
been an attentive listener.

'I will make her come, I warrant, presently,' said Margaret.

Hero, then taking Ursula with her into the orchard, said to her:
'Now, Ursula, when Beatrice comes, we will walk up and down this
alley, and our talk must be only of Benedick, and when I name him,
let it be your part to praise him more than ever man did merit. My
talk to you must be how Benedick is in love with Beatrice. Now
begin; for look where Beatrice like a lapwing runs close by the
ground, to hear our conference.'

They then began, Hero saying, as if in answer to something

which Ursula had said: 'No, truly, Ursula. She is too disdainful; her spirits are as coy as wild birds of the rock.'

'But are you sure,' said Ursula, 'that Benedick loves Beatrice so entirely?'

Hero replied, 'So says the prince and my lord Claudio, and they entreated me to acquaint her with it; but I persuaded them, if they loved Benedick, never to let Beatrice know of it.'

'Certainly,' replied Ursula, 'it were not good she knew his love, lest she made sport of it.'

'Why, to say truth,' said Hero, 'I never yet saw a man, how wise soever, or noble, young, or rarely featured, but she would dispraise him.'

'Sure, sure, such carping is not commendable,' said Ursula.

'No,' replied Hero, 'but who dare tell her so? If I should speak, she would mock me into air.'

'Oh, you wrong your cousin!' said Ursula. 'She cannot be so much without true judgement as to refuse so rare a gentleman as Signor Benedick.'

'He hath an excellent good name,' said Hero. 'Indeed, he is the first man in Italy, always excepting my dear Claudio.'

And now, Hero giving her attendant a hint that it was time to change the discourse, Ursula said, 'And when are you to be married, madam?'

Hero then told her that she was to be married to Claudio the next day, and desired she would go in with her and look at some new attire, as she wished to consult with her on what she would wear on the morrow.

Beatrice, who had been listening with breathless eagerness to this dialogue, when they went away exclaimed: 'What fire is in mine ears? Can this be true? Farewell, contempt and scorn, and maiden pride, adieu! Benedick, love on! I will requite you, taming my wild heart to your loving hand.'

It must have been a pleasant sight to see these old enemies converted into new and loving friends, and to behold their first meeting after being cheated into mutual liking by the merry artifice of the good-humoured prince. But a sad reverse in the fortunes of Hero must now be thought of. The morrow, which was to have been her wedding-day, brought sorrow on the heart of Hero and her good father, Leonato.

The prince had a half-brother, who came from the wars along with him to Messina. This brother (his name was Don John) was a melancholy, discontented man, whose spirits seemed to labour in the contriving of villainies. He hated the prince his brother, and he hated Claudio because he was the prince's friend, and determined to prevent Claudio's marriage with Hero, only for the malicious pleasure of making Claudio and the prince unhappy, for he knew the prince had set his heart upon this marriage almost as much as Claudio himself; and to effect this wicked purpose he employed one Borachio, a man as bad as himself, whom he encouraged with the offer of a great reward. This Borachio paid his court to Margaret, Hero's attendant; and Don John, knowing this, prevailed upon him to make Margaret promise to talk with him from her lady's chamber window that night, after Hero was asleep, and also to dress herself in Hero's clothes, the better to deceive Claudio into the belief that it was Hero; for that was the end he meant to compass by this wicked plot.

Don John then went to the prince and Claudio and told them that Hero was an imprudent lady, and that she talked with men from her chamber window at midnight. Now this was the evening before the wedding, and he offered to take them that night where they should themselves hear Hero discoursing with a man from her window; and they consented to go along with him, and Claudio said: 'If I see anything tonight why I should not marry her, tomorrow in the congregation, where I intended to wed her, there will I shame her.'

The prince also said, 'And as I assisted you to obtain her, I will join with you to disgrace her.'

When Don John brought them near Hero's chamber that night, they saw Borachio standing under the window, and they saw Margaret looking out of Hero's window and heard her talking with Borachio; and Margaret being dressed in the same clothes they had seen Hero wear, the prince and Claudio believed it was the lady Hero herself.

Nothing could equal the anger of Claudio when he had made (as he thought) this discovery. All his love for the innocent Hero was at once converted into hatred, and he resolved to expose her in the church, as he had said he would, the next day; and the prince agreed to this, thinking no punishment could be too severe for the naughty lady who talked with a man from her window the very night before she was going to be married to the noble Claudio.

The next day, when they were all met to celebrate the marriage, and Claudio and Hero were standing before the priest, and the priest, or friar, as he was called, was proceeding to pronounce the marriage ceremony, Claudio, in the most passionate language, proclaimed the guilt of the blameless Hero, who, amazed at the strange words he uttered, said, meekly: 'Is my lord well, that he does speak so wide?'

Leonato, in the utmost horror, said to the prince, 'My lord, why speak not you?'

'What should I speak?' said the prince. 'I stand dishonoured that have gone about to link my dear friend to an unworthy woman. Leonato, upon my honour, myself, my brother, and this grieved Claudio did see and hear her last night at midnight talk with a man at her chamber window.'

Benedick, in astonishment at what he heard, said, 'This looks not like a nuptial.'

'True, O God!' replied the heart-struck Hero; and then this hapless lady sank down in a fainting fit, to all appearance dead.

The prince and Claudio left the church without staying to see if Hero would recover, or at all regarding the distress into which they had thrown Leonato. So hard-hearted had their anger made them.

Benedick remained and assisted Beatrice to recover Hero from her swoon, saying, 'How does the lady?'

'Dead, I think,' replied Beatrice, in great agony, for she loved her cousin; and, knowing her virtuous principles, she believed nothing of what she had heard spoken against her.

Not so the poor old father. He believed the story of his child's shame, and it was piteous to hear him lamenting over her, as she lay like one dead before him, wishing she might never more open her eyes.

But the ancient friar was a wise man and full of observation on human nature, and he had attentively marked the lady's countenance when she heard herself accused and noted a thousand blushing shames to start into her face, and then he saw an angel-like whiteness bear away those blushes, and in her eye he saw a fire that did belie the error that the prince did speak against her maiden truth, and he said to the sorrowing father: 'Call me a fool; trust not my reading nor my observation; trust not my age, my reverence, nor my calling, if this sweet lady lie not guiltless here under some biting error.'

When Hero had recovered from the swoon into which she had fallen, the friar said to her, 'Lady, what man is he you are accused of?'

Hero replied, 'They know that do accuse me; I know of none.' Then turning to Leonato, she said, 'O my father, if you can prove that any man has ever conversed with me at hours unmeet, or that I yesternight changed words with any creature, refuse me, hate me, torture me to death.'

'There is,' said the friar, 'some strange misunderstanding in the prince and Claudio.' And then he counselled Leonato that he should report that Hero was dead; and he said that the deathlike swoon in which they had left Hero would make this easy of belief; and he also advised him that he should put on mourning, and erect a monument for her, and do all rites that appertain to a burial.

'What shall become of this?' said Leonato. 'What will this do?'

The friar replied: 'This report of her death shall change slander into pity; that is some good. But that is not all the good I hope for. When Claudio shall hear she died upon hearing his words, the idea of her life shall sweetly creep into his imagination. Then shall he mourn, if ever love had interest in his heart, and wish that he had not so accused her; yea, though he thought his accusation true.'

Benedick now said, 'Leonato, let the friar advise you; and though you know how well I love the prince and Claudio, yet on my honour I will not reveal this secret to them.'

Leonato, thus persuaded, yielded; and he said, sorrowfully, 'I am so grieved that the smallest twine may lead me.'

The kind friar then led Leonato and Hero away to comfort and console them, and Beatrice and Benedick remained alone; and this was the meeting from which their friends, who contrived the merry plot against them, expected so much diversion; those friends who were now overwhelmed with affliction and from whose minds all thoughts of merriment seemed forever banished.

Benedick was the first who spoke, and he said, 'Lady Beatrice, have you wept all this while?'

'Yea, and I will weep awhile longer,' said Beatrice.

'Surely,' said Benedick, 'I do believe your fair cousin is wronged.'

'Ah,' said Beatrice, 'how much might that man deserve of me who would right her!'

Benedick then said: 'Is there any way to show such friendship? I do love nothing in the world so well as you. Is not that strange?'

'It were as possible,' said Beatrice, 'for me to say I loved nothing in the world so well as you; but believe me not, and yet I lie not. I confess nothing, nor I deny nothing. I am sorry for my cousin.'

'By my sword,' said Benedick, 'you love me, and I protest I love you. Come, bid me do anything for you.'

'Kill Claudio,' said Beatrice.

'Ha! not for the world,' said Benedick; for he loved his friend Claudio and he believed he had been imposed upon.

'Is not Claudio a villain that has slandered, scorned, and dishonoured my cousin?' said Beatrice. 'Oh, that I were a man!'

'Hear me, Beatrice!' said Benedick.

But Beatrice would hear nothing in Claudio's defence, and she continued to urge on Benedick to revenge her cousin's wrongs; and she said: 'Talk with a man out of the window? a proper saying! Sweet Hero! she is wronged; she is slandered; she is undone. Oh, that I were a man for Claudio's sake! or that I had any friend who would be a man for my sake! But valour is melted into courtesies and compliments. I cannot be a man with wishing, therefore I will die a woman with grieving.'

'Tarry, good Beatrice,' said Benedick. 'By this hand I love you.'

'Use it for my love some other way than swearing by it,' said Beatrice.

'Think you on your soul that Claudio has wronged Hero?' asked Benedick.

'Yea,' answered Beatrice; 'as sure as I have a thought or a soul.'

'Enough,' said Benedick. 'I am engaged; I will challenge him. I will kiss your hand, and so leave you. By this hand Claudio shall render me a dear account! As you hear from me, so think of me. Go, comfort your cousin.'

While Beatrice was thus powerfully pleading with Benedick, and working his gallant temper, by the spirit of her angry words, to engage in the cause of Hero and fight even with his dear friend Claudio, Leonato was challenging the prince and Claudio to answer with their swords the injury they had done his child who he affirmed, had died for grief. But they respected his age and his sorrow, and they said: 'Nay, do not quarrel with us, good old man.'

And now came Benedick, and he also challenged Claudio to answer with his sword the injury he had done to Hero; and Claudio and the prince said to each other: 'Beatrice has set him on to do this.'

Claudio, nevertheless, must have accepted this challenge of Benedick had not the justice of Heaven at the moment brought to pass a better proof of the innocence of Hero than the uncertain fortune of a duel.

While the prince and Claudio were yet talking of the challenge of Benedick a magistrate brought Borachio as a prisoner before the prince. Borachio had been overheard talking with one of his companions of the mischief he had been employed by Don John to do.

Borachio made a full confession to the prince in Claudio's hearing that it was Margaret dressed in her lady's clothes that he had talked with from the window, whom they had mistaken for the lady Hero herself, and no doubt continued on the minds of Claudio and the prince of the innocence of Hero. If a suspicion had remained it must have been removed by the flight of Don John, who, finding his villainies were detected, fled from Messina to avoid the just anger of his brother.

The heart of Claudio was sorely grieved when he found he had falsely accused Hero, who, he thought, died upon hearing his cruel words; and the memory of his beloved Hero's image came over him in the rare semblance that he loved it first; and the prince, asking him if what he heard did not run like iron through his soul, he answered that he felt as if he had taken poison while Borachio was speaking.

And the repentant Claudio implored forgiveness of the old man Leonato for the injury he had done his child; and promised that, whatever penance Leonato would lay upon him for his fault in believing the false accusation against his betrothed wife, for her dear sake he would endure it.

The penance Leonato enjoined him was to marry the next morning a cousin of Hero's, who, he said, was now his heir, and in person very like Hero. Claudio, regarding the solemn promise he made to Leonato, said he would marry this unknown lady, even though she were an Ethiop. But his heart was very sorrowful, and he passed that night in tears and in remorseful grief at the tomb which Leonato had erected for Hero.

When the morning came the prince accompanied Claudio to the church, where the good friar and Leonato and his niece were already assembled, to celebrate a second nuptial; and Leonato presented to Claudio his promised bride. And she wore a mask, that Claudio might not discover her face. And Claudio said to the lady in the mask: 'Give me your hand, before this holy friar. I am your husband, if you will marry me.'

'And when I lived I was your other wife,' said this unknown lady; and, taking off her mask, she proved to be no niece (as was pretended), but Leonato's very daughter, the lady Hero herself. We may be sure that this proved a most agreeable surprise to Claudio, who thought her dead, so that he could scarcely for joy believe his eyes; and the prince, who was equally amazed at what he saw, exclaimed: 'Is not this Hero, Hero that was dead?''

Leonato replied, 'She died, my lord, but while her slander lived.'

The friar promised them an explanation of this seeming miracle, after the ceremony was ended, and was proceeding to marry them when he was interrupted by Benedick, who desired to be married at the same time to Beatrice. Beatrice making some demur to this match, and Benedick challenging her with her love for him, which he had learned from Hero, a pleasant explanation took place; and they found they had both been tricked into a belief of love, which had never existed, and had become lovers in truth by the power of a false jest. But the affection which a merry invention had cheated them into was grown too powerful to be shaken by a serious explanation; and since Benedick proposed to marry, he was resolved to think nothing to the purpose that the world could say against it; and he merrily kept up the jest and swore to Beatrice that he took her but for pity, and because he heard she was dying of love for him; and Beatrice protested that she yielded but upon great persuasion, and partly to save his life, for she heard he was in a consumption. So these two mad wits were reconciled and made a match of it, after Claudio and Hero were married; and to complete the history, Don John, the contriver of the villainy, was taken in his flight and brought back to Messina; and a brave punishment it was to this gloomy, discontented man to see the joy and feastings which, by the disappointment of his plots, took place in the palace in Messina.

As You Like It

During the time that France was divided into provinces (or duke-doms, as they were called) there reigned in one of these provinces a usurper who had deposed and banished his elder brother, the lawful duke.

The duke who was thus driven from his dominions retired with a few faithful followers to the forest of Arden; and here the good duke lived with his loving friends, who had put themselves into a voluntary exile for his sake, while their land and revenues enriched the false usurper; and custom soon made the life of careless ease they led here more sweet to them than the pomp and uneasy splendour of a courtier's life. Here they lived like the old Robin Hood of England, and to this forest many noble youths daily resorted from the court, and did fleet the time carelessly, as they did who lived in the golden age. In the summer they lay along under the fine shade of the large forest trees, marking the playful sports of the wild deer; and so fond were they of these poor dappled fools, who seemed to be the native inhabitants of the forest, that it grieved them to be forced to kill them to supply themselves with venison for their food. When the cold winds of winter made the duke feel the change of his adverse fortune, he would endure it patiently, and say: 'These chilling winds which blow upon my body are true counsellors; they do not flatter, but represent truly to me my condition; and though they bite sharply, their tooth is nothing like so keen as that of unkindness and ingratitude. I find that howsoever men speak against adversity, yet some sweet uses are to be extracted from it; like the jewel, precious for medicine, which is taken from the head of the venomous and despised toad.'

In this manner did the patient duke draw a useful moral from everything that he saw; and by the help of this moralising turn, in that life of his, remote from public haunts, he could find tongues in trees, books in the running brooks, sermons in stones, and good in everything.

The banished duke had an only daughter, named Rosalind, whom the usurper, Duke Frederick, when he banished her father, still retained in his court as a companion for his own daughter, Celia. A strict friendship subsisted between these ladies, which the disagreement between their fathers did not in the least interrupt, Celia striving by every kindness in her power to make amends to Rosalind for the injustice of her own father in deposing the father of Rosalind; and whenever the thoughts of her father's banishment, and her own dependence on the false usurper, made Rosalind melancholy, Celia's whole care was to comfort and console her.

One day, when Celia was talking in her usual kind manner to Rosalind, saying, 'I pray you, Rosalind, my sweet cousin, be merry,' a messenger entered from the duke, to tell them that if they wished to see a wrestling-match, which was just going to begin, they must come instantly to the court before the palace; and Celia, thinking it would amuse Rosalind, agreed to go and see it.

In those times wrestling, which is only practised now by country clowns, was a favourite sport even in the courts of princes, and before fair ladies and princesses. To this wrestling-match, therefore, Celia and Rosalind went. They found that it was likely to prove a very tragical sight; for a large and powerful man, who had been long practised in the art of wrestling and had slain many men in contests of this kind, was just going to wrestle with a very young man, who, from his extreme youth and inexperience in the art, the beholders all thought would certainly be killed.

When the duke saw Celia and Rosalind he said: 'How now, daughter and niece, are you crept hither to see the wrestling? You will take little delight in it, there is such odds in the men. In pity to this young man, I would wish to persuade him from wrestling. Speak to him, ladies, and see if you can move him.'

The ladies were well pleased to perform this humane office, and first Celia entreated the young stranger that he would desist from the attempt; and then Rosalind spoke so kindly to him, and with such feeling consideration for the danger he was about to undergo, that, instead of being persuaded by her gentle words to forgo his purpose, all his thoughts were bent to distinguish himself by his courage in this lovely lady's eyes. He refused the request of Celia and Rosalind in such graceful and modest words that they felt still more concern for him; he concluded his refusal with saying: 'I am sorry to deny such fair and excellent ladies anything. But let your fair eyes and gentle wishes go with me to my trial, wherein if I be conquered there is one shamed that was never gracious; if I am killed, there is one dead that is willing to die. I shall do my friends no wrong, for I have none to lament me; the world no injury, for in it I have nothing; for I only fill up a place in the world which may be better supplied when I have made it empty.'

And now the wrestling-match began. Celia wished the young stranger might not be hurt; but Rosalind felt most for him. The friendless state which he said he was in, and that he wished to die, made Rosalind think that he was, like herself, unfortunate; and she pitied him so much, and so deep an interest she took in his danger while he was wrestling, that she might almost be said at that moment to have fallen in love with him.

The kindness shown this unknown youth by these fair and noble ladies gave him courage and strength, so that he performed wonders; and in the end completely conquered his antagonist, who was so much hurt that for a while he was unable to speak or move.

The Duke Frederick was much pleased with the courage and skill shown by this young stranger; and desired to know his name and parentage, meaning to take him under his protection.

The stranger said his name was Orlando, and that he was the youngest son of Sir Rowland de Boys.

Sir Rowland de Boys, the father of Orlando, had been dead some years; but when he was living he had been a true subject and dear friend of the banished duke; therefore, when Frederick heard Orlando was the son of his banished brother's friend, all his liking for this brave young man was changed into displeasure and he left the place in very ill humour. Hating to hear the very name of any of his brother's friends, and yet still admiring the valour of the youth, he said, as he went out, that he wished Orlando had been the son of any other man.

Rosalind was delighted to hear that her new favourite was the son of her father's old friend; and she said to Celia, 'My father loved Sir Rowland de Boys, and if I had known this young man was his son I would have added tears to my entreaties before he should have ventured.'

The ladies then went up to him and, seeing him abashed by the sudden displeasure shown by the duke, they spoke kind and encouraging words to him; and Rosalind, when they were going away, turned back to speak some more civil things to the brave young son of her father's old friend, and taking a chain from off her neck, she said: 'Gentleman, wear this for me. I am out of suits with fortune, or I would give you a more valuable present.'

When the ladies were alone, Rosalind's talk being still of Orlando, Celia began to perceive her cousin had fallen in love with the handsome young wrestler, and she said to Rosalind: 'Is it possible you should fall in love so suddenly?'

Rosalind replied, 'The duke, my father, loved his father dearly.'

'But,' said Celia, 'does it therefore follow that you should love his son dearly? For then I ought to hate him, for my father hated his father; yet I do not hate Orlando.'

Frederick, being enraged at the sight of Sir Rowland de Boys's son, which reminded him of the many friends the banished duke had among the nobility, and having been for some time displeased with his niece because the people praised her for her virtues and pitied her for her good father's sake, his malice suddenly broke out against her; and while Celia and Rosalind were talking of Orlando, Frederick entered the room and with looks full of anger ordered Rosalind instantly to leave the palace and follow her father into banishment, telling Celia, who in vain pleaded for her, that he had only suffered Rosalind to stay upon her account.

'I did not then,' said Celia, 'entreat you to let her stay, for I was too young at that time to value her; but now that I know her worth, and that we so long have slept together, rose at the same instant, learned, played, and eat together, I cannot live out of her company.'

Frederick replied: 'She is too subtle for you; her smoothness, her very silence, and her patience speak to the people, and they pity her. You are a fool to plead for her, for you will seem more bright and virtuous when she is gone; therefore open not your lips in her favour, for the doom which I have passed upon her is irrevocable.'

When Celia found she could not prevail upon her father to let Rosalind remain with her, she generously resolved to accompany her; and, leaving her father's palace that night, she went along with her friend to seek Rosalind's father, the banished duke, in the forest of Arden.

Before they set out Celia considered that it would be unsafe for two young ladies to travel in the rich clothes they then wore; she therefore proposed that they should disguise their rank by dressing themselves like country maids. Rosalind said it would be a still greater protection if one of them was to be dressed like a man. And so it was quickly agreed on between them that, as Rosalind was the tallest, she should wear the dress of a young countryman, and Celia should be habited like a country lass, and that they should say they were brother and sister; and Rosalind said she would be called Ganymede, and Celia chose the name of Aliena.

In this disguise, and taking their money and jewels to defray their expenses, these fair princesses set out on their long travel; for the forest of Arden was a long way off, beyond the boundaries of the duke's dominions.

The lady Rosalind (or Ganymede, as she must now be called)

with her manly garb seemed to have put on a manly courage. The faithful friendship Celia had shown in accompanying Rosalind so many weary miles made the new brother, in recompense for this true love, exert a cheerful spirit, as if he were indeed Ganymede, the rustic and stout-hearted brother of the gentle village maiden, Aliena.

When at last they came to the forest of Arden they no longer found the convenient inns and good accommodations they had met with on the road, and, being in want of food and rest, Ganymede, who had so merrily cheered his sister with pleasant speeches and happy remarks all the way, now owned to Aliena that he was so weary he could find in his heart to disgrace his man's apparel and cry like a woman; and Aliena declared she could go no farther; and then again Ganymede tried to recollect that it was a man's duty to comfort and console a woman, as the weaker vessel; and to seem courageous to his new sister, he said: 'Come, have a good heart, my sister Aliena. We are now at the end of our travel, in the forest of Arden.'

But feigned manliness and forced courage would no longer support them; for, though they were in the forest of Arden, they knew not where to find the duke. And here the travel of these weary ladies might have come to a sad conclusion, for they might have lost themselves and perished for want of food, but, providentially, as they were sitting on the grass, almost dying with fatigue and hopeless of any relief, a countryman chanced to pass that way, and Ganymede once more tried to speak with a manly boldness, saying: 'Shepherd, if love or gold can in this desert place procure us entertainment, I pray you bring us where we may rest ourselves; for this young maid, my sister, is much fatigued with travelling, and faints for want of food.'

The man replied that he was only a servant to a shepherd, and that his master's house was just going to be sold, and therefore they would find but poor entertainment; but that if they would go with him they should be welcome to what there was. They followed the man, the near prospect of relief giving them fresh strength, and bought the house and sheep of the shepherd, and took the man who conducted them to the shepherd's house to wait on them; and being by this means so fortunately provided with a neat cottage, and well supplied with provisions, they agreed to stay here till they could learn in what part of the forest the duke dwelt.

When they were rested after the fatigue of their journey, they began to like their new way of life, and almost fancied themselves the shepherd and shepherdess they feigned to be. Yet sometimes Ganymede remembered he had once been the same Lady Rosalind who had so dearly loved the brave Orlando because he was the son of old Sir Rowland, her father's friend; and though Ganymede thought that Orlando was many miles distant, even so many weary miles as they had travelled, yet it soon appeared that Orlando was also in the forest of Arden. And in this manner this strange event came to pass.

Orlando was the youngest son of Sir Rowland de Boys, who, when he died, left him (Orlando being then very young) to the care of his eldest brother, Oliver, charging Oliver on his blessing to give his brother a good education and provide for him as became the dignity of their ancient house. Oliver proved an unworthy brother, and, disregarding the commands of his dying father, he never put his brother to school, but kept him at home untaught and entirely neglected. But in his nature and in the noble qualities of his mind Orlando so much resembled his excellent father that, without any advantages of education, he seemed like a youth who had been bred with the utmost care; and Oliver so envied the fine person and dignified manners of his untutored brother that at last he wished to destroy him, and to effect this he set on people to persuade him to wrestle with the famous wrestler who, as has been before related, had killed so many men. Now it was this cruel brother's neglect of him which made Orlando say he wished to die, being so friendless.

When, contrary to the wicked hopes he had formed, his brother proved victorious, his envy and malice knew no bounds, and he swore he would burn the chamber where Orlando slept. He was overheard making his vow by one that had been an old and faithful servant to their father, and that loved Orlando because he resembled Sir Rowland. This old man went out to meet him when he returned from the duke's palace, and when he saw Orlando the peril his dear young master was in made him break out into these passionate exclamations: 'O my gentle master, my sweet master! O you memory of old Sir Rowland! Why are you virtuous? Why are you gentle, strong, and valiant? And why would you be so fond to overcome the famous wrestler? Your praise is come too swiftly home before you.'

Orlando, wondering what all this meant, asked him what was the matter. And then the old man told him how his wicked brother, envying the love all people bore him, and now hearing the fame he had gained by his victory in the duke's palace, intended to destroy him by setting fire to his chamber that night, and in conclusion advised him to escape the danger he was in by instant flight; and knowing Orlando had no money, Adam (for that was the good old man's name) had brought out with him his own little hoard, and he said: 'I have five hundred crowns, the thrifty hire I saved under your father and laid by to be provision for me when my old limbs should become unfit for service. Take that, and He that doth the ravens feed be comfort to my age! Here is the gold. All this I give to you. Let me be your servant; though I look old I will do the service of a younger man in all your business and necessities.'

'O good old man!' said Orlando, 'how well appears in you the constant service of the old world! You are not for the fashion of these times. We will go along together, and before your youthful wages are spent I shall light upon some means for both our maintenance.'

Together, then, this faithful servant and his loved master set out; and Orlando and Adam travelled on, uncertain what course to pursue, till they came to the forest of Arden, and there they found themselves in the same distress for want of food that Ganymede and Aliena had been. They wandered on, seeking some human habitation, till they were almost spent with hunger and fatigue.

Adam at last said: 'O my dear master, I die for want of food. I can go no farther!' He then laid himself down, thinking to make that place his grave, and bade his dear master farewell.

Orlando, seeing him in this weak state, took his old servant up in his arms and carried him under the shelter of some pleasant trees;

and he said to him: 'Cheerly, old Adam. Rest your weary limbs here awhile, and do not talk of dying!'

Orlando then searched about to find some food, and he happened to arrive at that part of the forest where the duke was; and he and his friends were just going to eat their dinner, this royal duke being seated on the grass, under no other canopy than the shady covert of some large trees.

Orlando, whom hunger had made desperate, drew his sword, intending to take their meat by force, and said: 'Forbear and eat no more. I must have your food!'

The duke asked him if distress had made him so bold or if he were a rude despiser of good manners. On this Orlando said he was dying with hunger; and then the duke told him he was welcome to sit down and eat with them. Orlando, hearing him speak so gently, put up his sword and blushed with shame at the rude manner in which he had demanded their food.

'Pardon me, I pray you,' said he. 'I thought that all things had been savage here, and therefore I put on the countenance of stern command; but whatever men you are that in this desert, under the shade of melancholy boughs, lose and neglect the creeping hours of time, if ever you have looked on better days, if ever you have been where bells have knolled to church, if you have ever sat at any good man's feast, if ever from your eyelids you have wiped a tear and know what it is to pity or be pitied, may gentle speeches now move you to do me human courtesy!'

The duke replied: 'True it is that we are men (as you say) who have seen better days, and though we have now our habitation in this wild forest, we have lived in towns and cities and have with holy bell been knolled to church, have sat at good men's feasts, and from our eyes have wiped the drops which sacred pity has engendered; therefore sit you down and take of our refreshment as much as will minister to your wants.'

'There is an old poor man,' answered Orlando, 'who has limped after me many a weary step in pure love, oppressed at once with two sad infirmities, age and hunger; till he be satisfied I must not touch a bit.'

'Go, find him out and bring him hither,' said the duke. 'We will forbear to eat till you return.'

Then Orlando went like a doe to find its fawn and give it food; and presently returned, bringing Adam in his arms.

And the duke said, 'Set down your venerable burthen; you are both welcome.'

And they fed the old man and cheered his heart, and he revived and recovered his health and strength again.

The duke enquired who Orlando was; and when he found that he was the son of his old friend, Sir Rowland de Boys, he took him under his protection, and Orlando and his old servant lived with the duke in the forest.

Orlando arrived in the forest not many days after Ganymede and Aliena came there and (as has been before related) bought the shepherd's cottage.

Ganymede and Aliena were strangely surprised to find the name of Rosalind carved on the trees, and love-sonnets fastened to them, all addressed to Rosalind; and while they were wondering how this could be they met Orlando and they perceived the chain which Rosalind had given him about his neck.

Orlando little thought that Ganymede was the fair Princess Rosalind who, by her noble condescension and favour, had so won his heart that he passed his whole time in carving her name upon the trees and writing sonnets in praise of her beauty; but being much pleased with the graceful air of this pretty shepherd-youth, he entered into conversation with him, and he thought he saw a likeness in Ganymede to his beloved Rosalind, but that he had none of the dignified deportment of that noble lady; for Ganymede assumed the forward manners often seen in youths when they are between boys and men, and with much archness and humour talked to Orlando of a certain lover, 'who,' said she, 'haunts our forest, and spoils our young trees with carving Rosalind upon their barks; and he hangs odes upon hawthorns, and elegies on brambles, all praising this same Rosalind. If I could find this lover, I would give him some good counsel that would soon cure him of his love.'

Orlando confessed that he was the fond lover of whom he spoke, and asked Ganymede to give him the good counsel he talked of. The remedy Ganymede proposed, and the counsel he gave him, was that Orlando should come every day to the cottage where he and his sister Aliena dwelt.

'And then,' said Ganymede, 'I will feign myself to be Rosalind, and you shall feign to court me in the same manner as you would do if I was Rosalind, and then I will imitate the fantastic ways of whimsical ladies to their lovers, till I make you ashamed of your love; and this is the way I propose to cure you.'

Orlando had no great faith in the remedy, yet he agreed to come every day to Ganymede's cottage and feign a playful courtship; and every day Orlando visited Ganymede and Aliena, and Orlando called the shepherd Ganymede his Rosalind, and every day talked over all the fine words and flattering compliments which young men delight to use when they court their mistresses. It does not appear, however, that Ganymede made any progress in curing Orlando of his love for Rosalind.

Though Orlando thought all this was but a sportive play (not dreaming that Ganymede was his very Rosalind), yet the opportunity it gave him of saying all the fond things he had in his heart pleased his fancy almost as well as it did Ganymede's, who enjoyed the secret jest in knowing these fine love-speeches were all addressed to the right person.

In this manner many days passed pleasantly on with these young people; and the good-natured Aliena, seeing it made Ganymede happy, let him have his own way and was diverted at the mock-courtship, and did not care to remind Ganymede that the Lady Rosalind had not yet made herself known to the duke her father, whose place of resort in the forest they had learned from Orlando. Ganymede met the duke one day, and had some talk with him, and the duke asked of what parentage he came. Ganymede answered that he came of as good parentage as he did, which made the duke smile, for he did not suspect the pretty shepherd-boy came of royal lineage. Then seeing the duke look well and happy, Ganymede was content to put off all further explanation for a few days longer.

One morning, as Orlando was going to visit Ganymede, he saw a man lying asleep on the ground, and a large green snake had twisted itself about his neck. The snake, seeing Orlando approach, glided away among the bushes. Orlando went nearer, and then he discovered a lioness lie crouching, with her head on the ground, with a catlike watch, waiting until the sleeping man awaked (for it is said that lions will prey on nothing that is dead or sleeping). It seemed as if Orlando was sent by Providence to free the man from the danger of the snake and lioness; but when Orlando looked in the man's face he perceived that the sleeper who was exposed to this double peril was his own brother Oliver, who had so cruelly used him and had threatened to destroy him by fire, and he was almost tempted to leave him a prey to the hungry lioness; but brotherly affection and the gentleness of his nature soon overcame his first anger against his brother; and he drew his sword and attacked the lioness and slew her, and thus preserved his brother's life both from the venomous snake and from the furious lioness; but before Orlando could conquer the lioness she had torn one of his arms with her sharp claws.

While Orlando was engaged with the lioness, Oliver awaked, and, perceiving that his brother Orlando, whom he had so cruelly treated, was saving him from the fury of a wild beast at the risk of his own life, shame and remorse at once seized him, and he repented of his unworthy conduct and besought with many tears his brother's pardon for the injuries he had done him. Orlando rejoiced to see him so penitent, and readily forgave him. They embraced each other and from that hour Oliver loved Orlando with a true brotherly affection, though he had come to the forest bent on his destruction.

The wound in Orlando's arm having bled very much, he found himself too weak to go to visit Ganymede, and therefore he desired his brother to go and tell Ganymede, 'whom,' said Orlando, 'I in sport do call my Rosalind,' the accident which had befallen him.

Thither then Oliver went, and told to Ganymede and Aliena how Orlando had saved his life; and when he had finished the story of Orlando's bravery and his own providential escape he owned to them that he was Orlando's brother who had so cruelly used him; and then he told them of their reconciliation.

The sincere sorrow that Oliver expressed for his offences made such a lively impression on the kind heart of Aliena that she instantly fell in love with him; and Oliver observing how much she pitied the distress he told her he felt for his fault, he as suddenly fell in love with her. But while love was thus stealing into the hearts of Aliena and Oliver, he was no less busy with Ganymede, who, hearing of the danger Orlando had been in, and that he was wounded by the lioness, fainted; and when he recovered he pretended that he had counterfeited the swoon in the imaginary character of Rosalind, and Ganymede said to Oliver: 'Tell your brother Orlando how well I counterfeited a swoon.'

But Oliver saw by the paleness of his complexion that he did really faint, and, much wondering at the weakness of the young man, he said, 'Well, if you did counterfeit, take a good heart and counterfeit to be a man.'

'So I do,' replied Ganymede, truly, 'but I should have been a woman by right.'

Oliver made this visit a very long one, and when at last he returned back to his brother he had much news to tell him; for, besides the account of Ganymede's fainting at the hearing that Orlando was wounded, Oliver told him how he had fallen in love with the fair shepherdess Aliena, and that she had lent a favourable ear to his suit, even in this their first interview; and he talked to his brother, as of a thing almost settled, that he should marry Aliena, saying that he so well loved her that he would live here as a shepherd and settle his estate and house at home upon Orlando.

'You have my consent,' said Orlando. 'Let your wedding be tomorrow, and I will invite the duke and his friends. Go and persuade your shepherdess to agree to this. She is now alone, for, look, here comes her brother.'

Oliver went to Aliena, and Ganymede, whom Orlando had perceived approaching, came to enquire after the health of his wounded friend.

When Orlando and Ganymede began to talk over the sudden

love which had taken place between Oliver and Aliena, Orlando said he had advised his brother to persuade his fair shepherdess to be married on the morrow, and then he added how much he could wish to be married on the same day to his Rosalind.

Ganymede, who well approved of this arrangement, said that if Orlando really loved Rosalind as well as he professed to do, he should have his wish; for on the morrow he would engage to make Rosalind appear in her own person, and also that Rosalind should be willing to marry Orlando.

This seemingly wonderful event, which, as Ganymede was the Lady Rosalind, he could so easily perform, he pretended he would bring to pass by the aid of magic, which he said he had learned of an uncle who was a famous magician.

The fond lover Orlando, half believing and half doubting what he heard, asked Ganymede if he spoke in sober meaning.

'By my life I do,' said Ganymede. 'Therefore put on your best clothes, and bid the duke and your friends to your wedding, for if you desire to be married tomorrow to Rosalind, she shall be here.'

The next morning, Oliver having obtained the consent of Aliena, they came into the presence of the duke, and with them also came Orlando.

They being all assembled to celebrate this double marriage, and as yet only one of the brides appearing, there was much of wondering and conjecture, but they mostly thought that Ganymede was making a jest of Orlando.

The duke, hearing that it was his own daughter that was to be brought in this strange way, asked Orlando if he believed the shepherd-boy could really do what he had promised; and while Orlando was answering that he knew not what to think, Ganymede entered and asked the duke, if he brought his daughter, whether he would consent to her marriage with Orlando.

'That I would,' said the duke, 'if I had kingdoms to give with her.'

Ganymede then said to Orlando, 'And you say you will marry her if I bring her here.'

'That I would,' said Orlando, 'if I were king of many kingdoms.'

Ganymede and Aliena then went out together, and, Ganymede throwing off his male attire, and being once more dressed in woman's apparel, quickly became Rosalind without the power of magic; and Aliena, changing her country garb for her own rich clothes, was with as little trouble transformed into the lady Celia.

While they were gone, the duke said to Orlando that he thought the shepherd Ganymede very like his daughter Rosalind; and Orlando said he also had observed the resemblance.

They had no time to wonder how all this would end, for Rosalind and Celia, in their own clothes, entered, and, no longer pretending that it was by the power of magic that she came there, Rosalind threw herself on her knees before her father and begged his blessing. It seemed so wonderful to all present that she should so suddenly appear, that it might well have passed for magic; but Rosalind would no longer trifle with her father, and told him the story of her banishment, and of her dwelling in the forest as a shepherd-boy, her cousin Celia passing as her sister.

The duke ratified the consent he had already given to the marriage; and Orlando and Rosalind, Oliver and Celia, were married at the same time. And though their wedding could not be celebrated in this wild forest with any of the parade of splendour usual on such occasions, yet a happier wedding-day was never passed. And while they were eating their venison under the cool shade of the pleasant trees, as if nothing should be wanting to complete the felicity of this good duke and the true lovers, an unexpected messenger arrived to tell the duke the joyful news that his dukedom was restored to him.

The usurper, enraged at the flight of his daughter Celia, and hearing that every day men of great worth resorted to the forest of Arden to join the lawful duke in his exile, much envying that his brother should be so highly respected in his adversity, put himself at the head of a large force and advanced towards the forest, intending to seize his brother and put him with all his faithful followers to the sword; but by a wonderful interposition of Providence this bad brother was converted from his evil intention, for just as he entered the skirts of the wild forest he was met by an old religious man, a hermit, with whom he had much talk and who in the end completely turned his heart from his wicked design. Thenceforward he became a true penitent, and resolved, relinquishing his unjust dominion, to spend the remainder of his days in a religious house. The first act of his newly conceived penitence was to send a messenger to his brother (as has been related) to offer to restore to him his dukedom, which he had usurped so long, and with it the lands and revenues of his friends, the faithful followers of his adversity.

This joyful news, as unexpected as it was welcome, came opportunely to heighten the festivity and rejoicings at the wedding of the princesses. Celia complimented her cousin on this good fortune which had happened to the duke, Rosalind's father, and wished her joy very sincerely, though she herself was no longer heir to the dukedom, but by this restoration which her father had made, Rosalind was now the heir, so completely was the love of these two cousins unmixed with anything of jealousy or of envy.

The duke had now an opportunity of rewarding those true friends who had stayed with him in his banishment; and these worthy followers, though they had patiently shared his adverse fortune, were very well pleased to return in peace and prosperity to the palace of their lawful duke.

The Two Gentlemen of Verona

There lived in the city of Verona two young gentlemen, whose names were Valentine and Proteus, between whom a firm and uninterrupted friendship had long subsisted. They pursued their studies together, and their hours of leisure were always passed in each other's company, except when Proteus visited a lady he was in love with. And these visits to his mistress, and this passion of Proteus for the fair Julia, were the only topics on which these two friends disagreed; for Valentine, not being himself a lover, was sometimes a little weary of hearing his friend forever talking of his Julia, and then he would laugh at Proteus, and in pleasant terms ridicule the passion of love, and declare that no such idle fancies should ever enter his head, greatly preferring (as he said) the free and happy life he led to the anxious hopes and fears of the lover Proteus.

One morning Valentine came to Proteus to tell him that they must for a time be separated, for that he was going to Milan. Proteus, unwilling to part with his friend, used many arguments to prevail upon Valentine not to leave him. But Valentine said: 'Cease to persuade me, my loving Proteus. I will not, like a sluggard, wear out my youth in idleness at home. Home-keeping youths have ever homely wits. If your affection were not chained to the sweet glances of your honoured Julia, I would entreat you to accompany me, to see the wonders of the world abroad; but since you are a lover, love on still, and may your love be prosperous!'

They parted with mutual expressions of unalterable friendship.

'Sweet Valentine, adieu!' said Proteus. 'Think on me when you see some rare object worthy of notice in your travels, and wish me partaker of your happiness.'

Valentine began his journey that same day towards Milan; and when his friend had left him, Proteus sat down to write a letter to Julia, which he gave to her maid Lucetta to deliver to her mistress.

Julia loved Proteus as well as he did her, but she was a lady of a noble spirit, and she thought it did not become her maiden dignity too easily to be won; therefore she affected to be insensible of his passion and gave him much uneasiness in the prosecution of his suit.

And when Lucetta offered the letter to Julia she would not receive it, and chid her maid for taking letters from Proteus, and ordered her to leave the room. But she so much wished to see what was written in the letter that she soon called in her maid again; and when Lucetta returned she said, 'What o'clock is it?'

Lucetta, who knew her mistress more desired to see the letter than to know the time of day, without answering her question again offered the rejected letter. Julia, angry that her maid should thus take the liberty of seeming to know what she really wanted, tore the letter in pieces and threw it on the floor, ordering her maid once more out of the room. As Lucetta was retiring, she stopped to pick up the fragments of the torn letter; but Julia, who meant not so to part with them, said, in pretended anger, 'Go, get you gone, and let the papers lie; you would be fingering them to anger me.'

Julia then began to piece together as well as she could the torn fragments. She first made out these words, 'Love-wounded Proteus'; and lamenting over these and such like loving words, which she made out though they were all torn asunder, or, she said, *wounded* (the expression 'Love-wounded Proteus' giving her that idea), she talked to these kind words, telling them she would lodge them in her bosom as in a bed, till their wounds were healed, and that she would kiss each several piece to make amends.

In this manner she went on talking with a pretty, ladylike childishness, till, finding herself unable to make out the whole, and vexed at her own ingratitude in destroying such sweet and loving words, as she called them, she wrote a much kinder letter to Proteus than she had ever done before.

Proteus was greatly delighted at receiving this favourable answer to his letter. And while he was reading it he exclaimed, 'Sweet love! sweet lines! sweet life!'

In the midst of his raptures he was interrupted by his father. 'How now?' said the old gentleman. 'What letter are you reading there?'

'My lord,' replied Proteus, 'it is a letter from my friend Valentine, at Milan.'

'Lend me the letter,' said his father. 'Let me see what news.'

'There is no news, my lord,' said Proteus, greatly alarmed, 'but that he writes how well beloved he is of the Duke of Milan, who daily graces him with favours, and how he wishes me with him, the partner of his fortune.'

'And how stand you affected to his wish?' asked the father.

'As one relying on your lordship's will and not depending on his friendly wish,' said Proteus.

Now it had happened that Proteus's father had just been talking with a friend on this very subject. His friend had said he wondered his lordship suffered his son to spend his youth at home while most men were sending their sons to seek preferment abroad.

'Some,' said he, 'to the wars, to try their fortunes there, and some to discover islands far away, and some to study in foreign universities. And there is his companion Valentine; he is gone to the Duke of Milan's court. Your son is fit for any of these things, and it will be a great disadvantage to him in his riper age not to have travelled in his youth.'

Proteus's father thought the advice of his friend was very good, and upon Proteus telling him that Valentine 'wished him with him, the partner of his fortune', he at once determined to send his son to Milan; and without giving Proteus any reason for this sudden resolution, it being the usual habit of this positive old gentleman to command his son, not reason with him, he said: 'My will is the same as Valentine's wish.' And seeing his son look astonished, he added: 'Look not amazed, that I so suddenly resolve you shall spend some time in the Duke of Milan's court; for what I will I will, and there is an end. Tomorrow be in readiness to go. Make no excuses, for I am peremptory.'

Proteus knew it was of no use to make objections to his father, who never suffered him to dispute his will; and he blamed himself for telling his father an untruth about Julia's letter, which had brought upon him the sad necessity of leaving her.

Now that Julia found she was going to lose Proteus for so long a time she no longer pretended indifference; and they bade each other a mournful farewell, with many vows of love and constancy. Proteus and Julia exchanged rings, which they both promised to keep for ever in remembrance of each other; and thus, taking a sorrowful leave, Proteus set out on his journey to Milan, the abode of his friend Valentine.

Valentine was in reality what Proteus had feigned to his father, in high favour with the Duke of Milan; and another event had happened to him of which Proteus did not even dream, for Valentine had given up the freedom of which he used so much to boast, and was become as passionate a lover as Proteus.

She who had wrought this wondrous change in Valentine was the Lady Silvia, daughter of the Duke of Milan, and she also loved him; but they concealed their love from the duke, because, although he showed much kindness for Valentine and invited him every day to his palace, yet he designed to marry his daughter to a young courtier whose name was Thurio. Silvia despised this Thurio, for he had none of the fine sense and excellent qualities of Valentine.

These two rivals, Thurio and Valentine, were one day on a visit to Silvia, and Valentine was entertaining Silvia with turning everything Thurio said into ridicule, when the duke himself entered the room and told Valentine the welcome news of his friend Proteus's arrival.

Valentine said, 'If I had wished a thing, it would have been to have seen him here!' And then he highly praised Proteus to the duke, saying, 'My lord, though I have been a truant of my time, yet hath my friend made use and fair advantage of his days, and is complete in person and in mind, in all good grace to grace a gentleman.'

'Welcome him, then, according to his worth,' said the duke. 'Silvia, I speak to you, and you, Sir Thurio; for Valentine, I need not bid him do so.'

They were here interrupted by the entrance of Proteus, and Valentine introduced him to Silvia, saying, 'Sweet lady, entertain him to be my fellow-servant to your ladyship.'

When Valentine and Proteus had ended their visit, and were alone together, Valentine said: 'Now tell me how all does from whence you came? How does your lady, and how thrives your love?'

Proteus replied: 'My tales of love used to weary you. I know you joy not in a love discourse.'

'Aye, Proteus,' returned Valentine, 'but that life is altered now. I have done penance for condemning love. For in revenge of my contempt of love, love has chased sleep from my enthralled eyes. O gentle Proteus, Love is a mighty lord, and hath so humbled me that I confess there is no woe like his correction nor no such joy on earth as in his service. I now like no discourse except it be of love. Now I can break my fast, dine, sup, and sleep upon the very name of love.'

This acknowledgement of the change which love had made in the disposition of Valentine was a great triumph to his friend Proteus. But 'friend' Proteus must be called no longer, for the same all-powerful deity Love, of whom they were speaking (yea, even while they were talking of the change he had made in Valentine), was working in the heart of Proteus; and he, who had till this time been a pattern of true love and perfect friendship, was now, in one short interview with Silvia, become a false friend and a faithless lover; for at the first sight of Silvia all his love for Julia vanished away like a dream, nor did his long friendship for Valentine deter him from endeavouring to supplant him in her affections; and although, as it will always be, when people of dispositions naturally good become unjust, he had many scruples before he determined to forsake Julia and become the rival of Valentine, yet he at length overcame his sense of duty and yielded himself up, almost without remorse, to his new unhappy passion.

Valentine imparted to him in confidence the whole history of his love, and how carefully they had concealed it from the duke her father, and told him that, despairing of ever being able to obtain his consent, he had prevailed upon Silvia to leave her father's palace that night and go with him to Mantua; then he showed Proteus a ladder of ropes by help of which he meant to assist Silvia to get out of one of the windows of the palace after it was dark.

Upon hearing this faithful recital of his friend's dearest secrets, it is hardly possible to be believed, but so it was that Proteus resolved to go to the duke and disclose the whole to him.

This false friend began his tale with many artful speeches to the duke, such as that by the laws of friendship he ought to conceal what he was going to reveal, but that the gracious favour the duke had shown him, and the duty he owed his grace, urged him to tell that which else no worldly good should draw from him. He then told all he had heard from Valentine, not omitting the ladder of ropes and the manner in which Valentine meant to conceal them under a long cloak.

The duke thought Proteus quite a miracle of integrity, in that he preferred telling his friend's intention rather than he would conceal an unjust action; highly commended him, and promised him not to let Valentine know from whom he had learned this intelligence, but by some artifice to make Valentine betray the secret himself. For this purpose the duke awaited the coming of Valentine in the evening, whom he soon saw hurrying towards the palace, and he perceived somewhat was wrapped within his cloak, which he concluded was the rope ladder.

The duke, upon this, stopped him, saying, 'Whither away so fast, Valentine?'

'May it please your grace,' said Valentine, 'there is a messenger that stays to bear my letters to my friends, and I am going to deliver them.'

Now this falsehood of Valentine's had no better success in the event than the untruth Proteus told his father.

'Be they of much import?' said the duke.

'No more, my lord,' said Valentine, 'than to tell my father I am well and happy at your grace's court.'

'Nay then,' said the duke, 'no matter; stay with me a while. I wish your counsel about some affairs that concern me nearly.'

He then told Valentine an artful story, as a prelude to draw his secret from him, saying that Valentine knew he wished to match his daughter with Thurio, but that she was stubborn and disobedient to his commands.

'Neither regarding,' said he, 'that she is my child nor fearing me as if I were her father. And I may say to thee this pride of hers has drawn my love from her. I had thought my age should have been cherished by her childlike duty. I now am resolved to take a wife, and turn her out to whosoever will take her in. Let her beauty be her wedding dower, for me and my possessions she esteems not.'

Valentine, wondering where all this would end, made answer, 'And what would your grace have me to do in all this?'

'Why,' said the duke, 'the lady I would wish to marry is nice and coy and does not much esteem my aged eloquence. Besides, the fashion of courtship is much changed since I was young. Now I would willingly have you to be my tutor to instruct me how I am to woo.'

Valentine gave him a general idea of the modes of courtship then practised by young men when they wished to win a fair lady's love, such as presents, frequent visits, and the like.

The duke replied to this that the lady did refuse a present which he sent her, and that she was so strictly kept by her father that no man might have access to her by day.

'Why, then,' said Valentine, 'you must visit her by night.'

'But at night,' said the artful duke, who was now coming to the drift of his discourse, 'her doors are fast locked.'

Valentine then unfortunately proposed that the duke should get into the lady's chamber at night by means of a ladder of ropes, saying he would procure him one fitting for that purpose; and in conclusion advised him to conceal this ladder of ropes under such a cloak as that which he now wore.

'Lend me your cloak,' said the duke, who had feigned this long story on purpose to have a pretence to get off the cloak; so upon saying these words he caught hold of Valentine's cloak and, throwing it back, he discovered not only the ladder of ropes but also a letter of Silvia's, which he instantly opened and read; and this letter contained a full account of their intended elopement. The duke, after upbraiding Valentine for his ingratitude in thus returning the favour he had shown him, by endeavouring to steal away his daughter, banished him from the court and city of Milan for ever, and Valentine was forced to depart that night without even seeing Silvia.

While Proteus at Milan was thus injuring Valentine, Julia at Verona was regretting the absence of Proteus; and her regard for him at last so far overcame her sense of propriety that she resolved to leave Verona and seek her lover at Milan; and to secure herself from danger on the road she dressed her maiden Lucetta and herself in men's clothes, and they set out in this disguise, and arrived at Milan soon after Valentine was banished from that city through the treachery of Proteus.

Julia entered Milan about noon, and she took up her abode at an inn; and, her thoughts being all on her dear Proteus, she entered into conversation with the innkeeper – or host, as he was called – thinking by that means to learn some news of Proteus.

The host was greatly pleased that this handsome young gentleman (as he took her to be), who from his appearance he concluded was of high rank, spoke so familiarly to him, and, being a good-natured man, he was sorry to see him look so melancholy; and to amuse his young guest he offered to take him to hear some fine music, with which, he said, a gentleman that evening was going to serenade his mistress.

The reason Julia looked so very melancholy was, that she did not well know what Proteus would think of the imprudent step she had taken, for she knew he had loved her for her noble maiden pride and dignity of character, and she feared she should lower herself in his esteem; and this it was that made her wear a sad and thoughtful countenance.

She gladly accepted the offer of the host to go with him and hear the music; for she secretly hoped she might meet Proteus by the way.

But when she came to the palace whither the host conducted her, a very different effect was produced to what the kind host intended; for there, to her heart's sorrow, she beheld her lover, the inconstant Proteus, serenading the Lady Silvia with music, and addressing discourse of love and admiration to her. And Julia overheard Silvia from a window talk with Proteus, and reproach him for forsaking his own true lady, and for his ingratitude to his friend Valentine; and then Silvia left the window, not choosing to listen to his music and his fine speeches; for she was a faithful lady to her banished Valentine, and abhorred the ungenerous conduct of his false friend, Proteus.

Though Julia was in despair at what she had just witnessed, yet did she still love the truant Proteus; and hearing that he had lately parted with a servant, she contrived, with the assistance of her host, the friendly innkeeper, to hire herself to Proteus as a page; and Proteus knew not she was Julia, and he sent her with letters and presents to her rival, Silvia, and he even sent by her the very ring she gave him as a parting gift at Verona.

When she went to that lady with the ring she was most glad to find that Silvia utterly rejected the suit of Proteus; and Julia – or the page Sebastian, as she was called – entered into conversation with Silvia about Proteus's first love, the forsaken Lady Julia. She putting in (as one may say) a good word for herself, said she knew Julia; as well she might, being herself the Julia of whom she spoke; telling how fondly Julia loved her master, Proteus, and how his unkind neglect would grieve her. And then she with a pretty equivocation went on: 'Julia is about my height, and of my complexion, the colour of her eyes and hair the same as mine.' And indeed Julia looked a most beautiful youth in her boy's attire.

Silvia was moved to pity this lovely lady who was so sadly forsaken by the man she loved; and when Julia offered the ring which

Proteus had sent, refused it, saying: 'The more shame for him that he sends me that ring. I will not take it, for I have often heard him say his Julia gave it to him. I love thee, gentle youth, for pitying her, poor lady! Here is a purse; I give it you for Julia's sake.'

These comfortable words coming from her kind rival's tongue cheered the drooping heart of the disguised lady.

But to return to the banished Valentine, who scarce knew which way to bend his course, being unwilling to return home to his father a disgraced and banished man. As he was wandering over a lonely forest, not far distant from Milan, where he had left his heart's dear treasure, the Lady Silvia, he was set upon by robbers, who demanded his money.

Valentine told them that he was a man crossed by adversity, that he was going into banishment, and that he had no money, the clothes he had on being all his riches.

The robbers, hearing that he was a distressed man, and being struck with his noble air and manly behaviour, told him if he would live with them and be their chief, or captain, they would put themselves under his command; but that if he refused to accept their offer they would kill him.

Valentine, who cared little what became of himself, said he would consent to live with them and be their captain, provided they did no outrage on women or poor passengers.

Thus the noble Valentine became, like Robin Hood, of whom we read in ballads, a captain of robbers and outlawed banditti; and in this situation he was found by Silvia, and in this manner it came to pass.

Silvia, to avoid a marriage with Thurio, whom her father insisted upon her no longer refusing, came at last to the resolution of following Valentine to Mantua, at which place she had heard her lover had taken refuge; but in this account she was misinformed, for he still lived in the forest among the robbers, bearing the name of their captain, but taking no part in their depredations, and using the authority which they had imposed upon him in no other way than to compel them to show compassion to the travellers they robbed.

Silvia contrived to effect her escape from her father's palace in company with a worthy old gentleman whose name was Eglamour, whom she took along with her for protection on the road. She had to pass through the forest where Valentine and the banditti dwelt; and one of these robbers seized on Silvia, and would also have taken Eglamour, but he escaped.

The robber who had taken Silvia, seeing the terror she was in, bade her not be alarmed, for that he was only going to carry her to a cave where his captain lived, and that she need not be afraid, for their captain had an honourable mind and always showed humanity to women. Silvia found little comfort in hearing she was going to be carried as a prisoner before the captain of a lawless banditti.

'O Valentine,' she cried, 'this I endure for thee!'

But as the robber was conveying her to the cave of his captain he was stopped by Proteus, who, still attended by Julia in the disguise of a page, having heard of the flight of Silvia, had traced her steps to this forest. Proteus now rescued her from the hands of the robber; but scarce had she time to thank him for the service he had done her before he began to distress her afresh with his love suit; and while he was rudely pressing her to consent to marry him, and his page (the forlorn Julia) was standing beside him in great anxiety of mind, fearing lest the great service which Proteus had just done to Silvia should win her to show him some favour, they were all strangely surprised with the sudden appearance of Valentine, who, having heard his robbers had taken a lady prisoner, came to console and relieve her.

Proteus was courting Silvia, and he was so much ashamed of being caught by his friend that he was all at once seized with penitence and remorse; and he expressed such a lively sorrow for the injuries he had done to Valentine that Valentine, whose nature was noble and generous, even to a romantic degree, not only forgave and restored him to his former place in his friendship, but in a sudden flight of heroism he said: 'I freely do forgive you; and all the interest I have in Silvia I give it up to you.'

Julia, who was standing beside her master as a page, hearing this strange offer, and fearing Proteus would not be able with this new-found virtue to refuse Silvia, fainted; and they were all employed in recovering her, else would Silvia have been offended at being thus made over to Proteus, though she could scarcely think that Valentine would long persevere in this overstrained and too generous act of friendship. When Julia recovered from the fainting fit, she said: 'I had forgot, my master ordered me to deliver this ring to Silvia.'

Proteus, looking upon the ring, saw that it was the one he gave to Julia in return for that which he received from her and which he had sent by the supposed page to Silvia.

'How is this?' said he. 'This is Julia's ring. How came you by it, boy?'

Julia answered, 'Julia herself did give it me, and Julia herself hath brought it hither.'

Proteus, now looking earnestly upon her, plainly perceived that the page Sebastian was no other than the Lady Julia herself; and the proof she had given of her constancy and true love so wrought in him that his love for her returned into his heart, and he took again his own dear lady and joyfully resigned all pretensions to the Lady Silvia to Valentine, who had so well deserved her.

Proteus and Valentine were expressing their happiness in their reconciliation, and in the love of their faithful ladies, when they were surprised with the sight of the Duke of Milan and Thurio, who came there in pursuit of Silvia.

Thurio first approached, and attempted to seize Silvia, saying, 'Silvia is mine.'

Upon this Valentine said to him in a very spirited manner: 'Thurio, keep back. If once again you say that Silvia is yours, you shall embrace your death. Here she stands, take but possession of her with a touch! I dare you but to breathe upon my love.'

Hearing this threat, Thurio, who was a great coward, drew back, and said he cared not for her and that none but a fool would fight for a girl who loved him not.

The duke, who was a very brave man himself, said now, in great anger, 'The more base and degenerate in you to take such means for her as you have done and leave her on such slight conditions.'

Then turning to Valentine he said: 'I do applaud your spirit,

Valentine, and think you worthy of an empress's love. You shall have Silvia, for you have well deserved her.'

Valentine then with great humility kissed the duke's hand and accepted the noble present which he had made him of his daughter with becoming thankfulness, taking occasion of this joyful minute to entreat the good-humoured duke to pardon the thieves with whom he had associated in the forest, assuring him that when reformed and restored to society there would be found among them many good, and fit for great employment; for the most of them had been banished, like Valentine, for state offences, rather than for any black crimes they had been guilty of. To this the ready duke consented. And now nothing remained but that Proteus, the false friend, was ordained, by way of penance for his love-prompted faults, to be present at the recital of the whole story of his loves and falsehoods before the duke. And the shame of the recital to his awakened conscience was judged sufficient punishment; which being done, the lovers, all four, returned back to Milan, and their nuptials were solemnised in the presence of the duke, with high triumphs and feasting.

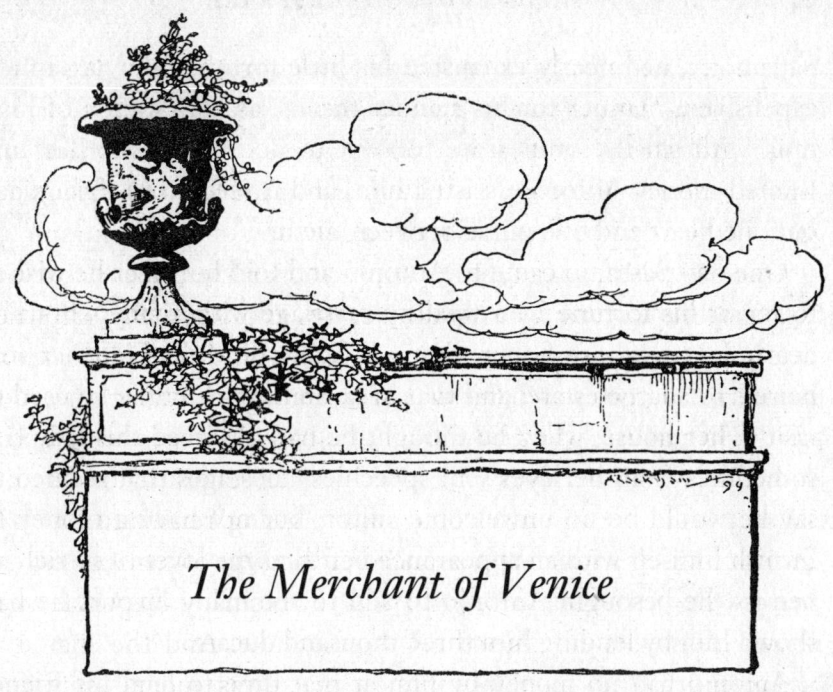

The Merchant of Venice

Shylock, the Jew, lived at Venice. He was a usurer who had amassed an immense fortune by lending money at great interest to Christian merchants. Shylock, being a hard-hearted man, exacted the payment of the money he lent with such severity that he was much disliked by all good men, and particularly by Antonio, a young merchant of Venice; and Shylock as much hated Antonio, because he used to lend money to people in distress, and would never take any interest for the money he lent; therefore there was great enmity between this covetous Jew and the generous merchant Antonio. Whenever Antonio met Shylock on the Rialto (or Exchange), he used to reproach him with his usuries and hard dealings, which the Jew would bear with seeming patience, while he secretly meditated revenge.

Antonio was the kindest man that lived, the best conditioned, and had the most unwearied spirit in doing courtesies; indeed, he was one in whom the ancient Roman honour more appeared than in any that drew breath in Italy. He was greatly beloved by all his fellow-citizens; but the friend who was nearest and dearest to his heart was Bassanio, a noble Venetian, who, having but a small patrimony, had nearly exhausted his little fortune by living in too expensive a manner for his slender means, as young men of high rank with small fortunes are too apt to do. Whenever Bassanio wanted money Antonio assisted him; and it seemed as if they had but one heart and one purse between them.

One day Bassanio came to Antonio and told him that he wished to repair his fortune by a wealthy marriage with a lady whom he dearly loved, whose father, that was lately dead, had left her sole heiress to a large estate; and that in her father's lifetime he used to visit at her house, when he thought he had observed this lady had sometimes from her eyes sent speechless messages that seemed to say he would be no unwelcome suitor; but not having money to furnish himself with an appearance befitting the lover of so rich an heiress, he besought Antonio to add to the many favours he had shown him by lending him three thousand ducats.

Antonio had no money by him at that time to lend his friend; but expecting soon to have some ships come home laden with merchandise, he said he would go to Shylock, the rich moneylender, and borrow the money upon the credit of those ships.

Antonio and Bassanio went together to Shylock, and Antonio asked the Jew to lend him three thousand ducats upon any interest he should require, to be paid out of the merchandise contained in his ships at sea.

On this, Shylock thought within himself: 'If I can once catch him on the hip, I will feed fat the ancient grudge I bear him. He hates our Jewish nation; he lends out money gratis; and among the merchants he rails at me and my well-earned bargains, which he calls interest. Cursed be my tribe if I forgive him!'

Antonio, finding he was musing within himself and did not answer, and being impatient for the money, said: 'Shylock, do you hear? Will you lend the money?'

To this question the Jew replied: 'Signor Antonio, on the Rialto many a time and often you have railed at me about my moneys and my usuries, and I have borne it with a patient shrug, for sufferance is the badge of all our tribe; and then you have called me unbeliever, cut-throat dog, and spit upon my Jewish garments, and spurned at me with your foot, as if I was a cur. Well, then, it now appears you need my help, and you come to me and say, *Shylock, lend me moneys.* Has a dog money? Is it possible a cur should lend three thousand ducats? Shall I bend low and say, "Fair sir, you spit upon me on Wednesday last; another time you called me dog, and for these courtesies I am to lend you moneys." '

Antonio replied: 'I am as like to call you so again, to spit on you again, and spurn you, too. If you will lend me this money, lend it not to me as to a friend, but rather lend it to me as to an enemy, that, if I break, you may with better face exact the penalty.'

'Why, look you,' said Shylock, 'how you storm! I would be friends with you and have your love. I will forget the shames you have put upon me. I will supply your wants and take no interest for my money.'

This seemingly kind offer greatly surprised Antonio; and then Shylock, still pretending kindness and that all he did was to gain Antonio's love, again said he would lend him the three thousand ducats, and take no interest for his money; only Antonio should go with him to a lawyer and there sign in merry sport a bond that, if he did not repay the money by a certain day, he would forfeit a pound of flesh, to be cut off from any part of his body that Shylock pleased.

'Content,' said Antonio. 'I will sign to this bond, and say there is much kindness in the Jew.'

Bassanio said Antonio should not sign to such a bond for him; but still Antonio insisted that he would sign it, for that before the day of payment came his ships would return laden with many times the value of the money.

Shylock, hearing this debate, exclaimed: 'O Father Abraham, what suspicious people these Christians are! Their own hard dealings teach them to suspect the thoughts of others. I pray you tell me this, Bassanio: if he should break his day, what should I gain by the exaction of the forfeiture? A pound of man's flesh, taken from a man, is not so estimable, profitable, neither, as the flesh of mutton or beef. I say, to buy his favour I offer this friendship: if he will take it, so; if not, adieu.'

At last, against the advice of Bassanio, who, notwithstanding all the Jew had said of his kind intentions, did not like his friend should run the hazard of this shocking penalty for his sake, Antonio signed the bond, thinking it really was (as the Jew said) merely in sport.

The rich heiress that Bassanio wished to marry lived near Venice, at a place called Belmont. Her name was Portia, and in the graces of her person and her mind she was nothing inferior to that Portia, of whom we read, who was Cato's daughter and the wife of Brutus.

Bassanio being so kindly supplied with money by his friend Antonio, at the hazard of his life, set out for Belmont with a splendid train and attended by a gentleman of the name of Gratiano.

Bassanio proving successful in his suit, Portia in a short time consented to accept of him for a husband.

Bassanio confessed to Portia that he had no fortune and that his high birth and noble ancestry were all that he could boast of; she, who loved him for his worthy qualities and had riches enough not to regard wealth in a husband, answered, with a graceful modesty, that she would wish herself a thousand times more fair, and ten thousand times more rich, to be more worthy of him; and then the accomplished Portia prettily dispraised herself and said she was an unlessoned girl, unschooled, unpractised, yet not so old but that she could learn, and that she would commit her gentle spirit to be directed and governed by him in all things; and she said: 'Myself and what is mine to you and yours is now converted. But yesterday, Bassanio, I was the lady of this fair mansion, queen of myself, and mistress over these servants; and now this house, these servants, and myself are yours, my lord; I give them with this ring,' presenting a ring to Bassanio.

Bassanio was so overpowered with gratitude and wonder at the gracious manner in which the rich and noble Portia accepted of a man of his humble fortunes that he could not express his joy and reverence to the dear lady who so honoured him, by anything but broken words of love and thankfulness; and, taking the ring, he vowed never to part with it.

Gratiano and Nerissa, Portia's waiting-maid, were in attendance upon their lord and lady when Portia so gracefully promised to become the obedient wife of Bassanio; and Gratiano, wishing Bassanio and the generous lady joy, desired permission to be married at the same time.

'With all my heart, Gratiano,' said Bassanio, 'if you can get a wife.'

Gratiano then said that he loved the Lady Portia's fair waiting-gentlewoman, Nerissa, and that she had promised to be his wife if her lady married Bassanio. Portia asked Nerissa if this was true. Nerissa replied: 'Madam, it is so, if you approve of it.'

Portia willingly consenting, Bassanio pleasantly said: 'Then our wedding-feast shall be much honoured by your marriage, Gratiano.'

The happiness of these lovers was sadly crossed at this moment by the entrance of a messenger, who brought a letter from Antonio containing fearful tidings. When Bassanio read Antonio's letter, Portia feared it was to tell him of the death of some dear friend, he looked so pale; and, enquiring what was the news which had so distressed him, he said: 'Oh, sweet Portia, here are a few of the unpleasantest words that ever blotted paper! Gentle lady, when I first imparted my love to you, I freely told you all the wealth I had ran in my veins; but I should have told you that I had less than nothing, being in debt.'

Bassanio then told Portia what has been here related, of his borrowing the money of Antonio, and of Antonio's procuring it of Shylock the Jew, and of the bond by which Antonio had engaged to forfeit a pound of flesh if it was not repaid by a certain day: and then Bassanio read Antonio's letter, the words of which were: '*Sweet Bassanio, my ships are all lost, my bond to the Jew is forfeited, and since in paying it is impossible I should live, I could wish to see you at my death; notwithstanding, use your pleasure. If your love for me do not persuade you to come, let not my letter.*'

'Oh, my dear love,' said Portia, 'despatch all business and begone; you shall have gold to pay the money twenty times over, before this kind friend shall lose a hair by my Bassanio's fault; and as you are so dearly bought, I will dearly love you.'

Portia then said she would be married to Bassanio before he set out, to give him a legal right to her money; and that same day they were married, and Gratiano was also married to Nerissa; and Bassanio and Gratiano, the instant they were married, set out in great haste for Venice, where Bassanio found Antonio in prison.

The day of payment being past, the cruel Jew would not accept of the money which Bassanio offered him, but insisted upon having a pound of Antonio's flesh. A day was appointed to try this shocking cause before the Duke of Venice, and Bassanio awaited in dreadful suspense the event of the trial.

When Portia parted with her husband she spoke cheeringly to him and bade him bring his dear friend along with him when he returned; yet she feared it would go hard with Antonio, and when she was left alone she began to think and consider within herself if she could by any means be instrumental in saving the life of her dear Bassanio's friend. And notwithstanding when she wished to honour her Bassanio she had said to him, with such a meek and wifelike grace, that she would submit in all things to be governed by his superior wisdom, yet being now called forth into action by the peril of her honoured husband's friend, she did nothing doubt her own powers, and by the sole guidance of her own true and perfect judgement at once resolved to go herself to Venice and speak in Antonio's defence.

Portia had a relation who was a counsellor in the law; to this gentleman, whose name was Bellario, she wrote, and, stating the case to him, desired his opinion, and that with his advice he would also send her the dress worn by a counsellor. When the messenger returned he brought letters from Bellario of advice how to proceed, and also everything necessary for her equipment.

Portia dressed herself and her maid Nerissa in men's apparel, and, putting on the robes of a counsellor, she took Nerissa along with her as her clerk; setting out immediately, they arrived at Venice on the very day of the trial. The cause was just going to be heard before the Duke and Senators of Venice in the Senate House when Portia entered this high court of justice and presented a letter from Bellario, in which that learned counsellor wrote to the duke, saying he would have come himself to plead for Antonio but that he was prevented by sickness, and he requested that the learned young Doctor Balthasar (so he called Portia) might be permitted to plead in his stead. This the Duke granted, much wondering at the youthful appearance of the stranger, who was prettily disguised by her counsellor's robes and her large wig.

And now began this important trial. Portia looked around her and she saw the merciless Jew; and she saw Bassanio, but he knew her not in her disguise. He was standing beside Antonio, in an agony of distress and fear for his friend.

The importance of the arduous task Portia had engaged in gave this tender lady courage, and she boldly proceeded in the duty she had undertaken to perform. And first of all she addressed herself to Shylock; and allowing that he had a right by the Venetian law to have the forfeit expressed in the bond, she spoke so sweetly of the noble quality of *mercy* as would have softened any heart but the unfeeling Shylock's, saying that it dropped as the gentle rain from heaven upon the place beneath; and how mercy was a double blessing, it blessed him that gave and him that received it; and how it became monarchs better than their crowns, being an attribute of God Himself; and that earthly power came nearest to God's in proportion as mercy tempered justice; and she bade Shylock remember that as we all pray for mercy, that same prayer should teach us to show mercy. Shylock only answered her by desiring to have the penalty forfeited in the bond.

'Is he not able to pay the money?' asked Portia.

Bassanio then offered the Jew the payment of the three thousand ducats as many times over as he should desire; which Shylock refusing, and still insisting upon having a pound of Antonio's flesh, Bassanio begged the learned young counsellor would endeavour to wrest the law a little, to save Antonio's life. But Portia gravely answered that laws once established must never be altered. Shylock, hearing Portia say that the law might not be altered, it seemed to him that she was pleading in his favour, and he said: 'A Daniel is come to judgment! O wise young judge, how I do honour you! How much elder are you than your looks!'

Portia now desired Shylock to let her look at the bond; and when she had read it she said: 'This bond is forfeited, and by this the Jew may lawfully claim a pound of flesh, to be by him cut off nearest

Antonio's heart.' Then she said to Shylock, 'Be merciful; take the money and bid me tear the bond.'

But no mercy would the cruel Shylock show; and he said, 'By my soul, I swear there is no power in the tongue of man to alter me.'

'Why, then, Antonio,' said Portia, 'you must prepare your bosom for the knife.' And while Shylock was sharpening a long knife with great eagerness to cut off the pound of flesh, Portia said to Antonio, 'Have you anything to say?'

Antonio with a calm resignation replied that he had but little to say, for that he had prepared his mind for death. Then he said to Bassanio: 'Give me your hand, Bassanio! Fare you well! Grieve not that I am fallen into this misfortune for you. Commend me to your honourable wife and tell her how I have loved you!'

Bassanio in the deepest affliction replied: 'Antonio, I am married to a wife who is as dear to me as life itself; but life itself, my wife, and all the world are not esteemed with me above your life. I would lose all, I would sacrifice all to this devil here, to deliver you.'

Portia hearing this, though the kind-hearted lady was not at all offended with her husband for expressing the love he owed to so true a friend as Antonio in these strong terms, yet could not help answering: 'Your wife would give you little thanks, if she were present, to hear you make this offer.'

And then Gratiano, who loved to copy what his lord did, thought he must make a speech like Bassanio's, and he said, in Nerissa's hearing, who was writing in her clerk's dress by the side of Portia: 'I have a wife whom I protest I love. I wish she were in heaven if she could but entreat some power there to change the cruel temper of this currish Jew.'

'It is well you wish this behind her back, else you would have but an unquiet house,' said Nerissa.

Shylock now cried out, impatiently: 'We trifle time. I pray pronounce the sentence.'

And now all was awful expectation in the court, and every heart was full of grief for Antonio.

Portia asked if the scales were ready to weigh the flesh; and she

Shylock was sharpening a long knife

said to the Jew, 'Shylock, you must have some surgeon by, lest he bleed to death.'

Shylock, whose whole intent was that Antonio should bleed to death, said, 'It is not so named in the bond.'

Portia replied: 'It is not so named in the bond, but what of that? It were good you did so much for charity.'

To this all the answer Shylock would make was, 'I cannot find it; it is not in the bond.'

'Then,' said Portia, 'a pound of Antonio's flesh is thine. The law allows it and the court awards it. And you may cut this flesh from off his breast. The law allows it and the court awards it.'

Again Shylock exclaimed: 'O wise and upright judge! A Daniel is come to judgment!' And then he sharpened his long knife again, and looking eagerly on Antonio, he said, 'Come, prepare!'

'Tarry a little, Jew,' said Portia. 'There is something else. This bond here gives you no drop of blood; the words expressly are, "a pound of flesh". If in the cutting off the pound of flesh you shed one drop of Christian blood, your lands and goods are by the law to be confiscated to the state of Venice.'

Now as it was utterly impossible for Shylock to cut off the pound of flesh without shedding some of Antonio's blood, this wise discovery of Portia's, that it was flesh and not blood that was named in the bond, saved the life of Antonio; and all admiring the wonderful sagacity of the young counsellor who had so happily thought of this expedient, plaudits resounded from every part of the Senate House; and Gratiano exclaimed, in the words which Shylock had used: 'O wise and upright judge! Mark, Jew, a Daniel is come to judgment!'

Shylock, finding himself defeated in his cruel intent, said, with a disappointed look, that he would take the money. And Bassanio, rejoiced beyond measure at Antonio's unexpected deliverance, cried out: 'Here is the money!'

But Portia stopped him, saying: 'Softly; there is no haste. The Jew shall have nothing but the penalty. Therefore prepare, Shylock, to cut off the flesh; but mind you shed no blood; nor do not cut off more nor less than just a pound; be it more or less by one poor

test

ter1er

scruple, nay, if the scale turn but by the weight of a single hair, you are condemned by the laws of Venice to die, and all your wealth is forfeited to the state.'

'Give me my money and let me go,' said Shylock.

'I have it ready,' said Bassanio. 'Here it is.'

Shylock was going to take the money, when Portia again stopped him, saying: 'Tarry, Jew. I have yet another hold upon you. By the laws of Venice your wealth is forfeited to the state for having conspired against the life of one of its citizens, and your life lies at the mercy of the duke; therefore, down on your knees and ask him to pardon you.'

The duke then said to Shylock: 'That you may see the difference of our Christian spirit, I pardon you your life before you ask it. Half your wealth belongs to Antonio, the other half comes to the state.'

The generous Antonio then said that he would give up his share of Shylock's wealth if Shylock would sign a deed to make it over at his death to his daughter and her husband; for Antonio knew that the Jew had an only daughter who had lately married against his consent a young Christian named Lorenzo, a friend of Antonio's, which had so offended Shylock that he had disinherited her.

The Jew agreed to this; and being thus disappointed in his revenge and despoiled of his riches, he said: 'I am ill. Let me go home. Send the deed after me, and I will sign over half my riches to my daughter.'

'Get thee gone, then,' said the duke, 'and sign it; and if you repent your cruelty and turn Christian, the state will forgive you the fine of the other half of your riches.'

The duke now released Antonio and dismissed the court. He then highly praised the wisdom and ingenuity of the young counsellor and invited him home to dinner.

Portia, who meant to return to Belmont before her husband, replied, 'I humbly thank your grace, but I must away directly.'

The duke said he was sorry he had not leisure to stay and dine with him, and, turning to Antonio, he added, 'Reward this gentleman; for in my mind you are much indebted to him.'

The duke and his senators left the court; and then Bassanio said to Portia: 'Most worthy gentleman, I and my friend Antonio have by your wisdom been this day acquitted of grievous penalties, and I beg you will accept of the three thousand ducats due unto the Jew.'

'And we shall stand indebted to you over and above,' said Antonio, 'in love and service evermore.'

Portia could not be prevailed upon to accept the money. But upon Bassanio still pressing her to accept of some reward, she said: 'Give me your gloves. I will wear them for your sake.' And then Bassanio taking off his gloves, she espied the ring which she had given him upon his finger. Now it was the ring the wily lady wanted to get from him to make a merry jest when she saw her Bassanio again, that made her ask him for his gloves; and she said, when she saw the ring, 'And for your love, I will take this ring from you.'

Bassanio was sadly distressed that the counsellor should ask him for the only thing he could not part with, and he replied, in great confusion, that he could not give him that ring, because it was his wife's gift and he had vowed never to part with it; but that he would give him the most valuable ring in Venice, and find it out by proclamation.

On this Portia affected to be affronted, and left the court, saying, 'You teach me, sir, how a beggar should be answered.'

'Dear Bassanio,' said Antonio, 'let him have the ring. Let my love and the great service he has done for me be valued against your wife's displeasure.'

Bassanio, ashamed to appear so ungrateful, yielded, and sent Gratiano after Portia with the ring; and then the 'clerk' Nerissa, who had also given Gratiano a ring, begged his ring, and Gratiano (not choosing to be outdone in generosity by his lord) gave it to her. And there was laughing among these ladies to think, when they got home, how they would tax their husbands with giving away their rings and swear that they had given them as a present to some woman.

Portia, when she returned, was in that happy temper of mind which never fails to attend the consciousness of having performed a good action. Her cheerful spirits enjoyed everything she saw: the moon never seemed to shine so bright before; and when that pleasant moon was hid behind a cloud, then a light which she saw from her house at Belmont as well pleased her charmed fancy, and she said to Nerissa: 'That light we see is burning in my hall. How far that little candle throws its beams! So shines a good deed in a naughty world.' And hearing the sound of music from her house, she said, 'Methinks that music sounds much sweeter than by day.'

And now Portia and Nerissa entered the house, and, dressing themselves in their own apparel, they awaited the arrival of their husbands, who soon followed them with Antonio; and Bassanio presenting his dear friend to the Lady Portia, the congratulations and welcomings of that lady were hardly over when they perceived Nerissa and her husband quarrelling in a corner of the room.

'A quarrel already?' said Portia. 'What is the matter?'

Gratiano replied, 'Lady, it is about a paltry gilt ring that Nerissa gave me, with words upon it like the poetry on a cutler's knife: *Love me, and leave me not.*'

'What does the poetry or the value of the ring signify?' said Nerissa. 'You swore to me, when I gave it to you, that you would keep it till the hour of death; and now you say you gave it to the lawyer's clerk. I know you gave it to a woman.'

'By this hand,' replied Gratiano, 'I gave it to a youth, a kind of boy, a little scrubbed boy, no higher than yourself; he was clerk to the young counsellor that by his wise pleading saved Antonio's life. This prating boy begged it for a fee, and I could not for my life deny him.'

Portia said: 'You were to blame, Gratiano, to part with your wife's first gift. I gave my Lord Bassanio a ring, and I am sure he would not part with it for all the world.'

Gratiano, in excuse for his fault, now said, 'My lord Bassanio gave his ring away to the counsellor, and then the boy, his clerk, that took some pains in writing, he begged my ring.'

Portia, hearing this, seemed very angry and reproached Bassanio for giving away her ring; and she said Nerissa had taught her what to believe, and that she knew some woman had the ring. Bassanio was very unhappy to have so offended his dear lady, and he said with great earnestness: 'No, by my honour, no woman had it, but a civil doctor who refused three thousand ducats of me and begged the ring, which when I denied him he went displeased away. What could I do, sweet Portia? I was so beset with shame for my seeming ingratitude that I was forced to send the ring after him. Pardon me, good lady. Had you been there, I think you would have begged the ring of me to give the worthy doctor.'

'Ah!' said Antonio, 'I am the unhappy cause of these quarrels.'

Portia bid Antonio not to grieve at that, for that he was welcome notwithstanding; and then Antonio said: 'I once did lend my body for Bassanio's sake; and but for him to whom your husband gave the ring I should have now been dead. I dare be bound again, my soul upon the forfeit, your lord will never more break his faith with you.'

'Then you shall be his surety,' said Portia. 'Give him this ring and bid him keep it better than the other.'

When Bassanio looked at this ring he was strangely surprised to find it was the same he gave away; and then Portia told him how she was the young counsellor, and Nerissa was her clerk; and Bassanio found, to his unspeakable wonder and delight, that it was by the noble courage and wisdom of his wife that Antonio's life was saved.

And Portia again welcomed Antonio, and gave him letters which by some chance had fallen into her hands, which contained an account of Antonio's ships, that were supposed lost, being safely arrived in the harbour. So these tragical beginnings of this rich merchant's story were all forgotten in the unexpected good fortune which ensued; and there was leisure to laugh at the comical adventure of the rings and the husbands that did not know their own wives, Gratiano merrily swearing, in a sort of rhyming speech, that

　－　While he lived, he'd fear no other thing
　　So sore, as keeping safe Nerissa's ring.

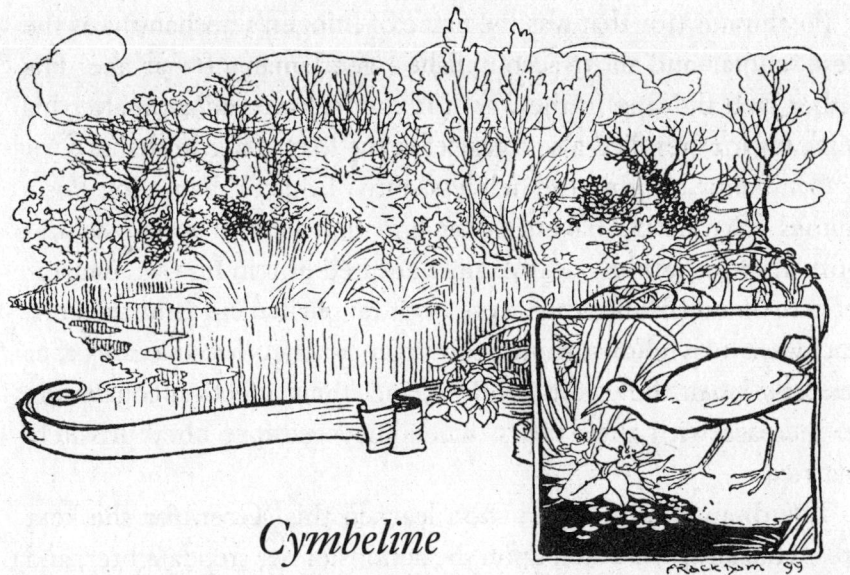

Cymbeline

During the time of Augustus Caesar, Emperor of Rome, there reigned in England (which was then called Britain) a king whose name was Cymbeline.

Cymbeline's first wife died when his three children (two sons and a daughter) were very young. Imogen, the eldest of these children, was brought up in her father's court; but by a strange chance the two sons of Cymbeline were stolen out of their nursery when the eldest was but three years of age and the youngest quite an infant; and Cymbeline could never discover what was become of them or by whom they were conveyed away.

Cymbeline was twice married. His second wife was a wicked, plotting woman, and a cruel stepmother to Imogen, Cymbeline's daughter by his first wife.

The queen, though she hated Imogen, yet wished her to marry a son of her own by a former husband (she also having been twice married), for by this means she hoped upon the death of Cymbeline to place the crown of Britain upon the head of her son Cloten; for she knew that, if the king's sons were not found, the Princess Imogen must be the king's heir. But this design was prevented by Imogen herself, who married without the consent or even knowledge of her father or the queen.

Posthumus (for that was the name of Imogen's husband) was the best scholar and most accomplished gentleman of that age. His father died fighting in the wars for Cymbeline, and soon after his birth his mother died also for grief at the loss of her husband.

Cymbeline, pitying the helpless state of this orphan, took Posthumus (Cymbeline having given him that name because he was born after his father's death), and educated him in his own court.

Imogen and Posthumus were both taught by the same masters, and were playfellows from their infancy; they loved each other tenderly when they were children, and, their affection continuing to increase with their years, when they grew up they privately married.

The disappointed queen soon learned this secret, for she kept spies constantly in watch upon the actions of her stepdaughter, and she immediately told the king of the marriage of Imogen with Posthumus.

Nothing could exceed the wrath of Cymbeline when he heard that his daughter had been so forgetful of her high dignity as to marry a subject. He commanded Posthumus to leave Britain and banished him from his native country for ever.

The queen, who pretended to pity Imogen for the grief she suffered at losing her husband, offered to procure them a private meeting before Posthumus set out on his journey to Rome, which place he had chosen for his residence in his banishment. This seeming kindness she showed the better to succeed in her future designs in regard to her son Cloten, for she meant to persuade Imogen, when her husband was gone, that her marriage was not lawful, being contracted without the consent of the king.

Imogen and Posthumus took a most affectionate leave of each other. Imogen gave her husband a diamond ring which had been her mother's, and Posthumus promised never to part with the ring; and he fastened a bracelet on the arm of his wife, which he begged she would preserve with great care, as a token of his love; they then bade each other farewell, with many vows of everlasting love and fidelity.

Imogen remained a solitary and dejected lady in her father's court, and Posthumus arrived at Rome, the place he had chosen for his banishment.

Posthumus fell into company at Rome with some gay young men of different nations, who were talking freely of ladies, each one praising the ladies of his own country and his own mistress. Posthumus, who had ever his own dear lady in his mind, affirmed that his wife, the fair Imogen, was the most virtuous, wise, and constant lady in the world.

One of those gentlemen, whose name was Iachimo, being offended that a lady of Britain should be so praised above the Roman ladies, his countrywomen, provoked Posthumus by seeming to doubt the constancy of his so highly praised wife; and at length, after much altercation, Posthumus consented to a proposal of Iachimo's that he (Iachimo) should go to Britain and endeavour to gain the love of the married Imogen. They then laid a wager that if Iachimo did not succeed in this wicked design he was to forfeit a large sum of money; but if he could win Imogen's favour, and prevail upon her to give him the bracelet which Posthumus had so earnestly desired she would keep as a token of his love, then the wager was to terminate with Posthumus giving to Iachimo the ring which was Imogen's love present when she parted with her husband. Such firm faith had Posthumus in the fidelity of Imogen that he thought he ran no hazard in this trial of her honour.

Iachimo, on his arrival in Britain, gained admittance and a courteous welcome from Imogen, as a friend of her husband; but when he began to make professions of love to her she repulsed him with disdain, and he soon found that he could have no hope of succeeding in his dishonourable design.

The desire Iachimo had to win the wager made him now have recourse to a stratagem to impose upon Posthumus, and for this purpose he bribed some of Imogen's attendants and was by them conveyed into her bedchamber, concealed in a large trunk, where he remained shut up till Imogen was retired to rest and had fallen asleep; and then, getting out of the trunk, he examined the chamber with great attention, and wrote down everything he saw there, and particularly noticed a mole which he observed upon Imogen's neck, and then softly unloosing the bracelet from her arm, which Post-humus had given to her, he retired into the chest again; and the next day he set off for Rome with great expedition, and boasted to Posthumus that Imogen had given him the bracelet, and likewise permitted him to pass a night in her chamber. And in this manner Iachimo told his false tale: 'Her bedchamber,' said he, 'was hung with tapestry of silk and silver, the story was *the proud Cleopatra when she met her Antony*, a piece of work most bravely wrought.'

'This is true,' said Posthumus; 'but this you might have heard spoken of without seeing.'

'Then the chimney,' said Iachimo, 'is south of the chamber, and the chimneypiece is *Diana bathing*; never saw I figures livelier expressed.'

'This is a thing you might have likewise heard,' said Posthumus; 'for it is much talked of.'

Iachimo as accurately described the roof of the chamber; and added, 'I had almost forgot her andirons; they were *two winking Cupids* made of silver, each on one foot standing.' He then took out the bracelet, and said: 'Know you this jewel, sir? She gave me this. She took it from her arm. I see her yet; her pretty action did outsell her gift, and yet enriched it, too. She gave it me, and said, *she prized it once*.' He last of all described the mole he had observed upon her neck.

Posthumus, who had heard the whole of this artful recital in an agony of doubt, now broke out into the most passionate exclamations against Imogen. He delivered up the diamond ring to Iachimo which he had agreed to forfeit to him if he obtained the bracelet from Imogen.

Posthumus then in a jealous rage wrote to Pisanio, a gentleman of Britain, who was one of Imogen's attendants, and had long been a faithful friend to Posthumus; and after telling him what proof he had of his wife's disloyalty, he desired Pisanio would take Imogen to Milford Haven, a seaport of Wales, and there kill her. And at the same time he wrote a deceitful letter to Imogen, desiring her to go with Pisanio, for that, finding he could live no longer without seeing her, though he was forbidden upon pain of death to return to Britain, he would come to Milford Haven, at which place he begged she would meet him. She, good, unsuspecting lady, who loved her husband above all things, and desired more than her life to see him, hastened her departure with Pisanio, and the same night she received the letter she set out.

When their journey was nearly at an end, Pisanio, who, though faithful to Posthumus, was not faithful to serve him in an evil deed, disclosed to Imogen the cruel order he had received.

Imogen, who, instead of meeting a loving and beloved husband, found herself doomed by that husband to suffer death, was afflicted beyond measure.

Pisanio persuaded her to take comfort and wait with patient fortitude for the time when Posthumus should see and repent his injustice. In the meantime, as she refused in her distress to return to her father's court, he advised her to dress herself in boy's clothes for more security in travelling; to which advice she agreed, and thought in that disguise she would go over to Rome and see her husband, whom, though he had used her so barbarously, she could not forget to love.

When Pisanio had provided her with her new apparel he left her to her uncertain fortune, being obliged to return to court; but before he departed he gave her a vial of cordial, which he said the queen had given him as a sovereign remedy in all disorders.

The queen, who hated Pisanio because he was a friend to Imogen and Posthumus, gave him this vial, which she supposed contained poison, she having ordered her physician to give her some poison, to try its effects (as she said) upon animals; but the physician, knowing her malicious disposition, would not trust her with real poison, but gave her a drug which would do no other mischief than causing a person to sleep with every appearance of death for a few hours. This mixture, which Pisanio thought a choice cordial, he gave to Imogen, desiring her, if she found herself ill upon the road, to take it; and so, with blessings and prayers for her safety and happy deliverance from her undeserved troubles, he left her.

Providence strangely directed Imogen's steps to the dwelling of her two brothers who had been stolen away in their infancy. Bellarius, who stole them away, was a lord in the court of

Cymbeline, and, having been falsely accused to the king of treason and banished from the court, in revenge he stole away the two sons of Cymbeline and brought them up in a forest, where he lived concealed in a cave. He stole them through revenge, but he soon loved them as tenderly as if they had been his own children, educated them carefully, and they grew up fine youths, their princely spirits leading them to bold and daring actions; and as they subsisted by hunting, they were active and hardy, and were always pressing their supposed father to let them seek their fortune in the wars.

At the cave where these youths dwelt it was Imogen's fortune to arrive. She had lost her way in a large forest through which her road lay to Milford Haven (from which she meant to embark for Rome); and being unable to find any place where she could purchase food, she was, with weariness and hunger, almost dying; for it is not merely putting on a man's apparel that will enable a young lady, tenderly brought up, to bear the fatigue of wandering about lonely forests like a man. Seeing this cave, she entered, hoping to find someone within of whom she could procure food. She found the cave empty, but, looking about, she discovered some cold meat, and her hunger was so pressing that she could not wait for an invitation, but sat down and began to eat.

'Ah,' said she, talking to herself, 'I see a man's life is a tedious one. How tired am I! For two nights together I have made the ground my bed. My resolution helps me, or I should be sick. When Pisanio showed me Milford Haven from the mountain-top, how near it seemed!' Then the thoughts of her husband and his cruel mandate came across her, and she said, 'My dear Posthumus, thou art a false one!'

The two brothers of Imogen, who had been hunting with their reputed father, Bellarius, were by this time returned home. Bellarius had given them the names of Polydore and Cadwal, and they knew no better, but supposed that Bellarius was their father; but the real names of these princes were Guiderius and Arviragus.

Bellarius entered the cave first, and, seeing Imogen, stopped them, saying: 'Come not in yet. It eats our victuals, or I should think it was a fairy.'

'What is the matter, sir?' said the young men.

'By Jupiter!' said Bellarius, again, 'there is an angel in the cave, or if not, an earthly paragon.' So beautiful did Imogen look in her boy's apparel.

She, hearing the sound of voices, came forth from the cave and addressed them in these words: 'Good masters, do not harm me. Before I entered your cave I had thought to have begged or bought what I have eaten. Indeed, I have stolen nothing, nor would I, though I had found gold strewed on the floor. Here is money for my meat, which I would have left on the board when I had made my meal, and parted with prayers for the provider.'

They refused her money with great earnestness.

'I see you are angry with me,' said the timid Imogen; 'but, sirs, if you kill me for my fault, know that I should have died if I had not made it.'

'Whither are you bound,' asked Bellarius, 'and what is your name?'

'Fidele is my name,' answered Imogen. 'I have a kinsman who is bound for Italy; he embarked at Milford Haven, to whom being going, almost spent with hunger, I am fallen into this offence.'

'Prithee, fair youth,' said old Bellarius, 'do not think us churls, nor measure our good minds by this rude place we live in. You are well encountered; it is almost night. You shall have better cheer before you depart, and thanks to stay and eat it. Boys, bid him welcome.'

The gentle youths, her brothers, then welcomed Imogen to their cave with many kind expressions, saying they would love her (or, as they said, *him*) as a brother; and they entered the cave, where (they having killed venison when they were hunting) Imogen delighted them with her neat housewifery, assisting them in preparing their supper; for, though it is not the custom now for young women of high birth to understand cookery, it was then, and Imogen excelled in this useful art; and, as her brothers prettily expressed it, Fidele cut their roots in characters, and sauced their broth, as if Juno had been sick and Fidele were her dieter.

'And then,' said Polydore to his brother, 'how angel-like he sings!'

They also remarked to each other that though Fidele smiled so sweetly, yet so sad a melancholy did overcloud his lovely face, as if grief and patience had together taken possession of him.

For these her gentle qualities (or perhaps it was their near relationship, though they knew it not) Imogen (or, as the boys called her, *Fidele*) became the doting-piece of her brothers, and she scarcely less loved them, thinking that but for the memory of her dear Posthumus she could live and die in the cave with these wild forest youths; and she gladly consented to stay with them till she was enough rested from the fatigue of travelling to pursue her way to Milford Haven.

When the venison they had taken was all eaten and they were going out to hunt for more, Fidele could not accompany them because she was unwell. Sorrow, no doubt, for her husband's cruel usage, as well as the fatigue of wandering in the forest, was the cause of her illness.

They then bid her farewell, and went to their hunt, praising all the way the noble parts and graceful demeanour of the youth Fidele.

Imogen was no sooner left alone than she recollected the cordial Pisanio had given her, and drank it off, and presently fell into a sound and deathlike sleep.

When Bellarius and her brothers returned from hunting, Polydore went first into the cave, and, supposing her asleep, pulled off his heavy shoes, that he might tread softly and not awake her (so did true gentleness spring up in the minds of these princely foresters); but he soon discovered that she could not be awakened by any noise, and concluded her to be dead, and Polydore lamented over her with dear and brotherly regret, as if they had never from their infancy been parted.

Bellarius also proposed to carry her out into the forest, and there celebrate her funeral with songs and solemn dirges, as was then the custom.

Imogen's two brothers then carried her to a shady covert, and there, laying her gently on the grass, they sang repose to her departed spirit, and, covering her over with leaves and flowers, Polydore said: 'While summer lasts and I live here, Fidele, I will daily strew thy grave. The pale primrose, that flower most like thy face; the bluebell, like thy clear veins; and the leaf of eglantine, which is not sweeter than was thy breath – all these will I strew over thee. Yea, and the furred moss in winter, when there are no flowers to cover thy sweet corse.'

When they had finished her funeral obsequies they departed, very sorrowful.

Imogen had not been long left alone when, the effect of the sleepy drug going off, she awaked, and easily shaking off the slight covering of leaves and flowers they had thrown over her, she arose, and, imagining she had been dreaming, she said: 'I thought I was a cave-keeper and cook to honest creatures. How came I here covered with flowers?'

Not being able to find her way back to the cave, and seeing nothing of her new companions, she concluded it was certainly all a dream; and once more Imogen set out on her weary pilgrimage, hoping at last she should find her way to Milford Haven, and thence get a passage in some ship bound for Italy; for all her thoughts were still with her husband, Posthumus, whom she intended to seek in the disguise of a page.

But great events were happening at this time, of which Imogen knew nothing; for a war had suddenly broken out between the Roman Emperor Augustus Caesar and Cymbeline, the King of Britain; and a Roman army had landed to invade Britain, and was advanced into the very forest over which Imogen was journeying. With this army came Posthumus.

Though Posthumus came over to Britain with the Roman army, he did not mean to fight on their side against his own countrymen, but intended to join the army of Britain and fight in the cause of his king who had banished him.

He still believed Imogen false to him; yet the death of her he had so fondly loved, and by his own orders, too (Pisanio having written him a letter to say he had obeyed his command, and that Imogen was dead), sat heavy on his heart, and therefore he returned to Britain, desiring either to be slain in battle or to be put to death by Cymbeline for returning home from banishment.

Imogen, before she reached Milford Haven, fell into the hands of the Roman army, and, her presence and deportment recommending her, she was made a page to Lucius, the Roman general.

Cymbeline's army now advanced to meet the enemy, and when they entered this forest Polydore and Cadwal joined the king's army. The young men were eager to engage in acts of valour, though they little thought they were going to fight for their own royal father; and old Bellarius went with them to the battle.

He had long since repented of the injury he had done to Cymbeline in carrying away his sons; and, having been a warrior in his youth, he gladly joined the army to fight for the king he had so injured.

And now a great battle commenced between the two armies, and the Britons would have been defeated, and Cymbeline himself killed, but for the extraordinary valour of Posthumus and Bellarius and the two sons of Cymbeline. They rescued the king and saved his life, and so entirely turned the fortune of the day that the Britons gained the victory.

When the battle was over, Posthumus, who had not found the death he sought for, surrendered himself up to one of the officers of Cymbeline, willing to suffer the death which was to be his punishment if he returned from banishment.

Imogen and the master she served were taken prisoners and brought before Cymbeline, as was also her old enemy, Iachimo, who was an officer in the Roman army. And when these prisoners were before the king, Posthumus was brought in to receive his sentence of death; and at this strange juncture of time Bellarius with Polydore and Cadwal were also brought before Cymbeline, to receive the rewards due to the great services they had by their valour done for the king. Pisanio, being one of the king's attendants, was likewise present.

Therefore there were now standing in the king's presence (but with very different hopes and fears) Posthumus and Imogen, with her new master the Roman general; the faithful servant Pisanio and the false friend Iachimo; and likewise the two lost sons of Cymbeline, with Bellarius, who had stolen them away.

The Roman general was the first who spoke; the rest stood silent before the king, though there was many a beating heart among them.

Imogen saw Posthumus, and knew him, though he was in the disguise of a peasant; but he did not know her in her male attire. And she knew Iachimo, and she saw a ring on his finger which she perceived to be her own, but she did not know him as yet to have been the author of all her troubles; and she stood before her own father a prisoner of war.

Pisanio knew Imogen, for it was he who had dressed her in the garb of a boy. 'It is my mistress,' thought he. 'Since she is living, let the time run on to good or bad.' Bellarius knew her, too, and softly said to Cadwal, 'Is not this boy revived from death?'

'One sand,' replied Cadwal, 'does not more resemble another than that sweet, rosy lad is like the dead Fidele.'

'The same dead thing alive,' said Polydore.

'Peace, peace,' said Bellarius. 'If it were he, I am sure he would have spoken to us.'

'But we saw him dead,' again whispered Polydore.

'Be silent,' replied Bellarius.

Posthumus waited in silence to hear the welcome sentence of his own death; and he resolved not to disclose to the king that he had saved his life in the battle, lest that should move Cymbeline to pardon him.

Lucius, the Roman general, who had taken Imogen under his protection as his page, was the first (as has been before said) who spoke to the king. He was a man of high courage and noble dignity, and this was his speech to the king: 'I hear you take no ransom for your prisoners, but doom them all to death. I am a Roman, and with a Roman heart will suffer death. But there is one thing for which I would entreat.' Then bringing Imogen before the king, he said: 'This boy is a Briton born. Let him be ransomed. He is my page. Never master had a page so kind, so duteous, so diligent on all occasions, so true, so nurselike. He hath done no Briton wrong, though he hath served a Roman. Save him, if you spare no one beside.'

Cymbeline looked earnestly on his daughter Imogen. He knew

her not in that disguise; but it seemed that all-powerful Nature spake in his heart, for he said: 'I have surely seen him; his face appears familiar to me. I know not why or wherefore I say, live, boy, but I give you your life; and ask of me what boon you will and I will grant it you. Yea, even though it be the life of the noblest prisoner I have.'

'I humbly thank your highness,' said Imogen.

What was then called granting a boon was the same as a promise to give any one thing, whatever it might be, that the person on whom that favour was conferred chose to ask for.

They all were attentive to hear what thing the page would ask for; and Lucius, her master, said to her: 'I do not beg my life, good lad, but I know that is what you will ask for.'

'No, no, alas!' said Imogen. 'I have other work in hand, good master. Your life I cannot ask for.'

This seeming want of gratitude in the boy astonished the Roman general.

Imogen then, fixing her eye on Iachimo, demanded no other boon than this: that Iachimo should be made to confess whence he had the ring he wore on his finger.

Cymbeline granted her this boon, and threatened Iachimo with the torture if he did not confess how he came by the diamond ring on his finger.

Iachimo then made a full acknowledgement of all his villainy, in telling, as has been before related, the whole story of his wager with Posthumus and how he had succeeded in imposing upon his credulity.

What Posthumus felt at hearing this proof of the innocence of his lady cannot be expressed. He instantly came forward and confessed to Cymbeline the cruel sentence which he had enjoined Pisanio to execute upon the princess, exclaiming, wildly: 'O Imogen, my queen, my life, my wife! O Imogen, Imogen, Imogen!'

Imogen could not see her beloved husband in this distress without discovering herself, to the unutterable joy of Posthumus, who was thus relieved from a weight of guilt and woe, and restored to the good graces of the dear lady he had so cruelly treated.

Cymbeline, almost as much overwhelmed as he with joy, at finding his lost daughter so strangely recovered, received her to her former place in his fatherly affection, and not only gave her husband Posthumus his life, but consented to acknowledge him for his son-in-law.

Bellarius chose this time of joy and reconciliation to make his confession. He presented Polydore and Cadwal to the king, telling him they were his two lost sons, Guiderius and Arviragus.

Cymbeline forgave old Bellarius; for who could think of punishments at a season of such universal happiness? To find his daughter living, and his lost sons in the persons of his young deliverers, that he had seen so bravely fight in his defence, was unlooked-for joy indeed!

Imogen was now at leisure to perform good services for her late master, the Roman general, Lucius, whose life the king, her father, readily granted at her request; and by the mediation of the same Lucius a peace was concluded between the Romans and the Britons which was kept inviolate many years.

How Cymbeline's wicked queen, through despair of bringing her projects to pass, and touched with remorse of conscience, sickened and died, having first lived to see her foolish son Cloten slain in a quarrel which he had provoked, are events too tragical to interrupt this happy conclusion by more than merely touching upon. It is sufficient that all were made happy who were deserving; and even the treacherous Iachimo, in consideration of his villainy having missed its final aim, was dismissed without punishment.

King Lear

Lear, King of Britain, had three daughters: Goneril, wife to the Duke of Albany; Regan, wife to the Duke of Cornwall; and Cordelia, a young maid, for whose love the King of France and Duke of Burgundy were joint suitors, and were at this time making stay for that purpose in the court of Lear.

The old king, worn out with age and the fatigues of government, he being more than fourscore years old, determined to take no further part in state affairs, but to leave the management to younger strengths, that he might have time to prepare for death, which must at no long period ensue. With this intent he called his three daughters to him, to know from their own lips which of them loved him best, that he might part his kingdom among them in such proportions as their affection for him should seem to deserve.

Goneril, the eldest, declared that she loved her father more than words could give out, that he was dearer to her than the light of her own eyes, dearer than life and liberty, with a deal of such professing stuff, which is easy to counterfeit where there is no real love, only a few fine words delivered with confidence being wanted in that case. The king, delighted to hear from her own mouth this assurance of her love, and thinking truly that her heart went with it, in a fit of fatherly fondness bestowed upon her and her husband one-third of his ample kingdom.

Then calling to him his second daughter he demanded what she had to say. Regan, who was made of the same hollow metal as her sister, was not a whit behind in her professions, but rather declared that what her sister had spoken came short of the love which she professed to bear for his highness; in so much that she found all other joys dead in comparison with the pleasure which she took in the love of her dear king and father.

Lear blessed himself in having such loving children, as he thought; and could do no less, after the handsome assurances which Regan had made, than bestow a third of his kingdom upon her and her husband, equal in size to that which he had already given away to Goneril.

Then turning to his youngest daughter, Cordelia, whom he called his joy, he asked what she had to say, thinking no doubt that she would glad his ears with the same loving speeches which her sisters had uttered, or rather that her expressions would be so much stronger than theirs, as she had always been his darling, and favoured by him above either of them. But Cordelia, disgusted with the flattery of her sisters, whose hearts she knew were far from their lips, and seeing that all their coaxing speeches were only intended to wheedle the old king out of his dominions, that they and their husbands might reign in his lifetime, made no other reply but this – that she loved his majesty according to her duty, neither more nor less.

The king, shocked with this appearance of ingratitude in his favourite child, desired her to consider her words and to mend her speech, lest it should mar her fortunes.

Cordelia then told her father that he was her father, that he had given her breeding, and loved her; that she returned those duties back as was most fit, and did obey him, love him, and most honour him. But that she could not frame her mouth to such large speeches as her sisters had done, or promise to love nothing else in the world. Why had her sisters husbands if (as they said) they had no love for anything but their father? If she should ever wed, she was sure the lord to whom she gave her hand would want half her love, half of her care and duty; she should never marry like her sisters, to love her father all.

Cordelia, who in earnest loved her old father even almost extravagantly as her sisters pretended to do, would have plainly told him so at any other time, in more daughter-like and loving terms, and without these qualifications, which did indeed sound a little ungracious; but after the crafty, flattering speeches of her sisters, which she had seen draw such extravagant rewards, she thought the handsomest thing she could do was to love and be silent. This put her affection out of suspicion of mercenary ends, and showed that she loved, but not for gain; and that her professions, the less ostentatious they were, had so much the more of truth and sincerity than her sisters'.

This plainness of speech, which Lear called pride, so enraged the old monarch – who in his best of times always showed much of spleen and rashness, and in whom the dotage incident to old age had so clouded over his reason that he could not discern truth from flattery, nor a gay painted speech from words that came from the heart – that in a fury of resentment he retracted the third part of his kingdom which yet remained, and which he had reserved for Cordelia, and gave it away from her, sharing it equally between her two sisters and their husbands, the Dukes of Albany and Cornwall, whom he now called to him and in presence of all his courtiers, bestowing a coronet between them, invested them jointly with all the power, revenue, and execution of government, only retaining to himself the name of king; all the rest of royalty he resigned, with this reservation, that himself, with a hundred knights for his attendants, was to be maintained by monthly course in each of his daughters' palaces in turn.

So preposterous a disposal of his kingdom, so little guided by reason, and so much by passion, filled all his courtiers with astonishment and sorrow; but none of them had the courage to interpose between this incensed king and his wrath, except the Earl of Kent, who was beginning to speak a good word for Cordelia, when the passionate Lear on pain of death commanded him to desist; but the good Kent was not so to be repelled. He had been ever loyal to Lear, whom he had honoured as a king, loved as a father, followed as a master; and he had never esteemed his life further than as a pawn to wage against his royal master's enemies, nor feared to lose it when Lear's safety was the motive; nor, now that Lear was most his own enemy, did this faithful servant of the king forget his old principles, but manfully opposed Lear to do Lear good; and was unmannerly only because Lear was mad. He had been a most faithful counsellor in times past to the king, and he besought him now that he would see with his eyes (as he had done in many weighty matters) and go by his advice still, and in his best consideration recall this hideous rashness; for he would answer with his life his judgement that Lear's youngest daughter did not love him least, nor were those empty-hearted whose low sound gave no token of hollowness. When power bowed to flattery, honour was bound to plainness. For Lear's threats, what could he do to him whose life was already at his service? That should not hinder duty from speaking.

The honest freedom of this good Earl of Kent only stirred up the king's wrath the more, and, like a frantic patient who kills his physician and loves his mortal disease, he banished this true servant, and allotted him but five days to make his preparations for departure; but if on the sixth his hated person was found within the realm of Britain, that moment was to be his death. And Kent bade farewell to the king, and said that, since he chose to show himself in such fashion, it was but banishment to stay there; and before he went he recommended Cordelia to the protection of the gods, the maid who had so rightly thought and so discreetly spoken; and only wished that her sisters' large speeches might be answered with deeds of love; and then he went, as he said, to shape his old course to a new country.

The King of France and Duke of Burgundy were now called in to hear the determination of Lear about his youngest daughter, and to know whether they would persist in their courtship to Cordelia, now that she was under her father's displeasure and had no fortune but her own person to recommend her. And the Duke of Burgundy declined the match, and would not take her to wife upon such conditions. But the King of France, understanding what the nature of the fault had been which had lost her the love of her father – that it was only a tardiness of speech and the not being able to frame her tongue to flattery like her sisters – took this young maid by the hand and, saying that her virtues were a dowry above a kingdom, bade Cordelia to take farewell of her sisters and of her father, though he had been unkind, and she should go with him and be queen of him and of fair France, and reign over fairer possessions than her sisters. And he called the Duke of Burgundy, in contempt, a waterish duke, because his love for this young maid had in a moment run all away like water.

Then Cordelia with weeping eyes took leave of her sisters, and besought them to love their father well and make good their professions; and they sullenly told her not to prescribe to them, for they knew their duty, but to strive to content her husband, who had taken her (as they tauntingly expressed it) as Fortune's alms. And Cordelia with a heavy heart departed, for she knew the cunning of her sisters and she wished her father in better hands than she was about to leave him in.

Cordelia was no sooner gone than the devilish dispositions of her sisters began to show themselves in their true favours. Even before the expiration of the first month, which Lear was to spend by agreement with his eldest daughter, Goneril, the old king began to find out the difference between promises and performances. This wretch, having got from her father all that he had to bestow, even to the giving away of the crown from off his head, began to grudge even those small remnants of royalty which the old man had reserved to himself, to please his fancy with the idea of being still a king. She could not bear to see him and his knights. Every time she met her father she put on a frowning countenance; and when the old man wanted to speak with her she would feign sickness or anything to get rid of the sight of him, for it was plain that she esteemed his old age a useless burden and his attendants an unnecessary expense; not only she herself slackened in her expressions of duty to the king, but by her example, and (it is to be feared) not without her private instructions, her very servants affected to treat him with neglect, and would either refuse to obey his orders or still more contemptuously pretend not to hear them. Lear could not but perceive this alteration in the behaviour of his daughter, but he shut his eyes against it as long as he could, as people commonly are unwilling to believe the unpleasant consequences which their own mistakes and obstinacy have brought upon them.

True love and fidelity are no more to be estranged by *ill*, than falsehood and hollow-heartedness can be conciliated by *good*, *usage*. This eminently appears in the instance of the good Earl of Kent, who, though banished by Lear, and his life made forfeit if he were found in Britain, chose to stay and abide all consequences as long as there was a chance of his being useful to the king his master. See to what mean shifts and disguises poor loyalty is forced to submit sometimes; yet it counts nothing base or unworthy so as it can but do service where it owes an obligation! In the disguise of a serving-man, all his greatness and pomp laid aside, this good earl proffered his services to the king, who, not knowing him to be Kent in that disguise, but pleased with a certain plainness, or rather bluntness, in his answers, which the earl put on (so different from that smooth, oily flattery which he had so much reason to be sick of, having found the effects not answerable in his daughter), a bargain was quickly struck, and Lear took Kent into his service by the name of Caius, as he called himself, never suspecting him to be his once great favourite, the high and mighty Earl of Kent.

This Caius quickly found means to show his fidelity and love to his royal master, for, Goneril's steward that same day behaving in a disrespectful manner to Lear, and giving him saucy looks and language, as no doubt he was secretly encouraged to do by his mistress, Caius, not enduring to hear so open an affront put upon his majesty, made no more ado, but presently tripped up his heels and laid the unmannerly slave in the kennel; for which friendly service Lear became more and more attached to him.

Nor was Kent the only friend Lear had. In his degree, and as far as so insignificant a personage could show his love, the poor fool, or jester, that had been of his palace while Lear had a palace, as it was the custom of kings and great personages at that time to keep a fool (as he was called) to make them sport after serious business – this poor fool clung to Lear after he had given away his crown, and by his witty sayings would keep up his good-humour, though he could not refrain sometimes from jeering at his master for his imprudence in uncrowing himself and giving all away to his daughters; at which time, as he rhymingly expressed it, these daughters –

> For sudden joy did weep,
>   And I for sorrow sung,
> That such a king should play bo-peep
>   And go the fools among.

And in such wild sayings, and scraps of songs, of which he had plenty, this pleasant, honest fool poured out his heart even in the presence of Goneril herself, in many a bitter taunt and jest which cut to the quick, such as comparing the king to the hedge sparrow, who feeds the young of the cuckoo till they grow old enough, and then has its head bit off for its pains; and saying that an ass may know when the cart draws the horse (meaning that Lear's daughters, that ought to go behind, now ranked before their father); and that Lear was no longer Lear, but the shadow of Lear. For which free speeches he was once or twice threatened to be whipped.

The coolness and falling off of respect which Lear had begun to perceive were not all which this foolish fond father was to suffer from his unworthy daughter. She now plainly told him that his staying in her palace was inconvenient so long as he insisted upon keeping up an establishment of a hundred knights; that this establishment was useless and expensive and only served to fill her court with riot and feasting; and she prayed him that he would lessen their number and keep none but old men about him, such as himself, and fitting his age.

Lear at first could not believe his eyes or ears, nor that it was his daughter who spoke so unkindly. He could not believe that she who had received a crown from him could seek to cut off his train and grudge him the respect due to his old age. But she persisting in her undutiful demand, the old man's rage was so excited that he called her a detested kite and said that she spoke an untruth; and so indeed she did, for the hundred knights were all men of choice behaviour and sobriety of manners, skilled in all particulars of duty, and not given to rioting or feasting, as she said. And he bid his horses to be prepared, for he would go to his other daughter, Regan, he and his hundred knights; and he spoke of ingratitude, and said it was a marble-hearted devil, and showed more hideous in a child than the sea-monster. And he cursed his eldest daughter, Goneril, so as was terrible to hear, praying that she might never have a child, or, if she had, that it might live to return that scorn and contempt upon her which she had shown to him; that she might feel how sharper than a serpent's tooth it was to have a thankless child. And Goneril's husband, the Duke of Albany, beginning to excuse himself for any share which Lear might suppose he had in the unkindness, Lear would not hear him out, but in a rage ordered his horses to be saddled and set out with his followers for the abode of Regan, his other daughter. And Lear thought to himself how small the fault of Cordelia (if it was a fault) now appeared in comparison with her sister's, and he wept; and then he was ashamed that such a creature as Goneril should have so much power over his manhood as to make him weep.

Regan and her husband were keeping their court in great pomp and state at their palace; and Lear despatched his servant Caius with letters to his daughter, that she might be prepared for his reception, while he and his train followed after. But it seems that Goneril had been beforehand with him, sending letters also to Regan, accusing her father of waywardness and ill-humours, and advising her not to receive so great a train as he was bringing with him. This messenger arrived at the same time with Caius, and Caius and he met, and who should it be but Caius's old enemy the steward, whom he had formerly tripped up by the heels for his saucy behaviour to Lear. Caius not liking the fellow's look, and, suspecting what he came for, began to revile him and challenged him to fight, which the fellow refusing, Caius, in a fit of honest passion, beat him soundly, as such a mischief-maker and carrier of wicked messages deserved; which coming to the ears of Regan and her husband, they ordered Caius to be put in the stocks, though he was a messenger from the king her father and in that character demanded the highest respect. So that the first thing the king saw when he entered the castle was his faithful servant Caius sitting in that disgraceful situation.

This was but a bad omen of the reception which he was to expect; but a worse followed when, upon enquiry for his daughter and her husband, he was told they were weary with travelling all night and could not see him; and when, lastly, upon his insisting in a positive and angry manner to see them, they came to greet him, whom should he see in their company but the hated Goneril, who had come to tell her own story and set her sister against the king her father!

This sight much moved the old man, and still more to see Regan take her by the hand; and he asked Goneril if she was not ashamed to look upon his old white beard. And Regan advised him to go home again with Goneril, and live with her peaceably, dismissing half of his attendants, and to ask her forgiveness; for he was old and wanted discretion, and must be ruled and led by persons that had more discretion than himself. And Lear showed how preposterous that would sound, if he were to go down on his knees and beg of his own daughter for food and raiment; and he argued against such an unnatural dependence, declaring his resolution never to return with her, but to stay where he was with Regan, he and his hundred knights; for he said that she had not forgot the half of the kingdom which he had endowed her with, and that her eyes were not fierce like Goneril's, but mild and kind. And he said that rather than return to Goneril, with half his train cut off, he would go over to France and beg a wretched pension of the king there, who had married his youngest daughter without a portion.

But he was mistaken in expecting kinder treatment of Regan than he had experienced from her sister Goneril. As if willing to outdo her sister in unfilial behaviour, she declared that she thought fifty knights too many to wait upon him; that five-and-twenty were enough. Then Lear, nigh heartbroken, turned to Goneril and said that he would go back with her, for her fifty doubled five-and-twenty, and so her love was twice as much as Regan's. But Goneril excused herself, and said, what need of so many as five-and twenty? or even ten? or five? when he might be waited upon by her servants or her sister's servants? So these two wicked daughters, as if they strove to exceed each other in cruelty to their old father, who had been so good to them, by little and little would have abated him of all his train, all respect (little enough for him that once commanded a kingdom) which was left him to show that he had once been a king! Not that a splendid train is essential to happiness, but from a king to a beggar is a hard change, from commanding millions to be without one attendant; and it was the ingratitude in his daughters' denying more than what he would suffer by the want of it, which pierced this poor king to the heart; in so much that, with this double ill-usage, and vexation for having so foolishly given away a kingdom, his wits began to be unsettled, and while he said he knew not what, he vowed revenge against those unnatural hags and to make examples of them that should be a terror to the earth!

While he was thus idly threatening what his weak arm could never execute, night came on, and a loud storm of thunder and lightning with rain; and his daughters still persisting in their resolution not to admit his followers, he called for his horses, and chose rather to encounter the utmost fury of the storm abroad than stay under the same roof with these ungrateful daughters; and they, saying that the injuries which wilful men procure to themselves are their just punishment, suffered him to go in that condition and shut their doors upon him.

The winds were high, and the rain and storm increased, when the old man sallied forth to combat with the elements, less sharp than his daughters' unkindness. For many miles about there was scarce a bush; and there upon a heath, exposed to the fury of the storm in a dark night, did King Lear wander out, and defy the winds and the thunder; and he bid the winds to blow the earth into the sea, or swell the waves of the sea till they drowned the earth, that no token might remain of any such ungrateful animal as man. The old king was now left with no other companion than the poor fool, who still abided with him, with his merry conceits striving to out-jest misfortune, saying it was but a naughty night to swim in, and truly the king had better go in and ask his daughter's blessing:

But he that has a little tiny wit –
With heigh ho, the wind and the rain!
Must make content with his fortunes fit
Though the rain it raineth every day,

and swearing it was a brave night to cool a lady's pride.

Thus poorly accompanied, this once great monarch was found by his ever-faithful servant the good Earl of Kent, now transformed to Caius, who ever followed close at his side, though the king did not know him to be the earl; and he said: 'Alas, sir, are you here? Creatures that love night love not such nights as these. This dreadful storm has driven the beasts to their hiding-places. Man's nature cannot endure the affliction or the fear.'

And Lear rebuked him and said these lesser evils were not felt where a greater malady was fixed. When the mind is at ease the body has leisure to be delicate, but the tempest in his mind did take all feeling else from his senses but of that which beat at his heart. And he spoke of filial ingratitude, and said it was all one as if the mouth should tear the hand for lifting food to it; for parents were hands and food and everything to children.

But the good Caius still persisting in his entreaties that the king would not stay out in the open air, at last persuaded him to enter a little wretched hovel which stood upon the heath, where the fool first entering, suddenly ran back terrified, saying that he had seen a spirit. But upon examination this spirit proved to be nothing more than a poor Bedlam beggar who had crept into this deserted hovel for shelter, and with his talk about devils frighted the fool, one of those poor lunatics who are either mad, or feign to be so, the better to extort charity from the compassionate country people, who go about the country calling themselves poor Tom and poor Turly-good, saying, 'Who gives anything to poor Tom?' sticking pins and

There upon a heath, exposed to the fury of the storm
in a dark night, did King Lear wander out

nails and sprigs of rosemary into their arms to make them bleed; and with horrible actions, partly by prayers, and partly with lunatic curses, they move or terrify the ignorant country folk into giving them alms. This poor fellow was such a one; and the king, seeing him in so wretched a plight, with nothing but a blanket about his loins to cover his nakedness, could not be persuaded but that the fellow was some father who had given all away to his daughters and brought himself to that pass; for nothing, he thought, could bring a man to such wretchedness but the having unkind daughters.

And from this and many such wild speeches which he uttered the good Caius plainly perceived that he was not in his perfect mind, but that his daughters' ill-usage had really made him go mad. And now the loyalty of this worthy Earl of Kent showed itself in more essential services than he had hitherto found opportunity to perform. For with the assistance of some of the king's attendants who remained loyal he had the person of his royal master removed at daybreak to the castle of Dover, where his own friends and influence, as Earl of Kent, chiefly lay; and himself, embarking for France, hastened to the court of Cordelia, and did there in such moving terms represent the pitiful condition of her royal father, and set out in such lively colours the inhumanity of her sisters, that this good and loving child with many tears besought the king, her husband, that he would give her leave to embark for England, with a sufficient power to subdue these cruel daughters and their husbands and restore the old king, her father, to his throne; which being granted, she set forth, and with a royal army landed at Dover.

Lear, having by some chance escaped from the guardians which the good Earl of Kent had put over him to take care of him in his lunacy, was found by some of Cordelia's train, wandering about the fields near Dover, in a pitiable condition, stark mad, and singing aloud to himself, with a crown upon his head which he had made of straw and nettles and other wild weeds that he had picked up in the cornfields. By the advice of the physicians, Cordelia, though earnestly desirous of seeing her father, was prevailed upon to put off the meeting till, by sleep and the operation of herbs which they gave him, he should be restored to greater composure. By the aid of these skilful physicians, to whom Cordelia promised all her gold and jewels for the recovery of the old king, Lear was soon in a condition to see his daughter.

A tender sight it was to see the meeting between this father and daughter; to see the struggles between the joy of this poor old king at beholding again his once darling child, and the shame at receiving such filial kindness from her whom he had cast off for so small a fault in his displeasure; both these passions struggling with the remains of his malady, which in his half-crazed brain some-times made him that he scarce remembered where he was or who it was that so kindly kissed him and spoke to him. And then he would beg the standers-by not to laugh at him if he were mistaken in thinking this lady to be his daughter Cordelia! And then to see him fall on his knees to beg pardon of his child; and she, good lady, kneeling all the while to ask a blessing of him, and telling him that it did not become him to kneel, but it was her duty, for she was his child, his true and very child Cordelia! And she kissed him (as she said) to kiss away all her sisters' unkindness, and said that they might be ashamed of themselves, to turn their old kind father with his white beard out into the cold air, when her enemy's dog, though it had bit her (as she prettily expressed it), should have stayed by her fire such a night as that, and warmed himself. And she told her father how she had come from France with purpose to bring him assistance; and he said that she must forget and forgive, for he was old and foolish and did not know what he did; but that to be sure she had great cause not to love him, but her sisters had none. And Cordelia said that she had no cause, no more than they had.

So we will leave this old king in the protection of his dutiful and loving child, where, by the help of sleep and medicine, she and her physicians at length succeeded in winding up the untuned and jarring senses which the cruelty of his other daughters had so violently shaken. Let us return to say a word or two about those cruel daughters.

These monsters of ingratitude, who had been so false to their old father, could not be expected to prove more faithful to their own husbands. They soon grew tired of paying even the appearance of duty and affection, and in an open way showed they had fixed their loves upon another. It happened that the object of their guilty loves was the same. It was Edmund, a natural son of the late Earl of Gloucester, who by his treacheries had succeeded in disinheriting his brother Edgar, the lawful heir, from his earldom, and by his wicked practices was now earl himself; a wicked man, and a fit object for the love of such wicked creatures as Goneril and Regan. It falling out about this time that the Duke of Cornwall, Regan's husband, died, Regan immediately declared her intention of wedding this Earl of Gloucester, which rousing the jealousy of her sister, to whom as well as to Regan this wicked earl had at sundry times professed love, Goneril found means to make away with her sister by poison; but being detected in her practices, and imprisoned by her husband, the Duke of Albany, for this deed, and for her guilty passion for the earl which had come to his ears, she, in a fit of disappointed love and rage, shortly put an end to her own life. Thus the justice of heaven at last overtook these wicked daughters.

While the eyes of all men were upon this event, admiring the justice displayed in their deserved deaths, the same eyes were suddenly taken off from this sight to admire at the mysterious ways of the same power in the melancholy fate of the young and virtuous daughter, the Lady Cordelia, whose good deeds did seem to deserve a more fortunate conclusion. But it is an awful truth that innocence and piety are not always successful in this world. The forces which Goneril and Regan had sent out under the command of the bad Earl of Gloucester were victorious, and Cordelia, by the practices of this wicked earl, who did not like that any should stand between him and the throne, ended her life in prison. Thus heaven took this innocent lady to itself in her young years, after showing her to the world an illustrious example of filial duty. Lear did not long survive this kind child.

Before he died, the good Earl of Kent, who had still attended his old master's steps from the first of his daughters' ill-usage to this sad period of his decay, tried to make him understand that it was he who had followed him under the name of Caius; but Lear's care-crazed brain at that time could not comprehend how that could be, or how Kent and Caius could be the same person, so Kent thought it needless to trouble him with explanations at such a time; and, Lear soon after expiring, this faithful servant to the king, between age and grief for his old master's vexations, soon followed him to the grave.

How the judgment of heaven overtook the bad Earl of Gloucester, whose treasons were discovered, and himself slain in single combat with his brother, the lawful earl, and how Goneril's husband, the Duke of Albany, who was innocent of the death of Cordelia, and had never encouraged his lady in her wicked proceedings against her father, ascended the throne of Britain after the death of Lear, it is needless here to narrate, Lear and his three daughters being dead, whose adventures alone concern our story.

Macbeth

When Duncan the Meek reigned King of Scotland there lived a great thane, or lord, called Macbeth. This Macbeth was a near kinsman to the king, and in great esteem at court for his valour and conduct in the wars, an example of which he had lately given in defeating a rebel army assisted by the troops of Norway in terrible numbers.

The two Scottish generals, Macbeth and Banquo, returning victorious from this great battle, their way lay over a blasted heath, where they were stopped by the strange appearance of three figures like women, except that they had beards, and their withered skins and wild attire made them look not like any earthly creatures. Macbeth first addressed them, when they, seemingly offended, laid each one her choppy finger upon her skinny lips, in token of silence; and the first of them saluted Macbeth with the title of Thane of Glamis. The general was not a little startled to find himself known by such creatures; but how much more, when the second of them followed up that salute by giving him the title of Thane of Cawdor, to which honour he had no pretensions; and again the third bid him, 'All hail! that shalt be king hereafter!' Such a prophetic greeting might well amaze him, who knew that while the king's sons lived he could not hope to succeed to the throne. Then turning to Banquo, they pronounced him, in a sort of riddling terms, to be *lesser than Macbeth, and greater! Not so happy, but much happier!* and prophesied that though he should never reign, yet his sons after him should be kings in Scotland. They then turned into air and vanished; by which the generals knew them to be the weird sisters, or witches.

While they stood pondering on the strangeness of this adventure there arrived certain messengers from the king, who were empowered by him to confer upon Macbeth the dignity of Thane of Cawdor. An event so miraculously corresponding with the prediction of the witches astonished Macbeth, and he stood wrapped in amazement, unable to make reply to the messengers; and in that point of time swelling hopes arose in his mind that the prediction of the third witch might in like manner have its accomplishment, and that he should one day reign king in Scotland.

Turning to Banquo, he said, 'Do you not hope that your children shall be kings, when what the witches promised to me has so wonderfully come to pass?'

'That hope,' answered the general, 'might enkindle you to aim at the throne; but oftentimes these ministers of darkness tell us truths in little things, to betray us into deeds of greatest consequence.'

But the wicked suggestions of the witches had sunk too deep into the mind of Macbeth to allow him to attend to the warnings of the good Banquo. From that time he bent all his thoughts how to compass the throne of Scotland.

Macbeth had a wife, to whom he communicated the strange prediction of the weird sisters and its partial accomplishment. She was a bad, ambitious woman, and so as her husband and herself could arrive at greatness she cared not much by what means. She spurred on the reluctant purpose of Macbeth, who felt compunction at the thoughts of blood, and did not cease to represent the murder of the king as a step absolutely necessary to the fulfilment of the flattering prophecy.

It happened at this time that the king, who out of his royal condescension would oftentimes visit his principal nobility upon gracious terms, came to Macbeth's house, attended by his two sons, Malcolm and Donalbain, and a numerous train of thanes and attendants, the more to honour Macbeth for the triumphal success of his wars.

The castle of Macbeth was pleasantly situated and the air about it was sweet and wholesome, which appeared by the nests which the martlet, or swallow, had built under all the jutting friezes and buttresses of the building, wherever it found a place of advantage; for where those birds most breed and haunt the air is observed to be delicate. The king entered, well pleased with the place, and not less so with the attentions and respect of his honoured hostess, Lady Macbeth, who had the art of covering treacherous purposes with smiles, and could look like the innocent flower while she was indeed the serpent under it.

The king, being tired with his journey, went early to bed, and in his stateroom two grooms of his chamber (as was the custom) slept beside him. He had been unusually pleased with his reception, and had made presents before he retired to his principal officers; and among the rest had sent a diamond to Lady Macbeth, greeting her by the name of his most kind hostess.

Now was the middle of night, when over half the world nature seems dead, and wicked dreams abuse men's minds asleep, and none but the wolf and the murderer are abroad. This was the time when Lady Macbeth waked to plot the murder of the king. She would not have undertaken a deed so abhorrent to her sex but that she feared her husband's nature, that it was too full of the milk of human kindness to do a contrived murder. She knew him to be ambitious, but withal to be scrupulous, and not yet prepared for that height of crime which commonly in the end accompanies inordinate ambition. She had won him to consent to the murder, but she doubted his resolution; and she feared that the natural tenderness of his disposition (more humane than her own) would come between and defeat the purpose. So with her own hands armed with a dagger she approached the king's bed, having taken care to ply the grooms of his chamber so with wine that they slept intoxicated and careless of their charge. There lay Duncan in a sound sleep after the fatigues of his journey, and as she viewed him earnestly there was something in his face, as he slept, which resembled her own father, and she had not the courage to proceed.

She returned to confer with her husband. His resolution had begun to stagger. He considered that there were strong reasons against the deed. In the first place, he was not only a subject, but a near kinsman to the king; and he had been his host and entertainer that day, whose duty, by the laws of hospitality, it was to shut the door against his murderers, not bear the knife himself. Then he considered how just and merciful a king this Duncan had been, how clear of offence to his subjects, how loving to his nobility, and in particular to him; that such kings are the peculiar care of heaven, and their subjects doubly bound to revenge their deaths. Besides, by the favours of the king, Macbeth stood high in the opinion of all sorts of men, and how would those honours be stained by the reputation of so foul a murder!

In these conflicts of the mind Lady Macbeth found her husband inclining to the better part and resolving to proceed no further. But she, being a woman not easily shaken from her evil purpose, began to pour in at his ears words which infused a portion of her own spirit into his mind, assigning reason upon reason why he should not shrink from what he had undertaken; how easy the deed was; how soon it would be over; and how the action of one short night would give to all their nights and days to come sovereign sway and royalty! Then she threw contempt on his change of purpose, and accused him of fickleness and cowardice; and declared that she had given suck, and knew how tender it was to love the babe that milked her, but she would, while it was smiling in her face, have plucked it from her breast and dashed its brains out if she had so sworn to do it as he had sworn to perform that murder. Then she added, how practicable it was to lay the guilt of the deed upon the drunken, sleepy grooms. And with the valour of her tongue she so chastised his sluggish resolutions that he once more summoned up courage to the bloody business.

So, taking the dagger in his hand, he softly stole in the dark to the room where Duncan lay; and as he went he thought he saw another dagger in the air, with the handle towards him, and on the blade and at the point of it drops of blood; but when he tried to grasp at it it was nothing but air, a mere phantasm proceeding from his own hot and oppressed brain and the business he had in hand.

Getting rid of this fear, he entered the king's room, whom he despatched with one stroke of his dagger. Just as he had done the murder one of the grooms who slept in the chamber laughed in his sleep, and the other cried, 'Murder,' which woke them both.

But they said a short prayer; one of them said, 'God bless us!' and the other answered, 'Amen'; and addressed themselves to sleep again. Macbeth, who stood listening to them, tried to say 'Amen' when the fellow said 'God bless us!' but, though he had most need of a blessing, the word stuck in his throat and he could not pronounce it.

Again he thought he heard a voice which cried: 'Sleep no more! Macbeth doth murder sleep, the innocent sleep, that nourishes life.' Still it cried, 'Sleep no more!' to all the house. 'Glamis hath murdered sleep, and therefore Cawdor shall sleep no more, Macbeth shall sleep no more.'

With such horrible imaginations Macbeth returned to his listening wife, who began to think he had failed of his purpose and that the deed was somehow frustrated. He came in so distracted a state that she reproached him with his want of firmness and sent him to wash his hands of the blood which stained them, while she took his dagger, with purpose to stain the cheeks of the grooms with blood, to make it seem their guilt.

Morning came, and with it the discovery of the murder, which could not be concealed; and though Macbeth and his lady made great show of grief, and the proofs against the grooms (the dagger being produced against them and their faces smeared with blood) were sufficiently strong, yet the entire suspicion fell upon Macbeth, whose inducements to such a deed were so much more forcible than such poor silly grooms could be supposed to have; and Duncan's two sons fled. Malcolm, the eldest, sought for refuge in the English court; and the youngest, Donalbain, made his escape to Ireland.

The king's sons, who should have succeeded him, having thus

vacated the throne, Macbeth as next heir was crowned king, and thus the prediction of the weird sisters was literally accomplished.

Though placed so high, Macbeth and his queen could not forget the prophecy of the weird sisters that, though Macbeth should be king, yet not his children, but the children of Banquo, should be kings after him. The thought of this, and that they had defiled their hands with blood, and done so great crimes, only to place the posterity of Banquo upon the throne, so rankled within them that they determined to put to death both Banquo and his son, to make void the predictions of the weird sisters, which in their own case had been so remarkably brought to pass.

For this purpose they made a great supper, to which they invited all the chief thanes; and among the rest, with marks of particular respect, Banquo and his son Fleance were invited. The way by which Banquo was to pass to the palace at night was beset by murderers appointed by Macbeth, who stabbed Banquo; but in the scuffle Fleance escaped. From that Fleance descended a race of monarchs who afterwards filled the Scottish throne, ending with James the Sixth of Scotland and the First of England, under whom the two crowns of England and Scotland were united.

At supper, the queen, whose manners were in the highest degree affable and royal, played the hostess with a gracefulness and attention which conciliated everyone present, and Macbeth discoursed freely with his thanes and nobles, saying that all that was honourable in the country was under his roof, if he had but his good friend Banquo present, whom yet he hoped he should rather have to chide for neglect than to lament for any mischance. Just at these words the ghost of Banquo, whom he had caused to be murdered, entered the room and placed himself on the chair which Macbeth was about to occupy. Though Macbeth was a bold man, and one that could have faced the devil without trembling, at this horrible sight his cheeks turned white with fear and he stood quite unmanned, with his eyes fixed upon the ghost. His queen and all the nobles, who saw nothing, but perceived him gazing (as they thought) upon an empty chair, took it for a fit of distraction; and she reproached him, whispering that it was but the same fancy which made him see the dagger in the air when he was about to kill Duncan. But Macbeth continued to see the ghost, and gave no heed to all they could say, while he addressed it with distracted words, yet so significant that his queen, fearing the dreadful secret would be disclosed, in great haste dismissed the guests, excusing the infirmity of Macbeth as a disorder he was often troubled with.

To such dreadful fancies Macbeth was subject. His queen and he had their sleeps afflicted with terrible dreams, and the blood of Banquo troubled them not more than the escape of Fleance, whom now they looked upon as father to a line of kings who should keep their posterity out of the throne. With these miserable thoughts they found no peace, and Macbeth determined once more to seek out the weird sisters and know from them the worst.

He sought them in a cave upon the heath, where they, who knew by foresight of his coming, were engaged in preparing their dreadful charms by which they conjured up infernal spirits to reveal to them futurity. Their horrid ingredients were toads, bats, and serpents, the eye of a newt and the tongue of a dog, the leg of a lizard and the wing of the night-owl, the scale of a dragon, the tooth of a wolf, the maw of the ravenous salt-sea shark, the mummy of a witch, the root of the poisonous hemlock (this to have effect must be digged in the dark), the gall of a goat, and the liver of a Jew, with slips of the yew tree that roots itself in graves, and the finger of a dead child. All these were set on to boil in a great kettle, or cauldron, which, as fast as it grew too hot, was cooled with a baboon's blood. To these they poured in the blood of a sow that had eaten her young, and they threw into the flame the grease that had sweaten from a murderer's gibbet. By these charms they bound the infernal spirit to answer their questions.

It was demanded of Macbeth whether he would have his doubts resolved by them or by their masters, the spirits.

He, nothing daunted by the dreadful ceremonies which he saw, boldly answered: 'Where are they? Let me see them.'

And they called the spirits, which were three. And the first arose in the likeness of an armed head, and he called Macbeth by name and bid him beware of the Thane of Fife; for which caution Macbeth thanked him; for Macbeth had entertained a jealousy of Macduff, the Thane of Fife.

And the second spirit arose in the likeness of a bloody child, and he called Macbeth by name and bid him have no fear, but laugh to scorn the power of man, for none of woman born should have power to hurt him; and he advised him to be bloody, bold, and resolute.

'Then live, Macduff!' cried the king. 'What need I fear thee? But yet I will make assurance doubly sure. Thou shalt not live, that I may tell pale-hearted fear it lies, and sleep in spite of thunder.'

That spirit being dismissed, a third arose in the form of a child crowned, with a tree in his hand. He called Macbeth by name and comforted him against conspiracies, saying that he should never be vanquished until the wood of Birnam to Dunsinane hill should come against him.

'Sweet bodements! good!' cried Macbeth; 'who can unfix the forest, and move it from its earthbound roots? I see I shall live the usual period of man's life, and not be cut off by a violent death. But my heart throbs to know one thing. Tell me, if your art can tell so much, if Banquo's issue shall ever reign in this kingdom?'

Here the cauldron sank into the ground, and a noise of music was heard, and eight shadows, like kings, passed by Macbeth, and Banquo last, who bore a glass which showed the figures of many more, and Banquo, all bloody, smiled upon Macbeth, and pointed to them; by which Macbeth knew that these were the posterity of Banquo, who should reign after him in Scotland; and the witches, with a sound of soft music, and with dancing, making a show of duty and welcome to Macbeth, vanished. And from this time the thoughts of Macbeth were all bloody and dreadful.

The first thing he heard when he got out of the witches' cave was that Macduff, Thane of Fife, had fled to England to join the army which was forming against him under Malcolm, the eldest son of the late king, with intent to displace Macbeth and set Malcolm, the right heir, upon the throne. Macbeth, stung with rage, set upon the castle of Macduff and put his wife and children, whom the thane had left behind, to the sword, and extended the slaughter to all who claimed the least relationship to Macduff.

These and such-like deeds alienated the minds of all his chief nobility from him. Such as could fled to join with Malcolm and Macduff, who were now approaching with a powerful army which they had raised in England; and the rest secretly wished success to their arms, though, for fear of Macbeth, they could take no active part. His recruits went on slowly. Everybody hated the tyrant; nobody loved or honoured him; but all suspected him; and he began to envy the condition of Duncan, whom he had murdered, who slept soundly in his grave, against whom treason had done its worst. Steel nor poison, domestic malice nor foreign levies, could hurt him any longer.

While these things were acting, the queen, who had been the sole partner in his wickedness, in whose bosom he could sometimes seek a momentary repose from those terrible dreams which afflicted them both nightly, died, it is supposed, by her own hands, unable to bear the remorse of guilt and public hate; by which event he was left alone, without a soul to love or care for him, or a friend to whom he could confide his wicked purposes.

He grew careless of life and wished for death; but the near approach of Malcolm's army roused in him what remained of his ancient courage, and he determined to die (as he expressed it) 'with armour on his back'. Besides this, the hollow promises of the witches had filled him with a false confidence, and he remembered the sayings of the spirits, that none of woman born was to hurt him, and that he was never to be vanquished till Birnam wood should come to Dunsinane, which he thought could never be. So he shut himself up in his castle, whose impregnable strength was such as defied a siege. Here he sullenly waited the approach of Malcolm. When, upon a day, there came a messenger to him, pale and shaking with fear, almost unable to report that which he had seen; for he averred, that as he stood upon his watch on the hill he looked towards Birnam, and to his thinking the wood began to move!

'Liar and slave!' cried Macbeth. 'If thou speakest false, thou shalt hang alive upon the next tree, till famine end thee. If thy tale be true, I care not if thou dost as much by me'; for Macbeth now began to faint in resolution, and to doubt the equivocal speeches of the spirits. He was not to fear till Birnam wood should come to Dunsinane; and now a wood did move! 'However,' said he, 'if this which he avouches be true, let us arm and out. There is no flying hence, nor staying here. I begin to be weary of the sun, and wish my life at an end.' With these desperate speeches he sallied forth upon the besiegers, who had now come up to the castle.

The strange appearance which had given the messenger an idea of a wood moving is easily solved. When the besieging army marched through the wood of Birnam, Malcolm, like a skilful general, instructed his soldiers to hew down every one a bough and bear it before him, by way of concealing the true numbers of his host. This marching of the soldiers with boughs had at a distance the appearance which had frightened the messenger. Thus were the words of the spirit brought to pass, in a sense different from that in which Macbeth had understood them, and one great hold of his confidence was gone.

And now a severe skirmishing took place, in which Macbeth, though feebly supported by those who called themselves his friends, but in reality hated the tyrant and inclined to the party of Malcolm and Macduff, yet fought with the extreme of rage and valour, cutting to pieces all who were opposed to him, till he came to where Macduff was fighting. Seeing Macduff, and remembering the caution of the spirit who had counselled him to avoid Macduff, above all men, he would have turned, but Macduff, who had been seeking him through the whole fight, opposed his turning, and a fierce contest ensued, Macduff giving him many foul reproaches for the murder of his wife and children. Macbeth, whose soul was charged enough with blood of that family already, would still have declined the combat; but Macduff still urged him to it, calling him tyrant, murderer, hell-hound, and villain.

Then Macbeth remembered the words of the spirit, how none of woman born should hurt him; and, smiling confidently, he said to Macduff: 'Thou losest thy labour, Macduff. As easily thou mayest impress the air with thy sword as make me vulnerable. I bear a charmed life, which must not yield to one of woman born.'

'Despair thy charm,' said Macduff, 'and let that lying spirit whom thou hast served tell thee that Macduff was never born of woman, never as the ordinary manner of men is to be born, but was untimely taken from his mother.'

'Accursed be the tongue which tells me so,' said the trembling Macbeth, who felt his last hold of confidence give way; 'and let never man in future believe the lying equivocations of witches and juggling spirits who deceive us in words which have double senses, and, while they keep their promise literally, disappoint our hopes with a different meaning. I will not fight with thee.'

'Then live!' said the scornful Macduff. 'We will have a show of thee, as men show monsters, and a painted board, on which shall be written, "Here men may see the tyrant!" '

'Never,' said Macbeth, whose courage returned with despair; 'I will not live to kiss the ground before young Malcolm's feet, and to be baited with the curses of the rabble. Though Birnam wood be come to Dunsinane, and thou opposed to me, who wast never born of woman, yet will I try the last.'

With these frantic words he threw himself upon Macduff, who, after a severe struggle, in the end overcame him, and, cutting off his head, made a present of it to the young and lawful king, Malcolm, who took upon him the government which, by the machinations of the usurper, he had so long been deprived of, and ascended the throne of Duncan the Meek among the acclamations of the nobles and the people.

All's Well that Ends Well

Bertram, Count of Rousillon, had newly come to his title and estate by the death of his father. The King of France loved the father of Bertram, and when he heard of his death he sent for his son to come immediately to his royal court in Paris, intending, for the friendship he bore the late count, to grace young Bertram with his especial favour and protection.

Bertram was living with his mother, the widowed countess, when Lafeu, an old lord of the French court, came to conduct him to the king. The King of France was an absolute monarch and the invitation to court was in the form of a royal mandate, or positive command, which no subject, of what high dignity soever, might disobey; therefore, though the countess, in parting with this dear son, seemed a second time to bury her husband, whose loss she had so lately mourned, yet she dared not to keep him a single day, but gave instant orders for his departure. Lafeu, who came to fetch him, tried to comfort the countess for the loss of her late lord and her son's sudden absence; and he said, in a courtier's flattering manner, that the king was so kind a prince, she would find in his majesty a husband, and that he would be a father to her son; meaning only that the good king would befriend the fortunes of Bertram. Lafeu told the countess that the king had fallen into a sad malady, which was pronounced by his physicians to be incurable. The lady expressed great sorrow on hearing this account of the king's ill health, and said she wished the father of Helena (a young gentlewoman who was present in attendance upon her) were living, for that she doubted not he could have cured his majesty of his disease. And she told Lafeu something of the history of Helena, saying she was the only daughter of the famous physician, Gerard de Narbon, and that he had recommended his daughter to her care when he was dying, so that since his death she had taken Helena under her protection; then the countess praised the virtuous disposition and excellent qualities of Helena, saying she inherited these virtues from her worthy father. While she was speaking, Helena wept in sad and mournful silence, which made the countess gently reprove her for too much grieving for her father's death.

Bertram now bade his mother farewell. The countess parted with this dear son with tears and many blessings, and commended him to the care of Lafeu, saying: 'Good my lord, advise him, for he is an unseasoned courtier.'

Bertram's last words were spoken to Helena, but they were words of mere civility, wishing her happiness; and he concluded his short farewell to her with saying: 'Be comfortable to my mother, your mistress, and make much of her.'

Helena had long loved Bertram, and when she wept in sad and mournful silence the tears she shed were not for Gerard de Narbon. Helena loved her father, but in the present feeling of a deeper love, the object of which she was about to lose, she had forgotten the very form and features of her dead father, her imagination presenting no image to her mind but Bertram's.

Helena had long loved Bertram, yet she always remembered that he was the Count of Rousillon, descended from the most ancient family in France. She of humble birth. Her parents of no note at all. His ancestors all noble. And therefore she looked up to the high-born Bertram as to her master and to her dear lord, and dared not form any wish but to live his servant, and, so living, to die his vassal.

So great the distance seemed to her between his height of dignity and her lowly fortunes that she would say: 'It were all one that I should love a bright particular star, and think to wed it, Bertram is so far above me.'

Bertram's absence filled her eyes with tears and her heart with sorrow; for though she loved without hope, yet it was a pretty comfort to her to see him every hour, and Helena would sit and look upon his dark eye, his arched brow, and the curls of his fine hair till she seemed to draw his portrait on the tablet of her heart, that heart too capable of retaining the memory of every line in the features of that loved face.

Gerard de Narbon, when he died, left her no other portion than some prescriptions of rare and well-proved virtue, which, by deep study and long experience in medicine, he had collected as sovereign and almost infallible remedies. Among the rest there was one set down as an approved medicine for the disease under which Lafeu said the king at that time languished; and when Helena heard of the king's complaint, she, who till now had been so humble and so hopeless, formed an ambitious project in her mind to go herself to Paris and undertake the cure of the king. But though Helena was the possessor of this choice prescription, it was unlikely, as the king as well as his physicians was of opinion that his disease was incurable, that they would give credit to a poor unlearned virgin if she should offer to perform a cure. The firm hopes that Helena had of succeeding, if she might be permitted to make the trial, seemed more than even her father's skill warranted, though he was the most famous physician of his time; for she felt a strong faith that this good medicine was sanctified by all the luckiest stars in heaven to be the legacy that should advance her fortune, even to the high dignity of being Count Rousillon's wife.

Bertram had not been long gone when the countess was informed by her steward that he had overheard Helena talking to herself, and that he understood, from some words she uttered, she was in love with Bertram and thought of following him to Paris. The countess dismissed the steward with thanks, and desired him to tell Helena she wished to speak with her. What she had just heard of

Helena brought the remembrance of days long past into the mind of the countess; those days, probably, when her love for Bertram's father first began; and she said to herself: 'Even so it was with me when I was young. Love is a thorn that belongs to the rose of youth; for in the season of youth, if ever we are Nature's children, these faults are ours, though then we think not they are faults.'

While the countess was thus meditating on the loving errors of her own youth, Helena entered, and she said to her, 'Helena, you know I am a mother to you.'

Helena replied, 'You are my honourable mistress.'

'You are my daughter,' said the countess again. 'I say I am your mother. Why do you start and look pale at my words?'

With looks of alarm and confused thoughts, fearing the countess suspected her love, Helena still replied, 'Pardon me, madam, you are not my mother; the Count Rousillon cannot be my brother, nor I your daughter.'

'Yet, Helena,' said the countess, 'you might be my daughter-in-law; and I am afraid that is what you mean to be, the words *mother* and *daughter* so disturb you. Helena, do you love my son?'

'Good madam, pardon me,' said the affrighted Helena.

Again the countess repeated her question. 'Do you love my son?'

'Do not you love him, madam?' said Helena.

The countess replied: 'Give me not this evasive answer, Helena. Come, come, disclose the state of your affections, for your love has to the full appeared.'

Helena, on her knees now, owned her love, and with shame and terror implored the pardon of her noble mistress; and with words expressive of the sense she had of the inequality between their fortunes she protested Bertram did not know she loved him, comparing her humble, unaspiring love to a poor Indian who adores the sun that looks upon his worshipper but knows of him no more. The countess asked Helena if she had not lately an intent to go to Paris. Helena owned the design she had formed in her mind when she heard Lafeu speak of the king's illness.

'This was your motive for wishing to go to Paris,' said the countess, 'was it? Speak truly.'

Helena honestly answered, 'My lord your son made me to think of this; else Paris, and the medicine and the king had from the conversation of my thoughts been absent then.'

The countess heard the whole of this confession without saying a word either of approval or of blame, but she strictly questioned Helena as to the probability of the medicine being useful to the king. She found that it was the most prized by Gerard de Narbon of all he possessed, and that he had given it to his daughter on his deathbed; and remembering the solemn promise she had made at that awful hour in regard to this young maid, whose destiny, and the life of the king himself, seemed to depend on the execution of a project (which, though conceived by the fond suggestions of a loving maiden's thoughts, the countess knew not but it might be the unseen workings of Providence to bring to pass the recovery of the king and to lay the foundation of the future fortunes of Gerard de Narbon's daughter), free leave she gave to Helena to pursue her own way, and generously furnished her with ample means and suitable attendants; and Helena set out for Paris with the blessings of the countess and her kindest wishes for her success.

Helena arrived at Paris, and by the assistance of her friend, the old Lord Lafeu, she obtained an audience of the king. She had still many difficulties to encounter, for the king was not easily prevailed on to try the medicine offered him by this fair young doctor. But she told him she was Gerard de Narbon's daughter (with whose fame the king was well acquainted), and she offered the precious medicine as the darling treasure which contained the essence of all her father's long experience and skill, and she boldly engaged to forfeit her life if it failed to restore his majesty to perfect health in the space of two days. The king at length consented to try it, and in two days' time Helena was to lose her life if the king did not recover; but if she succeeded, he promised to give her the choice of any man throughout all France (the princes only excepted) whom she could like for a husband; the choice of a husband being the fee Helena demanded if she cured the king of his disease.

Helena did not deceive herself in the hope she conceived of the efficacy of her father's medicine. Before two days were at an end the king was restored to perfect health, and he assembled all the young noblemen of his court together, in order to confer the promised reward of a husband upon his fair physician; and he desired Helena to look round on this youthful parcel of noble bachelors and choose her husband. Helena was not slow to make her choice, for among these young lords she saw the Count Rousillon, and, turning to Bertram, she said: 'This is the man. I dare not say, my lord, I take you, but I give me and my service ever whilst I live into your guiding power.'

'Why, then,' said the king, 'young Bertram, take her; she is your wife.'

Bertram did not hesitate to declare his dislike to this present of the king's of the self-offered Helena, who, he said, was a poor physician's daughter, bred at his father's charge, and now living a dependant on his mother's bounty.

Helena heard him speak these words of rejection and of scorn, and she said to the king: 'That you are well, my lord, I am glad. Let the rest go.'

But the king would not suffer his royal command to be so slighted, for the power of bestowing their nobles in marriage was one of the many privileges of the kings of France, and that same day Bertram was married to Helena, a forced and uneasy marriage to Bertram, and of no promising hope to the poor lady, who, though she gained the noble husband she had hazarded her life to obtain, seemed to have won but a splendid blank, her husband's love not being a gift in the power of the King of France to bestow.

Helena was no sooner married than she was desired by Bertram to apply to the king for him for leave of absence from court; and when she brought him the king's permission for his departure, Bertram told her that he was not prepared for this sudden marriage, it had much unsettled him, and therefore she must not wonder at the course he should pursue. If Helena wondered not, she grieved when she found it was his intention to leave her. He ordered her to go home to his mother. When Helena heard this unkind command, she replied: 'Sir, I can nothing say to this but that I am your most obedient servant, and shall ever with true observance seek to eke out that desert wherein my homely stars have failed to equal my great fortunes.'

But this humble speech of Helena's did not at all move the haughty Bertram to pity his gentle wife, and he parted from her without even the common civility of a kind farewell.

Back to the countess then Helena returned. She had accomplished the purport of her journey, she had preserved the life of the king, and she had wedded her heart's dear lord, the Count Rousillon; but she returned back a dejected lady to her noble mother-in-law, and as soon as she entered the house she received a letter from Bertram which almost broke her heart.

The good countess received her with a cordial welcome, as if she had been her son's own choice and a lady of a high degree, and she spoke kind words to comfort her for the unkind neglect of Bertram in sending his wife home on her bridal day alone. But this gracious reception failed to cheer the sad mind of Helena, and she said: 'Madam, my lord is gone, for ever gone.'

She then read these words out of Bertram's letter: '*When you can get the ring from my finger, which never shall come off, then call me husband, but in such a Then I write a Never.*'

'This is a dreadful sentence!' said Helena.

The countess begged her to have patience, and said, now Bertram was gone, she should be her child and that she deserved a lord that twenty such rude boys as Bertram might tend upon, and hourly call her mistress. But in vain by respectful condescension and kind flattery this matchless mother tried to soothe the sorrows of her daughter-in-law.

Helena still kept her eyes fixed upon the letter, and cried out in an agony of grief: '*Till I have no wife, I have nothing in France.*' The countess asked her if she found those words in the letter.

'Yes, madam,' was all poor Helena could answer.

The next morning Helena was missing. She left a letter to be delivered to the countess after she was gone, to acquaint her with the reason of her sudden absence. In this letter she informed her that she was so much grieved at having driven Bertram from his native country and his home, that to atone for her offence, she had undertaken a pilgrimage to the shrine of St Jaques le Grand, and concluded with requesting the countess to inform her son that the wife he so hated had left his house for ever.

Bertram, when he left Paris, went to Florence, and there became an officer in the Duke of Florence's army, and after a successful war, in which he distinguished himself by many brave actions, Bertram received letters from his mother containing the acceptable tidings that Helena would no more disturb him; and he was preparing to return home, when Helena herself, clad in her pilgrim's weeds, arrived at the city of Florence.

Florence was a city through which the pilgrims used to pass on their way to St Jaques le Grand; and when Helena arrived at this city she heard that a hospitable widow dwelt there who used to receive into her house the female pilgrims that were going to visit the shrine of that saint, giving them lodging and kind entertainment. To this good lady, therefore, Helena went, and the widow gave her a courteous welcome and invited her to see whatever was curious in that famous city, and told her that if she would like to see the duke's army she would take her where she might have a full view of it.

'And you will see a countryman of yours,' said the widow. 'His name is Count Rousillon, who has done worthy service in the duke's wars.' Helena wanted no second invitation, when she found Bertram was to make part of the show. She accompanied her hostess; and a sad and mournful pleasure it was to her to look once more upon her dear husband's face.

'Is he not a handsome man?' said the widow.

'I like him well,' replied Helena, with great truth.

All the way they walked the talkative widow's discourse was all of Bertram. She told Helena the story of Bertram's marriage, and how he had deserted the poor lady his wife and entered into the duke's army to avoid living with her. To this account of her own misfortunes Helena patiently listened, and when it was ended the history of Bertram was not yet done, for then the widow began another tale, every word of which sank deep into the mind of Helena; for the story she now told was of Bertram's love for her daughter.

Though Bertram did not like the marriage forced on him by the king, it seems he was not insensible to love, for since he had been stationed with the army at Florence he had fallen in love with Diana, a fair young gentlewoman, the daughter of this widow who was Helena's hostess; and every night, with music of all sorts, and songs composed in praise of Diana's beauty, he would come under her window and solicit her love; and all his suit to her was that she would permit him to visit her by stealth after the family were retired to rest. But Diana would by no means be persuaded to grant this improper request, nor give any encouragement to his suit, knowing him to be a married man; for Diana had been brought up under the counsels of a prudent mother, who, though she was now in reduced circumstances, was well born and descended from the noble family of the Capulets.

All this the good lady related to Helena, highly praising the virtuous principles of her discreet daughter, which she said were entirely owing to the excellent education and good advice she had given her; and she further said that Bertram had been particularly importunate with Diana to admit him to the visit he so much desired that night, because he was going to leave Florence early the next morning.

Though it grieved Helena to hear of Bertram's love for the widow's daughter, yet from this story the ardent mind of Helena conceived a project (nothing discouraged at the ill success of her former one) to recover her truant lord. She disclosed to the widow that she was Helena, the deserted wife of Bertram, and requested that her kind hostess and her daughter would suffer this visit from Bertram to take place, and allow her to pass herself upon Bertram for Diana, telling them her chief motive for desiring to have this secret meeting with her husband was to get a ring from him, which, he had said, if ever she was in possession of he would acknowledge her as his wife.

The widow and her daughter promised to assist her in this affair, partly moved by pity for this unhappy, forsaken wife and partly won over to her interest by the promises of reward which Helena made them, giving them a purse of money in earnest of her future favour.

In the course of that day Helena caused information to be sent to Bertram that she was dead, hoping that, when he thought himself free to make a second choice by the news of her death, he would offer marriage to her in her feigned character of Diana. And if she could obtain the ring and this promise, too, she doubted not she should make some future good come of it.

In the evening, after it was dark, Bertram was admitted into Diana's chamber, and Helena was there ready to receive him. The flattering compliments and love discourse he addressed to Helena were precious sounds to her though she knew they were meant for Diana; and Bertram was so well pleased with her that he made her a solemn promise to be her husband, and to love her for ever; which she hoped would be prophetic of a real affection, when he should know it was his own wife, the despised Helena, whose conversation had so delighted him.

Bertram never knew how sensible a lady Helena was, else perhaps he would not have been so regardless of her; and seeing her every day, he had entirely overlooked her beauty; a face we are accustomed to see constantly losing the effect which is caused by the first sight either of beauty or of plainness; and of her understanding it was impossible he should judge, because she felt such reverence, mixed with her love for him, that she was always silent in his presence. But now that her future fate, and the happy ending of all her love-projects, seemed to depend on her leaving a favourable impression on the mind of Bertram from this night's interview, she exerted all her wit to please him; and the simple graces of her lively conversation and the endearing sweetness of her manners so charmed Bertram that he vowed she should be his wife. Helena begged the ring from off his finger as a token of his regard, and he gave it to her; and in return for this ring, which it was of such importance to her to possess, she gave him another ring, which was one the king had made her a present of. Before it was light in the morning she sent Bertram away; and he immediately set out on his journey towards his mother's house.

Helena prevailed on the widow and Diana to accompany her to Paris, their further assistance being necessary to the full accomplishment of the plan she had formed. When they arrived there, they found the king was gone upon a visit to the Countess of Rousillon, and Helena followed the king with all the speed she could make.

The king was still in perfect health, and his gratitude to her who had been the means of his recovery was so lively in his mind that the moment he saw the Countess of Rousillon he began to talk of Helena, calling her a precious jewel that was lost by the folly of her son; but seeing the subject distressed the countess, who sincerely lamented the death of Helena, he said: 'My good lady, I have forgiven and forgotten all.'

But the good-natured old Lafeu, who was present, and could not bear that the memory of his favourite Helena should be so lightly passed over, said, 'This I must say, the young lord did great offence to his majesty, his mother, and his lady; but to himself he did the greatest wrong of all, for he has lost a wife whose beauty astonished all eyes, whose words took all ears captive, whose deep perfection made all hearts wish to serve her.'

The king said: 'Praising what is lost makes the remembrance dear. Well – call him hither'; meaning Bertram, who now presented himself before the king, and on his expressing deep sorrow for the injuries he had done to Helena the king, for his dead father's and his admirable mother's sake, pardoned him and restored him once more to his favour. But the gracious countenance of the king was soon changed towards him, for he perceived that Bertram wore the very ring upon his finger which he had given to Helena; and he well remembered that Helena had called all the saints in heaven to witness she would never part with that ring unless she sent it to the king himself upon some great disaster befalling her; and Bertram, on the king's questioning him how he came by the ring, told an improbable story of a lady throwing it to him out of a window, and denied ever having seen Helena since the day of their marriage. The king, knowing Bertram's dislike to his wife, feared he had destroyed her, and he ordered his guards to seize Bertram, saying: 'I am wrapped in dismal thinking, for I fear the life of Helena was foully snatched.'

At this moment Diana and her mother entered and presented a petition to the king, wherein they begged his majesty to exert his royal power to compel Bertram to marry Diana, he having made her a solemn promise of marriage. Bertram, fearing the king's anger, denied he had made any such promise; and then Diana produced the ring (which Helena had put into her hands) to confirm the truth of her words; and she said that she had given Bertram the ring he then wore, in exchange for that, at the time he vowed to marry her. On hearing this the king ordered the guards to seize her also; and, her account of the ring differing from Bertram's, the king's suspicions were confirmed, and he said if they did not confess how they came by this ring of Helena's they should be both put to death. Diana requested her mother might be permitted to fetch the jeweller of whom she bought the ring, which, being granted, the widow went out, and presently returned, leading in Helena herself.

The good countess, who in silent grief had beheld her son's danger, and had even dreaded that the suspicion of his having destroyed his wife might possibly be true, finding her dear Helena, whom she loved with even a maternal affection, was still living, felt a delight she was hardly able to support; and the king, scarce believing for joy that it was Helena, said: 'Is this indeed the wife of Bertram that I see?'

Helena, feeling herself yet an unacknowledged wife, replied, 'No, my good lord, it is but the shadow of a wife you see; the name and not the thing.'

Bertram cried out: 'Both, both! Oh pardon!'

'O my lord,' said Helena, 'when I personated this fair maid I found you wondrous kind; and look, here is your letter!' reading to him in a joyful tone those words which she had once repeated so sorrowfully, 'When from my finger you can get this ring – This is done; it was to me you gave the ring. Will you be mine, now you are doubly won?'

Bertram replied, 'If you can make it plain that you were the lady I talked with that night I will love you dearly, ever, ever dearly.'

This was no difficult task, for the widow and Diana came with

Helena to prove this fact; and the king was so well pleased with Diana for the friendly assistance she had rendered the dear lady he so truly valued for the service she had done him that he promised her also a noble husband, Helena's history giving him a hint that it was a suitable reward for kings to bestow upon fair ladies when they perform notable services.

Thus Helena at last found that her father's legacy was indeed sanctified by the luckiest stars in heaven; for she was now the beloved wife of her dear Bertram, the daughter-in-law of her noble mistress, and herself the Countess of Rousillon.

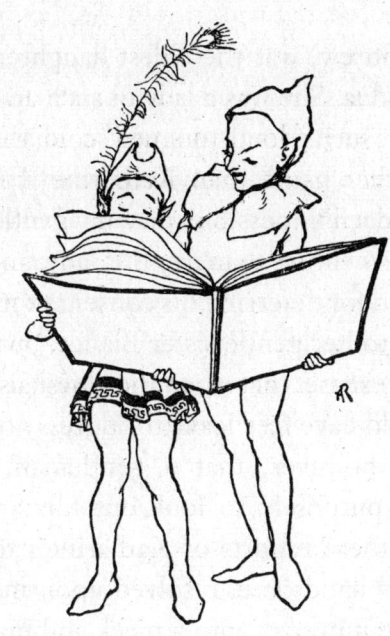

The Taming of the Shrew

Katharine, the Shrew, was the eldest daughter of Baptista, a rich gentleman of Padua. She was a lady of such an ungovernable spirit and fiery temper, such a loud-tongued scold, that she was known in Padua by no other name than Katharine the Shrew. It seemed very unlikely, indeed impossible, that any gentleman would ever be found who would venture to marry this lady, and therefore Baptista was much blamed for deferring his consent to many excellent offers that were made to her gentle sister Bianca, putting off all Bianca's suitors with this excuse, that when the eldest sister was fairly off his hands they should have free leave to address young Bianca.

It happened, however, that a gentleman, named Petruchio, came to Padua purposely to look out for a wife, who, nothing discouraged by these reports of Katharine's temper, and hearing she was rich and handsome, resolved upon marrying this famous termagant, and taming her into a meek and manageable wife. And truly none was so fit to set about this herculean labour as Petruchio, whose spirit was as high as Katharine's, and he was a witty and most happy-tempered humourist, and withal so wise, and of such a true judgement, that he well knew how to feign a passionate and furious deportment when his spirits were so calm that himself could have laughed merrily at his own angry feigning, for his natural temper

was careless and easy; the boisterous airs he assumed when he
became the husband of Katharine being but in sport, or, more
properly speaking, affected by his excellent discernment, as the
only means to overcome, in her own way, the passionate ways of
the furious Katharine.

A-courting, then, Petruchio went to Katharine the Shrew; and
first of all he applied to Baptista, her father, for leave to woo his
gentle daughter Katharine, as Petruchio called her, saying, archly,
that, having heard of her bashful modesty and mild behaviour, he
had come from Verona to solicit her love. Her father, though
he wished her married, was forced to confess Katharine would ill
answer this character, it being soon apparent of what manner of
gentleness she was composed, for her music-master rushed into the
room to complain that the gentle Katharine, his pupil, had broken
his head with her lute for presuming to find fault with her per-
formance; which, when Petruchio heard, he said: 'It is a brave
wench. I love her more than ever, and long to have some chat with
her.' And hurrying the old gentleman for a positive answer, he said:
'My business is in haste, Signor Baptista. I cannot come every day
to woo. You knew my father. He is dead, and has left me heir to all
his lands and goods. Then tell me, if I get your daughter's love,
what dowry you will give with her.'

Baptista thought his manner was somewhat blunt for a lover; but,
being glad to get Katharine married, he answered that he would
give her twenty thousand crowns for her dowry, and half his estate
at his death. So this odd match was quickly agreed on and Baptista
went to apprise his shrewish daughter of her lover's addresses, and
sent her in to Petruchio to listen to his suit.

In the meantime Petruchio was settling with himself the mode
of courtship he should pursue; and he said: 'I will woo her with
some spirit when she comes. If she rails at me, why, then I will tell
her she sings as sweetly as a nightingale; and if she frowns, I will
say she looks as clear as roses newly washed with dew. If she will
not speak a word, I will praise the eloquence of her language; and if
she bids me leave her, I will give her thanks as if she bid me stay
with her a week.'

Now the stately Katharine entered, and Petruchio first addressed her with: 'Good morrow, Kate, for that is your name, I hear.'

Katharine, not liking this plain salutation, said, disdainfully, 'They call me Katharine who do speak to me.'

'You lie,' replied the lover; 'for you are called plain Kate, and bonny Kate, and sometimes Kate the Shrew; but, Kate, you are the prettiest Kate in Christendom, and therefore, Kate, hearing your mildness praised in every town, I am come to woo you for my wife.'

A strange courtship they made of it. She in loud and angry terms showing him how justly she had gained the name of Shrew, while he still praised her sweet and courteous words, till at length, hearing her father coming, he said (intending to make as quick a wooing as possible): 'Sweet Katharine, let us set this idle chat aside, for your father has consented that you shall be my wife, your dowry is agreed on, and whether you will or no I will marry you.'

And now Baptista entering, Petruchio told him his daughter had received him kindly and that she had promised to be married the next Sunday. This Katharine denied, saying she would rather see him hanged on Sunday, and reproached her father for wishing to wed her to such a madcap ruffian as Petruchio. Petruchio desired her father not to regard her angry words, for they had agreed she should seem reluctant before him, but that when they were alone he had found her very fond and loving; and he said to her: 'Give me your hand, Kate. I will go to Venice to buy you apparel against our wedding-day. Provide the feast, father, bid the wedding guests. I will be sure to bring rings, fine array, and rich clothes, that my Katharine may be fine. And kiss me, Kate, for we will be married on Sunday.'

On the Sunday all the wedding guests were assembled, but they waited long before Petruchio came, and Katharine wept for vexation to think that Petruchio had only been making a jest of her. At last, however, he appeared; but he brought none of the bridal finery he had promised Katharine, nor was he dressed himself like a bridegroom, but in strange, disordered attire, as if he meant to make a sport of the serious business he came about; and his servant and the very horses on which they rode were in like manner in mean and fantastic fashion habited.

Petruchio could not be persuaded to change his dress. He said Katharine was to be married to him, and not to his clothes. And, finding it was in vain to argue with him, to the church they went, he still behaving in the same mad way, for when the priest asked Petruchio if Katharine should be his wife, he swore so loud that she should, that, all amazed, the priest let fall his book, and as he stooped to take it up this mad-brained bridegroom gave him such a cuff that down fell the priest and his book again. And all the while they were being married he stamped and swore so that the high-spirited Katharine trembled and shook with fear. After the ceremony was over, while they were yet in the church, he called for wine, and drank a loud health to the company, and threw a sop which was at the bottom of the glass full in the sexton's face, giving no other reason for this strange act than that the sexton's beard grew thin and hungerly, and seemed to ask the sop as he was drinking. Never sure was there such a mad marriage; but Petruchio did but put this wildness on the better to succeed in the plot he had formed to tame his shrewish wife.

Baptista had provided a sumptuous marriage feast, but when they returned from church, Petruchio, taking hold of Katharine, declared his intention of carrying his wife home instantly, and no remonstrance of his father-in-law, or angry words of the enraged Katharine, could make him change his purpose. He claimed a husband's right to dispose of his wife as he pleased, and away he hurried Katharine off; he seeming so daring and resolute that no one dared attempt to stop him.

Petruchio mounted his wife upon a miserable horse, lean and lank, which he had picked out for the purpose, and, himself and his servant no better mounted, they journeyed on through rough and miry ways, and ever when this horse of Katharine's stumbled he would storm and swear at the poor jaded beast, who could scarce crawl under his burthen, as if he had been the most passionate man alive.

At length, after a weary journey, during which Katharine had heard nothing but the wild ravings of Petruchio at the servant and the horses, they arrived at his house. Petruchio welcomed her kindly to her home, but he resolved she should have neither rest nor food that night. The tables were spread, and supper soon served; but Petruchio, pretending to find fault with every dish, threw the meat about the floor, and ordered the servants to remove it away; and all this he did, as he said, in love for his Katharine, that she might not eat meat that was not well dressed. And when Katharine, weary and supperless, retired to rest, he found the same fault with the bed, throwing the pillows and bedclothes about the room, so that she was forced to sit down in a chair, where if she chanced to drop asleep, she was presently awakened by the loud voice of her husband storming at the servants for the ill-making of his wife's bridal-bed.

The next day Petruchio pursued the same course, still speaking kind words to Katharine, but, when she attempted to eat, finding fault with everything that was set before her, throwing the breakfast on the floor as he had done the supper; and Katharine, the haughty Katharine, was fain to beg the servants would bring her secretly a morsel of food; but they, being instructed by Petruchio, replied they dared not give her anything unknown to their master.

'Ah,' said she, 'did he marry me to famish me? Beggars that come to my father's door have food given them. But I, who never knew what it was to entreat for anything, am starved for want of food, giddy for want of sleep, with oaths kept waking, and with brawling fed; and that which vexes me more than all, he does it under the name of perfect love, pretending that if I sleep or eat, it were present death to me.'

Here the soliloquy was interrupted by the entrance of Petruchio. He, not meaning she should be quite starved, had brought her a small portion of meat, and he said to her: 'How fares my sweet Kate? Here, love, you see how diligent I am. I have dressed your meat myself. I am sure this kindness merits thanks. What, not a word? Nay, then you love not the meat, and all the pains I have taken is to no purpose.' He then ordered the servant to take the dish away.

Extreme hunger, which had abated the pride of Katharine, made her say, though angered to the heart, 'I pray you let it stand.'

But this was not all Petruchio intended to bring her to, and he replied, 'The poorest service is repaid with thanks, and so shall mine before you touch the meat.'

On this Katharine brought out a reluctant 'I thank you, sir.'

And now he suffered her to make a slender meal, saying: 'Much good may it do your gentle heart, Kate. Eat apace! And now, my honey love, we will return to your father's house and revel it as bravely as the best, with silken coats and caps and golden rings, with ruffs and scarfs and fans and double change of finery.' And to make her believe he really intended to give her these gay things, he called in a tailor and a haberdasher, who brought some new clothes he had ordered for her, and then, giving her plate to the servant to take away, before she had half satisfied her hunger, he said: 'What, have you dined?'

The haberdasher presented a cap, saying, 'Here is the cap your worship bespoke.' On which Petruchio began to storm afresh, saying the cap was moulded in a porringer and that it was no bigger than a cockle or walnut shell, desiring the haberdasher to take it away and make it bigger.

Katharine said, 'I will have this; all gentlewomen wear such caps as these.'

'When you are gentle,' replied Petruchio, 'you shall have one, too, and not till then.'

The meat Katharine had eaten had a little revived her fallen spirits, and she said: 'Why, sir, I trust I may have leave to speak, and speak I will. I am no child, no babe. Your betters have endured to hear me say my mind; and if you cannot, you had better stop your ears.'

Petruchio would not hear these angry words, for he had happily discovered a better way of managing his wife than keeping up a jangling argument with her; therefore his answer was: 'Why, you say true; it is a paltry cap, and I love you for not liking it.'

'Love me, or love me not,' said Katharine, 'I like the cap, and I will have this cap or none.'

'You say you wish to see the gown,' said Petruchio, still affecting to misunderstand her.

The tailor then came forward and showed her a fine gown he had made for her. Petruchio, whose intent was that she should have neither cap nor gown, found as much fault with that.

'Oh, mercy, Heaven!' said he, 'what stuff is here! What, do you call this a sleeve? it is like a demi-cannon, carved up and down like an apple tart.'

The tailor said, 'You bid me make it according to the fashion of the times'; and Katharine said she never saw a better-fashioned gown. This was enough for Petruchio, and privately desiring these people might be paid for their goods, and excuses made to them for the seemingly strange treatment he bestowed upon them, he with fierce words and furious gestures drove the tailor and the haberdasher out of the room; and then, turning to Katharine, he said: 'Well, come, my Kate, we will go to your father's even in these mean garments we now wear.'

And then he ordered his horses, affirming they should reach Baptista's house by dinner-time, for that it was but seven o'clock. Now it was not early morning, but the very middle of the day, when he spoke this; therefore Katharine ventured to say, though modestly, being almost overcome by the vehemence of his manner: 'I dare assure you, sir, it is two o'clock, and will be supper-time before we get there.'

But Petruchio meant that she should be so completely subdued that she should assent to everything he said before he carried her to her father; and therefore, as if he were lord even of the sun and could command the hours, he said it should be what time he pleased to have it, before he set forward. 'For,' he said, 'whatever I say or do, you still are crossing it. I will not go today, and when I go, it shall be what o'clock I say it is.'

Another day Katharine was forced to practise her newly found obedience, and not till he had brought her proud spirit to such a perfect subjection that she dared not remember there was such a word as contradiction would Petruchio allow her to go to her father's house; and even while they were upon their journey thither she was in danger of being turned back again, only because she happened to hint it was the sun when he affirmed the moon shone brightly at noonday.

'Now, by my mother's son,' said he, 'and that is myself, it shall be the moon, or stars, or what I list, before I journey to your father's house.' He then made as if he were going back again. But Katharine, no longer Katharine the Shrew, but the obedient wife, said, 'Let us go forward, I pray, now we have come so far, and it shall be the sun, or moon, or what you please; and if you please to call it a rush candle henceforth, I vow it shall be so for me.'

This he was resolved to prove, therefore he said again, 'I say it is the moon.'

'I know it is the moon,' replied Katharine.

'You lie. It is the blessed sun,' said Petruchio.

'Then it is the blessed sun,' replied Katharine; 'but sun it is not when you say it is not. What you will have it named, even so it is, and so it ever shall be for Katharine.'

Now then he suffered her to proceed on her journey; but further to try if this yielding humour would last, he addressed an old gentleman they met on the road as if he had been a young woman, saying to him, 'Good morrow, gentle mistress'; and asked Katharine if she had ever beheld a fairer gentlewoman, praising the red and white of the old man's cheeks, and comparing his eyes to two bright stars; and again he addressed him, saying, 'Fair, lovely maid, once more good-day to you!' and said to his wife, 'Sweet Kate, embrace her for her beauty's sake.'

The now completely vanquished Katharine quickly adopted her husband's opinion, and made her speech in like sort to the old gentleman, saying to him: 'Young budding virgin, you are fair and fresh and sweet. Whither are you going, and where is your dwelling? Happy are the parents of so fair a child.'

'Why, how now, Kate,' said Petruchio. 'I hope you are not mad. This is a man, old and wrinkled, faded and withered, and not a maiden, as you say he is.'

On this Katharine said, 'Pardon me, old gentleman; the sun has so dazzled my eyes that everything I look on seemeth green. Now I perceive you are a reverend father. I hope you will pardon me for my sad mistake.'

'Do, good old grandsire,' said Petruchio, 'and tell us which way you are travelling. We shall be glad of your good company, if you are going our way.'

The old gentleman replied: 'Fair sir, and you, my merry mistress, your strange encounter has much amazed me. My name is Vincentio, and I am going to visit a son of mine who lives at Padua.'

Then Petruchio knew the old gentleman to be the father of Lucentio, a young gentleman who was to be married to Baptista's younger daughter, Bianca, and he made Vincentio very happy by telling him the rich marriage his son was about to make; and they all journeyed on pleasantly together till they came to Baptista's house, where there was a large company assembled to celebrate the wedding of Bianca and Lucentio, Baptista having willingly consented to the marriage of Bianca when he had got Katharine off his hands.

When they entered, Baptista welcomed them to the wedding feast, and there was present also another newly married pair.

Lucentio, Bianca's husband, and Hortensio, the other new-married man, could not forbear sly jests, which seemed to hint at the shrewish disposition of Petruchio's wife, and these fond bridegrooms seemed highly pleased with the mild tempers of the ladies they had chosen, laughing at Petruchio for his less fortunate choice. Petruchio took little notice of their jokes till the ladies were retired after dinner, and then he perceived Baptista himself joined in the laugh against him, for when Petruchio affirmed that his wife would prove more obedient than theirs, the father of Katharine said, 'Now, in good sadness, son Petruchio, I fear you have got the veriest shrew of all.'

'Well,' said Petruchio, 'I say no, and therefore, for assurance that I speak the truth, let us each one send for his wife, and he whose wife is most obedient to come at first when she is sent for shall win a wager which we will propose.'

To this the other two husbands willingly consented, for they were confident that their gentle wives would prove more obedient than the headstrong Katharine, and they proposed a wager of twenty crowns. But Petruchio merrily said he would lay as much as that upon his hawk or hound, but twenty times as much upon his wife.

THE TAMING OF THE SHREW

Lucentio and Hortensio raised the wager to a hundred crowns, and Lucentio first sent his servant to desire Bianca would come to him. But the servant returned, and said: 'Sir, my mistress sends you word she is busy and cannot come.'

'How,' said Petruchio, 'does she say she is busy and cannot come? Is that an answer for a wife?'

Then they laughed at him, and said it would be well if Katharine did not send him a worse answer. And now it was Hortensio's turn to send for his wife; and he said to his servant, 'Go, and entreat my wife to come to me.'

'Oh ho! entreat her!' said Petruchio.

'Nay, then, she needs must come.'

'I am afraid, sir,' said Hortensio, 'your wife will not be entreated.' But presently this civil husband looked a little blank when the servant returned without his mistress; and he said to him: 'How now? Where is my wife?'

'Sir,' said the servant, 'my mistress says you have some goodly jest in hand, and therefore she will not come. She bids you come to her.'

'Worse and worse!' said Petruchio. And then he sent his servant, saying, 'Sirrah, go to your mistress and tell her I command her to come to me.'

The company had scarcely time to think she would not obey this summons when Baptista, all in amaze, exclaimed: 'Now, by my *holidame*, here comes Katharine!'

And she entered, saying meekly to Petruchio, 'What is your will, sir, that you send for me?'

'Where is your sister and Hortensio's wife?' said he.

Katharine replied, 'They sit conferring by the parlour fire.'

'Go, fetch them hither!' said Petruchio.

Away went Katharine without reply to perform her husband's command.

'Here is a wonder,' said Lucentio, 'if you talk of a wonder.'

'And so it is,' said Hortensio. 'I marvel what it bodes.'

'Marry, peace it bodes,' said Petruchio, 'and love, and quiet life, and right supremacy; and, to be short, everything that is sweet and happy.'

Katharine's father, overjoyed to see this reformation in his daughter, said: 'Now, fair befall thee, son Petruchio! You have won the wager, and I will add another twenty thousand crowns to her dowry, as if she were another daughter, for she is changed as if she had never been.'

'Nay,' said Petruchio, 'I will win the wager better yet, and show more signs of her new-built virtue and obedience.' Katharine now entering with the two ladies, he continued: 'See where she comes, and brings your froward wives as prisoners to her womanly persuasion. Katharine, that cap of yours does not become you; off with that bauble, and throw it underfoot.'

Katharine instantly took off her cap and threw it down.

'Lord!' said Hortensio's wife, 'may I never have a cause to sigh till I am brought to such a silly pass!'

And Bianca, she too said, 'Fie! What foolish duty call you this?'

On this Bianca's husband said to her, 'I wish your duty were as foolish, too! The wisdom of your duty, fair Bianca, has cost me a hundred crowns since dinner-time.'

'The more fool you,' said Bianca, 'for laying on my duty.'

'Katharine,' said Petruchio, 'I charge you tell these headstrong women what duty they owe their lords and husbands.'

And to the wonder of all present, the reformed shrewish lady spoke as eloquently in praise of the wifelike duty of obedience as she had practised it implicitly in a ready submission to Petruchio's will. And Katharine once more became famous in Padua, not as heretofore as Katharine the Shrew, but as Katharine the most obedient and duteous wife in Padua.

The Comedy of Errors

The states of Syracuse and Ephesus being at variance, there was a cruel law made at Ephesus, ordaining that if any merchant of Syracuse was seen in the city of Ephesus he was to be put to death, unless he could pay a thousand marks for the ransom of his life.

Aegeon, an old merchant of Syracuse, was discovered in the streets of Ephesus, and brought before the duke, either to pay this heavy fine or receive sentence of death.

Aegeon had no money to pay the fine, and the duke, before he pronounced the sentence of death upon him, desired him to relate the history of his life, and to tell for what cause he had ventured to come to the city of Ephesus, which it was death for any Syracusan merchant to enter.

Aegeon said that he did not fear to die, for sorrow had made him weary of his life, but that a heavier task could not have been imposed upon him than to relate the events of his unfortunate life. He then began his own history, in the following words: 'I was born at Syracuse, and brought up to the profession of a merchant. I married a lady, with whom I lived very happily, but, being obliged to go to Epidamnum, I was detained there by my business six months, and then, finding I should be obliged to stay some time longer, I sent for my wife, who, as soon as she arrived, was brought to bed of two sons, and what was very strange, they were both so exactly alike that it was impossible to distinguish the one from the other. At the same time that my wife was brought to bed of these twin boys a poor woman in the inn where my wife lodged was brought to bed of two sons, and these twins were as much like each other as my two sons were. The parents of these children being exceeding poor, I bought the two boys and brought them up to attend upon my sons.

'My sons were very fine children, and my wife was not a little proud of two such boys; and she daily wishing to return home, I unwillingly agreed, and in an evil hour we got on shipboard, for we had not sailed above a league from Epidamnum before a dreadful storm arose, which continued with such violence that the sailors, seeing no chance of saving the ship, crowded into the boat to save their own lives, leaving us alone in the ship, which we every moment expected would be destroyed by the fury of the storm.

'The incessant weeping of my wife and the piteous complaints of the pretty babes, who, not knowing what to fear, wept for fashion, because they saw their mother weep, filled me with terror for them, though I did not for myself fear death; and all my thoughts were bent to contrive means for their safety. I tied my youngest son to the end of a small spire mast, such as seafaring men provide against storms; at the other end I bound the youngest of the twin slaves, and at the same time I directed my wife how to fasten the other children in like manner to another mast. She thus having the care of the eldest two children, and I of the younger two, we bound ourselves separately to these masts with the children; and but for this contrivance we had all been lost, for the ship split on a mighty rock and was dashed in pieces; and we, clinging to these slender masts, were supported above the water, where I, having the care of two children, was unable to assist my wife, who, with the other children, was soon separated from me; but while they were yet in my sight they were taken up by a boat of fishermen, from Corinth (as I supposed), and, seeing them in safety, I had no care but to struggle with the wild sea-waves, to preserve my dear son and the youngest slave. At length we, in our turn, were taken up by a ship, and the sailors, knowing me, gave us kind welcome and assistance and landed us in safety at Syracuse; but from that sad hour I have never known what became of my wife and eldest child.

'My youngest son, and now my only care, when he was eighteen years of age, began to be inquisitive after his mother and his brother, and often importuned me that he might take his attendant, the young slave, who had also lost his brother, and go in search of them. At length I unwillingly gave consent, for, though I anxiously desired to hear tidings of my wife and eldest son, yet in sending my younger one to find them I hazarded the loss of him also. It is now seven years since my son left me; five years have I passed in travelling through the world in search of him. I have been in farthest Greece, and through the bounds of Asia, and, coasting homeward, I landed here in Ephesus, being unwilling to leave any place unsought that harbours men; but this day must end the story of my life, and happy should I think myself in my death if I were assured my wife and sons were living.'

Here the hapless Aegeon ended the account of his misfortunes; and the duke, pitying this unfortunate father who had brought upon himself this great peril by his love for his lost son, said if it were not against the laws, which his oath and dignity did not permit him to alter, he would freely pardon him; yet, instead of dooming him to instant death, as the strict letter of the law required, he would give him that day to try if he could beg or borrow the money to pay the fine.

This day of grace did seem no great favour to Aegeon, for, not knowing any man in Ephesus, there seemed to him but little chance that any stranger would lend or give him a thousand marks to pay the fine; and, helpless and hopeless of any relief, he retired from the presence of the duke in the custody of a jailer.

Aegeon supposed he knew no person in Ephesus; but at the time he was in danger of losing his life through the careful search he was making after his youngest son, that son, and his eldest son also, were in the city of Ephesus.

Aegeon's sons, besides being exactly alike in face and person, were both named alike, being both called Antipholus, and the two twin slaves were also both named Dromio. Aegeon's youngest son,

Antipholus of Syracuse, he whom the old man had come to Ephesus to seek, happened to arrive at Ephesus with his slave Dromio that very same day that Aegeon did; and he being also a merchant of Syracuse, he would have been in the same danger that his father was, but by good fortune he met a friend who told him the peril an old merchant of Syracuse was in, and advised him to pass for a merchant of Epidamnum. This Antipholus agreed to do, and he was sorry to hear one of his own countrymen was in this danger, but he little thought this old merchant was his own father.

The eldest son of Aegeon (who must be called Antipholus of Ephesus, to distinguish him from his brother Antipholus of Syracuse) had lived at Ephesus twenty years, and, being a rich man, was well able to have paid the money for the ransom of his father's life; but Antipholus knew nothing of his father, being so young when he was taken out of the sea with his mother by the fishermen that he only remembered he had been so preserved; but he had no recollection of either his father or his mother, the fishermen who took up this Antipholus and his mother and the young slave Dromio having carried the two children away from her (to the great grief of that unhappy lady), intending to sell them.

Antipholus and Dromio were sold by them to Duke Menaphon, a famous warrior, who was uncle to the Duke of Ephesus, and he carried the boys to Ephesus when he went to visit the duke, his nephew.

The Duke of Ephesus, taking a liking to young Antipholus, when he grew up made him an officer in his army, in which he distinguished himself by his great bravery in the wars, where he saved the life of his patron, the duke, who rewarded his merit by marrying him to Adriana, a rich lady of Ephesus, with whom he was living (his slave Dromio still attending him) at the time his father came there.

Antipholus of Syracuse, when he parted with his friend, who advised him to say he came from Epidamnum, gave his slave Dromio some money to carry to the inn where he intended to dine, and in the meantime he said he would walk about and view the city and observe the manners of the people.

Dromio was a pleasant fellow, and when Antipholus was dull and melancholy he used to divert himself with the odd humours and merry jests of his slave, so that the freedoms of speech he allowed in Dromio were greater than is usual between masters and their servants.

When Antipholus of Syracuse had sent Dromio away, he stood awhile thinking over his solitary wanderings in search of his mother and his brother, of whom in no place where he landed could he hear the least tidings; and he said sorrowfully to himself, 'I am like a drop of water in the ocean which, seeking to find its fellow-drop, loses itself in the wide sea, So I, unhappily, to find a mother and a brother, do lose myself.'

While he was thus meditating on his weary travels, which had hitherto been so useless, Dromio (as he thought) returned. Antipholus, wondering that he came back so soon, asked him where he had left the money. Now it was not his own Dromio, but the twin brother that lived with Antipholus of Ephesus, that he spoke to. The two Dromios and the two Antipholuses were still as much alike as Aegeon had said they were in their infancy; therefore no wonder Antipholus thought it was his own slave returned, and asked him why he came back so soon.

Dromio replied: 'My mistress sent me to bid you come to dinner. The capon burns, and the pig falls from the spit, and the meat will be all cold if you do not come home.'

'These jests are out of season,' said Antipholus. 'Where did you leave the money?'

Dromio still answering that his mistress had sent him to fetch Antipholus to dinner, 'What mistress?' said Antipholus.

'Why, your worship's wife, sir!' replied Dromio.

Antipholus having no wife, he was very angry with Dromio, and said: 'Because I familiarly sometimes chat with you, you presume to jest with me in this free manner. I am not in a sportive humour now. Where is the money? We being strangers here, how dare you trust so great a charge from your own custody?'

Dromio, hearing his master, as he thought him, talk of their being strangers, supposing Antipholus was jesting, replied, merrily:

'I pray you, sir, jest as you sit at dinner. I had no charge but to fetch you home to dine with my mistress and her sister.'

Now Antipholus lost all patience, and beat Dromio, who ran home and told his mistress that his master had refused to come to dinner and said that he had no wife.

Adriana, the wife of Antipholus of Ephesus, was very angry when she heard that her husband said he had no wife; for she was of a jealous temper, and she said her husband meant that he loved another lady better than herself; and she began to fret, and say unkind words of jealousy and reproach of her husband; and her sister Luciana, who lived with her, tried in vain to persuade her out of her groundless suspicions.

Antipholus of Syracuse went to the inn, and found Dromio with the money in safety there, and, seeing his own Dromio, he was going again to chide him for his free jests, when Adriana came up to him, and, not doubting but it was her husband she saw, she began to reproach him for looking strange upon her (as well he might, never having seen this angry lady before); and then she told him how well he loved her before they were married, and that now he loved some other lady instead of her.

'How comes it now, my husband,' said she, 'oh, how comes it that I have lost your love?'

'Plead you to me, fair dame?' said the astonished Antipholus.

It was in vain he told her he was not her husband and that he had been in Ephesus but two hours. She insisted on his going home with her, and Antipholus at last, being unable to get away, went with her to his brother's house, and dined with Adriana and her sister, the one calling him husband and the other brother, he, all amazed, thinking he must have been married to her in his sleep, or that he was sleeping now. And Dromio, who followed them, was no less surprised, for the cook-maid, who was his brother's wife, also claimed him for her husband.

While Antipholus of Syracuse was dining with his brother's wife, his brother, the real husband, returned home to dinner with his slave Dromio; but the servants would not open the door, because their mistress had ordered them not to admit any company; and when they repeatedly knocked, and said they were Antipholus and Dromio, the maids laughed at them, and said that Antipholus was at dinner with their mistress, and Dromio was in the kitchen, and though they almost knocked the door down, they could not gain admittance, and at last Antipholus went away very angry, and strangely surprised at hearing a gentleman was dining with his wife.

When Antipholus of Syracuse had finished his dinner, he was so perplexed at the lady's still persisting in calling him husband, and at hearing that Dromio had also been claimed by the cookmaid, that he left the house as soon as he could find any pretence to get away; for though he was very much pleased with Luciana, the sister, yet the jealous-tempered Adriana he disliked very much, nor was Dromio at all better satisfied with his fair wife in the kitchen; therefore both master and man were glad to get away from their new wives as fast as they could.

The moment Antipholus of Syracuse had left the house he was met by a goldsmith, who, mistaking him, as Adriana had done, for Antipholus of Ephesus, gave him a gold chain, calling him by his name; and when Antipholus would have refused the chain, saying it did not belong to him, the goldsmith replied he made it by his own orders, and went away, leaving the chain in the hands of Antipholus, who ordered his man Dromio to get his things on board a ship, not choosing to stay in a place any longer where he met with such strange adventures that he surely thought himself bewitched.

The goldsmith who had given the chain to the wrong Antipholus was arrested immediately after for a sum of money he owed; and Antipholus, the married brother, to whom the goldsmith thought he had given the chain, happened to come to the place where the officer was arresting the goldsmith, who, when he saw Antipholus, asked him to pay for the gold chain he had just delivered to him, the price amounting to nearly the same sum as that for which he had been arrested. Antipholus denying the having received the chain, and the goldsmith persisting to declare that he had but a few minutes before given it to him, they disputed this matter a long time, both thinking they were right; for Antipholus knew the goldsmith never gave him the chain, and so like were the two brothers, the goldsmith was as certain he had delivered the chain into his hands, till at last the officer took the goldsmith away to prison for the debt he owed, and at the same time the goldsmith made the officer arrest Antipholus for the price of the chain; so that at the conclusion of their dispute Antipholus and the merchant were both taken away to prison together.

As Antipholus was going to prison, he met Dromio of Syracuse, his brother's slave, and, mistaking him for his own, he ordered him to go to Adriana his wife, and tell her to send the money for which he was arrested. Dromio, wondering that his master should send him back to the strange house where he dined, and from which he had just before been in such haste to depart, did not dare to reply, though he came to tell his master the ship was ready to sail, for he saw Antipholus was in no humour to be jested with. Therefore he went away, grumbling within himself that he must return to Adriana's house, 'Where,' said he, 'Dowsabel claims me for a husband. But I must go, for servants must obey their masters' commands.'

Adriana gave him the money, and as Dromio was returning he met Antipholus of Syracuse, who was still in amaze at the surprising adventures he met with, for, his brother being well known in Ephesus, there was hardly a man he met in the streets but saluted him as an old acquaintance. Some offered him money which they said was owing to him, some invited him to come and see them, and some gave him thanks for kindnesses they said he had done them, all mistaking him for his brother. A tailor showed him some silks he had bought for him, and insisted upon taking measure of him for some clothes.

Antipholus began to think he was among a nation of sorcerers and witches, and Dromio did not at all relieve his master from his bewildered thoughts by asking him how he got free from the officer who was carrying him to prison, and giving him the purse of gold which Adriana had sent to pay the debt with. This talk of Dromio's of the arrest and of a prison, and of the money he had brought from Adriana, perfectly confounded Antipholus, and he said,

'This fellow Dromio is certainly distracted, and we wander here in illusions,' and, quite terrified at his own confused thoughts, he cried out, 'Some blessed power deliver us from this strange place!'

And now another stranger came up to him, and she was a lady, and she, too, called him Antipholus, and told him he had dined with her that day, and asked him for a gold chain which she said he had promised to give her. Antipholus now lost all patience, and, calling her a sorceress, he denied that he had ever promised her a chain, or dined with her, or had even seen her face before that moment. The lady persisted in affirming he had dined with her and had promised her a chain, which Antipholus still denying, she further said that she had given him a valuable ring, and if he would not give her the gold chain, she insisted upon having her own ring again. On this Antipholus became quite frantic, and again calling her sorceress and witch, and denying all knowledge of her or her ring, ran away from her, leaving her astonished at his words and his wild looks, for nothing to her appeared more certain than that he had dined with her, and that she had given him a ring in consequence of his promising to make her a present of a gold chain. But this lady had fallen into the same mistake the others had done, for she had taken him for his brother; the married Antipholus had done all the things she taxed this Antipholus with.

When the married Antipholus was denied entrance into his house (those within supposing him to be already there) he had gone away very angry, believing it to be one of his wife's jealous freaks, to which she was very subject, and, remembering that she had often falsely accused him of visiting other ladies, he, to be revenged on her for shutting him out of his own house, determined to go and dine with this lady, and she receiving him with great civility, and his wife having so highly offended him, Antipholus promised to give her a gold chain which he had intended as a present for his wife; it was the same chain which the goldsmith by mistake had given to his brother. The lady liked so well the thoughts of having a fine gold chain that she gave the married Antipholus a ring; which when, as she supposed (taking his brother for him), he denied, and said he did not know her, and left her in such a wild passion, she began to think he was certainly out of his senses; and presently she resolved to go and tell Adriana that her husband was mad. And while she was telling it to Adriana he came, attended by the jailer (who allowed him to come home to get the money to pay the debt), for the purse of money which Adriana had sent by Dromio and he had delivered to the other Antipholus.

Adriana believed the story the lady told her of her husband's madness must be true when he reproached her for shutting him out of his own house; and remembering how he had protested all dinner-time that he was not her husband and had never been in Ephesus till that day, she had no doubt that he was mad; she therefore paid the jailer the money, and, having discharged him, she ordered her servants to bind her husband with ropes, and had him conveyed into a dark room, and sent for a doctor to come and cure him of his madness, Antipholus all the while hotly exclaiming against this false accusation, which the exact likeness he bore to his brother had brought upon him. But his rage only the more confirmed them in the belief that he was mad; and Dromio persisting in the same story, they bound him also and took him away along with his master.

Soon after Adriana had put her husband into confinement a servant came to tell her that Antipholus and Dromio must have broken loose from their keepers, for that they were both walking at liberty in the next street. On hearing this Adriana ran out to fetch him home, taking some people with her to secure her husband again; and her sister went along with her. When they came to the gates of a convent in their neighbourhood, there they saw Antipholus and Dromio, as they thought, being again deceived by the likeness of the twin brothers.

Antipholus of Syracuse was still beset with the perplexities this likeness had brought upon him. The chain which the goldsmith had given him was about his neck, and the goldsmith was reproaching him for denying that he had it and refusing to pay for it, and Antipholus was protesting that the goldsmith freely gave him the chain in the morning, and that from that hour he had never seen the goldsmith again.

And now Adriana came up to him and claimed him as her lunatic husband who had escaped from his keepers, and the men she brought with her were going to lay violent hands on Antipholus and Dromio; but they ran into the convent, and Antipholus begged the abbess to give him shelter in her house.

And now came out the lady abbess herself to enquire into the cause of this disturbance. She was a grave and venerable lady, and wise to judge of what she saw, and she would not too hastily give up the man who had sought protection in her house; so she strictly questioned the wife about the story she told of her husband's madness, and she said: 'What is the cause of this sudden distemper of your husband's? Has he lost his wealth at sea? Or is it the death of some dear friend that has disturbed his mind?'

Adriana replied that no such things as these had been the cause.

'Perhaps,' said the abbess, 'he has fixed his affections on some other lady than you, his wife, and that has driven him to this state.'

Adriana said she had long thought the love of some other lady was the cause of his frequent absences from home.

Now it was not his love for another, but the teasing jealousy of his wife's temper, that often obliged Antipholus to leave his home; and the abbess (suspecting this from the vehemence of Adriana's manner), to learn the truth, said: 'You should have reprehended him for this.'

'Why, so I did,' replied Adriana.

'Aye,' said the abbess, 'but perhaps not enough.'

Adriana, willing to convince the abbess that she had said enough to Antipholus on this subject, replied: 'It was the constant subject of our conversation; in bed I would not let him sleep for speaking of it. At table I would not let him eat for speaking of it. When I was alone with him I talked of nothing else; and in company I gave him frequent hints of it. Still all my talk was how vile and bad it was in him to love any lady better than me.'

The lady abbess, having drawn this full confession from the jealous Adriana, now said: 'And therefore comes it that your husband is mad. The venomous clamour of a jealous woman is a more deadly poison than a mad dog's tooth. It seems his sleep was hindered by your railing; no wonder that his head is light; and his meat was sauced with your upbraidings; unquiet meals make ill digestions, and that has thrown him into this fever. You say his sports were disturbed by your brawls; being debarred from the enjoyment of society and recreation, what could ensue but dull melancholy and comfortless despair? The consequence is, then, that your jealous fits have made your husband mad.'

Luciana would have excused her sister, saying she always reprehended her husband mildly; and she said to her sister, 'Why do you hear these rebukes without answering them?'

But the abbess had made her so plainly perceive her fault that she could only answer, 'She has betrayed me to my own reproof.'

Adriana, though ashamed of her own conduct, still insisted on having her husband delivered up to her; but the abbess would suffer no person to enter her house, nor would she deliver up this unhappy man to the care of the jealous wife, determining herself to use gentle means for his recovery, and she retired into her house again, and ordered her gates to be shut against them.

During the course of this eventful day, in which so many errors had happened from the likeness the twin brothers bore to each other, old Aegeon's day of grace was passing away, it being now near sunset; and at sunset he was doomed to die if he could not pay the money.

The place of his execution was near this convent, and here he arrived just as the abbess retired into the convent; the duke attending in person, that, if any offered to pay the money, he might be present to pardon him.

Adriana stopped this melancholy procession, and cried out to the duke for justice, telling him that the abbess had refused to deliver up her lunatic husband to her care. While she was speaking, her real husband and his servant, Dromio, who had got loose, came before the duke to demand justice, complaining that his wife had confined him on a false charge of lunacy, and telling in what manner he had broken his bands and eluded the vigilance of his keepers. Adriana was strangely surprised to see her husband when she thought he had been within the convent.

Aegeon, seeing his son, concluded this was the son who had left him to go in search of his mother and his brother, and he felt secure that this dear son would readily pay the money demanded for his ransom. He therefore spoke to Antipholus in words of fatherly affection, with joyful hope that he should now be released. But, to the utter astonishment of Aegeon, his son denied all knowledge of him, as well he might, for this Antipholus had never seen his father since they were separated in the storm in his infancy. But while the poor old Aegeon was in vain endeavouring to make his son acknowledge him, thinking surely that either his griefs and the anxieties he had suffered had so strangely altered him that his son did not know him or else that he was ashamed to acknowledge his father in his misery – in the midst of this perplexity the lady abbess and the other Antipholus and Dromio came out, and the wondering Adriana saw two husbands and two Dromios standing before her.

And now these riddling errors, which had so perplexed them all, were clearly made out. When the duke saw the two Antipholuses and the two Dromios both so exactly alike, he at once conjectured aright of these seeming mysteries, for he remembered the story Aegeon had told him in the morning; and he said these men must be the two sons of Aegeon and their twin slaves.

But now an unlooked-for joy indeed completed the history of Aegeon; and the tale he had in the morning told in sorrow, and under sentence of death, before the setting sun went down was brought to a happy conclusion, for the venerable lady abbess made herself known to be the long-lost wife of Aegeon and the fond mother of the two Antipholuses.

When the fishermen took the eldest Antipholus and Dromio away from her, she entered a nunnery, and by her wise and virtuous conduct she was at length made lady abbess of this convent and in discharging the rites of hospitality to an unhappy stranger she had unknowingly protected her own son.

Joyful congratulations and affectionate greetings between these long-separated parents and their children made them for a while forget that Aegeon was yet under sentence of death. When they were become a little calm, Antipholus of Ephesus offered the duke the ransom money for his father's life; but the duke freely pardoned Aegeon, and would not take the money. And the duke went with the abbess and her newly found husband and children into the convent, to hear this happy family discourse at leisure of the blessed ending of their adverse fortunes. And the two Dromios' humble joy must not be forgotten; they had their congratulations and greetings, too, and each Dromio pleasantly complimented his brother on his good looks, being well pleased to see his own person (as in a glass) show so handsome in his brother.

Adriana had so well profited by the good counsel of her mother-in-law that she never after cherished unjust suspicions nor was jealous of her husband.

Antipholus of Syracuse married the fair Luciana, the sister of his brother's wife; and the good old Aegeon, with his wife and sons, lived at Ephesus many years. Nor did the unravelling of these perplexities so entirely remove every ground of mistake for the future but that sometimes, to remind them of adventures past, comical blunders would happen, and the one Antipholus, and the one Dromio, be mistaken for the other, making altogether a pleasant and diverting comedy of errors.

Measure for Measure

In the city of Vienna there once reigned a duke of such a mild and gentle temper that he suffered his subjects to neglect the laws with impunity; and there was in particular one law the existence of which was almost forgotten, the duke never having put it in force during his whole reign. This was a law dooming any man to the punishment of death who should live with a woman that was not his wife; and this law, through the lenity of the duke, being utterly disregarded, the holy institution of marriage became neglected, and complaints were every day made to the duke by the parents of the young ladies in Vienna that their daughters had been seduced from their protection and were living as the companions of single men.

The good duke perceived with sorrow this growing evil among his subjects; but he thought that a sudden change in himself from the indulgence he had hitherto shown, to the strict severity requisite to check this abuse, would make his people (who had hitherto loved him) consider him as a tyrant; therefore he determined to absent himself awhile from his dukedom and depute another to the full exercise of his power, that the law against these dishonourable lovers might be put in effect, without giving offence by an unusual severity in his own person.

Angelo, a man who bore the reputation of a saint in Vienna for his strict and rigid life, was chosen by the duke as a fit person to undertake this important charge; and when the duke imparted his design to Lord Escalus, his chief counsellor, Escalus said: 'If any man in Vienna be of worth to undergo such ample grace and honour, it is Lord Angelo.'

And now the duke departed from Vienna under pretence of making a journey into Poland, leaving Angelo to act as the lord deputy in his absence; but the duke's absence was only a feigned one, for he privately returned to Vienna, habited like a friar, with the intent to watch unseen the conduct of the saintly-seeming Angelo.

It happened just about the time that Angelo was invested with his new dignity that a gentleman, whose name was Claudio, had seduced a young lady from her parents; and for this offence, by command of the new lord deputy, Claudio was taken up and committed to prison, and by virtue of the old law which had been so long neglected Angelo sentenced Claudio to be beheaded. Great interest was made for the pardon of young Claudio, and the good old Lord Escalus himself interceded for him.

'Alas!' said he, 'this gentleman whom I would save had an honourable father, for whose sake I pray you pardon the young man's transgression.'

But Angelo replied: 'We must not make a scarecrow of the law, setting it up to frighten birds of prey, till custom, finding it harmless, makes it their perch and not their terror. Sir, he must die.'

Lucio, the friend of Claudio, visited him in the prison, and Claudio said to him: 'I pray you, Lucio, do me this kind service. Go to my sister Isabel, who this day proposes to enter the convent of Saint Clare; acquaint her with the danger of my state; implore her that she make friends with the strict deputy; bid her go herself to Angelo. I have great hopes in that; for she can discourse with prosperous art, and well she can persuade; besides, there is a speechless dialect in youthful sorrow such as moves men.'

Isabel, the sister of Claudio, had, as he said, that day entered upon her novitiate in the convent, and it was her intent, after passing through her probation as a novice, to take the veil, and she was enquiring of a nun concerning the rules of the convent when they heard the voice of Lucio, who, as he entered that religious house, said, 'Peace be in this place!'

'Who is it that speaks?' said Isabel.

'It is a man's voice,' replied the nun. 'Gentle Isabel, go to him, and learn his business; you may, I may not. When you have taken the veil, you must not speak with men but in the presence of the prioress; then if you speak you must not show your face, or if you show your face you must not speak.'

'And have you nuns no further privileges?' said Isabel.

'Are not these large enough?' replied the nun.

'Yes, truly,' said Isabel. 'I speak not as desiring more, but rather wishing a more strict restraint upon the sisterhood, the votarists of Saint Clare.'

Again they heard the voice of Lucio, and the nun said: 'He calls again. I pray you answer him.'

Isabel then went out to Lucio, and in answer to his salutation, said: 'Peace and Prosperity! Who is it that calls?'

Then Lucio, approaching her with reverence, said: 'Hail, virgin, if such you be, as the roses on your cheeks proclaim you are no less! Can you bring me to the sight of Isabel, a novice of this place, and the fair sister to her unhappy brother Claudio?'

'Why her unhappy brother?' said Isabel, 'let me ask! for I am that Isabel and his sister.'

'Fair and gentle lady,' he replied, 'your brother kindly greets you by me; he is in prison.'

'Woe is me! for what?' said Isabel.

Lucio then told her Claudio was imprisoned for seducing a young maiden. 'Ah,' said she, 'I fear it is my cousin Juliet.'

Juliet and Isabel were not related, but they called each other cousin in remembrance of their school-days' friendship; and as Isabel knew that Juliet loved Claudio, she feared she had been led by her affection for him into this transgression.

'She it is,' replied Lucio.

'Why, then, let my brother marry Juliet,' said Isabel.

Lucio replied that Claudio would gladly marry Juliet, but that the lord deputy had sentenced him to die for his offence. 'Unless,' said he, 'you have the grace by your fair prayer to soften Angelo, and that is my business between you and your poor brother.'

'Alas!' said Isabel, 'what poor ability is there in me to do him good? I doubt I have no power to move Angelo.'

'Our doubts are traitors,' said Lucio, 'and make us lose the good we might often win, by fearing to attempt it. Go to Lord Angelo! When maidens sue and kneel and weep men give like gods.'

'I will see what I can do,' said Isabel. 'I will but stay to give the prioress notice of the affair, and then I will go to Angelo. Commend me to my brother. Soon at night I will send him word of my success.'

Isabel hastened to the palace and threw herself on her knees before Angelo, saying, 'I am a woeful suitor to your honour, if it will please your honour to hear me.'

'Well, what is your suit?' said Angelo.

She then made her petition in the most moving terms for her brother's life.

But Angelo said, 'Maiden, there is no remedy; your brother is sentenced, and he must die.'

'Oh, just but severe law!' said Isabel. 'I had a brother then. Heaven keep your honour!' and she was about to depart.

But Lucio, who had accompanied her, said: 'Give it not over so; return to him again, entreat him, kneel down before him, hang upon his gown. You are too cold; if you should need a pin, you could not with a more tame tongue desire it.'

Then again Isabel on her knees implored for mercy.

'He is sentenced,' said Angelo. 'It is too late.'

'Too late!' said Isabel. 'Why, no! I that do speak a word may call it back again. Believe this, my lord, no ceremony that to great ones belongs, not the king's crown, nor the deputed sword, the marshal's truncheon, nor the judge's robe, becomes them with one half so good a grace as mercy does.'

'Pray you begone,' said Angelo.

But still Isabel entreated; and she said: 'If my brother had been as you, and you as he, you might have slipped like him, but he, like you, would not have been so stern. I would to heaven I had your power and you were Isabel. Should it then be thus? No, I would tell you what it were to be a judge, and what a prisoner.'

'Be content, fair maid!' said Angelo: 'it is the law, not I, condemns your brother. Were he my kinsman, my brother, or my son, it should be thus with him. He must die tomorrow.'

'Tomorrow?' said Isabel. 'Oh, that is sudden! Spare him, spare him. He is not prepared for death. Even for our kitchens we kill the fowl in season; shall we serve heaven with less respect than we minister to our gross selves? Good, good, my lord, bethink you, none have died for my brother's offence, though many have committed it. So you would be the first that gives this sentence and he the first that suffers it. Go to your own bosom, my lord; knock there, and ask your heart what it does know that is like my brother's fault; if it confess a natural guiltiness such as his is, let it not sound a thought against my brother's life!'

Her last words more moved Angelo than all she had before said, for the beauty of Isabel had raised a guilty passion in his heart and he began to form thoughts of dishonourable love, such as Claudio's crime had been, and the conflict in his mind made him to turn away from Isabel; but she called him back, saying: 'Gentle my lord, turn back. Hark, how I will bribe you. Good my lord, turn back!'

'How! bribe me?' said Angelo, astonished that she should think of offering him a bribe.

'Aye,' said Isabel, 'with such gifts that heaven itself shall share with you; not with golden treasures, or those glittering stones whose price is either rich or poor as fancy values them, but with true prayers that shall be up to heaven before sunrise – prayers from preserved souls, from fasting maids whose minds are dedicated to nothing temporal.'

'Well, come to me tomorrow,' said Angelo.

And for this short respite of her brother's life, and for this permission that she might be heard again, she left him with the joyful hope that she should at last prevail over his stern nature. And as she went away she said: 'Heaven keep your honour safe! Heaven save your honour!' Which, when Angelo heard, he said within his heart, 'Amen, I would be saved from thee and from thy virtues.'

And then, affrighted at his own evil thoughts, he said: 'What is this? What is this? Do I love her, that I desire to hear her speak again and feast upon her eyes? What is it I dream on? The cunning enemy of mankind, to catch a saint, with saints does bait the hook. Never could an immodest woman once stir my temper, but this virtuous woman subdues me quite. Even till now, when men were fond, I smiled and wondered at them.'

In the guilty conflict in his mind Angelo suffered more that night than the prisoner he had so severely sentenced; for in the prison Claudio was visited by the good duke, who, in his friar's habit, taught the young man the way to heaven, preaching to him the words of penitence and peace. But Angelo felt all the pangs of irresolute guilt, now wishing to seduce Isabel from the paths of innocence and honour, and now suffering remorse and horror for a crime as yet but intentional. But in the end his evil thoughts prevailed; and he who had so lately started at the offer of a bribe resolved to tempt this maiden with so high a bribe as she might not be able to resist, even with the precious gift of her dear brother's life.

When Isabel came in the morning Angelo desired she might be admitted alone to his presence; and being there, he said to her, if she would yield to him her virgin honour and transgress even as Juliet had done with Claudio, he would give her her brother's life.

'For,' said he, 'I love you, Isabel.'

'My brother,' said Isabel, 'did so love Juliet, and yet you tell me he shall die for it.'

'But,' said Angelo, 'Claudio shall not die if you will consent to visit me by stealth at night, even as Juliet left her father's house at night to come to Claudio.'

Isabel, in amazement at his words, that he should tempt her to the same fault for which he passed sentence upon her brother, said, 'I would do as much for my poor brother as for myself; that is, were I under sentence of death, the impression of keen whips I would wear as rubies, and go to my death as to a bed that longing I had been sick for, ere I would yield myself up to this shame.' And then she told him she hoped he only spoke these words to try her virtue.

But he said, 'Believe me, on my honour, my words express my purpose.'

Isabel, angered to the heart to hear him use the word honour to express such dishonourable purposes, said: 'Ha! little honour to be much believed; and most pernicious purpose. I will proclaim thee, Angelo, look for it! Sign me a present pardon for my brother, or I will tell the world aloud what man thou art!'

'Who will believe you, Isabel?' said Angelo; 'my unsoiled name, the austereness of my life, my word vouched against yours, will outweigh your accusation. Redeem your brother by yielding to my will, or he shall die tomorrow. As for you, say what you can, my false will overweigh your true story. Answer me tomorrow.'

'To whom should I complain? Did I tell this, who would believe me?' said Isabel, as she went towards the dreary prison where her brother was confined. When she arrived there her brother was in pious conversation with the duke, who in his friar's habit had also visited Juliet and brought both these guilty lovers to a proper sense of their fault; and unhappy Juliet with tears and a true remorse confessed that she was more to blame than Claudio, in that she willingly consented to his dishonourable solicitations.

As Isabel entered the room where Claudio was confined, she said, 'Peace be here, grace, and good company!'

'Who is there?' said the disguised duke. 'Come in; the wish deserves a welcome.'

'My business is a word or two with Claudio,' said Isabel.

Then the duke left them together, and desired the provost who had the charge of the prisoners to place him where he might overhear their conversation.

'Now, sister, what is the comfort?' said Claudio.

Isabel told him he must prepare for death on the morrow.

'Is there no remedy?' said Claudio.

'Yes, brother,' replied Isabel, 'there is; but such a one as if you consented to it would strip your honour from you and leave you naked.'

'Let me know the point,' said Claudio.

'Oh, I do fear you, Claudio!' replied his sister; 'and I quake, lest you should wish to live, and more respect the trifling term of six or seven winters added to your life than your perpetual honour! Do you dare to die? The sense of death is most in apprehension, and the poor beetle that we tread upon feels a pang as great as when a giant dies.'

'Why do you give me this shame?' said Claudio. 'Think you I can fetch a resolution from flowery tenderness? If I must die, I will encounter darkness as a bride and hug it in my arms.'

'There spoke my brother,' said Isabel; 'there my father's grave did utter forth a voice! Yes, you must die; yet would you think it, Claudio, this outward sainted deputy, if I would yield to him my virgin honour, would grant your life? Oh, were it but my life, I would lay it down for your deliverance as frankly as a pin!'

'Thanks, dear Isabel,' said Claudio.

'Be ready to die tomorrow,' said Isabel.

'Death is a fearful thing,' said Claudio.

'And shamed life a hateful,' replied his sister.

But the thoughts of death now overcame the constancy of Claudio's temper, and terrors, such as the guilty only at their deaths do know, assailing him, he cried out: 'Sweet sister, let me live! The sin you do to save a brother's life, nature dispenses with the deed so far that it becomes a virtue.'

'O faithless coward! O dishonest wretch!' said Isabel. 'Would you preserve your life by your sister's shame? Oh, fie, fie, fie! I thought, my brother, you had in you such a mind of honour that, had you twenty heads to render up on twenty blocks, you would have yielded them up all before your sister should stoop to such dishonour.'

'Nay, hear me, Isabel!' said Claudio.

But what he would have said in defence of his weakness in desiring to live by the dishonour of his virtuous sister was interrupted by the entrance of the duke; who said: 'Claudio, I have overheard what has passed between you and your sister. Angelo had never the purpose to corrupt her; what he said, has only been to make trial of her virtue. She, having the truth of honour in her, has given him that gracious denial which he is most ill glad to receive.

There is no hope that he will pardon you; therefore pass your hours in prayer, and make ready for death.'

Then Claudio repented of his weakness, and said: 'Let me ask my sister's pardon! I am so out of love with life that I will sue to be rid of it.' And Claudio retired, overwhelmed with shame and sorrow for his fault.

The duke, being now alone with Isabel, commended her virtuous resolution, saying, 'The hand that made you fair has made you good.'

'Oh,' said Isabel, 'how much is the good duke deceived in Angelo! If ever he return, and I can speak to him, I will discover his government.' Isabel knew not that she was even now making the discovery she threatened.

The duke replied: 'That shall not be much amiss; yet as the matter now stands, Angelo will repel your accusation; therefore lend an attentive ear to my advisings. I believe that you may most righteously do a poor wronged lady a merited benefit, redeem your brother from the angry law, do no stain to your own most gracious person, and much please the absent duke, if peradventure he shall ever return to have notice of this business.'

Isabel said she had a spirit to do anything he desired, provided it was nothing wrong.

'Virtue is bold and never fearful,' said the duke: and then he asked her, if she had ever heard of Mariana, the sister of Frederick, the great soldier who was drowned at sea.

'I have heard of the lady,' said Isabel, 'and good words went with her name.'

'This lady,' said the duke, 'is the wife of Angelo; but her marriage dowry was on board the vessel in which her brother perished, and mark how heavily this befell to the poor gentlewoman! for, besides the loss of a most noble and renowned brother, who in his love towards her was ever most kind and natural, in the wreck of her fortune she lost the affections of her husband, the well-seeming Angelo, who, pretending to discover some dishonour in this honourable lady (though the true cause was the loss of her dowry), left her in her tears and dried not one of them with his comfort. His unjust unkindness, that in all reason should have quenched her love, has, like an impediment in the current, made it more unruly, and Mariana loves her cruel husband with the full continuance of her first affection.'

The duke then more plainly unfolded his plan. It was that Isabel should go to Lord Angelo and seemingly consent to come to him as he desired at midnight; that by this means she would obtain the promised pardon; and that Mariana should go in her stead to the appointment, and pass herself upon Angelo in the dark for Isabel.

'Nor, gentle daughter,' said the feigned friar, 'fear you to this thing. Angelo is her husband, and to bring them thus together is no sin.'

Isabel, being pleased with this project, departed to do as he directed her; and he went to apprise Mariana of their intention. He had before this time visited this unhappy lady in his assumed character, giving her religious instruction and friendly consolation, at which times he had learned her sad story from her own lips; and now she, looking upon him as a holy man, readily consented to be directed by him in this undertaking.

When Isabel returned from her interview with Angelo, to the house of Mariana, where the duke had appointed her to meet him, he said: 'Well met, and in good time. What is the news from this good deputy?'

Isabel related the manner in which she had settled the affair. 'Angelo,' said she, 'has a garden surrounded with a brick wall, on the western side of which is a vineyard, and to that vineyard is a gate.' And then she showed to the duke and Mariana two keys that Angelo had given her; and she said: 'This bigger key opens the vineyard gate; this other a little door which leads from the vineyard to the garden. There I have made my promise at the dead of the night to call upon him, and have got from him his word of assurance for my brother's life. I have taken a due and wary note of the place; and with whispering and most guilty diligence he showed me the way twice over.'

'Are there no other tokens agreed upon between you, that Mariana must observe?' said the duke.

'No, none,' said Isabel, 'only to go when it is dark. I have told him my time can be but short; for I have made him think a servant comes along with me, and that this servant is persuaded I come about my brother.'

The duke commended her discreet management, and she, turning to Mariana, said, 'Little have you to say to Angelo, when you depart from him, but soft and low, "*Remember now my brother!*" '

Mariana was that night conducted to the appointed place by Isabel, who rejoiced that she had, as she supposed, by this device preserved both her brother's life and her own honour. But that her brother's life was safe the duke was not well satisfied, and therefore at midnight he again repaired to the prison, and it was well for Claudio that he did so, else would Claudio have that night been beheaded; for soon after the duke entered the prison an order came from the cruel deputy commanding that Claudio should be beheaded and his head sent to him by five o'clock in the morning. But the duke persuaded the provost to put off the execution of Claudio, and to deceive Angelo by sending him the head of a man who died that morning in the prison. And to prevail upon the provost to agree to this, the duke, whom still the provost suspected not to be anything more or greater than he seemed, showed the provost a letter written with the duke's hand, and sealed with his seal, which when the provost saw, he concluded this friar must have some secret order from the absent duke, and therefore he consented to spare Claudio; and he cut off the dead man's head and carried it to Angelo.

Then the duke in his own name wrote to Angelo a letter saying that certain accidents had put a stop to his journey and that he should be in Vienna by the following morning, requiring Angelo to meet him at the entrance of the city, there to deliver up his authority; and the duke also commanded it to be proclaimed that if any of his subjects craved redress for injustice they should exhibit their petitions in the street on his first entrance into the city.

Early in the morning Isabel came to the prison, and the duke, who there awaited her coming, for secret reasons thought it good to tell her that Claudio was beheaded; therefore when Isabel enquired if Angelo had sent the pardon for her brother, he said: 'Angelo has released Claudio from this world. His head is off and sent to the deputy.'

The much-grieved sister cried out, 'O unhappy Claudio, wretched Isabel, injurious world, most wicked Angelo!'

The seeming friar bid her take comfort, and when she was become a little calm he acquainted her with the near prospect of the duke's return and told her in what manner she should proceed in preferring her complaint against Angelo; and he bade her not fear if the cause should seem to go against her for a while. Leaving Isabel sufficiently instructed, he next went to Mariana and gave her counsel in what manner she also should act.

Then the duke laid aside his friar's habit, and in his own royal robes, amid a joyful crowd of his faithful subjects assembled to greet his arrival, entered the city of Vienna, where he was met by Angelo, who delivered up his authority in the proper form.

And there came Isabel, in the manner of a petitioner for redress, and said: 'Justice, most royal duke! I am the sister of one Claudio, who, for the seducing a young maid, was condemned to lose his head. I made my suit to Lord Angelo for my brother's pardon. It were needless to tell your grace how I prayed and kneeled, how he repelled me, and how I replied; for this was of much length. The vile conclusion I now begin with grief and pain to utter. Angelo would not, but by my yielding to his dishonourable love, release my brother; and after much debate within myself my sisterly remorse overcame my virtue, and I did yield to him. But the next morning betimes, Angelo, forfeiting his promise, sent a warrant for my poor brother's head!'

The duke affected to disbelieve her story; and Angelo said that grief for her brother's death, who had suffered by the due course of the law, had disordered her senses.

And now another suitor approached, which was Mariana; and Mariana said: 'Noble prince, as there comes light from heaven and truth from breath, as there is sense in truth and truth in virtue, I am this man's wife, and, my good lord, the words of Isabel are false, for the night she says she was with Angelo I passed that night with him in the garden-house. As this is true let me in safety rise, or else forever be fixed here a marble monument.'

Then did Isabel appeal for the truth of what she had said to Friar Lodowick, that being the name the duke had assumed in his disguise. Isabel and Mariana had both obeyed his instructions in what they said, the duke intending that the innocence of Isabel should be plainly proved in that public manner before the whole city of Vienna; but Angelo little thought that it was from such a cause that they thus differed in their story, and he hoped from their contradictory evidence to be able to clear himself from the accusation of Isabel; and he said, assuming the look of offended innocence: 'I did but smile till now; but, good my lord, my patience here is touched, and I perceive these poor, distracted women are but the instruments of some greater one who sets them on. Let me have way, my lord, to find this practice out.'

'Aye, with all my heart,' said the duke, 'and punish them to the height of your pleasure. You, Lord Escalus, sit with Lord Angelo, lend him your pains to discover this abuse; the friar is sent for that set them on, and when he comes do with your injuries as may seem best in any chastisement. I for a while will leave you, but stir not you, Lord Angelo, till you have well determined upon this slander.' The duke then went away, leaving Angelo well pleased to be deputed judge and umpire in his own cause. But the duke was absent only while he threw off his royal robes and put on his friar's habit; and in that disguise again he presented himself before Angelo and Escalus. And the good old Escalus, who thought Angelo had been falsely accused, said to the supposed friar, 'Come, sir, did you set these women on to slander Lord Angelo?'

He replied: 'Where is the duke? It is he who should hear me speak.'

Escalus said: 'The duke is in us, and we will hear you. Speak justly.'

'Boldly, at least,' retorted the friar; and then he blamed the duke for leaving the cause of Isabel in the hands of him she had accused, and spoke so freely of many corrupt practices he had observed while, as he said, he had been a looker-on in Vienna, that Escalus threatened him with the torture for speaking words against the state and for censuring the conduct of the duke, and ordered him to be taken away to prison. Then, to the amazement of all present, and to the utter confusion of Angelo, the supposed friar threw off his disguise, and they saw it was the duke himself.

The duke first addressed Isabel. He said to her: 'Come hither, Isabel. Your friar is now your prince, but with my habit I have not changed my heart. I am still devoted to your service.'

'Oh, give me pardon,' said Isabel, 'that I, your vassal, have employed and troubled your unknown sovereignty.'

He answered that he had most need of forgiveness from her for not having prevented the death of her brother for not yet would he tell her that Claudio was living; meaning first to make a further trial of her goodness.

Angelo now knew the duke had been a secret witness of his bad deeds, and he said: 'O my dread lord, I should be guiltier than my guiltiness, to think I can be undiscernible, when I perceive your grace, like power divine, has looked upon my actions. Then, good prince, no longer prolong my shame, but let my trial be my own confession. Immediate sentence and death is all the grace I beg.'

The duke replied: 'Angelo, thy faults are manifest. We do condemn thee to the very block where Claudio stooped to death, and with like haste away with him; and for his possessions, Mariana, we do instate and widow you withal, to buy you a better husband.'

'O my dear lord,' said Mariana, 'I crave no other, nor no better man!' And then on her knees, even as Isabel had begged the life of Claudio, did this kind wife of an ungrateful husband beg the life of Angelo; and she said: 'Gentle my liege, O good my lord! Sweet Isabel, take my part! Lend me your knees and all my life to come I will lend you all my life, to do you service!'

The duke said: 'Against all sense you importune her. Should Isabel kneel down to beg for mercy, her brother's ghost would break his paved bed and take her hence in horror.'

Still Mariana said: 'Isabel, sweet Isabel, do but kneel by me, hold up your hand, say nothing! I will speak all. They say best men are moulded out of faults, and for the most part become much the better for being a little bad. So may my husband. O Isabel! will you not lend a knee?'

The duke then said, 'He dies for Claudio.' But much pleased was the good duke when his own Isabel, from whom he expected all gracious and honourable acts, kneeled down before him, and said: 'Most bounteous sir, look, if it please you, on this man condemned, as if my brother lived. I partly think a due sincerity governed his deeds till he did look on me. Since it is so, let him not die! My brother had but justice in that he did the thing for which he died.'

The duke, as the best reply he could make to this noble petitioner for her enemy's life, sending for Claudio from his prison house, where he lay doubtful of his destiny, presented to her this lamented brother living; and he said to Isabel: 'Give me your hand, Isabel. For your lovely sake I pardon Claudio. Say you will be mine, and he shall be my brother, too.'

By this time Lord Angelo perceived he was safe; and the duke, observing his eye to brighten up a little, said: 'Well, Angelo, look that you love your wife; her worth has obtained your pardon. Joy to you, Mariana! Love her, Angelo! I have confessed her and know her virtue.'

Angelo remembered, when dressed in a little brief authority, how hard his heart had been, and felt how sweet is mercy.

The duke commanded Claudio to marry Juliet, and offered himself again to the acceptance of Isabel, whose virtuous and noble conduct had won her prince's heart. Isabel, not having taken the veil, was free to marry; and the friendly offices, while hid under the disguise of a humble friar, which the noble duke had done for her, made her with grateful joy accept the honour he offered her; and when she became Duchess of Vienna the excellent example of the virtuous Isabel worked such a complete reformation among the young ladies of that city, that from that time none ever fell into the transgression of Juliet, the repentant wife of the reformed Claudio. And the mercy-loving duke long reigned with his beloved Isabel, the happiest of husbands and of princes.

Twelfth Night
or, What you will

Sebastian and his sister Viola, a young gentleman and lady of Messaline, were twins, and (which was accounted a great wonder) from their birth they so much resembled each other that, but for the difference in their dress, they could not be known apart. They were both born in one hour, and in one hour they were both in danger of perishing, for they were shipwrecked on the coast of Illyria, as they were making a sea-voyage together. The ship on board of which they were split on a rock in a violent storm, and a very small number of the ship's company escaped with their lives. The captain of the vessel, with a few of the sailors that were saved, got to land in a small boat, and with them they brought Viola safe on shore, where she, poor lady, instead of rejoicing at her own deliverance, began to lament her brother's loss; but the captain comforted her with the assurance that he had seen her brother, when the ship split, fasten himself to a strong mast, on which, as long as he could see anything of him for the distance, he perceived him borne up above the waves. Viola was much consoled by the hope this account gave her, and now considered how she was to dispose of herself in a strange country, so far from home; and she asked the captain if he knew anything of Illyria.

'Aye, very well, madam,' replied the captain, 'for I was born not three hours' travel from this place.'

'Who governs here?' said Viola. The captain told her Illyria was governed by Orsino, a duke noble in nature as well as dignity.

Viola said, she had heard her father speak of Orsino, and that he was unmarried then.

'And he is so now,' said the captain; 'or was so very late for, but a month ago, I went from here, and then it was the general talk (as you know what great ones do, the people will prattle of) that Orsino sought the love of fair Olivia, a virtuous maid, the daughter of a count who died twelve months ago, leaving Olivia to the protection of her brother, who shortly after died also; and for the love of this dear brother, they say, she has abjured the sight and company of men.'

Viola, who was herself in such a sad affliction for her brother's loss, wished she could live with this lady who so tenderly mourned a brother's death. She asked the captain if he could introduce her to Olivia, saying she would willingly serve this lady. But he replied this would be a hard thing to accomplish, because the Lady Olivia would admit no person into her house since her brother's death, not even the duke himself. Then Viola formed another project in her mind, which was, in a man's habit, to serve the Duke Orsino as a page. It was a strange fancy in a young lady to put on male attire and pass for a boy; but the forlorn and unprotected state of Viola, who was young and of uncommon beauty, alone, and in a foreign land, must plead her excuse.

She having observed a fair behaviour in the captain, and that he showed a friendly concern for her welfare, entrusted him with her design, and he readily engaged to assist her. Viola gave him money and directed him to furnish her with suitable apparel, ordering her clothes to be made of the same colour and in the same fashion her brother Sebastian used to wear, and when she was dressed in her manly garb she looked so exactly like her brother that some strange errors happened by means of their being mistaken for each other, for, as will afterwards appear, Sebastian was also saved.

Viola's good friend, the captain, when he had transformed this pretty lady into a gentleman, having some interest at court, got her presented to Orsino under the feigned name of Cesario. The duke was wonderfully pleased with the address and graceful deportment of this handsome youth, and made Cesario one of his pages, that being the office Viola wished to obtain; and she so well fulfilled the duties of her new station, and showed such a ready observance and faithful attachment to her lord, that she soon became his most favoured attendant. To Cesario Orsino confided the whole history of his love for the Lady Olivia. To Cesario he told the long and unsuccessful suit he had made to one who, rejecting his long services and despising his person, refused to admit him to her presence; and for the love of this lady who had so unkindly treated him the noble Orsino, forsaking the sports of the field and all manly exercises in which he used to delight, passed his hours in ignoble sloth, listening to the effeminate sounds of soft music, gentle airs, and passionate love-songs; and neglecting the company of the wise and learned lords with whom he used to associate, he was now all day long conversing with young Cesario. Unmeet companion no doubt his grave courtiers thought Cesario was for their once noble master, the great Duke Orsino.

It is a dangerous matter for young maidens to be the confidantes of handsome young dukes; which Viola too soon found, to her sorrow, for all that Orsino told her he endured for Olivia she presently perceived she suffered for the love of him, and much it moved her wonder that Olivia could be so regardless of this her peerless lord and master, whom she thought no one could behold without the deepest admiration, and she ventured gently to hint to Orsino, that it was a pity he should affect a lady who was so blind to his worthy qualities; and she said: 'If a lady were to love you, my lord, as you love Olivia (and perhaps there may be one who does), if you could not love her in return, would you not tell her that you could not love, and must she not be content with this answer?'

But Orsino would not admit of this reasoning, for he denied that it was possible for any woman to love as he did. He said no woman's heart was big enough to hold so much love, and therefore it was unfair to compare the love of any lady for him to his love for Olivia. Now, though Viola had the utmost deference for the duke's opinions, she could not help thinking this was not quite true, for she thought her heart had full as much love in it as Orsino's had; and she said: 'Ah, but I know, my lord.'

'What do you know, Cesario?' said Orsino.

'Too well I know,' replied Viola, 'what love women may owe to men. They are as true of heart as we are. My father had a daughter loved a man, as I perhaps, were I a woman, should love your lordship.'

'And what is her history?' said Orsino.

'A blank, my lord,' replied Viola. 'She never told her love, but let concealment, like a worm in the bud, feed on her damask cheek. She pined in thought, and with a green and yellow melancholy she sat like Patience on a monument, smiling at Grief.'

The duke enquired if this lady died of her love, but to this question Viola returned an evasive answer; as probably she had feigned the story, to speak words expressive of the secret love and silent grief she suffered for Orsino.

While they were talking, a gentleman entered whom the duke had sent to Olivia, and he said, 'So please you, my lord, I might not be admitted to the lady, but by her handmaid she returned you this answer: Until seven years hence the element itself shall not behold her face; but like a cloistress she will walk veiled, watering her chamber with her tears for the sad remembrance of her dead brother.'

On hearing this the duke exclaimed, 'Oh, she that has a heart of this fine frame, to pay this debt of love to a dead brother, how will she love when the rich golden shaft has touched her heart!'

And then he said to Viola: 'You know, Cesario, I have told you all the secrets of my heart; therefore, good youth, go to Olivia's house. Be not denied access; stand at her doors and tell her there your fixed foot shall grow till you have audience.'

'And if I do speak to her, my lord, what then?' said Viola.

'Oh, then,' replied Orsino, 'unfold to her the passion of my love. Make a long discourse to her of my dear faith. It will well become you to act my woes, for she will attend more to you than to one of graver aspect.'

Away then went Viola; but not willingly did she undertake this courtship, for she was to woo a lady to become a wife to him she wished to marry; but, having undertaken the affair, she performed it with fidelity, and Olivia soon heard that a youth was at her door who insisted upon being admitted to her presence.

'I told him,' said the servant, 'that you were sick. He said he knew you were, and therefore he came to speak with you. I told him that you were asleep. He seemed to have a foreknowledge of that, too, and said that therefore he must speak with you. What is to be said to him, lady? for he seems fortified against all denial, and will speak with you, whether you will or no.'

Olivia, curious to see who this peremptory messenger might be, desired he might be admitted, and, throwing her veil over her face, she said she would once more hear Orsino's embassy, not doubting but that he came from the duke, by his importunity. Viola, entering, put on the most manly air she could assume, and, affecting the fine courtier language of great men's pages, she said to the veiled lady: 'Most radiant, exquisite, and matchless beauty, I pray you tell me if you are the lady of the house; for I should be sorry to cast away my speech upon another; for besides that it is excellently well penned, I have taken great pains to learn it.'

'Whence come you, sir?' said Olivia.

'I can say little more than I have studied,' replied Viola, 'and that question is out of my part.'

'Are you a comedian?' said Olivia.

'No,' replied Viola; 'and yet I am not that which I play,' meaning that she, being a woman, feigned herself to be a man. And again she asked Olivia if she were the lady of the house.

Olivia said she was; and then Viola, having more curiosity to see her rival's features than haste to deliver her master's message, said, 'Good madam, let me see your face.' With this bold request Olivia was not averse to comply, for this haughty beauty, whom the Duke

Orsino had loved so long in vain, at first sight conceived a passion for the supposed page, the humble Cesario.

When Viola asked to see her face, Olivia said, 'Have you any commission from your lord and master to negotiate with my face?' And then, forgetting her determination to go veiled for seven long years, she drew aside her veil, saying: 'But I will draw the curtain and show the picture. Is it not well done?'

Viola replied: 'It is beauty truly mixed; the red and white upon your cheeks is by Nature's own cunning hand laid on. You are the most cruel lady living if you lead these graces to the grave and leave the world no copy.'

'Oh, sir,' replied Olivia, 'I will not be so cruel. The world may have an inventory of my beauty. As, *item*, two lips, indifferent red; *item*, two grey eyes with lids to them; one neck; one chin; and so forth. Were you sent here to praise me?'

Viola replied, 'I see what you are: you are too proud, but you are fair. My lord and master loves you. Oh, such a love could but be recompensed though you were crowned the queen of beauty; for Orsino loves you with adoration and with tears, with groans that thunder love, and sighs of fire.'

'Your lord,' said Olivia, 'knows well my mind. I cannot love him; yet I doubt not he is virtuous; I know him to be noble and of high estate, of fresh and spotless youth. All voices proclaim him learned, courteous, and valiant; yet I cannot love him. He might have taken his answer long ago.'

'If I did love you as my master does,' said Viola, 'I would make me a willow cabin at your gates, and call upon your name. I would write complaining sonnets on Olivia, and sing them in the dead of the night. Your name should sound among the hills, and I would make Echo, the babbling gossip of the air, cry out "*Olivia*". Oh, you should not rest between the elements of earth and air, but you should pity me.'

'You might do much,' said Olivia. 'What is your parentage?'

Viola replied: 'Above my fortunes, yet my state is well. I am a gentleman.'

Olivia now reluctantly dismissed Viola, saying: 'Go to your master and tell him I cannot love him. Let him send no more, unless perchance you come again to tell me how he takes it.'

And Viola departed, bidding the lady farewell by the name of Fair Cruelty. When she was gone Olivia repeated the words, '*Above my fortunes, yet my state is well. I am a gentleman.*' And she said aloud, 'I will be sworn he is; his tongue, his face, his limbs, action, and spirit plainly show he is a gentleman.' And then she wished Cesario was the duke; and, perceiving the fast hold he had taken on her affections, she blamed herself for her sudden love; but the gentle blame which people lay upon their own faults has no deep root, and presently the noble Lady Olivia so far forgot the inequality between her fortunes and those of this seeming page, as well as the maidenly reserve which is the chief ornament of a lady's character, that she resolved to court the love of young Cesario, and sent a servant after him with a diamond ring, under the pretence that he had left it with her as a present from Orsino. She hoped by thus artfully making Cesario a present of the ring she should give him some intimation of her design; and truly it did make Viola suspect; for, knowing that Orsino had sent no ring by her, she began to recollect that Olivia's looks and manner were expressive of admiration, and she presently guessed her master's mistress had fallen in love with her.

'Alas!' said she, 'the poor lady might as well love a dream. Disguise I see is wicked, for it has caused Olivia to breathe as fruitless sighs for me as I do for Orsino.'

Viola returned to Orsino's palace, and related to her lord the ill success of the negotiation, repeating the command of Olivia that the duke should trouble her no more. Yet still the duke persisted in hoping that the gentle Cesario would in time be able to persuade her to show some pity, and therefore he bade him he should go to her again the next day. In the meantime, to pass away the tedious interval, he commanded a song which he loved to be sung; and he said: 'My good Cesario, when I heard that song last night, methought it did relieve my passion much. Mark it, Cesario, it is old and plain. The spinsters and the knitters when they sit in the sun, and the young maids that weave their thread with bone, chant this song. It is silly, yet I love it, for it tells of the innocence of love in the old times.'

SONG

Come away, come away, Death,
　　And in sad cypress let me be laid;
Fly away, fly away, breath,
　　I am slain by a fair cruel maid.
My shroud of white stuck all with yew, O prepare it!
My part of death no one so true did share it.
　　Not a flower, not a flower sweet,
　　　　On my black coffin let there be strewn:
　　Not a friend, not a friend greet
　　　　My poor corpse, where my bones shall be thrown.
A thousand thousand sighs to save, lay me O where
Sad true lover never find my grave, to weep there!

Viola did not fail to mark the words of the old song, which in such true simplicity described the pangs of unrequited love, and she bore testimony in her countenance of feeling what the song expressed. Her sad looks were observed by Orsino, who said to her: 'My life upon it, Cesario, though you are so young, your eye has looked upon some face that it loves. Has it not, boy?'

'A little, with your leave,' replied Viola.

'And what kind of woman, and of what age is she?' said Orsino.

'Of your age and of your complexion, my lord,' said Viola; which made the duke smile to hear this fair young boy loved a woman so much older than himself and of a man's dark complexion; but Viola secretly meant Orsino, and not a woman like him.

When Viola made her second visit to Olivia she found no difficulty in gaining access to her. Servants soon discover when their ladies delight to converse with handsome young messengers; and the instant Viola arrived the gates were thrown wide open, and the duke's page was shown into Olivia's apartment with great respect. And when Viola told Olivia that she was come once more to plead in her lord's behalf, this lady said: 'I desired you never to speak of him again; but if you would undertake another suit, I had rather hear you solicit, than music from the spheres.'

This was pretty plain speaking, but Olivia soon explained herself still more plainly, and openly confessed her love; and when she saw displeasure with perplexity expressed in Viola's face, she said: 'Oh, what a deal of scorn looks beautiful in the contempt and anger of his lip! Cesario, by the roses of the spring, by maidhood, honour, and by truth, I love you so that, in spite of your pride, I have neither wit nor reason to conceal my passion.'

But in vain the lady wooed. Viola hastened from her presence, threatening never more to come to plead Orsino's love; and all the reply she made to Olivia's fond solicitation was, a declaration of a resolution *'Never to love any woman'*.

No sooner had Viola left the lady than a claim was made upon her valour. A gentleman, a rejected suitor of Olivia, who had learned how that lady had favoured the duke's messenger, challenged him to fight a duel. What should poor Viola do, who, though she carried a manlike outside, had a true woman's heart and feared to look on her own sword?

When she saw her formidable rival advancing towards her with his sword drawn she began to think of confessing that she was a woman; but she was relieved at once from her terror, and the shame of such a discovery, by a stranger that was passing by, who made up to them, and as if he had been long known to her and were her dearest friend said to her opponent: 'If this young gentleman has done offence, I will take the fault on me; and if you offend him, I will for his sake defy you.'

Before Viola had time to thank him for his protection, or to enquire the reason of his kind interference, her new friend met with an enemy where his bravery was of no use to him; for the officers of justice coming up in that instant, apprehended the stranger in the duke's name, to answer for an offence he had committed some years before; and he said to Viola: 'This comes with seeking you.' And then he asked her for a purse, saying: 'Now my necessity makes me ask for my purse, and it grieves me much more for what I cannot do for you than for what befalls myself. You stand amazed, but be of comfort.'

His words did indeed amaze Viola, and she protested she knew him not, nor had ever received a purse from him; but for the kindness he had just shown her she offered him a small sum of money, being nearly the whole she possessed. And now the stranger spoke severe things, charging her with ingratitude and unkindness. He said: 'This youth whom you see here I snatched from the jaws of death, and for his sake alone I came to Illyria and have fallen into this danger.'

But the officers cared little for harkening to the complaints of their prisoner, and they hurried him off, saying, 'What is that to us?' And as he was carried away, he called Viola by the name of Sebastian, reproaching the supposed Sebastian for disowning his friend, as long as he was within hearing. When Viola heard herself called Sebastian, though the stranger was taken away too hastily for her to ask an explanation, she conjectured that this seeming mystery might arise from her being mistaken for her brother, and she began to cherish hopes that it was her brother whose life this man said he had preserved. And so indeed it was. The stranger, whose name was Antonio, was a sea-captain. He had taken Sebastian up into his ship when, almost exhausted with fatigue, he was floating on the mast to which he had fastened himself in the storm. Antonio conceived such a friendship for Sebastian that he resolved to accompany him whithersoever he went; and when the youth expressed a curiosity to visit Orsino's court, Antonio, rather than part from him, came to Illyria, though he knew, if his person should be known there, his life would be in danger, because in a sea-fight he had once dangerously wounded the Duke Orsino's nephew. This was the offence for which he was now made a prisoner.

Antonio and Sebastian had landed together but a few hours before Antonio met Viola. He had given his purse to Sebastian, desiring him to use it freely if he saw anything he wished to purchase, telling him he would wait at the inn while Sebastian went to view the town; but, Sebastian not returning at the time appointed, Antonio had ventured out to look for him, and Viola being dressed the same, and in face so exactly resembling her brother, Antonio drew his sword (as he thought) in defence of the youth he had saved, and when Sebastian (as he supposed) disowned him, and denied him his own purse, no wonder he accused him of ingratitude.

Viola, when Antonio was gone, fearing a second invitation to fight, slunk home as fast as she could. She had not been long gone, when her adversary thought he saw her return; but was her brother Sebastian, who happened to arrive at this place, and he said, 'Now, sir, have I met with you again? There's for you'; and struck him a, blow, Sabastian was no coward; he returned the blow with interest, and drew his sword.

A lady now put a stop to this duel, for Olivia came out of the house, and she too mistaking Sebastian for Cesario, invited him to come into her house, expressing much sorrow at the rude attack he had met with. Though Sebastian was as much surprised at the courtesy of this lady as at the rudeness of his unknown foe, yet he went very willingly into the house, and Olivia was delighted to mid Cesario (as she thought him) become more sensible of her attentions; for though their features were exactly the same, there was none of the contempt and anger to be seen in his face, which she had complained of when she told her love to Cesario.

Sebastian did not at all object to the fondness the lady lavished on him. He seemed to take it in very good part, yet he wondered how it had come to pass, and he was rather inclined to think Olivia was not in her right senses; but perceiving that she was mistress of a fine house, and that she ordered her affairs and seemed to govern her family discreetly, and that in all but her sudden love for him she appeared in the full possession of her reason, he well approved of the courtship; and Olivia finding Cesario in this good humour, and fearing he might change his mind, proposed that, as she had a priest in the house, they should be instantly married. Sebastian assented to this proposal; and when the marriage ceremony was over, he left his lady for a short time, intending to go and tell his friend Antonio the good fortune that he had met with. In the meantime Orsino came to visit Olivia: and at the moment he arrived before Olivia's house, the officers of justice brought their prisoner, Antonio, before the duke. Viola was with Orsino, her master; and when Antonio saw Viola, whom he still imagined to be Sebastian, he told the duke in what manner he had rescued this youth from the perils of the sea; and after fully relating all the kindness he had really shown to Sebastian, he ended his complaint with *saying*, that for three months, both day and night, this ungrateful youth had been with him. But now the Lady Olivia coming forth from her house, the duke could no longer attend to Antonio's story; and he said, 'Here comes the countess: now Heaven walks on earth! but for thee, fellow, thy words are madness. Three months has this youth attended on me:' and then he ordered Antonio to be taken aside. But Orsino's heavenly countess soon gave the duke cause to accuse Cesario as much of ingratitude as Antonio had done, for all the words he could hear Olivia speak were words of kindness to Cesario: and when he found his page had obtained this high place in Olivia's favour, he threatened him with all the terrors of his just revenge; and as he was going to depart, he called Viola to follow him, saying, 'Come, boy, with me. My thoughts are ripe for mischief.' Though it seemed in his jealous rage he was going to doom Viola to instant death, yet her love made her no longer a coward, and she said she would most joyfully suffer death to give her master ease. But Olivia would not so lose her husband, and she cried, 'Where goes my Cesario?' Viola replied, "After him I love more than my life.' Olivia, however, prevented their departure by loudly proclaiming that Cesario was her husband, and sent for the priest, who declared that not two hours had passed since he had married the Lady Olivia to this young man. In vain Viola protested she was not married to Olivia; the evidence of that lady and the priest made Orsino believe that his page had robbed him of the treasure he prized above his life. But thinking that it was past recall, he was bidding farewell to his faithless mistress, and the *young dissembler* her husband, as he called Viola, warning her never to come in his sight again, when (as it seemed to them) a miracle appeared! for another Cesario entered, and addressed Olivia as his wife. This new Cesario was Sebastian, the real husband of Olivia; and when their wonder had a little ceased at seeing two persons with the same face, the same voice, and the same habit, the brother and sister began to question each other; for Viola could scarce be persuaded that her brother was living, and Sebastian knew not how to account for the sister he supposed drowned being found in the habit of a young man. But Viola presently acknowledged that she was indeed Viola, and his sister, under that disguise.

When all the errors were cleared up which the extreme likeness between this brother and sister had occasioned, they laughed at the Lady Olivia for the pleasant mistake she had made in falling in love with a woman; and Olivia showed no dislike to her exchange, when she found she had wedded the brother instead of the sister.

The hopes of Orsino were forever at an end by this marriage of Olivia, and with his hopes, all his fruitless love seemed to vanish away, and all his thoughts were fixed on the event of his favourite, young Cesario, being changed into a fair lady. He viewed Viola with great attention, and he remembered how very handsome he had always thought Cesario was, and he concluded she would look very beautiful in a woman's attire; and then he remembered how often she had said 'she loved him', which at the time seemed only the dutiful expressions of a faithful page; but now he guessed that something more was meant, for many of her pretty sayings, which were like riddles to him, came now into his mind, and he no sooner remembered all these things than he resolved to make Viola his wife; and he said to her (he still could not help calling her Cesario and boy): 'Boy, you have said to me a thousand times that you should never love a woman like to me, and for the faithful service you have done for me so much beneath your soft and tender breeding, and since you have called me master so long, you shall now be your master's mistress, and Orsino's true duchess.'

Olivia, perceiving Orsino was making over that heart, which she had so ungraciously rejected, to Viola, invited them to enter her house and offered the assistance of the good priest who had married her to Sebastian in the morning to perform the same ceremony in the remaining part of the day for Orsino and Viola. Thus the twin brother and sister were both wedded on the same day, the storm and shipwreck which had separated them being the means of bringing to pass their high and mighty fortunes. Viola was the wife of Orsino, the Duke of Illyria, and Sebastian the husband of the rich and noble countess, the Lady Olivia.

Timon of Athens

Timon, a lord of Athens, in the enjoyment of a princely fortune, affected a humour of liberality which knew no limits. His almost infinite wealth could not flow in so fast but he poured it out faster upon all sorts and degrees of people. Not the poor only tasted of his bounty, but great lords did not disdain to rank themselves among his dependants and followers. His table was resorted to by all the luxurious feasters, and his house was open to all comers and goers at Athens. His large wealth combined with his free and prodigal nature to subdue all hearts to his love; men of all minds and dispositions tendered their services to Lord Timon, from the glass-faced flatterer whose face reflects as in a mirror the present humour of his patron, to the rough and unbending cynic who, affecting a contempt of men's persons and an indifference to worldly things, yet could not stand out against the gracious manners and munificent soul of Lord Timon, but would come (against his nature) to partake of his royal entertainments and return most rich in his own estimation if he had received a nod or a salutation from Timon.

If a poet had composed a work which wanted a recommendatory introduction to the world, he had no more to do but to dedicate it to Lord Timon, and the poem was sure of sale, besides a present purse from the patron, and daily access to his house and table. If a painter had a picture to dispose of he had only to take it to Lord Timon and pretend to consult his taste as to the merits of it; nothing more was wanting to persuade the liberal-hearted lord to buy it. If a jeweller had a stone of price, or a mercer rich, costly stuffs, which for their costliness lay upon his hands, Lord Timon's house was a ready mart always open, where they might get off their wares or their jewellery at any price, and the good-natured lord would thank them into the bargain, as if they had done him a piece of courtesy in letting him have the refusal of such precious commodities. So that by this means his house was thronged with superfluous purchases, of no use but to swell uneasy and ostentatious pomp; and his person was still more inconveniently beset with a crowd of these idle visitors, lying poets, painters, sharking tradesmen, lords, ladies, needy courtiers, and expectants, who continually filled his lobbies, raining their fulsome flatteries in whispers in his ears, sacrificing to him with adulation as to a god, making sacred the very stirrup by which he mounted his horse, and seeming as though they drank the free air but through his permission and bounty.

Some of these daily dependants were young men of birth who (their means not answering to their extravagance) had been put in prison by creditors and redeemed thence by Lord Timon; these young prodigals thenceforward fastened upon his lordship, as if by common sympathy he were necessarily endeared to all such spendthrifts and loose livers, who, not being able to follow him in his wealth, found it easier to copy him in prodigality and copious spending of what was their own. One of these flesh-flies was Ventidius, for whose debts, unjustly contracted, Timon but lately had paid down the sum of five talents.

But among this confluence, this great flood of visitors, none were more conspicuous than the makers of presents and givers of gifts. It was fortunate for these men if Timon took a fancy to a dog or a horse, or any piece of cheap furniture which was theirs. The thing so praised, whatever it was, was sure to be sent the next morning with the compliments of the giver for Lord Timon's acceptance, and apologies for the unworthiness of the gift; and this dog or horse, or whatever it might be, did not fail to produce from Timon's bounty, who would not be outdone in gifts, perhaps twenty dogs or horses, certainly presents of far richer worth, as these pretended donors knew well enough, and that their false presents were but the putting out of so much money at large and speedy interest. In this way Lord Lucius had lately sent to Timon a present of four milk-white horses, trapped in silver, which this cunning lord had observed Timon upon some occasion to commend; and another lord, Lucullus, had bestowed upon him in the same pretended way of free gift a brace of greyhounds whose make and fleetness Timon had been heard to admire; these presents the easy-hearted lord accepted without suspicion of the dishonest views of the presenters; and the givers of course were rewarded with some rich return, a diamond or some jewel of twenty times the value of their false and mercenary donation.

Sometimes these creatures would go to work in a more direct way, and with gross and palpable artifice, which yet the credulous Timon was too blind to see, would affect to admire and praise something that Timon possessed, a bargain that he had bought, or some late purchase, which was sure to draw from this yielding and soft-hearted lord a gift of the thing commended, for no service in the world done for it but the easy expense of a little cheap and obvious flattery. In this way Timon but the other day had given to one of these mean lords the bay courser which he himself rode upon, because his lordship had been pleased to say that it was a handsome beast and went well; and Timon knew that no man ever justly praised what he did not wish to possess. For Lord Timon weighed his friends' affection with his own, and so fond was he of bestowing, that he could have dealt kingdoms to these supposed friends and never have been weary.

Not that Timon's wealth all went to enrich these wicked flatterers; he could do noble and praiseworthy actions; and when a servant of his once loved the daughter of a rich Athenian, but could not hope to obtain her by reason that in wealth and rank the maid was so far above him, Lord Timon freely bestowed upon his servant three Athenian talents, to make his fortune equal with the dowry which the father of the young maid demanded of him who should be her husband. But for the most part, knaves and parasites had the command of his fortune, false friends whom he did not know to be such, but, because they flocked around his person, he thought they must needs love him; and because they smiled and flattered him, he thought surely that his conduct was approved by all the wise and good. And when he was feasting in the midst of all these flatterers and mock friends, when they were eating him up and draining his fortunes dry with large draughts of richest wines drunk to his health and prosperity, he could not perceive the difference of a friend from a flatterer, but to his deluded eyes (made proud with the sight) it seemed a precious comfort to have so many like brothers commanding one another's fortunes (though it was his own fortune which paid all the costs), and with joy they would run over at the spectacle of such, as it appeared to him, truly festive and fraternal meeting.

But while he thus outwent the very heart of kindness, and poured out his bounty, as if Plutus, the god of gold, had been but his steward; while thus he proceeded without care or stop, so senseless of expense that he would neither enquire how he could maintain it nor cease his wild flow of riot – his riches, which were not infinite, must needs melt away before a prodigality which knew no limits. But who should tell him so? His flatterers? They had an interest in shutting his eyes. In vain did his honest steward Flavius try to represent to him his condition, laying his accounts before him, begging of him, praying of him, with an importunity that on any other occasion would have been unmannerly in a servant, beseeching him with tears to look into the state of his affairs. Timon would still put him off, and turn the discourse to something else; for nothing is so deaf to remonstrance as riches turned to poverty, nothing is so unwilling to believe its situation, nothing so incredulous to its own true state, and hard to give credit to a reverse. Often had this good steward, this honest creature, when all the rooms of Timon's great house had been choked up with riotous feeders at his master's cost, when the floors have wept with drunken spilling of wine, and every apartment has blazed with lights and resounded with music and feasting, often had he retired by himself to some solitary spot, and wept faster than the wine ran from the wasteful casks within, to see the mad bounty of his lord, and to think, when the means were gone which brought him praises from all sorts of people, how quickly the breath would be gone of which the praise was made; praises won in feasting would be lost in fasting, and at one cloud of winter-showers these flies would disappear.

But now the time was come that Timon could shut his ears no longer to the representations of this faithful steward. Money must be had; and when he ordered Flavius to sell some of his land for that purpose, Flavius informed him, what he had in vain endeavoured at several times before to make him listen to, that most of his land was already sold or forfeited, and that all he possessed at present was not enough to pay the one-half of what he owed. Struck with wonder at this presentation, Timon hastily replied: 'My lands extend from Athens to Lacedoemon.'

'O my good lord,' said Flavius, 'the world is but a world, and has bounds. Were it all yours to give in a breath, how quickly were it gone!'

Timon consoled himself that no villainous bounty had yet come from him, that if he had given his wealth away unwisely, it had not been bestowed to feed his vices, but to cherish his friends; and he bade the kind-hearted steward (who was weeping) to take comfort in the assurance that his master could never lack means while he had so many noble friends; and this infatuated lord persuaded himself that he had nothing to do but to send and borrow, to use every man's fortune (that had ever tasted his bounty) in this extremity, as freely as his own. Then with a cheerful look, as if confident of the trial, he severally despatched messengers to Lord Lucius, to Lords Lucullus and Sempronius, men upon whom he had lavished his gifts in past times without measure or moderation; and to Ventidius, whom he had lately released out of prison by paying his debts, and who, by the death of his father, was now come into the possession of an ample fortune and well enabled to requite Timon's courtesy; to request of Ventidius the return of those five talents which he had paid for him, and of each of those noble lords the loan of fifty talents; nothing doubting that their gratitude would supply his wants (if he needed it) to the amount of five hundred times fifty talents.

Lucullus was the first applied to. This mean lord had been dreaming overnight of a silver bason and cup, and when Timon's servant was announced his sordid mind suggested to him that this was surely a making out of his dream, and that Timon had sent him such a present. But when he understood the truth of the matter, and that Timon wanted money, the quality of his faint and watery friendship showed itself, for with many protestations he vowed to the servant that he had long foreseen the ruin of his master's affairs, and many a time had he come to dinner to tell him of it, and had come again to supper to try to persuade him to spend less, but he would take no counsel nor warning by his coming. And true it was that he had been a constant attender (as he said) at Timon's feasts, as he had in greater things tasted his bounty; but that he ever came with that intent, or gave good counsel or reproof to Timon, was a base, unworthy lie, which he suitably followed up with meanly offering the servant a bribe to go home to his master and tell him that he had not found Lucullus at home.

As little success had the messenger who was sent to Lord Lucius. This lying lord, who was full of Timon's meat and enriched almost to bursting with Timon's costly presents, when he found the wind changed, and the fountain of so much bounty suddenly stopped, at first could hardly believe it; but on its being confirmed he affected great regret that he should not have it in his power to serve Lord Timon, for, unfortunately (which was a base falsehood), he had made a great purchase the day before, which had quite disfurnished him of the means at present, the more beast he, he called himself, to put it out of his power to serve so good a friend; and he counted it one of his greatest afflictions that his ability should fail him to pleasure such an honourable gentleman.

Who can call any man friend that dips in the same dish with him? Just of this metal is every flatterer. In the recollection of everybody Timon had been a father to this Lucius, had kept up his credit with his purse; Timon's money had gone to pay the wages of his servants, to pay the hire of the labourers who had sweat to build the fine houses which Lucius's pride had made necessary to him. Yet – oh, the monster which man makes himself when he proves ungrateful! – this Lucius now denied to Timon a sum which, in respect of what Timon had bestowed on him, was less than charitable men afford to beggars.

Sempronius, and everyone of these mercenary lords to whom Timon applied in their turn, returned the same evasive answer or direct denial; even Ventidius, the redeemed and now rich Ventidius, refused to assist him with the loan of those five talents which Timon had not lent but generously given him in his distress.

Now was Timon as much avoided in his poverty as he had been courted and resorted to in his riches. Now the same tongues which had been loudest in his praises, extolling him as bountiful, liberal, and open-handed, were not ashamed to censure that very bounty as folly, that liberality as profuseness, though it had shown itself folly in nothing so truly as in the selection of such unworthy creatures as themselves for its objects. Now was Timon's princely mansion forsaken and become a shunned and hated place, a place for men to pass by, not a place, as formerly, where every passenger must stop and taste of his wine and good cheer; now, instead of being thronged with feasting and tumultuous guests, it was beset with impatient and clamorous creditors, usurers, extortioners, fierce and intolerable in their demands, pleading bonds, interest, mortgages; iron-hearted men that would take no denial nor putting off, that Timon's house was now his jail, which he could not pass, nor go in nor out for them; one demanding his due of fifty talents, another bringing in a bill of five thousand crowns, which, if he would tell out his blood by drops and pay them so, he had not enough in his body to discharge, drop by drop.

In this desperate and irremediable state (as it seemed) of his affairs, the eyes of all men were suddenly surprised at a new and incredible lustre which this setting sun put forth. Once more Lord Timon proclaimed a feast, to which he invited his accustomed guests – lords, ladies, all that was great or fashionable in Athens.

Lord Lucius and Lucullus came, Ventidius, Sempronius, and the
rest. Who more sorry now than these fawning wretches, when they
found (as they thought) that Lord Timon's poverty was all pretence
and had been only put on to make trial of their loves, to think that
they should not have seen through the artifice at the time and have
had the cheap credit of obliging his lordship? Yet who more glad to
find the fountain of that noble bounty which they had thought
dried up, still fresh and running? They came dissembling, protesting, expressing deepest sorrow and shame, that when his
lordship sent to them they should have been so unfortunate as
to want the present means to oblige so honourable a friend. But
Timon begged them not to give such trifles a thought, for he had
altogether forgotten it. And these base, fawning lords, though they
had denied him money in his adversity, yet could not refuse their
presence at this new blaze of his returning prosperity. For the
swallow follows not summer more willingly than men of these dispositions follow the good fortunes of the great, nor more willingly
leaves winter than these shrink from the first appearance of a
reverse. Such summer birds are men. But now with music and state
the banquet of smoking dishes was served up; and when the guests
had a little done admiring whence the bankrupt Timon could find
means to furnish so costly a feast, some doubting whether the scene
which they saw was real, as scarce trusting their own eyes, at a
signal given the dishes were uncovered and Timon's drift appeared.
Instead of those varieties and far-fetched dainties which they
expected, that Timon's epicurean table in past times had so liberally
presented, now appeared under the covers of these dishes a
preparation more suitable to Timon's poverty – nothing but a little
smoke and lukewarm water, fit feast for this knot of mouth-friends,
whose professions were indeed smoke, and their hearts lukewarm
and slippery as the water with which Timon welcomed his
astonished guests, bidding them, 'Uncover, dogs, and lap'; and,
before they could recover their surprise, sprinkling it in their faces,
that they might have enough, and throwing dishes and all after
them, who now ran huddling out, lords, ladies, with their caps
snatched up in haste, a splendid confusion, Timon pursuing them,

still calling them what they were, 'smooth smiling parasites, destroyers under the mask of courtesy, affable wolves, meek bears, fools of fortune, feast-friends, time-flies'. They, crowding out to avoid him, left the house more willingly than they had entered it; some losing their gowns and caps, and some their jewels in the hurry, all glad to escape out of the presence of such a mad lord, and from the ridicule of his mock banquet.

This was the last feast which ever Timon made, and in it he took farewell of Athens and the society of men; for, after that, he betook himself to the woods, turning his back upon the hated city and upon all mankind, wishing the walls of that detestable city might sink, and the houses fall upon their owners, wishing all plagues which infest humanity – war, outrage, poverty, diseases – might fasten upon its inhabitants, praying the just gods to confound all Athenians, both young and old, high and low; so wishing, he went to the woods, where he said he should find the unkindest beast much kinder than mankind. He stripped himself naked, that he might retain no fashion of a man, and dug a cave to live in, and lived solitary in the manner of a beast, eating the wild roots and drinking water, flying from the face of his kind, and choosing rather to herd with wild beasts, as more harmless and friendly than man.

What a change from Lord Timon the rich, Lord Timon the delight of mankind, to Timon the naked, Timon the man-hater! Where were his flatterers now? Where were his attendants and retinue? Would the bleak air, that boisterous servitor, be his chamberlain, to put his shirt on warm? Would those stiff trees that had outlived the eagle turn young and airy pages to him, to skip on his errands when he bade them? Would the cool brook, when it was iced with winter, administer to him his warm broths and caudles when sick of an overnight's surfeit? Or would the creatures that lived in those wild woods come and lick his hand and flatter him?

Here on a day, when he was digging for roots, his poor sustenance, his spade struck against something heavy, which proved to be gold, a great heap which some miser had probably buried in a time of alarm, thinking to have come again and taken it from its prison, but died before the opportunity had arrived, without making any man privy to the concealment; so it lay, doing neither good nor harm, in the bowels of the earth, its mother, as if it had never come thence, till the accidental striking of Timon's spade against it once more brought it to light.

Here was a mass of treasure which, if Timon had retained his old mind, was enough to have purchased him friends and flatterers again; but Timon was sick of the false world and the sight of gold was poisonous to his eyes; and he would have restored it to the earth, but that, thinking of the infinite calamities which by means of gold happen to mankind, how the lucre of it causes robberies, oppression, injustice, briberies, violence, and murder, among men, he had a pleasure in imagining (such a rooted hatred did he bear to his species) that out of this heap, which in digging he had discovered, might arise some mischief to plague mankind. And some soldiers passing through the woods near to his cave at that instant, which proved to be a part of the troops of the Athenian captain Alcibiades, who, upon some disgust taken against the senators of Athens (the Athenians were ever noted to be a thankless and ungrateful people, giving disgust to their generals and best friends), was marching at the head of the same triumphant army which he had formerly headed in their defence, to war against them. Timon, who liked their business well, bestowed upon their captain the gold to pay his soldiers, requiring no other service from him than that he should with his conquering army lay Athens level with the ground, and burn, slay, kill all her inhabitants; not sparing the old men for their white beards, for (he said) they were usurers, nor the young children for their seeming innocent smiles, for those (he said) would live, if they grew up, to be traitors; but to steel his eyes and ears against any sights or sounds that might awaken compassion; and not to let the cries of virgins, babes, or mothers hinder him from making one universal massacre of the city, but to confound them all in his conquest; and when he had conquered, he prayed that the gods would confound him also, the conqueror. So thoroughly did Timon hate Athens, Athenians, and all mankind.

While he lived in this forlorn state, leading a life more brutal than human, he was suddenly surprised one day with the appearance of a man standing in an admiring posture at the door of his cave. It was Flavius, the honest steward, whom love and zealous affection to his master had led to seek him out at his wretched dwelling and to offer his services; and the first sight of his master, the once noble Timon, in that abject condition, naked as he was born, living in the manner of a beast among beasts, looking like his own sad ruins and a monument of decay, so affected this good servant that he stood speechless, wrapped up in horror and confounded. And when he found utterance at last to his words, they were so choked with tears that Timon had much ado to know him again, or to make out who it was that had come (so contrary to the experience he had had of mankind) to offer him service in extremity. And being in the form and shape of a man, he suspected him for a traitor, and his tears for false; but the good servant by so many tokens confirmed the truth of his fidelity, and made it clear that nothing but love and zealous duty to his once dear master had brought him there, that Timon was forced to confess that the world contained one honest man; yet, being in the shape and form of a man, he could not look upon his man's face without abhorrence, or hear words uttered from his man's lips without loathing; and this singly honest man was forced to depart, because he was a man, and because, with a heart more gentle and compassionate than is usual to man, he bore man's detested form and outward feature.

But greater visitants than a poor steward were about to interrupt the savage quiet of Timon's solitude. For now the day was come when the ungrateful lords of Athens sorely repented the injustice which they had done to the noble Timon. For Alcibiades, like an incensed wild boar, was raging at the walls of their city, and with his hot siege threatened to lay fair Athens in the dust. And now the memory of Lord Timon's former prowess and military conduct came fresh into their forgetful minds, for Timon had been their general in past times, and a valiant and expert soldier, who alone of all the Athenians was deemed able to cope with a besieging army such as then threatened them, or to drive back the furious approaches of Alcibiades.

A deputation of the senators was chosen in this emergency to wait upon Timon. To him they come in their extremity, to whom, when he was in extremity, they had shown but small regard; as if they presumed upon his gratitude whom they had disobliged, and had derived a claim to his courtesy from their own most discourteous and unpiteous treatment.

Now they earnestly beseech him, implore him with tears, to return and save that city from which their ingratitude had so lately driven him; now they offer him riches, power, dignities, satisfaction for past injuries, and public honours, and the public love; their persons, lives, and fortunes to be at his disposal, if he will but come back and save them. But Timon the naked, Timon the man-hater, was no longer Lord Timon, the lord of bounty, the flower of valour, their defence in war, their ornament in peace. If Alcibiades killed his countrymen, Timon cared not. If he sacked fair Athens, and slew her old men and her infants, Timon would rejoice. So he told them; and that there was not a knife in the unruly camp which he did not prize above the reverendest throat in Athens.

This was all the answer he vouchsafed to the weeping, disappointed senators; only at parting he bade them commend him to his countrymen, and tell them that to ease them of their griefs and anxieties, and to prevent the consequences of fierce Alcibiades's wrath, there was yet a way left, which he would teach them, for he had yet so much affection left for his dear countrymen as to be willing to do them a kindness before his death. These words a little revived the senators, who hoped that his kindness for their city was returning. Then Timon told them that he had a tree, which grew near his cave, which he should shortly have occasion to cut down, and he invited all his friends in Athens, high or low, of whatsoever degree, who wished to shun affliction, to come and take a taste of his tree before he cut it down; meaning that they might come and hang themselves on it and escape affliction that way.

And this was the last courtesy, of all his noble bounties, which Timon showed to mankind, and this the last sight of him which his countrymen had, for not many days after, a poor soldier, passing by the sea-beach which was at a little distance from the woods which

Timon frequented, found a tomb on the verge of the sea, with an inscription upon it purporting that it was the grave of Timon the man-hater, who 'While he lived, did hate all living men, and, dying, wished a plague might consume all caitiffs left!'

Whether he finished his life by violence, or whether mere distaste of life and the loathing he had for mankind brought Timon to his conclusion, was not clear, yet all men admired the fitness of his epitaph and the consistency of his end, dying, as he had lived, a hater of mankind. And some there were who fancied a conceit in the very choice which he had made of the sea-beach for his place of burial, where the vast sea might weep for ever upon his grave, as in contempt of the transient and shallow tears of hypocritical and deceitful mankind.

Romeo and Juliet

The two chief families in Verona were the rich Capulets and the Montagues. There had been an old quarrel between these families, which was grown to such a height, and so deadly was the enmity between them, that it extended to the remotest kindred, to the followers and retainers of both sides, in so much that a servant of the house of Montague could not meet a servant of the house of Capulet, nor a Capulet encounter with a Montague by chance, but fierce words and sometimes bloodshed ensued; and frequent were the brawls from such accidental meetings, which disturbed the happy quiet of Verona's streets.

Old Lord Capulet made a great supper, to which many fair ladies and many noble guests were invited. All the admired beauties of Verona were present, and all comers were made welcome if they were not of the house of Montague. At this feast of Capulets, Rosaline, beloved of Romeo, son to the old Lord Montague, was present; and though it was dangerous for a Montague to be seen in this assembly, yet Benvolio, a friend of Romeo, persuaded the young lord to go to this assembly in the disguise of a mask, that he might see his Rosaline, and, seeing her, compare her with some choice beauties of Verona, who (he said) would make him think his swan a crow. Romeo had small faith in Benvolio's words; nevertheless, for the love of Rosaline, he was persuaded to go. For Romeo was a sincere and passionate lover, and one that lost his sleep for love and fled society to be alone, thinking on Rosaline, who disdained him and never requited his love with the least show of courtesy or affection; and Benvolio wished to cure his friend of this love by showing him diversity of ladies and company. To this feast of Capulets, then, young Romeo, with Benvolio and their friend Mercutio, went masked. Old Capulet bid them welcome and told them that ladies who had their toes unplagued with corns would dance with them. And the old man was light-hearted and merry, and said that he had worn a mask when he was young and could have told a whispering tale in a fair lady's ear. And they fell to dancing, and Romeo was suddenly struck with the exceeding beauty of a lady who danced there, who seemed to him to teach the torches to burn bright, and her beauty to show by night like a rich jewel worn by a blackamoor; beauty too rich for use, too dear for earth! like a snowy dove trooping with crows (he said), so richly did her beauty and perfections shine above the ladies her companions. While he uttered these praises he was overheard by Tybalt, a nephew of Lord Capulet, who knew him by his voice to be Romeo. And this Tybalt, being of a fiery and passionate temper, could not endure that a Montague should come under cover of a mask, to fleer and scorn (as he said) at their solemnities. And he stormed and raged exceedingly, and would have struck young Romeo dead. But his uncle, the old Lord Capulet, would not suffer him to do any injury at that time, both out of respect to his guests and because Romeo had borne himself like a gentleman and all tongues in Verona bragged of him to be a virtuous and well-governed youth. Tybalt, forced to be patient against his will, restrained himself, but swore that this vile Montague should at another time dearly pay for his intrusion.

The dancing being done, Romeo watched the place where the lady stood; and under favour of his masking habit, which might seem to excuse in part the liberty, he presumed in the gentlest manner to take her by the hand, calling it a shrine, which if he profaned by touching it, he was a blushing pilgrim and would kiss it for atonement.

'Good pilgrim,' answered the lady, 'your devotion shows by far too mannerly and too courtly. Saints have hands which pilgrims may touch but kiss not.'

'Have not saints lips, and pilgrims, too?' said Romeo.

'Aye,' said the lady, 'lips which they must use in prayer.'

'Oh, then, my dear saint,' said Romeo, 'hear my prayer, and grant it, lest I despair.'

In such like allusions and loving conceits they were engaged when the lady was called away to her mother. And Romeo, enquiring who her mother was, discovered that the lady whose peerless beauty he was so much struck with was young Juliet, daughter and heir to the Lord Capulet, the great enemy of the Montagues; and that he had unknowingly engaged his heart to his foe. This troubled him, but it could not dissuade him from loving. As little rest had Juliet when she found that the gentle man that she had been talking with was Romeo and a Montague, for she had been suddenly smit with the same hasty and inconsiderate passion for Romeo which he had conceived for her; and a prodigious birth of love it seemed to her, that she must love her enemy and that her affections should settle there, where family considerations should induce her chiefly to hate.

It being midnight, Romeo with his companions departed; but they soon missed him, for, unable to stay away from the house where he had left his heart, he leaped the wall of an orchard which was at the back of Juliet's house. Here he had not been long, ruminating on his new love, when Juliet appeared above at a window, through which her exceeding beauty seemed to break like the light of the sun in the east; and the moon, which shone in the orchard with a faint light, appeared to Romeo as if sick and pale with grief at the superior lustre of this new sun. And she leaning her cheek upon her hand, he passionately wished himself a glove upon that hand, that he might touch her cheek. She all this while thinking herself alone, fetched a deep sigh, and exclaimed: 'Ah me!'

Romeo, enraptured to hear her speak, said, softly and unheard by her, 'Oh, speak again, bright angel, for such you appear, being over my head, like a winged messenger from heaven whom mortals fall back to gaze upon.'

She, unconscious of being overheard, and full of the new passion which that night's adventure had given birth to, called upon her lover by name (whom she supposed absent). 'O Romeo, Romeo!' said she, 'wherefore art thou Romeo? Deny thy father and refuse thy name, for my sake; or if thou wilt not, be but my sworn love, and I no longer will be a Capulet.'

Romeo, having this encouragement, would fain have spoken, but he was desirous of hearing more; and the lady continued her passionate discourse with herself (as she thought), still chiding Romeo for being Romeo and a Montague, and wishing him some other name, or that he would put away that hated name, and for that name which was no part of himself he should take all herself. At this loving word Romeo could no longer refrain, but, taking up the dialogue as if her words had been addressed to him personally, and not merely in fancy, he bade her call him Love, or by whatever other name she pleased, for he was no longer Romeo, if that name was displeasing to her. Juliet, alarmed to hear a man's voice in the garden, did not at first know who it was that by favour of the night and darkness had thus stumbled upon the discovery of her secret; but when he spoke again, though her ears had not yet drunk a hundred words of that tongue's uttering, yet so nice is a lover's hearing that she immediately knew him to be young Romeo, and she expostulated with him on the danger to which he had exposed himself by climbing the orchard walls, for if any of her kinsmen should find him there it would be death to him, being a Montague.

'Alack!' said Romeo, 'there is more peril in your eye than in twenty of their swords. Do you but look kind upon me, lady, and I am proof against their enmity. Better my life should be ended by their hate than that hated life should be prolonged to live without your love.'

'How came you into this place,' said Juliet, 'and by whose direction?'

'Love directed me,' answered Romeo. 'I am no pilot, yet wert thou as far apart from me as that vast shore which is washed with the farthest sea, I should venture for such merchandise.'

A crimson blush came over Juliet's face, yet unseen by Romeo by reason of the night, when she reflected upon the discovery which she had made, yet not meaning to make it, of her love to Romeo. She would fain have recalled her words, but that was impossible; fain would she have stood upon form, and have kept her lover at a distance, as the custom of discreet ladies is, to frown and be perverse and give their suitors harsh denials at first; to stand off, and affect a coyness or indifference where they most love, that their lovers may not think them too lightly or too easily won; for the difficulty of attainment increases the value of the object. But there was no room in her case for denials, or puttings off, or any of the customary arts of delay and protracted courtship. Romeo had heard from her own tongue, when she did not dream that he was near her, a confession of her love. So with an honest frankness which the novelty of her situation excused she confirmed the truth of what he had before heard, and, addressing him by the name of *fair Montague* (love can sweeten a sour name), she begged him not to impute her easy yielding to levity or an unworthy mind, but that he must lay the fault of it (if it were a fault) upon the accident of the night which had so strangely discovered her thoughts. And she added, that though her behaviour to him might not be sufficiently prudent, measured by the custom of her sex, yet that she would prove more true than many whose prudence was dissembling, and their modesty artificial cunning.

Romeo was beginning to call the heavens to witness that nothing was farther from his thoughts than to impute a shadow of dishonour to such an honoured lady, when she stopped him, begging him not to swear; for although she joyed in him, yet she had no joy of that night's contract – it was too rash, too unadvised, too sudden. But he being urgent with her to exchange a vow of love with him that night, she said that she already had given him hers before he requested it, meaning, when he overheard her confession; but she would retract what she then bestowed, for the pleasure of giving it again, for her bounty was as infinite as the sea, and her love as deep. From this loving conference she was called away by her nurse, who slept with her and thought it time for her to be in bed, for it was near to daybreak; but, hastily returning, she said three or four words more to Romeo the purport of which was, that if his love was indeed honourable, and his purpose marriage, she would send a messenger to him tomorrow to appoint a time for their marriage, when she would lay all her fortunes at his feet and follow him as her lord through the world. While they were settling this point Juliet was repeatedly called for by her nurse, and went in and returned, and went and returned again, for she seemed as jealous of Romeo going from her as a young girl of her bird, which she will let hop a little from her hand and pluck it back with a silken thread; and Romeo was as loath to part as she, for the sweetest music to lovers is the sound of each other's tongues at night. But at last they parted, wishing mutually sweet sleep and rest for that night.

The day was breaking when they parted, and Romeo, who was too full of thoughts of his mistress and that blessed meeting to allow him to sleep, instead of going home, bent his course to a monastery hard by, to find Friar Lawrence. The good friar was already up at his devotions, but, seeing young Romeo abroad so early, he conjectured rightly that he had not been abed that night, but that some distemper of youthful affection had kept him waking. He was right in imputing the cause of Romeo's wakefulness to love, but he made a wrong guess at the object, for he thought that his love for Rosaline had kept him waking. But when Romeo revealed his new passion for Juliet, and requested the assistance of the friar to marry them that day, the holy man lifted up his eyes and hands in a sort of wonder at the sudden change in Romeo's affections, for he had been privy to all Romeo's love for Rosaline and his many complaints of her disdain; and he said that young men's love lay not truly in their hearts, but in their eyes. But Romeo replying that he himself had often chidden him for doting on Rosaline, who could not love him again, whereas Juliet both loved and was beloved by him, the friar assented in some measure to his reasons; and thinking that a matrimonial alliance between young Juliet and Romeo might happily be the means of making up the long breach between the Capulets and the Montagues, which no one more lamented than this good friar who was a friend to both the families and had often interposed his mediation to make up the quarrel without effect; partly moved by policy, and partly by his fondness for young Romeo, to whom he could deny nothing, the old man consented to join their hands in marriage.

Now was Romeo blessed indeed, and Juliet, who knew his intent from a messenger which she had despatched according to promise, did not fail to be early at the cell of Friar Lawrence, where their hands were joined in holy marriage, the good friar praying the heavens to smile upon that act, and in the union of this young Montague and young Capulet, to bury the old strife and long dissensions of their families.

The ceremony being over, Juliet hastened home, where she stayed, impatient for the coming of night, at which time Romeo promised to come and meet her in the orchard, where they had met the night before; and the time between seemed as tedious to her as the night before some great festival seems to an impatient child that has got new finery which it may not put on till the morning.

That same day, about noon, Romeo's friends, Benvolio and Mercutio, walking through the streets of Verona, were met by a party of the Capulets with the impetuous Tybalt at their head. This was the same angry Tybalt who would have fought with Romeo at old Lord Capulet's feast. He, seeing Mercutio, accused him bluntly of associating with Romeo, a Montague. Mercutio, who had as much fire and youthful blood in him as Tybalt, replied to this accusation with some sharpness; and in spite of all Benvolio could say to moderate their wrath a quarrel was beginning when, Romeo himself passing that way, the fierce Tybalt turned from Mercutio to Romeo, and gave him the disgraceful appellation of villain. Romeo wished to avoid a quarrel with Tybalt above all men, because he was the kinsman of Juliet and much beloved by her; besides, this young Montague had never thoroughly entered into the family quarrel, being by nature wise and gentle, and the name of a Capulet, which was his dear lady's name, was now rather a charm to allay resentment than a watchword to excite fury. So he tried to reason with Tybalt, whom he saluted mildly by the name of *good Capulet*, as if he, though a Montague, had some secret pleasure in uttering that name; but Tybalt, who hated all Montagues as he hated hell, would hear no reason, but drew his weapon; and Mercutio, who knew not of Romeo's secret motive for desiring peace with Tybalt, but looked upon his present forbearance as a sort of calm dishonourable submission, with many disdainful words provoked Tybalt to the prosecution of his first quarrel with him; and Tybalt and Mercutio fought, till Mercutio fell, receiving his death's wound while Romeo and Benvolio were vainly endeavouring to part the combatants. Mercutio being dead, Romeo kept his temper no longer, but returned the scornful appellation of villain which Tybalt had given him, and they fought till Tybalt was slain by Romeo. This deadly broil falling out in the midst of Verona at noonday, the news of it quickly brought a crowd of citizens to the spot and among them the Lords Capulet and Montague, with their wives; and soon after arrived the prince himself, who, being related to Mercutio, whom Tybalt had slain, and having had the peace of his government often disturbed by these brawls of Montagues and Capulets, came determined to put the law in strictest force against those who should be found to be offenders. Benvolio, who had been eyewitness to the fray, was commanded by the prince to relate the origin of it; which he did, keeping as near the truth as he could without injury to Romeo, softening and excusing the part which his friends took in it. Lady Capulet, whose extreme grief for the loss of her kinsman Tybalt made her keep no bounds in her revenge, exhorted the prince to do strict justice upon his murderer, and to pay no attention to Benvolio's representation, who, being Romeo's friend and a Montague, spoke partially. Thus she pleaded against her new son-in-law, but she knew not yet that he was her son-in-law and Juliet's husband. On the other hand was to be seen Lady Montague pleading for her child's life, and arguing with some justice that Romeo had done nothing worthy of punishment in taking the life of Tybalt, which was already forfeited to the law by his having slain Mercutio. The prince, unmoved by the passionate exclamations of these women, on a careful examination of the facts pronounced his sentence, and by that sentence Romeo was banished from Verona.

Heavy news to young Juliet, who had been but a few hours a

bride and now by this decree seemed everlastingly divorced! When the tidings reached her, she at first gave way to rage against Romeo, who had slain her dear cousin. She called him a beautiful tyrant, a fiend angelical, a ravenous dove, a lamb with a wolf's nature, a serpent-heart hid with a flowering face, and other, like contradictory names, which denoted the struggles in her mind between her love and her resentment. But in the end love got the mastery, and the tears which she shed for grief that Romeo had slain her cousin turned to drops of joy that her husband lived whom Tybalt would have slain. Then came fresh tears, and they were altogether of grief for Romeo's banishment. That word was more terrible to her than the death of many Tybalts.

Romeo, after the fray, had taken refuge in Friar Lawrence's cell, where he was first made acquainted with the prince's sentence, which seemed to him far more terrible than death. To him it appeared there was no world out of Verona's walls, no living out of the sight of Juliet. Heaven was there where Juliet lived, and all beyond was purgatory, torture, hell. The good friar would have applied the consolation of philosophy to his griefs; but this frantic young man would hear of none, but like a madman he tore his hair and threw himself all along upon the ground, as he said, to take the measure of his grave. From this unseemly state he was roused by a message from his dear lady which a little revived him; and then the friar took the advantage to expostulate with him on the unmanly weakness which he had shown. He had slain Tybalt, but would he also slay himself, slay his dear lady, who lived but in his life? The noble form of man, he said, was but a shape of wax when it wanted the courage which should keep it firm. The law had been lenient to him that instead of death, which he had incurred, had pronounced by the prince's mouth only banishment. He had slain Tybalt, but Tybalt would have slain him – there was a sort of happiness in that. Juliet was alive and (beyond all hope) had become his dear wife; therein he was most happy. All these blessings, as the friar made them out to be, did Romeo put from him like a sullen misbehaved wench. And the friar bade him beware, for such as despaired (he said) died miserable. Then when Romeo was a little calmed he counselled him that he should go that night and secretly take his leave of Juliet, and thence proceed straightway to Mantua, at which place he should sojourn till the friar found fit occasion to publish his marriage, which might be a joyful means of reconciling their families; and then he did not doubt but the prince would be moved to pardon him, and he would return with twenty times more joy than he went forth with grief. Romeo was convinced by these wise counsels of the friar, and took his leave to go and seek his lady, proposing to stay with her that night, and by daybreak pursue his journey alone to Mantua; to which place the good friar promised to send him letters from time to time, acquainting him with the state of affairs at home.

That night Romeo passed with his dear wife, gaining secret admission to her chamber from the orchard in which he had heard her confession of love the night before. That had been a night of unmixed joy and rapture; but the pleasures of this night and the delight which these lovers took in each other's society were sadly allayed with the prospect of parting and the fatal adventures of the past day. The unwelcome daybreak seemed to come too soon, and when Juliet heard the morning song of the lark she would have persuaded herself that it was the nightingale, which sings by night; but it was too truly the lark which sang, and a discordant and unpleasing note it seemed to her; and the streaks of day in the east too certainly pointed out that it was time for these lovers to part. Romeo took his leave of his dear wife with a heavy heart, promising to write to her from Mantua every hour in the day; and when he had descended from her chamber window, as he stood below her on the ground, in that sad foreboding state of mind in which she was, he appeared to her eyes as one dead in the bottom of a tomb. Romeo's mind misgave him in like manner. But now he was forced hastily to depart, for it was death for him to be found within the walls of Verona after daybreak.

This was but the beginning of the tragedy of this pair of star-crossed lovers. Romeo had not been gone many days before the old Lord Capulet proposed a match for Juliet. The husband he had chosen for her, not dreaming that she was married already, was

Count Paris, a gallant, young, and noble gentleman, no unworthy suitor to the young Juliet if she had never seen Romeo.

The terrified Juliet was in a sad perplexity at her father's offer. She pleaded her youth unsuitable to marriage, the recent death of Tybalt, which had left her spirits too weak to meet a husband with any face of joy, and how indecorous it would show for the family of the Capulets to be celebrating a nuptial feast when his funeral solemnities were hardly over. She pleaded every reason against the match but the true one, namely, that she was married already. But Lord Capulet was deaf to all her excuses, and in a peremptory manner ordered her to get ready, for by the following Thursday she should be married to Paris. And having found her a husband, rich, young, and noble, such as the proudest maid in Verona might joyfully accept, he could not bear that out of an affected coyness, as he construed her denial, she should oppose obstacles to her own good fortune.

In this extremity Juliet applied to the friendly friar, always a counsellor in distress, and he asking her if she had resolution to undertake a desperate remedy, and she answering that she would go into the grave alive rather than marry Paris, her own dear husband living, he directed her to go home, and appear merry, and give her consent to marry Paris, according to her father's desire, and on the next night, which was the night before the marriage, to drink off the contents of a vial which he then gave her, the effect of which would be that for two-and-forty hours after drinking it she should appear cold and lifeless, and when the bridegroom came to fetch her in the morning he would find her to appearance dead; that then she would be borne, as the manner in that country was, uncovered on a bier, to be buried in the family vault; that if she could put off womanish fear, and consent to this terrible trial, in forty-two hours after swallowing the liquid (such was its certain operation) she would be sure to awake, as from a dream; and before she should awake he would let her husband know their drift, and he should come in the night and bear her thence to Mantua. Love, and the dread of marrying Paris, gave young Juliet strength to undertake this horrible adventure; and she took the vial of the friar, promising to observe his directions.

Going from the monastery, she met the young Count Paris, and, modestly dissembling, promised to become his bride. This was joyful news to the Lord Capulet and his wife. It seemed to put youth into the old man; and Juliet, who had displeased him exceedingly by her refusal of the count, was his darling again, now she promised to be obedient. All things in the house were in a bustle against the approaching nuptials. No cost was spared to prepare such festival rejoicings as Verona had never before witnessed.

On the Wednesday night Juliet drank off the potion. She had many misgivings lest the friar, to avoid the blame which might be imputed to him for marrying her to Romeo, had given her poison; but then he was always known for a holy man. Then lest she should awake before the time that Romeo was to come for her; whether the terror of the place, a vault full of dead Capulets' bones, and where Tybalt, all bloody, lay festering in his shroud, would not be enough to drive her distracted. Again she thought of all the stories she had heard of spirits haunting the places where their bodies were bestowed. But then her love for Romeo and her aversion for Paris returned, and she desperately swallowed the draught and became insensible.

When young Paris came early in the morning with music to awaken his bride, instead of a living Juliet her chamber presented the dreary spectacle of a lifeless corse. What death to his hopes! What confusion then reigned through the whole house! Poor Paris lamenting his bride, whom most detestable death had beguiled him of, had divorced from him even before their hands were joined. But still more piteous it was to hear the mournings of the old Lord and Lady Capulet, who having but this one, one poor loving child to rejoice and solace in, cruel death had snatched her from their sight, just as these careful parents were on the point of seeing her advanced (as they thought) by a promising and advantageous match. Now all things that were ordained for the festival were turned from their properties to do the office of a black funeral. The wedding cheer served for a sad burial feast, the bridal hymns were changed for sullen dirges, the sprightly instruments to melancholy bells, and the flowers that should have been strewed in the bride's path now served but to strew her corse. Now, instead of a priest to marry her, a priest was needed to bury her, and she was borne to church indeed, not to augment the cheerful hopes of the living, but to swell the dreary numbers of the dead.

Bad news, which always travels faster than good, now brought the dismal story of his Juliet's death to Romeo, at Mantua, before the messenger could arrive who was sent from Friar Lawrence to apprise him that these were mock funerals only, and but the shadow and representation of death, and that his dear lady lay in the tomb but for a short while, expecting when Romeo would come to release her from that dreary mansion. Just before, Romeo had been unusually joyful and light-hearted. He had dreamed in the night that he was dead (a strange dream, that gave a dead man leave to think) and that his lady came and found him dead, and breathed such life with kisses in his lips that he revived and was an emperor! And now that a messenger came from Verona, he thought surely it was to confirm some good news which his dreams had presaged. But when the contrary to this flattering vision appeared, and that it was his lady who was dead in truth, whom he could not revive by any kisses, he ordered horses to be got ready, for he determined that night to visit Verona and to see his lady in her tomb. And as mischief is swift to enter into the thoughts of desperate men, he called to mind a poor apothecary, whose shop in Mantua he had lately passed, and from the beggarly appearance of the man, who seemed famished, and the wretched show in his show of empty boxes ranged on dirty shelves, and other tokens of extreme wretchedness, he had said at the time (perhaps having some misgivings that his own disastrous life might haply meet with a conclusion so desperate): 'If a man were to need poison, which by the law of Mantua it is death to sell, here lives a poor wretch who would sell it him.'

These words of his now came into his mind and he sought out the apothecary, who after some pretended scruples, Romeo offering him gold, which his poverty could not resist, sold him a poison which, if he swallowed, he told him, if he had the strength of twenty men, would quickly despatch him.

With this poison he set out for Verona, to have a sight of his dear lady in her tomb, meaning, when he had satisfied his sight, to swallow the poison and be buried by her side. He reached Verona at midnight, and found the churchyard in the midst of which was situated the ancient tomb of the Capulets. He had provided a light, and a spade, and wrenching-iron, and was proceeding to break open the monument when he was interrupted by a voice, which by the name of *vile Montague* bade him desist from his unlawful business. It was the young Count Paris, who had come to the tomb of Juliet at that unseasonable time of night to strew flowers and to weep over the grave of her that should have been his bride. He knew not what an interest Romeo had in the dead, but, knowing him to be a Montague and (as he supposed) a sworn foe to all the Capulets, he judged that he was come by night to do some villainous shame to the dead bodies; therefore in an angry tone he bade him desist; and as a criminal, condemned by the laws of Verona to die if he were found within the walls of the city, he would have apprehended him. Romeo urged Paris to leave him, and warned him by the fate of Tybalt, who lay buried there, not to provoke his anger or draw down another sin upon his head by forcing him to kill him. But the count in scorn refused his warning, and laid hands on him as a felon, which, Romeo resisting, they fought, and Paris fell. When Romeo, by the help of a light, came to see who it was that he had slain, that it was Paris, who (he learned in his way from Mantua) should have married Juliet, he took the dead youth by the hand, as one whom misfortune had made a companion, and said that he would bury him in a triumphal grave, meaning in Juliet's grave, which he now opened. And there lay his lady, as one whom death had no power upon to change a feature or complexion, in her matchless beauty; or as if death were amorous, and the lean, abhorred monster kept her there for his delight; for she lay yet fresh and blooming, as she had fallen to sleep when she swallowed that benumbing potion; and near her lay Tybalt in his bloody shroud, whom Romeo seeing, begged pardon of his lifeless corse, and for Juliet's sake called him *cousin*, and said that he was about to do him a favour by putting his enemy to death. Here

Romeo took his last leave of his lady's lips, kissing them; and here he shook the burden of his cross stars from his weary body, swallowing that poison which the apothecary had sold him, whose operation was fatal and real, not like that dissembling potion which Juliet had swallowed, the effect of which was now nearly expiring, and she about to awake to complain that Romeo had not kept his time, or that he had come too soon.

For now the hour was arrived at which the friar had promised that she should awake; and he, having learned that his letters which he had sent to Mantua, by some unlucky detention of the messenger, had never reached Romeo, came himself, provided with a pickaxe and lantern, to deliver the lady from her confinement; but he was surprised to find a light already burning in the Capulets' monument, and to see swords and blood near it, and Romeo and Paris lying breathless by the monument.

Before he could entertain a conjecture, to imagine how these fatal accidents had fallen out, Juliet awoke out of her trance, and, seeing the friar near her, she remembered the place where she was, and the occasion of her being there, and asked for Romeo, but the friar, hearing a noise, bade her come out of that place of death and of unnatural sleep, for a greater power than they could contradict had thwarted their intents; and, being frightened by the noise of people coming, he fled. But when Juliet saw the cup closed in her true love's hands, she guessed that poison had been the cause of his end, and she would have swallowed the dregs if any had been left, and she kissed his still warm lips to try if any poison yet did hang upon them; then hearing a nearer noise of people coming, she quickly unsheathed a dagger which she wore, and, stabbing herself, died by her true Romeo's side.

The watch by this time had come up to the place. A page belonging to Count Paris, who had witnessed the fight between his master and Romeo, had given the alarm, which had spread among the citizens, who went up and down the streets of Verona confusedly exclaiming, 'A Paris! a Romeo! a Juliet!' as the rumour had imperfectly reached them, till the uproar brought Lord Montague and Lord Capulet out of their beds, with the prince, to enquire into the causes of the disturbance. The friar had been apprehended by some of the watch, coming from the churchyard, trembling, sighing, and weeping in a suspicious manner. A great multitude being assembled at the Capulets' monument, the friar was demanded by the prince to deliver what he knew of these strange and disastrous accidents.

And there, in the presence of the old Lords Montague and Capulet, he faithfully related the story of their children's fatal love, the part he took in promoting their marriage, in the hope in that union to end the long quarrels between their families; how Romeo, there dead, was husband to Juliet, and Juliet, there dead, was Romeo's faithful wife; how, before he could find a fit opportunity to divulge their marriage, another match was projected for Juliet, who, to avoid the crime of a second marriage, swallowed the sleeping-draught (as he advised), and all thought her dead; how meantime he wrote to Romeo to come and take her thence when the force of the potion should cease, and by what unfortunate miscarriage of the messenger the letters never reached Romeo. Further than this the friar could not follow the story, nor knew more than that, coming himself to deliver Juliet from that place of death, he found the Count Paris and Romeo slain. The remainder of the transactions was supplied by the narration of the page who had seen Paris and Romeo fight, and by the servant who came with Romeo from Verona, to whom this faithful lover had given letters to be delivered to his father in the event of his death, which made good the friar's words, confessing his marriage with Juliet, imploring the forgiveness of his parents, acknowledging the buying of the poison of the poor apothecary and his intent in coming to the monument to die and lie with Juliet. All these circumstances agreed together to clear the friar from any hand he could be supposed to have in these complicated slaughters, further than as the unintended consequences of his own well-meant, yet too artificial and subtle contrivances.

And the prince, turning to these old lords, Montague and Capulet, rebuked them for their brutal and irrational enmities, and showed them what a scourge heaven had laid upon such offences, that it had found means even through the love of their children to punish their unnatural hate. And these old rivals, no longer enemies, agreed to bury their long strife in their children's graves; and Lord Capulet requested Lord Montague to give him his hand, calling him by the name of brother, as if in acknowledgement of the union of their families by the marriage of the young Capulet and Montague; and saying that Lord Montague's hand (in token of reconcilement) was all he demanded for his daughter's jointure. But Lord Montague said he would give him more, for he would raise her a statue of pure gold that, while Verona kept its name, no figure should be so esteemed for its richness and workmanship as that of the true and faithful Juliet. And Lord Capulet in return said that he would raise another statue to Romeo. So did these poor old lords, when it was too late, strive to outgo each other in mutual courtesies; while so deadly had been their rage and enmity in past times that nothing but the fearful overthrow of their children (poor sacrifices to their quarrels and dissensions) could remove the rooted hates and jealousies of the noble families.

Hamlet, Prince of Denmark

Gertrude, Queen of Denmark, becoming a widow by the sudden death of King Hamlet, in less than two months after his death married his brother Claudius, which was noted by all people at the time for a strange act of indiscretion, or unfeelingness, or worse; for this Claudius did no way resemble her late husband in the qualities of his person or his mind, but was as contemptible in outward appearance as he was base and unworthy in disposition; and suspicions did not fail to arise in the minds of some that he had privately made away with his brother, the late king, with the view of marrying his widow and ascending the throne of Denmark, to the exclusion of young Hamlet, the son of the buried king and lawful successor to the throne.

But upon no one did this unadvised action of the queen make such impression as upon this young prince, who loved and venerated the memory of his dead father almost to idolatry, and, being of a nice sense of honour and a most exquisite practiser of propriety himself, did sorely take to heart this unworthy conduct of his mother Gertrude; in so much that, between grief for his father's death and shame for his mother's marriage, this young prince was overclouded with a deep melancholy, and lost all his mirth and all his good looks; all his customary pleasure in books forsook him, his princely exercises and sports, proper to his youth, were no longer acceptable; he grew weary of the world, which seemed to him an unweeded garden, where all the wholesome flowers were choked up and nothing but weeds could thrive. Not that the prospect of exclusion from the throne, his lawful inheritance, weighed so much upon his spirits, though that to a young and high-minded prince was a bitter wound and a sore indignity; but what so galled him and took away all his cheerful spirits was that his mother had shown herself so forgetful to his father's memory, and such a father! who had been to her so loving and so gentle a husband! and then she always appeared as loving and obedient a wife to him, and would hang upon him as if her affection grew to him. And now within two months, or, as it seemed to young Hamlet, less than two months, she had married again, married his uncle, her dear husband's brother, in itself a highly improper and unlawful marriage, from the nearness of relationship, but made much more so by the indecent haste with which it was concluded and the unkingly character of the man whom she had chosen to be the partner of her throne and bed. This it was which more than the loss of ten kingdoms dashed the spirits and brought a cloud over the mind of this honourable young prince.

In vain was all that his mother Gertrude or the king could do to contrive to divert him; he still appeared in court in a suit of deep black, as mourning for the king his father's death, which mode of dress he had never laid aside, not even in compliment to his mother upon the day she was married, nor could he be brought to join in any of the festivities or rejoicings of that (as appeared to him) disgraceful day.

What mostly troubled him was an uncertainty about the manner of his father's death. It was given out by Claudius that a serpent had stung him; but young Hamlet had shrewd suspicions that Claudius himself was the serpent; in plain English, that he had murdered him for his crown, and that the serpent who stung his father did now sit on the throne.

How far he was right in this conjecture and what he ought to think of his mother, how far she was privy to this murder and whether by her consent or knowledge, or without, it came to pass, were the doubts which continually harassed and distracted him.

A rumour had reached the ear of young Hamlet that an apparition, exactly resembling the dead king his father, had been seen by the soldiers upon watch, on the platform before the palace at midnight, for two or three nights successively. The figure came constantly clad in the same suit of armour, from head to foot, which the dead king was known to have worn. And they who saw it (Hamlet's bosom friend Horatio was one) agreed in their testimony as to the time and manner of its appearance that it came just as the clock struck twelve; that it looked pale, with a face more of sorrow than of anger; that its beard was grisly, and the colour a *sable silvered*, as they had seen it in his lifetime; that it made no answer when they spoke to it; yet once they thought it lifted up its head and addressed itself to motion, as if it were about to speak; but in that moment the morning cock crew and it shrank in haste away, and vanished out of their sight.

The young prince, strangely amazed at their relation, which was too consistent and agreeing with itself to disbelieve, concluded that it was his father's ghost which they had seen, and determined to take his watch with the soldiers that night, that he might have a chance of seeing it; for he reasoned with himself that such an appearance did not come for nothing, but that the ghost had something to impart, and though it had been silent hitherto, yet it would speak to him. And he waited with impatience for the coming of night.

When night came he took his stand with Horatio, and Marcellus, one of the guard, upon the platform, where this apparition was accustomed to walk; and it being a cold night, and the air unusually raw and nipping, Hamlet and Horatio and their companion fell into some talk about the coldness of the night, which was suddenly broken off by Horatio announcing that the ghost was coming.

At the sight of his father's spirit Hamlet was struck with a sudden surprise and fear. He at first called upon the angels and heavenly ministers to defend them, for he knew not whether it were a good spirit or bad, whether it came for good or evil; but he gradually assumed more courage; and his father (as it seemed to him) looked upon him so piteously, and as it were desiring to have conversation with him, and did in all respects appear so like himself as he was when he lived, that Hamlet could not help addressing him. He called him by his name, 'Hamlet, King, Father!' and conjured him that he would tell the reason why he had left his grave, where they had seen him quietly bestowed, to come again and visit the earth and the moonlight; and besought him that he would let them know if there was anything which they could do to give peace to his spirit. And the ghost beckoned to Hamlet, that he should go with him to some more removed place where they might be alone; and Horatio and Marcellus would have dissuaded the young prince from following it, for they feared lest it should be some evil spirit who would tempt him to the neighbouring sea or to the top of some dreadful cliff, and there put on some horrible shape which might deprive the prince of his reason. But their counsels and entreaties could not alter Hamlet's determination, who cared too little about life to fear the losing of it; and as to his soul, he said, what could the spirit do to that, being a thing immortal as itself? And he felt as hardy as a lion, and, bursting from them, who did all they could to hold him, he followed whithersoever the spirit led him.

And when they were alone together, the spirit broke silence and told him that he was the ghost of Hamlet, his father, who had been cruelly murdered, and he told the manner of it; that it was done by his own brother Claudius, Hamlet's uncle, as Hamlet had already but too much suspected, for the hope of succeeding to his bed and crown. That as he was sleeping in his garden, his custom always in the afternoon, his treasonous brother stole upon him in his sleep and poured the juice of poisonous henbane into his ears, which has such an antipathy to the life of man that, swift as quicksilver, it courses through all the veins of the body, baking up the blood and spreading a crust-like leprosy all over the skin. Thus sleeping, by a brother's hand he was cut off at once from his crown, his queen, and his life; and he adjured Hamlet, if he did ever his dear father love, that he would revenge his foul murder. And the ghost lamented to his son that his mother should so fall off from virtue as to prove false to the wedded love of her first husband and to marry his murderer; but he cautioned Hamlet, howsoever he proceeded in his revenge against his wicked uncle, by no means to act any violence against the person of his mother, but to leave her to heaven, and to the stings and thorns of conscience. And Hamlet promised to observe the ghost's direction in all things, and the ghost vanished.

And when Hamlet was left alone he took up a solemn resolution that all he had in his memory, all that he had ever learned by books or observation, should be instantly forgotten by him, and nothing live in his brain but the memory of what the ghost had told him and enjoined him to do. And Hamlet related the particulars of the conversation which had passed to none but his dear friend Horatio; and he enjoined both to him and Marcellus the strictest secrecy as to what they had seen that night.

The terror which the sight of the ghost had left upon the senses of Hamlet, he being weak and dispirited before, almost unhinged his mind and drove him beside his reason. And he, fearing that it would continue to have this effect, which might subject him to observation and set his uncle upon his guard, if he suspected that he was meditating anything against him, or that Hamlet really knew more of his father's death than he professed, took up a strange resolution, from that time to counterfeit as if he were really and truly mad; thinking that he would be less an object of suspicion when his uncle should believe him incapable of any serious project, and that his real perturbation of mind would be best covered and pass concealed under a disguise of pretended lunacy.

From this time Hamlet affected a certain wildness and strangeness in his apparel, his speech, and behaviour, and did so excellently counterfeit the madman that the king and queen were both deceived, and not thinking his grief for his father's death a sufficient cause to produce such a distemper, for they knew not of the appearance of the ghost, they concluded that his malady was love and they thought they had found out the object.

Before Hamlet fell into the melancholy way which has been

related he had dearly loved a fair maid called Ophelia, the daughter of Polonius, the king's chief counsellor in affairs of state. He had sent her letters and rings, and made many tenders of his affection to her, and importuned her with love in honourable fashion; and she had given belief to his vows and importunities. But the melancholy which he fell into latterly had made him neglect her, and from the time he conceived the project of counterfeiting madness he affected to treat her with unkindness and a sort of rudeness; but she, good lady, rather than reproach him with being false to her, persuaded herself that it was nothing but the disease in his mind, and no settled unkindness, which had made him less observant of her than formerly; and she compared the faculties of his once noble mind and excellent understanding, impaired as they were with the deep melancholy that oppressed him, to sweet bells which in themselves are capable of most exquisite music, but when jangled out of tune, or rudely handled, produce only a harsh and unpleasing sound.

Though the rough business which Hamlet had in hand, the revenging of his father's death upon his murderer, did not suit with the playful state of courtship, or admit of the society of so idle a passion as love now seemed to him, yet it could not hinder but that soft thoughts of his Ophelia would come between, and in one of these moments, when he thought that his treatment of this gentle lady had been unreasonably harsh, he wrote her a letter full of wild starts of passion, and in extravagant terms, such as agreed with his supposed madness, but mixed with some gentle touches of affection, which could not but show to this honoured lady that a deep love for her yet lay at the bottom of his heart. He bade her to doubt the stars were fire, and to doubt that the sun did move, to doubt truth to be a liar, but never to doubt that he loved; with more of such extravagant phrases. This letter Ophelia dutifully showed to her father, and the old man thought himself bound to communicate it to the king and queen, who from that time supposed that the true cause of Hamlet's madness was love. And the queen wished that the good beauties of Ophelia might be the happy cause of his wildness, for so she hoped that her virtues might happily restore him to his accustomed way again, to both their honours.

But Hamlet's malady lay deeper than she supposed, or than could be so cured. His father's ghost, which he had seen, still haunted his imagination, and the sacred injunction to revenge his murder gave him no rest till it was accomplished. Every hour of delay seemed to him a sin and a violation of his father's commands. Yet how to compass the death of the king, surrounded as he constantly was with his guards, was no easy matter. Or if it had been, the presence of the queen, Hamlet's mother, who was generally with the king, was a restraint upon his purpose, which he could not break through. Besides, the very circumstance that the usurper was his mother's husband, filled him with some remorse and still blunted the edge of his purpose. The mere act of putting a fellow-creature to death was in itself odious and terrible to a disposition naturally so gentle as Hamlet's was. His very melancholy, and the dejection of spirits he had so long been in, produced an irresoluteness and wavering of purpose which kept him from proceeding to extremities. Moreover, he could not help having some scruples upon his mind, whether the spirit which he had seen was indeed his father, or whether it might not be the devil, who he had heard has power to take any form he pleases, and who might have assumed his father's shape only to take advantage of his weakness and his melancholy, to drive him to the doing of so desperate an act as murder. And he determined that he would have more certain grounds to go upon than a vision, or apparition, which might be a delusion.

While he was in this irresolute mind there came to the court certain players, in whom Hamlet formerly used to take delight, and particularly to hear one of them speak a tragical speech, describing the death of old Priam, King of Troy, with the grief of Hecuba his queen. Hamlet welcomed his old friends, the players, and remembering how that speech had formerly given him pleasure, requested the player to repeat it; which he did in so lively a manner, setting forth the cruel murder of the feeble old king, with the destruction of his people and city by fire, and the mad grief of the old queen, running barefoot up and down the palace, with a poor clout upon that head where a crown had been, and with nothing but a blanket upon her loins, snatched up in haste, where she had worn a royal robe; that not only it drew tears from all that stood by, who thought they saw the real scene, so lively was it represented, but even the player himself delivered it with a broken voice and real tears. This put Hamlet upon thinking, if that player could so work himself up to passion by a mere fictitious speech, to weep for one that he had never seen, for Hecuba, that had been dead so many hundred years, how dull was he, who having a real motive and cue for passion, a real king and a dear father murdered, was yet so little moved that his revenge all this while had seemed to have slept in dull and muddy forgetfulness! and while he meditated on actors and acting, and the powerful effects which a good play, represented to the life, has upon the spectator, he remembered the instance of some murderer, who, seeing a murder on the stage, was by the mere force of the scene and resemblance of circumstances so affected that on the spot he confessed the crime which he had committed. And he determined that these players should play something like the murder of his father before his uncle, and he would watch narrowly what effect it might have upon him, and from his looks he would be able to gather with more certainty if he were the murderer or not. To this effect he ordered a play to be prepared, to the representation of which he invited the king and queen.

The story of the play was of a murder done in Vienna upon a duke. The duke's name was Gonzago, his wife's Baptista. The play showed how one Lucianus, a near relation to the duke, poisoned him in his garden for his estate, and how the murderer in a short time after got the love of Gonzago's wife.

At the representation of this play, the king, who did not know the trap which was laid for him, was present, with his queen and the whole court; Hamlet sitting attentively near him to observe his looks. The play began with a conversation between Gonzago and his wife, in which the lady made many protestations of love, and of never marrying a second husband if she should outlive Gonzago, wishing she might be accursed if she ever took a second husband, and adding that no woman did so but those wicked women who kill their first husbands. Hamlet observed the king his uncle change colour at this expression, and that it was as bad as wormwood both to him and to the queen. But when Lucianus, according to the story, came to poison Gonzago sleeping in the garden, the strong resemblance which it bore to his own wicked act upon the late king, his brother, whom he had poisoned in his garden, so struck upon the conscience of this usurper that he was unable to sit out the rest of the play, but on a sudden calling for lights to his chamber, and affecting or partly feeling a sudden sickness, he abruptly left the theatre. The king being departed, the play was given over. Now Hamlet had seen enough to be satisfied that the words of the ghost were true and no illusion; and in a fit of gaiety, like that which comes over a man who suddenly has some great doubt or scruple resolved, he swore to Horatio that he would take the ghost's word for a thousand pounds. But before he could make up his resolution as to what measures of revenge he should take, now he was certainly informed that his uncle was his father's murderer, he was sent for by the queen his mother, to a private conference in her closet.

It was by desire of the king that the queen sent for Hamlet, that she might signify to her son how much his late behaviour had displeased them both, and the king, wishing to know all that passed at that conference, and thinking that the too partial report of a mother might let slip some part of Hamlet's words, which it might much import the king to know, Polonius, the old counsellor of state, was ordered to plant himself behind the hangings in the queen's closet, where he might, unseen, hear all that passed. This artifice was particularly adapted to the disposition of Polonius, who was a man grown old in crooked maxims and policies of state, and delighted to get at the knowledge of matters in an indirect and cunning way.

Hamlet being come to his mother, she began to tax him in the roundest way with his actions and behaviour, and she told him that he had given great offence to *his father*, meaning the king, his uncle, whom, because he had married her, she called Hamlet's father. Hamlet, sorely indignant that she should give so dear and honoured a name as father seemed to him to a wretch who was indeed no better than the murderer of his true father, with some sharpness replied: 'Mother, *you* have much offended *my father*.'

The queen said that was but an idle answer.

'As good as the question deserved,' said Hamlet.

The queen asked him if he had forgotten who it was he was speaking to.

'Alas!' replied Hamlet, 'I wish I could forget. You are the queen, your husband's brother's wife; and you are my mother. I wish you were not what you are.'

'Nay, then,' said the queen, 'if you show me so little respect, I will set those to you that can speak,' and was going to send the king or Polonius to him.

But Hamlet would not let her go, now he had her alone, till he had tried if his words could not bring her to some sense of her wicked life; and, taking her by the wrist, he held her fast, and made her sit down. She, affrighted at his earnest manner, and fearful lest in his lunacy he should do her a mischief, cried out; and a voice was heard from behind the hangings, 'Help, help, the queen!' which Hamlet hearing, and verily thinking that it was the king himself there concealed, he drew his sword and stabbed at the place where the voice came from, as he would have stabbed a rat that ran there, till, the voice ceasing, he concluded the person to be dead. But when he dragged forth the body it was not the king, but Polonius, the old, officious counsellor, that had planted himself as a spy behind the hangings.

'Oh, me!' exclaimed the queen, 'what a rash and bloody deed have you done!'

'A bloody deed, mother,' replied Hamlet, 'but not so bad as yours, who killed a king, and married his brother.'

Hamlet had gone too far to leave off here. He was now in the humour to speak plainly to his mother, and he pursued it. And though the faults of parents are to be tenderly treated by their children, yet in the case of great crimes the son may have leave to speak even to his own mother with some harshness, so as that harshness is meant for her good and to turn her from her wicked ways, and not done for the purpose of upbraiding. And now this virtuous prince did in moving terms represent to the queen the heinousness of her offence in being so forgetful of the dead king, his father, as in so short a space of time to marry with his brother and reputed murderer. Such an act as, after the vows which she had sworn to her first husband, was enough to make all vows of women suspected and all virtue to be accounted hypocrisy, wedding contracts to be less than gamesters' oaths, and religion to be a mockery and a mere form of words. He said she had done such a deed that the heavens blushed at it, and the earth was sick of her because of it. And he showed her two pictures, the one of the late king, her first husband, and the other of the present king, her second husband, and he bade her mark the difference; what a grace was on the brow of his father, how like a god he looked! the curls of Apollo, the forehead of Jupiter, the eye of Mars, and a posture like to Mercury newly alighted on some heaven-kissing hill! this man, he said, *had been* her husband. And then he showed her whom she had got in his stead; how like a blight or a mildew he looked, for so he had blasted his wholesome brother. And the queen was sore ashamed that he should so turn her eyes inward upon her soul, which she now saw so black and deformed. And he asked her how she could continue to live with this man, and be a wife to him, who had murdered her first husband and got the crown by as false means as a thief – and just as he spoke the ghost of his father, such as he was in his lifetime and such as he had lately seen it, entered the room, and Hamlet, in great terror, asked what it would have; and the ghost said that it came to remind him of the revenge he had promised, which Hamlet seemed to have forgot; and the ghost bade him speak to his mother, for the grief and terror she was in would else kill her. It then vanished, and was seen by none but Hamlet, neither could he by pointing to where it stood, or by any description, make his mother perceive it, who was terribly frightened all this while to hear him conversing, as it seemed to her, with nothing; and she imputed it to the disorder of his mind. But Hamlet begged her not to flatter her wicked soul in such a manner as to think that it was his madness, and not her own offences, which had brought his father's spirit again on the earth. And he bade her feel his pulse, how temperately it beat, not like a madman's. And he begged of her, with tears, to confess herself to heaven for what was past, and for the future to avoid the company of the king and be no more as a wife to him; and when she should show herself a mother to him, by respecting his father's memory, he would ask a blessing of her as a son. And she promising to observe his directions, the conference ended.

And now Hamlet was at leisure to consider who it was that in his unfortunate rashness he had killed; and when he came to see that it was Polonius, the father of the Lady Ophelia whom he so dearly loved, he drew apart the dead body, and, his spirits being now a little quieter, he wept for what he had done.

The unfortunate death of Polonius gave the king a pretence for sending Hamlet out of the kingdom. He would willingly have put him to death, fearing him as dangerous; but he dreaded the people, who loved Hamlet, and the queen, who, with all her faults, doted upon the prince, her son. So this subtle king, under pretence of providing for Hamlet's safety, that he might not be called to account for Polonius's death, caused him to be conveyed on board a ship bound for England, under the care of two courtiers, by whom he despatched letters to the English court, which in that time was in subjection and paid tribute to Denmark, requiring, for special reasons there pretended, that Hamlet should be put to death as soon as he landed on English ground. Hamlet, suspecting some treachery, in the nighttime secretly got at the letters, and, skilfully erasing his own name, he in the stead of it put in the names of those two courtiers, who had the charge of him, to be put to death; then sealing up the letters, he put them into their place again. Soon after the ship was attacked by pirates, and a sea-fight commenced, in the course of which Hamlet, desirous to show his valour, with sword in hand singly boarded the enemy's vessel; while his own ship, in a cowardly manner, bore away; and leaving him to his fate, the two courtiers made the best of their way to England, charged with those letters the sense of which Hamlet had altered to their own deserved destruction.

The pirates who had the prince in their power showed themselves gentle enemies, and, knowing whom they had got prisoner, in the hope that the prince might do them a good turn at court in recompense for any favour they might show him, they set Hamlet on shore at the nearest port in Denmark. From that place Hamlet wrote to the king, acquainting him with the strange chance which had brought him back to his own country and saying that on the next day he should present himself before his majesty. When he got home a sad spectacle offered itself the first thing to his eyes.

This was the funeral of the young and beautiful Ophelia, his once dear mistress. The wits of this young lady had begun to turn ever since her poor father's death. That he should die a violent death, and by the hands of the prince whom she loved, so affected this tender young maid that in a little time she grew perfectly distracted, and would go about giving flowers away to the ladies of the court, and saying that they were for her father's burial, singing songs about love and about death, and sometimes such as had no meaning at all, as if she had no memory of what happened to her. There was a willow which grew slanting over a brook, and reflected its leaves on the stream. To this brook she came one day when she was unwatched, with garlands she had been making, mixed up of daisies and nettles, flowers and weeds together, and clambering up to hang her garland upon the boughs of the willow, a bough broke and precipitated this fair young maid, garland, and all that she had gathered, into the water, where her clothes bore her up for a while, during which she chanted scraps of old tunes, like one insensible to her own distress, or as if she were a creature natural to that element; but long it was not before her garments, heavy with the wet, pulled her in from her melodious singing to a muddy and miserable death. It was the funeral of this fair maid which her brother Laertes was celebrating, the king and queen and whole court being present, when Hamlet arrived. He knew not what all this show imported, but stood on one side, not inclining to interrupt the ceremony. He saw the flowers strewed upon her grave, as the custom was in maiden burials, which the queen herself threw in; and as she threw them she said: 'Sweets to the sweet! I thought to have decked thy bride bed, sweet maid, not to have strewed thy grave. Thou shouldst have been my Hamlet's wife.'

And he heard her brother wish that violets might spring from her grave; and he saw him leap into the grave all frantic with grief, and bid the attendants pile mountains of earth upon him, that he might be buried with her. And Hamlet's love for this fair maid came back to him, and he could not bear that a brother should show so much transport of grief, for he thought that he loved Ophelia better than forty thousand brothers. Then discovering himself, he leaped into the grave where Laertes was, all as frantic or more frantic than he, and Laertes, knowing him to be Hamlet, who had been the cause of his father's and his sister's death, grappled him by the throat as an enemy, till the attendants parted them; and Hamlet, after the funeral, excused his hasty act in throwing himself into the grave as if to brave Laertes; but he said he could not bear that anyone should seem to outgo him in grief for the death of the fair Ophelia. And for the time these two noble youths seemed reconciled.

But out of the grief and anger of Laertes for the death of his father and Ophelia the king, Hamlet's wicked uncle, contrived destruction for Hamlet. He set on Laertes, under cover of peace and recon-ciliation, to challenge Hamlet to a friendly trial of skill at fencing, which Hamlet accepting, a day was appointed to try the match. At this match all the court was present, and Laertes, by direction of the king, prepared a poisoned weapon. Upon this match great wagers were laid by the courtiers, as both Hamlet and Laertes were known to excel at this sword play; and Hamlet, taking up the foils, chose one, not at all suspecting the treachery of Laertes, or being careful to examine Laertes's weapon, who, instead of a foil or blunted sword, which the laws of fencing require, made use of one with a point, and poisoned. At first Laertes did but play with Hamlet, and suffered him to gain some advantages, which the dissembling king magnified and extolled beyond measure, drinking to Hamlet's success and wagering rich bets upon the issue. But after a few passes Laertes, growing warm, made a deadly thrust at Hamlet with his poisoned weapon, and gave him a mortal blow. Hamlet, incensed, but not knowing the whole of the treachery, in the scuffle exchanged his own innocent weapon for Laertes's deadly one, and with a thrust of Laertes's own sword repaid Laertes home, who was thus justly caught in his own treachery. In this instant the queen shrieked out that she was poisoned. She had inadvertently drunk out of a bowl which the king had prepared for Hamlet, in case that, being warm in fencing, he should call for drink; into this the treacherous king had infused a deadly poison, to make sure of Hamlet, if Laertes had failed. He had forgotten to warn the queen of the bowl, which she drank of, and immediately died, exclaiming with her last breath that she was poisoned. Hamlet, suspecting some treachery, ordered the doors to be shut while he sought it out. Laertes told him to seek no farther, for he was the traitor; and feeling his life go away with the wound which Hamlet had given him, he made confession of the treachery he had used and how he had fallen a victim to it: and he told Hamlet of the envenomed point, and said that Hamlet had not half an hour to live, for no medicine could cure him; and begging forgiveness of Hamlet, he died, with his last words accusing the king of being the contriver of the mischief. When Hamlet saw his end draw near, there being yet some venom left upon the sword, he suddenly turned upon his false uncle and thrust the point of it to his heart, fulfilling the promise which he had made to his father's spirit, whose injunction was now accomplished and his foul murder revenged upon the murderer. Then Hamlet, feeling his breath fail and life departing, turned to his dear friend Horatio, who had been spectator of this fatal tragedy; and with his dying breath requested him that he would live to tell his story to the world (for Horatio had made a motion as if he would slay himself to accompany the prince in death), and Horatio promised that he would make a true report as one that was privy to all the circumstances. And, thus satisfied, the noble heart of Hamlet cracked; and Horatio and the bystanders with many tears commended the spirit of this sweet prince to the guardianship of angels. For Hamlet was a loving and a gentle prince and greatly beloved for his many noble and princelike qualities; and if he had lived, would no doubt have proved a most royal and complete king to Denmark.

Othello

Brabantio, the rich senator of Venice, had a fair daughter, the gentle Desdemona. She was sought to by divers suitors, both on account of her many virtuous qualities and for her rich expectations. But among the suitors of her own clime and complexion she saw none whom she could affect, for this noble lady, who regarded the mind more than the features of men, with a singularity rather to be admired than imitated had chosen for the object of her affections a Moor, a black, whom her father loved and often invited to his house.

Neither is Desdemona to be altogether condemned for the unsuitableness of the person whom she selected for her lover. Bating that Othello was black, the noble Moor wanted nothing which might recommend him to the affections of the greatest lady. He was a soldier, and a brave one; and by his conduct in bloody wars against the Turks had risen to the rank of general in the Venetian service, and was esteemed and trusted by the state.

He had been a traveller, and Desdemona (as is the manner of ladies) loved to hear him tell the story of his adventures, which he would run through from his earliest recollection; the battles, sieges, and encounters which he had passed through; the perils he had been exposed to by land and by water; his hair-breadth escapes, when he had entered a breach or marched up to the mouth of a cannon; and how he had been taken prisoner by the insolent enemy, and sold to slavery; how he demeaned himself in that state, and how he escaped: all these accounts, added to the narration of the strange things he had seen in foreign countries, the vast wilderness and romantic caverns, the quarries, the rocks and mountains whose heads are in the clouds; of the savage nations, the cannibals who are man-eaters, and a race of people in Africa whose heads do grow beneath their shoulders. These travellers' stories would so enchain the attention of Desdemona that if she were called off at any time by household affairs she would despatch with all haste that business, and return, and with a greedy ear devour Othello's discourse. And once he took advantage of a pliant hour and drew from her a prayer that he would tell her the whole story of his life at large, of which she had heard so much, but only by parts. To which he consented, and beguiled her of many a tear when he spoke of some distressful stroke which his youth had suffered.

His story being done, she gave him for his pains a world of sighs. She swore a pretty oath that it was all passing strange, and pitiful, wondrous pitiful. She wished (she said) she had not heard it, yet she wished that heaven had made her such a man; and then she thanked him, and told him, if he had a friend who loved her, he had only to teach him how to tell his story and that would woo her. Upon this hint, delivered not with more frankness than modesty, accompanied with certain bewitching prettiness and blushes, which Othello could not but understand, he spoke more openly of his love, and in this golden opportunity gained the consent of the generous Lady Desdemona privately to marry him.

Neither Othello's colour nor his fortune was such that it could be hoped Brabantio would accept him for a son-in-law. He had left his daughter free; but he did expect that, as the manner of noble Venetian ladies was, she would choose ere long a husband of senatorial rank or expectations; but in this he was deceived. Desdemona loved the Moor, though he was black, and devoted her heart and fortunes to his valiant parts and qualities. So was her heart subdued to an implicit devotion to the man she had selected for a husband that his very colour, which to all but this discerning lady would have proved an insurmountable objection, was by her esteemed above all the white skins and clear complexions of the young Venetian nobility, her suitors.

Their marriage, which, though privately carried, could not long be kept a secret, came to the ears of the old man, Brabantio, who appeared in a solemn council of the senate as an accuser of the Moor Othello, who by spells and witchcraft (he maintained) had seduced the affections of the fair Desdemona to marry him, without the consent of her father, and against the obligations of hospitality.

At this juncture of time it happened that the state of Venice had immediate need of the services of Othello, news having arrived that the Turks with mighty preparation had fitted out a fleet, which was bending its course to the island of Cyprus, with intent to regain that strong post from the Venetians, who then held it; in this emergency the state turned its eyes upon Othello, who alone was deemed adequate to conduct the defence of Cyprus against the Turks. So that Othello, now summoned before the senate, stood in their presence at once as a candidate for a great state employment and as a culprit charged with offences which by the laws of Venice were made capital.

The age and senatorial character of old Brabantio commanded a most patient hearing from that grave assembly; but the incensed father conducted his accusation with so much intemperance, producing likelihoods and allegations for proofs, that, when Othello was called upon for his defence, he had only to relate a plain tale of the course of his love; which he did with such an artless eloquence, recounting the whole story of his wooing as we have related it above, and delivered his speech with so noble a plainness (the evidence of truth) that the duke, who sat as chief judge, could not help confessing that a tale so told would have won his daughter, too, and the spells and conjurations which Othello had used in his courtship plainly appeared to have been no more than the honest arts of men in love, and the only witchcraft which he had used the faculty of telling a soft tale to win a lady's ear.

This statement of Othello was confirmed by the testimony of the

Lady Desdemona herself, who appeared in court and, professing a duty to her father for life and education, challenged leave of him to profess a yet higher duty to her lord and husband, even so much as her mother had shown in preferring him (Brabantio) above *her* father.

The old senator, unable to maintain his plea, called the Moor to him with many expressions of sorrow, and, as an act of necessity, bestowed upon him his daughter, whom, if he had been free to withhold her (he told him), he would with all his heart have kept from him; adding that he was glad at soul that he had no other child, for this behaviour of Desdemona would have taught him to be a tyrant and hang clogs on them for her desertion.

This difficulty being got over, Othello, to whom custom had rendered the hardships of a military life as natural as food and rest are to other men, readily undertook the management of the wars in Cyprus; and Desdemona, preferring the honour of her lord (though with danger) before the indulgence of those idle delights in which new-married people usually waste their time, cheerfully consented to his going.

No sooner were Othello and his lady landed in Cyprus than news arrived that a desperate tempest had dispersed the Turkish fleet, and thus the island was secure from any immediate apprehension of an attack. But the war which Othello was to suffer was now beginning; and the enemies which malice stirred up against his innocent lady proved in their nature more deadly than strangers or infidels.

Among all the general's friends no one possessed the confidence of Othello more entirely than Cassio. Michael Cassio was a young soldier, a Florentine, gay, amorous, and of pleasing address, favourite qualities with women; he was handsome and eloquent, and exactly such a person as might alarm the jealousy of a man advanced in years (as Othello in some measure was) who had married a young and beautiful wife; but Othello was as free from jealousy as he was noble, and as incapable of suspecting as of doing a base action. He had employed this Cassio in his love affair with Desdemona, and Cassio had been a sort of go-between in his suit; for Othello, fearing

that himself had not those soft parts of conversation which please
ladies, and finding these qualities in his friend, would often depute
Cassio to go (as he phrased it) a-courting for him, such innocent
simplicity being rather an honour than a blemish to the character of
the valiant Moor. So that no wonder if, next to Othello himself (but
at far distance, as beseems a virtuous wife), the gentle Desdemona
loved and trusted Cassio. Nor had the marriage of this couple made
any difference in their behaviour to Michael Cassio. He frequented
their house, and his free and rattling talk was no unpleasing variety
to Othello, who was himself of a more serious temper; for such
tempers are observed often to delight in their contraries, as a relief
from the oppressive excess of their own; and Desdemona and Cassio
would talk and laugh together, as in the days when he went a-
courting for his friend.

Othello had lately promoted Cassio to be the lieutenant, a place
of trust, and nearest to the general's person. This promotion gave
great offence to Iago, an older officer who thought he had a better
claim than Cassio, and would often ridicule Cassio as a fellow fit
only for the company of ladies and one that knew no more of the
art of war or how to set an army in array for battle than a girl. Iago
hated Cassio, and he hated Othello as well for favouring Cassio
as for an unjust suspicion, which he had lightly taken up against
Othello, that the Moor was too fond of Iago's wife Emilia. From
these imaginary provocations the plotting mind of Iago conceived a
horrid scheme of revenge, which should involve Cassio, the Moor,
and Desdemona in one common ruin.

Iago was artful, and had studied human nature deeply, and he
knew that of all the torments which afflict the mind of man (and
far beyond bodily torture) the pains of jealousy were the most
intolerable and had the sorest sting. If he could succeed in making
Othello jealous of Cassio he thought it would be an exquisite plot
of revenge and might end in the death of Cassio or Othello, or
both; he cared not.

The arrival of the general and his lady in Cyprus, meeting with
news of the dispersion of the enemy's fleet, made a sort of holiday
in the island. Everybody gave himself up to feasting and making

merry. Wine flowed in abundance, and cups went round to the health of the black Othello and his lady the fair Desdemona.

Cassio had the direction of the guard that night, with a charge from Othello to keep the soldiers from excess in drinking, that no brawl might arise to fright the inhabitants or disgust them with the new-landed forces. That night Iago began his deep-laid plans of mischief. Under colour of loyalty and love to the general, he enticed Cassio to make rather too free with the bottle (a great fault in an officer upon guard). Cassio for a time resisted, but he could not long hold out against the honest freedom which Iago knew how to put on, but kept swallowing glass after glass (as Iago still plied him with drink and encouraging songs), and Cassio's tongue ran over in praise of the Lady Desdemona, whom he again and again toasted, affirming that she was a most exquisite lady. Until at last the enemy which he put into his mouth stole away his brains; and upon some provocation given him by a fellow whom Iago had set on, swords were drawn, and Montano, a worthy officer, who interfered to appease the dispute, was wounded in the scuffle. The riot now began to be general, and Iago, who had set on foot the mischief, was foremost in spreading the alarm, causing the castle bell to be rung (as if some dangerous mutiny instead of a slight drunken quarrel had arisen). The alarm-bell ringing awakened Othello, who, dressing in a hurry and coming to the scene of action, questioned Cassio of the cause.

Cassio was now come to himself, the effect of the wine having a little gone off, but was too much ashamed to reply; and Iago, pretending a great reluctance to accuse Cassio, but, as it were, forced into it by Othello, who insisted to know the truth, gave an account of the whole matter (leaving out his own share in it, which Cassio was too far gone to remember) in such a manner as, while he seemed to make Cassio's offence less, did indeed make it appear greater than it was. The result was that Othello, who was a strict observer of discipline, was compelled to take away Cassio's place of lieutenant from him.

Thus did Iago's first artifice succeed completely; he had now undermined his hated rival and thrust him out of his place; but a further use was hereafter to be made of the adventure of this disastrous night.

Cassio, whom this misfortune had entirely sobered, now lamented to his seeming friend Iago that he should have been such a fool as to transform himself into a beast. He was undone, for how could he ask the general for his place again? He would tell him he was a drunkard. He despised himself. Iago, affecting to make light of it, said that he, or any man living, might be drunk upon occasion; it remained now to make the best of a bad bargain. The general's wife was now the general, and could do anything with Othello; that he were best to apply to the Lady Desdemona to mediate for him with her lord; that she was of a frank, obliging disposition and would readily undertake a good office of this sort and set Cassio right again in the general's favour; and then this crack in their love would be made stronger than ever. A good advice of Iago, if it had not been given for wicked purposes, which will after appear.

Cassio did as Iago advised him, and made application to the Lady Desdemona, who was easy to be won over in any honest suit; and she promised Cassio that she should be his solicitor with her lord, and rather die than give up his cause. This she immediately set about in so earnest and pretty a manner that Othello, who was mortally offended with Cassio, could not put her off. When he pleaded delay, and that it was too soon to pardon such an offender, she would not be beat back, but insisted that it should be the next night, or the morning after, or the next morning to that at farthest. Then she showed how penitent and humbled poor Cassio was, and that his offence did not deserve so sharp a check. And when Othello still hung back: 'What! my lord,' said she, 'that I should have so much to do to plead for Cassio, Michael Cassio, that came a-courting for you, and oftentimes, when I have spoken in dispraise of you has taken your part! I count this but a little thing to ask of you. When I mean to try your love indeed I shall ask a weighty matter.'

Othello could deny nothing to such a pleader, and only requesting that Desdemona would leave the time to him, promised to receive Michael Cassio again in favour.

It happened that Othello and Iago had entered into the room where Desdemona was, just as Cassio, who had been imploring her intercession, was departing at the opposite door; and Iago, who was full of art, said in a low voice, as if to himself, 'I like not that.' Othello took no great notice of what he said; indeed, the conference which immediately took place with his lady put it out of his head; but he remembered it afterwards. For when Desdemona was gone, Iago, as if for mere satisfaction of his thought, questioned Othello whether Michael Cassio, when Othello was courting his lady, knew of his love. To this the general answering in the affirmative, and adding, that he had gone between them very often during the courtship, Iago knitted his brow, as if he had got fresh light on some terrible matter, and cried, 'Indeed!' This brought into Othello's mind the words which Iago had let fall upon entering the room and seeing Cassio with Desdemona; and he began to think there was some meaning in all this, for he deemed Iago to be a just man, and full of love and honesty, and what in a false knave would be tricks in him seemed to be the natural workings of an honest mind, big with something too great for utterance. And Othello prayed Iago to speak what he knew and to give his worst thoughts words.

'And what,' said Iago, 'if some thoughts very vile should have intruded into my breast, as where is the palace into which foul things do not enter?' Then Iago went on to say, what a pity it were if any trouble should arise to Othello out of his imperfect observations; that it would not be for Othello's peace to know his thoughts; that people's good names were not to be taken away for slight suspicions; and when Othello's curiosity was raised almost to distraction with these hints and scattered words, Iago, as if in earnest care for Othello's peace of mind, besought him to beware of jealousy. With such art did this villain raise suspicions in the unguarded Othello, by the very caution which he pretended to give him against suspicion.

'I know,' said Othello, 'that my wife is fair, loves company and feasting, is free of speech, sings, plays, and dances well; but where virtue is, these qualities are virtuous. I must have proof before I think her dishonest.'

Then Iago, as if glad that Othello was slow to believe ill of his lady, frankly declared that he had no proof, but begged Othello to see her behaviour well, when Cassio was by; not to be jealous nor too secure neither, for that he (Iago) knew the dispositions of the Italian ladies, his countrywomen, better than Othello could do; and that in Venice the wives let heaven see many pranks they dared not show their husbands. Then he artfully insinuated that Desdemona deceived her father in marrying with Othello, and carried it so closely that the poor old man thought that witchcraft had been used. Othello was much moved with this argument, which brought the matter home to him, for if she had deceived her father why might she not deceive her husband?

Iago begged pardon for having moved him; but Othello, assuming an indifference, while he was really shaken with inward grief at Iago's words, begged him to go on, which Iago did with many apologies, as if unwilling to produce anything against Cassio, whom he called his friend. He then came strongly to the point and reminded Othello how Desdemona had refused many suitable matches of her own clime and complexion, and had married him, a Moor, which showed unnatural in her and proved her to have a headstrong will; and when her better judgement returned, how probable it was she should fall upon comparing Othello with the fine forms and clear white complexions of the young Italians her countrymen. He concluded with advising Othello to put off his reconcilement with Cassio a little longer, and in the meanwhile to note with what earnestness Desdemona should intercede in his behalf; for that much would be seen in that. So mischievously did this artful villain lay his plots to turn the gentle qualities of this innocent lady into her destruction, and make a net for her out of her own goodness to entrap her, first setting Cassio on to entreat her mediation, and then out of that very mediation contriving stratagems for her ruin.

The conference ended with Iago's begging Othello to account his wife innocent until he had more decisive proof; and Othello promised to be patient; but from that moment the deceived Othello never tasted content of mind. Poppy, nor the juice of mandragora, nor all the sleeping potions in the world, could ever again restore to him that sweet rest which he had enjoyed but yesterday. His occupation sickened upon him. He no longer took delight in arms. His heart, that used to be roused at the sight of troops and banners and battle array, and would stir and leap at the sound of a drum or a trumpet or a neighing warhorse, seemed to have lost all that pride and ambition which are a soldier's virtue; and his military ardour and all his old joys forsook him. Sometimes he thought his wife honest, and at times he thought her not so; sometimes he thought Iago just, and at times he thought him not so; then he would wish that he had never known of it; he was not the worse for her loving Cassio, so long as he knew it not. Torn to pieces with these distracting thoughts, he once laid hold on Iago's throat and demanded proof of Desdemona's guilt, or threatened instant death for his having belied her. Iago, feigning indignation that his honesty should be taken for a vice, asked Othello if he had not sometimes seen a handkerchief spotted with strawberries in his wife's hand. Othello answered that he had given her such a one, and that it was his first gift.

'That same handkerchief,' said Iago, 'did I see Michael Cassio this day wipe his face with.'

'If it be as you say,' said Othello, 'I will not rest till a wide revenge swallow them up; and first, for a token of your fidelity, I expect that Cassio shall be put to death within three days; and for that fair devil [meaning his lady] I will withdraw and devise some swift means of death for her.'

Trifles light as air are to the jealous proofs as strong as holy writ. A handkerchief of his wife's seen in Cassio's hand was motive enough to the deluded Othello to pass sentence of death upon them both, without once enquiring how Cassio came by it. Desdemona had never given such a present to Cassio, nor would this constant lady have wronged her lord with doing so naughty a thing as giving his presents to another man; both Cassio and Desdemona were innocent of any offence against Othello; but the wicked Iago, whose spirits never slept in contrivance of villainy, had made his wife (a good, but a weak woman) steal this handkerchief from Desdemona, under pretence of getting the work copied, but in reality to drop it in Cassio's way, where he might find it, and give a handle to Iago's suggestion that it was Desdemona's present.

Othello, soon after meeting his wife, pretended that he had a headache (as he might indeed with truth), and desired her to lend him her handkerchief to hold to his temples. She did so.

'Not this,' said Othello, 'but that handkerchief I gave you.'

Desdemona had it not about her (for indeed it was stolen, as we have related).

'How?' said Othello, 'this is a fault indeed. That handkerchief an Egyptian woman gave to my mother; the woman was a witch and could read people's thoughts. She told my mother while she kept it it would make her amiable and my father would love her; but if she lost it or gave it away, my father's fancy would turn and he would loathe her as much as he had loved her. She, dying, gave it to me, and bade me, if I ever married, to give it to my wife. I did so. Take heed of it. Make it a darling as precious as your eye.'

'Is it possible?' said the frighted lady.

' 'Tis true,' continued Othello; 'it is a magical handkerchief; a sibyl that had lived in the world two hundred years, in a fit of prophetic fury worked it; the silkworms that furnished the silk were hallowed, and it was dyed in a mummy of maidens' hearts conserved.'

Desdemona, hearing the wondrous virtues of the handkerchief, was ready to die with fear, for she plainly perceived she had lost it, and with it, she feared, the affections of her husband. Then Othello started and looked as if he were going to do some rash thing, and still he demanded the handkerchief, which when she could not produce, she tried to divert her husband from too serious thoughts, and cheerfully told him she saw all his talk about the handkerchief was only to put her off from her suit about Michael Cassio, whom she went on to praise (as Iago had foretold), till Othello in perfect distraction burst out of the room, and then Desdemona, though unwillingly, began to suspect that her lord was jealous.

What cause she could have ministered to him she knew not, and then she accused herself for accusing the noble Othello, and thought, to be sure, that some untoward news from Venice or some state troubles had puddled his spirits and made his temper not so sweet as formerly. And she said, 'Men are not gods, and we must not look for that observance from them when they are married which they show us on the bridal day.' And she beshrewed herself for so unkindly judging of his unkindness.

Again Othello and Desdemona met, and he accused her more plainly of being unfaithful and of loving another man, but he did not name whom. And Othello wept, and Desdemona said, 'Alas! the heavy day! why do you weep?' And Othello told her he could have borne all sorts of evils with fortitude – poverty, and disease, and disgrace – but her infidelity had broken his heart. And he called her a weed that looked so fair and smelled so sweet that the sense ached at it; and wished she had never been born. And when he had left her this innocent lady was so stupefied with wonder at her lord's untrue suspicion of her that a weightlike sleep came over her, and she only desired her attendant to make her bed and to lay her wedding-sheets upon it, saying that when people teach their babes they do it by gentle means and easy tasks, and Othello might have chid her so; for in good faith she was but a child when she was chidden. And this was all the complaint which this gentle lady made.

Desdemona being retired to bed, expecting her lord would follow her, soon fell into a slumber, the effect of her troubled spirits, when Othello entered the chamber, full of the black purpose which he had meditated, of putting his lady to death. But when he saw her asleep he thought he would not shed her blood, nor scar that white skin of hers, more white than alabaster. But he was resolved she should die, else (as he said) she would live to betray more men as she had done him. Then he kissed her for the last time (as he said), and that kiss was so sweet that he must needs kiss her again; and he wept, but he said they were cruel tears.

Desdemona was awakened with his kisses, and she looked upon Othello, and she saw him gnaw his under lip and roll his eyes, and she knew he was always fatal when he looked so; and he bade her prepare for death and to say her prayers, for he would not kill her soul. And this innocent wife, as she lay at his mercy, begged for compassion and to know her fault, and then he named Cassio, and the handkerchief which (he said) she had given him; and as the guiltless lady was proceeding to clear herself he suddenly would hear no more, but, covering her up in the bedclothes, stifled her till she died.

In this instant of time was brought into the house Cassio, wounded and bleeding, whom Iago had set one of his creatures on to assassinate; but the fellow not succeeding in his attempt to kill Cassio (whom he wounded, but not mortally), and being himself killed by Iago to prevent discovery, in his pockets were found certain letters, which made the guilt of Iago, and the innocence of Cassio, clear beyond all doubt; and Cassio now came to beg pardon of Othello, and to ask wherein he had offended him, that he had employed Iago to murder him.

This discovery was as a thunderstroke to Othello, who now plainly saw that he was no better than a murderer, and that his wife (poor innocent lady) had been ever faithful to him; the extreme anguish of which discovery making life insupportable, he fell upon his sword, and throwing himself upon the body of his dear injured lady, expired.

These rash acts raised much passion of horror and amazement in the bystanders, for Othello had borne a fair reputation, and till he was wrought upon by the arts of a villain, which his own noble nature never gave him leave to suspect, he was a loving and a doting husband. He had loved not wisely, but too well; and his manly eyes (when he learned his mistake), though not used to weep on every small occasion, dropped tears as fast as the Arabian trees their gum. And when he was dead all his former merits and his valiant acts were remembered. Nothing now remained for his successor but to put the utmost censure of the law in force against Iago, who was executed with strict tortures; and to send word to the state of Venice of the lamentable death of their renowned general.

Pericles, Prince of Tyre

Pericles, Prince of Tyre, became a voluntary exile from his dominions, to avert the dreadful calamities which Antiochus, the wicked emperor of Greece, threatened to bring upon his subjects and city of Tyre, in revenge for a discovery which the prince had made of a shocking deed which the emperor had done in secret; as commonly it proves dangerous to pry into the hidden crimes of great ones. Leaving the government of his people in the hands of his able and honest minister, Helicanus, Pericles set sail from Tyre, thinking to absent himself till the wrath of Antiochus, who was mighty, should be appeased.

The first place which the prince directed his course to was Tarsus, and hearing that the city of Tarsus was at that time suffering under a severe famine, he took with him a store of provisions for its relief. On his arrival he found the city reduced to the utmost distress; and, he coming like a messenger from heaven with his unhoped-for succour, Cleon, the governor of Tarsus, welcomed him with boundless thanks. Pericles had not been here many days before letters came from his faithful minister, warning him that it was not safe for him to stay at Tarsus, for Antiochus knew of his abode, and by secret emissaries despatched for that purpose sought his life. Upon receipt of these letters Pericles put out to sea again, amid the blessings and prayers of a whole people who had been fed by his bounty.

He had not sailed far when his ship was overtaken by a dreadful storm, and every man on board perished except Pericles, who was cast by the sea-waves naked on an unknown shore, where he had not wandered long before he met with some poor fishermen, who invited him to their homes, giving him clothes and provisions. The fishermen told Pericles the name of their country was Pentapolis, and that their king was Simonides, commonly called the good Simonides, because of his peaceable reign and good government. From them he also learned that King Simonides had a fair young daughter, and that the following day was her birthday, when a grand tournament was to be held at court, many princes and knights being come from all parts to try their skill in arms for the love of Thaisa, this fair princess. While the prince was listening to this account, and secretly lamenting the loss of his good armour, which disabled him from making one among these valiant knights, another fisherman brought in a complete suit of armour that he had taken out of the sea with his fishing-net, which proved to be the very armour he had lost. When Pericles beheld his own armour he said: 'Thanks, Fortune; after all my crosses you give me somewhat to repair myself. This armour was bequeathed to me by my dead father, for whose dear sake I have so loved it that whithersoever I went I still have kept it by me, and the rough sea that parted it from me, having now become calm, hath given it back again, for which I thank it, for, since I have my father's gift again, I think my shipwreck no misfortune.'

The next day Pericles, clad in his brave father's armour, repaired to the royal court of Simonides, where he performed wonders at the tournament, vanquishing with ease all the brave knights and valiant princes who contended with him in arms for the honour of Thaisa's love. When brave warriors contended at court tournaments for the love of kings' daughters, if one proved sole victor over all the rest, it was usual for the great lady for whose sake these deeds of valour were undertaken to bestow all her respect upon the conqueror, and Thaisa did not depart from this custom, for she presently dismissed all the princes and knights whom Pericles had vanquished, and distinguished him by her especial favour and regard, crowning him with the wreath of victory, as king of that day's happiness; and Pericles became a most passionate lover of this beauteous princess from the first moment he beheld her.

The good Simonides so well approved of the valour and noble qualities of Pericles, who was indeed a most accomplished gentleman and well learned in all excellent arts, that though he knew not the rank of this royal stranger (for Pericles for fear of Antiochus gave out that he was a private gentleman of Tyre), yet did not Simonides disdain to accept of the valiant unknown for a son-in-law, when he perceived his daughter's affections were firmly fixed upon him.

Pericles had not been many months married to Thaisa before he received intelligence that his enemy Antiochus was dead, and that his subjects of Tyre, impatient of his long absence, threatened to revolt and talked of placing Helicanus upon his vacant throne. This news came from Helicanus himself, who, being a loyal subject to his royal master, would not accept of the high dignity offered him, but sent to let Pericles know their intentions, that he might return home and resume his lawful right. It was matter of great surprise and joy to Simonides to find that his son-in-law (the obscure knight) was the renowned Prince of Tyre; yet again he regretted that he was not the private gentleman he supposed him to be, seeing that he must now part both with his admired son-in-law and his beloved daughter, whom he feared to trust to the perils of the sea, because Thaisa was with child; and Pericles himself wished her to remain with her father till after her confinement; but the poor lady so earnestly desired to go with her husband that at last they consented, hoping she would reach Tyre before she was brought to bed.

The sea was no friendly element to unhappy Pericles, for long before they reached Tyre another dreadful tempest arose, which so terrified Thaisa that she was taken ill, and in a short space of time her nurse, Lychorida, came to Pericles with a little child in her arms, to tell the prince the sad tidings that his wife died the moment her little babe was born. She held the babe towards its father, saying: 'Here is a thing too young for such a place. This is the child of your dead queen.'

No tongue can tell the dreadful sufferings of Pericles when he heard his wife was dead. As soon as he could speak he said: 'O you gods, why do you make us love your goodly gifts and then snatch those gifts away?'

'Patience, good sir,' said Lychorida, 'here is all that is left alive of our dead queen, a little daughter, and for your child's sake be more manly. Patience, good sir, even for the sake of this precious charge.'

Pericles took the newborn infant in his arms, and he said to the little babe: 'Now may your life be mild, for a more blusterous birth had never babe! May your condition be mild and gentle, for you have had the rudest welcome that ever prince's child did meet with! May that which follows be happy, for you have had as chiding a nativity as fire, air, water, earth, and heaven could make to herald you from the womb! Even at the first, your loss,' meaning in the death of her mother, 'is more than all the joys, which you shall find upon this earth to which you are come a new visitor, shall be able to recompense.'

The storm still continuing to rage furiously, and the sailors having a superstition that while a dead body remained in the ship the storm would never cease, they came to Pericles to demand that his queen should be thrown overboard; and they said: 'What courage, sir? God save you!'

'Courage enough,' said the sorrowing prince. 'I do not fear the storm; it has done to me its worst; yet for the love of this poor infant, this fresh new seafarer, I wish the storm was over.'

'Sir,' said the sailors, 'your queen must overboard. The sea works high, the wind is loud, and the storm will not abate till the ship be cleared of the dead.'

Though Pericles knew how weak and unfounded this superstition was, yet he patiently submitted, saying: 'As you think meet. Then she must overboard, most wretched queen!'

And now this unhappy prince went to take a last view of his dear wife, and as he looked on his Thaisa he said: 'A terrible childbed hast thou had, my dear; no light, no fire; the unfriendly elements forget thee utterly, nor have I time to bring thee hallowed to thy grave, but must cast thee scarcely coffined into the sea, where for a monument upon thy bones the humming waters must overwhelm thy corpse, lying with simple shells. O Lychorida, bid Nestor bring me spices, ink, and paper, my casket and my jewels, and bid Nicandor bring me the satin coffin. Lay the babe upon the pillow, and go about this suddenly, Lychorida, while I say a priestly fare-well to my Thaisa.'

They brought Pericles a large chest, in which (wrapped in a satin shroud) he placed his queen, and sweet-smelling spices he strewed over her, and beside her he placed rich jewels, and a written paper telling who she was and praying if haply anyone should find the chest which contained the body of his wife they would give her burial; and then with his own hands he cast the chest into the sea. When the storm was over, Pericles ordered the sailors to make for Tarsus. 'For,' said Pericles, 'the babe cannot hold out till we come to Tyre. At Tarsus I will leave it at careful nursing.'

After that tempestuous night when Thaisa was thrown into the sea, and while it was yet early morning, as Cerimon, a worthy gentleman of Ephesus and a most skilful physician, was standing by the seaside, his servants brought to him a chest, which they said the sea-waves had thrown on the land.

'I never saw,' said one of them, 'so huge a billow as cast it on our shore.'

Cerimon ordered the chest to be conveyed to his own house, and when it was opened he beheld with wonder the body of a young and lovely lady; and the sweet-smelling spices and rich casket of jewels made him conclude it was some great person who was thus strangely entombed. Searching farther, he discovered a paper, from which he learned that the corpse which lay as dead before him had been a queen, and wife to Pericles, Prince of Tyre; and much admiring at the strangeness of that accident, and more pitying the husband who had lost this sweet lady, he said: 'If you are living, Pericles, you have a heart that even cracks with woe.' Then, observing attentively Thaisa's face, he saw how fresh and unlike death her looks were, and he said, 'They were too hasty that threw you into the sea'; for he did not believe her to be dead. He ordered a fire to be made, and proper cordials to be brought, and soft music to be played, which might help to calm her amazed spirits if she should revive; and he said to those who crowded round her, wondering at what they saw, 'O, I pray you, gentlemen, give her air; this queen will live; she has not been entranced above five hours; and see, she begins to blow into life again; she is alive; behold, her eyelids move; this fair creature will live to make us weep to hear her fate.'

Thaisa had never died, but after the birth of her little baby had fallen into a deep swoon which made all that saw her conclude her to be dead; and now by the care of this kind gentleman she once more revived to light and life; and, opening her eyes, she said: 'Where am I? Where is my lord? What world is this?'

By gentle degrees Cerimon let her understand what had befallen her; and when he thought she was enough recovered to bear the sight he showed her the paper written by her husband, and the jewels; and she looked on the paper and said: 'It is my lord's writing. That I was shipped at sea I well remember, but whether there delivered of my babe, by the holy gods I cannot rightly say; but since my wedded lord I never shall see again, I will put on a vestal livery and never more have joy.'

'Madam,' said Cerimon, 'if you purpose as you speak, the temple of Diana is not far distant from hence; there you may abide as a vestal. Moreover, if you please, a niece of mine shall there attend you.' This proposal was accepted with thanks by Thaisa; and when she was perfectly recovered, Cerimon placed her in the temple of Diana, where she became a vestal or priestess of that goddess, and passed her days in sorrowing for her husband's supposed loss, and in the most devout exercises of those times.

Pericles carried his young daughter (whom he named Marina, because she was born at sea) to Tarsus, intending to leave her with Cleon, the governor of that city, and his wife Dionysia, thinking, for the good he had done to them at the time of their famine, they would be kind to his little motherless daughter. When Cleon saw Prince Pericles and heard of the great loss which had befallen him he said, 'Oh, your sweet queen, that it had pleased Heaven you could have brought her hither to have blessed my eyes with the sight of her!'

Pericles replied: 'We must obey the powers above us. Should I rage and roar as the sea does in which my Thaisa lies, yet the end must be as it is. My gentle babe, Marina here, I must charge your charity with her. I leave her the infant of your care, beseeching you to give her princely training.' And then turning to Cleon's wife, Dionysia, he said, 'Good madam, make me blessed in your care in bringing up my child.'

And she answered, 'I have a child myself who shall not be more dear to my respect than yours, my lord.'

And Cleon made the like promise, saying: 'Your noble services, Prince Pericles, in feeding my whole people with your corn (for which in their prayers they daily remember you) must in your child be thought on. If I should neglect your child, my whole people that were by you relieved would force me to my duty; but if to that I need a spur, the gods revenge it on me and mine to the end of generation.'

Pericles, being thus assured that his child would be carefully attended to, left her to the protection of Cleon and his wife Dionysia, and with her he left the nurse, Lychorida. When he went away the little Marina knew not her loss, but Lychorida wept sadly at parting with her royal master.

'Oh, no tears, Lychorida,' said Pericles; 'no tears; look to your little mistress, on whose grace you may depend hereafter.'

Pericles arrived in safety at Tyre, and was once more settled in the quiet possession of his throne, while his woeful queen, whom he thought dead, remained at Ephesus. Her little babe Marina, whom this hapless mother had never seen, was brought up by Cleon in a manner suitable to her high birth. He gave her the most careful education, so that by the time Marina attained the age of fourteen years the most deeply learned men were not more studied in the learning of those times than was Marina. She sang like one immortal, and danced as goddess-like, and with her needle she was so skilful that she seemed to compose nature's own shapes in birds, fruits, or flowers, the natural roses being scarcely more like to each other than they were to Marina's silken flowers. But when she had gained from education all these graces which made her the general wonder, Dionysia, the wife of Cleon, became her mortal enemy from jealousy, by reason that her own daughter, from the slowness of her mind, was not able to attain to that perfection wherein Marina excelled; and finding that all praise was bestowed on Marina, while her daughter, who was of the same age and had been educated with the same care as Marina, though not with the same success, was in comparison disregarded, she formed a project to remove Marina out of the way, vainly imagining that her untoward daughter would be more respected when Marina was no more seen. To encompass this she employed a man to murder Marina, and she well timed her wicked design, when Lychorida, the faithful nurse, had just died. Dionysia was discoursing with the man she had commanded to commit this murder when the young Marina was weeping over the dead Lychorida. Leonine, the man she employed to do this bad deed, though he was a very wicked man, could hardly be persuaded to undertake it, so had Marina won all hearts to love her. He said: 'She is a goodly creature!'

'The fitter then the gods should have her,' replied her merciless enemy. 'Here she comes weeping for the death of her nurse Lychorida. Are you resolved to obey me?'

Leonine, fearing to disobey her, replied, 'I am resolved.' And so, in that one short sentence, was the matchless Marina doomed to an untimely death. She now approached, with a basket of flowers in her hand, which she said she would daily strew over the grave of good Lychorida. The purple violet and the marigold should as a carpet hang upon her grave, while summer days did last.

'Alas for me,' she said, 'poor unhappy maid, born in a tempest, when my mother died. This world to me is like a lasting storm, hurrying me from my friends.'

'How now, Marina,' said the dissembling Dionysia, 'do you weep alone? How does it chance my daughter is not with you? Do not sorrow for Lychorida; you have a nurse in me. Your beauty is quite changed with this unprofitable woe. Come, give me your flowers –

the sea air will spoil them – and walk with Leonine; the air is fine, and will enliven you. Come, Leonine, take her by the arm and walk with her.'

'No, madam,' said Marina, 'I pray you let me not deprive you of your servant'; for Leonine was one of Dionysia's attendants.

'Come, come,' said this artful woman, who wished for a pretence to leave her alone with Leonine, 'I love the prince, your father, and I love you. We every day expect your father here; and when he comes and finds you so changed by grief from the paragon of beauty we reported you, he will think we have taken no care of you. Go, I pray you, walk, and be cheerful once again. Be careful of that excellent complexion which stole the hearts of old and young.'

Marina, being thus importuned, said, 'Well, I will go, but yet I have no desire to it.'

As Dionysia walked away she said to Leonine, *'Remember what I have said!'* shocking words, for their meaning was that he should remember to kill Marina.

Marina looked towards the sea, her birthplace, and said, 'Is the wind westerly that blows?'

'Southwest,' replied Leonine.

'When I was born the wind was north,' said she; and then the storm and tempest and all her father's sorrows, and her mother's death, came full into her mind, and she said, 'My father, as Lychorida told me, did never fear, but cried, *Courage, good seamen*, to the sailors, galling his princely hands with the ropes, and, clasping to the masts, he endured a sea that almost split the deck.'

'When was this?' said Leonine.

'When I was born,' replied Marina. 'Never were wind and waves more violent.' And then she described the storm, the action of the sailors, the boatswain's whistle, and the loud call of the master, 'which,' said she, 'trebled the confusion of the ship.'

Lychorida had so often recounted to Marina the story of her hapless birth that these things seemed ever present to her imagination. But here Leonine interrupted her with desiring her to say her prayers. 'What mean you?' said Marina, who began to fear, she knew not why.

'If you require a little space for prayer, I grant it,' said Leonine; 'but be not tedious; the gods are quick of ear and I am sworn to do my work in haste.'

'Will you kill me?' said Marina. 'Alas! why?'

'To satisfy my lady,' replied Leonine.

'Why would she have me killed?' said Marina. 'Now, as I can remember, I never hurt her in all my life. I never spake bad word nor did any ill turn to any living creature. Believe me now, I never killed a mouse nor hurt a fly. I trod upon a worm once against my will, but I wept for it. How have I offended?'

The murderer replied, 'My commission is not to reason on the deed, but to do it.' And he was just going to kill her when certain pirates happened to land at that very moment, who, seeing Marina, bore her off as a prize to their ship.

The pirate who had made Marina his prize carried her to Mitylene and sold her for a slave, where; though in that humble condition, Marina soon became known throughout the whole city of Mitylene for her beauty and her virtues, and the person to whom she was sold became rich by the money she earned for him. She taught music, dancing, and fine needleworks, and the money she got by her scholars she gave to her master and mistress; and the fame of her learning and her great industry came to the knowledge of Lysimachus, a young nobleman who was governor of Mitylene, and Lysimachus went himself to the house where Marina dwelt, to see this paragon of excellence whom all the city praised so highly. Her conversation delighted Lysimachus beyond measure, for, though he had heard much of this admired maiden, he did not expect to find her so sensible a lady, so virtuous, and so good, as he perceived Marina to be; and he left her, saying he hoped she would persevere in her industrious and virtuous course, and that if ever she heard from him again it should be for her good. Lysimachus thought Marina such a miracle for sense, fine breeding, and excellent qualities, as well as for beauty and all outward graces, that he wished to marry her, and, notwithstanding her humble situation, he hoped to find that her birth was noble; but ever when they asked her parentage she would sit still and weep.

Meantime, at Tarsus, Leonine, fearing the anger of Dionysia, told her he had killed Marina; and that wicked woman gave out that she was dead, and made a pretended funeral for her, and erected a stately monument; and shortly after Pericles, accompanied by his loyal minister Helicanus, made a voyage from Tyre to Tarsus, on purpose to see his daughter, intending to take her home with him. And he never having beheld her since he left her an infant in the care of Cleon and his wife, how did this good prince rejoice at the thought of seeing this dear child of his buried queen! But when they told him Marina was dead, and showed the monument they had erected for her, great was the misery this most wretched father endured, and, not being able to bear the sight of that country where his last hope and only memory of his dear Thaisa was entombed, he took ship and hastily departed from Tarsus. From the day he entered the ship a dull and heavy melancholy seized him. He never spoke, and seemed totally insensible to everything around him.

Sailing from Tarsus to Tyre, the ship in its course passed by Mitylene, where Marina dwelt; the governor of which place, Lysimachus, observing this royal vessel from the shore, and desirous of knowing who was on board, went in a barge to the side of the ship, to satisfy his curiosity. Helicanus received him very courteously and told him that the ship came from Tyre, and that they were conducting thither Pericles, their prince. 'A man sir,' said Helicanus, 'who has not spoken to anyone these three months, nor taken any sustenance, but just to prolong his grief; it would be tedious to repeat the whole ground of his distemper, but the main springs from the loss of a beloved daughter and a wife.'

Lysimachus begged to see this afflicted prince, and when he beheld Pericles he saw he had been once a goodly person, and he said to him: 'Sir king, all hail! The gods preserve you! Hail, royal sir!'

But in vain Lysimachus spoke to him. Pericles made no answer, nor did he appear to perceive any stranger approached. And then Lysimachus bethought him of the peerless maid Marina, that haply with her sweet tongue she might win some answer from the silent prince; and with the consent of Helicanus he sent for Marina, and when she entered the ship in which her own father sat motionless with grief, they welcomed her on board as if they had known she was their princess; and they cried: 'She is a gallant lady.'

Lysimachus was well pleased to hear their commendations, and he said: 'She is such a one that, were I well assured she came of noble birth, I would wish no better choice and think me rarely blessed in a wife.' And then he addressed her in courtly terms, as if the lowly seeming maid had been the high-born lady he wished to find her, calling her *fair and beautiful Marina*, telling her a great prince on board that ship had fallen into a sad and mournful silence; and, as if Marina had the power of conferring health and felicity, he begged she would undertake to cure the royal stranger of his melancholy.

'Sir,' said Marina, 'I will use my utmost skill in his recovery, provided none but I and my maid be suffered to come near him.'

She, who at Mitylene had so carefully concealed her birth, ashamed to tell that one of royal ancestry was now a slave, first began to speak to Pericles of the wayward changes in her own fate, telling him from what a high estate herself had fallen. As if she had known it was her royal father she stood before, all the words she spoke were of her own sorrows; but her reason for so doing was that she knew nothing more wins the attention of the unfortunate than the recital of some sad calamity to match their own. The sound of her sweet voice aroused the drooping prince; he lifted up his eyes, which had been so long fixed and motionless; and Marina, who was the perfect image of her mother, presented to his amazed sight the features of his dead queen. The long silent prince was once more heard to speak.

'My dearest wife,' said the awakened Pericles, 'was like this maid, and such a one might my daughter have been. My queen's square brows, her stature to an inch, as wandlike straight, as silver-voiced, her eyes as jewel-like. Where do you live, young maid? Report your parentage. I think you said you had been tossed from wrong to injury, and that you thought your griefs would equal mine, if both were opened.'

'Some such thing I said,' replied Marina, 'and said no more than what my thoughts did warrant me as likely.'

'Tell me your story,' answered Pericles. 'If I find you have known the thousandth part of my endurance you have borne your sorrows like a man and I have suffered like a girl; yet you do look like Patience gazing on kings' graves and smiling extremely out of act. How lost you your name, my most kind virgin? Recount your story, I beseech you. Come, sit by me.'

How was Pericles surprised when she said her name was *Marina*, for he knew it was no usual name, but had been invented by himself for his own child to signify *Sea-born*.

'Oh, I am mocked,' said he, 'and you are sent hither by some incensed god to make the world laugh at me.'

'Patience, good sir,' said Marina, 'or I must cease here.'

'Nay,' said Pericles, 'I will be patient. You little know how you do startle me, to call yourself Marina.'

'The name,' she replied, 'was given me by one that had some power, my father and a king.'

'How, a king's daughter!' said Pericles, 'and called Marina! But are you flesh and blood? Are you no fairy? Speak on. Where were you born, and wherefore called Marina?'

She replied: 'I was called Marina because I was born at sea. My mother was the daughter of a king; she died the minute I was born, as my good nurse Lychorida has often told me, weeping. The king, my father, left me at Tarsus till the cruel wife of Cleon sought to murder me. A crew of pirates came and rescued me and brought me here to Mitylene. But, good sir, why do you weep? It may be you think me an impostor. But indeed, sir, I am the daughter to King Pericles, if good King Pericles be living.'

Then Pericles, terrified as he seemed at his own sudden joy, and doubtful if this could be real, loudly called for his attendants, who rejoiced at the sound of their beloved king's voice; and he said to Helicanus: 'O Helicanus, strike me, give me a gash, put me to present pain, lest this great sea of joys rushing upon me overbear the shores of my mortality. Oh, come hither, thou that wast born at sea, buried at Tarsus, and found at sea again. O Helicanus, down on your knees, thank the holy gods! This is Marina. Now blessings on thee, my child! Give me fresh garments, mine own Helicanus!

She is not dead at Tarsus as she should have been by the savage Dionysia. She shall tell you all, when you shall kneel to her and call her your very princess. Who is this?' (observing Lysimachus for the first time).

'Sir,' said Helicanus, 'it is the governor of Mitylene, who, hearing of your melancholy, came to see you.'

'I embrace you, sir,' said Pericles. 'Give me my robes! I am well with beholding. O heaven bless my girl! But hark, what music is that?' – for now, either sent by some kind god or by his own delighted fancy deceived, he seemed to hear soft music.

'My lord, I hear none,' replied Helicanus.

'None?' said Pericles. 'Why, it is the music of the spheres.'

As there was no music to be heard, Lysimachus concluded that the sudden joy had unsettled the prince's understanding, and he said, 'It is not good to cross him; let him have his way.' And then they told him they heard the music; and he now complaining of a drowsy slumber coming over him, Lysimachus persuaded him to rest on a couch, and, placing a pillow under his head, he, quite overpowered with excess of joy, sank into a sound sleep, and Marina watched in silence by the couch of her sleeping parent.

While he slept, Pericles dreamed a dream which made him resolve to go to Ephesus. His dream was that Diana, the goddess of the Ephesians, appeared to him and commanded him to go to her temple at Ephesus, and there before her altar to declare the story of his life and misfortunes; and by her silver bow she swore that if he performed her injunction he should meet with some rare felicity. When he awoke, being miraculously refreshed, he told his dream, and that his resolution was to obey the bidding of the goddess.

Then Lysimachus invited Pericles to come on shore and refresh himself with such entertainment as he should find at Mitylene, which courteous offer Pericles accepting, agreed to tarry with him for the space of a day or two. During which time we may well suppose what feastings, what rejoicings, what costly shows and entertainments the governor made in Mitylene to greet the royal father of his dear Marina, whom in her obscure fortunes he had so respected. Nor did Pericles frown upon Lysimachus's suit, when he understood how he had honoured his child in the days of her low estate, and that Marina showed herself not averse to his proposals; only he made it a condition, before he gave his consent, that they should visit with him the shrine of the Ephesian Diana; to whose temple they shortly after all three undertook a voyage; and, the goddess herself filling their sails with prosperous winds, after a few weeks they arrived in safety at Ephesus.

There was standing near the altar of the goddess, when Pericles with his train entered the temple, the good Cerimon (now grown very aged), who had restored Thaisa, the wife of Pericles, to life; and Thaisa, now a priestess of the temple, was standing before the altar; and though the many years he had passed in sorrow for her loss had much altered Pericles, Thaisa thought she knew her husband's features, and when he approached the altar and began to speak, she remembered his voice, and listened to his words with wonder and a joyful amazement. And these were the words that Pericles spoke before the altar: 'Hail, Diana! to perform thy just commands I here confess myself the Prince of Tyre, who, frighted from my country, at Pentapolis wedded the fair Thaisa. She died at sea in childbed, but brought forth a maid-child called Marina. She at Tarsus was nursed with Dionysia, who at fourteen years thought to kill her, but her better stars brought her to Mitylene, by whose shores as I sailed her good fortunes brought this maid on board, where by her most clear remembrance she made herself known to be my daughter.'

Thaisa, unable to bear the transports which his words had raised in her, cried out, 'You are, you are, O royal Pericles' and fainted.

'What means this woman?' said Pericles. 'She dies! Gentlemen, help.'

'Sir,' said Cerimon, 'if you have told Diana's altar true, this is your wife.'

'Reverend gentleman, no,' said Pericles. 'I threw her overboard with these very arms.'

Cerimon then recounted how, early one tempestuous morning, this lady was thrown upon the Ephesian shore; how, opening the coffin, he found therein rich jewels and a paper; how, happily, he recovered her and placed her here in Diana's temple.

And now Thaisa, being restored from her swoon, said: 'O my lord, are you not Pericles? Like him you speak, like him you are. Did you not name a tempest, a birth, and death?'

He, astonished, said, 'The voice of dead Thaisa!'

'That Thaisa am I,' she replied, 'supposed dead and drowned.'

'O true Diana!' exclaimed Pericles, in a passion of devout astonishment.

'And now,' said Thaisa, 'I know you better. Such a ring as I see on your finger did the king my father give you when we with tears parted from him at Pentapolis.'

'Enough, you gods!' cried Pericles. 'Your present kindness makes my past miseries sport. Oh, come, Thaisa, be buried a second time within these arms.'

And Marina said, 'My heart leaps to be gone into my mother's bosom.'

Then did Pericles show his daughter to her mother, saying, 'Look who kneels here, flesh of thy flesh, thy burthen at sea, and called Marina because she was yielded there.'

'Blessed and my own!' said Thaisa. And while she hung in rapturous joy over her child Pericles knelt before the altar, saying: 'Pure Diana, bless thee for thy vision. For this I will offer oblations nightly to thee.'

And then and there did Pericles, with the consent of Thaisa, solemnly affiance their daughter, the virtuous Marina, to the well-deserving Lysimachus in marriage.

Thus have we seen in Pericles, his queen, and daughter, a famous example of virtue assailed by calamity (through the sufferance of heaven, to teach patience and constancy to men), under the same guidance becoming finally successful and triumphing over chance and change. In Helicanus we have beheld a notable pattern of truth, of faith, and loyalty, who, when he might have succeeded to a throne, chose rather to recall the rightful owner to his possession than to become great by another's wrong. In the worthy Cerimon, who restored Thaisa to life, we are instructed how goodness, directed by knowledge, in bestowing benefits upon mankind approaches to the nature of the gods. It only remains to be told that Dionysia, the wicked wife of Cleon, met with an end proportionable to her deserts. The inhabitants of Tarsus, when her cruel attempt upon Marina was known, rising in a body to revenge the daughter of their benefactor, and setting fire to the palace of Cleon, burned both him and her and their whole household, the gods seeming well pleased that so foul a murder, though but intentional and never carried into act, should be punished in a way befitting its enormity.

TALES FROM THE ARABIAN NIGHTS

Tales from
the Arabian Nights

EDITED BY
Andrew Lang

with illustrations by
H. J. FORD

CONTENTS

Preface

The stories in the fairy books have generally been such as old women in country places tell to their grandchildren. Nobody knows how old they are, or who told them first. The children of Ham, Shem and Japhet may have listened to them in the Ark, on wet days. Hector's little boy may have heard them in Troy Town, for it is certain that Homer knew them, and that some of them were written down in Egypt about the time of Moses.

People in different countries tell them differently, but they are always the same stories, really, whether among little Zulus, at the Cape, or little Eskimo, near the North Pole. The changes are only in matters of manners and customs; such as wearing clothes or not, meeting lions who talk in the warm countries, or talking bears in the cold countries. There are plenty of kings and queens in the fairy tales, just because long ago there were plenty of kings in the country. A gentleman who would be a squire now was a kind of king in Scotland in very old times, and the same in other places. These old stories, never forgotten, were taken down in writing in different ages, but mostly in this century, in all sorts of languages. These ancient stories are the contents of the fairy books.

Now 'The Arabian Nights', some of which, but not nearly all, are given in this volume, are only fairy tales of the East. The people of Asia, Arabia, and Persia told them in their own way, not for children, but for grown-up people. There were no novels then, nor any printed books, of course; but there were people whose profession it was to amuse men and women by telling tales. They dressed the fairy stories up, and made the characters good Mahommedans, living in Bagdad or India. The events were often supposed to happen in the reign of the great caliph, or ruler of the Faithful, Haroun al Raschid, who lived in Bagdad in 786–808 AD. The vizir who accompanies the caliph was also a real person of the great family of the barmecides. He was put to death by the caliph in a very cruel way, nobody ever knew why. The stories must have been told in their present shape a good long while after the caliph died, when nobody knew very exactly what had really happened. At last some storyteller thought of writing down the tales, and fixing them into a kind of framework, as if they had all been narrated to a cruel sultan by his wife. Probably the tales were written down about the time when Edward I was fighting Robert Bruce. But changes were made in them at different times, and a great deal that is very dull and stupid was put in, and plenty of verses. Neither the verses nor the dull pieces are given in this book.

People in France and England knew almost nothing about 'The Arabian Nights' till the reigns of Queen Anne and George I, when they were translated into French by Monsieur Galland. Grown-up people were then very fond of fairy tales, and they thought these Arab stories the best that they had ever read. They were delighted with ghouls (who lived among the tombs) and geni, who seemed to be a kind of ogres, and with princesses who work magic spells, and with peris, who are Arab fairies. Sindbad had adventures which perhaps came out of the Odyssey of Homer; in fact, all the East had contributed its wonders, and sent them to Europe in one parcel. Young men once made a noise at Monsieur Galland's windows in the dead of night, and asked him to tell them one of his marvellous tales. Nobody talked of anything but dervishes and viziers, rocs and peris. The stories were translated from French into all languages, and only Bishop Atterbury complained that the tales were not likely to be true, and had no moral. The bishop was presently banished for being on the side of Prince Charlie's father, and had leisure to repent of being so solemn.

In this book 'The Arabian Nights' are translated from the French version of Monsieur Galland, who dropped out the poetry and a great deal of what the Arabian authors thought funny, though it seems wearisome to us. In this book the stories are shortened here and there, and omissions are made of pieces only suitable for Arabs and old gentlemen. The translations are by the writers of the tales in the fairy books, and the pictures are by Mr Ford.

I can remember reading 'The Arabian Nights' when I was six years old, in dirty yellow old volumes of small type with no pictures, and I hope children who read them with Mr Ford's pictures will be as happy as I was then in the company of Aladdin and Sindbad the Sailor.

Introduction

In the chronicles of the ancient dynasty of the Sassanidae, who reigned for about four hundred years, from Persia to the borders of China, beyond the great river Ganges itself, we read the praises of one of the kings of this race, who was said to be the best monarch of his time. His subjects loved him, and his neighbours feared him, and when he died he left his kingdom in a more prosperous and powerful condition than any king had done before him.

The two sons who survived him loved each other tenderly, and it was a real grief to the elder, Schahriar, that the laws of the empire forbade him to share his dominions with his brother Schahzeman. Indeed, after ten years, during which this state of things had not ceased to trouble him, Schahriar cut off the country of Great Tartary from the Persian Empire and made his brother king.

Now the Sultan Schahriar had a wife whom he loved more than all the world, and his greatest happiness was to surround her with splendour, and to give her the finest dresses and the most beautiful jewels. It was therefore with the deepest shame and sorrow that he accidentally discovered, after several years, that she had deceived him completely, and her whole conduct turned out to have been so bad, that he felt himself obliged to carry out the law of the land, and order the grand-vizir to put her to death. The blow was so heavy that his mind almost gave way, and he declared that he was quite sure that at bottom all women were as wicked as the sultana, if you could only find them out, and that the fewer the world contained the better. So every evening he married a fresh wife and had her strangled the following morning before the grand-vizir, whose duty it was to provide these unhappy brides for the sultan. The poor man fulfilled his task with reluctance, but there was no escape, and every day saw a girl married and a wife dead.

This behaviour caused the greatest horror in the town, where nothing was heard but cries and lamentations. In one house was a father weeping for the loss of his daughter, in another perhaps a mother trembling for the fate of her child; and instead of the blessings that had formerly been heaped on the sultan's head, the air was now full of curses.

The grand-vizir himself was the father of two daughters, of whom the elder was called Scheherazade, and the younger Dinarzade. Dinarzade had no particular gifts to distinguish her from other girls, but her sister was clever and courageous in the highest degree. Her father had given her the best masters in philosophy, medicine, history and the fine arts, and besides all this, her beauty excelled that of any girl in the kingdom of Persia.

One day, when the grand-vizir was talking to his eldest daughter, who was his delight and pride, Scheherazade said to him, 'Father, I have a favour to ask of you. Will you grant it to me?'

'I can refuse you nothing,' replied he, 'that is just and reasonable.'

'Then listen,' said Scheherazade. 'I am determined to stop this barbarous practice of the sultan's, and to deliver the girls and mothers from the awful fate that hangs over them.'

'It would be an excellent thing to do,' returned the grand-vizir, 'but how do you propose to accomplish it?'

'My father,' answered Scheherazade, 'it is you who have to provide the sultan daily with a fresh wife, and I implore you, by all the affection you bear me, to allow the honour to fall upon me.'

'Have you lost your senses?' cried the grand-vizir, starting back in horror. 'What has put such a thing into your head? You ought to know by this time what it means to be the sultan's bride!'

'Yes, my father, I know it well,' replied she, 'and I am not afraid to think of it. If I fail, my death will be a glorious one, and if I succeed I shall have done a great service to my country.'

'It is of no use,' said the grand-vizir, 'I shall never consent. If the sultan was to order me to plunge a dagger in your heart, I should have to obey. What a task for a father! Ah, if you do not fear death, fear at any rate the anguish you would cause me.'

Scheherazade, Dinarzade and the sultan

'Once again, my father,' said Scheherazade, 'will you grant me what I ask?'

'What, are you still so obstinate?' exclaimed the grand-vizir. 'Why are you so resolved upon your own ruin?'

But the maiden absolutely refused to attend to her father's words, and at length, in despair, the grand-vizir was obliged to give way, and went sadly to the palace to tell the sultan that the following evening he would bring him Scheherazade.

The sultan received this news with the greatest astonishment.

'How have you made up your mind,' he asked, 'to sacrifice your own daughter to me?'

'Sire,' answered the grand-vizir, 'it is her own wish. Even the sad fate that awaits her could not hold her back.'

'Let there be no mistake, vizir,' said the sultan. 'Remember you will have to take her life yourself. If you refuse, I swear that your head shall pay forfeit.'

'Sire,' returned the vizir. 'Whatever the cost, I will obey you. Though a father, I am also your subject.' So the sultan told the grand-vizir he might bring his daughter as soon as he liked.

The vizir took back this news to Scheherazade, who received it as if it had been the most pleasant thing in the world. She thanked her father warmly for yielding to her wishes, and, seeing him still bowed down with grief, told him that she hoped he would never repent having allowed her to marry the sultan. Then she went to prepare herself for the marriage, and begged that her sister Dinarzade should be sent for to speak to her.

When they were alone, Scheherazade addressed her thus: 'My dear sister; I want your help in a very important affair. My father is going to take me to the palace to celebrate my marriage with the sultan. When his highness receives me, I shall beg him, as a last favour, to let you sleep in our chamber, so that I may have your company during the last night I am alive. If, as I hope, he grants me my wish, be sure that you wake me an hour before the dawn, and speak to me in these words: "My sister, if you are not asleep, I beg you, before the sun rises, to tell me one of your charming stories." Then I shall begin, and I hope by this means to deliver the people from the terror that reigns over them.' Dinarzade replied that she would do with pleasure what her sister wished.

When the usual hour arrived the grand-vizir conducted Scheherazade to the palace, and left her alone with the sultan, who bade her raise her veil and was amazed at her beauty. But seeing her eyes full of tears, he asked what was the matter. 'Sire,' replied Scheherazade, 'I have a sister who loves me as tenderly as I love her. Grant me the favour of allowing her to sleep this night in the same room, as it is the last we shall be together.' Schahriar consented to Scheherazade's petition and Dinarzade was sent for.

An hour before daybreak Dinarzade awoke, and exclaimed, as

she had promised, 'My dear sister, if you are not asleep, tell me I pray you, before the sun rises, one of your charming stories. It is the last time that I shall have the pleasure of hearing you.'

Scheherazade did not answer her sister, but turned to the sultan. 'Will your highness permit me to do as my sister asks?' said she.

'Willingly,' he answered. So Scheherazade began.

The Story of the Merchant
and the Genius

Sire, there was once upon a time a merchant who possessed great wealth, in land and merchandise, as well as in ready money. He was obliged from time to time to take journeys to arrange his affairs. One day, having to go a long way from home, he mounted his horse, taking with him a small wallet in which he had put a few biscuits and dates, because he had to pass through the desert where no food was to be got. He arrived without any mishap, and, having finished his business, set out on his return. On the fourth day of his journey, the heat of the sun being very great, he turned out of his road to rest under some trees. He found at the foot of a large walnut-tree a fountain of clear and running water. He dismounted, fastened his horse to a branch of the tree, and sat by the fountain, after having taken from his wallet some of his dates and biscuits. When he had finished this frugal meal he washed his face and hands in the fountain.

When he was thus employed he saw an enormous genius, white with rage, coming towards him, with a scimitar in his hand.

'Arise,' he cried in a terrible voice, 'and let me kill you as you have killed my son!'

As he uttered these words he gave a frightful yell. The merchant, quite as much terrified at the hideous face of the monster as at his words, answered him tremblingly, 'Alas, good sir, what can I have done to you to deserve death?'

'I shall kill you,' repeated the genius, 'as you have killed my son.'

'But,' said the merchant, 'how can I have killed your son? I do not know him, and I have never even seen him.'

'When you arrived here did you not sit down on the ground?' asked the genius, 'and did you not take some dates from your wallet, and whilst eating them did not you throw the stones about?'

'Yes,' said the merchant, 'I certainly did so.'

'Then,' said the genius, 'I tell you you have killed my son, for whilst you were throwing about the stones, my son passed by, and one of them struck him in the eye and killed him. So I shall kill you.'

'Ah, sir, forgive me!' cried the merchant.

'I will have no mercy on you,' answered the genius.

'But I killed your son quite unintentionally, so I implore you to spare my life.'

'No,' said the genius, 'I shall kill you as you killed my son,' and so saying, he seized the merchant by the arm, threw him on the ground, and lifted his sabre to cut off his head.

The merchant, protesting his innocence, bewailed his wife and children, and tried pitifully to avert his fate. The genius, with his raised scimitar, waited till he had finished, but was not in the least touched.

Scheherazade, at this point, seeing that it was day, and knowing that the sultan always rose very early to attend the council, stopped speaking.

'Indeed, sister,' said Dinarzade, 'this is a wonderful story.'

'The rest is still more wonderful,' replied Scheherazade, 'and you would say so, if the sultan would allow me to live another day, and would give me leave to tell it to you the next night.'

Schahriar, who had been listening to Scheherazade with pleasure, said to himself, 'I will wait till tomorrow; I can always have her killed when I have heard the end of her story.'

All this time the grand-vizir was in a terrible state of anxiety. But he was much delighted when he saw the sultan enter the council-chamber without giving the terrible command that he was expecting.

The next morning, before the day broke, Dinarzade said to her sister, 'Dear sister, if you are awake I pray you to go on with your story.'

The sultan did not wait for Scheherazade to ask his leave. 'Finish,' said he, 'the story of the genius and the merchant. I am curious to hear the end.' So Scheherazade went on with the story. This happened every morning. The sultana told a story, and the sultan let her live to finish it.

When the merchant saw that the genius was determined to cut off his head, he said: 'One word more, I entreat you. Grant me a little delay; just a short time to go home and bid my wife and children farewell, and to make my will. When I have done this I will come back here, and you shall kill me.'

'But,' said the genius, 'if I grant you the delay you ask, I am afraid that you will not come back.'

'I give you my word of honour,' answered the merchant, 'that I will come back without fail.'

'How long do you require?' asked the genius.

'I ask you for a year's grace,' replied the merchant. 'I promise you that tomorrow twelvemonth, I shall be waiting under these trees to give myself up to you.'

On this the genius left him near the fountain and disappeared.

The merchant, having recovered from his fright, mounted his horse and went on his road.

When he arrived home his wife and children received him with the greatest joy. But instead of embracing them he began to weep so bitterly that they soon guessed that something terrible was the matter.

'Tell us, I pray you,' said his wife, 'what has happened.'

'Alas!' answered her husband, 'I have only a year to live.'

Then he told them what had passed between him and the genius, and how he had given his word to return at the end of a year to be killed. When they heard this sad news they were in despair, and wept much.

The next day the merchant began to settle his affairs, and first of all to pay his debts. He gave presents to his friends, and large alms to the poor. He set his slaves at liberty, and provided for his wife and children. The year soon passed away, and he was obliged to depart. When he tried to say goodbye he was quite overcome with grief, and with difficulty tore himself away. At length he reached the place where he had first seen the genius, on the very day that he had appointed. He dismounted, and sat down at the edge of the fountain, where he awaited the genius in terrible suspense.

Whilst he was thus waiting an old man leading a hind came

The genius and the merchants

towards him. They greeted one another, and then the old man said to him, 'May I ask, brother, what brought you to this desert place, where there are so many evil genii about? To see these beautiful trees one would imagine it was inhabited, but it is a dangerous place to stop long in.'

The merchant told the old man why he was obliged to come there. He listened in astonishment.

'This is a most marvellous affair. I should like to be a witness of your interview with the genius.' So saying he sat down by the merchant.

While they were talking another old man came up, followed by two black dogs. He greeted them, and asked what they were doing in this place. The old man who was leading the hind told him the adventure of the merchant and the genius. The second old man had no sooner heard the story than he, too, decided to stay there to see what would happen. He sat down by the others, and was talking, when a third old man arrived. He asked why the merchant who was with them looked so sad. They told him the story, and he also resolved to see what would pass between the genius and the merchant, so waited with the rest.

They soon saw in the distance a thick smoke, like a cloud of dust. This smoke came nearer and nearer, and then, all at once, it vanished, and they saw the genius, who, without speaking to them, approached the merchant, sword in hand, and, taking him by the arm, said, 'Get up and let me kill you as you killed my son.'

The merchant and the three old men began to weep and groan.

Then the old man leading the hind threw himself at the monster's feet and said, 'O Prince of the Genii, I beg of you to stay your fury and to listen to me. I am going to tell you my story and that of the hind I have with me, and if you find it more marvellous than that of the merchant whom you are about to kill, I hope that you will do away with a third part of his punishment?'

The genius considered some time, and then he said, 'Very well, I agree to this.'

The Story of the First Old Man and of the Hind

I am now going to begin my story (said the old man), so please attend.

This hind that you see with me is my wife. We have no children of our own, therefore I adopted the son of a favourite slave, and determined to make him my heir.

My wife, however, took a great dislike to both mother and child, which she concealed from me till too late. When my adopted son was about ten years old I was obliged to go on a journey. Before I went I entrusted to my wife's keeping both the mother and child, and begged her to take care of them during my absence, which lasted a whole year. During this time she studied magic in order to carry out her wicked scheme. When she had learnt enough she took my son into a distant place and changed him into a calf. Then she gave him to my steward, and told him to look after a calf she had bought. She also changed the slave into a cow, which she sent to my steward.

When I returned I enquired after my slave and the child. 'Your slave is dead,' she said, 'and as for your son, I have not seen him for two months, and I do not know where he is.'

I was grieved to hear of my slave's death, but as my son had only disappeared, I thought I should soon find him. Eight months, however, passed, and still no tidings of him; then the feast of Bairam came.

To celebrate it I ordered my steward to bring me a very fat cow to sacrifice. He did so. The cow that he brought was my unfortunate slave. I bound her, but just as I was about to kill her she began to low most piteously, and I saw that her eyes were streaming with tears. It seemed to me most extraordinary, and, feeling a movement of pity, I ordered the steward to lead her away and bring another. My wife, who was present, scoffed at my compassion, which made her malice of no avail. 'What are you doing?' she cried. 'Kill this cow. It is the best we have to sacrifice.'

To please her, I tried again, but again the animal's lows and tears disarmed me.

'Take her away,' I said to the steward, 'and kill her; I cannot.'

The steward killed her, but on skinning her found that she was nothing but bones, although she appeared so fat. I was vexed.

'Keep her for yourself,' I said to the steward, 'and if you have a fat calf, bring that in her stead.'

In a short time he brought a very fat calf, which, although I did not know it, was my son. It tried hard to break its cord and come to me. It threw itself at my feet, with its head on the ground, as if it wished to excite my pity, and to beg me not to take away its life.

I was even more surprised and touched at this action than I had been at the tears of the cow.

'Go,' I said to the steward, 'take back this calf, take great care of it, and bring me another in its place instantly.'

As soon as my wife heard me speak this she at once cried out, 'What are you doing, husband? Do not sacrifice any calf but this.'

'Wife,' I answered, 'I will not sacrifice this calf,' and in spite of all her remonstrances, I remained firm.

I had another calf killed; this one was led away. The next day the steward asked to speak to me in private.

'I have come,' he said, 'to tell you some news which I think you will like to hear. I have a daughter who knows magic. Yesterday, when I was leading back the calf which you refused to sacrifice, I noticed that she smiled, and then directly afterwards began to cry. I asked her why she did so.'

'Father,' she answered, 'this calf is the son of our master. I smile with joy at seeing him still alive, and I weep to think of his mother, who was sacrificed yesterday as a cow. These changes have been wrought by our master's wife, who hated the mother and son.'

'At these words, O genius,' continued the old man, 'I leave you to imagine my astonishment. I went immediately with the steward to speak with his daughter myself. First of all I went to the stable to

The calf begs for its life

see my son, and he replied in his dumb way to all my caresses. When the steward's daughter came I asked her if she could change my son back to his proper shape.'

'Yes, I can,' she replied, 'on two conditions. One is that you will give him to me for a husband, and the other is that you will let me punish the woman who changed him into a calf.'

'To the first condition,' I answered, 'I agree with all my heart, and I will give you an ample dowry. To the second I also agree, I only beg you to spare her life.'

'That I will do,' she replied; 'I will treat her as she treated your son.'

Then she took a vessel of water and pronounced over it some words I did not understand; then, on throwing the water over him, he became immediately a young man once more.

'My son, my dear son,' I exclaimed, kissing him in a transport of joy. 'This kind maiden has rescued you from a terrible enchantment, and I am sure that out of gratitude you will marry her.'

He consented joyfully, but before they were married, the young girl changed my wife into a hind, and it is she whom you see before you. I wished her to have this form rather than a stranger one, so that we could see her in the family without repugnance.

Since then my son has become a widower and has gone travelling. I am now going in search of him, and not wishing to confide my wife to the care of other people, I am taking her with me. Is this not a most marvellous tale?

'It is indeed,' said the genius, 'and because of it I grant to you the third part of the punishment of this merchant.'

When the first old man had finished his story, the second, who was leading the two black dogs, said to the genius, 'I am going to tell you what happened to me, and I am sure that you will find my story even more astonishing than the one to which you have just been listening. But when I have related it, will you grant me also the third part of the merchant's punishment?'

'Yes,' replied the genius, 'provided that your story surpasses that of the hind.'

With this agreement the second old man began in this way.

The Story of the Second Old Man and of the Two Black Dogs

Great prince of the genii, you must know that we are three brothers – these two black dogs and myself. Our father died, leaving us each a thousand sequins. With this sum we all three took up the same profession, and became merchants. A short time after we had opened our shops, my eldest brother, one of these two dogs, resolved to travel in foreign countries for the sake of merchandise. With this intention he sold all he had and bought merchandise suitable to the voyages he was about to make. He set out, and was away a whole year. At the end of this time a beggar came to my shop. 'Good-day,' I said. 'Good-day,' he answered; 'is it possible that you do not recognise me?' Then I looked at him closely and saw he was my brother. I made him come into my house, and asked him how he had fared in his enterprise.

'Do not question me,' he replied, 'see me, you see all I have. It would but renew my trouble to tell of all the misfortunes that have befallen me in a year, and have brought me to this state.'

I shut up my shop, paid him every attention, taking him to the bath, giving him my most beautiful robes. I examined my accounts, and found that I had doubled my capital – that is, that I now possessed two thousand sequins. I gave my brother half, saying: 'Now, brother, you can forget your losses.' He accepted them with joy, and we lived together as we had before.

Some time afterwards my second brother wished also to sell his business and travel. My eldest brother and I did all we could to dissuade him, but it was of no use. He joined a caravan and set out. He came back at the end of a year in the same state as his elder brother. I took care of him, and as I had a thousand sequins to spare I gave them to him, and he reopened his shop.

One day, my two brothers came to me to propose that we should make a journey and trade. At first I refused to go. 'You travelled,' I said, 'and what did you gain?' But they came to me repeatedly, and after having held out for five years I at last gave way. But when they had made their preparation, and they began to buy the merchandise we needed, they found they had spent every piece of the thousand sequins I had given them. I did not reproach them. I divided my six thousand sequins with them, giving a thousand to each and keeping one for myself, and the other three I buried in a corner of my house. We bought merchandise, loaded a vessel with it, and set forth with a favourable wind.

After two months' sailing we arrived at a seaport, where we disembarked and did a great trade. Then we bought the merchandise of the country, and were just going to sail once more, when I was stopped on the shore by a beautiful though poorly dressed woman. She came up to me, kissed my hand, and implored me to marry her, and take her on board. At first I refused, but she begged so hard and promised to be such a good wife to me, that at last I consented. I got her some beautiful dresses, and after having married her, we embarked and set sail. During the voyage, I discovered so many good qualities in my wife that I began to love her more and more. But my brothers began to be jealous of my prosperity, and set to work to plot against my life. One night when we were sleeping they threw my wife and myself into the sea. My wife, however, was a fairy, and so she did not let me drown, but transported me to an island. When the day dawned, she said to me,

'When I saw you on the seashore I took a great fancy to you, and wished to try your good nature, so I presented myself in the disguise you saw. Now I have rewarded you by saving your life. But I am very angry with your brothers, and I shall not rest till I have taken their lives.'

I thanked the fairy for all that she had done for me, but I begged her not to kill my brothers.

I appeased her wrath, and in a moment she transported me from the island where we were to the roof of my house, and she disappeared a moment afterwards. I went down, and opened the doors, and dug up the three thousand sequins which I had buried. I went to the place where my shop was, opened it, and received from my fellow-merchants congratulations on my return. When I went home, I saw two black dogs who came to meet me with sorrowful faces. I was much astonished, but the fairy who reappeared said to me,

'Do not be surprised to see these dogs; they are your two brothers. I have condemned them to remain for ten years in these shapes.' Then having told me where I could hear news of her, she vanished.

The ten years are nearly passed, and I am on the road to find her. As in passing I met this merchant and the old man with the hind, I stayed with them.

This is my history, O prince of genii! Do you not think it is a most marvellous one?

'Yes, indeed,' replied the genius, 'and I will give up to you the third of the merchant's punishment.'

Then the third old man made the genius the same request as the other two had done, and the genius promised him the last third of the merchant's punishment if his story surpassed both the others.

So he told his story to the genius, but I cannot tell you what it was, as I do not know.

But I do know that it was even more marvellous than either of the others, so that the genius was astonished, and said to the third old man, 'I will give up to you the third part of the merchant's punishment. He ought to thank all three of you for having interested yourselves in his favour. But for you, he would be here no longer.'

So saying, he disappeared, to the great joy of the company. The merchant did not fail to thank his friends, and then each went on his way. The merchant returned to his wife and children, and passed the rest of his days happily with them.

'But, sire,' added Scheherazade, 'however beautiful are the stories I have just told you, they cannot compare with the story of the Fisherman.'

The Story of the Fisherman

Sire, there was once upon a time a fisherman so old and so poor that he could scarcely manage to support his wife and three children. He went every day to fish very early, and each day he made a rule not to throw his nets more than four times. He started out one morning by moonlight and came to the seashore. He undressed and threw his nets, and as he was drawing them towards the bank he felt a great weight. He though he had caught a large fish, and he felt very pleased. But a moment afterwards, seeing that instead of a fish he only had in his nets the carcase of an ass, he was much disappointed.

Vexed with having such a bad haul, when he had mended his nets, which the carcase of the ass had broken in several places, he threw them a second time. In drawing them in he again felt a great weight, so that he thought they were full of fish. But he only found a large basket full of rubbish. He was much annoyed.

'O Fortune,' he cried, 'do not trifle thus with me, a poor fisherman, who can hardly support his family!'

So saying, he threw away the rubbish, and after having washed his nets clean of the dirt, he threw them for the third time. But he only drew in stones, shells, and mud. He was almost in despair.

Then he threw his nets for the fourth time. When he thought he had a fish he drew them in with a great deal of trouble. There was no fish however, but he found a yellow pot, which by its weight seemed full of something, and he noticed that it was fastened and sealed with lead, with the impression of a seal. He was delighted. 'I will sell it to the founder,' he said; 'with the money I shall get for it I shall buy a measure of wheat.'

He examined the jar on all sides; he shook it to see if it would rattle. But he heard nothing, and so, judging from the impression of the seal and the lid, he thought there must be something precious inside. To find out, he took his knife, and with a little trouble he opened it. He turned it upside down, but nothing came out, which surprised him very much. He set it in front of him, and whilst he was looking at it attentively, such a thick smoke came out that he had to step back a pace or two. This smoke rose up to the clouds, and stretching over the sea and the shore, formed a thick mist, which caused the fisherman much astonishment. When all the smoke was out of the jar it gathered itself together, and became a thick mass in which appeared a genius, twice as large as the largest giant. When he saw such a terrible-looking monster, the fisherman would like to have run away, but he trembled so with fright that he could not move a step.

'Great king of the genii,' cried the monster, 'I will never again disobey you!'

At these words the fisherman took courage.

'What is this you are saying, great genius? Tell me your history and how you came to be shut up in that vase.'

At this, the genius looked at the fisherman haughtily. 'Speak to me more civilly,' he said, 'before I kill you.'

'Alas! why should you kill me?' cried the fisherman. 'I have just freed you; have you already forgotten that?'

'No,' answered the genius; 'but that will not prevent me from killing you; and I am only going to grant you one favour, and that is to choose the manner of your death.'

'But what have I done to you?' asked the fisherman.

'I cannot treat you in any other way,' said the genius, 'and if you would know why, listen to my story.

'I rebelled against the king of the genii. To punish me, he shut me up in this vase of copper, and he put on the leaden cover his seal, which is enchantment enough to prevent my coming out. Then he had the vase thrown into the sea. During the first period of my captivity I vowed that if anyone should free me before a hundred years were passed, I would make him rich even after his death. But that century passed, and no one freed me. In the second century I vowed that I would give all the treasures in the world to my deliverer; but he never came.

The genius comes out of the jar

'In the third, I promised to make him a king, to be always near him, and to grant him three wishes every day; but that century passed away as the other two had done, and I remained in the same plight. At last I grew angry at being captive for so long, and I vowed that if anyone would release me I would kill him at once, and would only allow him to choose in what manner he should die. So you see, as you have freed me today, choose in what way you will die.'

The fisherman was very unhappy. 'What an unlucky man I am to have freed you! I implore you to spare my life.'

'I have told you,' said the genius, 'that it is impossible. Choose quickly; you are wasting time.'

The fisherman began to devise a plot.

'Since I must die,' he said, 'before I choose the manner of my death, I conjure you on your honour to tell me if you really were in that vase?'

'Yes, I was,' answered the genius.

'I really cannot believe it,' said the fisherman. 'That vase could not contain one of your feet even, and how could your whole body go in? I cannot believe it unless I see you do the thing.'

Then the genius began to change himself into smoke, which, as before, spread over the sea and the shore, and which, then collecting itself together, began to go back into the vase slowly and evenly till there was nothing left outside. Then a voice came from the vase which said to the fisherman, 'Well, unbelieving fisherman, here I am in the vase; do you believe me now?'

The fisherman instead of answering took the lid of lead and shut it down quickly on the vase.

'Now, O genius,' he cried, 'ask pardon of me, and choose by what death you will die! But no, it will be better if I throw you into the sea whence I drew you out, and I will build a house on the shore to warn fishermen who come to cast their nets here, against fishing up such a wicked genius as you are, who vows to kill the man who frees you.'

At these words the genius did all he could to get out, but he could not, because of the enchantment of the lid.

Then he tried to get out by cunning.

'If you will take off the cover,' he said, 'I will repay you.'

'No,' answered the fisherman, 'if I trust myself to you I am afraid you will treat me as a certain Greek king treated the physician Douban. Listen, and I will tell you.'

The Story of the Greek King and the Physician Douban

In the country of Zouman, in Persia, there lived a Greek king. This king was a leper, and all his doctors had been unable to cure him, when a very clever physician came to his court.

He was very learned in all languages, and knew a great deal about herbs and medicines.

As soon as he was told of the king's illness he put on his best robe and presented himself before the king. 'Sire,' said he, 'I know that no physician has been able to cure your majesty, but if you will follow my instructions, I will promise to cure you without any medicines or outward application.'

The king listened to this proposal.

'If you are clever enough to do this,' he said, 'I promise to make you and your descendants rich for ever.'

The physician went to his house and made a polo club, the handle of which he hollowed out, and put in it the drug he wished to use. Then he made a ball, and with these things he went the next day to the king.

He told him that he wished him to play at polo. Accordingly the king mounted his horse and went into the place where he played. There the physician approached him with the bat he had made, saying, 'Take this, sire, and strike the ball till you feel your hand and whole body in a glow. When the remedy that is in the handle of the club is warmed by your hand it will penetrate throughout your body. The you must return to your palace, bathe, and go to sleep, and when you awake tomorrow morning you will be cured.'

The king took the club and urged his horse after the ball which he had thrown. He struck it, and then it was hit back by the courtiers who were playing with him. When he felt very hot he stopped playing, and went back to the palace, went into the bath, and did all that the physician had said. The next day when he arose he found, to his great joy and astonishment, that he was completely cured. When he entered his audience-chamber all his courtiers, who were eager to see if the wonderful cure had been effected, were overwhelmed with joy.

The physician Douban entered the hall and bowed low to the ground. The king, seeing him, called him, made him sit by his side, and showed him every mark of honour.

That evening he gave him a long and rich robe of state, and presented him with two thousand sequins. The following day he continued to load him with favours.

Now the king had a grand-vizir who was avaricious, and envious, and a very bad man. He grew extremely jealous of the physician, and determined to bring about his ruin.

In order to do this he asked to speak in private with the king, saying that he had a most important communication to make.

'What is it?' asked the king.

'Sire,' answered the grand-vizir, 'it is most dangerous for a monarch to confide in a man whose faithfulness is not proved, You do not know that this physician is not a traitor come here to assassinate you.'

'I am sure,' said the king, 'that this man is the most faithful and virtuous of men. If he wished to take my life, why did he cure me? Cease to speak against him. I see what it is, you are jealous of him; but do not think that I can be turned against him. I remember well what a vizir said to King Sindbad, his master, to prevent him from putting the prince, his son, to death.'

What the Greek king said excited the vizir's curiosity, and he said to him, 'Sire, I beg your majesty to have the condescension to tell me what the vizir said to King Sindbad.'

'This vizir,' he replied, 'told King Sindbad that one ought not believe everything that a mother-in-law says, and told him this story.'

The Story of the Husband and the Parrot

A good man had a beautiful wife, whom he loved passionately, and never left if possible. One day, when he was obliged by important business to go away from her, he went to a place where all kinds of birds are sold and bought a parrot. This parrot not only spoke well, but it had the gift of telling all that had been done before it. He brought it home in a cage, and asked his wife to put it in her room, and take great care of it while he was away. Then he departed. On his return he asked the parrot what had happened during his absence, and the parrot told him some things which made him scold his wife.

She thought that one of her slaves must have been telling tales of her, but they told her it was the parrot, and she resolved to revenge herself on him.

When her husband next went away for one day, she told one slave to turn under the bird's cage a hand-mill; another to throw water down from above the cage, and a third to take a mirror and turn it in front of its eyes, from left to right by the light of a candle. The slaves did this for part of the night, and did it very well.

The next day when the husband came back he asked the parrot what he had seen. The bird replied, 'My good master, the lightning, thunder and rain disturbed me so much all night long, that I cannot tell you what I have suffered.'

The husband, who knew that it had neither rained nor thundered in the night, was convinced that the parrot was not speaking the truth, so he took him out of the cage and threw him so roughly on the ground that he killed him. Nevertheless he was sorry afterwards, for he found that the parrot had spoken the truth.

'When the Greek king,' said the fisherman to the genius, 'had finished the story of the parrot, he added to the vizir, "And so, vizir,

I shall not listen to you, and I shall take care of the physician, in case I repent as the husband did when he had killed the parrot." But the vizir was determined. "Sire," he replied, "the death of the parrot was nothing. But when it is a question of the life of a king it is better to sacrifice the innocent than save the guilty. It is no uncertain thing, however. The physician, Douban, wishes to assassinate you. My zeal prompts me to disclose this to your majesty. If I am wrong, I deserve to be punished as a vizir was once punished." "What had the vizir done," said the Greek king, "to merit the punishment?" "I will tell your majesty, if you will do me the honour to listen," answered the vizir.'

The Story of the Vizir
who was Punished

There was once upon a time a king who had a son who was very fond of hunting. He often allowed him to indulge in this pastime, but he had ordered his grand-vizir always to go with him, and never to lose sight of him. One day the huntsman roused a stag, and the prince, thinking that the vizir was behind, gave chase, and rode so hard that he found himself alone. He stopped, and having lost sight of it, he turned to rejoin the vizir, who had not been careful enough to follow him. But he lost his way. Whilst he was trying to find it, he saw on the side of the road a beautiful lady who was crying bitterly. He drew his horse's rein, and asked her who she was and what she was doing in this place, and if she needed help. 'I am the daughter of an Indian king,' she answered, 'and whilst riding in the country I fell asleep and tumbled off. My horse has run away, and I do not know what has become of him.'

The young prince had pity on her, and offered to take her behind him, which he did. As they passed by a ruined building the lady dismounted and went in. The prince also dismounted and followed her. To his great surprise, he heard her saying to someone inside, 'Rejoice my children; I am bringing you a nice fat youth.' And other voices replied, 'Where is he, mamma, that we may eat him at once, as we are very hungry?'

The prince at once saw the danger he was in. He now knew that the lady who said she was the daughter of an Indian king was an ogress, who lived in desolate places, and who by a thousand wiles surprised and devoured passers-by. He was terrified, and threw himself on his horse. The pretended princess appeared at this moment, and seeing that she had lost her prey, she said to him, 'Do not be afraid. What do you want?'

'I am lost,' he answered, 'and I am looking for the road.'

'Keep straight on,' said the ogress, 'and you will find it.'

The prince could hardly believe his ears, and rode off as hard as he could. He found his way, and arrived safe and sound at his father's house, where he told him of the danger he had run because of the grand-vizir's carelessness. The king was very angry, and had him strangled immediately.

'Sire,' went on the vizir to the Greek king, 'to return to the physician, Douban. If you do not take care, you will repent of having trusted him. Who knows what this remedy, with which he has cured you, may not in time have a bad effect on you?'

The Greek king was naturally very weak, and did not perceive the wicked intention of his vizir, nor was he firm enough to keep to his first resolution.

'Well, vizir,' he said, 'you are right. Perhaps he did come to take my life. He might do it by the mere smell of one of his drugs. I must see what can be done.'

'The best means, sire, to put your life in security, is to send for him at once, and to cut off his head directly he comes,' said the vizir.

'I really think,' replied the king, 'that will be the best way.'

He then ordered one of his ministers to fetch the physician, who came at once.

'I have had you sent for,' said the king, 'in order to free myself from you by taking your life.'

The physician was beyond measure astonished when he heard he was to die.

'What crimes have I committed, your majesty?'

'I have learnt,' replied the king, 'that you are a spy, and intend to kill me. But I will be first, and kill you. Strike,' he added to an executioner who was by, 'and rid me of this assassin.'

At this cruel order the physician threw himself on his knees. 'Spare my life,' he cried, 'and yours will be spared.'

The fisherman stopped here to say to the genius: 'You see what passed between the Greek king and the physician has just passed between us two. The Greek king,' he went on, 'had no mercy on him, and the executioner bound his eyes.'

All those present begged for his life, but in vain.

The prince falls in with the ogress

The physician on his knees, and bound, said to the king: 'At least let me put my affairs in order, and leave my books to persons who will make good use of them. There is one which I should like to present to your majesty. It is very precious, and ought to be kept carefully in your treasury. It contains many curious things, the chief being that when you cut off my head, if your majesty will turn to the sixth leaf, and read the third line of the left-hand page, my head will answer all the questions you like to ask it.'

The king, eager to see such a wonderful thing, put off his execution to the next day, and sent him under a strong guard to his house. There the physician put his affairs in order, and the next day there was a great crowd assembled in the hall to see his death, and the doings after it. The physician went up to the foot of the throne with a large book in his hand. He carried a basin, on which he spread the covering of the book, and presenting it to the king, said: 'Sire, take this book, and when my head is cut off, let it be placed in the basin on the covering of this book; as soon as it is there, the blood will cease to flow. Then open the book, and my head will answer your questions. But, sire, I implore your mercy, for I am innocent.'

'Your prayers are useless, and if it were only to hear your head speak when you are dead, you should die.'

So saying, he took the book from the physician's hands, and ordered the executioner to do his duty.

The head was so cleverly cut off that it fell into the basin, and directly the blood ceased to flow. Then, to the great astonishment of the king, the eyes opened, and the head said, 'Your majesty, open the book.' The king did so, and finding that the first leaf stuck against the second, he put his finger in his mouth, to turn it more easily. He did the same thing till he reached the sixth page, and not seeing any writing on it, 'Physician,' he said, 'there is no writing.'

'Turn over a few more pages,' answered the head. The king went on turning, still putting his finger in his mouth, till the poison in which each page was dipped took effect. His sight failed him, and he fell at the foot of his throne.

When the physician's head saw that the poison had taken effect, and that the king had only a few more minutes to live, 'Tyrant,' it cried, 'see how cruelty and injustice are punished.'

Scarcely had it uttered these words than the king died, and the head lost also the little life that had remained in it.

That is the end of the story of the Greek king, and now let us return to the fisherman and the genius.

The king turns over the leaves of the book

'If the Greek king,' said the fisherman, 'had spared the physician, he would not have thus died. The same thing applies to you. Now I am going to throw you into the sea.'

'My friend,' said the genius, 'do not do such a cruel thing. Do not treat me as Imma treated Ateca.'

'What did Imma do to Ateca?' asked the fisherman.

'Do you think I can tell you while I am shut up in here?' replied the genius. 'Let me out, and I will make you rich.'

The hope of being no longer poor made the fisherman give way.

'If you will give me your promise to do this, I will open the lid. I do not think you will dare to break your word.'

The genius promised, and the fisherman lifted the lid. He came out at once in smoke, and then, having resumed his proper form, the first thing he did was to kick the vase into the sea. This frightened the fisherman, but the genius laughed and said, 'Do not be afraid; I only did it to frighten you, and to show you that I intend to keep my word; take your nets and follow me.'

He began to walk in front of the fisherman, who followed him with some misgivings. They passed in front of the town, and went up a mountain and then down into a great plain, where there was a large lake lying between four hills.

When they reached the lake the genius said to the fisherman, 'Throw your nets and catch fish.'

The fisherman did as he was told, hoping for a good catch, as he saw plenty of fish. What was his astonishment at seeing that there were four quite different kinds, some white, some red, some blue, and some yellow. He caught four, one of each colour. As he had never seen any like them he admired them very much, and he was very pleased to think how much money he would get for them.

'Take these fish and carry them to the sultan, who will give you more money for them than you have ever had in your life. You can come every day to fish in this lake, but be careful not to throw your nets more than once every day, otherwise some harm will happen to you. If you follow my advice carefully you will find it good.'

Saying these words, he struck his foot against the ground, which opened, and when he had disappeared, it closed immediately.

The fisherman resolved to obey the genius exactly, so he did not cast his nets a second time, but walked into the town to sell his fish at the palace.

When the sultan saw the fish he was much astonished. He looked at them one after the other, and when he had admired them long enough, 'Take these fish,' he said to his first vizir, 'and give them to the clever cook the Emperor of the Greeks sent me. I think they must be as good as they are beautiful.'

The vizir took them himself to the cook, saying, 'Here are four fish that have been brought to the sultan. He wants you to cook them.'

Then he went back to the sultan, who told him to give the fisherman four hundred gold pieces. The fisherman, who had never before possessed such a large sum of money at once, could hardly believe his good fortune. He at once relieved the needs of his family, and made good use of it.

But now we must return to the kitchen, which we shall find in great confusion. The cook, when she had cleaned the fish, put them in a pan with some oil to fry them. When she thought them cooked enough on one side she turned them on the other. But scarcely had she done so when the walls of the kitchen opened, and there came out a young and beautiful damsel. She was dressed in an Egyptian dress of flowered satin, and she wore earrings, and a necklace of white pearls, and bracelets of gold set with rubies, and she held a wand of myrtle in her hand.

She went up to the pan, to the great astonishment of the cook, who stood motionless at the sight of her. She struck one of the fish with her rod, 'Fish, fish,' said she, 'are you doing your duty?' The fish answered nothing, and then she repeated her question, whereupon they all raised their heads together and answered very distinctly, 'Yes, yes. If you reckon, we reckon. If you pay your debts, we pay ours. If you fly, we conquer, and we are content.'

When they had spoken the girl upset the pan, and entered the opening in the wall, which at once closed, and appeared the same as before.

When the cook had recovered from her fright she lifted up the fish which had fallen into the ashes, but she found them as black as cinders, and not fit to serve up to the sultan. She began to cry.

'Alas! what shall I say to the sultan? He will be so angry with me, and I know he will not believe me!'

Whilst she was crying the grand-vizir came in and asked if the fish were ready. She told him all that had happened, and he was much surprised. He sent at once for the fisherman, and when he came said to him, 'Fisherman, bring me four more fish like you

The girl upsets the frying-pan

have brought already, for an accident has happened to them so that they cannot be served up to the sultan.'

The fisherman did not say what the genius had told him, but he excused himself from bringing them that day on account of the length of the way, and he promised to bring them next day.

In the night he went to the lake, cast his nets, and on drawing them in found four fish, which were like the others, each of a different colour.

He went back at once and carried them to the grand-vizir as he had promised.

He then took them to the kitchen and shut himself up with the cook, who began to cook them as she had done the four others on the previous day. When she was about to turn them on the other side, the wall opened, the damsel appeared, addressed the same words to the fish, received the same answer, and then overturned the pan and disappeared.

The grand-vizir was filled with astonishment. 'I shall tell the sultan all that has happened,' said he. And he did so.

The sultan was very much astounded, and wished to see this marvel for himself. So he sent for the fisherman, and asked him to procure four more fish. The fisherman asked for three days, which were granted, and he then cast his nets in the lake, and again caught four different coloured fish. The sultan was delighted to see he had got them, and gave him again four hundred gold pieces.

As soon as the sultan had the fish he had them carried to his room with all that was needed to cook them.

Then he shut himself up with the grand-vizir, who began to prepare them and cook them. When they were done on one side he turned them over on the other. Then the wall of the room opened, but instead of the maiden a black slave came out. He was enormously tall, and carried a large green stick with which he touched the fish, saying in a terrible voice, 'Fish, fish, are you doing your duty?' To these words the fish lifting up their heads replied, 'Yes, yes. If you reckon, we reckon. If you pay your debts, we pay ours. If you fly, we conquer, and are content.'

The black slave overturned the pan in the middle of the room, and the fish were turned to cinders. Then he stepped proudly back into the wall, which closed round him.

'After having seen this,' said the sultan, 'I cannot rest. These fish signify some mystery I must clear up.'

He sent for the fisherman. 'Fisherman,' he said, 'the fish you have brought us have caused me some anxiety. Where did you get them from?'

'Sire,' he answered, 'I got them from a lake which lies in the middle of four hills beyond yonder mountains.'

'Do you know this lake?' asked the sultan of the grand-vizir.

'No; though I have hunted many times round that mountain, I have never heard of it,' said the vizir.

As the fisherman said it was only three hours' journey away, the sultan ordered his whole court to mount and ride thither, and the fisherman led them.

They climbed the mountain, and then, on the other side, saw the lake as the fisherman had described. The water was so clear that they could see the four kinds of fish swimming about in it. They looked at them for some time, and then the sultan ordered them to make a camp by the edge of the water.

When night came the sultan called his vizir, and said to him, 'I have resolved to clear up this mystery. I am going out alone, and do you stay here in my tent, and when my ministers come tomorrow, say I am not well, and cannot see them. Do this each day till I return.'

The grand-vizir tried to persuade the sultan not to go, but in vain. The sultan took off his state robe and put on his sword, and when he saw all was quiet in the camp he set forth alone.

He climbed one of the hills, and then crossed the great plain, till, just as the sun rose, he beheld far in front of him a large building. When he came near to it he saw it was a splendid palace of beautiful black polished marble, covered with steel as smooth as a mirror.

He went to the gate, which stood half open, and went in, as nobody came when he knocked. He passed through a magnificent courtyard and still saw no one, though he called aloud several times.

He entered large halls where the carpets were of silk, the lounges and sofas covered with tapestry from Mecca, and the hangings of the most beautiful Indian stuffs of gold and silver. Then he found himself in a splendid room, with a fountain supported by golden lions. The water out of the lions' mouths turned into diamonds and pearls, and the leaping water almost touched a most beautifully painted dome. The palace was surrounded on three sides by magnificent gardens, little lakes, and woods. Birds sang in the trees, which were netted over to keep them always there.

Still the sultan saw no one, till he heard a plaintive cry, and a voice which said, 'Oh that I could die, for I am too unhappy to wish to live any longer!'

The sultan looked round to discover who it was who thus bemoaned his fate, and at last saw a handsome young man, richly clothed, who was sitting on a throne raised slightly from the ground. His face was very sad.

The sultan approached him and bowed to him. The young man bent his head very low, but did not rise.

'Sire,' he said to the sultan, 'I cannot rise and do you the reverence that I am sure should be paid to your rank.'

'Sir,' answered the sultan, 'I am sure you have a good reason for not doing so, and having heard your cry of distress, I am come to offer you my help. Whose is this palace, and why is it thus empty?'

Instead of answering the young man lifted up his robe, and showed the sultan that, from the waist downwards, he was a block of black marble.

The sultan was horrified, and begged the young man to tell him his story.

'Willingly I will tell you my sad history,' said the young man.

The Story of the Young King
of the Black Isles

You must know, sire, that my father was Mahmoud, the king of this country, the Black Isles, so called from the four little mountains which were once islands, while the capital was the place where now the great lake lies. My story will tell you how these changes came about.

My father died when he was sixty-six, and I succeeded him. I married my cousin, whom I loved tenderly, and I thought she loved me too. But one afternoon, when I was half asleep, and was being fanned by two of her maids, I heard one say to the other, 'What a pity it is that our mistress no longer loves our master! I believe she would like to kill him if she could, for she is an enchantress.'

I soon found by watching that they were right, and when I mortally wounded a favourite slave of hers for a great crime, she begged that she might build a palace in the garden, where she wept and bewailed him for two years.

At last I begged her to cease grieving for him, for although he could not speak or move, by her enchantments she just kept him alive. She turned upon me in a rage, and said over me some magic words, and I instantly became as you see me now, half man and half marble.

Then this wicked enchantress changed the capital, which was a very populous and flourishing city, into the lake and desert plain you saw. The fish of four colours which are in it are the different races who lived in the town; the four hills are the four islands which give the name to my kingdom. All this the enchantress told me to add to my troubles. And this is not all. Every day she comes and beats me with a whip of buffalo hide.

When the young king had finished his sad story he burst once more into tears, and the sultan was much moved.

I became half man and half marble

'Tell me,' he cried, 'where is this wicked woman, and where is the miserable object of her affection, whom she just manages to keep alive?'

'Where she lives I do not know,' answered the unhappy prince, 'but she goes every day at sunrise to see if the slave can yet speak to her, after she has beaten me.'

'Unfortunate king,' said the sultan, 'I will do what I can to avenge you.'

So he consulted with the young king over the best way to bring this about, and they agreed their plan should be put in effect the next day.

The sultan then rested, and the young king gave himself up to happy hopes of release. The next day the sultan arose, and then went to the palace in the garden where the black slave was. He drew his sword and destroyed the little life that remained in him, and then threw the body down a well. He then lay down on the couch where the slave had been, and waited for the enchantress.

She went first to the young king, whom she beat with a hundred blows.

Then she came to the room where she thought her wounded slave was, but where the sultan really lay.

She came near his couch and said, 'Are you better today, my dear slave? Speak but one word to me.'

'How can I be better,' answered the sultan, imitating the language of the Ethiopians, 'when I can never sleep for the cries and groans of your husband?'

'What joy to hear you speak!' answered the queen. 'Do you wish him to regain his proper shape?'

'Yes,' said the sultan; 'hasten to set him at liberty, so that I may no longer hear his cries.'

The queen at once went out and took a cup of water, and said over it some words that made it boil as if it were on the fire. Then she threw it over the prince, who at once regained his own form. He was filled with joy, but the enchantress said, 'Hasten away from this place and never come back, lest I kill you.'

So he hid himself to see the end of the sultan's plan.

The enchantress went back to the Palace of Tears and said, 'Now I have done what you wished.'

'What you have done,' said the sultan, 'is not enough to cure me. Every day at midnight all the people whom you have changed into fish lift their heads out of the lake and cry for vengeance. Go quickly, and give them their proper shape.'

The enchantress hurried away and said some words over the lake.

The fish then became men, women, and children, and the houses and shops were once more filled. The sultan's suite, who had encamped by the lake, were not a little astonished to see themselves in the middle of a large and beautiful town.

As soon as she had disenchanted it the queen went back to the palace.

'Are you quite well now?' she said.

'Come near,' said the sultan. 'Nearer still.'

She obeyed. Then he sprang up, and with one blow of his sword he cut her in two. Then he went and found the prince.

'Rejoice,' he said, 'your cruel enemy is dead.'

The prince thanked him again and again.

'And now,' said the sultan. 'I will go back to my capital, which I am glad to find is so near yours.'

'So near mine!' said the King of the Black Isles.

'Do you know it is a whole year's journey from here? You came here in a few hours because it was enchanted. But I will accompany you on your journey.'

'It will give me much pleasure if you will escort me,' said the sultan, 'and as I have no children, I will make you my heir.'

The sultan and the prince set out together, the sultan laden with rich presents from the King of the Black Isles.

The day after he reached his capital the sultan assembled his court and told them all that had befallen him, and told them how he intended to adopt the young king as his heir.

Then he gave each man presents in proportion to his rank.

As for the fisherman, as he was the first cause of the deliverance of the young prince, the sultan gave him much money, and made him and his family happy for the rest of their days.

The Story of the Three Calenders, Sons of Kings, and of Five Ladies of Bagdad

In the reign of the Caliph Haroun-al-Raschid, there lived at Bagdad a porter who, in spite of his humble calling, was an intelligent and sensible man. One morning he was sitting in his usual place with his basket before him, waiting to be hired, when a tall young lady, covered with a long muslin veil, came up to him and said, 'Pick up your basket and follow me.' The porter, who was greatly pleased by her appearance and voice, jumped up at once, poised his basket on his head, and accompanied the lady, saying to himself as he went, 'Oh, happy day! Oh, lucky meeting!'

The lady soon stopped before a closed door, at which she knocked. It was opened by an old man with a long white beard, to whom the lady held out money without speaking. The old man, who seemed to understand what she wanted, vanished into the house, and returned bringing a large jar of wine, which the porter placed in his basket. Then the lady signed to him to follow, and they went their way.

The next place she stopped at was a fruit and flower shop, and here she bought a large quantity of apples, apricots, peaches, and other things, with lilies, jasmine, and all sorts of sweet-smelling plants. From this shop she went to a butcher's, a grocer's, and a poulterer's, till at last the porter exclaimed in despair, 'My good lady, if you had only told me you were going to buy enough provisions to stock a town, I would have brought a horse, or rather a camel.' The lady laughed, and told him she had not finished yet, but after choosing various kinds of scents and spices from a druggist's store, she halted before a magnificent palace, at the door of which she knocked gently. The porteress who opened it was of such beauty that the eyes of the man were quite dazzled, and he was the more astonished as he saw clearly that she was no slave. The

The man is astonished at the beauty of the porteress

lady who had led him hither stood watching him with amusement, till the porteress exclaimed, 'Why don't you come in, my sister? This poor man is so heavily weighed down that he is ready to drop.'

When they were both inside the door was fastened, and they all three entered a large court, surrounded by an open-work gallery. At one end of the court was a platform, and on the platform stood an amber throne supported by four ebony columns, garnished with pearls and diamonds. In the middle of the court stood a marble basin filled with water from the mouth of a golden lion.

The porter looked about him, noticing and admiring everything; but his attention was specially attracted by a third lady sitting on the throne, who was even more beautiful than the other two. By the respect shown to her by the others, he judged that she must be the eldest, and in this he was right. This lady's name was Zobeida, the porteress was Sadie, and the housekeeper was Amina. At a word from Zobeida, Sadie and Amina took the basket from the porter, who was glad enough to be relieved from its weight; and when it was emptied, paid him handsomely for its use. But instead of taking up his basket and going away, the man still lingered, till Zobeida enquired what he was waiting for, and if he expected more money. 'Oh, madam,' returned he, 'you have already given me too much, and I fear I may have been guilty of rudeness in not taking my departure at once. But, if you will pardon my saying so, I was lost in astonishment at seeing such beautiful ladies by themselves. A company of women without men is, however, as dull as a company of men without women.' And after telling some stories to prove his point, he ended by entreating them to let him stay and make a fourth at their dinner.

The ladies were rather amused at the man's assurances and after some discussion it was agreed that he should be allowed to stay, as his society might prove entertaining. 'But listen, friend,' said Zobeida, 'if we grant your request, it is only on condition that you behave with the utmost politeness, and that you keep the secret of our way of living, which chance has revealed to you.' Then they all sat down to table, which had been covered by Amina with the dishes she had bought.

After the first few mouthfuls Amina poured some wine into a golden cup. She first drank herself, according to the Arab custom, and then filled it for her sisters. When it came to the porter's turn he kissed Amina's hand, and sang a song, which he composed at the moment in praise of the wine. The three ladies were pleased with the song, and then sang themselves, so that the repast was a merry one, and lasted much longer than usual.

At length, seeing that the sun was about to set, Sadie said to the porter, 'Rise and go; it is now time for us to separate.'

'Oh, madam,' replied he, 'how can you desire me to quit you in the state in which I am? Between the wine I have drunk, and the pleasure of seeing you, I should never find the way to my house. Let me remain here till morning, and when I have recovered my senses I will go when you like.'

'Let him stay,' said Amina, who had before proved herself his friend. 'It is only just, as he has given us so much amusement.'

'If you wish it, my sister,' replied Zobeida; 'but if he does, I must make a new condition. Porter,' she continued, turning to him, 'if you remain, you must promise to ask no questions about anything you may see. If you do, you may perhaps hear what you don't like.'

This being settled, Amina brought in supper, and lit up the hall with a number of sweet-smelling tapers. They then sat down again at the table, and began with fresh appetites to eat, drink, sing, and recite verses. In fact, they were all enjoying themselves mightily when they heard a knock at the outer door, which Sadie rose to open. She soon returned saying that three calenders, all blind in the right eye, and all with their heads, faces, and eyebrows clean shaved, begged for admittance, as they were newly arrived in Bagdad, and night had already fallen. 'They seem to have pleasant manners,' she added, 'but you have no idea how funny they look. I am sure we should find their company diverting.'

Zobeida and Amina made some difficulty about admitting the newcomers, and Sadie knew the reason of their hesitation. But she urged the matter so strongly that Zobeida was at last forced to consent. 'Bring them in, then,' said she, 'but make them understand that they are not to make remarks about what does not concern them, and be sure to make them read the inscription over the door.' For on the door was written in letters of gold, 'Whoso meddles in affairs that are no business of his, will hear truths that will not please him.'

The three calenders bowed low on entering, and thanked the ladies for their kindness and hospitality. The ladies replied with words of welcome, and they were all about to seat themselves when the eyes of the calenders fell on the porter, whose dress was not so very unlike their own, though he still wore all the hair that nature had given him. 'This,' said one of them, 'is apparently one of our Arab brothers, who has rebelled against our ruler.'

The porter, although half asleep from the wine he had drunk, heard the words, and without moving cried angrily to the calender, 'Sit down and mind your own business. Did you not read the inscription over the door? Everybody is not obliged to live in the same way.'

'Do not be so angry, my good man,' replied the calender; 'we should be very sorry to displease you'; so the quarrel was smoothed over, and supper began in good earnest. When the calenders had satisfied their hunger, they offered to play to their hostesses, if there were any instruments in the house. The ladies were delighted at the idea, and Sadie went to see what she could find, returning in a few moments laden with two different kinds of flutes and a tambourine. Each calender took the one he preferred, and began to play a well-known air, while the ladies sang the words of the song. These words were the gayest and liveliest possible, and every now and then the singers had to stop to indulge the laughter which almost choked them. In the midst of all their noise, a knock was heard at the door.

Now early that evening the caliph secretly left the palace, accompanied by his grand-vizir, Giafar, and Mesrour, chief of the eunuchs, all three wearing the dresses of merchants. Passing down the street, the caliph had been attracted by the music of instruments and the sound of laughter, and had ordered his vizir to go and knock at the door of the house, as he wished to enter. The vizir replied that the ladies who lived there seemed to be entertaining their friends, and he thought his master would do well not to intrude on them; but the caliph had taken it into his head to see for himself, and insisted on being obeyed.

The knock was answered by Sadie, with a taper in her hand, and the vizir, who was surprised at her beauty, bowed low before her, and said respectfully, 'Madam, we are three merchants who have lately arrived from Moussoul, and, owing to a misadventure which befell us this very night, only reached our inn to find that the doors were closed to us till tomorrow morning. Not knowing what to do, we wandered in the streets till we happened to pass your house, when, seeing lights and hearing the sound of voices, we resolved to ask you to give us shelter till the dawn. If you will grant us this favour, we will, with your permission, do all in our power to help you spend the time pleasantly.'

Sadie answered the merchant that she must first consult her sisters; and after having talked over the matter with them, she returned to tell him that he and his two friends would be welcome to join their company. They entered and bowed politely to the ladies and their guests. Then Zobeida, as the mistress, came forward and said gravely, 'You are welcome here, but I hope you will allow me to beg one thing of you – have as many eyes as you like, but no tongues; and ask no questions about anything you see, however strange it may appear to you.'

'Madam,' returned the vizir, 'you shall be obeyed. We have quite enough to please and interest us without troubling ourselves about that with which we have no concern.' Then they all sat down, and drank to the health of the newcomers.

While the vizir, Giafar, was talking to the ladies the caliph was occupied in wondering who they could be, and why the three calenders had each lost his right eye. He was burning to enquire the reason of it all, but was silenced by Zobeida's request, so he tried to rouse himself and to take his part in the conversation, which was very lively, the subject of discussion being the many different sorts of pleasures that there were in the world. After some time the calenders got up and performed some curious dances, which delighted the rest of the company.

When they had finished Zobeida rose from her seat, and, taking Amina by the hand, she said to her, 'My sister, our friends will excuse us if we seem to forget their presence and fulfil our nightly task.' Amina understood her sister's meaning, and collecting the dishes, glasses, and musical instruments, she carried them away, while Sadie swept the hall and put everything in order. Having done this she begged the calenders to sit on a sofa on one side of the room, and the caliph and his friends to place themselves opposite. As to the porter, she requested him to come and help her and her sister.

Shortly after Amina entered carrying a seat, which she put down in the middle of the empty space. She next went over to the door of a closet and signed to the porter to follow her. He did so, and soon reappeared leading two black dogs by a chain, which he brought into the centre of the hall. Zobeida then got up from her seat between the calenders and the caliph and walked slowly across to where the porter stood with the dogs. 'We must do our duty,' she said with a deep sigh, pushing back her sleeves, and, taking a whip from Sadie, she said to the man, 'Take one of those dogs to my sister Amina and give me the other.'

The porter did as he was bid, but as he led the dog to Zobeida it uttered piercing howls, and gazed up at her with looks of entreaty. But Zobeida took no notice, and whipped the dog till she was out of breath. She then took the chain from the porter, and, raising the dog on its hind legs, they looked into each other's eyes sorrowfully till tears began to fall from both. Then Zobeida took her handkerchief and wiped the dog's eyes tenderly, after which she kissed it, then, putting the chain into the porter's hand she said, 'Take it back to the closet and bring me the other.'

The same ceremony was gone through with the second dog, and all the while the whole company looked on with astonishment. The caliph in particular could hardly contain himself, and made signs to the vizir to ask what it all meant. But the vizir pretended not to see, and turned his head away.

Zobeida remained for some time in the middle of the room, till at last Sadie went up to her and begged her to sit down, as she also had her part to play. At these words Amina fetched a lute from a case of yellow satin and gave it to Sadie, who sang several songs to its accompaniment. When she was tired she said to Amina, 'My sister, I can do no more; come, I pray you, and take my place.'

Amina struck a few chords and then broke into a song, which she sang with so much ardour that she was quite overcome, and sank gasping on a pile of cushions, tearing open her dress as she did so to

Zobeida prepares to whip the dog

give herself some air. To the amazement of all present, her neck, instead of being as smooth and white as her face, was a mass of scars.

The calenders and the caliph looked at each other, and whispered together, unheard by Zobeida and Sadie, who were tending their fainting sister.

'What does it all mean?' asked the caliph.

'We know no more than you,' said the calender to whom he had spoken.

'What! You do not belong to the house?'

'My lord,' answered all the calenders together, 'we came here for the first time an hour before you.'

They then turned to the porter to see if he could explain the mystery, but the porter was no wiser than they were themselves. At length the caliph could contain his curiosity no longer, and declared that he would compel the ladies to tell them the meaning of their strange conduct. The vizir, foreseeing what would happen, implored him to remember the condition their hostesses had imposed, and added in a whisper that if his highness would only wait till morning he could as caliph summon the ladies to appear before him. But the caliph, who was not accustomed to be contradicted, rejected this advice, and it was resolved after a little more talking that the question should be put by the porter. Suddenly Zobeida turned round, and seeing their excitement she said, 'What is the matter – what are you all discussing so earnestly?'

'Madam,' answered the porter, 'these gentlemen entreat you to explain to them why you should first whip the dogs and then cry over them, and also how it happens that the fainting lady is covered with scars. They have requested me, madam, to be their mouth-piece.'

'Is it true, gentlemen,' asked Zobeida, drawing herself up, 'that you have charged this man to put me that question?'

'It is,' they all replied, except Giafar, who was silent.

'Is this,' continued Zobeida, growing more angry every moment, 'is this the return you make for the hospitality I have shown you? Have you forgotten the one condition on which you were allowed to enter the house? Come quickly,' she added, clapping her hands three times, and the words were hardly uttered when seven black slaves, each armed with a sabre, burst in and stood over the seven men, throwing them on the ground, and preparing themselves, on a sign from their mistress, to cut off their heads.

The seven culprits all thought their last hour had come, and the caliph repented bitterly that he had not taken the vizir's advice. But they made up their minds to die bravely, all except the porter, who loudly enquired of Zobeida why he was to suffer for other people's faults, and declared that these misfortunes would never have happened if it had not been for the calenders, who always brought ill-luck. He ended by imploring Zobeida not to confound the innocent with the guilty and to spare his life.

In spite of her anger, there was something so comic in the groans of the porter that Zobeida could not refrain from laughing. But putting him aside she addressed the others a second time, saying, 'Answer me; who are you? Unless you tell me truly you have not another moment to live. I can hardly think you are men of any position, whatever country you belong to. If you were, you would have had more consideration for us.'

The caliph, who was naturally very impatient, suffered far more than either of the others at feeling that his life was at the mercy of a justly offended lady, but when he heard her question he began to breathe more freely, for he was convinced that she had only to learn his name and rank for all danger to be over. So he whispered hastily to the vizir, who was next to him, to reveal their secret. But the vizir, wiser than his master, wished to conceal from the public the affront they had received, and merely answered, 'After all, we have only got what we deserved.'

Meanwhile Zobeida had turned to the three calenders and enquired if, as they were all blind, they were brothers.

'No, madam,' replied one, 'we are no blood relations at all, only brothers by our mode of life.'

'And you,' she asked, addressing another, 'were you born blind of one eye?'

'No, madam,' returned he, 'I became blind through a most

surprising adventure, such as probably has never happened to anybody. After that I shaved my head and eyebrows and put on the dress in which you see me now.'

Zobeida put the same question to the other two calenders, and received the same answer.

'But,' added the third, 'it may interest you, madam, to know that we are not men of low birth, but are all three sons of kings, and of kings, too, whom the world holds in high esteem.'

At these words Zobeida's anger cooled down, and she turned to her slaves and said, 'You can give them a little more liberty, but do not leave the hall. Those that will tell us their histories and their reasons for coming here shall be allowed to leave unhurt; those who refuse – ' And she paused, but in a moment the porter, who understood that he had only to relate his story to set himself free from this terrible danger, immediately broke in,

'Madam, you know already how I came here, and what I have to say will soon be told. Your sister found me this morning in the place where I always stand waiting to be hired. She bade me follow her to various shops, and when my basket was quite full we returned to this house, when you had the goodness to permit me to remain, for which I shall be eternally grateful. That is my story.'

He looked anxiously to Zobeida, who nodded her head and said, 'You can go; and take care we never meet again.'

'Oh, madam,' cried the porter, 'let me stay yet a little while. It is not just that the others should have heard my story and that I should not hear theirs,' and without waiting for permission he seated himself on the end of the sofa occupied by the ladies, whilst the rest crouched on the carpet, and the slaves stood against the wall.

Then one of the calenders, addressing himself to Zobeida as the principal lady, began his story.

The Story of the First Calender, Son of a King

In order, madam, to explain how I came to lose my right eye, and to wear the dress of a calender, you must first know that I am the son of a king. My father's only brother reigned over the neighbouring country, and had two children, a daughter and a son, who were of the same age as myself.

As I grew up, and was allowed more liberty, I went every year to pay a visit to my uncle's court, and usually stayed there about two months. In this way my cousin and I became very intimate, and were much attached to each other. The very last time I saw him he seemed more delighted to see me than ever, and gave a great feast in my honour. When we had finished eating, he said to me, 'My cousin, you would never guess what I have been doing since your last visit to us! Directly after your departure I set a number of men to work on a building after my own design. It is now completed, and ready to be lived in. I should like to show it to you, but you must first swear two things: to be faithful to me, and to keep my secret.'

Of course I did not dream of refusing him anything he asked, and gave the promise without the least hesitation. He then bade me wait an instant, and vanished, returning in a few moments with a richly dressed lady of great beauty, but as he did not tell me her name, I thought it was better not to enquire. We all three sat down to table and amused ourselves with talking of all sorts of indifferent things, and with drinking each other's health. Suddenly the prince said to me, 'Cousin, we have no time to lose; be so kind as to conduct this lady to a certain spot, where you will find a domelike tomb, newly built. You cannot mistake it. Go in, both of you, and wait till I come. I shall not be long.'

As I had promised I prepared to do as I was told, and giving my hand to the lady, I escorted her, by the light of the moon, to the place of which the prince had spoken. We had barely reached it when he joined us himself, carrying a small vessel of water, a pick-axe, and a little bag containing plaster.

With the pickaxe he at once began to destroy the empty sepulchre in the middle of the tomb. One by one he took the stones and piled them up in a corner. When he had knocked down the whole sepulchre he proceeded to dig at the earth, and beneath where the sepulchre had been I saw a trap-door. He raised the door and I caught sight of the top of a spiral staircase; then he said, turning to the lady, 'Madam, this is the way that will lead you down to the spot which I told you of.'

The lady did not answer, but silently descended the staircase, the prince following her. At the top, however, he looked at me. 'My cousin,' he exclaimed, 'I do not know how to thank you for your kindness. Farewell.'

'What do you mean?' I cried. 'I don't understand.'

'No matter,' he replied, 'go back by the path that you came.'

He would say no more, and, greatly puzzled, I returned to my room in the palace and went to bed. When I woke, and considered my adventure, I thought that I must have been dreaming, and sent a servant to ask if the prince was dressed and could see me. But on hearing that he had not slept at home I was much alarmed, and hastened to the cemetery, where, unluckily, the tombs were all so alike that I could not discover which was the one I was in search of, though I spent four days in looking for it.

You must know that all this time the king, my uncle, was absent on a hunting expedition, and as no one knew when he would be back, I at last decided to return home, leaving the ministers to make my excuses. I longed to tell them what had become of the prince, about whose fate they felt the most dreadful anxiety, but the oath I had sworn kept me silent.

On my arrival at my father's capital, I was astonished to find a large detachment of guards drawn up before the gate of the palace; they surrounded me directly I entered. I asked the officers in command the reason of this strange behaviour, and was horrified to

The king's son begs for his life

learn that the army had mutinied and put to death the king, my father, and had placed the grand-vizir on the throne. Further, that by his orders I was placed under arrest.

Now this rebel vizir had hated me from my boyhood, because once, when shooting at a bird with a bow, I had shot out his eye by accident. Of course I not only sent a servant at once to offer him my regrets and apologies, but I made them in person. It was all of no use. He cherished an undying hatred towards me, and lost no occasion of showing it. Having once got me in his power I felt he could show no mercy, and I was right. Mad with triumph and fury he came to me in my prison and tore out my right eye. That is how I lost it.

My persecutor, however, did not stop here. He shut me up in a large case and ordered his executioner to carry me into a desert place, to cut off my head, and then to abandon my body to the birds of prey. The case, with me inside it, was accordingly placed on a horse, and the executioner, accompanied by another man, rode into the country until they found a spot suitable for the purpose. But their hearts were not so hard as they seemed, and my tears and prayers made them waver.

'Forsake the kingdom instantly,' said the executioner at last, 'and take care never to come back, for you will not only lose your head, but make us lose ours.' I thanked him gratefully, and tried to console myself for the loss of my eye by thinking of the other misfortunes I had escaped.

After all I had gone through, and my fear of being recognised by some enemy, I could only travel very slowly and cautiously, generally resting in some out-of-the-way place by day, and walking as far as I was able by night, but at length I arrived in the kingdom of my uncle, of whose protection I was sure.

I found him in great trouble about the disappearance of his son, who had, he said, vanished without leaving a trace; but his own grief did not prevent him sharing mine. We mingled our tears, for the loss of one was the loss of the other, and then I made up my mind that it was my duty to break the solemn oath I had sworn to the prince. I therefore lost no time in telling my uncle everything I knew, and I observed that even before I had ended his sorrow appeared to be lightened a little.

'My dear nephew,' he said, 'your story gives me some hope. I was aware that my son was building a tomb, and I think I can find the spot. But as he wished to keep the matter secret, let us go alone and seek the place ourselves.'

He then bade me disguise myself, and we both slipped out of a garden door which opened on to the cemetery. It did not take long for us to arrive at the scene of the prince's disappearance, or to discover the tomb I had sought so vainly before. We entered it, and found the trap-door which led to the staircase, but we had great difficulty in raising it, because the prince had fastened it down underneath with the plaster he had brought with him.

My uncle went first, and I followed him. When we reached the bottom of the stairs we stepped into a sort of anteroom, filled with such a dense smoke that it was hardly possible to see anything. However, we passed through the smoke into a large chamber, which at first seemed quite empty. The room was brilliantly lighted, and in another moment we perceived a sort of platform at one end, on which were the bodies of the prince and a lady, both half burned, as if they had been dragged out of a fire before it had quite consumed them.

This horrible sight turned me faint, but, to my surprise, my uncle did not show so much surprise as anger.

'I knew,' he said, 'that my son was tenderly attached to this lady, whom it was impossible he should ever marry. I tried to turn his thoughts, and presented to him the most beautiful princesses, but he cared for none of them, and, as you see, they have now been united by a horrible death in an underground tomb.' But, as he spoke, his anger melted into tears, and again I wept with him.

When he recovered himself he drew me to him. 'My dear nephew,' he said, embracing me, 'you have come to me to take his place, and I will do my best to forget that I ever had a son who could act in so wicked a manner.' Then he turned and went up the stairs.

We reached the palace without anyone having noticed our absence, when, shortly after, a clashing of drums, and cymbals, and the blare of trumpets burst upon our astonished ears. At the same time a thick cloud of dust on the horizon told of the approach of a great army. My heart sank when I perceived that the commander was the vizir who had dethroned my father, and was come to seize the kingdom of my uncle.

The capital was utterly unprepared to stand a siege, and seeing that resistance was useless, at once opened its gates. My uncle fought hard for his life, but was soon overpowered, and when he fell I managed to escape through a secret passage, and took refuge with an officer whom I knew I could trust.

Persecuted by ill-fortune, and stricken with grief, there seemed to be only one means of safety left to me. I shaved my beard and my eyebrows, and put on the dress of a calender, in which it was easy for me to travel without being known. I avoided the towns till I reached the kingdom of the famous and powerful Caliph Haroun-al-Raschid, when I had no further reason to fear my enemies. It was my intention to come to Bagdad and to throw myself at the feet of his highness, who would, I felt certain, be touched by my sad story, and would grant me, besides, his help and protection.

After a journey which lasted some months I arrived at length at the gates of this city. It was sunset, and I paused for a little to look about me, and to decide which way to turn my steps. I was still debating on this subject when I was joined by this other calender, who stopped to greet me. 'You, like me, appear to be a stranger,' I said. He replied that I was right, and before he could say more the third calender came up. He, also, was newly arrived in Bagdad, and being brothers in misfortune, we resolved to cast in our lots together, and to share whatever fate might have in store.

By this time it had grown late, and we did not know where to spend the night. But our lucky star having guided us to this door, we took the liberty of knocking and of asking for shelter, which was given to us at once with the best grace in the world.

This, madam, is my story.

'I am satisfied,' replied Zobeida; 'you can go when you like.'

The calender, however, begged leave to stay and to hear the histories of his two friends and of the three other persons of the company, which he was allowed to do.

The Story of the Second Calender, Son of a King

'Madam,' said the young man, addressing Zobeida, 'if you wish to know how I lost my right eye, I shall have to tell you the story of my whole life.'

I was scarcely more than a baby, when the king my father, finding me unusually quick and clever for my age, turned his thoughts to my education. I was taught first to read and write, and then to learn the Koran, which is the basis of our holy religion, and the better to understand it, I read with my tutors the ablest commentators on its teaching, and committed to memory all the traditions respecting the Prophet, which have been gathered from the mouth of those who were his friends. I also learnt history, and was instructed in poetry, versification, geography, chronology, and in all the outdoor exercises in which every prince should excel. But what I liked best of all was writing Arabic characters, and in this I soon surpassed my masters, and gained a reputation in this branch of knowledge that reached as far as India itself.

Now the Sultan of the Indies, curious to see a young prince with such strange tastes, sent an ambassador to my father, laden with rich presents, and a warm invitation to visit his court. My father, who was deeply anxious to secure the friendship of so powerful a monarch, and held besides that a little travel would greatly improve my manners and open my mind, accepted gladly, and in a short time I had set out for India with the ambassador, attended only by a small suite on account of the length of the journey, and the badness of the roads. However, as was my duty, I took with me ten camels, laden with rich presents for the sultan.

We had been travelling for about a month, when one day we saw a cloud of dust moving swiftly towards us; and as soon as it came near, we found that the dust concealed a band of fifty robbers. Our men barely numbered half, and as we were also hampered by the camels, there was no use in fighting, so we tried to overawe them by informing them who we were, and whither we were going. The robbers, however, only laughed, and declared that was none of their business, and, without more words, attacked us brutally. I defended myself to the last, wounded though I was, but at length, seeing that resistance was hopeless, and that the ambassador and all our followers were made prisoners, I put spurs to my horse and rode away as fast as I could, till the poor beast fell dead from a wound in his side. I managed to jump off without any injury, and looked about to see if I was pursued. But for the moment I was safe, for, as I imagined, the robbers were all engaged in quarrelling over their booty.

I found myself in a country that was quite new to me, and dared not return to the main road lest I should again fall into the hands of the robbers. Luckily my wound was only a slight one, and after binding it up as well as I could, I walked on for the rest of the day, till I reached a cave at the foot of a mountain, where I passed the night in peace, making my supper off some fruits I had gathered on the way.

I wandered about for a whole month without knowing where I was going, till at length I found myself on the outskirts of a beautiful city, watered by winding streams, which enjoyed an eternal spring. My delight at the prospect of mixing once more with human beings was somewhat damped at the thought of the miserable object I must seem. My face and hands had been burned nearly black; my clothes were all in rags, and my shoes were in such a state that I had been forced to abandon them altogether.

I entered the town, and stopped at a tailor's shop to enquire where I was. The man saw I was better than my condition, and begged me to sit down, and in return I told him my whole story. The tailor listened with attention, but his reply, instead of giving me consolation, only increased my trouble.

'Beware,' he said, 'of telling anyone what you have told me, for the prince who governs the kingdom is your father's greatest enemy, and he will be rejoiced to find you in his power.'

I thanked the tailor for his counsel, and said I would do whatever he advised; then, being very hungry, I gladly ate of the food he put before me, and accepted his offer of a lodging in his house.

In a few days I had quite recovered from the hardships I had undergone, and then the tailor, knowing that it was the custom for the princes of our religion to learn a trade or profession so as to provide for themselves in times of ill-fortune, enquired if there was anything I could do for my living. I replied that I had been educated as a grammarian and a poet, but that my great gift was writing.

'All that is of no use here,' said the tailor. 'Take my advice, put on a short coat, and as you seem hardy and strong, go into the woods and cut firewood, which you will sell in the streets. By this means you will earn your living, and be able to wait till better times come. The hatchet and the cord shall be my present.'

This counsel was very distasteful to me, but I thought I could not do otherwise than adopt it. So the next morning I set out with a company of poor woodcutters, to whom the tailor had introduced me. Even on the first day I cut enough wood to sell for a tolerable sum, and very soon I became more expert, and had made enough money to repay the tailor all he had lent me.

I had been a woodcutter for more than a year, when one day I wandered further into the forest than I had ever done before, and reached a delicious green glade, where I began to cut wood. I was hacking at the root of a tree, when I beheld an iron ring fastened to a trapdoor of the same metal. I soon cleared away the earth, and pulling up the door, found a staircase, which I hastily made up my mind to go down, carrying my hatchet with me by way of protection. When I reached the bottom I discovered that I was in a huge palace, as brilliantly lighted as any palace above ground that I had ever seen, with a long gallery supported by pillars of jasper, ornamented with capitals of gold. Down this gallery a lady came to meet me, of such beauty that I forgot everything else, and thought only of her.

To save her all the trouble possible, I hastened towards her, and bowed low.

'Who are you? Who are you?' she said. 'A man or a genius?'

'A man, madam,' I replied; 'I have nothing to do with genii.'

'By what accident do you come here?' she asked again with a sigh. 'I have been in this place now for five and twenty years, and you are the first man who has visited me.'

Emboldened by her beauty and gentleness, I ventured to reply, 'Before, madam, I answer your question, allow me to say how grateful I am for this meeting, which is not only a consolation to me in my own heavy sorrow, but may perhaps enable me to render your lot happier,' and then I told her who I was, and how I had come there.

'Alas, prince,' she said, with a deeper sigh than before, 'you have guessed rightly in supposing me an unwilling prisoner in this gorgeous place. I am the daughter of the King of the Ebony Isle, of whose fame you surely must have heard. At my father's desire I was married to a prince who was my own cousin; but on my very wedding day, I was snatched up by a genius, and brought here in a faint. For a long while I did nothing but weep, and would not suffer the genius to come near me; but time teaches us submission, and I have now got accustomed to his presence, and if clothes and jewels could content me, I have them in plenty. Every tenth day, for five and twenty years, I have received a visit from him, but in case I should need his help at any other time, I have only to touch a talisman that stands at the entrance of my chamber. It wants still five days to his next visit, and I hope that during that time you will do me the honour to be my guest.'

I was too much dazzled by her beauty to dream of refusing her offer, and accordingly the princess had me conducted to the bath, and a rich dress befitting my rank was provided for me. Then a feast of the most delicate dishes was served in a room hung with embroidered Indian fabrics.

Next day, when we were at dinner, I could maintain my patience no longer, and implored the princess to break her bonds, and return with me to the world which was lighted by the sun.

'What you ask is impossible,' she answered; 'but stay here with me instead, and we can be happy, and all you will have to do is to betake yourself to the forest every tenth day, when I am expecting my master the genius. He is very jealous, as you know, and will not suffer a man to come near me.'

'Princess,' I replied, 'I see it is only fear of the genius that makes you act like this. For myself, I dread him so little that I mean to break his talisman in pieces! Awful though you think him, he shall feel the weight of my arm, and I herewith take a solemn vow to stamp out the whole race.'

The princess, who realised the consequences of such audacity, entreated me not to touch the talisman. 'If you do, it will be the ruin of both of us,' said she; 'I know genii much better than you.' But the wine I had drunk had confused my brain; I gave one kick to the talisman, and it fell into a thousand pieces.

Hardly had my foot touched the talisman when the air became as dark as night, a fearful noise was heard, and the palace shook to its very foundations. In an instant I was sobered, and understood what I had done. 'Princess!' I cried, 'what is happening?'

'Alas!' she exclaimed, forgetting all her own terrors in anxiety for me, 'fly, or you are lost.'

I followed her advice and dashed up the staircase, leaving my hatchet behind me. But I was too late. The palace opened and the genius appeared, who, turning angrily to the princess, asked indignantly, 'What is the matter, that you have sent for me like this?'

'A pain in my heart,' she replied hastily, 'obliged me to seek the aid of this little bottle. Feeling faint, I slipped and fell against the talisman, which broke. That is really all.'

'You are an impudent liar!' cried the genius. 'How did this hatchet and those shoes get here?'

'I never saw them before,' she answered, 'and you came in such a hurry that you may have picked them up on the road without knowing it.' To this the genius only replied by insults and blows. I could hear the shrieks and groans of the princess, and having by this time taken off my rich garments and put on those in which I had arrived the previous day, I lifted the trap, found myself once more in the forest, and returned to my friend the tailor, with a light load of wood and a heart full of shame and sorrow.

The tailor, who had been uneasy at my long absence, was

delighted to see me; but I kept silence about my adventure, and as soon as possible retired to my room to lament in secret over my folly. While I was thus indulging my grief my host entered, and said, 'There is an old man downstairs who has brought your hatchet and slippers, which he picked up on the road, and now restores to you, as he found out from one of your comrades where you lived. You had better come down and speak to him yourself.' At this speech I changed colour, and my legs trembled under me. The tailor noticed my confusion, and was just going to enquire the reason when the door of the room opened, and the old man appeared, carrying with him my hatchet and shoes.

'I am a genius,' he said, 'the son of the daughter of Eblis, prince of the genii. Is not this hatchet yours, and these shoes?' Without waiting for an answer – which, indeed, I could hardly have given him, so great was my fright – he seized hold of me, and darted up into the air with the quickness of lightning, and then, with equal swiftness, dropped down towards the earth. When he touched the ground, he rapped it with his foot; it opened, and we found ourselves in the enchanted palace, in the presence of the beautiful princess of the Ebony Isle. But how different she looked from what she was when I had last seen her, for she was lying stretched on the ground covered with blood, and weeping bitterly.

'Traitress!' cried the genius, 'is not this man your lover?'

She lifted up her eyes slowly, and looked sadly at me. 'I never saw him before,' she answered slowly. 'I do not know who he is.'

'What!' exclaimed the genius, 'you owe all your sufferings to him, and yet you dare to say he is a stranger to you!'

'But if he really is a stranger to me,' she replied, 'why should I tell a lie and cause his death?'

'Very well,' said the genius, drawing his sword, 'take this, and cut off his head.'

'Alas,' answered the princess, 'I am too weak even to hold the sabre. And supposing that I had the strength, why should I put an innocent man to death?'

'You condemn yourself by your refusal,' said the genius; then turning to me, he added, 'and you, do you not know her?'

The genius commands the young man to slay the princess

'How should I?' I replied, resolved to imitate the princess in her fidelity. 'How should I, when I never saw her before?'

'Cut her head off, then, if she is a stranger to you, and I shall believe you are speaking the truth, and will set you at liberty.'

'Certainly,' I answered, taking the sabre in my hands, and making a sign to the princess to fear nothing, as it was my own life that I was about to sacrifice, and not hers. But the look of gratitude she gave me shook my courage, and I flung the sabre to the earth.

'I should not deserve to live,' I said to the genius, 'if I were such a coward as to slay a lady who is not only unknown to me, but who is at this moment half dead herself. Do with me as you will – I am in your power – but I refuse to obey your cruel command.'

'I see,' said the genius, 'that you have both made up your minds to brave me, but I will give you a sample of what you may expect.' So saying, with one sweep of his sabre he cut off a hand of the princess, who was just able to lift the other to wave me an eternal farewell. Then I lost consciousness for several minutes.

When I came to myself I implored the genius to keep me no longer in this state of suspense, but to lose no time in putting an end to my sufferings. The genius, however, paid no attention to my prayers, but said sternly, 'That is the way in which a genius treats the woman who has betrayed him. If I chose, I could kill you also; but I will be merciful, and content myself with changing you into a dog, an ass, a lion, or a bird – whichever you prefer.'

I caught eagerly at these words, as giving me a faint hope of softening his wrath. 'O genius!' I cried, 'as you wish to spare my life, be generous, and spare it altogether. Grant my prayer, and pardon my crime, as the best man in the whole world forgave his neighbour who was eaten up with envy of him.' Contrary to my hopes, the genius seemed interested in my words, and said he would like to hear the story of the two neighbours; and as I think, madam, it may please you, I will tell it to you also.

The Story of the Envious Man and of Him who was Envied

In a town of moderate size, two men lived in neighbouring houses; but they had not been there very long before one man took such a hatred of the other, and envied him so bitterly, that the poor man determined to find another home, hoping that when they no longer met every day his enemy would forget all about him. So he sold his house and the little furniture it contained, and moved into the capital of the country, which was luckily at no great distance. About half a mile from this city he bought a nice little place, with a large garden and a fair-sized court, in the centre of which stood an old well.

In order to live a quieter life, the good man put on the robe of a dervish, and divided his house into a quantity of small cells, where he soon established a number of other dervishes. The fame of his virtue gradually spread abroad, and many people, including several of the highest quality, came to visit him and ask his prayers.

Of course it was not long before his reputation reached the ears of the man who envied him, and this wicked wretch resolved never to rest till he had in some way worked ill to the dervish whom he hated. So he left his house and his business to look after themselves, and betook himself to the new dervish monastery, where he was welcomed by the founder with all the warmth imaginable. The excuse he gave for his appearance was that he had come to consult the chief of the dervishes on a private matter of great importance. 'What I have to say must not be overheard,' he whispered; 'command, I beg of you, that your dervishes retire into their cells, as night is approaching, and meet me in the court.'

The dervish did as he was asked without delay, and directly they were alone together the envious man began to tell a long story, edging, as they walked to and fro, always nearer to the well, and when they were quite close, he seized the dervish and dropped him in. He then ran off triumphantly, without having been seen by anyone, and congratulating himself that the object of his hatred was dead, and would trouble him no more.

But in this he was mistaken! The old well had long been inhabited (unknown to mere human beings) by a set of fairies and genii, who caught the dervish as he fell, so that he received no hurt. The dervish himself could see nothing, but he took for granted that something strange had happened, or he must certainly have been dashed against the side of the well and been killed. He lay quite still, and in a moment he heard a voice saying, 'Can you guess who this man is that we have saved from death?'

'No,' replied several other voices.

And the first speaker answered, 'I will tell you. This man, from pure goodness of heart, forsook the town where he lived and came to dwell here, in the hope of curing one of his neighbours of the envy he felt towards him. But his character soon won him the esteem of all, and the envious man's hatred grew, till he came here with the deliberate intention of causing his death. And this he would have done, without our help, the very day before the sultan has arranged to visit this holy dervish, and to entreat his prayers for the princess, his daughter.'

'But what is the matter with the princess that she needs the dervish's prayers?' asked another voice.

'She has fallen into the power of the genius Maimoum, the son of Dimdim,' replied the first voice. 'But it would be quite simple for this holy chief of the dervishes to cure her if he only knew! In his convent there is a black cat which has a tiny white tip to its tail. Now to cure the princess the dervish must pull out seven of these white hairs, burn three, and with their smoke perfume the head of the princess. This will deliver her so completely that Maimoum, the son of Dimdim, will never dare to approach her again.'

The fairies and genii ceased talking, but the dervish did not forget a word of all they had said; and when morning came he perceived a place in the side of the well which was broken, and where he could easily climb out.

The dervishes, who could not imagine what had become of him, were enchanted at his reappearance. He told them of the attempt on his life made by his guest of the previous day, and then retired into his cell. He was soon joined here by the black cat of which the voice had spoken, who came as usual to say good-morning to his master. He took him on his knee and seized the opportunity to pull seven white hairs out of his tail, and put them on one side till they were needed.

The sun had not long risen before the sultan, who was anxious to leave nothing undone that might deliver the princess, arrived with a large suite at the gate of the monastery, and was received by the dervishes with profound respect. The sultan lost no time in declaring the object of his visit, and leading the chief of the dervishes aside, he said to him, 'Noble scheik, you have guessed perhaps what I have come to ask you?'

'Yes, sire,' answered the dervish; 'if I am not mistaken, it is the illness of the princess which has procured me this honour.'

'You are right,' returned the sultan, 'and you will give me fresh life if you can by your prayers deliver my daughter from the strange malady that has taken possession of her.'

'Let your highness command her to come here, and I will see what I can do.'

The sultan, full of hope, sent orders at once that the princess was to set out as soon as possible, accompanied by her usual staff of attendants. When she arrived, she was so thickly veiled that the dervish could not see her face, but he desired a brazier to be held over her head, and laid the seven hairs on the burning coals. The instant they were consumed, terrific cries were heard, but no one could tell from whom they proceeded. Only the dervish guessed that they were uttered by Maimoum the son of Dimdim, who felt the princess escaping him.

All this time she had seemed unconscious of what she was doing, but now she raised her hand to her veil and uncovered her face. 'Where am I?' she said in a bewildered manner; 'and how did I get here?'

The sultan was so delighted to hear these words that he not only embraced his daughter, but kissed the hand of the dervish. Then, turning to his attendants who stood round, he said to them, 'What reward shall I give to the man who has restored me my daughter?'

They all replied with one accord that he deserved the hand of the princess.

'That is my own opinion,' said he, 'and from this moment I declare him to be my son-in-law.'

Shortly after these events, the grand-vizir died, and his post was given to the dervish. But he did not hold it for long, for the sultan fell a victim to an attack of illness, and as he had no sons, the soldiers and priests declared the dervish heir to the throne, to the great joy of all the people.

One day, when the dervish, who had now become sultan, was making a royal progress with his court, he perceived the envious man standing in the crowd. He made a sign to one of his vizirs, and whispered in his ear, 'Fetch me that man who is standing out there, but take great care not to frighten him.' The vizir obeyed, and when the envious man was brought before the sultan, the monarch said to him, 'My friend, I am delighted to see you again.' Then turning to an officer, he added, 'Give him a thousand pieces of gold out of my treasury, and twenty waggonloads of merchandise out of my private stores, and let an escort of soldiers accompany him home.' He then took leave of the envious man, and went on his way.

Now when I had ended my story, I proceeded to show the genius how to apply it to himself. 'O genius,' I said, 'you see that this sultan was not content with merely forgiving the envious man for the attempt on his life; he heaped rewards and riches upon him.'

But the genius had made up his mind, and could not be softened. 'Do not imagine that you are going to escape so easily,' he said. 'All I can do is to give you bare life; you will have to learn what happens to people who interfere with me.'

As he spoke he seized me violently by the arm; the roof of the palace opened to make way for us, and we mounted up so high into the air that the earth looked like a little cloud. Then, as before, he came down with the swiftness of lightning, and we touched the ground on a mountain top.

Then he stooped and gathered a handful of earth, and murmured some words over it, after which he threw the earth in my face, saying as he did so, 'Quit the form of a man, and assume that of a monkey.' This done, he vanished, and I was in the likeness of an ape, and in a country I had never seen before.

However there was no use in stopping where I was, so I came down the mountain and found myself in a flat plain which was bounded by the sea. I travelled towards it, and was pleased to see a vessel moored about half a mile from shore. There were no waves, so I broke off the branch of a tree, and dragging it down to the water's edge, sat across it, while, using two sticks for oars, I rowed myself towards the ship.

The deck was full of people, who watched my progress with interest, but when I seized a rope and swung myself on board, I found that I had only escaped death at the hands of the genius to perish by those of the sailors, lest I should bring ill-luck to the vessel and the merchants. 'Throw him into the sea!' cried one. 'Knock him on the head with a hammer,' exclaimed another. 'Let me shoot him with an arrow,' said a third; and certainly somebody would have had his way if I had not flung myself at the captain's feet and grasped tight hold of his dress. He appeared touched by my action and patted my head, and declared that he would take me under his protection, and that no one should do me any harm.

At the end of about fifty days we cast anchor before a large town, and the ship was immediately surrounded by a multitude of small boats filled with people, who had come either to meet their friends or from simple curiosity. Among others, one boat contained several officials, who asked to see the merchants on board, and informed them that they had been sent by the sultan in token of welcome, and to beg them each to write a few lines on a roll of paper. 'In order to explain this strange request,' continued the officers, 'it is necessary that you should know that the grand-vizir, lately dead, was celebrated for his beautiful handwriting, and the sultan is anxious to find a similar talent in his successor. Hitherto the search has been a failure, but his highness has not yet given up hope.'

One after another the merchants set down a few lines upon the roll, and when they had all finished, I came forward, and snatched the paper from the man who held it. At first they all thought I was going to throw it into the sea, but they were quieted when they saw I held it with great care, and great was their surprise when I made signs that I too wished to write something.

'Let him do it if he wants to,' said the captain. 'If he only makes a mess of the paper, you may be sure I will punish him for it. But if, as I hope, he really can write, for he is the cleverest monkey I ever saw, I will adopt him as my son. The one I lost had not nearly so much sense!'

No more was said, and I took the pen and wrote the six sorts of writing in use among the Arabs, and each sort contained an original verse or couplet, in praise of the sultan. And not only did my handwriting completely eclipse that of the merchants, but it is hardly too much to say that none so beautiful had ever before been seen in that country. When I had ended the officials took the roll and returned to the sultan.

As soon as the monarch saw my writing he did not so much as look at the samples of the merchants, but desired his officials to take the finest and most richly caparisoned horse in his stables, together with the most magnificent dress they could procure, and to put it on the person who had written those lines, and bring him to court.

The officials began to laugh when they heard the sultan's command, but as soon as they could speak they said, 'Deign, your highness, to excuse our mirth, but those lines were not written by a man but by a monkey.'

'A monkey!' exclaimed the sultan.

'Yes, sire,' answered the officials. 'They were written by a monkey in our presence.'

'Then bring me the monkey,' he replied, 'as fast as you can.'

The sultan's officials returned to the ship and showed the royal order to the captain.

'He is the master,' said the good man, and desired that I should be sent for.

Then they put on me the gorgeous robe and rowed me to land, where I was placed on the horse and led to the palace. Here the sultan was awaiting me in great state surrounded by his court.

All the way along the streets I had been the object of curiosity to a vast crowd, which had filled every doorway and every window, and it was amidst their shouts and cheers that I was ushered into the presence of the sultan.

I approached the throne on which he was seated and made him three low bows, then prostrated myself at his feet to the surprise of everyone, who could not understand how it was possible that a monkey should be able to distinguish a sultan from other people, and to pay him the respect due to his rank. However, excepting the usual speech, I omitted none of the common forms attending a royal audience.

When it was over the sultan dismissed all the court, keeping with him only the chief of the eunuchs and a little slave. He then passed into another room and ordered food to be brought, making signs to me to sit at table with him and eat. I rose from my seat, kissed the ground, and took my place at the table, eating, as you may suppose, with care and in moderation.

Before the dishes were removed I made signs that writing materials, which stood in one corner of the room, should be laid in front of me. I then took a peach and wrote on it some verses in praise of the sultan, who was speechless with astonishment; but when I did the same thing on a glass from which I had drunk he murmured to himself, 'Why, a man who could do as much would be cleverer than any other man, and this is only a monkey!'

Supper being over chessmen were brought, and the sultan signed to me to know if I would play with him. I kissed the ground and laid my hand on my head to show that I was ready to show myself worthy of the honour. He beat me the first game, but I won the second and third, and seeing that this did not quite please I dashed off a verse by way of consolation.

The sultan was so enchanted with all the talents of which I had given proof that he wished me to exhibit some of them to other people. So turning to the chief of the eunuchs he said, 'Go and beg my daughter, Queen of Beauty, to come here. I will show her something she has never seen before.'

The chief of the eunuchs bowed and left the room, ushering in a few moments later the princess, Queen of Beauty. Her face was uncovered, but the moment she set foot in the room she threw her veil over her head. 'Sire,' she said to her father, 'what can you be thinking of to summon me like this into the presence of a man?'

'I do not understand you,' replied the sultan. 'There is nobody here but the eunuch, who is your own servant, the little slave, and myself, yet you cover yourself with your veil and reproach me for having sent for you, as if I had committed a crime.'

'Sire,' answered the princess, 'I am right and you are wrong. This monkey is really no monkey at all, but a young prince who has been turned into a monkey by the wicked spells of a genius, son of the daughter of Eblis.'

As will be imagined, these words took the sultan by surprise, and he looked at me to see how I should take the statement of the princess. As I was unable to speak, I placed my hand on my head to show that it was true.

'But how do you know this, my daughter?' asked he.

'Sire,' replied Queen of Beauty, 'the old lady who took care of me in my childhood was an accomplished magician, and she taught me seventy rules of her art, by means of which I could, in the twinkling of an eye, transplant your capital into the middle of the ocean. Her art likewise teaches me to recognise at first sight all persons who are enchanted, and tells me by whom the spell was wrought.'

'My daughter,' said the sultan, 'I really had no idea you were so clever.'

'Sire,' replied the princess, 'there are many out-of-the-way things it is as well to know, but one should never boast of them.'

'Well,' asked the sultan, 'can you tell me what must be done to disenchant the young prince?'

'Certainly; and I can do it.'

'Then restore him to his former shape,' cried the sultan. 'You could give me no greater pleasure, for I wish to make him my grand-vizir, and to give him to you for your husband.'

The princess veils herself when she sees the monkey

'As your highness pleases,' replied the princess.

Queen of Beauty rose and went to her chamber, from which she fetched a knife with some Hebrew words engraven on the blade. She then desired the sultan, the chief of the eunuchs, the little slave, and myself to descend into a secret court of the palace, and placed us beneath a gallery which ran all round, she herself standing in the centre of the court. Here she traced a large circle and in it wrote several words in Arab characters.

When the circle and the writing were finished she stood in the middle of it and repeated some verses from the Koran. Slowly the air grew dark, and we felt as if the earth was about to crumble away, and our fright was by no means diminished at seeing the genius, son of the daughter of Eblis, suddenly appear under the form of a colossal lion.

'Dog,' cried the princess when she first caught sight of him, 'you think to strike terror into me by daring to present yourself before me in this hideous shape.'

'And you,' retorted the lion, 'have not feared to break our treaty that engaged solemnly we should never interfere with each other.'

'Accursed genius!' exclaimed the princess, 'it is you by whom that treaty was first broken.'

'I will teach you how to give me so much trouble,' said the lion, and opening his huge mouth he advanced to swallow her. But the princess expected something of the sort and was on her guard. She bounded on one side, and seizing one of the hairs of his mane repeated two or three words over it. In an instant it became a sword, and with a sharp blow she cut the lion's body into two pieces. These pieces vanished no one knew where, and only the lion's head remained, which was at once changed into a scorpion. Quick as thought the princess assumed the form of a serpent and gave battle to the scorpion, who, finding he was getting the worst of it, turned himself into an eagle and took flight. But in a moment the serpent had become an eagle more powerful still, who soared up in the air and after him, and then we lost sight of them both.

We all remained where we were quaking with anxiety, when the ground opened in front of us and a black and white cat leapt out, its

She cut the lion's body into two pieces

hair standing on end, and miaowing frightfully. At its heels was a
wolf, who had almost seized it, when the cat changed itself into a
worm, and, piercing the skin of a pomegranate which had tumbled
from a tree, hid itself in the fruit. The pomegranate swelled till it
grew as large as a pumpkin, and raised itself on to the roof of the
gallery, from which it fell into the court and was broken into bits.
While this was taking place the wolf, who had transformed himself
into a cock, began to swallow the seed of the pomegranate as fast as
he could. When all were gone he flew towards us, flapping his
wings as if to ask if we saw any more, when suddenly his eye fell on
one which lay on the bank of the little canal that flowed through

the court; he hastened towards it, but before he could touch it the seed rolled into the canal and became a fish. The cock flung himself in after the fish and took the shape of a pike, and for two hours they chased each other up and down under the water, uttering horrible cries, but we could see nothing. At length they rose from the water in their proper forms, but darting such flames of fire from their mouths that we dreaded lest the palace should catch fire. Soon, however, we had much greater cause for alarm, as the genius, having shaken off the princess, flew towards us. Our fate would have been sealed if the princess, seeing our danger, had not attracted the attention of the genius to herself. As it was, the sultan's beard was singed and his face scorched, the chief of the eunuchs was burned to a cinder, while a spark deprived me of the sight of one eye. Both I and the sultan had given up all hope of a rescue, when there was a shout of 'Victory, victory!' from the princess, and the genius lay at her feet a great heap of ashes.

Exhausted though she was, the princess at once ordered the little slave, who alone was uninjured, to bring her a cup of water, which she took in her hand. First repeating some magic words over it, she dashed it into my face saying, 'If you are only a monkey by enchantment, resume the form of the man you were before.' In an instant I stood before her the same man I had formerly been, though having lost the sight of one eye.

I was about to fall on my knees and thank the princess but she did not give me time. Turning to the sultan, her father, she said, 'Sire, I have gained the battle, but it has cost me dear. The fire has penetrated to my heart, and I have only a few moments to live. This would not have happened if I had only noticed the last pomegranate seed and eaten it like the rest. It was the last struggle of the genius, and up to that time I was quite safe. But having let this chance slip I was forced to resort to fire, and in spite of all his experience I showed the genius that I knew more than he did. He is dead and in ashes, but my own death is approaching fast.'

'My daughter,' cried the sultan, 'how sad is my condition! I am only surprised I am alive at all! The eunuch is consumed by the flames, and the prince whom you have delivered has lost the sight of

'I burn, I burn!'

one eye.' He could say no more, for sobs choked his voice, and we all wept together.

Suddenly the princess shrieked, 'I burn, I burn!' and death came to free her from her torments.

I have no words, madam, to tell you of my feelings at this terrible sight. I would rather have remained a monkey all my life than let my benefactress perish in this shocking manner. As for the sultan, he was quite inconsolable, and his subjects, who had dearly loved the princess, shared his grief. For seven days the whole nation mourned, and then the ashes of the princess were buried with great pomp, and a superb tomb was raised over her.

As soon as the sultan recovered from the severe illness which had seized him after the death of the princess he sent for me and plainly, though politely, informed me that my presence would always remind him of his loss, and he begged that I would instantly quit his kingdom, and on pain of death never return to it. I was, of course, bound to obey, and not knowing what was to become of me I shaved my beard and eyebrows and put on the dress of a calender. After wandering aimlessly through several countries, I resolved to come to Bagdad and request an audience of the Commander of the Faithful.

And that, madam, is my story.

The other calender then told his story.

The Story of the Third Calender,
Son of a King

My story, said the third calender, is quite different from those of my two friends. It was fate that deprived them of the sight of their right eyes, but mine was lost by my own folly.

My name is Agib, and I am the son of a king called Cassib, who reigned over a large kingdom, which had for its capital one of the finest seaport towns in the world.

When I succeeded to my father's throne my first care was to visit the provinces on the mainland, and then to sail to the numerous islands which lay off the shore, in order to gain the hearts of my subjects. These voyages gave me such a taste for sailing that I soon determined to explore more distant seas, and commanded a fleet of large ships to be got ready without delay. When they were properly fitted out I embarked on my expedition.

For forty days wind and weather were all in our favour, but the next night a terrific storm arose, which blew us hither and thither for ten days, till the pilot confessed that he had quite lost his bearings. Accordingly a sailor was sent up to the masthead to try to catch a sight of land, and reported that nothing was to be seen but the sea and sky, except a huge mass of blackness that lay astern.

On hearing this the pilot grew white, and, beating his breast, he cried, 'Oh, sir, we are lost, lost!' till the ship's crew trembled at they knew not what. When he had recovered himself a little, and was able to explain the cause of his terror, he replied, in answer to my question, that we had drifted far out of our course, and that the following day about noon we should come near that mass of darkness, which, said he, is nothing but the famous Black Mountain. This mountain is composed of adamant, which attracts to itself all the iron and nails in your ship; and as we are helplessly drawn nearer, the force of attraction will become so great that the iron and nails will fall out of the ships and cling to the mountain, and the ships will sink to the bottom with all that are in them. This it is that causes the side of the mountain towards the sea to appear of such a dense blackness.

As may be supposed – continued the pilot – the mountain sides are very rugged, but on the summit stands a brass dome supported on pillars, and bearing on top the figure of a brass horse, with a rider on his back. This rider wears a breastplate of lead, on which strange signs and figures are engraved, and it is said that as long as this statue remains on the dome, vessels will never cease to perish at the foot of the mountain.

So saying, the pilot began to weep afresh, and the crew, fearing their last hour had come, made their wills, each one in favour of his fellow.

At noon next day, as the pilot had foretold, we were so near to the Black Mountain that we saw all the nails and iron fly out of the ships and dash themselves against the mountain with a horrible noise. A moment after the vessels fell asunder and sank, the crews with them. I alone managed to grasp a floating plank, and was driven ashore by the wind, without even a scratch. What was my joy on finding myself at the bottom of some steps which led straight up the mountain, for there was not another inch to the right or the left where a man could set his foot. And, indeed, even the steps themselves were so narrow and so steep that, if the lightest breeze had arisen, I should certainly have been blown into the sea.

When I reached the top I found the brass dome and the statue exactly as the pilot had described, but was too wearied with all I had gone through to do more than glance at them, and, flinging myself under the dome, was asleep in an instant. In my dreams an old man appeared to me and said, 'Hearken, Agib! As soon as thou art awake dig up the ground underfoot, and thou shalt find a bow of brass and three arrows of lead. Shoot the arrows at the statue, and the rider shall tumble into the sea, but the horse will fall down by thy side, and thou shalt bury him in the place from which thou tookest the bow and arrows. This being done the sea will rise and cover the mountain, and on it thou wilt perceive the figure of a metal man seated in a boat, having an oar in each hand. Step on board and let him conduct thee; but if thou wouldest behold thy kingdom again, see that thou takest not the name of Allah into thy mouth.'

Having uttered these words the vision left me, and I woke, much comforted. I sprang up and drew the bow and arrows out of the ground, and with the third shot the horseman fell with a great crash into the sea, which instantly began to rise, so rapidly, that I had hardly time to bury the horse before the boat approached me. I stepped silently in and sat down, and the metal man pushed off, and rowed without stopping for nine days, after which land appeared on the horizon. I was so overcome with joy at this sight that I forgot all the old man had told me, and cried out, 'Allah be praised! Allah be praised!'

The words were scarcely out of my mouth when the boat and man sank from beneath me, and left me floating on the surface. All that day and the next night I swam and floated alternately, making as well as I could for the land which was nearest to me. At last my strength began to fail, and I gave myself up for lost, when the wind suddenly rose, and a huge wave cast me on a flat shore. Then, placing myself in safety, I hastily spread my clothes out to dry in the sun, and flung myself on the warm ground to rest.

Next morning I dressed myself and began to look about me. There seemed to be no one but myself on the island, which was covered with fruit trees and watered with streams, but seemed a long distance from the mainland which I hoped to reach. Before, however, I had time to feel cast down, I saw a ship making directly for the island, and not knowing whether it would contain friends or foes, I hid myself in the thick branches of a tree.

The sailors ran the ship into a creek, where ten slaves landed, carrying spades and pickaxes. In the middle of the island they stopped, and after digging some time, lifted up what seemed to be a trap-door. They then returned to the vessel two or three times for furniture and provisions, and finally were accompanied by an old man, leading a handsome boy of fourteen or fifteen years of age. They all disappeared down the trap-door, and after remaining below for a few minutes came up again, but without the boy, and

The overthrow of the brazen horseman

let down the trap-door, covering it with earth as before. This done, they entered the ship and set sail.

As soon as they were out of sight, I came down from my tree, and went to the place where the boy had been buried. I dug up the earth till I reached a large stone with a ring in the centre. This, when removed, disclosed a flight of stone steps which led to a large room richly furnished and lighted by tapers. On a pile of cushions, covered with tapestry, sat the boy. He looked up, startled and frightened at the sight of a stranger in such a place, and to soothe his fears, I at once spoke: 'Be not alarmed, sir, whoever you may be. I am a king, and the son of a king, and will do you no hurt. On the contrary, perhaps I have been sent here to deliver you out of this tomb, where you have been buried alive.'

Hearing my words, the young man recovered himself, and when I had ended, he said, 'The reasons, prince, that have caused me to be buried in this place are so strange that they cannot but surprise you. My father is a rich merchant, owning much land and many ships, and has great dealings in precious stones, but he never ceased mourning that he had no child to inherit his wealth.

'At length one day he dreamed that the following year a son would be born to him, and when this actually happened, he consulted all the wise men in the kingdom as to the future of the infant. One and all they said the same thing. I was to live happily till I was fifteen, when a terrible danger awaited me, which I should hardly escape. If, however, I should succeed in doing so, I should live to a great old age. And, they added, when the statue of the brass horse on the top of the mountain of adamant is thrown into the sea by Agib, the son of Cassib, then beware, for fifty days later your son shall fall by his hand!

'This prophecy struck the heart of my father with such woe, that he never got over it, but that did not prevent him from attending carefully to my education till I attained, a short time ago, my fifteenth birthday. It was only yesterday that the news reached him that ten days previously the statue of brass had been thrown into the sea, and he at once set about hiding me in this underground chamber, which was built for the purpose, promising to fetch me out when the forty days have passed. For myself, I have no fears, as Prince Agib is not likely to come here to look for me.'

I listened to his story with an inward laugh as to the absurdity of my ever wishing to cause the death of this harmless boy, whom I hastened to assure of my friendship and even of my protection; begging him, in return, to convey me in his father's ship to my own country. I need hardly say that I took special care not to inform him that I was the Agib whom he dreaded.

The day passed in conversation on various subjects, and I found him a youth of ready wit and of some learning. I took on myself the duties of a servant, held the basin and water for him when he washed, prepared the dinner and set it on the table. He soon grew to love me, and for thirty-nine days we spent as pleasant an existence as could be expected underground.

The morning of the fortieth dawned, and the young man when he woke gave thanks in an outburst of joy that the danger was passed. 'My father may be here at any moment,' said he, 'so make me, I pray you, a bath of hot water, that I may bathe, and change my clothes, and be ready to receive him.'

So I fetched the water as he asked, and washed and rubbed him, after which he lay down again and slept a little. When he opened his eyes for the second time, he begged me to bring him a melon and some sugar, that he might eat and refresh himself.

I soon chose a fine melon out of those which remained, but could find no knife to cut it with. 'Look in the cornice over my head,' said he, 'and I think you will see one.' It was so high above me, that I had some difficulty in reaching it, and catching my foot in the covering of the bed, I slipped, and fell right upon the young man, the knife going straight into his heart.

At this awful sight I shrieked aloud in my grief and pain. I threw myself on the ground and rent my clothes and tore my hair with sorrow. Then, fearing to be punished as his murderer by the unhappy father, I raised the great stone which blocked the staircase, and quitting the underground chamber, made everything fast as before.

Scarcely had I finished when, looking out to sea, I saw the vessel heading for the island, and, feeling that it would be useless for me to protest my innocence, I again concealed myself among the branches of a tree that grew near by.

The old man and his slaves pushed off in a boat directly the ship touched land, and walked quickly towards the entrance to the underground chamber; but when they were near enough to see that the earth had been disturbed, they paused and changed colour. In silence they all went down and called to the youth by name; then for a moment I heard no more. Suddenly a fearful scream rent the air, and the next instant the slaves came up the steps, carrying with them the body of the old man, who had fainted from sorrow! Laying him down at the foot of the tree in which I had taken shelter, they did their best to recover him, but it took a long while. When at last he revived, they left him to dig a grave, and then laying the young man's body in it, they threw in the earth.

This ended, the slaves brought up all the furniture that remained below, and put it on the vessel, and breaking some boughs to weave a litter, they laid the old man on it, and carried him to the ship, which spread its sails and stood out to sea.

So once more I was quite alone, and for a whole month I walked daily over the island, seeking for some chance of escape. At length one day it struck me that my prison had grown much larger, and that the mainland seemed to be nearer. My heart beat at this thought, which was almost too good to be true. I watched a little longer: there was no doubt about it, and soon there was only a tiny stream for me to cross.

Even when I was safe on the other side I had a long distance to go on the mud and sand before I reached dry ground, and very tired I was, when far in front of me I caught sight of a castle of red copper, which, at first sight, I took to be a fire. I made all the haste I could, and after some miles of hard walking stood before it, and gazed at it in astonishment, for it seemed to me the most wonderful building I had ever beheld. While I was still staring at it, there came towards me a tall old man, accompanied by ten young men, all handsome, and all blind of the right eye.

Now in its way, the spectacle of ten men walking together, all

THE STORY OF THE THIRD CALENDER

blind of the right eye, is as uncommon as that of a copper castle, and I was turning over in my mind what could be the meaning of this strange fact, when they greeted me warmly, and enquired what had brought me there. I replied that my story was somewhat long, but that if they would take the trouble to sit down, I should be happy to tell it them. When I had finished, the young men begged that I would go with them to the castle, and I joyfully accepted their offer. We passed through what seemed to me an endless number of rooms, and came at length into a large hall, furnished with ten small blue sofas for the ten young men, which served as beds as well as chairs, and with another sofa in the middle for the old man. As none of the sofas could hold more than one person, they bade me place myself on the carpet, and to ask no questions about anything I should see.

After a little while the old man rose and brought in supper, which I ate heartily, for I was very hungry. Then one of the young men begged me to repeat my story, which had struck them all with astonishment, and when I had ended, the old man was bidden to 'do his duty', as it was late, and they wished to go to bed. At these words he rose, and went to a closet, from which he brought out ten basins, all covered with blue stuff. He set one before each of the young men, together with a lighted taper.

When the covers were taken off the basins, I saw they were filled with ashes, coal-dust, and lampblack. The young men mixed these all together, and smeared the whole over their heads and faces. They then wept and beat their breasts, crying, 'This is the fruit of idleness, and of our wicked lives.'

This ceremony lasted nearly the whole night, and when it stopped they washed themselves carefully, and put on fresh clothes, and lay down to sleep.

All this while I had refrained from questions, though my curiosity almost seemed to burn a hole in me, but the following day, when we went out to walk, I said to them, 'Gentlemen, I must disobey your wishes, for I can keep silence no more. You do not appear to lack wit, yet you do such actions as none but madmen could be capable of. Whatever befalls me I cannot forbear asking, "Why do you daub your faces with black, and how is it you are all blind of one eye?"'

But they only answered that such questions were none of my business, and that I should do well to hold my peace.

During that day we spoke of other things, but when night came, and the same ceremony was repeated, I implored them most earnestly to let me know the meaning of it all.

'It is for your own sake,' replied one of the young men, 'that we have not granted your request, and to preserve you from our unfortunate fate. If, however, you wish to share our destiny we will delay no longer.'

I answered that whatever might be the consequence I wished to have my curiosity satisfied, and that I would take the result on my own head. He then assured me that, even when I had lost my eye, I should be unable to remain with them, as their number was complete, and could not be added to. But to this I replied that, though I should be grieved to part company with such honest gentlemen, I would not be turned from my resolution on that account.

On hearing my determination my ten hosts then took a sheep and killed it, and handed me a knife, which they said I should by and by find useful. 'We must sew you into this sheepskin,' said they, 'and then leave you. A fowl of monstrous size, called a roc, will appear in the air, taking you to be a sheep. He will snatch you up and carry you into the sky, but be not alarmed, for he will bring you safely down and lay you on the top of a mountain. When you are on the ground cut the skin with the knife and throw it off. As soon as the roc sees you he will fly away from fear, but you must walk on till you come to a castle covered with plates of gold, studded with jewels. Enter boldly at the gate, which always stands open, but do not ask us to tell you what we saw or what befell us there, for that you will learn for yourself. This only we may say, that it cost us each our right eye, and has imposed upon us our nightly penance.'

After the young gentlemen had been at the trouble of sewing the sheepskin on me they left me, and retired to the hall. In a few minutes the roc appeared, and bore me off to the top of the mountain in his huge claws as lightly as if I had been a feather, for this great white bird is so strong that he has been known to carry even an elephant to his nest in the hills.

The young men sew up Agib in the sheepskin

The moment my feet touched the ground I took out my knife and cut the threads that bound me, and the sight of me in my proper clothes so alarmed the roc that he spread his wings and flew away. Then I set out to seek the castle.

I found it after wandering about for half a day, and never could I have imagined anything so glorious. The gate led into a square court, into which opened a hundred doors, ninety-nine of them being of rare woods and one of gold. Through each of these doors I caught glimpses of splendid gardens or of rich storehouses.

Entering one of the doors which was standing open I found

myself in a vast hall where forty young ladies, magnificently dressed, and of perfect beauty, were reclining. As soon as they saw me they rose and uttered words of welcome, and even forced me to take possession of a seat that was higher than their own, though my proper place was at their feet. Not content with this, one brought me splendid garments, while another filled a basin with scented water and poured it over my hands, and the rest busied themselves with preparing refreshments. After I had eaten and drunk of the most delicate food and rarest wines, the ladies crowded round me and begged me to tell them all my adventures.

By the time I had finished night had fallen, and the ladies lighted up the castle with such a prodigious quantity of tapers that even day could hardly have been brighter. We then sat down to a supper of dried fruits and sweetmeats, after which some sang and others danced. I was so well amused that I did not notice how the time was passing, but at length one of the ladies approached and informed me it was midnight, and that, as I must be tired, she would conduct me to the room that had been prepared for me. Then, bidding me good-night, I was left to sleep.

I spent the next thirty-nine days in much the same way as the first, but at the close of that time the ladies appeared (as was their custom) in my room one morning to enquire how I had slept, and instead of looking cheerful and smiling they were in floods of tears. 'Prince,' said they, 'we must leave you, and never was it so hard to part from any of our friends. Most likely we shall never see you again, but if you have sufficient self-command perhaps we may yet look forward to a meeting.'

'Ladies,' I replied, 'what is the meaning of these strange words – I pray you to tell me?'

'Know then,' answered one of them, 'that we are all princesses – each a king's daughter. We live in this castle together, in the way that you have seen, but at the end of every year secret duties call us away for the space of forty days. The time has now come; but before we depart, we will leave you our keys, so that you may not lack entertainment during our absence. But one thing we would ask of you. The Golden Door, alone, forbear to open, as you value

Agib entertained by the ladies

your own peace, and the happiness of your life. That door once unlocked, we must bid you farewell for ever.'

Weeping, I assured them of my prudence, and after embracing me tenderly, they went their ways.

Every day I opened two or three fresh doors, each of which contained behind it so many curious things that I had no chance of feeling dull, much as I regretted the absence of the ladies. Sometimes it was an orchard, whose fruit far exceeded in bigness any that grew in my father's garden. Sometimes it was a court planted with roses, jessamine, daffodils, hyacinths and anemones, and a thousand other flowers of which I did not know the names. Or again, it would be an aviary, fitted with all kinds of singing birds, or a treasury heaped up with precious stones; but whatever I might see, all was perfect of its own sort.

Thirty-nine days passed away more rapidly than I could have conceived possible, and the following morning the princesses were to return to the castle. But alas! I had explored every corner, save only the room that was shut in by the Golden Door, and I had no longer anything to amuse myself with. I stood before the forbidden

TALES FROM THE ARABIAN NIGHTS

place for some time, gazing at its beauty; then a happy inspiration struck me, that because I unlocked the door it was not necessary that I should enter the chamber. It would be enough for me to stand outside and view whatever hidden wonders might be therein.

Thus arguing against my own conscience, I turned the key, when a smell rushed out that, pleasant though it was, overcame me completely, and I fell fainting across the threshold. Instead of being warned by this accident, directly I came to myself I went for a few moments into the air to shake off the effects of the perfume, and then entered boldly. I found myself in a large, vaulted room, lighted by tapers, scented with aloes and ambergris, standing in golden candlesticks, whilst gold and silver lamps hung from the ceiling.

Though objects of rare workmanship lay heaped around me, I paid them scant attention, so much was I struck by a great black horse which stood in one corner, the handsomest and best-shaped animal I had ever seen. His saddle and bridle were of massive gold, curiously wrought; one side of his trough was filled with clean barley and sesame, and the other with rose water. I led the animal into the open air, and then jumped on his back, shaking the reins as I did so, but as he never stirred, I touched him lightly with a switch I had picked up in his stable. No sooner did he feel the stroke, than he spread his wings (which I had not perceived before), and flew up with me straight into the sky. When he had reached a prodigious height, he next darted back to earth, and alighted on the terrace belonging to a castle, shaking me violently out of the saddle as he did so, and giving me such a blow with his tail, that he knocked out my right eye.

Half-stunned as I was with all that had happened to me, I rose to my feet, thinking as I did so of what had befallen the ten young men, and watching the horse which was soaring into the clouds. I left the terrace and wandered on till I came to a hall, which I knew to have been the one from which the roc had taken me, by the ten blue sofas against the wall.

The ten young men were not present when I first entered, but came in soon after, accompanied by the old man. They greeted me

The black horse leaves Agib on the terrace

kindly, and bewailed my misfortune, though, indeed, they had expected nothing less. 'All that has happened to you,' they said, 'we also have undergone, and we should be enjoying the same happiness still, had we not opened the Golden Door while the princesses were absent. You have been no wiser than we, and have suffered the same punishment. We would gladly receive you among us, to perform such penance as we do, but we have already told you that this is impossible. Depart, therefore, from hence and go to the Court of Bagdad, where you shall meet with him that can decide your destiny.' They told me the way I was to travel, and I left them.

On the road I caused my beard and eyebrows to be shaved, and put on a calender's habit. I have had a long journey, but arrived this evening in the city, where I met my brother calenders at the gate, being strangers like myself. We wondered much at one another, to see we were all blind of the same eye, but we had no leisure to discourse at length of our common calamities. We had only so much time as to come hither to implore those favours which you have been generously pleased to grant us.

He finished, and it was Zobeida's turn to speak: 'Go wherever you please,' she said, addressing all three. 'I pardon you all, but you must depart immediately out of this house.'

The Seven Voyages of
Sindbad the Sailor

In the times of the Caliph Haroun-al-Raschid there lived in Bagdad
a poor porter named Hindbad, who on a very hot day was sent to
carry a heavy load from one end of the city to the other. Before he
had accomplished half the distance he was so tired that, finding
himself in a quiet street where the pavement was sprinkled with
rose water, and a cool breeze was blowing, he set his burden upon
the ground, and sat down to rest in the shade of a grand house.
Very soon he decided that he could not have chosen a pleasanter
place; a delicious perfume of aloes wood and pastilles came from
the open windows and mingled with the scent of the rose water
which steamed up from the hot pavement. Within the palace he
heard some music, as of many instruments cunningly played, and
the melodious warble of nightingales and other birds, and by
this, and the appetising smell of many dainty dishes of which he
presently became aware, he judged that feasting and merry-making
were going on. He wondered who lived in this magnificent house
which he had never seen before, the street in which it stood being
one which he seldom had occasion to pass. To satisfy his curiosity
he went up to some splendidly dressed servants who stood at
the door, and asked one of them the name of the master of the
mansion.

'What,' replied he, 'do you live in Bagdad, and not know that
here lives the noble Sindbad the Sailor, that famous traveller who
sailed over every sea upon which the sun shines?'

The porter, who had often heard people speak of the immense
wealth of Sindbad, could not help feeling envious of one whose lot
seemed to be as happy as his own was miserable. Casting his eyes up
to the sky he exclaimed aloud,

'Consider, Mighty Creator of all things, the differences between

Hindbad curses his fate

Sindbad's life and mine. Every day I suffer a thousand hardships and misfortunes, and have hard work to get even enough bad barley bread to keep myself and my family alive, while the lucky Sindbad spends money right and left and lives upon the fat of the land! What has he done that you should give him this pleasant life – what have I done to deserve so hard a fate?'

So saying he stamped upon the ground like one beside himself with misery and despair. Just at this moment a servant came out of the palace, and taking him by the arm said, 'Come with me, the noble Sindbad, my master, wishes to speak to you.'

Hindbad was not a little surprised at this summons, and feared that his unguarded words might have drawn upon him the displeasure of Sindbad, so he tried to excuse himself upon the pretext that he could not leave the burden which had been entrusted to him in the street. However the lackey promised him that it should be taken care of, and urged him to obey the call so pressingly that at last the porter was obliged to yield.

He followed the servant into a vast room, where a great company was seated round a table covered with all sorts of delicacies. In the place of honour sat a tall, grave man whose long white beard gave him a venerable air. Behind his chair stood a crowd of attendants eager to minister to his wants. This was the famous Sindbad himself. The porter, more than ever alarmed at the sight of so much magnificence, tremblingly saluted the noble company. Sindbad, making a sign to him to approach, caused him to be seated at his right hand, and himself heaped choice morsels upon his plate, and poured out for him a draught of excellent wine, and presently, when the banquet drew to a close, spoke to him familiarly, asking his name and occupation.

'My lord,' replied the porter, 'I am called Hindbad.'

'I am glad to see you here,' continued Sindbad. 'And I will answer for the rest of the company that they are equally pleased, but I wish you to tell me what it was that you said just now in the street.' For Sindbad, passing by the open window before the feast began, had heard his complaint and therefore had sent for him.

At this question Hindbad was covered with confusion, and hanging down his head, replied, 'My lord, I confess that, overcome by weariness and ill-humour, I uttered indiscreet words, which I pray you to pardon me.'

'Oh!' replied Sindbad, 'do not imagine that I am so unjust as to blame you. On the contrary, I understand your situation and can pity you. Only you appear to be mistaken about me, and I wish to set you right. You doubtless imagine that I have acquired all the wealth and luxury that you see me enjoy without difficulty or danger, but this is far indeed from being the case. I have only reached this happy state after having for years suffered every possible kind of toil and danger.

'Yes, my noble friends,' he continued, addressing the company, 'I assure you that my adventures have been strange enough to deter even the most avaricious men from seeking wealth by traversing the seas. Since you have, perhaps, heard but confused accounts of my seven voyages, and the dangers and wonders that I have met with by sea and land, I will now give you a full and true account of them, which I think you will be well pleased to hear.'

As Sindbad was relating his adventures chiefly on account of the porter, he ordered, before beginning his tale, that the burden which had been left in the street should be carried by some of his own servants to the place for which Hindbad had set out at first, while he remained to listen to the story.

The First Voyage of Sindbad

I had inherited considerable wealth from my parents, and being young and foolish I at first squandered it recklessly upon every kind of pleasure, but presently, finding that riches speedily take to themselves wings if managed as badly as I was managing mine, and remembering also that to be old and poor is misery indeed, I began to bethink me of how I could make the best of what still remained to me. I sold all my household goods by public auction, and joined a company of merchants who traded by sea, embarking with them at Balsora in a ship which we had fitted out between us.

We set sail and took our course towards the East Indies by the Persian Gulf, having the coast of Persia upon our left hand and upon our right the shores of Arabia Felix. I was at first much troubled by the uneasy motion of the vessel, but speedily recovered my health, and since that hour have been no more plagued by seasickness.

From time to time we landed at various islands, where we sold or exchanged our merchandise, and one day, when the wind dropped suddenly, we found ourselves becalmed close to a small island like a green meadow, which only rose slightly above the surface of the water. Our sails were furled, and the captain gave permission to all who wished to land for a while and amuse themselves. I was among the number, but when after strolling about for some time we lighted a fire and sat down to enjoy the repast which we had brought with us, we were startled by a sudden and violent trembling of the island, while at the same moment those left upon the ship set up an outcry bidding us come on board for our lives, since what we had taken for an island was nothing but the back of a sleeping whale. Those who were nearest to the boat threw themselves into it, others sprang into the sea, but before I could save myself the whale plunged suddenly into the depths of the ocean, leaving me clinging to a piece of the wood which we had brought to make our fire. Meanwhile a breeze had sprung up, and in the confusion that ensued on board our vessel in hoisting the sails and taking up those who were in the boat and clinging to its sides, no one missed me and I was left at the mercy of the waves. All that day I floated up and down, now beaten this way, now that, and when night fell I despaired for my life; but, weary and spent as I was, I clung to my frail support, and great was my joy when the morning light showed me that I had drifted against an island.

The cliffs were high and steep, but luckily for me some tree-roots protruded in places, and by their aid I climbed up at last, and stretched myself upon the turf at the top, where I lay, more dead than alive, till the sun was high in the heavens. By that time I was very hungry, but after some searching I came upon some eatable herbs, and a spring of clear water, and much refreshed I set out to explore the island. Presently I reached a great plain where a grazing horse was tethered, and as I stood looking at it I heard voices talking apparently underground, and in a moment a man appeared who asked me how I came upon the island. I told him my adventures, and heard in return that he was one of the grooms of Mihrage, the king of the island, and that each year they came to feed their master's horses in this plain. He took me to a cave where his companions were assembled, and when I had eaten of the food they set before me, they bade me think myself fortunate to have come upon them when I did, since they were going back to their master on the morrow, and without their aid I could certainly never have found my way to the inhabited part of the island.

Early the next morning we accordingly set out, and when we reached the capital I was graciously received by the king, to whom I related my adventures, upon which he ordered that I should be well cared for and provided with such things as I needed. Being a merchant I sought out men of my own profession, and particularly those who came from foreign countries, as I hoped in this way to hear news from Bagdad, and find out some means of returning thither, for the capital was situated upon the seashore, and visited by vessels from all parts of the world. In the meantime I heard many curious things, and answered many questions concerning my own country, for I talked willingly with all who came to me. Also to while away the time of waiting I explored a little island named Cassel, which belonged to King Mihrage, and which was supposed to be inhabited by a spirit named Deggial. Indeed, the sailors assured me that often at night the playing of timbals could be heard upon it. However, I saw nothing strange upon my voyage, saving some fish that were full two hundred cubits long, but were fortunately more in dread of us than even we were of them, and fled from us if we did but strike upon a board to frighten them. Other fishes there were only a cubit long which had heads like owls.

One day after my return, as I went down to the quay, I saw a ship which had just cast anchor, and was discharging her cargo, while the merchants to whom it belonged were busily directing the removal of it to their warehouses. Drawing nearer I presently noticed that my own name was marked upon some of the packages, and after having carefully examined them, I felt sure that they were indeed those which I had put on board our ship at Balsora. I then recognised the captain of the vessel, but as I was certain that he believed me to be dead, I went up to him and asked who owned the packages that I was looking at.

'There was on board my ship,' he replied, 'a merchant of Bagdad named Sindbad. One day he and several of my other passengers landed upon what we supposed to be an island, but which was really an enormous whale floating asleep upon the waves. No sooner did it feel upon its back the heat of the fire which had been kindled, than it plunged into the depths of the sea. Several of the people who were upon it perished in the waters, and among others this unlucky Sindbad. This merchandise is his, but I have resolved to dispose of it for the benefit of his family if I should ever chance to meet with them.'

'Captain,' said I, 'I am that Sindbad whom you believe to be dead, and these are my possessions!'

When the captain heard these words he cried out in amazement, 'Lackaday! and what is the world coming to? In these days there is not an honest man to be met with. Did I not with my own eyes see

Sindbad drown, and now you have the audacity to tell me that you are he! I should have taken you to be a just man, and yet for the sake of obtaining that which does not belong to you, you are ready to invent this horrible falsehood.'

'Have patience, and do me the favour to hear my story,' said I.

'Speak then,' replied the captain, 'I'm all attention.'

So I told him of my escape and of my fortunate meeting with the king's grooms, and how kindly I had been received at the palace. Very soon I began to see that I had made some impression upon him, and after the arrival of some of the other merchants, who showed great joy at once more seeing me alive, he declared that he also recognised me.

Throwing himself upon my neck he exclaimed, 'Heaven be praised that you have escaped from so great a danger. As to your goods, I pray you take them, and dispose of them as you please.' I thanked him, and praised his honesty, begging him to accept several bales of merchandise in token of my gratitude, but he would take nothing. Of the choicest of my goods I prepared a present for King Mihrage, who was at first amazed, having known that I had lost my all. However, when I had explained to him how my bales had been miraculously restored to me, he graciously accepted my gifts, and in return gave me many valuable things. I then took leave of him, and exchanging my merchandise for sandal and aloes wood, camphor, nutmegs, cloves, pepper, and ginger, I embarked upon the same vessel and traded so successfully upon our homeward voyage that I arrived in Balsora with about one hundred thousand sequins. My family received me with as much joy as I felt upon seeing them once more. I bought land and slaves, and built a great house in which I resolved to live happily, and in the enjoyment of all the pleasures of life to forget my past sufferings.

Here Sindbad paused, and commanded the musicians to play again, while the feasting continued until evening. When the time came for the porter to depart, Sindbad gave him a purse containing one hundred sequins, saying, 'Take this, Hindbad, and go home, but tomorrow come again and you shall hear more of my adventures.'

The porter retired quite overcome by so much generosity, and you may imagine that he was well received at home, where his wife and children thanked their lucky stars that he had found such a benefactor.

The next day Hindbad, dressed in his best, returned to the voyager's house, and was received with open arms. As soon as all the guests had arrived the banquet began as before, and when they had feasted long and merrily, Sindbad addressed them thus: 'My friends, I beg that you will give me your attention while I relate the adventures of my second voyage, which you will find even more astonishing than the first.'

The Second Voyage of Sindbad

I had resolved, as you know, on my return from my first voyage, to spend the rest of my days quietly in Bagdad, but very soon I grew tired of such an idle life and longed once more to find myself upon the sea.

I procured, therefore, such goods as were suitable for the places I intended to visit, and embarked for the second time in a good ship with other merchants whom I knew to be honourable men. We went from island to island, often making excellent bargains, until one day we landed at a spot which, though covered with fruit trees and abounding in springs of excellent water, appeared to possess neither houses nor people. While my companions wandered here and there gathering flowers and fruit I sat down in a shady place, and, having heartily enjoyed the provisions and the wine I had brought with me, I fell asleep, lulled by the murmur of a clear brook which flowed close by.

How long I slept I know not, but when I opened my eyes and started to my feet I perceived with horror that I was alone and that the ship was gone. I rushed to and fro like one distracted, uttering cries of despair, and when from the shore I saw the vessel under full sail just disappearing upon the horizon, I wished bitterly enough that I had been content to stay at home in safety. But since wishes could do me no good, I presently took courage and looked about me for a means of escape. When I had climbed a tall tree I first of all directed my anxious glances towards the sea; but, finding nothing hopeful there, I turned landward, and my curiosity was excited by a huge dazzling white object, so far off that I could not make out what it might be.

Descending from the tree I hastily collected what remained of my provisions and set off as fast as I could go towards it. As I drew near it seemed to me to be a white ball of immense size and height,

THE SECOND VOYAGE OF SINDBAD

and when I could touch it, I found it marvellously smooth and soft. As it was impossible to climb it – for it presented no foothold – I walked round about it seeking some opening, but there was none. I counted, however, that it was at least fifty paces round. By this time the sun was near setting, but quite suddenly it fell dark, something like a huge black cloud came swiftly over me, and I saw with amazement that it was a bird of extraordinary size which was hovering near. Then I remembered that I had often heard the sailors speak of a wonderful bird called a roc, and it occurred to me that the white object which had so puzzled me must be its egg.

Sure enough the bird settled slowly down upon it, covering it with its wings to keep it warm, and I cowered close beside the egg in such a position that one of the bird's feet, which was as large as the trunk of a tree, was just in front of me. Taking off my turban I bound myself securely to it with the linen in the hope that the roc, when it took flight next morning, would bear me away with it from the desolate island. And this was precisely what did happen. As soon as the dawn appeared the bird rose into the air carrying me up and up till I could no longer see the earth, and then suddenly it descended so swiftly that I almost lost consciousness. When I became aware that the roc had settled and that I was once again upon solid ground, I hastily unbound my turban from its foot and freed myself, and that not a moment too soon; for the bird, pouncing upon a huge snake, killed it with a few blows from its powerful beak, and seizing it up rose into the air once more and soon disappeared from my view. When I had looked about me I began to doubt if I had gained anything by quitting the desolate island.

The valley in which I found myself was deep and narrow, and surrounded by mountains which towered into the clouds, and were so steep and rocky that there was no way of climbing up their sides. As I wandered about, seeking anxiously for some means of escaping from this trap, I observed that the ground was strewed with diamonds, some of them of an astonishing size. This sight gave me great pleasure, but my delight was speedily damped when I saw also numbers of horrible snakes so long and so large that the smallest of them could have swallowed an elephant with ease. Fortunately for me they seemed to hide in caverns of the rocks by day, and only came out by night, probably because of their enemy the roc.

All day long I wandered up and down the valley, and when it grew dusk I crept into a little cave, and having blocked up the entrance to it with a stone, I ate part of my little store of food and lay down to sleep, but all through the night the serpents crawled to and fro, hissing horribly, so that I could scarcely close my eyes for terror. I was thankful when the morning light appeared, and when I judged by the silence that the serpents had retreated to their dens I came tremblingly out of my cave and wandered up and down the valley once more, kicking the diamonds contemptuously out of my path, for I felt that they were indeed vain things to a man in my situation. At last, overcome with weariness, I sat down upon a rock, but I had hardly closed my eyes when I was startled by something which fell to the ground with a thud close beside me.

It was a huge piece of fresh meat, and as I stared at it several more pieces rolled over the cliffs in different places. I had always thought that the stories the sailors told of the famous valley of diamonds, and of the cunning way which some merchants had devised for getting at the precious stones, were mere travellers' tales invented to give pleasure to the hearers, but now I perceived that they were surely true. These merchants came to the valley at the time when the eagles, which keep their eyries in the rocks, had hatched their young. The merchants then threw great lumps of meat into the valley. These, falling with so much force upon the diamonds, were sure to take up some of the precious stones with them, when the eagles pounced upon the meat and carried it off to their nests to feed their hungry broods. Then the merchants, scaring away the parent birds with shouts and outcries, would secure their treasures. Until this moment I had looked upon the valley as my grave, for I had seen no possibility of getting out of it alive, but now I took courage and began to devise a means of escape. I began by picking up all the largest diamonds I could find and storing them carefully in the leathern wallet which had held my provisions; this I tied

Sindbad carried off by the roc

securely to my belt. I then chose the piece of meat which seemed most suited to my purpose, and with the aid of my turban bound it firmly to my back; this done I laid down upon my face and awaited the coming of the eagles. I soon heard the flapping of their mighty wings above me, and had the satisfaction of feeling one of them seize upon my piece of meat, and me with it, and rise slowly towards his nest, into which he presently dropped me. Luckily for me the merchants were on the watch, and setting up their usual outcries they rushed to the nest scaring away the eagle. Their amazement was great when they discovered me, and also their disappointment, and with one accord they fell to abusing me for having robbed them of their usual profit. Addressing myself to the one who seemed most aggrieved, I said: 'I am sure, if you knew all that I have suffered, you would show more kindness towards me, and as for diamonds, I have enough here of the very best for you and me and all your company.' So saying I showed them to him. The others all crowded round me, wondering at my adventures and admiring the device by which I had escaped from the valley, and when they had led me to their camp and examined my diamonds, they assured me that in all the years that they had carried on their trade they had seen no stones to be compared with them for size and beauty.

I found that each merchant chose a particular nest, and took his chance of what he might find in it. So I begged the one who owned the nest to which I had been carried to take as much as he would of my treasure, but he contented himself with one stone, and that by no means the largest, assuring me that with such a gem his fortune was made, and he need toil no more. I stayed with the merchants several days, and then as they were journeying homewards I gladly accompanied them. Our way lay across high mountains infested with frightful serpents, but we had the good luck to escape them and came at last to the seashore. Thence we sailed to the isle of Rohat where the camphor trees grow to such a size that a hundred men could shelter under one of them with ease. The sap flows from an incision made high up in the tree into a vessel hung there to receive it, and soon hardens into the substance called camphor, but the tree itself withers up and dies when it has been so treated.

Sindbad in the valley of serpents

In this same island we saw the rhinoceros, an animal which is smaller than the elephant and larger than the buffalo. It has one horn about a cubit long which is solid, but has a furrow from the base to the tip. Upon it is traced in white lines the figure of a man. The rhinoceros fights with the elephant, and transfixing him with his horn carries him off upon his head, but becoming blinded with the blood of his enemy, he falls helpless to the ground, and then comes the roc, and clutches them both up in his talons and takes them to feed his young. This doubtless astonishes you, but if you do not believe my tale go to Rohat and see for yourself. For fear of wearying you I pass over in silence many other wonderful things which we saw in this island. Before we left I exchanged one of my diamonds for much goodly merchandise by which I profited greatly on our homeward way. At last we reached Balsora, whence I hastened to Bagdad, where my first action was to bestow large sums of money upon the poor, after which I settled down to enjoy tranquilly the riches I had gained with so much toil and pain.

Having thus related the adventures of his second voyage, Sindbad again bestowed a hundred sequins upon Hindbad, inviting him to come again on the following day and hear how he fared upon his third voyage. The other guests also departed to their homes, but all returned at the same hour next day, including the porter, whose former life of hard work and poverty had already begun to seem to him like a bad dream. Again after the feast was over did Sindbad claim the attention of his guests and began the account of his third voyage.

The Third Voyage of Sindbad

After a very short time the pleasant easy life I led made me quite forget the perils of my two voyages. Moreover, as I was still in the prime of life, it pleased me better to be up and doing. So once more providing myself with the rarest and choicest merchandise of Bagdad, I conveyed it to Balsora, and set sail with other merchants of my acquaintance for distant lands. We had touched at many ports and made much profit, when one day upon the open sea we were caught by a terrible wind which blew us completely out of our reckoning, and lasting for several days finally drove us into harbour on a strange island.

'I would rather have come to anchor anywhere than here,' quoth our captain. 'This island and all adjoining it are inhabited by hairy savages, who are certain to attack us, and whatever these dwarfs may do we dare not resist, since they swarm like locusts, and if one of them is killed the rest will fall upon us, and speedily make an end of us.'

These words caused great consternation among all the ship's company, and only too soon we were to find out that the captain spoke truly. There appeared a vast multitude of hideous savages, not more than two feet high and covered with reddish fur. Throwing themselves into the waves they surrounded our vessel. Chattering meanwhile in a language we could not understand, and clutching at ropes and gangways, they swarmed up the ship's side with such speed and agility that they almost seemed to fly.

You may imagine the rage and terror that seized us as we watched them, neither daring to hinder them nor able to speak a word to deter them from their purpose, whatever it might be. Of this we were not left long in doubt. Hoisting the sails, and cutting the cable of the anchor, they sailed our vessel to an island which lay a little further off, where they drove us ashore; then taking possession of her, they made off to the place from which they had come, leaving us helpless upon a shore avoided with horror by all mariners for a reason which you will soon learn.

Turning away from the sea we wandered miserably inland, finding as we went various herbs and fruits which we ate, feeling that we might as well live as long as possible though we had no hope of escape. Presently we saw in the far distance what seemed to us to be a splendid palace, towards which we turned our weary steps, but when we reached it we saw that it was a castle, lofty, and strongly built. Pushing back the heavy ebony doors we entered the court-yard, but upon the threshold of the great hall beyond it we paused, frozen with horror, at the sight which greeted us. On one side lay a huge pile of bones – human bones, and on the other numberless spits for roasting! Overcome with despair we sank trembling to the ground, and lay there without speech or motion. The sun was setting when a loud noise aroused us, the door of the hall was violently burst open and a horrible giant entered. He was as tall as a palm tree, and perfectly black, and had one eye, which flamed like a burning coal in the middle of his forehead. His teeth were long and sharp and grinned horribly, while his lower lip hung down upon his chest, and he had ears like elephant's ears, which covered his shoulders, and nails like the claws of some fierce bird.

At this terrible sight our senses left us and we lay like dead men. When at last we came to ourselves the giant sat examining us attentively with his fearful eye. Presently when he had looked at us enough he came towards us, and stretching out his hand took me by the back of the neck, turning me this way and that, but feeling that I was mere skin and bone he set me down again and went on to the next, whom he treated in the same fashion; at last he came to the captain, and finding him the fattest of us all, he took him up in one hand and stuck him upon a spit and proceeded to kindle a huge fire at which he presently roasted him. After the giant had supped he lay down to sleep, snoring like the loudest thunder, while we lay shivering with horror the whole night through, and when day broke he awoke and went out, leaving us in the castle.

When we believed him to be really gone we started up bemoaning our horrible fate, until the hall echoed with our despairing cries.

The giant enters

Though we were many and our enemy was alone it did not occur to us to kill him, and indeed we should have found that a hard task, even if we had thought of it, and no plan could we devise to deliver ourselves. So at last, submitting to our sad fate, we spent the day in wandering up and down the island eating such fruits as we could find, and when night came we returned to the castle, having sought in vain for any other place of shelter. At sunset the giant returned, supped upon one of our unhappy comrades, slept and snored till dawn, and then left us as before. Our condition seemed to us so frightful that several of my companions thought it would be better to leap from the cliffs and perish in the waves at once, rather than await so miserable an end; but I had a plan of escape which I now unfolded to them, and which they at once agreed to attempt.

'Listen, my brothers,' I added. 'You know that plenty of drift-wood lies along the shore. Let us make several rafts, and carry them to a suitable place. If our plot succeeds, we can wait patiently for the chance of some passing ship which would rescue us from this fatal island. If it fails, we must quickly take to our rafts; frail as they are, we have more chance of saving our lives with them than we have if we remain here.'

All agreed with me, and we spent the day in building rafts, each capable of carrying three persons. At nightfall we returned to the castle, and very soon in came the giant, and one more of our number was sacrificed. But the time of our vengeance was at hand! As soon as he had finished his horrible repast he lay down to sleep as before, and when we heard him begin to snore I, and nine of the boldest of my comrades, rose softly, and took each a spit, which we made red-hot in the fire, and then at a given signal we plunged it with one accord into the giant's eye, completely blinding him. Uttering a terrible cry, he sprang to his feet clutching in all directions to try to seize one of us, but we had all fled different ways as soon as the deed was done, and thrown ourselves flat upon the ground in corners where he was not likely to touch us with his feet.

After a vain search he fumbled about till he found the door, and fled out of it howling frightfully. As for us, when he was gone we made haste to leave the fatal castle, and, stationing ourselves beside

The giants hurl rocks at Sindbad and his companions

our rafts, we waited to see what would happen. Our idea was that if, when the sun rose, we saw nothing of the giant, and no longer heard his howls, which still came faintly through the darkness, growing more and more distant, we should conclude that he was dead, and that we might safely stay upon the island and need not risk our lives upon the frail rafts. But alas! morning light showed us our enemy approaching us, supported on either hand by two giants nearly as large and fearful as himself, while a crowd of others followed close upon their heels. Hesitating no longer we clambered upon our rafts and rowed with all our might out to sea. The giants, seeing their prey escaping them, seized up huge pieces of rock, and wading into the water hurled them after us with such good aim that all the rafts except the one I was upon were swamped, and their luckless crews drowned, without our being able to do anything to help them. Indeed I and my two companions had all we could do to keep our own raft beyond the reach of the giants, but by dint of hard rowing we at last gained the open sea. Here we were at the mercy of the winds and waves, which tossed us to and fro all that day and night, but the next morning we found ourselves near an island, upon which we gladly landed.

There we found delicious fruits, and having satisfied our hunger we presently lay down to rest upon the shore. Suddenly we were aroused by a loud rustling noise, and starting up, saw that it was caused by an immense snake which was gliding towards us over the sand. So swiftly it came that it had seized one of my comrades before he had time to fly, and in spite of his cries and struggles speedily crushed the life out of him in its mighty coils and proceeded to swallow him. By this time my other companion and I were running for our lives to some place where we might hope to be safe from this new horror, and seeing a tall tree we climbed up into it, having first provided ourselves with a store of fruit off the surrounding bushes. When night came I fell asleep, but only to be awakened once more by the terrible snake, which after hissing horribly round the tree at last reared itself up against it, and finding my sleeping comrade who was perched just below me, it swallowed him also, and crawled away leaving me half dead with terror.

When the sun rose I crept down from the tree with hardly a hope of escaping the dreadful fate which had overtaken my comrades; but life is sweet, and I determined to do all I could to save myself. All day long I toiled with frantic haste and collected quantities of dry brushwood, reeds and thorns, which I bound with faggots, and making a circle of them under my tree I piled them firmly one upon another until I had a kind of tent in which I crouched like a mouse in a hole when she sees the cat coming. You may imagine what a fearful night I passed, for the snake returned eager to devour me, and glided round and round my frail shelter seeking an entrance. Every moment I feared that it would succeed in pushing aside some of the faggots, but happily for me they held together, and when it grew light my enemy retired, baffled and hungry, to his den. As for me I was more dead than alive! Shaking with fright and half suffocated by the poisonous breath of the monster, I came out of my tent and crawled down to the sea, feeling that it would be better to plunge from the cliffs and end my life at once than pass such another night of horror. But to my joy and relief I saw a ship sailing by, and by shouting wildly and waving my turban I managed to attract the attention of her crew.

A boat was sent to rescue me, and very soon I found myself on board surrounded by a wondering crowd of sailors and merchants eager to know by what chance I found myself in that desolate island. After I had told my story they regaled me with the choicest food the ship afforded, and the captain, seeing that I was in rags, generously bestowed upon me one of his own coats. After sailing about for some time and touching at many ports we came at last to the island of Salahat, where sandal wood grows in great abundance. Here we anchored, and as I stood watching the merchants disembarking their goods and preparing to sell or exchange them, the captain came up to me and said,

'I have here, brother, some merchandise belonging to a passenger of mine who is dead. Will you do me the favour to trade with it, and when I meet with his heirs I shall be able to give them the money, though it will be only just that you shall have a portion for your trouble.'

I consented gladly, for I did not like standing by idle. Whereupon he pointed the bales out to me, and sent for the person whose duty it was to keep a list of the goods that were upon the ship. When this man came he asked in what name the merchandise was to be registered.

'In the name of Sindbad the Sailor,' replied the captain.

At this I was greatly surprised, but looking carefully at him I recognised him to be the captain of the ship upon which I had made my second voyage, though he had altered much since that time. As for him, believing me to be dead it was no wonder that he had not recognised me.

'So, captain,' said I, 'the merchant who owned those bales was called Sindbad?'

'Yes,' he replied. 'He was so named. He belonged to Bagdad, and joined my ship at Balsora, but by mischance he was left behind upon a desert island where we had landed to fill up our water-casks, and it was not until four hours later that he was missed. By that time the wind had freshened, and it was impossible to put back for him.'

'You suppose him to have perished then?' said I.

'Alas! yes,' he answered.

'Why, captain!' I cried, 'look well at me. I am that Sindbad who fell asleep upon the island and awoke to find himself abandoned!'

The captain stared at me in amazement, but was presently convinced that I was indeed speaking the truth, and rejoiced greatly at my escape.

'I am glad to have that piece of carelessness off my conscience at any rate,' said he. 'Now take your goods, and the profit I have made for you upon them, and may you prosper in future.'

I took them gratefully, and as we went from one island to another I laid in stores of cloves, cinnamon, and other spices. In one place I saw a tortoise which was twenty cubits long and as many broad, also a fish that was like a cow and had skin so thick that it was used to make shields. Another I saw that was like a camel in shape and colour. So by degrees we came back to Balsora, and I returned to Bagdad with so much money that I could not myself count it, besides treasures without end. I gave largely to the poor, and bought much land to add to what I already possessed, and thus ended my third voyage.

When Sindbad had finished his story he gave another hundred sequins to Hindbad, who then departed with the other guests, but next day when they had all reassembled, and the banquet was ended, their host continued his adventures.

The Fourth Voyage of Sindbad

Rich and happy as I was after my third voyage, I could not make up my mind to stay at home altogether. My love of trading, and the pleasure I took in anything that was new and strange, made me set my affairs in order, and begin my journey through some of the Persian provinces, having first sent off stores of goods to await my coming in the different places I intended to visit. I took ship at a distant seaport, and for some time all went well, but at last, being caught in a violent hurricane, our vessel became a total wreck in spite of all our worthy captain could do to save her, and many of our company perished in the waves. I, with a few others, had the good fortune to be washed ashore clinging to pieces of the wreck, for the storm had driven us near an island, and scrambling up beyond the reach of the waves we threw ourselves down quite exhausted, to wait for morning.

At daylight we wandered inland, and soon saw some huts, to which we directed our steps. As we drew near their black inhabitants swarmed out in great numbers and surrounded us, and we were led to their houses, and as it were divided among our captors. I with five others was taken into a hut, where we were made to sit upon the ground, and certain herbs were given to us, which the blacks made signs to us to eat. Observing that they themselves did not touch them, I was careful only to pretend to taste my portion; but my companions, being very hungry, rashly ate up all that was set before them, and very soon I had the horror of seeing them become perfectly mad. Though they chattered incessantly I could not understand a word they said, nor did they heed when I spoke to them. The savages now produced large bowls full of rice prepared with coconut oil, of which my crazy comrades ate eagerly, but I only tasted a few grains, understanding clearly that the object of our captors was to fatten us speedily for their own eating, and this was exactly what happened. My unlucky companions having lost their reason, felt neither anxiety nor fear, and ate greedily all that was offered them. So they were soon fat and there was an end of them, but I grew leaner day by day, for I ate but little, and even that little did me no good by reason of my fear of what lay before me. However, as I was so far from being a tempting morsel, I was allowed to wander about freely, and one day, when all the blacks had gone off upon some expedition leaving only an old man to guard me, I managed to escape from him and plunged into the forest, running faster the more he cried to me to come back, until I had completely distanced him.

For seven days I hurried on, resting only when the darkness stopped me, and living chiefly upon coconuts, which afforded me both meat and drink, and on the eighth day I reached the seashore and saw a party of white men gathering pepper, which grew abundantly all about. Reassured by the nature of their occupation, I advanced towards them and they greeted me in Arabic, asking who I was and whence I came. My delight was great on hearing this familiar speech, and I willingly satisfied their curiosity, telling them how I had been shipwrecked, and captured by the blacks. 'But these savages devour men!' said they. 'How did you escape?' I repeated to them what I have just told you, at which they were mightily astonished. I stayed with them until they had collected as much pepper as they wished, and then they took me back to their own country and presented me to their king, by whom I was hospitably received. To him also I had to relate my adventures, which surprised him much, and when I had finished he ordered that I should be supplied with food and raiment and treated with consideration.

The island on which I found myself was full of people, and abounded in all sorts of desirable things, and a great deal of traffic went on in the capital, where I soon began to feel at home and contented. Moreover, the king treated me with special favour, and in consequence of this everyone, whether at the court or in the town, sought to make life pleasant to me. One thing I remarked which I thought very strange; this was that, from the greatest to the least, all men rode their horses without bridle or stirrups. I one day presumed to ask his majesty why he did not use them, to which he replied, 'You speak to me of things of which I have never before heard!' This gave me an idea. I found a clever workman, and made him cut out under my direction the foundation of a saddle, which I wadded and covered with choice leather, adorning it with rich gold embroidery. I then got a locksmith to make me a bit and a pair of spurs after a pattern that I drew for him, and when all these things were completed I presented them to the king and showed him how to use them. When I had saddled one of his horses he mounted it and rode about quite delighted with the novelty, and to show his gratitude he rewarded me with large gifts. After this I had to make saddles for all the principal officers of the king's household, and as they all gave me rich presents I soon became very wealthy and quite an important person in the city.

One day the king sent for me and said, 'Sindbad, I am going to ask a favour of you. Both I and my subjects esteem you, and wish you to end your days amongst us. Therefore I desire that you will marry a rich and beautiful lady whom I will find for you, and think no more of your own country.'

As the king's will was law I accepted the charming bride he presented to me, and lived happily with her. Nevertheless I had every intention of escaping at the first opportunity, and going back to Bagdad. Things were thus going prosperously with me when it happened that the wife of one of my neighbours, with whom I had struck up quite a friendship, fell ill, and presently died. I went to his house to offer my consolations, and found him in the depths of woe.

'Heaven preserve you,' said I, 'and send you a long life!'

'Alas!' he replied, 'what is the good of saying that when I have but an hour left to live!'

'Come, come!' said I, 'surely it is not so bad as all that. I trust that you may be spared to me for many years.'

'I hope,' answered he, 'that your life may be long, but as for me, all is finished. I have set my house in order, and today I shall be buried with my wife. This has been the law upon our island from the earliest ages – the living husband goes to the grave with his dead wife, the living wife with her dead husband. So did our fathers, and so must we do. The law changes not, and all must submit to it!'

As he spoke the friends and relations of the unhappy pair began to assemble. The body, decked in rich robes and sparkling with jewels, was laid upon an open bier, and the procession started, taking its way to a high mountain at some distance from the city, the wretched husband, clothed from head to foot in a black mantle, following mournfully.

When the place of interment was reached the corpse was lowered, just as it was, into a deep pit. Then the husband, bidding farewell to all his friends, stretched himself upon another bier, upon which were laid seven little loaves of bread and a pitcher of water, and he also was let down-down-down to the depths of the horrible cavern, and then a stone was laid over the opening, and the melancholy company wended its way back to the city.

You may imagine that I was no unmoved spectator of these proceedings; to all the others it was a thing to which they had been accustomed from their youth up; but I was so horrified that I could not help telling the king how it struck me.

'Sire,' I said, 'I am more astonished than I can express to you at the strange custom which exists in your dominions of burying the living with the dead. In all my travels I have never before met with so cruel and horrible a law.'

'What would you have, Sindbad?' he replied. 'It is the law for everybody. I myself should be buried with the queen if she were the first to die.'

'But, your majesty,' said I, 'dare I ask if this law applies to foreigners also?'

'Why, yes,' replied the king smiling, in what I could but consider a very heartless manner, 'they are no exception to the rule if they have married in the country.'

When I heard this I went home much cast down, and from that time forward my mind was never easy. If only my wife's little finger ached I fancied she was going to die, and sure enough before very long she fell really ill and in a few days breathed her last. My dismay was great, for it seemed to me that to be buried alive was even a worse fate than to be devoured by cannibals, nevertheless there was no escape. The body of my wife, arrayed in her richest robes and decked with all her jewels, was laid upon the bier. I followed it, and after me came a great procession, headed by the king and all his nobles, and in this order we reached the fatal mountain, which was one of a lofty chain bordering the sea.

Here I made one more frantic effort to excite the pity of the king and those who stood by, hoping to save myself even at this last moment, but it was of no avail. No one spoke to me, they even appeared to hasten over their dreadful task, and I speedily found myself descending into the gloomy pit, with my seven loaves and pitcher of water beside me. Almost before I reached the bottom the stone was rolled into its place above my head, and I was left to my fate. A feeble ray of light shone into the cavern through some chink, and when I had the courage to look about me I could see that I was in a vast vault, bestrewn with bones and bodies of the dead. I even fancied that I heard the expiring sighs of those who, like myself, had come into this dismal place alive. All in vain did I shriek aloud with rage and despair, reproaching myself for the love of gain and adventure which had brought me to such a pass, but at length, growing calmer, I took up my bread and water, and wrapping my face in my mantle I groped my way towards the end of the cavern, where the air was fresher.

Here I lived in darkness and misery until my provisions were exhausted, but just as I was nearly dead from starvation the rock was rolled away overhead and I saw that a bier was being lowered into the cavern, and that the corpse upon it was a man. In a moment my mind was made up, the woman who followed had nothing to expect but a lingering death; I should be doing her a service if I shortened her misery. Therefore when she descended, already insensible from terror, I was ready armed with a huge bone, one blow from which left her dead, and I secured the bread and water which gave me a hope of life. Several times did I have recourse to this desperate expedient, and I know not how long I had been a prisoner when one day I fancied that I heard something near me, which breathed

Sindbad lowered into the cavern

loudly. Turning to the place from which the sound came I dimly saw a shadowy form which fled at my movement, squeezing itself through a cranny in the wall. I pursued it as fast as I could, and found myself in a narrow crack among the rocks, along which I was just able to force my way. I followed it for what seemed to me many miles, and at last saw before me a glimmer of light which grew clearer every moment until I emerged upon the sea shore with a joy which I cannot describe. When I was sure that I was not dreaming, I realised that it was doubtless some little animal which had found its way into the cavern from the sea, and when disturbed had fled, showing me a means of escape which I could never have discovered for myself. I hastily surveyed my surroundings, and saw that I was safe from all pursuit from the town.

The mountains sloped sheer down to the sea, and there was no road across them. Being assured of this I returned to the cavern, and amassed a rich treasure of diamonds, rubies, emeralds, and jewels of all kinds which strewed the ground. These I made up into bales, and stored them into a safe place upon the beach, and then waited hopefully for the passing of a ship. I had looked out for two days, however, before a single sail appeared, so it was with much delight that I at last saw a vessel not very far from the shore, and by waving my arms and uttering loud cries succeeded in attracting the attention of her crew. A boat was sent off to me, and in answer to the questions of the sailors as to how I came to be in such a plight, I replied that I had been shipwrecked two days before, but had managed to scramble ashore with the bales which I pointed out to them. Luckily for me they believed my story, and without even looking at the place where they found me, took up my bundles, and rowed me back to the ship. Once on board, I soon saw that the captain was too much occupied with the difficulties of navigation to pay much heed to me, though he generously made me welcome, and would not even accept the jewels with which I offered to pay my passage. Our voyage was prosperous, and after visiting many lands, and collecting in each place great store of goodly merchandise, I found myself at last in Bagdad once more with unheard-of riches of every description. Again I gave large sums of money to the poor, and enriched all the mosques in the city, after which I gave myself up to my friends and relations, with whom I passed my time in feasting and merriment.

Here Sindbad paused, and all his hearers declared that the adventures of his fourth voyage had pleased them better than anything they had heard before. They then took their leave, followed by Hindbad, who had once more received a hundred sequins, and with the rest had been bidden to return next day for the story of the fifth voyage.

When the time came all were in their places, and when they had eaten and drunk of all that was set before them Sindbad began his tale.

The Fifth Voyage of Sindbad

Not even all that I had gone through could make me contented with a quiet life. I soon wearied of its pleasures, and longed for change and adventure. Therefore I set out once more, but this time in a ship of my own, which I built and fitted out at the nearest seaport. I wished to be able to call at whatever port I chose, taking my own time; but as I did not intend carrying enough goods for a full cargo, I invited several merchants of different nations to join me. We set sail with the first favourable wind, and after a long voyage upon the open seas we landed upon an unknown island which proved to be uninhabited. We determined, however, to explore it, but had not gone far when we found a roc's egg, as large as the one I had seen before and evidently very nearly hatched, for the beak of the young bird had already pierced the shell. In spite of all I could say to deter them, the merchants who were with me fell upon it with their hatchets, breaking the shell, and killing the young roc. Then lighting a fire upon the ground they hacked morsels from the bird, and proceeded to roast them while I stood by aghast.

Scarcely had they finished their ill-omened repast, when the air above us was darkened by two mighty shadows. The captain of my ship, knowing by experience what this meant, cried out to us that the parent birds were coming, and urged us to get on board with all speed. This we did, and the sails were hoisted, but before we had made any way the rocs reached their despoiled nest and hovered about it, uttering frightful cries when they discovered the mangled remains of their young one. For a moment we lost sight of them, and were flattering ourselves that we had escaped, when they reappeared and soared into the air directly over our vessel, and we saw that each held in its claws an immense rock ready to crush us. There was a moment of breathless suspense, then one bird loosed

The first roc aims a stone at the ship

its hold and the huge block of stone hurtled through the air, but thanks to the presence of mind of the helmsman, who turned our ship violently in another direction, it fell into the sea close beside us, cleaving it asunder till we could nearly see the bottom. We had hardly time to draw a breath of relief before the other rock fell with a mighty crash right in the midst of our luckless vessel, smashing it into a thousand fragments, and crushing, or hurling into the sea, passengers and crew. I myself went down with the rest, but had the good fortune to rise unhurt, and by holding on to a piece of driftwood with one hand and swimming with the other I kept myself afloat and was presently washed up by the tide on to an island. Its shores were steep and rocky, but I scrambled up safely and threw myself down to rest upon the green turf.

When I had somewhat recovered I began to examine the spot in which I found myself, and truly it seemed to me that I had reached a garden of delights. There were trees everywhere, and they were laden with flowers and fruit, while a crystal stream wandered in and out under their shadow. When night came I slept sweetly in a cosy nook, though the remembrance that I was alone in a strange land made me sometimes start up and look around me in alarm, and then I wished heartily that I had stayed at home at ease. However, the morning sunlight restored my courage, and I once more wandered among the trees, but always with some anxiety as to what I might see next. I had penetrated some distance into the island when I saw an old man bent and feeble sitting upon the river bank, and at first I took him to be some shipwrecked mariner like myself. Going up to him I greeted him in a friendly way, but he only nodded his head at me in reply. I then asked what he did there, and he made signs to me that he wished to get across the river to gather some fruit, and seemed to beg me to carry him on my back. Pitying his age and feebleness, I took him up, and wading across the stream I bent down that he might more easily reach the bank, and bade him get down. But instead of allowing himself to be set upon his feet (even now it makes me laugh to think of it!), this creature who had seemed to me so decrepit leaped nimbly upon my shoulders, and hooking his legs round my neck gripped me so tightly that I was well-nigh choked, and so overcome with terror that I fell insensible to the ground. When I recovered my enemy was still in his place, though he had released his hold enough to allow me breathing space, and seeing me revive he prodded me adroitly first with one foot and then with the other, until I was forced to get up and stagger about with him under the trees while he gathered and ate the choicest fruits. This went on all day, and even at night, when I threw myself down half dead with weariness, the terrible old man held on tight to my neck, nor did he fail to greet the first glimmer of morning light by drumming upon me with his heels, until I perforce awoke and resumed my dreary march with rage and bitterness in my heart.

It happened one day that I passed a tree under which lay several dry gourds, and catching one up I amused myself with scooping out its contents and pressing into it the juice of several bunches of grapes which hung from every bush. When it was full I left it propped in the fork of a tree, and a few days later, carrying the hateful old man that way, I snatched at my gourd as I passed it and had the satisfaction of a draught of excellent wine so good and refreshing that I even forgot my detestable burden, and began to sing and caper.

The old monster was not slow to perceive the effect which my draught had produced and that I carried him more lightly than usual, so he stretched out his skinny hand and seizing the gourd first tasted its contents cautiously, then drained them to the very last drop. The wine was strong and the gourd capacious, so he also began to sing after a fashion, and soon I had the delight of feeling the iron grip of his goblin legs unclasp, and with one vigorous effort I threw him to the ground, from which he never moved again. I was so rejoiced to have at last got rid of this uncanny old man that I ran leaping and bounding down to the sea shore, where, by the greatest good luck, I met with some mariners who had anchored off the island to enjoy the delicious fruits, and to renew their supply of water.

They heard the story of my escape with amazement, saying, 'You fell into the hands of the Old Man of the Sea, and it is a mercy that he did not strangle you as he has everyone else upon whose shoulders he has managed to perch himself. This island is well known as the scene of his evil deeds, and no merchant or sailor who lands upon it cares to stray far away from his comrades.' After we had talked for a while they took me back with them on board their ship, where the captain received me kindly, and we soon set sail, and after several days reached a large and prosperous-looking town where all the houses were built of stone. Here we anchored, and one of the merchants, who had been very friendly to me on the way, took me ashore with him and showed me a lodging set apart for strange merchants. He then provided me with a large sack, and pointed out to me a party of others equipped in like manner.

'Go with them,' said he, 'and do as they do, but beware of losing sight of them, for if you strayed your life would be in danger.'

With that he supplied me with provisions, and bade me farewell, and I set out with my new companions. I soon learnt that the object of our expedition was to fill our sacks with coconuts, but when at length I saw the trees and noted their immense height and the slippery smoothness of their slender trunks, I did not at all understand how we were to do it. The crowns of the coco-palms were all alive with monkeys, big and little, which skipped from one to the other with surprising agility, seeming to be curious about us and disturbed at our appearance, and I was at first surprised when my companions after collecting stones began to throw them at the lively creatures, which seemed to me quite harmless. But very soon I saw the reason of it and joined them heartily, for the monkeys, annoyed and wishing to pay us back in our own coin, began to tear the nuts from the trees and cast them at us with angry and spiteful gestures, so that after very little labour our sacks were filled with the fruit which we could not otherwise have obtained.

As soon as we had as many as we could carry we went back to the town, where my friend bought my share and advised me to continue the same occupation until I had earned money enough to carry me to my own country. This I did, and before long had amassed a considerable sum. Just then I heard that there was a trading ship ready to sail, and taking leave of my friend I went on

The Old Man of the Sea

board, carrying with me a goodly store of coconuts; and we sailed first to the islands where pepper grows, then to Comari where the best aloes wood is found, and where men drink no wine by an unalterable law. Here I exchanged my nuts for pepper and good aloes wood, and went a-fishing for pearls with some of the other merchants, and my divers were so lucky that very soon I had an immense number, and those very large and perfect. With all these treasures I came joyfully back to Bagdad, where I disposed of them for large sums of money, of which I did not fail as before to give the tenth part to the poor, and after that I rested from my labours and comforted myself with all the pleasures that my riches could give me.

Having thus ended his story, Sindbad ordered that one hundred sequins should be given to Hindbad, and the guests then withdrew; but after the next day's feast he began the account of his sixth voyage as follows.

The Sixth Voyage of Sindbad

It must be a marvel to you how, after having five times met with shipwreck and unheard-of perils, I could again tempt fortune and risk fresh trouble. I am even surprised myself when I look back, but evidently it was my fate to rove, and after a year of repose I prepared to make a sixth voyage, regardless of the entreaties of my friends and relations, who did all they could to keep me at home. Instead of going by the Persian Gulf, I travelled a considerable way overland, and finally embarked from a distant Indian port with a captain who meant to make a long voyage. And truly he did so, for we fell in with stormy weather which drove us completely out of our course, so that for many days neither captain nor pilot knew where we were, nor where we were going. When they did at last discover our position we had small ground for rejoicing, for the captain, casting his turban upon the deck and tearing his beard, declared that we were in the most dangerous spot upon the whole wide sea, and had been caught by a current which was at that minute sweeping us to destruction. It was too true! In spite of all the sailors could do we were driven with frightful rapidity towards the foot of a mountain, which rose sheer out of the sea, and our vessel was dashed to pieces upon the rocks at its base, not, however, until we had managed to scramble on shore, carrying with us the most precious of our possessions. When we had done this the captain said to us: 'Now we are here we may as well begin to dig our graves at once, since from this fatal spot no shipwrecked mariner has ever returned.'

This speech discouraged us much, and we began to lament over our sad fate.

The mountain formed the seaward boundary of a large island, and the narrow strip of rocky shore upon which we stood was strewn with the wreckage of a thousand gallant ships, while the bones of the luckless mariners shone white in the sunshine, and we shuddered to think how soon our own would be added to the heap. All around, too, lay vast quantities of the costliest merchandise, and treasures were heaped in every cranny of the rocks, but all these things only added to the desolation of the scene. It struck me as a very strange thing that a river of clear fresh water, which gushed out from the mountain not far from where we stood, instead of flowing into the sea as rivers generally do, turned off sharply, and flowed out of sight under a natural archway of rock, and when I went to examine it more closely I found that inside the cave the walls were thick with diamonds, and rubies, and masses of crystal, and the floor was strewn with ambergris. Here, then, upon this desolate shore we abandoned ourselves to our fate, for there was no possibility of scaling the mountain, and if a ship had appeared it could only have shared our doom. The first thing our captain did was to divide equally amongst us all the food we possessed, and then the length of each man's life depended on the time he could make his portion last. I myself could live upon very little.

Nevertheless, by the time I had buried the last of my companions my stock of provisions was so small that I hardly thought I should live long enough to dig my own grave, which I set about doing, while I regretted bitterly the roving disposition which was always bringing me into such straits, and thought longingly of all the comfort and luxury that I had left. But luckily for me the fancy took me to stand once more beside the river where it plunged out of sight in the depths of the cavern, and as I did so an idea struck me. This river which hid itself underground doubtless emerged again at some distant spot. Why should I not build a raft and trust myself to its swiftly flowing waters? If I perished before I could reach the light of day once more I should be no worse off than I was now, for death stared me in the face, while there was always the possibility that, as I was born under a lucky star, I might find myself safe and sound in some desirable land. I decided at any rate to risk it, and speedily built myself a stout raft of driftwood with strong cords, of which enough and to spare lay strewn upon the beach. I then made up many packages of rubies, emeralds, rock crystal, ambergris, and precious stuffs, and bound them upon my raft, being careful to preserve the balance, and then I seated myself upon it, having two small oars that I had fashioned laid ready to my hand, and loosed the cord which held it to the bank. Once out in the current my raft flew swiftly under the gloomy archway, and I found myself in total darkness, carried smoothly forward by the rapid river. On I went as it seemed to me for many nights and days. Once the channel became so small that I had a narrow escape of being crushed against the rocky roof, and after that I took the precaution of lying flat upon my precious bales. Though I only ate what was absolutely necessary to keep myself alive, the inevitable moment came when, after swallowing my last morsel of food, I began to wonder if I must after all die of hunger. Then, worn out with anxiety and fatigue, I fell into a deep sleep, and when I again opened my eyes I was once more in the light of day; a beautiful country lay before me, and my raft, which was tied to the river bank, was surrounded by friendly-looking black men. I rose and saluted them, and they spoke to me in return, but I could not understand a word of their language. Feeling perfectly bewildered by my sudden return to life and light, I murmured to myself in Arabic, 'Close thine eyes, and while thou sleepest heaven will change thy fortune from evil to good.'

One of the natives, who understood this tongue, then came forward saying: 'My brother, be not surprised to see us; this is our land, and as we came to get water from the river we noticed your raft floating down it, and one of us swam out and brought you to the shore. We have waited for your awakening; tell us now whence you come and where you were going by that dangerous way?'

I replied that nothing would please me better than to tell them, but that I was starving, and would fain eat something first. I was soon supplied with all I needed, and having satisfied my hunger I told them faithfully all that had befallen me. They were lost in wonder at my tale when it was interpreted to them, and said that adventures so surprising must be related to their king only by the man to whom they had happened. So, procuring a horse, they mounted me upon it, and we set out, followed by several strong men carrying my raft just as it was upon their shoulders. In this order we marched into the city of Serendib, where the natives presented me to their king, whom I saluted in the Indian fashion, prostrating myself at his feet and kissing the ground; but the monarch bade me rise and sit beside him, asking first what was my name.

'I am Sindbad,' I replied, 'whom men call "the Sailor", for I have voyaged much upon many seas.'

'And how come you here?' asked the king.

I told my story, concealing nothing, and his surprise and delight were so great that he ordered my adventures to be written in letters of gold and laid up in the archives of his kingdom.

Presently my raft was brought in and the bales opened in his presence, and the king declared that in all his treasury there were no such rubies and emeralds as those which lay in great heaps before him. Seeing that he looked at them with interest, I ventured to say that I myself and all that I had were at his disposal, but he answered me smiling: 'Nay, Sindbad. Heaven forbid that I should covet your riches; I will rather add to them, for I desire that you shall not leave my kingdom without some tokens of my good will.' He then commanded his officers to provide me with a suitable lodging at his expense, and sent slaves to wait upon me and carry my raft and my bales to my new dwelling place. You may imagine that I praised his generosity and gave him grateful thanks, nor did I fail to present myself daily in his audience chamber, and for the rest of my time I amused myself in seeing all that was most worthy of attention in the city. The island of Serendib being situated on the equinoctial line, the days and nights there are of equal length. The chief city is placed at the end of a beautiful valley, formed by the highest mountain in the world, which is in the middle of the island. I had the curiosity to ascend to its very summit, for this was the place to which Adam was banished out of Paradise. Here are found rubies and many precious things, and rare plants grow abundantly, with cedar trees and coco-palms. On the seashore and at the mouths of the rivers the divers seek for pearls, and in some valleys diamonds are plentiful. After many days I petitioned the king that I might return to my own country, to which he graciously consented.

Moreover, he loaded me with rich gifts, and when I went to take leave of him he entrusted me with a royal present and a letter to the Commander of the Faithful, our sovereign lord, saying, 'I pray you give these to the Caliph Haroun-al-Raschid, and assure him of my friendship.'

I accepted the charge respectfully, and soon embarked upon the vessel which the king himself had chosen for me. The king's letter was written in blue characters upon a rare and precious skin of yellowish colour, and these were the words of it: 'The King of the Indies, before whom walk a thousand elephants, who lives in a palace, of which the roof blazes with a hundred thousand rubies, and whose treasure house contains twenty thousand diamond crowns, to the Caliph Haroun-al-Raschid sends greeting. Though the offering we present to you is unworthy of your notice, we pray you to accept it as a mark of the esteem and friendship which we cherish for you, and of which we gladly send you this token, and we ask of you a like regard if you deem us worthy of it. Adieu, brother.'

The present consisted of a vase carved from a single ruby, six inches high and as thick as my finger; this was filled with the choicest pearls, large, and of perfect shape and lustre; secondly, a huge snake skin, with scales as large as a sequin, which would preserve from sickness those who slept upon it. Then quantities of aloes wood, camphor, and pistachio-nuts; and lastly, a beautiful slave girl, whose robes glittered with precious stones.

After a long and prosperous voyage we landed at Balsora, and I made haste to reach Bagdad, and taking the king's letter I presented myself at the palace gate, followed by the beautiful slave, and various members of my own family, bearing the treasure.

As soon as I had declared my errand I was conducted into the presence of the caliph, to whom, after I had made my obeisance, I gave the letter and the king's gift, and when he had examined them he demanded of me whether the Prince of Serendib was really as rich and powerful as he claimed to be.

'Commander of the Faithful,' I replied, again bowing humbly before him, 'I can assure your majesty that he has in no way exaggerated his wealth and grandeur. Nothing can equal the magnificence of his palace. When he goes abroad his throne is prepared upon the back of an elephant, and on either side of him ride his ministers, his favourites, and courtiers. On his elephant's neck sits an officer, his golden lance in his hand, and behind him stands another bearing a pillar of gold, at the top of which is an emerald as long as my hand. A thousand men in cloth of gold, mounted upon richly caparisoned elephants, go before him, and as the procession moves onward the officer who guides his elephant cries aloud, "Behold the mighty monarch, the powerful and valiant Sultan of the Indies, whose palace is covered with a hundred thousand rubies, who possesses twenty thousand diamond crowns. Behold a monarch greater than Solomon and Mihrage in all their glory!"

'Then the one who stands behind the throne answers: "This king, so great and powerful, must die, must die, must die!"

'And the first takes up the chant again, "All praise to him who lives for evermore."

'Further, my lord, in Serendib no judge is needed, for to the king himself his people come for justice.'

The caliph was well satisfied with my report.

'From the king's letter,' said he, 'I judged that he was a wise man. It seems that he is worthy of his people, and his people of him.'

So saying he dismissed me with rich presents, and I returned in peace to my own house.

When Sindbad had done speaking his guests withdrew, Hindbad having first received a hundred sequins, but all returned next day to hear the story of the seventh voyage, Sindbad thus began.

The Seventh and Last Voyage

After my sixth voyage I was quite determined that I would go to sea no more. I was now of an age to appreciate a quiet life, and I had run risks enough. I only wished to end my days in peace.

One day, however, when I was entertaining a number of my friends, I was told that an officer of the caliph wished to speak to me, and when he was admitted he bade me follow him into the presence of Haroun-al-Raschid, which I accordingly did. After I had saluted him, the caliph said: 'I have sent for you, Sindbad, because I need your services. I have chosen you to bear a letter and a gift to the King of Serendib in return for his message of friendship.'

The caliph's commandment fell upon me like a thunderbolt.

'Commander of the Faithful,' I answered, 'I am ready to do all that your majesty commands, but I humbly pray you to remember that I am utterly disheartened by the unheard-of sufferings I have undergone. Indeed, I have made a vow never again to leave Bagdad.'

With this I gave him a long account of some of my strangest adventures, to which he listened patiently.

'I admit,' said he, 'that you have indeed had some extraordinary experiences, but I do not see why they should hinder you from doing as I wish. You have only to go straight to Serendib and give my message, then you are free to come back and do as you will. But go you must; my honour and dignity demand it.'

Seeing that there was no help for it, I declared myself willing to obey; and the caliph, delighted at having got his own way, gave me a thousand sequins for the expenses of the voyage. I was soon ready to start, and taking the letter and the present I embarked at Balsora, and sailed quickly and safely to Serendib. Here, when I had disclosed my errand, I was well received, and brought into the presence of the king, who greeted me with joy.

'Welcome, Sindbad,' he cried. 'I have thought of you often, and rejoice to see you once more.'

After thanking him for the honour that he did me, I displayed the caliph's gifts. First a bed with complete hangings all cloth of gold, which cost a thousand sequins, and another like to it of crimson stuff. Fifty robes of rich embroidery, a hundred of the finest white linen from Cairo, Suez, Cufa, and Alexandria. Then more beds of different fashion, and an agate vase carved with the figure of a man aiming an arrow at a lion, and finally a costly table, which had once belonged to King Solomon. The King of Serendib received with satisfaction the assurance of the caliph's friendliness toward him, and now my task being accomplished I was anxious to depart, but it was some time before the king would think of letting me go. At last, however, he dismissed me with many presents, and I lost no time in going on board a ship, which sailed at once, and for four days all went well. On the fifth day we had the misfortune to fall in with pirates, who seized our vessel, killing all who resisted, and making prisoners of those who were prudent enough to submit at once, of whom I was one. When they had despoiled us of all we possessed, they forced us to put on vile raiment, and sailing to a distant island there sold us for slaves. I fell into the hands of a rich merchant, who took me home with him, and clothed and fed me well, and after some days sent for me and questioned me as to what I could do.

I answered that I was a rich merchant who had been captured by pirates, and therefore I knew no trade.

'Tell me,' said he, 'can you shoot with a bow?'

I replied that this had been one of the pastimes of my youth, and that doubtless with practice my skill would come back to me.

Upon this he provided me with a bow and arrows, and mounting me with him upon his own elephant took the way to a vast forest which lay far from the town. When we had reached the wildest part of it we stopped, and my master said to me: 'This forest swarms with elephants. Hide yourself in this great tree, and shoot at all that pass you. When you have succeeded in killing one come and tell me.'

So saying he gave me a supply of food, and returned to the town, and I perched myself high up in the tree and kept watch. That night

I saw nothing, but just after sunrise the next morning a large herd of elephants came crashing and trampling by. I lost no time in letting fly several arrows, and at last one of the great animals fell to the ground dead, and the others retreated, leaving me free to come down from my hiding place and run back to tell my master of my success, for which I was praised and regaled with good things. Then we went back to the forest together and dug a mighty trench in which we buried the elephant I had killed, in order that when it became a skeleton my master might return and secure its tusks.

For two months I hunted thus, and no day passed without my securing, an elephant. Of course I did not always station myself in the same tree, but sometimes in one place, sometimes in another. One morning as I watched the coming of the elephants I was surprised to see that, instead of passing the tree I was in, as they usually did, they paused, and completely surrounded it, trumpeting horribly, and shaking the very ground with their heavy tread, and when I saw that their eyes were fixed upon me I was terrified, and my arrows dropped from my trembling hand. I had indeed good reason for my terror when, an instant later, the largest of the animals wound his trunk round the stem of my tree, and with one mighty effort tore it up by the roots, bringing me to the ground entangled in its branches. I thought now that my last hour was surely come; but the huge creature, picking me up gently enough, set me upon its back, where I clung more dead than alive, and followed by the whole herd turned and crashed off into the dense forest. It seemed to me a long time before I was once more set upon my feet by the elephant, and I stood as if in a dream watching the herd, which turned and trampled off in another direction, and were soon hidden in the dense underwood. Then, recovering myself, I looked about me, and found that I was standing upon the side of a great hill, strewn as far as I could see on either hand with bones and tusks of elephants. 'This then must be the elephants' burying place,' I said to myself, 'and they must have brought me here that I might cease to persecute them, seeing that I want nothing but their tusks, and here lie more than I could carry away in a lifetime.'

Whereupon I turned and made for the city as fast as I could go,

Sindbad left by the elephants in their burial-place

not seeing a single elephant by the way, which convinced me that they had retired deeper into the forest to leave the way open to the Ivory Hill, and I did not know how sufficiently to admire their sagacity. After a day and a night I reached my master's house, and was received by him with joyful surprise.

'Ah! poor Sindbad,' he cried, 'I was wondering what could have become of you. When I went to the forest I found the tree newly uprooted, and the arrows lying beside it, and I feared I should never see you again. Pray tell me how you escaped death.'

I soon satisfied his curiosity, and the next day we went together to the Ivory Hill, and he was overjoyed to find that I had told him nothing but the truth. When we had loaded our elephant with as many tusks as it could carry and were on our way back to the city, he said: 'My brother – since I can no longer treat as a slave one who has enriched me thus – take your liberty and may heaven prosper you. I will no longer conceal from you that these wild elephants have killed numbers of our slaves every year. No matter what good advice we gave them, they were caught sooner or later. You alone have escaped the wiles of these animals, therefore you must be under the special protection of heaven. Now through you the whole town will be enriched without further loss of life, therefore you shall not only receive your liberty, but I will also bestow a fortune upon you.'

To which I replied, 'Master, I thank you, and wish you all prosperity. For myself I only ask liberty to return to my own country.'

'It is well,' he answered, 'the monsoon will soon bring the ivory ships hither, then I will send you on your way with somewhat to pay your passage.'

So I stayed with him till the time of the monsoon, and every day we added to our store of ivory till all his warehouses were overflowing with it. By this time the other merchants knew the secret, but there was enough and to spare for all. When the ships at last arrived my master himself chose the one in which I was to sail, and put on board for me a great store of choice provisions, also ivory in abundance, and all the costliest curiosities of the country, for which I could not thank him enough, and so we parted. I left the ship at the first port we came to, not feeling at ease upon the sea after all that had happened to me by reason of it, and having disposed of my ivory for much gold, and bought many rare and costly presents, I loaded my pack animals, and joined a caravan of merchants. Our journey was long and tedious, but I bore it patiently, reflecting that at least I had not to fear tempests, nor pirates, nor serpents, nor any of the other perils from which I had suffered before, and at length we reached Bagdad. My first care was to present myself before the caliph, and give him an account of my embassy. He assured me that my long absence had disquieted him much, but he had nevertheless hoped for the best. As to my adventure among the elephants he heard it with amazement, declaring that he could not have believed it had not my truthfulness been well known to him.

By his orders this story and the others I had told him were written by his scribes in letters of gold, and laid up among his treasures. I took my leave of him, well satisfied with the honours and rewards he bestowed upon me; and since that time I have rested from my labours, and given myself up wholly to my family and my friends.

Thus Sindbad ended the story of his seventh and last voyage, and turning to Hindbad he added: 'Well, my friend, and what do you think now? Have you ever heard of anyone who has suffered more, or had more narrow escapes than I have? Is it not just that I should now enjoy a life of ease and tranquillity?'

Hindbad drew near, and kissing his hand respectfully, replied, 'Sir, you have indeed known fearful perils; my troubles have been nothing compared to yours. Moreover, the generous use you make of your wealth proves that you deserve it. May you live long and happily in the enjoyment in it.'

Sindbad then gave him a hundred sequins, and henceforward counted him among his friends; also he caused him to give up his profession as a porter, and to eat daily at his table that he might all his life remember Sindbad the Sailor.

The Little Hunchback

In the kingdom of Kashgar, which is, as everybody knows, situated on the frontiers of Great Tartary, there lived long ago a tailor and his wife who loved each other very much. One day, when the tailor was hard at work, a little hunchback came and sat at the entrance of the shop, and began to sing and play his tambourine. The tailor was amused with the antics of the fellow, and thought he would take him home to divert his wife. The hunchback having agreed to his proposal, the tailor closed his shop and they set off together.

When they reached the house they found the table ready laid for supper, and in a very few minutes all three were sitting before a beautiful fish which the tailor's wife had cooked with her own hands. But unluckily, the hunchback happened to swallow a large bone, and, in spite of all the tailor and his wife could do to help him, died of suffocation in an instant. Besides being very sorry for the poor man, the tailor and his wife were very much frightened on their own account, for if the police came to hear of it the worthy couple ran the risk of being thrown into prison for wilful murder. In order to prevent this dreadful calamity they both set about inventing some plan which would throw suspicion on someone else, and at last they made up their minds that they could do no better than select a Jewish doctor who lived close by as the author of the crime. So the tailor picked up the hunchback by his head while his wife took his feet and carried him to the doctor's house. Then they knocked at the door, which opened straight on to a steep staircase. A servant soon appeared, feeling her way down the dark staircases and enquired what they wanted.

'Tell your master,' said the tailor, 'that we have brought a very sick man for him to cure; and,' he added, holding out some money, 'give him this in advance, so that he may not feel he is wasting his time.' The servant remounted the stairs to give the message to the doctor, and the moment she was out of sight the tailor and his wife carried the body swiftly after her, propped it up at the top of the staircase, and ran home as fast as their legs could carry them.

Now the doctor was so delighted at the news of a patient (for he was young, and had not many of them), that he was transported with joy.

'Get a light,' he called to the servant, 'and follow me as fast as you can!' and rushing out of his room he ran towards the staircase. There he nearly fell over the body of the hunchback, and without knowing what it was gave it such a kick that it rolled right to the bottom, and very nearly dragged the doctor after it. 'A light! a light!' he cried again, and when it was brought and he saw what he had done he was almost beside himself with terror.

'Holy Moses!' he exclaimed, 'why did I not wait for the light? I have killed the sick man whom they brought me; and if the sacred Ass of Esdras does not come to my aid I am lost! It will not be long before I am led to jail as a murderer.'

Agitated though he was, and with reason, the doctor did not forget to shut the house door, lest some passers-by might chance to see what had happened. He then took up the corpse and carried it into his wife's room, nearly driving her crazy with fright.

'It is all over with us!' she wailed, 'if we cannot find some means of getting the body out of the house. Once let the sun rise and we can hide it no longer! How were you driven to commit such a terrible crime?'

'Never mind that,' returned the doctor, 'the thing is to find a way out of it.'

For a long while the doctor and his wife continued to turn over in their minds a way of escape, but could not find any that seemed good enough. At last the doctor gave it up altogether and resigned himself to bear the penalty of his misfortune.

But his wife, who had twice his brains, suddenly exclaimed, 'I have thought of something! Let us carry the body on the roof of the house and lower it down the chimney of our neighbour the Mussulman.' Now this Mussulman was employed by the sultan, and furnished his table with oil and butter. Part of his house was

The death of the hunchback

occupied by a great storeroom, where rats and mice held high revel.

The doctor jumped at his wife's plan, and they took up the hunchback, and passing cords under his armpits they let him down into the purveyor's bedroom so gently that he really seemed to be leaning against the wall. When they felt he was touching the ground they drew up the cords and left him.

Scarcely had they got back to their own house when the purveyor entered his room. He had spent the evening at a wedding feast, and had a lantern in his hand. In the dim light it cast he was astonished to see a man standing in his chimney, but being naturally courageous he seized a stick and made straight for the supposed thief. 'Ah!' he cried, 'so it is you, and not the rats and mice, who steal my butter. I'll take care that you don't want to come back!'

So saying he struck him several hard blows. The corpse fell on the floor, but the man only redoubled his blows, till at length it occurred to him it was odd that the thief should lie so still and make no resistance. Then, finding he was quite dead, a cold fear took possession of him. 'Wretch that I am,' said he, 'I have murdered a man. Ah, my revenge has gone too far. Without the help of Allah I am undone! Cursed be the goods which have led me to my ruin.' And already he felt the rope round his neck.

But when he had got over the first shock he began to think of some way out of the difficulty, and seizing the hunchback in his arms he carried him out into the street, and leaning him against the wall of a shop he stole back to his own house, without once looking behind him.

A few minutes before the sun rose, a rich Christian merchant, who supplied the palace with all sorts of necessaries, left his house, after a night of feasting, to go to the bath. Though he was very drunk, he was yet sober enough to know that the dawn was at hand, and that all good Mussulmen would shortly be going to prayer. So he hastened his steps lest he should meet someone on his way to the mosque, who, seeing his condition, would send him to prison as a drunkard. In his haste he jostled against the hunchback, who fell heavily upon him, and the merchant, thinking he was being attacked by a thief, knocked him down with one blow of his fist. He then called loudly for help, beating the fallen man all the while.

The chief policeman of the quarter came running up, and found a Christian ill-treating a Mussulman. 'What are you doing?' he asked indignantly.

'He tried to rob me,' replied the merchant, 'and very nearly choked me.'

'Well, you have had your revenge,' said the man, catching hold of his arm. 'Come, be off with you!'

As he spoke he held out his hand to the hunchback to help him up, but the hunchback never moved. 'Oho!' he went on, looking closer, 'so this is the way a Christian has the impudence to treat a

Mussulman!' and seizing the merchant in a firm grasp he took him to the inspector of police, who threw him into prison till the judge should be out of bed and ready to attend to his case. All this brought the merchant to his senses, but the more he thought of it the less he could understand how the hunchback could have died merely from the blows he had received.

The merchant was still pondering on this subject when he was summoned before the chief of police and questioned about his crime, which he could not deny. As the hunchback was one of the sultan's private jesters, the chief of police resolved to defer sentence of death until he had consulted his master. He went to the palace to demand an audience, and told his story to the sultan, who only answered,

'There is no pardon for a Christian who kills a Mussulman. Do your duty.'

So the chief of police ordered a gallows to be erected, and sent criers to proclaim in every street in the city that a Christian was to be hanged that day for having killed a Mussulman.

When all was ready the merchant was brought from prison and led to the foot of the gallows. The executioner knotted the cord firmly round the unfortunate man's neck and was just about to swing him into the air, when the sultan's purveyor dashed through the crowd, and cried, panting, to the hangman,

'Stop, stop, don't be in such a hurry. It was not he who did the murder, it was I.'

The chief of police, who was present to see that everything was in order, put several questions to the purveyor, who told him the whole story of the death of the hunchback, and how he had carried the body to the place where it had been found by the Christian merchant.

'You are going,' he said to the chief of police, 'to kill an innocent man, for it is impossible that he should have murdered a creature who was dead already. It is bad enough for me to have slain a Mussulman without having it on my conscience that a Christian who is guiltless should suffer through my fault.'

Now the purveyor's speech had been made in a loud voice, and was heard by all the crowd, and even if he had wished it, the chief of police could not have escaped setting the merchant free.

'Loose the cords from the Christian's neck,' he commanded, turning to the executioner, 'and hang this man in his place, seeing that by his own confession he is the murderer.'

The hangman did as he was bid, and was tying the cord firmly, when he was stopped by the voice of the Jewish doctor beseeching him to pause, for he had something very important to say. When he had fought his way through the crowd and reached the chief of police,

'Worshipful sir,' he began, 'this Mussulman whom you desire to hang is unworthy of death; I alone am guilty. Last night a man and a woman who were strangers to me knocked at my door, bringing with them a patient for me to cure. The servant opened it, but having no light was hardly able to make out their faces, though she readily agreed to wake me and to hand me the fee for my services. While she was telling me her story they seem to have carried the sick man to the top of the staircase and then left him there. I jumped up in a hurry without waiting for a lantern, and in the darkness I fell against something, which tumbled headlong down the stairs and never stopped till it reached the bottom. When I examined the body I found it was quite dead, and the corpse was that of a hunchback Mussulman. Terrified at what we had done, my wife and I took the body on the roof and let it down the chimney of our neighbour the purveyor, whom you were just about to hang. The purveyor, finding him in his room, naturally thought he was a thief, and struck him such a blow that the man fell down and lay motionless on the floor. Stooping to examine him, and finding him stone dead, the purveyor supposed that the man had died from the blow he had received; but of course this was a mistake, as you will see from my account, and I only am the murderer; and although I am innocent of any wish to commit a crime, I must suffer for it all the same, or else have the blood of two Mussulmen on my conscience. Therefore send away this man, I pray you, and let me take his place, as it is I who am guilty.'

On hearing the declaration of the Jewish doctor, the chief of police commanded that he should be led to the gallows, and the sultan's purveyor go free. The cord was placed round the Jew's neck, and his feet had already ceased to touch the ground when the voice of the tailor was heard beseeching the executioner to pause one moment and to listen to what he had to say.

'Oh, my lord,' he cried, turning to the chief of police, 'how nearly have you caused the death of three innocent people! But if you will only have the patience to listen to my tale, you shall know who is the real culprit. If someone has to suffer, it must be me! Yesterday, at dusk, I was working in my shop with a light heart when the little hunchback, who was more than half drunk, came and sat in the doorway. He sang me several songs, and then I invited him to finish the evening at my house. He accepted my invitation, and we went away together. At supper I helped him to a slice of fish, but in eating it a bone stuck in his throat, and in spite of all we could do he died in a few minutes. We felt deeply sorry for his death, but fearing lest we should be held responsible, we carried the corpse to the house of the Jewish doctor. I knocked, and desired the servant to beg her master to come down as fast as possible and see a sick man whom we had brought for him to cure; and in order to hasten his movements I placed a piece of money in her hand as the doctor's fee. Directly she had disappeared I dragged the body to the top of the stairs, and then hurried away with my wife back to our house. In descending the stairs the doctor accidentally knocked over the corpse, and finding him dead believed that he himself was the murderer. But now you know the truth set him free, and let me die in his stead.'

The chief of police and the crowd of spectators were lost in astonishment at the strange events to which the death of the hunchback had given rise.

'Loosen the Jewish doctor,' said he to the hangman, 'and string up the tailor instead, since he has made confession of his crime. Really, one cannot deny that this is a very singular story, and it deserves to be written in letters of gold.'

The executioner speedily untied the knots which confined the doctor, and was passing the cord round the neck of the tailor, when the Sultan of Kashgar, who had missed his jester, happened to make enquiry of his officers as to what had become of him.

'Sire,' replied they, 'the hunchback having drunk more than was good for him, escaped from the palace and was seen wandering about the town, where this morning he was found dead. A man was arrested for having caused his death, and held in custody till a gallows was erected. At the moment that he was about to suffer punishment, first one man arrived, and then another, each accusing themselves of the murder, and this went on for a long time, and at the present instant the chief of police is engaged in questioning a man who declares that he alone is the true assassin.'

The Sultan of Kashgar no sooner heard these words than he ordered an usher to go to the chief of police and to bring all the persons concerned in the hunchback's death, together with the corpse, that he wished to see once again. The usher hastened on his errand, but was only just in time, for the tailor was positively swinging in the air, when his voice fell upon the silence of the crowd, commanding the hangman to cut down the body. The hangman, recognising the usher as one of the king's servants, cut down the tailor, and the usher, seeing the man was safe, sought the chief of police and gave him the sultan's message. Accordingly, the chief of police at once set out for the palace, taking with him the tailor, the doctor, the purveyor, and the merchant, who bore the dead hunchback on their shoulders.

When the procession reached the palace the chief of police prostrated himself at the feet of the sultan, and related all that he knew of the matter. The sultan was so much struck by the circumstances that he ordered his private historian to write down an exact account of what had passed, so that in the years to come the miraculous escape of the four men who had thought themselves murderers might never be forgotten.

The sultan asked everybody concerned in the hunchback's affair to tell him their stories. Among others was a prating barber, whose tale of one of his brothers follows.

The Story of the Barber's Fifth Brother

As long as our father lived Alnaschar was very idle. Instead of working for his bread he was not ashamed to ask for it every evening, and to support himself next day on what he had received the night before. When our father died, worn out by age, he only left seven hundred silver drachmas to be divided amongst us, which made one hundred for each son. Alnaschar, who had never possessed so much money in his life, was quite puzzled to know what to do with it. After reflecting upon the matter for some time he decided to lay it out on glasses, bottles, and things of that sort, which he would buy from a wholesale merchant. Having bought his stock he next proceeded to look out for a small shop in a good position, where he sat down at the open door, his wares being piled up in an uncovered basket in front of him, waiting for a customer among the passers-by.

In this attitude he remained seated, his eyes fixed on the basket, but his thoughts far away. Unknown to himself he began to talk out loud, and a tailor, whose shop was next door to his, heard quite plainly what he was saying.

'This basket,' said Alnaschar to himself, 'has cost me a hundred drachmas – all that I possess in the world. Now in selling the contents piece by piece I shall turn two hundred, and these hundreds I shall again lay out in glass, which will produce four hundred. By this means I shall in course of time make four thousand drachmas, which will easily double themselves. When I have got ten thousand I will give up the glass trade and become a jeweller, and devote all my time to trading in pearls, diamonds, and other precious stones. At last, having all the wealth that heart can desire, I will buy a beautiful country house, with horses and slaves, and then I will lead a merry life and entertain my friends. At my feasts I will send for musicians and dancers from the neighbouring town to amuse my guests. In spite of my riches I shall not, however, give up trade till I have amassed a capital of a hundred thousand drachmas, when, having become a man of much consideration, I shall request the hand of the grand-vizir's daughter, taking care to inform the worthy father that I have heard favourable reports of her beauty and wit, and that I will pay down on our wedding day three thousand gold pieces. Should the vizir refuse my proposal, which after all is hardly to be expected, I will seize him by the beard and drag him to my house.

'When I shall have married his daughter I will give her ten of the best eunuchs that can be found for her service. Then I shall put on my most gorgeous robes, and mounted on a horse with a saddle of fine gold, and its trappings blazing with diamonds, followed by a train of slaves, I shall present myself at the house of the grand-vizir, the people casting down their eyes and bowing low as I pass along. At the foot of the grand-vizir's staircase I shall dismount, and while my servants stand in a row to right and left I shall ascend the stairs, at the head of which the grand-vizir will be waiting to receive me. He will then embrace me as his son-in-law, and giving me his seat will place himself below me. This being done (as I have every reason to expect), two of my servants will enter, each bearing a purse containing a thousand pieces of gold. One of these I shall present to him saying, "Here are the thousand gold pieces that I offered for your daughter's hand, and here," I shall continue, holding out the second purse, "are another thousand to show you that I am a man who is better than his word." After hearing of such generosity the world will talk of nothing else.

'I shall return home with the same pomp as I set out, and my wife will send an officer to compliment me on my visit to her father, and I shall confer on the officer the honour of a rich dress and a handsome gift. Should she send one to me I shall refuse it and dismiss the bearer. I shall never allow my wife to leave her rooms on any pretext whatever without my permission, and my visits to her will be marked by all the ceremony calculated to inspire respect. No establishment will be better ordered than mine, and I shall take care always to be dressed in a manner suitable to my position. In the evening, when we retire to our apartments, I shall sit in the place of honour, where I shall assume a grand demeanour and speak little, gazing straight before me, and when my wife, lovely as the full moon, stands humbly in front of my chair I shall pretend not to see her. Then her women will say to me, "Respected lord and master, your wife and slave is before you waiting to be noticed. She is mortified that you never deign to look her way; she is tired of standing so long. Beg her, we pray you, to be seated." Of course I shall give no signs of even hearing this speech, which will vex them mightily. They will throw themselves at my feet with lamentations, and at length I will raise my head and throw a care-less glance at her, then I shall go back to my former attitude. The women will think that I am displeased at my wife's dress and will lead her away to put on a finer one, and I on my side shall replace the one I am wearing with another yet more splendid. They will then return to the charge, but this time it will take much longer before they persuade me even to look at my wife. It is as well to begin on my wedding-day as I mean to go on for the rest of our lives.

'The next day she will complain to her mother of the way she has been treated, which will fill my heart with joy. Her mother will come to seek me, and, kissing my hands with respect, will say, "My lord" (for she could not dare to risk my anger by using the familiar title of "son-in-law"), "My lord, do not, I implore you, refuse to look upon my daughter or to approach her. She only lives to please you, and loves you with all her soul." But I shall pay no more heed to my mother-in-law's words than I did to those of the women. Again she will beseech me to listen to her entreaties, throwing herself this time at my feet, but all to no purpose. Then, putting a glass of wine into my wife's hand, she will say to her, "There, present that to him yourself, he cannot have the cruelty to reject anything offered by so beautiful a hand," and my wife will take it and offer it to me tremblingly with tears in her eyes, but I shall look in the other direction. This will cause her to weep still more, and she will hold out the glass cry "Adorable husband, never shall I cease my prayers till you have done me the favour to drink." Sick of her importunities, these words will goad me to fury. I shall dart an angry look at her and give her a sharp blow on the cheek, at the same time giving her a kick so violent that she will stagger across the room and fall on to the sofa.'

My brother, pursued the barber, was so much absorbed in his dreams that he actually did give a kick with his foot, which unluckily hit the basket of glass. It fell into the street and was instantly broken into a thousand pieces.

His neighbour the tailor, who had been listening to his visions, broke into a loud fit of laughter as he saw this sight.

'Wretched man!' he cried, 'you ought to die of shame at behaving so to a young wife who has done nothing to you. You must be a brute for her tears and prayers not to touch your heart. If I were the grand-vizir I would order you a hundred blows from a bullock whip, and would have you led round the town accompanied by a herald who should proclaim your crimes.'

The accident, so fatal to all his profits, had restored my brother to his senses, and seeing that the mischief had been caused by his own insufferable pride, he rent his clothes and tore his hair, and lamented himself so loudly that the passers-by stopped to listen. It was a Friday, so these were more numerous than usual. Some pitied Alnaschar, others only laughed at him, but the vanity which had gone to his head had disappeared with his basket of glass, and he was loudly bewailing his folly when a lady, evidently a person of consideration, rode by on a mule. She stopped and enquired what was the matter, and why the man wept. They told her that he was a poor man who had laid out all his money on this basket of glass, which was now broken. On hearing the cause of these loud wails the lady turned to her attendant and said to him, 'Give him what-ever you have got with you.' The man obeyed, and placed in my brother's hands a purse containing five hundred pieces of gold. Alnaschar almost died of joy on receiving it. He blessed the lady a thousand times, and, shutting up his shop where he had no longer anything to do, he returned home.

He was still absorbed in contemplating his good fortune, when a knock came to his door, and on opening it he found an old woman standing outside.

Alnaschar kicks over the basket

'My son,' she said, 'I have a favour to ask of you. It is the hour of prayer and I have not yet washed myself. Let me, I beg you, enter your house, and give me water.'

My brother, although the old woman was a stranger to him, did not hesitate to do as she wished. He gave her a vessel of water and then went back to his place and his thoughts, and with his mind busy over his last adventure, he put his gold into a long and narrow purse, which he could easily carry in his belt. During this time the old woman was busy over her prayers, and when she had finished she came and prostrated herself twice before my brother, and then rising called down endless blessings on his head. Observing her shabby clothes, my brother thought that her gratitude was in reality a hint that he should give her some money to buy some new ones, so he held out two pieces of gold. The old woman started back in surprise as if she had received an insult. 'Good heavens!' she exclaimed, 'what is the meaning of this? Is it possible that you take me, my lord, for one of those miserable creatures who force their way into houses to beg for alms? Take back your money. I am thankful to say I do not need it, for I belong to a beautiful lady who is very rich and gives me everything I want.'

My brother was not clever enough to detect that the old woman had merely refused the two pieces of money he had offered her in order to get more, but he enquired if she could procure him the pleasure of seeing this lady.

'Willingly,' she replied; 'and she will be charmed to marry you, and to make you the master of all her wealth. So pick up your money and follow me.'

Delighted at the thought that he had found so easily both a fortune and a beautiful wife, my brother asked no more questions, but concealing his purse, with the money the lady had given him, in the folds of his dress, he set out joyfully with his guide.

They walked for some distance till the old woman stopped at a large house, where she knocked. The door was opened by a young Greek slave, and the old woman led my brother across a well-paved court into a well-furnished hall. Here she left him to inform her mistress of his presence, and as the day was hot he flung himself on a pile of cushions and took off his heavy turban. In a few minutes there entered a lady, and my brother perceived at the first glance that she was even more beautiful and more richly dressed than he had expected. He rose from his seat, but the lady signed to him to sit down again and placed herself beside him. After the usual compliments had passed between them she said, 'We are not comfortable here, let us go into another room,' and passing into a smaller chamber, apparently communicating with no other, she continued to talk to him for some time. Then rising hastily she left him, saying, 'Stay where you are, I will come back in a moment.'

He waited as he was told, but instead of the lady there entered a huge black slave with a sword in his hand. Approaching my brother with an angry countenance he exclaimed, 'What business have you here?' His voice and manner were so terrific that Alnaschar had not strength to reply, and allowed his gold to be taken from him, and even sabre cuts to be inflicted on him without making any resistance. As soon as he was let go, he sank on the ground powerless to move, though he still had possession of his senses. Thinking he was dead, the black ordered the Greek slave to bring him some salt, and between them they rubbed it into his wounds, thus giving him acute agony, though he had the presence of mind to give no sign of life. They then left him, and their place was taken by the old woman, who dragged him to a trap-door and threw him down into a vault filled with the bodies of murdered men.

At first the violence of his fall caused him to lose consciousness, but luckily the salt which had been rubbed into his wounds had by its smarting preserved his life, and little by little he regained his strength. At the end of two days he lifted the trap-door during the night and hid himself in the courtyard till daybreak, when he saw the old woman leave the house in search of more prey. Luckily she did not observe him, and when she was out of sight he stole from this nest of assassins and took refuge in my house.

I dressed his wounds and tended him carefully, and when a month had passed he was as well as ever. His one thought was how to be revenged on that wicked old hag, and for this purpose he had a purse made large enough to contain five hundred gold pieces, but filled it instead with bits of glass. This he tied round him with his sash, and, disguising himself as an old woman, he took a sabre, which he hid under his dress.

One morning as he was hobbling through the streets he met his old enemy prowling to see if she could find anyone to decoy. He went up to her and, imitating the voice of a woman, he said, 'Do you happen to have a pair of scales you could lend me? I have just come from Persia and have brought with me five hundred gold pieces, and I am anxious to see if they are the proper weight.'

'Good woman,' replied the old hag, 'you could not have asked anyone better. My son is a money-changer, and if you will follow me he will weigh them for you himself. Only we must be quick or he will have gone to his shop.' So saying she led the way to the same house as before, and the door was opened by the same Greek slave.

Again my brother was left in the hall, and the pretended son appeared under the form of the black slave. 'Miserable crone,' he said to my brother, 'get up and come with me,' and turned to lead the way to the place of murder. Alnaschar rose too, and drawing the sabre from under his dress dealt the black such a blow on his neck that his head was severed from his body. My brother picked up the head with one hand, and seizing the body with the other dragged it to the vault, when he threw it in and sent the head after it. The Greek slave, supposing that all had passed as usual, shortly arrived with the basin of salt, but when she beheld Alnaschar with the sabre in his hand she let the basin fall and turned to fly. My brother, however, was too quick for her, and in another instant her head was rolling from her shoulders. The noise brought the old woman running to see what was the matter, and he seized her before she had time to escape. 'Wretch!' he cried, 'do you know me?'

'Who are you, my lord?' she replied trembling all over. 'I have never seen you before.'

'I am he whose house you entered to offer your hypocritical prayers. Don't you remember now?'

She flung herself on her knees to implore mercy, but he cut her in four pieces.

There remained only the lady, who was quite ignorant of all that was taking place around her. He sought her through the house, and when at last he found her, she nearly fainted with terror at the sight of him. She begged hard for life, which he was generous enough to give her, but he bade her to tell him how she had got into partnership with the abominable creatures he had just put to death.

'I was once,' replied she, 'the wife of an honest merchant, and that old woman, whose wickedness I did not know, used occasionally to visit me. "Madam," she said to me one day, "we have a grand wedding at our house today. If you would do us the honour to be present, I am sure you would enjoy yourself." I allowed myself to be persuaded, put on my richest dress, and took a purse with a hundred pieces of gold. Once inside the doors I was kept by force by that dreadful black, and it is now three years that I have been here, to my great grief.'

'That horrible black must have amassed great wealth,' remarked my brother.

'Such wealth,' returned she, 'that if you succeed in carrying it all away it will make you rich for ever. Come and let us see how much there is.'

She led Alnaschar into a chamber filled with coffers packed with gold, which he gazed at with an admiration he was powerless to conceal. 'Go,' she said, 'and bring men to carry them away.'

My brother did not wait to be told twice, and hurried out into the streets, where he soon collected ten men. They all came back to the house, but what was his surprise to find the door open, and the room with the chests of gold quite empty. The lady had been cleverer than himself, and had made the best use of her time. However, he tried to console himself by removing all the beautiful furniture, which more than made up for the five hundred gold pieces he had lost.

Unluckily, on leaving the house, he forgot to lock the door, and the neighbours, finding the place empty, informed the police, who next morning arrested Alnaschar as a thief. My brother tried to bribe them to let him off, but far from listening to him they tied his hands, and forced him to walk between them to the presence of the judge. When they had explained to the official the cause of complaint, he asked Alnaschar where he had obtained all the furniture that he had taken to his house the day before.

'Sir,' replied Alnaschar, 'I am ready to tell you the whole story, but give, I pray you, your word, that I shall run no risk of punishment.'

'That I promise,' said the judge. So my brother began at the beginning and related all his adventures, and how he had avenged himself on those who had betrayed him. As to the furniture, he entreated the judge at least to allow him to keep part to make up for

The lady shows Alnaschar the coffers packed with gold

the five hundred pieces of gold which had been stolen from him.

The judge, however, would say nothing about this, and lost no time in sending men to fetch away all that Alnaschar had taken from the house. When everything had been moved and placed under his roof he ordered my brother to leave the town and never more to enter it on peril of his life, fearing that if he returned he might seek justice from the caliph. Alnaschar obeyed, and was on his way to a neighbouring city when he fell in with a band of robbers, who stripped him of his clothes and left him naked by the roadside. Hearing of his plight, I hurried after him to console him for his misfortunes, and to dress him in my best robe. I then brought him back disguised, under cover of night, to my house, where I have since given him all the care I bestow on my other brothers.

The Story of the Barber's Sixth Brother

There now remains for me to relate to you the story of my sixth brother, whose name was Schacabac. Like the rest of us, he inherited a hundred silver drachmas from our father, which he thought was a large fortune, but through ill-luck, he soon lost it all, and was driven to beg. As he had a smooth tongue and good manners, he really did very well in his new profession, and he devoted himself specially to making friends with the servants in big houses, so as to gain access to their masters.

One day he was passing a splendid mansion, with a crowd of servants lounging in the courtyard. He thought that from the appearance of the house it might yield him a rich harvest, so he entered and enquired to whom it belonged.

'My good man, where do you come from?' replied the servant. 'Can't you see for yourself that it can belong to nobody but a barmecide?' for the barmecides were famed for their liberality and generosity. My brother, hearing this, asked the porters, of whom there were several, if they would give him alms. They did not refuse, but told him politely to go in, and speak to the master himself.

My brother thanked them for their courtesy and entered the building, which was so large that it took him some time to reach the apartments of the barmecide. At last, in a room richly decorated with paintings, he saw an old man with a long white beard, sitting on a sofa, who received him with such kindness that my brother was emboldened to make his petition.

'My lord,' he said, 'you behold in me a poor man who only lives by the help of persons as rich and as generous as you.'

Before he could proceed further, he was stopped by the astonishment shown by the barmecide. 'Is it possible,' he cried, 'that while I am in Bagdad, a man like you should be starving? That is a state of things that must at once be put an end to! Never shall it be said that I have abandoned you, and I am sure that you, on your part, will never abandon me.'

'My lord,' answered my brother, 'I swear that I have not broken my fast this whole day.'

'What, you are dying of hunger?' exclaimed the barmecide. 'Here, slave; bring water, that we may wash our hands before meat!' No slave appeared, but my brother remarked that the barmecide did not fail to rub his hands as if the water had been poured over them.

Then he said to my brother, 'Why don't you wash your hands too?' and Schacabac, supposing that it was a joke on the part of the barmecide (though he could see none himself), drew near, and imitated his motion.

When the barmecide had done rubbing his hands, he raised his voice, and cried, 'Set food before us at once, we are very hungry.' No food was brought, but the barmecide pretended to help himself from a dish, and carry a morsel to his mouth, saying as he did so, 'Eat, my friend, eat, I entreat. Help yourself as freely as if you were at home! For a starving man, you seem to have a very small appetite.'

'Excuse me, my lord,' replied Schacabac, imitating his gestures as before, 'I really am not losing time, and I do full justice to the repast.'

'How do you like this bread?' asked the barmecide. 'I find it particularly good myself.'

'Oh, my lord,' answered my brother, who beheld neither meat nor bread, 'never have I tasted anything so delicious.'

'Eat as much as you want,' said the barmecide. 'I bought the woman who makes it for five hundred pieces of gold, so that I might never be without it.'

After ordering a variety of dishes (which never came) to be placed on the table, and discussing the merits of each one, the barmecide declared that having dined so well, they would now proceed to take their wine. To this my brother at first objected, declaring that it was forbidden; but on the barmecide insisting that it was out of the question that he should drink by himself, he consented to take a little. The barmecide, however, pretended to fill their glasses so often, that my brother feigned that the wine had gone into his head, and struck the barmecide such a blow on the head, that he fell to the ground. Indeed, he raised his hand to strike him a second time, when the barmecide cried out that he was mad, upon which my brother controlled himself, and apologised and protested that it was all the fault of the wine he had drunk. At this the barmecide, instead of being angry, began to laugh, and embraced him heartily. 'I have long been seeking,' he exclaimed, 'a man of your description, and henceforth my house shall be yours. You have had the good grace to fall in with my humour, and to pretend to eat and to drink when nothing was there. Now you shall be rewarded by a really good supper.'

Then he clapped his hands, and all the dishes were brought that they had tasted in imagination before and during the repast, slaves sang and played on various instruments. All the while Schacabac was treated by the barmecide as a familiar friend, and dressed in a garment out of his own wardrobe.

Twenty years passed by, and my brother was still living with the barmecide, looking after his house, and managing his affairs. At the end of that time his generous benefactor died without heirs, so all his possessions went to the prince. They even despoiled my brother of those that rightly belonged to him, and he, now as poor as he had ever been in his life, decided to cast in his lot with a caravan of pilgrims who were on their way to Mecca. Unluckily, the caravan was attacked and pillaged by the Bedouins, and the pilgrims were taken prisoners. My brother became the slave of a man who beat him daily, hoping to drive him to offer a ransom, although, as Schacabac pointed out, it was quite useless trouble, as his relations were as poor as himself. At length the Bedouin grew tired of tormenting, and sent him on a camel to the top of a high barren mountain, where he left him to take his chance. A passing caravan, on its way to Bagdad, told me where he was to be found, and I hurried to his rescue, and brought him in a deplorable condition back to the town.

'This,' – continued the barber, – 'is the tale I related to the caliph, who, when I had finished, burst into fits of laughter.

'Well were you called "the Silent", said he; "no name was ever

The barmecide's feast

better deserved. But for reasons of my own, which it is not necessary to mention, I desire you to leave the town, and never to come back."

'I had of course no choice but to obey, and travelled about for several years until I heard of the death of the caliph, when I hastily returned to Bagdad, only to find that all my brothers were dead. It was at this time that I rendered to the young cripple the important service of which you have heard, and for which, as you know, he showed such profound ingratitude, that he preferred rather to leave Bagdad than to run the risk of seeing me. I sought him long from place to place, but it was only today, when I expected it least, that I came across him, as much irritated with me as ever.' – So saying the tailor went on to relate the story of the lame man and the barber, which has already been told.

'When the barber,' he continued, 'had finished his tale, we came to the conclusion that the young man had been right, when he had accused him of being a great chatter-box. However, we wished to keep him with us, and share our feast, and we remained at table till the hour of afternoon prayer. Then the company broke up, and I went back to work in my shop.

'It was during this interval that the little hunchback, half drunk already, presented himself before me, singing and playing on his drum. I took him home, to amuse my wife, and she invited him to supper. While eating some fish, a bone got into his throat, and in spite of all we could do, he died shortly. It was all so sudden that we lost our heads, and in order to divert suspicion from ourselves, we carried the body to the house of a Jewish physician. He placed it in the chamber of the purveyor, and the purveyor propped it up in the street, where it was thought to have been killed by the merchant.

'This, sire, is the story which I was obliged to tell to satisfy your highness. It is now for you to say if we deserve mercy or punishment; life or death?'

The Sultan of Kashgar listened with an air of pleasure which filled the tailor and his friends with hope. 'I must confess,' he exclaimed, 'that I am much more interested in the stories of the barber and his brothers, and of the lame man, than in that of my own jester. But before I allow you all four to return to your own homes, and have the corpse of the hunchback properly buried, I should like to see this barber who has earned your pardon. And as he is in this town, let an usher go with you at once in search of him.'

The usher and the tailor soon returned, bringing with them an old man who must have been at least ninety years of age. 'O Silent One,' said the sultan, 'I am told that you know many strange stories. Will you tell some of them to me?'

'Never mind my stories for the present,' replied the barber, 'but will your highness graciously be pleased to explain why this Jew, this Christian, and this Mussulman, as well as this dead body, are all here?'

'What business is that of yours?' asked the sultan with a smile; but seeing that the barber had some reasons for his question, he commanded that the tale of the hunchback should be told him.

'It is certainly most surprising,' cried he, when he had heard it all, 'but I should like to examine the body.' He then knelt down, and took the head on his knees, looking at it attentively. Suddenly he burst into such loud laughter that he fell right backwards, and when he had recovered himself enough to speak, he turned to the sultan. 'The man is no more dead than I am,' he said; 'watch me.' As he spoke he drew a small case of medicines from his pocket and rubbed the neck of the hunchback with some ointment made of balsam. Next he opened the dead man's mouth, and by the help of a pair of pincers drew the bone from his throat. At this the hunchback sneezed, stretched himself and opened his eyes.

The sultan and all those who saw this operation did not know which to admire most, the constitution of the hunchback who had apparently been dead for a whole night and most of one day, or the skill of the barber, whom everyone now began to look upon as a great man. His highness desired that the history of the hunchback should be written down, and placed in the archives beside that of the barber, so that they might be associated in people's minds to the end of time. And he did not stop there; for in order to wipe out the memory of what they had undergone, he commanded that the tailor, the doctor, the purveyor and the merchant, should each be clothed in his presence with a robe from his own wardrobe before they returned home. As for the barber, he bestowed on him a large pension, and kept him near his own person.

The Adventures of Prince Camaralzaman and the Princess Badoura

Some twenty days' sail from the coast of Persia lies the isle of the children of Khaledan. The island is divided into several provinces, in each of which are large flourishing towns, and the whole forms an important kingdom. It was governed in former days by a king named Schahzaman, who, with good right, considered himself one of the most peaceful, prosperous, and fortunate monarchs on the earth. In fact, he had but one grievance, which was that none of his four wives had given him an heir.

This distressed him so greatly that one day he confided his grief to the grand-vizir, who, being a wise counsellor, said: 'Such matters are indeed beyond human aid. Allah alone can grant your desire, and I should advise you, sire, to send large gifts to those holy men who spend their lives in prayer, and to beg for their intercessions. Who knows whether their petitions may not be answered!'

The king took his vizir's advice, and the result of so many prayers for an heir to the throne was that a son was born to him the following year.

Schahzaman sent noble gifts as thank offerings to all the mosques and religious houses, and great rejoicings were celebrated in honour of the birth of the little prince, who was so beautiful that he was named Camaralzaman, or 'Moon of the Century'.

Prince Camaralzaman was brought up with extreme care by an excellent governor and all the cleverest teachers, and he did such credit to them that when he was grown up, a more charming and accomplished young man was not to be found. Whilst he was still a youth the king, his father, who loved him dearly, had some thoughts of abdicating in his favour. As usual he talked over his plans with his grand-vizir, who, though he did not approve the idea, would not state all his objections.

'Sire,' he replied, 'the prince is still very young for the cares of state. Your majesty fears his growing idle and careless, and doubtless you are right. But how would it be if he were first to marry? This would attach him to his home, and your majesty might give him a share in your counsels, so that he might gradually learn how to wear a crown, which you can give up to him whenever you find him capable of wearing it.'

The vizir's advice once more struck the king as being good, and he sent for his son, who lost no time in obeying the summons, and standing respectfully with downcast eyes before the king asked for his commands.

'I have sent for you,' said the king, 'to say that I wish you to marry. What do you think about it?'

The prince was so much overcome by these words that he remained silent for some time. At length he said: 'Sire, I beg you to pardon me if I am unable to reply as you might wish. I certainly did not expect such a proposal as I am still so young, and I confess that the idea of marrying is very distasteful to me. Possibly I may not always be in this mind, but I certainly feel that it will require some time to induce me to take the step which your majesty desires.'

This answer greatly distressed the king, who was sincerely grieved by his objection to marriage. However he would not have recourse to extreme measures, so he said: 'I do not wish to force you; I will give you time to reflect, but remember that such a step is necessary, for a prince such as you who will someday be called to rule over a great kingdom.'

From this time Prince Camaralzaman was admitted to the royal council, and the king showed him every mark of favour.

At the end of a year the king took his son aside, and said: 'Well, my son, have you changed your mind on the subject of marriage, or do you still refuse to obey my wish?'

The prince was less surprised but no less firm than on the former occasion, and begged his father not to press the subject, adding that it was quite useless to urge him any longer.

This answer much distressed the king, who again confided his trouble to his vizir.

'I have followed your advice,' he said; 'but Camaralzaman declines to marry, and is more obstinate than ever.'

'Sire,' replied the vizir, 'much is gained by patience, and your majesty might regret any violence. Why not wait another year and then inform the prince in the midst of the assembled council that the good of the state demands his marriage? He cannot possibly refuse again before so distinguished an assemblage, and in our immediate presence.'

The sultan ardently desired to see his son married at once, but he yielded to the vizir's arguments and decided to wait. He then visited the prince's mother, and after telling her of his disappointment and of the further respite he had given his son, he added: 'I know that Camaralzaman confides more in you than he does in me. Pray speak very seriously to him on this subject, and make him realise that he will most seriously displease me if he remains obstinate, and that he will certainly regret the measures I shall be obliged to take to enforce my will.'

So the first time the Sultana Fatima saw her son she told him she had heard of his refusal to marry, adding how distressed she felt that he should have vexed his father so much. She asked what reasons he could have for his objections to obey.

'Madam,' replied the prince, 'I make no doubt that there are as many good, virtuous, sweet, and amiable women as there are others very much the reverse. Would that all were like you! But what revolts me is the idea of marrying a woman without knowing anything at all about her. My father will ask the hand of the daughter of some neighbouring sovereign, who will give his consent to our union. Be she fair or frightful, clever or stupid, good or bad, I must marry her, and am left no choice in the matter. How am I to know that she will not be proud, passionate, contemptuous, and recklessly extravagant, or that her disposition will in any way suit mine?'

'But, my son,' urged Fatima, 'you surely do not wish to be the last of a race which has reigned so long and so gloriously over this kingdom?'

'Madam,' said the prince, 'I have no wish to survive the king, my father, but should I do so I will try to reign in such a manner as may be considered worthy of my predecessors.'

These and similar conversations proved to the sultan how useless it was to argue with his son, and the year elapsed without bringing any change in the prince's ideas.

At length a day came when the sultan summoned him before the council, and there informed him that not only his own wishes but the good of the empire demanded his marriage, and desired him to give his answer before the assembled ministers.

At this Camaralzaman grew so angry and spoke with so much heat that the king, naturally irritated at being opposed by his son in full council, ordered the prince to be arrested and locked up in an old tower, where he had nothing but a very little furniture, a few books, and a single slave to wait on him.

Camaralzaman, pleased to be free to enjoy his books, showed himself very indifferent to his sentence.

When night came he washed himself, performed his devotions, and, having read some pages of the Koran, lay down on a couch, without putting out the light near him, and was soon asleep.

Now there was a deep well in the tower in which Prince Camaralzaman was imprisoned, and this well was a favourite resort of the fairy Maimoune, daughter of Damriat, chief of a legion of genii. Towards midnight Maimoune floated lightly up from the well, intending, according to her usual habit, to roam about the upper world as curiosity or accident might prompt.

The light in the prince's room surprised her, and without disturbing the slave, who slept across the threshold, she entered the room, and approaching the bed was still more astonished to find it occupied. The prince lay with his face half hidden by the coverlet. Maimoune lifted it a little and beheld the most beautiful youth she had ever seen.

'What a marvel of beauty he must be when his eyes are open!' she thought. 'What can he have done to deserve to be treated like this?'

She could not weary gazing at Camaralzaman, but at length, having softly kissed his brow and each cheek, she replaced the coverlet and resumed her flight through the air.

She could not weary gazing at Camaralzaman

As she entered the middle region she heard the sound of great wings coming towards her, and shortly met one of the race of bad genii. This genie, whose name was Danhasch, recognised Maimoune with terror, for he knew the supremacy which her goodness gave her over him. He would gladly have avoided her altogether, but they were so near that he must either be prepared to fight or yield to her, so he at once addressed her in a conciliatory tone: 'Good Maimoune, swear to me by Allah to do me no harm, and on my side I will promise not to injure you.'

'Accursed genie!' replied Maimoune, 'what harm can you do me? But I will grant your power and give the promise you ask. And now tell me what you have seen and done tonight.'

'Fair lady,' said Danhasch, 'you meet me at the right moment to hear something really interesting. I must tell you that I come from the furthest end of China, which is one of the largest and most powerful kingdoms in the world. The present king has one only daughter, who is so perfectly lovely that neither you, nor I, nor any other creature could find adequate terms in which to describe her marvellous charms. You must therefore picture to yourself the most perfect features, joined to a brilliant and delicate complexion, and an enchanting expression, and even then imagination will fall short of the reality.

'The king, her father, has carefully shielded this treasure from the vulgar gaze, and has taken every precaution to keep her from the sight of everyone except the happy mortal he may choose to be her husband. But in order to give her variety in her confinement he has built her seven palaces such as have never been seen before. The first palace is entirely composed of rock crystal, the second of bronze, the third of fine steel, the fourth of another and more precious species of bronze, the fifth of touchstone, the sixth of silver, and the seventh of solid gold. They are all most sumptuously furnished, whilst the gardens surrounding them are laid out with exquisite taste. In fact, neither trouble nor cost has been spared to make this retreat agreeable to the princess. The report of her wonderful beauty has spread far and wide, and many powerful kings have sent embassies to ask her hand in marriage. The king has always received these embassies graciously, but says that he will never oblige the princess to marry against her will, and as she regularly declines each fresh proposal, the envoys have had to leave as disappointed in the result of their missions as they were gratified by their magnificent receptions.'

"Sire," said the princess to her father, "you wish me to marry, and I know you desire to please me, for which I am very grateful. But, indeed, I have no inclination to change my state, for where could I find so happy a life amidst so many beautiful and delightful surroundings? I feel that I could never be as happy with any husband as I am here, and I beg you not to press one on me."

'At last an embassy came from a king so rich and powerful that the King of China felt constrained to urge this suit on his daughter. He told her how important such an alliance would be, and pressed her to consent. In fact, he pressed her so persistingly that the princess at length lost her temper and quite forgot the respect due to her father. "Sire," cried she angrily, "do not speak further of this or any other marriage or I will plunge this dagger in my breast and so escape from all these importunities."

'The King of China was extremely indignant with his daughter and replied: "You have lost your senses and you must be treated accordingly." So he had her shut in one set of rooms in one of her palaces, and only allowed her ten old women, of whom her nurse was the head, to wait on her and keep her company. He next sent letters to all the kings who had sued for the princess's hand, begging they would think of her no longer, as she was quite insane, and he desired his various envoys to make it known that anyone who could cure her should have her to wife.

'Fair Maimoune,' continued Danhasch, 'this is the present state of affairs. I never pass a day without going to gaze on this incomparable beauty, and I am sure that if you would only accompany me you would think the sight well worth the trouble, and own that you never saw such loveliness before.'

The fairy only answered with a peal of laughter, and when at length she had control of her voice she cried, 'Oh, come, you are making game of me! I thought you had something really interesting to tell me instead of raving about some unknown damsel. What would you say if you could see the prince I have just been looking at and whose beauty is really transcendent? That is something worth talking about, you would certainly quite lose your head.'

'Charming Maimoune,' asked Danhasch, 'may I enquire who and what is the prince of whom you speak?'

'Know,' replied Maimoune, 'that he is in much the same case as your princess. The king, his father, wanted to force him to marry, and on the prince's refusal to obey he has been imprisoned in an old tower where I have just seen him.'

'I don't like to contradict a lady,' said Danhasch, 'but you must really permit me to doubt any mortal being is as beautiful as my princess.'

'Hold your tongue,' cried Maimoune. 'I repeat that it is possible.'

'Well, I don't wish to seem obstinate,' replied Danhasch; 'the best plan to test the truth of what I say will be for you to let me take you to see the princess for yourself.'

'There is no need for that,' retorted Maimoune; 'we can satisfy ourselves in another way. Bring your princess here and lay her down beside my prince. We can then compare them at leisure, and decide which is in the right.'

Danhasch readily consented, and after having the tower where the prince was confined pointed out to him, and making a wager with Maimoune as to the result of the comparison, he flew off to China to fetch the princess.

In an incredibly short time Danhasch returned, bearing the sleeping princess. Maimoune led him to the prince's room, and the rival beauty was placed beside him.

When the prince and princess lay thus side by side, an animated dispute as to their respective charms arose between the fairy and the genius. Danhasch began by saying: 'Now you see that my princess is more beautiful than your prince. Can you doubt any longer?'

'Doubt! Of course I do!' exclaimed Maimoune. 'Why, you must be blind not to see how much my prince excels your princess. I do not deny that your princess is very handsome, but only look and you must own that I am in the right.'

'There is no need for me to look longer,' said Danhasch; 'my first impression will remain the same; but of course, charming Maimoune, I am ready to yield to you if you insist on it.'

'By no means,' replied Maimoune. 'I have no idea of being under any obligation to an accursed genius like you. I refer the matter to an umpire, and shall expect you to submit to his verdict.'

Danhasch readily agreed, and on Maimoune striking the floor with her foot it opened, and a hideous, humpbacked, lame, squinting genius, with six horns on his head, hands like claws, emerged. As soon as he beheld Maimoune he threw himself at her feet and asked her commands.

'Rise, Caschcasch,' said she. 'I summoned you to judge between me and Danhasch. Glance at that couch, and say without any partiality whether you think the youth or the maiden lying there the more beautiful.'

Caschcasch looked at the prince and princess with every token of surprise and admiration. At length, having gazed long without being able to come to a decision, he said,

'Madam, I must confess that I should deceive you were I to declare one to be handsomer than the other. There seems to me only one way in which to decide the matter, and that is to wake one after the other and judge which of them expresses the greater admiration for the other.'

This advice pleased Maimoune and Danhasch, and the fairy at once transformed herself into the shape of a gnat and settling on Camaralzaman's throat stung him so sharply that he awoke. As he did so his eyes fell on the Princess of China. Surprised at finding a lady so near him, he raised himself on one arm to look at her. The youth and beauty of the princess at once awoke a feeling to which his heart had as yet been a stranger, and he could not restrain his delight.

'What loveliness! What charms! Oh, my heart, my soul!' he exclaimed, as he kissed her forehead, her eyes and mouth in a way which would certainly have roused her had not the genie's enchantments kept her asleep.

'How, fair lady!' he cried, 'you do not wake at the signs of

Caschcasch is unable to decide which is the fairer

Camaralzaman's love? Be you who you may, he is not unworthy of you.'

It then suddenly occurred to him, that perhaps this was the bride his father had destined for him, and that the king had probably had her placed in this room in order to see how far Camaralzaman's aversion to marriage would withstand her charms.

'At all events,' he thought, 'I will take this ring as a remembrance of her.' So saying he drew off a fine ring which the princess wore on her finger, and replaced it by one of his own. After which he lay down again and was soon fast asleep.

Then Danhasch, in his turn, took the form of a gnat and bit the princess on her lip.

She started up, and was not a little amazed at seeing a young man beside her. From surprise she soon passed to admiration, and then to delight on perceiving how handsome and fascinating he was.

'Why,' cried she, 'was it you my father wished me to marry? How unlucky that I did not know sooner! I should not have made him so angry. But wake up! wake up! for I know I shall love you with all my heart.'

So saying she shook Camaralzaman so violently that nothing but the spells of Maimoune could have prevented his waking.

'Oh!' cried the princess. 'Why are you so drowsy?' So saying she took his hand and noticed her own ring on his finger, which made her wonder still more. But as he still remained in a profound slumber she pressed a kiss on his cheek and soon fell fast asleep too.

Then Maimoune turning to the genie said: 'Well, are you satisfied that my prince surpasses your princess? Another time pray believe me when I assert anything.'

Then turning to Caschcasch: 'My thanks to you, and now do you and Danhasch bear the princess back to her own home.'

The two genii hastened to obey, and Maimoune returned to her well.

On waking next morning the first thing Prince Camaralzaman did was to look round for the lovely lady he had seen at night, and the next to question the slave who waited on him about her. But the slave persisted so strongly that he knew nothing of any lady, and still less of how she got into the tower, that the prince lost all patience, and after giving him a good beating tied a rope round him and ducked him in the well till the unfortunate man cried out that he would tell everything. Then the prince drew him up all dripping wet, but the slave begged leave to change his clothes first, and as soon as the prince consented hurried off just as he was to the palace. Here he found the king talking to the grand-vizir of all the anxiety his son had caused him. The slave was admitted at once and cried: 'Alas, sire! I bring sad news to your majesty. There can be no doubt that the prince has completely lost his senses. He declares that he saw a lady sleeping on his couch last night, and the state you see me in proves how violent contradiction makes him.' He then gave a minute account of all the prince had said and done.

The king, much moved, begged the vizir to examine into this new misfortune, and the latter at once went to the tower, where he found the prince quietly reading a book. After the first exchange of greetings the vizir said: 'I feel really very angry with your slave for alarming his majesty by the news he brought him.'

'What news?' asked the prince.

'Ah!' replied the vizir, 'something absurd, I feel sure, seeing how I find you.'

'Most likely,' said the prince; 'but now that you are here I am glad of the opportunity to ask you where is the lady who slept in this room last night?'

The grand-vizir felt beside himself at this question.

'Prince!' he exclaimed, 'how would it be possible for any man, much less a woman, to enter this room at night without walking over your slave on the threshold? Pray consider the matter, and you will realise that you have been deeply impressed by some dream.'

But the prince angrily insisted on knowing who and where the lady was, and was not to be persuaded by all the vizir's protestations to the contrary that the plot had not been one of his making. At last, losing patience, he seized the vizir by the beard and loaded him with blows.

'Stop, prince,' cried the unhappy vizir, 'stay and hear what I have to say.'

Camaralzaman ill-treats the grand-vizir

The prince, whose arm was getting tired, paused.

'I confess, prince,' said the vizir, 'that there is some foundation for what you say. But you know well that a minister has to carry out his master's orders. Allow me to go and to take to the king any message you may choose to send.'

'Very well,' said the prince; 'then go and tell him that I consent to marry the lady whom he sent or brought here last night. Be quick and bring me back his answer.'

The vizir bowed to the ground and hastened to leave the room and tower.

'Well,' asked the king as soon as he appeared, 'and how did you find my son?'

'Alas, sire,' was the reply, 'the slave's report is only too true!'

He then gave an exact account of his interview with Camaralzaman and of the prince's fury when told that it was not possible for any lady to have entered his room, and of the treatment he himself had received. The king, much distressed, determined to clear up the matter himself, and, ordering the vizir to follow him, set out to visit his son.

The prince received his father with profound respect, and the king, making him sit beside him, asked him several questions, to which Camaralzaman replied with much good sense. At last the king said: 'My son, pray tell me about the lady who, it is said, was in your room last night.'

'Sire,' replied the prince, 'pray do not increase my distress in this matter, but rather make me happy by giving her to me in marriage. However much I may have objected to matrimony formerly, the sight of this lovely girl has overcome all my prejudices, and I will gratefully receive her from your hands.'

The king was almost speechless on hearing his son, but after a time assured him most solemnly that he knew nothing whatever about the lady in question, and had not connived at her appearance. He then desired the prince to relate the whole story to him.

Camaralzaman did so at great length, showed the ring, and implored his father to help to find the bride he so ardently desired.

'After all you tell me,' remarked the king, 'I can no longer doubt your word; but how and whence the lady came, or why she should have stayed so short a time I cannot imagine. The whole affair is indeed mysterious. Come, my dear son, let us wait together for happier days.'

So saying the king took Camaralzaman by the hand and led him back to the palace, where the prince took to his bed and gave himself up to despair, and the king shutting himself up with his son entirely neglected the affairs of state.

The prime minister, who was the only person admitted, felt it his duty at last to tell the king how much the court and all the people complained of his seclusion, and how bad it was for the nation. He urged the sultan to remove with the prince to a lovely little island close by, whence he could easily attend public audiences, and where the charming scenery and fine air would do the invalid so much good as to enable him to bear his father's occasional absence.

The king approved the plan, and as soon as the castle on the island could be prepared for their reception he and the prince arrived there, Schahzaman never leaving his son except for the prescribed public audiences twice a week.

Whilst all this was happening in the capital of Schahzaman the two genii had carefully borne the Princess of China back to her own palace and replaced her in bed. On waking next morning she first turned from one side to another and then, finding herself alone, called loudly for her women.

'Tell me,' she cried, 'where is the young man I love so dearly, and who slept near me last night?'

'Princess,' exclaimed the nurse, 'we cannot tell what you allude to without more explanation.'

'Why,' continued the princess, 'the most charming and beautiful young man lay sleeping beside me last night. I did my utmost to wake him, but in vain.'

'Your royal highness wishes to make game of us,' said the nurse. 'Is it your pleasure to rise?'

'I am quite in earnest,' persisted the princess, 'and I want to know where he is.'

'But, princess,' expostulated the nurse, 'we left you quite alone last night, and we have seen no one enter your room since then.'

At this the princess lost all patience, and taking the nurse by her hair she boxed her ears soundly, crying out: 'You shall tell me, you old witch, or I'll kill you.'

The nurse had no little trouble in escaping, and hurried off to the queen, to whom she related the whole story with tears in her eyes.

'You see, madam,' she concluded, 'that the princess must be out of her mind. If only you will come and see her, you will be able to judge for yourself.'

The queen hurried to her daughter's apartments, and after tenderly embracing her, asked her why she had treated her nurse so badly.

'Madam,' said the princess, 'I perceive that your majesty wishes to make game of me, but I can assure you that I will never marry anyone except the charming young man whom I saw last night. You must know where he is, so pray send for him.'

The queen was much surprised by these words, but when she declared that she knew nothing whatever of the matter the princess lost all respect, and answered that if she were not allowed to marry as she wished she should kill herself, and it was in vain that the queen tried to pacify her and bring her to reason.

The king himself came to hear the rights of the matter, but the princess only persisted in her story, and as a proof showed the ring on her finger. The king hardly knew what to make of it all, but ended by thinking that his daughter was more crazy than ever, and without further argument he had her placed in still closer confinement, with only her nurse to wait on her and a powerful guard to keep the door.

Then he assembled his council, and having told them the sad state of things, added: 'If any of you can succeed in curing the princess, I will give her to him in marriage, and he shall be my heir.'

An elderly emir present, fired with the desire to possess a young and lovely wife and to rule over a great kingdom, offered to try the magic arts with which he was acquainted.

'You are welcome to try,' said the king, 'but I make one condition, which is, that should you fail you will lose your life.'

The King of China looks at the ring on the princess's finger

The emir accepted the condition, and the king led him to the princess, who, veiling her face, remarked, 'I am surprised, sire, that you should bring an unknown man into my presence.'

'You need not be shocked,' said the king; 'this is one of my emirs who asks your hand in marriage.'

'Sire,' replied the princess, 'this is not the one you gave me before and whose ring I wear. Permit me to say that I can accept no other.'

The emir, who had expected to hear the princess talk nonsense, finding how calm and reasonable she was, assured the king that he could not venture to undertake a cure, but placed his head at his majesty's disposal, on which the justly irritated monarch promptly had it cut off.

This was the first of many suitors for the princess whose inability to cure her cost them their lives.

Now it happened that after things had been going on in this way for some time the nurse's son Marzavan returned from his travels. He had been in many countries and learnt many things, including astrology. Needless to say that one of the first things his mother told him was the sad condition of the princess, his foster-sister. Marzavan asked if she could not manage to let him see the princess without the king's knowledge.

After some consideration his mother consented, and even persuaded the eunuch on guard to make no objection to Marzavan's entering the royal apartment.

The princess was delighted to see her foster-brother again, and after some conversation she confided to him all her history and the cause of her imprisonment.

Marzavan listened with downcast eyes and the utmost attention. When she had finished speaking he said,

'If what you tell me, princess, is indeed the case, I do not despair of finding comfort for you. Take patience yet a little longer. I will set out at once to explore other countries, and when you hear of my return be sure that he for whom you sigh is not far off.' So saying, he took his leave and started next morning on his travels.

Marzavan journeyed from city to city and from one island and province to another, and wherever he went he heard people talk of the strange story of the Princess Badoura, as the Princess of China was named.

After four months he reached a large populous seaport town named Torf, and here he heard no more of the Princess Badoura but a great deal of Prince Camaralzaman, who was reported ill, and whose story sounded very similar to that of the Princess Badoura.

Marzavan was rejoiced, and set out at once for Prince Camaral-zaman's residence. The ship on which he embarked had a prosperous voyage till she got within sight of the capital of King Schahzaman, but when just about to enter the harbour she suddenly struck on a rock, and foundered within sight of the palace where the prince was living with his father and the grand-vizir.

Marzavan, who swam well, threw himself into the sea and managed to land close to the palace, where he was kindly received, and after having a change of clothing given him was brought before the grand-vizir. The vizir was at once attracted by the young man's superior air and intelligent conversation, and perceiving that he had gained much experience in the course of his travels, he said, 'Ah, how I wish you had learnt some secret which might enable you to cure a malady which has plunged this court into affliction for some time past!'

Marzavan replied that if he knew what the illness was he might possibly be able to suggest a remedy, on which the vizir related to him the whole history of Prince Camaralzaman.

On hearing this Marzavan rejoiced inwardly, for he felt sure that he had at last discovered the object of the Princess Badoura's infatuation. However, he said nothing, but begged to be allowed to see the prince.

On entering the royal apartment the first thing which struck him was the prince himself, who lay stretched out on his bed with his eyes closed. The king sat near him, but, without paying any regard to his presence, Marzavan exclaimed, 'Heavens! what a striking likeness!' And, indeed, there was a good deal of resemblance between the features of Camaralzaman and those of the Princess of China.

These words caused the prince to open his eyes with languid curiosity, and Marzavan seized this moment to pay him his compliments, contriving at the same time to express the condition of the Princess of China in terms unintelligible, indeed, to the sultan and his vizir, but which left the prince in no doubt that his visitor could give him some welcome information.

The prince begged his father to allow him the favour of a private interview with Marzavan, and the king was only too pleased to find his son taking an interest in anyone or anything. As soon as they were left alone Marzavan told the prince the story of the Princess Badoura and her sufferings, adding, 'I am convinced that you alone can cure her; but before starting on so long a journey you must be well and strong, so do your best to recover as quickly as may be.'

These words produced a great effect on the prince, who was so much cheered by the hopes held out that he declared he felt able to get up and be dressed. The king was overjoyed at the result of Marzavan's interview, and ordered public rejoicings in honour of the prince's recovery.

Before long the prince was quite restored to his original state of health, and as soon as he felt himself really strong he took Marzavan aside and said: 'Now is the time to perform your promise. I am so impatient to see my beloved princess once more that I am sure I shall fall ill again if we do not start soon. The one obstacle is my father's tender care of me, for, as you may have noticed, he cannot bear me out of his sight.'

'Prince,' replied Marzavan, 'I have already thought over the matter, and this is what seems to me the best plan. You have not been out of doors since my arrival. Ask the king's permission to go with me for two or three days' hunting, and when he has given leave order two good horses to be held ready for each of us. Leave all the rest to me.'

Next day the prince seized a favourable opportunity for making his request, and the king gladly granted it on condition that only one night should be spent out for fear of too great fatigue after such a long illness.

Next morning Prince Camaralzaman and Marzavan were off betimes, attended by two grooms leading the two extra horses. They hunted a little by the way, but took care to get as far from the towns as possible. At nightfall they reached an inn, where they supped and slept till midnight. Then Marzavan awoke and roused the prince without disturbing anyone else. He begged the prince to give him the coat he had been wearing and to put on another which they had brought with them. They mounted their second horses, and Marzavan led one of the grooms' horses by the bridle.

By daybreak our travellers found themselves where four cross roads met in the middle of the forest. Here Marzavan begged the prince to wait for him, and leading the groom's horse into a dense part of the wood he cut its throat, dipped the prince's coat in its blood, and having rejoined the prince threw the coat on the ground where the roads parted.

In answer to Camaralzaman's enquiries as to the reason for this, Marzavan replied that the only chance they had of continuing their journey was to divert attention by creating the idea of the prince's death. 'Your father will doubtless be plunged in the deepest grief,' he went on, 'but his joy at your return will be all the greater.'

The prince and his companion now continued their journey by land and sea, and as they had brought plenty of money to defray their expenses they met with no needless delays. At length they reached the capital of China, where they spent three days in a suitable lodging to recover from their fatigues.

During this time Marzavan had an astrologer's dress prepared for the prince. They then went to the baths, after which the prince put on the astrologer's robe and was conducted within sight of the king's palace by Marzavan, who left him there and went to consult his mother, the princess's nurse.

Meantime the prince, according to Marzavan's instructions, advanced close to the palace gates and there proclaimed aloud: 'I am an astrologer and I come to restore health to the Princess Badoura, daughter of the high and mighty King of China, on the conditions laid down by his majesty of marrying her should I succeed, or of losing my life if I fail.'

It was some little time since anyone had presented himself to run the terrible risk involved in attempting to cure the princess, and a crowd soon gathered round the prince. On perceiving his youth, good looks, and distinguished bearing, everyone felt pity for him.

'What are you thinking of, sir,' exclaimed some; 'why expose yourself to certain death? Are not the heads you see exposed on the town wall sufficient warning? For mercy's sake give up this mad idea and retire whilst you can.'

But the prince remained firm, and only repeated his cry with greater assurance, to the horror of the crowd.

'He is resolved to die!' they cried; 'may heaven have pity on him!'

Camaralzaman now called out for the third time, and at last the grand-vizir himself came out and fetched him in.

The prime minister led the prince to the king, who was much struck by the noble air of this new adventurer, and felt such pity for the fate so evidently in store for him, that he tried to persuade the young man to renounce his project.

But Camaralzaman politely yet firmly persisted in his intentions, and at length the king desired the eunuch who had the guard of the princess's apartments to conduct the astrologer to her presence.

The eunuch led the way through long passages, and Camaralzaman followed rapidly, in haste to reach the object of his desires. At last they came to a large hall which was the anteroom to the princess's chamber, and here Camaralzaman said to the eunuch: 'Now you shall choose. Shall I cure the princess in her own presence, or shall I do it from here without seeing her?'

The eunuch, who had expressed many contemptuous doubts as they came along of the newcomer's powers, was much surprised and said: 'If you really can cure, it is immaterial when you do it. Your fame will be equally great.'

'Very well,' replied the prince: 'then, impatient though I am to see the princess, I will effect the cure where I stand, the better to convince you of my power.' He accordingly drew out his writing case and wrote as follows – 'Adorable princess! The enamoured Camaralzaman has never forgotten the moment when, contemplating your sleeping beauty, he gave you his heart. As he was at that time deprived of the happiness of conversing with you, he ventured to give you his ring as a token of his love, and to take yours in exchange, which he now encloses in this letter. Should you deign to return it to him he will be the happiest of mortals, if not he will cheerfully resign himself to death, seeing he does so for love of you. He awaits your reply in your anteroom.'

Having finished this note the prince carefully enclosed the ring in it without letting the eunuch see it, and gave him the letter, saying: 'Take this to your mistress, my friend, and if on reading it and seeing its contents she is not instantly cured, you may call me an impudent impostor.'

The eunuch at once passed into the princess's room, and handing her the letter said: 'Madam, a new astrologer has arrived, who declares that you will be cured as soon as you have read this letter and seen what it contains.'

The princess took the note and opened it with languid indifference. But no sooner did she see her ring than, barely glancing at the writing, she rose hastily and with one bound reached the doorway and pushed back the hangings. Here she and the prince recognised each other, and in a moment they were locked in each other's arms, where they tenderly embraced, wondering how they came to meet at last after so long a separation. The nurse, who had hastened after her charge, drew them back to the inner room, where the princess restored her ring to Camaralzaman.

'Take it back,' she said, 'I could not keep it without returning yours to you, and I am resolved to wear that as long as I live.'

Meantime the eunuch had hastened back to the king. 'Sire,' he cried, 'all the former doctors and astrologers were mere quacks. This man has cured the princess without even seeing her.' He then told all to the king, who, overjoyed, hastened to his daughter's apartments, where, after embracing her, he placed her hand in that of the prince, saying: 'Happy stranger, I keep my promise, and give you my daughter to wife, be you who you may. But, if I am not much mistaken, your condition is above what you appear to be.'

The prince thanked the king in the warmest and most respectful terms, and added: 'As regards my person, your majesty has rightly guessed that I am not an astrologer. It is but a disguise which I assumed in order to merit your illustrious alliance. I am myself a prince, my name is Camaralzaman, and my father is Schahzaman, King of the Isles of the Children of Khaledan.' He then told his whole history, including the extraordinary manner of his first seeing and loving the Princess Badoura.

Badoura recognises Camaralzaman

When he had finished the king exclaimed: 'So remarkable a story must not be lost to posterity. It shall be inscribed in the archives of my kingdom and published everywhere abroad.'

The wedding took place next day amidst great pomp and rejoicings. Marzavan was not forgotten, but was given a lucrative post at court, with a promise of further advancement.

The prince and princess were now entirely happy, and months slipped by unconsciously in the enjoyment of each other's society.

One night, however, Prince Camaralzaman dreamt that he saw his father lying at the point of death, and saying: 'Alas! my son whom I loved so tenderly, has deserted me and is now causing my death.'

The prince woke with such a groan as to startle the princess, who asked what was the matter.

'Ah!' cried the prince, 'at this very moment my father is perhaps no more!' and he told his dream.

The princess said but little at the time, but next morning she went to the king, and kissing his hand said: 'I have a favour to ask of your majesty, and I beg you to believe that it is in no way prompted by my husband. It is that you will allow us both to visit my father-in-law King Schahzaman.'

Sorry though the king felt at the idea of parting with his daughter, he felt her request to be so reasonable that he could not refuse it, and made but one condition, which was that she should only spend one year at the court of King Schahzaman, suggesting that in future the young couple should visit their respective parents alternately.

The princess brought this good news to her husband, who thanked her tenderly for this fresh proof of her affection.

All preparations for the journey were now pressed forwards, and when all was ready the king accompanied the travellers for some days, after which he took an affectionate leave of his daughter, and charging the prince to take every care of her, returned to his capital.

The prince and princess journeyed on, and at the end of a month reached a huge meadow interspersed with clumps of big trees which cast a most pleasant shade. As the heat was great, Camaralzaman thought it well to encamp in this cool spot. Accordingly the tents were pitched, and the princess entering hers whilst the prince was giving his further orders, removed her girdle, which she placed beside her, and desiring her women to leave her, lay down and was soon asleep.

When the camp was all in order the prince entered the tent and, seeing the princess asleep, he sat down near her without speaking. His eyes fell on the girdle, which he took up, and whilst inspecting the precious stones set in it he noticed a little pouch sewn to the girdle and fastened by a loop. He touched it and felt something hard within. Curious as to what this might be, he opened the pouch and found a cornelian engraved with various figures and strange characters.

'This cornelian must be something very precious,' thought he, 'or my wife would not wear it on her person with so much care.'

In truth it was a talisman which the Queen of China had given her daughter, telling her it would ensure her happiness as long as she carried it about her.

The better to examine the stone the prince stepped to the open doorway of the tent. As he stood there holding it in the open palm of his hand, a bird suddenly swooped down, picked the stone up in its beak and flew away with it.

Imagine the prince's dismay at losing a thing by which his wife evidently set such store!

The bird having secured its prey flew off some yards and alighted on the ground, holding the talisman it its beak. Prince Camaralzaman advanced, hoping the bird would drop it, but as soon as he approached the thief fluttered on a little further still. He continued his pursuit till the bird suddenly swallowed the stone and took a longer flight than before. The prince then hoped to kill it with a stone, but the more hotly he pursued the further flew the bird.

In this fashion he was led on by hill and dale through the entire day, and when night came the tiresome creature roosted on the top of a very high tree where it could rest in safety.

The prince in despair at all his useless trouble began to think whether he had better return to the camp. 'But,' thought he, 'how shall I find my way back? Must I go up hill or down? I should

The bird flies off with the talisman

certainly lose my way in the dark, even if my strength held out.'
Overwhelmed by hunger, thirst, fatigue and sleep, he ended by
spending the night at the foot of the tree.

Next morning Camaralzaman woke up before the bird left its
perch, and no sooner did it take flight than he followed it again with
as little success as the previous day, only stopping to eat some herbs
and fruit he found by the way. In this fashion he spent ten days,
following the bird all day and spending the night at the foot of a
tree, whilst it roosted on the topmost bough. On the eleventh day
the bird and the prince reached a large town, and as soon as they
were close to its walls the bird took a sudden and higher flight and
was shortly completely out of sight, whilst Camaralzaman felt in
despair at having to give up all hopes of ever recovering the talisman
of the Princess Badoura.

Much cast down, he entered the town, which was built near the
sea and had a fine harbour. He walked about the streets for a long
time, not knowing where to go, but at length as he walked near the
seashore he found a garden door open and walked in.

The gardener, a good old man, who was at work, happened to look up, and, seeing a stranger, whom he recognised by his dress as a Mussulman, he told him to come in at once and to shut the door.

Camaralzaman did as he was bid, and enquired why this precaution was taken.

'Because,' said the gardener, 'I see that you are a stranger and a Mussulman, and this town is almost entirely inhabited by idolaters, who hate and persecute all of our faith. It seems almost a miracle that has led you to this house, and I am indeed glad that you have found a place of safety.'

Camaralzaman warmly thanked the kind old man for offering him shelter, and was about to say more, but the gardener interrupted him with: 'Leave compliments alone. You are weary and must be hungry. Come in, eat, and rest.' So saying he led the prince into his cottage, and after satisfying his hunger begged to learn the cause of his arrival.

Camaralzaman told him all without disguise, and ended by enquiring the shortest way to his father's capital. 'For,' added he, 'if I tried to rejoin the princess, how should I find her after eleven days' separation. Perhaps, indeed, she may be no longer alive!' At this terrible thought he burst into tears.

The gardener informed Camaralzaman that they were quite a year's land journey to any Mahomedan country, but that there was a much shorter route by sea to the Ebony Island, from whence the Isles of the Children of Khaledan could be easily reached, and that a ship sailed once a year for the Ebony Island by which he might get so far as his very home.

'If only you had arrived a few days sooner,' he said, 'you might have embarked at once. As it is you must now wait till next year, but if you care to stay with me I offer you my house, such as it is, with all my heart.'

Prince Camaralzaman thought himself lucky to find some place of refuge, and gladly accepted the gardener's offer. He spent his days working in the garden, and his nights thinking of and sighing for his beloved wife.

Let us now see what had become during this time of the Princess Badoura.

On first waking she was much surprised not to find the prince near her. She called her women and asked if they knew where he was, and whilst they were telling her that they had seen him enter the tent, but had not noticed his leaving it, she took up her belt and perceived that the little pouch was open and the talisman gone.

She at once concluded that her husband had taken it and would shortly bring it back. She waited for him till evening rather impatiently, and wondering what could have kept him from her so long. When night came without him she felt in despair and abused the talisman and its maker roundly. In spite of her grief and anxiety however, she did not lose her presence of mind, but decided on a courageous, though very unusual step.

Only the princess and her women knew of Camaralzaman's disappearance, for the rest of the party were sleeping or resting in their tents. Fearing some treason should the truth be known, she ordered her women not to say a word which would give rise to any suspicion, and proceeded to change her dress for one of her husband's, to whom, as has been already said, she bore a strong likeness.

In this disguise she looked so like the prince that when she gave orders next morning to break up the camp and continue the journey no one suspected the change. She made one of her women enter her litter, whilst she herself mounted on horseback and the march began.

After a protracted journey by land and sea the princess, still under the name and disguise of Prince Camaralzaman, arrived at the capital of the Ebony Island whose king was named Armanos.

No sooner did the king hear that the ship which was just in port had on board the son of his old friend and ally than he hurried to meet the supposed prince, and had him and his retinue brought to the palace, where they were lodged and entertained sumptuously.

After three days, finding that his guest, to whom he had taken a great fancy, talked of continuing his journey, King Armanos said to him: 'Prince, I am now an old man, and unfortunately I have no son to whom to leave my kingdom. It has pleased heaven to give me only one daughter, who possesses such great beauty and charm that I could only give her to a prince as highly born and as accomplished as yourself. Instead, therefore, of returning to your own country, take my daughter and my crown and stay with us. I shall feel that I have a worthy successor, and shall cheerfully retire from the fatigues of government.'

The king's offer was naturally rather embarrassing to the Princess Badoura. She felt that it was equally impossible to confess that she had deceived him, or to refuse the marriage on which he had set his heart; a refusal which might turn all his kindness to hatred and persecution.

All things considered, she decided to accept, and after a few moments' silence said with a blush, which the king attributed to modesty: 'Sire, I feel so great an obligation for the good opinion your majesty has expressed for my person and of the honour you do me, that, though I am quite unworthy of it, I dare not refuse. But, sire, I can only accept such an alliance if you give me your promise to assist me with your counsels.'

The marriage being thus arranged, the ceremony was fixed for the following day, and the princess employed the intervening time in informing the officers of her suite of what had happened, assuring them that the Princess Badoura had given her full consent to the marriage. She also told her women, and bade them keep her secret well.

King Armanos, delighted with the success of his plans, lost no time in assembling his court and council, to whom he presented his successor, and placing his future son-in-law on the throne made everyone do homage and take oaths of allegiance to the new king.

At night the whole town was filled with rejoicings, and with much pomp the Princess Haiatelnefous (this was the name of the king's daughter) was conducted to the palace of the Princess Badoura.

Now Badoura had thought much of the difficulties of her first interview with King Armanos's daughter, and she felt the only thing to do was at once to take her into her confidence.

Accordingly, as soon as they were alone she took Haiatelnefous by the hand and said: 'Princess, I have a secret to tell you, and must throw myself on your mercy. I am not Prince Camaralzaman, but a princess like yourself and his wife, and I beg you to listen to my story, then I am sure you will forgive my imposture, in consideration of my sufferings.'

She then related her whole history, and at its close Haiatelnefous embraced her warmly, and assured her of her entire sympathy and affection.

The two princesses now planned out their future action, and agreed to combine to keep up the deception and to let Badoura continue to play a man's part until such time as there might be news of the real Camaralzaman.

Whilst these things were passing in the Ebony Island Prince Camaralzaman continued to find shelter in the gardener's cottage in the town of the idolaters.

Early one morning the gardener said to the prince: 'Today is a public holiday, and the people of the town not only do not work themselves but forbid others to do so. You had better therefore take a good rest whilst I go to see some friends, and as the time is near for the arrival of the ship of which I told you I will make enquiries about it, and try to bespeak a passage for you.' He then put on his best clothes and went out, leaving the prince, who strolled into the garden and was soon lost in thoughts of his dear wife and their sad separation.

As he walked up and down he was suddenly disturbed in his reverie by the noise two large birds were making in a tree.

Camaralzaman stood still and looked up, and saw that the birds were fighting so savagely with beaks and claws that before long one fell dead to the ground, whilst the conqueror spread his wings and flew away. Almost immediately two other larger birds, who had been watching the duel, flew up and alighted, one at the head and the other at the feet of the dead bird. They stood there some time sadly shaking their heads, and then dug up a grave with their claws in which they buried him.

As soon as they had filled in the grave the two flew off, and ere long returned, bringing with them the murderer, whom they held, one by a wing and the other by a leg, with their beaks, screaming and struggling with rage and terror. But they held tight, and having brought him to his victim's grave, they proceeded to kill him, after which they tore open his body, scattered the insides and once more flew away.

The prince, who had watched the whole scene with much interest, now drew near the spot where it happened, and glancing at the dead bird he noticed something red lying near which had evidently fallen out of its inside. He picked it up, and what was his surprise when he recognised the Princess Badoura's talisman which had been the cause of many misfortunes. It would be impossible to describe his joy; he kissed the talisman repeatedly, wrapped it up, and carefully tied it round his arm. For the first time since his separation from the princess he had a good night, and next morning he was up at daybreak and went cheerfully to ask what work he should do.

The gardener told him to cut down an old fruit tree which had quite died away, and Camaralzaman took an axe and fell to vigorously. As he was hacking at one of the roots the axe struck on something hard. On pushing away the earth he discovered a large slab of bronze, under which was disclosed a staircase with ten steps. He went down them and found himself in a roomy kind of cave in which stood fifty large bronze jars, each with a cover on it. The prince uncovered one after another, and found them all filled with gold dust. Delighted with his discovery he left the cave, replaced the slab, and having finished cutting down the tree waited for the gardener's return.

The gardener had heard the night before that the ship about which he was enquiring would start ere long, but the exact date not being yet known he had been told to return next day for further information. He had gone therefore to enquire, and came back with good news beaming in his face.

'My son,' said he, 'rejoice and hold yourself ready to start in three days' time. The ship is to set sail, and I have arranged all about your passage with the captain.'

'You could not bring me better news,' replied Camaralzaman,

Camaralzaman watches the birds

'and in return I have something pleasant to tell you. Follow me and see the good fortune which has befallen you.'

He then led the gardener to the cave, and having shown him the treasure stored up there, said how happy it made him that heaven should in this way reward his kind host's many virtues and compensate him for the privations of many years.

'What do you mean?' asked the gardener. 'Do you imagine that I should appropriate this treasure? It is yours, and I have no right whatever to it. For the last eighty years I have dug up the ground here without discovering anything. It is clear that these riches are intended for you, and they are much more needed by a prince like yourself than by an old man like me, who am near my end and require nothing. This treasure comes just at the right time, when you are about to return to your own country, where you will make good use of it.'

But the prince would not hear of this suggestion, and finally after much discussion they agreed to divide the gold. When this was done the gardener said: 'My son, the great thing now is to arrange how you can best carry off this treasure as secretly as possible for fear of losing it. There are no olives in the Ebony Island, and those imported from here fetch a high price. As you know, I have a good stock of the olives which grew in this garden. Now you must take fifty jars, fill each half full of gold dust and fill them up with the olives. We will then have them taken on board ship when you embark.'

The prince took this advice, and spent the rest of the day filling the fifty jars, and fearing lest the precious talisman might slip from his arm and be lost again, he took the precaution of putting it in one of the jars, on which he made a mark so as to be able to recognise it. When night came the jars were all ready, and the prince and his host went to bed.

Whether in consequence of his great age, or of the fatigues and excitement of the previous day, I do not know, but the gardener passed a very bad night. He was worse next day, and by the morning of the third day was dangerously ill. At daybreak the ship's captain and some of his sailors knocked at the garden door and asked for the passenger who was to embark.

'I am he,' said Camaralzaman, who had opened the door. 'The gardener who took my passage is ill and cannot see you, but please come in and take these jars of olives and my bag, and I will follow as soon as I have taken leave of him.'

The sailors did as he asked, and the captain before leaving charged Camaralzaman to lose no time, as the wind was fair, and he wished to set sail at once.

As soon as they were gone the prince returned to the cottage to bid farewell to his old friend, and to thank him once more for all his kindness. But the old man was at his last gasp, and had barely murmured his confession of faith when he expired.

Camaralzaman was obliged to stay and pay him the last offices, so having dug a grave in the garden he wrapped the kind old man up and buried him. He then locked the door, gave up the key to the

The talisman is discovered in one of the jars

owner of the garden, and hurried to the quay only to hear that the ship had sailed long ago, after waiting three hours for him.

It may well be believed that the prince felt in despair at this fresh misfortune, which obliged him to spend another year in a strange and distasteful country. Moreover, he had once more lost the Princess Badoura's talisman, which he feared he might never see again. There was nothing left for him but to hire the garden as the old man had done, and to live on in the cottage. As he could not well cultivate the garden by himself, he engaged a lad to help him, and to secure the rest of the treasure he put the remaining gold dust into fifty more jars, filling them up with olives so as to have them ready for transport.

Whilst the prince was settling down to this second year of toil and privation, the ship made a rapid voyage and arrived safely at the Ebony Island.

As the palace of the new king, or rather of the Princess Badoura, overlooked the harbour, she saw the ship entering it and asked what vessel it was coming in so gaily decked with flags, and was told that it was a ship from the Island of the Idolaters which yearly brought rich merchandise.

The princess, ever on the lookout for any chance of news of her beloved husband, went down to the harbour attended by some officers of the court, and arrived just as the captain was landing. She sent for him and asked many questions as to his country, voyage, what passengers he had, and what his vessel was laden with. The captain answered all her questions, and said that his passengers consisted entirely of traders who brought rich stuffs from various countries, fine muslins, precious stones, musk, amber, spices, drugs, olives, and many other things.

As soon as he mentioned olives, the princess, who was very partial to them, exclaimed: 'I will take all you have on board. Have them unloaded and we will make our bargain at once, and tell the other merchants to let me see all their best wares before showing them to other people.'

'Sire,' replied the captain, 'I have on board fifty very large pots of olives. They belong to a merchant who was left behind, as in spite of waiting for him he delayed so long that I was obliged to set sail without him.'

'Never mind,' said the princess, 'unload them all the same, and we will arrange the price.'

The captain accordingly sent his boat off to the ship and it soon returned laden with the fifty pots of olives. The princess asked what they might be worth.

'Sire,' replied the captain, 'the merchant is very poor. Your majesty will not overpay him if you give him a thousand pieces of silver.'

'In order to satisfy him and as he is so poor,' said the princess, 'I will order a thousand pieces of gold to be given you, which you will be sure to remit to him.'

So saying she gave orders for the payment and returned to the palace, having the jars carried before her. When evening came the Princess Badoura retired to the inner part of the palace, and going to the apartments of the Princess Haiatelnefous she had the fifty jars of olives brought to her. She opened one to let her friend taste the olives and to taste them herself, but great was her surprise when, on pouring some into a dish, she found them all powdered with gold dust. 'What an adventure! how extraordinary!' she cried. Then she had the other jars opened, and was more and more surprised to find the olives in each jar mixed with gold dust.

But when at length her talisman was discovered in one of the jars her emotion was so great that she fainted away. The Princess Haiatelnefous and her women hastened to restore her, and as soon as she recovered consciousness she covered the precious talisman with kisses.

Then, dismissing the attendants, she said to her friend: 'You will have guessed, my dear, that it was the sight of this talisman which has moved me so deeply. This was the cause of my separation from my dear husband, and now, I am convinced, it will be the means of our reunion.'

As soon as it was light next day the Princess Badoura sent for the captain, and made further enquiries about the merchant who owned the olive jars she had bought.

In reply the captain told her all he knew of the place where the young man lived, and how, after engaging his passage, he came to be left behind.

'If that is the case,' said the princess, 'you must set sail at once and go back for him. He is a debtor of mine and must be brought here at once, or I will confiscate all your merchandise. I shall now give orders to have all the warehouses where your cargo is placed under the royal seal, and they will only be opened when you have brought me the man I ask for. Go at once and obey my orders.'

The captain had no choice but to do as he was bid, so hastily provisioning his ship he started that same evening on his return voyage.

When, after a rapid passage, he gained sight of the Island of Idolaters, he judged it better not to enter the harbour, but casting anchor at some distance he embarked at night in a small boat with six active sailors and landed near Camaralzaman's cottage.

The prince was not asleep, and as he lay awake moaning over all the sad events which had separated him from his wife, he thought he heard a knock at the garden door. He went to open it, and was immediately seized by the captain and sailors, who without a word of explanation forcibly bore him off to the boat, which took them back to the ship without loss of time. No sooner were they on board than they weighed anchor and set sail.

Camaralzaman, who had kept silence till then, now asked the captain (whom he had recognised) the reason for this abduction.

'Are you not a debtor of the King of the Ebony Island?' asked the captain.

'I? Why, I never even heard of him before, and never set foot in his kingdom!' was the answer.

'Well, you must know better than I,' said the captain. 'You will soon see him now, and meantime be content where you are and have patience.'

The return voyage was as prosperous as the former one, and though it was night when the ship entered the harbour, the captain lost no time in landing with his passenger, whom he conducted to the palace, where he begged an audience with the king.

Directly the Princess Badoura saw the prince she recognised him in spite of his shabby clothes. She longed to throw herself on his neck, but restrained herself, feeling it was better for them both that she should play her part a little longer. She therefore desired one of her officers to take care of him and to treat him well. Next she ordered another officer to remove the seals from the warehouse, whilst she presented the captain with a costly diamond, and told him to keep the thousand pieces of gold paid for the olives, as she would arrange matters with the merchant himself.

She then returned to her private apartments, where she told the Princess Haiatelnefous all that had happened, as well as her plans for the future, and begged her assistance, which her friend readily promised.

Next morning she ordered the prince to be taken to the bath and clothed in a manner suitable to an emir or governor of a province. He was then introduced to the council, where his good looks and grand air drew the attention of all on him. Princess Badoura, delighted to see him looking himself once more, turned to the other emirs, saying: 'My lords, I introduce to you a new colleague, Camaralzaman, whom I have known on my travels and who, I can assure you, you will find well deserves your regard and admiration.'

Camaralzaman was much surprised at hearing the king – whom he never suspected of being a woman in disguise – asserting their acquaintance, for he felt sure he had never seen her before. However he received all the praises bestowed on him with becoming modesty, and prostrating himself, said: 'Sire, I cannot find words in which to thank your majesty for the great honour conferred on me. I can but assure you that I will do all in my power to prove myself worthy of it.'

On leaving the council the prince was conducted to a splendid house which had been prepared for him, where he found a full establishment and well-filled stables at his orders. On entering his study his steward presented him with a coffer filled with gold pieces for his current expenses. He felt more and more puzzled by such good fortune, and little guessed that the Princess of China was the cause of it.

After a few days the Princess Badoura promoted Camaralzaman to the post of grand treasurer, an office which he filled with so much integrity and benevolence as to win universal esteem.

He would now have thought himself the happiest of men had it not been for that separation which he never ceased to bewail. He had no clue to the mystery of his present position, for the princess, out of compliment to the old king, had taken his name, and was generally known as King Armanos the younger, few people remembering that on her first arrival she went by another name.

At length the princess felt that the time had come to put an end to her own and the prince's suspense, and having arranged all her plans with the Princess Haiatelnefous, she informed Camaralzaman that she wished his advice on some important business, and, to avoid being disturbed, desired him to come to the palace that evening.

The prince was punctual, and was received in the private apartment, when, having ordered her attendants to withdraw, the princess took from a small box the talisman, and, handing it to Camaralzaman, said: 'Not long ago an astrologer gave me this talisman. As you are universally well informed, you can perhaps tell me what is its use.'

Camaralzaman took the talisman and, holding it to the light, cried with surprise, 'Sire, you ask me the use of this talisman. Alas! hitherto it has been only a source of misfortune to me, being the cause of my separation from the one I love best on earth. The story is so sad and strange that I am sure your majesty will be touched by it if you will permit me to tell it you.'

'I will hear it some other time,' replied the princess. 'Meanwhile I fancy it is not quite unknown to me. Wait here for me. I will return shortly.'

So saying she retired to another room, where she hastily changed her masculine attire for that of a woman, and, after putting on the girdle she wore the day they parted, returned to Camaralzaman.

The prince recognised her at once, and, embracing her with the utmost tenderness, cried, 'Ah, how can I thank the king for this delightful surprise?'

'Do not expect ever to see the king again,' said the princess, as she wiped the tears of joy from her eyes, 'in me you see the king. Let us sit down, and I will tell you all about it.'

She then gave a full account of all her adventures since their parting, and dwelt much on the charms and noble disposition of the Princess Haiatelnefous, to whose friendly assistance she owed so much. When she had done she asked to hear the prince's story, and in this manner they spent most of the night.

Next morning the princess resumed her woman's clothes, and as soon as she was ready she desired the chief eunuch to beg King Armanos to come to her apartments.

When the king arrived great was his surprise at finding a strange lady in company of the grand treasurer who had no actual right to enter the private apartment. Seating himself he asked for the king.

'Sire,' said the princess, 'yesterday I was the king, today I am only the Princess of China and wife to the real Prince Camaralzaman, son of King Schahzaman, and I trust that when your majesty shall have heard our story you will not condemn the innocent deception I have been obliged to practise.'

The king consented to listen, and did so with marked surprise.

At the close of her narrative the princess said, 'Sire, as our religion allows a man to have more than one wife, I would beg your majesty to give your daughter, the Princess Haiatelnefous, in marriage to Prince Camaralzaman. I gladly yield to her the precedence and title of queen in recognition of the debt of gratitude which I owe her.'

King Armanos heard the princess with surprise and admiration, then, turning to Camaralzaman, he said, 'My son, as your wife, the Princess Badoura (whom I have hitherto looked on as my son-in-law), consents to share your hand and affections with my daughter, I have only to ask if this marriage is agreeable to you, and if you will consent to accept the crown which the Princess Badoura deserves to wear all her life, but which she prefers to resign for love of you.'

'Sire,' replied Camaralzaman, 'I can refuse your majesty nothing.'

Accordingly Camaralzaman was duly proclaimed king, and as duly married with all pomp to the Princess Haiatelnefous, with whose beauty, talents, and affections he had every reason to be pleased.

The two queens lived in true sisterly harmony together, and after a time each presented King Camaralzaman with a son, whose births were celebrated throughout the kingdom with the utmost rejoicing.

Noureddin and the Fair Persian

Balsora was the capital of a kingdom long tributary to the caliph. During the time of the Caliph Haroun-al-Raschid the king of Balsora, who was his cousin, was called Zinebi. Not thinking one vizir enough for the administration of his estates he had two, named Khacan and Saouy.

Khacan was kind, generous, and liberal, and took pleasure in obliging, as far as in him lay, those who had business with him. Throughout the entire kingdom there was no one who did not esteem and praise him as he deserved.

Saouy was quite a different character, and repelled everyone with whom he came in contact; he was always gloomy, and, in spite of his great riches, so miserly that he denied himself even the necessaries of life. What made him particularly detested was the great aversion he had to Khacan, of whom he never ceased to speak evil to the king.

One day, while the king amused himself talking with his two vizirs and other members of the council, the conversation turned on female slaves. While some declared that it sufficed for a slave to be beautiful, others, and Khacan was among the number, maintained that beauty alone was not enough, but that it must be accompanied by wit, wisdom, modesty, and, if possible, knowledge.

The king not only declared himself to be of this opinion, but charged Khacan to procure him a slave who should fulfil all these conditions. Saouy, who had been of the opposite side, and was jealous of the honour done to Khacan, said, 'Sire, it will be very difficult to find a slave as accomplished as your majesty desires, and, if she is to be found, she will be cheap if she cost less than 10,000 gold pieces.'

'Saouy,' answered the king, 'you seem to find that a very great sum. For you it may be so, but not for me.'

And forthwith he ordered his grand treasurer, who was present, to send 10,000 gold pieces to Khacan for the purchase of the slave.

As soon, then, as Khacan returned home he sent for the dealers in female slaves, and charged them directly they had found such a one as he described to inform him. They promised to do their utmost, and no day passed that they did not bring a slave for his inspection, but none was found without some defect.

At length, early one morning, while Khacan was on his way to the king's palace, a dealer, throwing himself in his way, announced eagerly that a Persian merchant, arrived late the previous evening, had a slave to sell whose wit and wisdom were equal to her incomparable beauty.

Khacan, overjoyed at this news, gave orders that the slave should be brought for his inspection on his return from the palace. The dealer appearing at the appointed hour, Khacan found the slave beautiful beyond his expectations, and immediately gave her the name of 'The Fair Persian'.

Being a man of great wisdom and learning, he perceived in the short conversation he had with her that he would seek in vain another slave to surpass her in any of the qualities required by the king, and therefore asked the dealer what price the merchant put upon her.

'Sir,' was the answer, 'for less than 10,000 gold pieces he will not let her go; he declares that, what with masters for her instruction, and for bodily exercises, not to speak of clothing and nourishment, he has already spent that sum upon her. She is in every way fit to be the slave of a king; she plays every musical instrument, she sings, she dances, she makes verses, in fact there is no accomplishment in which she does not excel.'

Khacan, who was better able to judge of her merits than the dealer, wishing to bring the matter to a conclusion, sent for the merchant, and said to him, 'It is not for myself that I wish to buy your slave, but for the king. Her price, however, is too high.'

'Sir,' replied the merchant, 'I should esteem it an honour to present her to his majesty, did it become a merchant to do such a thing. I ask no more than the sum it has cost me to make her such as she is.'

The beautiful Persian is brought to Khacan

Khacan, not wishing to bargain, immediately had the sum counted out, and given to the merchant, who before withdrawing said: 'Sir, as she is destined for the king, I would have you observe that she is extremely tired with the long journey, and before presenting her to his majesty you would do well to keep her a fortnight in your own house, and to see that a little care is bestowed upon her. The sun has tanned her complexion, but when she has been two or three times to the bath, and is fittingly dressed, you will see how much her beauty will be increased.'

Khacan thanked the merchant for his advice, and determined to follow it. He gave the beautiful Persian an apartment near to that of his wife, whom he charged to treat her as befitting a lady destined for the king, and to order for her the most magnificent garments.

Before bidding adieu to the fair Persian, he said to her: 'No happiness can be greater than what I have procured for you; judge for yourself, you now belong to the king. I have, however, to warn you of one thing. I have a son, who, though not wanting in sense, is young, foolish, and headstrong, and I charge you to keep him at a distance.'

The Persian thanked him for his advice, and promised to profit by it.

Noureddin – for so the vizir's son was named – went freely in and out of his mother's apartments. He was young, well-made and agreeable, and had the gift of charming all with whom he came in contact. As soon as he saw the beautiful Persian, though aware that she was destined for the king, he let himself be carried away by her charms, and determined at once to use every means in his power to retain her for himself. The Persian was equally captivated by Noureddin, and said to herself: 'The vizir does me too great honour in buying me for the king. I should esteem myself very happy if he would give me to his son.'

Noureddin availed himself of every opportunity to gaze upon her beauty, to talk and laugh with her, and never would have left her side if his mother had not forced him.

Some time having elapsed, on account of the long journey, since the beautiful Persian had been to the bath, five or six days after her purchase the vizir's wife gave orders that the bath should be heated for her, and that her own female slaves should attend her there, and afterwards should array her in a magnificent dress that had been prepared for her.

Her toilet completed, the beautiful Persian came to present herself to the vizir's wife, who hardly recognised her, so greatly was her beauty increased. Kissing her hand, the beautiful slave said: 'Madam, I do not know how you find me in this dress that you have had prepared for me; your women assure me that it suits me so well that they hardly knew me. If it is the truth they tell me, and not flattery, it is to you I owe the transformation.'

'My daughter,' answered the vizir's wife, 'they do not flatter you. I myself hardly recognised you. The improvement is not due to the dress alone, but largely to the beautifying effects of the bath. I am so struck by its results, that I would try it on myself.'

Acting forthwith on this decision she ordered two little slaves during her absence to watch over the beautiful Persian, and not to allow Noureddin to enter should he come.

She had no sooner gone than he arrived, and not finding his mother in her apartment, would have sought her in that of the Persian. The two little slaves barred the entrance, saying that his mother had given orders that he was not to be admitted. Taking each by an arm, he put them out of the anteroom, and shut the door. Then they rushed to the bath, informing their mistress with shrieks and tears that Noureddin had driven them away by force and gone in.

This news caused great consternation to the lady, who, dressing herself as quickly as possible, hastened to the apartment of the fair Persian, to find that Noureddin had already gone out. Much astonished to see the vizir's wife enter in tears, the Persian asked what misfortune had happened.

'What!' exclaimed the lady, 'you ask me that, knowing that my son Noureddin has been alone with you?'

'But, madam,' enquired the Persian, 'what harm is there in that?'

'How! Has my husband not told you that you are destined for the king?'

Noureddin gets rid of the two little slaves

'Certainly, but Noureddin has just been to tell me that his father has changed his mind and has bestowed me upon him. I believed him, and so great is my affection for Noureddin that I would willingly pass my life with him.'

'Would to heaven,' exclaimed the wife of the vizir, 'that what you say were true; but Noureddin has deceived you, and his father will sacrifice him in vengeance for the wrong he has done.'

So saying, she wept bitterly, and all her slaves wept with her.

Khacan, entering shortly after this, was much astonished to find his wife and her slaves in tears, and the beautiful Persian greatly perturbed. He enquired the cause, but for some time no answer was forthcoming. When his wife was at length sufficiently calm to inform him of what had happened, his rage and mortification knew no bounds. Wringing his hands and rending his beard, he exclaimed: 'Wretched son! thou destroyest not only thyself but thy father. The king will shed not only thy blood but mine.' His wife tried to console him, saying: 'Do not torment thyself. With the sale of my jewels I will obtain 10,000 gold pieces, and with this sum you will buy another slave.'

'Do not suppose,' replied her husband, 'that it is the loss of the money that affects me. My honour is at stake, and that is more precious to me than all my wealth. You know that Saouy is my mortal enemy. He will relate all this to the king, and you will see the consequences that will ensue.'

'My lord,' said his wife, 'I am quite aware of Saouy's baseness, and that he is capable of playing you this malicious trick. But how can he or anyone else know what takes place in this house? Even if you are suspected and the king accuses you, you have only to say that, after examining the slave, you did not find her worthy of his majesty. Reassure yourself, and send to the dealers, saying that you are not satisfied, and wish them to find you another slave.'

This advice appearing reasonable, Khacan decided to follow it, but his wrath against his son did not abate. Noureddin dared not appear all that day, and fearing to take refuge with his usual associates in case his father should seek him there, he spent the day in a secluded garden where he was not known. He did not return home till after his father had gone to bed, and went out early next morning before the vizir awoke, and these precautions he kept up during an entire month.

His mother, though knowing very well that he returned to the house every evening, dare not ask her husband to pardon him. At length she took courage and said: 'My lord, I know that a son could not act more basely towards his father than Noureddin has done towards you, but after all will you now pardon him? Do you not consider the harm you may be doing yourself, and fear that malicious people, seeking the cause of your estrangement, may guess the real one?'

'Madam,' replied the vizir, 'what you say is very just, but I cannot pardon Noureddin before I have mortified him as he deserves.'

'He will be sufficiently punished,' answered the lady, 'if you do as I suggest. In the evening, when he returns home, lie in wait for him and pretend that you will slay him. I will come to his aid, and while pointing out that you only yield his life at my supplications, you can force him to take the beautiful Persian on any conditions you please.' Khacan agreed to follow this plan, and everything took place as arranged. On Noureddin's return Khacan pretended to be about to slay him, but yielding to his wife's intercession, said to his son: 'You owe your life to your mother. I pardon you on her intercession, and on the conditions that you take the beautiful Persian for your wife, and not your slave, that you never sell her, nor put her away.'

Noureddin, not hoping for so great indulgence, thanked his father, and vowed to do as he desired. Khacan was at great pains frequently to speak to the king of the difficulties attending the commission he had given him, but some whispers of what had actually taken place did reach Saouy's ears.

More than a year after these events the minister took a chill, leaving the bath while still heated to go out on important business. This resulted in inflammation of the lungs, which rapidly increased. The vizir, feeling that his end was at hand, sent for Noureddin, and charged him with his dying breath never to part with the beautiful Persian.

Shortly afterwards he expired, leaving universal regret through-out the kingdom; rich and poor alike followed him to the grave. Noureddin showed every mark of the deepest grief at his father's death, and for long refused to see anyone. At length a day came when, one of his friends being admitted, urged him strongly to be consoled, and to resume his former place in society. This advice Noureddin was not slow to follow, and soon he formed a little society of ten young men all about his own age, with whom he spent all his time in continual feasting and merrymaking.

Sometimes the fair Persian consented to appear at these festivities, but she disapproved of this lavish expenditure, and did not scruple to warn Noureddin of the probable consequences. He, however, only laughed at her advice, saying that his father had always kept him in too great constraint, and that now he rejoiced at his new-found liberty.

What added to the confusion in his affairs was that he refused to look into his accounts with his steward, sending him away every time he appeared with his book.

'See only that I live well,' he said, 'and do not disturb me about anything else.'

Not only did Noureddin's friends constantly partake of his hospitality, but in every way they took advantage of his generosity; everything of his that they admired, whether land, houses, baths, or any other source of his revenue, he immediately bestowed on them. In vain the Persian protested against the wrong he did himself; he continued to scatter with the same lavish hand.

Throughout one entire year Noureddin did nothing but amuse himself, and dissipate the wealth his father had taken such pains to acquire. The year had barely elapsed, when one day, as they sat at table, there came a knock at the door. The slaves having been sent away, Noureddin went to open it himself. One of his friends had risen at the same time, but Noureddin was before him, and finding the intruder to be the steward, he went out and closed the door. The friend, curious to hear what passed between them, hid himself behind the hangings, and heard the following words: 'My lord,' said the steward, 'I beg a thousand pardons for interrupting you, but what I have long foreseen has taken place. Nothing remains of the sums you gave me for your expenses, and all other sources of income are also at an end, having been transferred by you to others. If you wish me to remain in your service, furnish me with the necessary funds, else I must withdraw.'

So great was Noureddin's consternation that he had not a word to say in reply.

The friend, who had been listening behind the curtain, immediately hastened to communicate the news to the rest of the company.

'If this is so,' they said, 'we must cease to come here.'

Noureddin re-entering at that moment, they plainly saw, in spite of his efforts to dissemble, that what they had heard was the truth. One by one they rose, and each with a different excuse left the room, till presently he found himself alone, though little suspecting the resolution his friends had taken. Then, seeing the beautiful Persian, he confided to her the statement of the steward, with many expressions of regret for his own carelessness.

'Had I but followed your advice, beautiful Persian,' he said, 'all this would not have happened, but at least I have this consolation, that I have spent my fortune in the company of friends who will not desert me in an hour of need. Tomorrow I will go to them, and amongst them they will lend me a sum sufficient to start in some business.'

Accordingly next morning early Noureddin went to seek his ten friends, who all lived in the same street. Knocking at the door of the first and chief, the slave who opened it left him to wait in a hall while he announced his visit to his master. 'Noureddin!' he heard him exclaim quite audibly. 'Tell him, every time he calls, that I am not at home.' The same thing happened at the second door, and also at the third, and so on with all the ten. Noureddin, much mortified, recognised too late that he had confided in false friends, who abandoned him in his hour of need. Overwhelmed with grief, he sought consolation from the beautiful Persian.

'Alas, my lord,' she said, 'at last you are convinced of the truth of what I foretold. There is now no other resource left but to sell your slaves and your furniture.'

First then he sold the slaves, and subsisted for a time on the proceeds, after that the furniture was sold, and as much of it was valuable it sufficed for some time. Finally this resource also came to an end, and again he sought counsel from the beautiful Persian.

'My lord,' she said, 'I know that the late vizir, your father, bought me for 10,000 gold pieces, and though I have diminished in value since, I should still fetch a large sum. Do not therefore hesitate to sell me, and with the money you obtain go and establish yourself in business in some distant town.'

'Charming Persian,' answered Noureddin, 'how could I be guilty of such baseness? I would die rather than part from you whom I love better than my life.'

'My lord,' she replied, 'I am well aware of your love for me, which is only equalled by mine for you, but a cruel necessity obliges us to seek the only remedy.'

Noureddin, convinced at length of the truth of her words, yielded, and reluctantly led her to the slave market, where, showing her to a dealer named Hagi Hassan, he enquired her value.

Taking them into a room apart, Hagi Hassan exclaimed as soon as she had unveiled, 'My lord, is not this the slave your father bought for 10,000 pieces?'

On learning that it was so, he promised to obtain the highest possible price for her. Leaving the beautiful Persian shut up in the room alone, he went out to seek the slave merchants, announcing to them that he had found the pearl among slaves, and asking them to come and put a value upon her. As soon as they saw her they agreed that less than 4,000 gold pieces could not be asked. Hagi Hassan, then closing the door upon her, began to offer her for sale – calling out: 'Who will bid 4,000 gold pieces for the Persian slave?'

Before any of the merchants had bid, Saouy happened to pass that way, and judging that it must be a slave of extraordinary beauty, rode up to Hagi Hassan and desired to see her. Now it was not the custom to show a slave to a private bidder, but as no one dared to disobey the vizir his request was granted.

As soon as Saouy saw the Persian he was so struck by her beauty,

that he immediately wished to possess her, and not knowing that
she belonged to Noureddin, he desired Hagi Hassan to send for the
owner and to conclude the bargain at once.

Hagi Hassan then sought Noureddin, and told him that his slave
was going far below her value, and that if Saouy bought her he was
capable of not paying the money. 'What you must do,' he said, 'is to
pretend that you had no real intention of selling your slave, and
only swore you would in a fit of anger against her. When I present
her to Saouy as if with your consent you must step in, and with
blows begin to lead her away.'

Noureddin did as Hagi Hassan advised, to the great wrath of
Saouy, who riding straight at him endeavoured to take the beautiful
Persian from him by force. Noureddin letting her go, seized Saouy's
horse by the bridle, and, encouraged by the applause of the bystanders, dragged him to the ground, beat him severely, and left
him in the gutter streaming with blood. Then, taking the beautiful
Persian, he returned home amidst the acclamations of the people,
who detested Saouy so much that they would neither interfere in his
behalf nor allow his slaves to protect him.

Covered from head to foot with mire and streaming with blood
he rose, and leaning on two of his slaves went straight to the
palace, where he demanded an audience of the king, to whom he
related what had taken place in these words: 'May it please your
majesty, I had gone to the slave market to buy myself a cook.
While there I heard a slave being offered for 4,000 pieces. Asking
to see her, I found she was of incomparable beauty, and was being
sold by Noureddin, the son of your late vizir, to whom your
majesty will remember giving a sum of 10,000 gold pieces for the
purchase of a slave. This is the identical slave, whom instead of
bringing to your majesty he gave to his own son. Since the death of
his father this Noureddin has run through his entire fortune, has
sold all his possessions, and is now reduced to selling the slave.
Calling him to me, I said: "Noureddin, I will give you 10,000
gold pieces for your slave, whom I will present to the king. I will
interest him at the same time in your behalf, and this will be worth
much more to you than what extra money you might obtain from

Saouy tries to take the beautiful Persian from Noureddin

the merchants." "Bad old man," he exclaimed, "rather than sell my slave to you I would give her to a Jew." "But, Noureddin," I remonstrated, "you do not consider that in speaking thus you wrong the king, to whom your father owed everything." This remonstrance only irritated him the more. Throwing himself on me like a madman, he tore me from my horse, beat me to his heart's content, and left me in the state your majesty sees.'

So saying Saouy turned aside his head and wept bitterly.

The king's wrath was kindled against Noureddin. He ordered the captain of the guard to take with him forty men, to pillage Noureddin's house, to rase it to the ground, and to bring Noureddin and the slave to him. A doorkeeper, named Sangiar, who had been a slave of Khacan's, hearing this order given, slipped out of the king's apartment, and hastened to warn Noureddin to take flight instantly with the beautiful Persian. Then, presenting him with forty gold pieces, he disappeared before Noureddin had time to thank him.

As soon, then, as the fair Persian had put on her veil they fled together, and had the good fortune to get out of the town without being observed. At the mouth of the Euphrates they found a ship just about to start for Bagdad. They embarked, and immediately the anchor was raised and they set sail.

When the captain of the guard reached Noureddin's house he caused his soldiers to burst open the door and to enter by force, but no trace was to be found of Noureddin and his slave, nor could the neighbours give any information about them. When the king heard that they had escaped, he issued a proclamation that a reward of 1,000 gold pieces would be given to whoever would bring him Noureddin and the slave, but that, on the contrary, whoever hid them would be severely punished. Meanwhile Noureddin and the fair Persian had safely reached Bagdad. When the vessel had come to an anchor they paid five gold pieces for their passage and went ashore. Never having been in Bagdad before, they did not know where to seek a lodging. Wandering along the banks of the Tigris, they skirted a garden enclosed by a high wall. The gate was shut, but in front of it was an open vestibule with a sofa on either side. 'Here,' said Noureddin, 'let us pass the night,' and reclining on the sofas they soon fell asleep.

Now this garden belonged to the caliph. In the middle of it was a vast pavilion, whose superb saloon had eighty windows, each window having a lustre, lit solely when the caliph spent the evening there. Only the doorkeeper lived there, an old soldier named Scheih Ibrahim, who had strict orders to be very careful whom he admitted, and never to allow anyone to sit on the sofas by the door. It happened that evening that he had gone out on an errand. When he came back and saw two persons asleep on the sofas he was about to drive them out with blows, but drawing nearer he perceived that they were a handsome young man and beautiful young woman, and decided to awake them by gentler means. Noureddin, on being awoke, told the old man that they were strangers, and merely wished to pass the night there. 'Come with me,' said Scheih Ibrahim, 'I will lodge you better, and will show you a magnificent garden belonging to me.' So saying the doorkeeper led the way into the caliph's garden, the beauties of which filled them with wonder and amazement. Noureddin took out two gold pieces, and giving them to Scheih Ibrahim said: 'I beg you to get us something to eat that we may make merry together.' Being very avaricious, Scheih Ibrahim determined to spend only the tenth part of the money and to keep the rest to himself. While he was gone Noureddin and the Persian wandered through the gardens and went up the white marble staircase of the pavilion as far as the locked door of the saloon. On the return of Scheih Ibrahim they begged him to open it, and to allow them to enter and admire the magnificence within. Consenting, he brought not only the key, but a light, and immediately unlocked the door. Noureddin and the Persian entering, were dazzled with the magnificence they beheld. The paintings and furniture were of astonishing beauty, and between each window was a silver arm holding a candle.

Scheih Ibrahim spread the table in front of a sofa, and all three ate together. When they had finished eating Noureddin asked the old man to bring them a bottle of wine.

'Heaven forbid,' said Scheih Ibrahim, 'that I should come in contact with wine! I who have four times made the pilgrimage to Mecca, and have renounced wine for ever.'

'You would, however, do us a great service in procuring us some,' said Noureddin. 'You need not touch it yourself. Take the ass which is tied to the gate, lead it to the nearest wine-shop, and ask some passer-by to order two jars of wine; have them put in the ass's panniers, and drive him before you. Here are two pieces of gold for the expenses.'

At sight of the gold, Scheih Ibrahim set off at once to execute the commission. On his return, Noureddin said: 'We have still need of cups to drink from, and of fruit, if you can procure us some.' Scheih

526   TALES FROM THE ARABIAN NIGHTS

Ibrahim disappeared again, and soon returned with a table spread with cups of gold and silver, and every sort of beautiful fruit. Then he withdrew, in spite of repeated invitations to remain.

Noureddin and the beautiful Persian, finding the wine excellent, drank of it freely, and while drinking they sang. Both had fine voices, and Scheih Ibrahim listened to them with great pleasure – first from a distance, then he drew nearer, and finally put his head in at the door. Noureddin, seeing him, called to him to come in and keep them company. At first the old man declined, but was persuaded to enter the room, to sit down on the edge of the sofa nearest the door, and at last to draw closer and to seat himself by the beautiful Persian, who urged him so persistently to drink her health that at length he yielded, and took the cup she offered.

Now the old man only made a pretence of renouncing wine; he frequented wine-shops like other people, and had taken none of the precautions Noureddin had proposed. Having once yielded, he was easily persuaded to take a second cup, and a third, and so on till he no longer knew what he was doing. Till near midnight they continued drinking, laughing, and singing together.

About that time the Persian, perceiving that the room was lit by only one miserable tallow candle, asked Scheih Ibrahim to light some of the beautiful candles in the silver arms.

'Light them yourself,' answered the old man; 'you are younger than I, but let five or six be enough.'

She did not stop, however, till she had lit all the eighty, but Scheih Ibrahim was not conscious of this, and when, soon after that, Noureddin proposed to have some of the lustres lit, he answered: 'You are more capable of lighting them than I, but not more than three.'

Noureddin, far from contenting himself with three, lit all, and opened all the eighty windows.

The Caliph Haroun-al-Raschid, chancing at that moment to open a window in the saloon of his palace looking on the garden, was surprised to see the pavilion brilliantly illuminated. Calling the grand-vizir, Giafar, he said to him: 'Negligent vizir, look at the pavilion, and tell me why it is lit up when I am not there.'

The fair Persian lights the candles

When the vizir saw that it was as the caliph said, he trembled with fear, and immediately invented an excuse.

'Commander of the Faithful,' he said, 'I must tell you that four or five days ago Scheih Ibrahim told me that he wished to have an assembly of the ministers of his mosque, and asked permission to hold it in the pavilion. I granted his request, but forgot since to mention it to your majesty.'

'Giafar,' replied the caliph, 'you have committed three faults – first, in giving the permission; second, in not mentioning it to me; and third, in not investigating the matter more closely. For punishment I condemn you to spend the rest of the night with me in company of these worthy people. While I dress myself as a citizen, go and disguise yourself, and then come with me.'

When they reached the garden gate they found it open, to the great indignation of the caliph. The door of the pavilion being also open, he went softly upstairs, and looked in at the half-closed door of the saloon. Great was his surprise to see Scheih Ibrahim, whose sobriety he had never doubted, drinking and singing with a young man and a beautiful lady. The caliph, before giving way to his anger, determined to watch and see who the people were and what they did.

Presently Scheih Ibrahim asked the beautiful Persian if anything were wanting to complete her enjoyment of the evening.

'If only,' she said, 'I had an instrument upon which I might play.'

Scheih Ibrahim immediately took a lute from a cupboard and gave it to the Persian, who began to play on it, singing the while with such skill and taste that the caliph was enchanted. When she ceased he went softly downstairs and said to the vizir: 'Never have I heard a finer voice, nor the lute better played. I am determined to go in and make her play to me.'

'Commander of the Faithful,' said the vizir, 'if Scheih Ibrahim recognises you he will die of fright.'

'I should be sorry for that,' answered the caliph, 'and I am going to take steps to prevent it. Wait here till I return.'

Now the caliph had caused a bend in the river to form a lake in his garden. There the finest fish in the Tigris were to be found, but fishing was strictly forbidden. It happened that night, however, that a fisherman had taken advantage of the gate being open to go in and cast his nets. He was just about to draw them when he saw the caliph approaching. Recognising him at once in spite of his disguise, he threw himself at his feet imploring forgiveness.

'Fear nothing,' said the caliph, 'only rise up and draw thy nets.'

The fisherman did as he was told, and produced five or six fine fish, of which the caliph took the two largest. Then he desired the fisherman to change clothes with him, and in a few minutes the caliph was transformed into a fisherman, even to the shoes and the turban. Taking the two fish in his hand, he returned to the vizir, who, not recognising him, would have sent him about his business. Leaving the vizir at the foot of the stairs, the caliph went up and knocked at the door of the saloon. Noureddin opened it, and the caliph, standing on the threshold, said: 'Scheih Ibrahim, I am the fisher Kerim. Seeing that you are feasting with your friends, I bring you these fish.'

Noureddin and the Persian said that when the fishes were properly cooked and dressed they would gladly eat of them. The caliph then returned to the vizir, and they set to work in Scheih Ibrahim's house to cook the fish, of which they made so tempting a dish that Noureddin and the fair Persian ate of it with great relish. When they had finished Noureddin took thirty gold pieces (all that remained of what Sangiar had given him) and presented them to the caliph, who, thanking him, asked as a further favour if the lady would play him one piece on the lute. The Persian gladly consented, and sang and played so as to delight the caliph.

Noureddin, in the habit of giving to others whatever they admired, said, 'Fisherman, as she pleases you so much, take her; she is yours.'

The fair Persian, astounded that he should wish to part from her, took her lute, and with tears in her eyes sang her reproaches to its music.

The caliph (still in the character of fisherman) said to him, 'Sir, I perceive that this fair lady is your slave. Oblige me, I beg you, by relating your history.'

Noureddin willingly granted this request, and recounted

everything from the purchase of the slave down to the present moment.

'And where do you go now?' asked the caliph.

'Wherever the hand of Allah leads me,' said Noureddin.

'Then, if you will listen to me,' said the caliph, 'you will immediately return to Balsora. I will give you a letter to the king, which will ensure you a good reception from him.'

'It is an unheard-of thing,' said Noureddin, 'that a fisherman should be in correspondence with a king.'

'Let not that astonish you,' answered the caliph; 'we studied together, and have always remained the best of friends, though fortune, while making him a king, left me a humble fisherman.'

The caliph then took a sheet of paper, and wrote the following letter, at the top of which he put in very small characters this formula to show that he must be implicitly obeyed: – 'In the name of the Most Merciful God.

'Letter of the Caliph Haroun-al-Raschid to the King of Balsora.

'Haroun-al-Raschid, son of Mahdi, sends this letter to Mohammed Zinebi, his cousin. As soon as Noureddin, son of the Vizir Khacan, bearer of this letter, has given it to thee, and thou hast read it, take off thy royal mantle, put it on his shoulders, and seat him in thy place without fail. Farewell.'

The caliph then gave this letter to Noureddin, who immediately set off, with only what little money he possessed when Sangiar came to his assistance. The beautiful Persian, inconsolable at his departure, sank on a sofa bathed in tears.

When Noureddin had left the room, Scheih Ibrahim, who had hitherto kept silence, said: 'Kerim, for two miserable fish thou hast received a purse and a slave. I tell thee I will take the slave, and as to the purse, if it contains silver thou mayst keep one piece, if gold then I will take all and give thee what copper pieces I have in my purse.'

Now here it must be related that when the caliph went upstairs with the plate of fish he ordered the vizir to hasten to the palace and bring back four slaves bearing a change of raiment, who should wait outside the pavilion till the caliph should clap his hands.

Noureddin offers the fair Persian to the fisherman

Still personating the fisherman, the caliph answered: 'Scheih Ibrahim, whatever is in the purse I will share equally with you, but as to the slave I will keep her for myself. If you do not agree to these conditions you shall have nothing.'

The old man, furious at this insolence as he considered it, took a cup and threw it at the caliph, who easily avoided a missile from the hand of a drunken man. It hit against the wall, and broke into a thousand pieces. Scheih Ibrahim, still more enraged, then went out to fetch a stick. The caliph at that moment clapped his hands, and the vizir and the four slaves entering took off the fisherman's dress and put on him that which they had brought.

When Scheih Ibrahim returned, a thick stick in his hand, the caliph was seated on his throne, and nothing remained of the fisherman but his clothes in the middle of the room. Throwing himself on the ground at the caliph's feet, he said: 'Commander of the Faithful, your miserable slave has offended you, and craves forgiveness.'

The caliph came down from his throne, and said: 'Rise, I forgive thee.' Then turning to the Persian he said: 'Fair lady, now you know who I am; learn also that I have sent Noureddin to Balsora to be king, and as soon as all necessary preparations are made I will send you there to be queen. Meanwhile I will give you an apartment in my palace, where you will be treated with all honour.'

At this the beautiful Persian took courage, and the caliph was as good as his word, recommending her to the care of his wife Zobeida.

Noureddin made all haste on his journey to Balsora, and on his arrival there went straight to the palace of the king, of whom he demanded an audience. It was immediately granted, and holding the letter high above his head he forced his way through the crowd. While the king read the letter he changed colour. He would instantly have executed the caliph's order, but first he showed the letter to Saouy, whose interests were equally at stake with his own. Pretending that he wished to read it a second time, Saouy turned aside as if to seek a better light; unperceived by anyone he tore off the formula from the top of the letter, put it to his mouth, and swallowed it. Then, turning to the king, he said: 'Your majesty has no need to obey this letter. The writing is indeed that of the caliph, but the formula is absent. Besides, he has not sent an express with the patent, without which the letter is useless. Leave all to me, and I will take the consequences.'

The king not only listened to the persuasions of Saouy, but gave Noureddin into his hands. Such a severe bastinado was first administered to him, that he was left more dead than alive; then Saouy threw him into the darkest and deepest dungeon, and fed him only on bread and water. After ten days Saouy determined to put an end to Noureddin's life, but dared not without the king's authority. To gain this end, he loaded several of his own slaves with rich gifts, and presented himself at their head to the king, saying that they were from the new king on his coronation.

'What!' said the king; 'is that wretch still alive? Go and behead him at once. I authorise you.'

'Sire,' said Saouy, 'I thank your majesty for the justice you do me. I would further beg, as Noureddin publicly affronted me, that the execution might be in front of the palace, and that it might be proclaimed throughout the city, so that no one may be ignorant of it.'

The king granted these requests, and the announcement caused universal grief, for the memory of Noureddin's father was still fresh in the hearts of his people. Saouy, accompanied by twenty of his own slaves, went to the prison to fetch Noureddin, whom he mounted on a wretched horse without a saddle. Arrived at the palace, Saouy went in to the king, leaving Noureddin in the square, hemmed in not only by Saouy's slaves but by the royal guard, who had great difficulty in preventing the people from rushing in and rescuing Noureddin. So great was the indignation against Saouy that if anyone had set the example he would have been stoned on his way through the streets. Saouy, who witnessed the agitation of the people from the windows of the king's privy chambers, called to the executioner to strike at once. The king, however, ordered him to delay; not only was he jealous of Saouy's interference, but he had another reason. A troop of horsemen was seen at that moment riding at full gallop towards the square. Saouy suspected who they might be, and urged the king to give the signal for the execution

Noureddin led to execution

without delay, but this the king refused to do till he knew who the horsemen were.

Now, they were the Vizir Giafar and his suite arriving at full speed from Bagdad. For several days after Noureddin's departure with the letter the caliph had forgotten to send the express with the patent, without which the letter was useless. Hearing a beautiful voice one day in the women's part of the palace uttering lamentations, he was informed that it was the voice of the fair Persian, and suddenly calling to mind the patent, he sent for Giafar, and ordered him to make for Balsora with the utmost speed – if Noureddin were dead, to hang Saouy; if he were still alive, to bring him at once to Bagdad along with the king and Saouy.

Giafar rode at full speed through the square, and alighted at the steps of the palace, where the king came to greet him. The vizir's first question was whether Noureddin were still alive. The king replied that he was, and he was immediately led forth, though bound hand and foot. By the vizir's orders his bonds were immediately undone, and Saouy was tied with the same cords. Next day Giafar returned to Bagdad, bearing with him the king, Saouy, and Noureddin.

When the caliph heard what treatment Noureddin had received, he authorised him to behead Saouy with his own hands, but he declined to shed the blood of his enemy, who was forthwith handed over to the executioner. The caliph also desired Noureddin to reign over Balsora, but this, too, he declined, saying that after what had passed there he preferred never to return, but to enter the service of the caliph. He became one of his most intimate courtiers, and lived long in great happiness with the fair Persian. As to the king, the caliph contented himself with sending him back to Balsora, with the recommendation to be more careful in future in the choice of his vizir.

Aladdin and the Wonderful Lamp

There once lived a poor tailor, who had a son called Aladdin, a careless, idle boy who would do nothing but play all day long in the streets with little idle boys like himself. This so grieved the father that he died; yet, in spite of his mother's tears and prayers, Aladdin did not mend his ways. One day, when he was playing in the streets as usual, a stranger asked him his age, and if he were not the son of Mustapha the tailor.

'I am, sir,' replied Aladdin; 'but he died a long while ago.'

On this the stranger, who was a famous African magician, fell on his neck and kissed him, saying: 'I am your uncle, and knew you from your likeness to my brother. Go to your mother and tell her I am coming.'

Aladdin ran home, and told his mother of his newly found uncle.

'Indeed, child,' she said, 'your father had a brother, but I always thought he was dead.'

However, she prepared supper, and bade Aladdin seek his uncle, who came laden with wine and fruit. He presently fell down and kissed the place where Mustapha used to sit, bidding Aladdin's mother not to be surprised at not having seen him before, as he had been forty years out of the country. He then turned to Aladdin, and asked him his trade, at which the boy hung his head, while his mother burst into tears. On learning that Aladdin was idle and would learn no trade, he offered to take a shop for him and stock it with merchandise. Next day he bought Aladdin a fine suit of clothes, and took him all over the city, showing him the sights, and brought him home at nightfall to his mother, who was overjoyed to see her son so fine.

Next day the magician led Aladdin into some beautiful gardens a long way outside the city gates. They sat down by a fountain, and the magician pulled a cake from his girdle, which he divided between them. They then journeyed onwards till they almost reached the mountains. Aladdin was so tired that he begged to go back, but the magician beguiled him with pleasant stories, and led him on in spite of himself.

At last they came to two mountains divided by a narrow valley.

'We will go no farther,' said the false uncle. 'I will show you something wonderful; only do you gather up sticks while I kindle a fire.'

When it was lit the magician threw on it a powder he had about him, at the same time saying some magical words. The earth trembled a little and opened in front of them, disclosing a square flat stone with a brass ring in the middle to raise it by. Aladdin tried to run away, but the magician caught him and gave him a blow that knocked him down.

'What have I done, uncle?' he said piteously; whereupon the magician said more kindly: 'Fear nothing, but obey me. Beneath this stone lies a treasure which is to be yours, and no one else may touch it, so you must do exactly as I tell you.'

At the word treasure, Aladdin forgot his fears, and grasped the ring as he was told, saying the names of his father and grandfather. The stone came up quite easily and some steps appeared.

'Go down,' said the magician; 'at the foot of those steps you will find an open door leading into three large halls. Tuck up your gown and go through them without touching anything, or you will die instantly. These halls lead into a garden of fine fruit trees. Walk on till you come to a niche in a terrace where stands a lighted lamp. Pour out the oil it contains and bring it to me.'

He drew a ring from his finger and gave it to Aladdin, bidding him prosper.

Aladdin found everything as the magician had said, gathered some fruit off the trees, and, having got the lamp, arrived at the mouth of the cave. The magician cried out in a great hurry: 'Make haste and give me the lamp.' This Aladdin refused to do until he was out of the cave. The magician flew into a terrible passion, and throwing some more powder on the fire, he said something, and the stone rolled back into its place.

The magician left Persia for ever, which plainly showed that he was no uncle of Aladdin's, but a cunning magician who had read in his magic books of a wonderful lamp, which would make him the most powerful man in the world. Though he alone knew where to find it, he could only receive it from the hand of another. He had picked out the foolish Aladdin for this purpose, intending to get the lamp and kill him afterwards.

For two days Aladdin remained in the dark, crying and lamenting. At last he clasped his hands in prayer, and in so doing rubbed the ring, which the magician had forgotten to take from him. Immediately an enormous and frightful genie rose out of the earth, saying: 'What wouldst thou with me? I am the Slave of the Ring, and will obey thee in all things.'

Aladdin fearlessly replied: 'Deliver me from this place!' where-upon the earth opened, and he found himself outside. As soon as his eyes could bear the light he went home, but fainted on the threshold. When he came to himself he told his mother what had passed, and showed her the lamp and the fruits he had gathered in the garden, which were in reality precious stones. He then asked for some food.

'Alas! child,' she said, 'I have nothing in the house, but I have spun a little cotton and will go and sell it.'

Aladdin bade her keep her cotton, for he would sell the lamp instead. As it was very dirty she began to rub it, that it might fetch a higher price. Instantly a hideous genie appeared, and asked what she would have. She fainted away, but Aladdin, snatching the lamp, said boldly: 'Fetch me something to eat!'

The genie returned with a silver bowl, twelve silver plates containing rich meats, two silver cups, and two bottles of wine. Aladdin's mother, when she came to herself, said: 'Whence comes this splendid feast?'

'Ask not, but eat,' replied Aladdin.

So they sat at breakfast till it was dinner-time, and Aladdin told his mother about the lamp. She begged him to sell it, and have nothing to do with devils.

'No,' said Aladdin, 'since chance has made us aware of its virtues,

The Slave of the Ring appears to Aladdin

we will use it and the ring likewise, which I shall always wear on my finger.' When they had eaten all the genie had brought, Aladdin sold one of the silver plates, and so on till none were left. He then had recourse to the genie, who gave him another set of plates, and thus they lived for many years.

One day Aladdin heard an order from the sultan proclaiming that everyone was to stay at home and close his shutters while the princess, his daughter, went to and from the bath. Aladdin was seized by a desire to see her face, which was very difficult, as she always went veiled. He hid himself behind the door of the bath, and peeped through a chink. The princess lifted her veil as she went in, and looked so beautiful that Aladdin fell in love with her at first sight. He went home so changed that his mother was frightened. He told her he loved the princess so deeply that he could not live without her, and meant to ask her in marriage of her father. His mother, on hearing this, burst out laughing, but Aladdin at last prevailed upon her to go before the sultan and carry his request. She fetched a napkin and laid in it the magic fruits from the enchanted garden, which sparkled and shone like the most beautiful jewels. She took these with her to please the sultan, and set out, trusting in the lamp. The grand-vizir and the lords of council had just gone in as she entered the hall and placed herself in front of the sultan. He, however, took no notice of her. She went every day for a week, and stood in the same place.

When the council broke up on the sixth day the sultan said to his vizir: 'I see a certain woman in the audience-chamber every day carrying something in a napkin. Call her next time, that I may find out what she wants.'

Next day, at a sign from the vizir, she went up to the foot of the throne, and remained kneeling till the sultan said to her: 'Rise, good woman, and tell me what you want.'

She hesitated, so the sultan sent away all but the vizir, and bade her speak freely, promising to forgive her beforehand for anything she might say. She then told him of her son's violent love for the princess.

'I prayed him to forget her,' she said, 'but in vain; he threatened to do some desperate deed if I refused to go and ask your majesty for the hand of the princess. Now I pray you to forgive not me alone, but my son Aladdin.'

The sultan asked her kindly what she had in the napkin, whereupon she unfolded the jewels and presented them.

He was thunderstruck, and turning to the vizir said: 'What sayest thou? Ought I not to bestow the princess on one who values her at such a price?'

The vizir, who wanted her for his own son, begged the sultan to withhold her for three months, in the course of which he hoped his son would contrive to make him a richer present. The sultan granted this, and told Aladdin's mother that, though he consented to the marriage, she must not appear before him again for three months.

Aladdin waited patiently for nearly three months, but after two had elapsed his mother, going into the city to buy oil, found everyone rejoicing, and asked what was going on.

'Do you not know,' was the answer, 'that the son of the grand-vizir is to marry the sultan's daughter tonight?'

Breathless, she ran and told Aladdin, who was overwhelmed at first, but presently bethought him of the lamp. He rubbed it, and the genie appeared, saying: 'What is thy will?'

Aladdin replied: 'The sultan, as thou knowest, has broken his promise to me, and the vizir's son is to have the princess. My command is that tonight you bring hither the bride and bridegroom.'

'Master, I obey,' said the genie.

Aladdin then went to his chamber, where, sure enough at midnight the genie transported the bed containing the vizir's son and the princess.

'Take this new-married man,' he said, 'and put him outside in the cold, and return at daybreak.'

Whereupon the genie took the vizir's son out of bed, leaving Aladdin with the princess.

'Fear nothing,' Aladdin said to her; 'you are my wife, promised to me by your unjust father, and no harm shall come to you.'

The princess was too frightened to speak, and passed the most miserable night of her life, while Aladdin lay down beside her and slept soundly. At the appointed hour the genie fetched in the shivering bridegroom, laid him in his place, and transported the bed back to the palace.

Presently the sultan came to wish his daughter good-morning. The unhappy vizir's son jumped up and hid himself, while the princess would not say a word, and was very sorrowful.

The sultan sent her mother to her, who said: 'How comes it, child, that you will not speak to your father? What has happened?'

The princess sighed deeply, and at last told her mother how, during the night, the bed had been carried into some strange house, and what had passed there. Her mother did not believe her in the least, but bade her rise and consider it an idle dream.

The following night exactly the same thing happened, and next morning, on the princess's refusing to speak, the sultan threatened to cut off her head. She then confessed all, bidding him ask the vizir's son if it were not so. The sultan told the vizir to ask his son, who owned the truth, adding that, dearly as he loved the princess, he had rather die than go through another such fearful night, and wished to be separated from her. His wish was granted, and there was an end of feasting and rejoicing.

When the three months were over, Aladdin sent his mother to remind the sultan of his promise. She stood in the same place as before, and the sultan, who had forgotten Aladdin, at once remembered him, and sent for her. On seeing her poverty the sultan felt less inclined than ever to keep his word, and asked the vizir's advice, who counselled him to set so high a value on the princess that no man living could come up to it.

The sultan then turned to Aladdin's mother, saying: 'Good woman, a sultan must remember his promises, and I will remember mine, but your son must first send me forty basins of gold brimful of jewels, carried by forty black slaves, led by as many white ones, splendidly dressed. Tell him that I await his answer.' The mother of Aladdin bowed low and went home, thinking all was lost.

She gave Aladdin the message, adding: 'He may wait long enough for your answer!'

Aladdin's mother brings the slaves with the forty
basins of gold before the sultan

'Not so long, mother, as you think,' her son replied. 'I would do a great deal more than that for the princess.'

He summoned the genie, and in a few moments the eighty slaves arrived, and filled up the small house and garden.

Aladdin made them set out to the palace, two and two, followed by his mother. They were so richly dressed, with such splendid jewels in their girdles, that everyone crowded to see them and the basins of gold they carried on their heads.

They entered the palace, and, after kneeling before the sultan, stood in a half-circle round the throne with their arms crossed, while Aladdin's mother presented them to the sultan.

He hesitated no longer, but said: 'Good woman, return and tell your son that I wait for him with open arms.'

She lost no time in telling Aladdin, bidding him make haste. But Aladdin first called the genie.

'I want a scented bath,' he said, 'a richly embroidered habit, a horse surpassing the sultan's, and twenty slaves to attend me. Besides this, six slaves, beautifully dressed, to wait on my mother; and lastly, ten thousand pieces of gold in ten purses.'

No sooner said than done. Aladdin mounted his horse and passed through the streets, the slaves strewing gold as they went. Those who had played with him in his childhood knew him not, he had grown so handsome.

When the sultan saw him he came down from his throne, embraced him, and led him into a hall where a feast was spread, intending to marry him to the princess that very day.

But Aladdin refused, saying, 'I must build a palace fit for her,' and took his leave.

Once home he said to the genie: 'Build me a palace of the finest marble, set with jasper, agate, and other precious stones. In the middle you shall build me a large hall with a dome, its four walls of massy gold and silver, each side having six windows, whose lattices, all except one, which is to be left unfinished, must be set with diamonds and rubies. There must be stables and horses and grooms and slaves; go and see about it!'

The palace was finished by next day, and the genie carried him there and showed him all his orders faithfully carried out, even to the laying of a velvet carpet from Aladdin's palace to the sultan's. Aladdin's mother then dressed herself carefully, and walked to the palace with her slaves, while he followed her on horseback. The sultan sent musicians with trumpets and cymbals to meet them, so that the air resounded with music and cheers. She was taken to the princess, who saluted her and treated her with great honour. At night the princess said goodbye to her father, and set out on the carpet for Aladdin's palace, with his mother at her side, and followed by the hundred slaves. She was charmed at the sight of Aladdin, who ran to receive her.

'Princess,' he said, 'blame your beauty for my boldness if I have displeased you.'

She told him that, having seen him, she willingly obeyed her father in this matter. After the wedding had taken place Aladdin led her into the hall, where a feast was spread, and she supped with him, after which they danced till midnight.

Next day Aladdin invited the sultan to see the palace. On entering the hall with the four-and-twenty windows, with their rubies, diamonds, and emeralds, he cried: 'It is a world's wonder! There is only one thing that surprises me. Was it by accident that one window was left unfinished?'

'No, sir, by design,' returned Aladdin. 'I wished your majesty to have the glory of finishing this palace.'

The sultan was pleased, and sent for the best jewellers in the city. He showed them the unfinished window, and bade them fit it up like the others.

'Sir,' replied their spokesman, 'we cannot find jewels enough.'

The sultan had his own fetched, which they soon used, but to no purpose, for in a month's time the work was not half done. Aladdin, knowing that their task was vain, bade them undo their work and carry the jewels back, and the genie finished the window at his command. The sultan was surprised to receive his jewels again and visited Aladdin, who showed him the window finished. The sultan embraced him, the envious vizir meanwhile hinting that it was the work of enchantment.

Aladdin had won the hearts of the people by his gentle bearing. He was made captain of the sultan's armies, and won several battles for him, but remained modest and courteous as before, and lived thus in peace and content for several years.

But far away in Africa the magician remembered Aladdin, and by his magic arts discovered that Aladdin, instead of perishing miserably in the cave, had escaped, and had married a princess, with whom he was living in great honour and wealth. He knew that the poor tailor's son could only have accomplished this by means of the lamp, and travelled night and day till he reached the capital of China, bent on Aladdin's ruin. As he passed through the town he heard people talking everywhere about a marvellous palace.

'Forgive my ignorance,' he asked, 'what is this palace you speak of?'

'Have you not heard of Prince Aladdin's palace,' was the reply, 'the greatest wonder of the world? I will direct you if you have a mind to see it.'

The magician thanked him who spoke, and having seen the palace knew that it had been raised by the genie of the lamp, and became half mad with rage. He determined to get hold of the lamp, and again plunge Aladdin into the deepest poverty.

Unluckily, Aladdin had gone a-hunting for eight days, which gave the magician plenty of time. He bought a dozen copper lamps, put them into a basket, and went to the palace, crying: 'New lamps for old!' followed by a jeering crowd.

The princess, sitting in the hall of four-and-twenty windows, sent a slave to find out what the noise was about, who came back laughing, so that the princess scolded her.

'Madam,' replied the slave, 'who can help laughing to see an old fool offering to exchange fine new lamps for old ones?'

Another slave, hearing this, said: 'There is an old one on the cornice there which he can have.'

Now this was the magic lamp, which Aladdin had left there, as he could not take it out hunting with him. The princess, not knowing its value, laughingly bade the slave take it and make the exchange.

She went and said to the magician: 'Give me a new lamp for this.'

He snatched it and bade the slave take her choice, amid the jeers

The African magician gets the lamp from the slave

of the crowd. Little he cared, but left off crying his lamps, and went out of the city gates to a lonely place, where he remained till nightfall, when he pulled out the lamp and rubbed it. The genie appeared, and at the magician's command carried him, together with the palace and the princess in it, to a lonely place in Africa.

Next morning the sultan looked out of the window towards Aladdin's palace and rubbed his eyes, for it was gone. He sent for the vizir, and asked what had become of the palace. The vizir looked out too, and was lost in astonishment. He again put it down to enchantment, and this time the sultan believed him, and sent thirty men on horseback to fetch Aladdin in chains. They met him riding home, bound him, and forced him to go with them on foot. The people, however, who loved him, followed, armed, to see that he came to no harm. He was carried before the sultan, who ordered the executioner to cut off his head. The executioner made Aladdin kneel down, bandaged his eyes, and raised his scimitar to strike.

At that instant the vizir, who saw that the crowd had forced their way into the courtyard and were scaling the walls to rescue Aladdin, called to the executioner to stay his hand. The people, indeed, looked so threatening that the sultan gave way and ordered Aladdin to be unbound, and pardoned him in the sight of the crowd.

Aladdin now begged to know what he had done.

'False wretch!' said the sultan, 'come hither,' and showed him from the window the place where his palace had stood.

Aladdin was so amazed that he could not say a word.

'Where is my palace and my daughter?' demanded the sultan. 'For the first I am not so deeply concerned, but my daughter I must have, and you must find her or lose your head.'

Aladdin begged for forty days in which to find her, promising if he failed to return and suffer death at the sultan's pleasure. His prayer was granted, and he went forth sadly from the sultan's presence. For three days he wandered about like a madman, asking everyone what had become of his palace, but they only laughed and pitied him. He came to the banks of a river, and knelt down to say his prayers before throwing himself in. In so doing he rubbed the magic ring he still wore.

The genie he had seen in the cave appeared, and asked his will.

'Save my life, genie,' said Aladdin, 'and bring my palace back.'

'That is not in my power,' said the genie; 'I am only the slave of the ring; you must ask the slave of the lamp.'

'Even so,' said Aladdin 'but thou canst take me to the palace, and set me down under my dear wife's window.' He at once found himself in Africa, under the window of the princess, and fell asleep out of sheer weariness.

He was awakened by the singing of the birds, and his heart was lighter. He saw plainly that all his misfortunes were owing to the loss of the lamp, and vainly wondered who had robbed him of it.

That morning the princess rose earlier than she had done since she had been carried into Africa by the magician, whose company she was forced to endure once a day. She, however, treated him so harshly that he dared not live there altogether. As she was dressing, one of her women looked out and saw Aladdin. The princess ran and opened the window, and at the noise she made Aladdin looked up. She called to him to come to her, and great was the joy of these lovers at seeing each other again.

After he had kissed her Aladdin said: 'I beg of you, princess, in God's name, before we speak of anything else, for your own sake and mine, tell me what has become of an old lamp I left on the cornice in the hall of four-and-twenty windows, when I went a-hunting.'

'Alas!' she said 'I am the innocent cause of our sorrows,' and told him of the exchange of the lamp.

'Now I know,' cried Aladdin, 'that we have to thank the African magician for this! Where is the lamp?'

'He carries it about with him,' said the princess, 'I know, for he pulled it out of his breast to show me. He wishes me to break my faith with you and marry him, saying that you were beheaded by my father's command. He is forever speaking ill of you, but I only reply by my tears. If I persist, I doubt not that he will use violence.'

Aladdin comforted her, and left her for a while. He changed clothes with the first person he met in the town, and having bought a certain powder returned to the princess, who let him in by a little side door.

'Put on your most beautiful dress,' he said to her, 'and receive the magician with smiles, leading him to believe that you have forgotten me. Invite him to sup with you, and say you wish to taste the wine of his country. He will go for some, and while he is gone I will tell you what to do.'

She listened carefully to Aladdin, and when he left her arrayed herself gaily for the first time since she left China. She put on a girdle and headdress of diamonds, and seeing in a glass that she looked more beautiful than ever, received the magician, saying to his great amazement: 'I have made up my mind that Aladdin is dead, and that all my tears will not bring him back to me, so I am resolved to mourn no more, and have therefore invited you to sup with me; but I am tired of the wines of China, and would fain taste those of Africa.'

The magician flew to his cellar, and the princess put the powder Aladdin had given her in her cup. When he returned she asked him to drink her health in the wine of Africa, handing him her cup in exchange for his as a sign she was reconciled to him.

Before drinking the magician made her a speech in praise of her beauty, but the princess cut him short saying: 'Let me drink first, and you shall say what you will afterwards.' She set her cup to her lips and kept it there, while the magician drained his to the dregs and fell back lifeless.

The princess then opened the door to Aladdin, and flung her arms round his neck, but Aladdin put her away, bidding her to leave him, as he had more to do. He then went to the dead magician, took the lamp out of his vest, and bade the genie carry the palace and all in it back to China. This was done, and the princess in her chamber only felt two little shocks, and little thought she was at home again.

The sultan, who was sitting in his closet, mourning for his lost daughter, happened to look up, and rubbed his eyes, for there stood the palace as before! He hastened thither, and Aladdin received him in the hall of the four-and-twenty windows, with the princess at his side. Aladdin told him what had happened, and showed him the dead body of the magician, that he might believe. A ten days'

The death of the African magician

feast was proclaimed, and it seemed as if Aladdin might now live the rest of his life in peace; but it was not to be.

The African magician had a younger brother, who was, if possible, more wicked and more cunning than himself. He travelled to China to avenge his brother's death, and went to visit a pious woman called Fatima, thinking she might be of use to him. He entered her cell and clapped a dagger to her breast, telling her to rise and do his bidding on pain of death. He changed clothes with her, coloured his face like hers, put on her veil and murdered her, that she might tell no tales. Then he went towards the palace of Aladdin, and all the peoples thinking he was the holy woman, gathered round him, kissing his hands and begging his blessing. When he got to the palace there was such a noise going on round him that the princess bade her slave look out of the window and ask what was the matter. The slave said it was the holy woman, curing people by her touch of their ailments, whereupon the princess, who had long desired to see Fatima, sent for her. On coming to the princess the magician offered up a prayer for her health and prosperity. When he had done the princess made him sit by her, and begged him to stay with her always. The false Fatima, who wished for nothing better, consented, but kept his veil down for fear of discovery. The princess showed him the hall, and asked him what he thought of it.

'It is truly beautiful,' said the false Fatima. 'In my mind it wants but one thing.'

'And what is that?' said the princess.

'If only a roc's egg,' replied he, 'were hung up from the middle of this dome, it would be the wonder of the world.'

After this the princess could think of nothing but a roc's egg, and when Aladdin returned from hunting he found her in a very ill humour. He begged to know what was amiss, and she told him that all her pleasure in the hall was spoilt for the want of a roc's egg hanging from the dome.

'It that is all,' replied Aladdin, 'you shall soon be happy.'

He left her and rubbed the lamp, and when the genie appeared commanded him to bring a roc's egg. The genie gave such a loud and terrible shriek that the hall shook.

'Wretch!' he cried, 'is it not enough that I have done everything for you, but you must command me to bring my master and hang him up in the midst of this dome? You and your wife and your palace deserve to be burnt to ashes; but this request does not come from you, but from the brother of the African magician whom you destroyed. He is now in your palace disguised as the holy woman – whom he murdered. He it was who put that wish into your wife's head. Take care of yourself, for he means to kill you.' So saying the genie disappeared.

Aladdin went back to the princess, saying his head ached, and requesting that the holy Fatima should be fetched to lay her hands on it. But when the magician came near, Aladdin, seizing his dagger, pierced him to the heart.

'What have you done?' cried the princess. 'You have killed the holy woman!'

'Not so,' replied Aladdin, 'but a wicked magician,' and told her of how she had been deceived.

After this Aladdin and his wife lived in peace. He succeeded the sultan when he died, and reigned for many years, leaving behind him a long line of kings.

The Adventures of Haroun-al-Raschid, Caliph of Bagdad

The Caliph Haroun-al-Raschid sat in his palace, wondering if there was anything left in the world that could possibly give him a few hours' amusement, when Giafar the grand-vizir, his old and tried friend, suddenly appeared before him. Bowing low, he waited, as was his duty, till his master spoke, but Haroun-al-Raschid merely turned his head and looked at him, and sank back into his former weary posture.

Now Giafar had something of importance to say to the caliph, and had no intention of being put off by mere silence, so with another low bow in front of the throne, he began to speak.

'Commander of the Faithful,' said he, 'I have taken on myself to remind your Highness that you have undertaken secretly to observe for yourself the manner in which justice is done and order is kept throughout the city. This is the day you have set apart to devote to this object, and perhaps in fulfilling this duty you may find some distraction from the melancholy to which, as I see to my sorrow, you are a prey.'

'You are right,' returned the caliph, 'I had forgotten all about it. Go and change your coat, and I will change mine.'

A few moments later they both re-entered the hall, disguised as foreign merchants, and passed through a secret door, out into the open country. Here they turned towards the Euphrates, and crossing the river in a small boat, walked through that part of the town which lay along the further bank, without seeing anything to call for their interference. Much pleased with the peace and good order of the city, the caliph and his vizir made their way to a bridge, which led straight back to the palace, and had already crossed it, when they were stopped by an old and blind man, who begged for alms.

The caliph gave him a piece of money, and was passing on, but the blind man seized his hand, and held him fast.

'Charitable person,' he said, 'whoever you may be grant me yet another prayer. Strike me, I beg of you, one blow. I have deserved it richly, and even a more severe penalty.'

The caliph, much surprised at this request, replied gently: 'My good man, that which you ask is impossible. Of what use would my alms be if I treated you so ill?' And as he spoke he tried to loosen the grasp of the blind beggar.

'My lord,' answered the man, 'pardon my boldness and my persistence. Take back your money, or give me the blow which I crave. I have sworn a solemn oath that I will receive nothing without receiving chastisement, and if you knew all, you would feel that the punishment is not a tenth part of what I deserve.'

Moved by these words, and perhaps still more by the fact that he had other business to attend to, the caliph yielded, and struck him lightly on the shoulder. Then he continued his road, followed by the blessing of the blind man. When they were out of earshot, he said to the vizir, 'There must be something very odd to make that man act so – I should like to find out what is the reason. Go back to him; tell him who I am, and order him to come without fail to the palace tomorrow, after the hour of evening prayer.'

So the grand-vizir went back to the bridge; gave the blind beggar first a piece of money and then a blow, delivered the caliph's message, and rejoined his master.

They passed on towards the palace, but walking through a square, they came upon a crowd watching a young and well-dressed man who was urging a horse at full speed round the open space, using at the same time his spurs and whip so unmercifully that the animal was all covered with foam and blood. The caliph, astonished at this proceeding, enquired of a passer-by what it all meant, but no one could tell him anything, except that every day at the same hour the same thing took place.

Still wondering, he passed on, and for the moment had to content himself with telling the vizir to command the horseman also to appear before him at the same time as the blind man.

The next day, after evening prayer, the caliph entered the hall, and was followed by the vizir bringing with him the two men of whom we have spoken, and a third, with whom we have nothing to do. They all bowed themselves low before the throne and then the caliph bade them rise, and ask the blind man his name.

'Baba-Abdalla, your highness,' said he.

'Baba-Abdalla,' returned the caliph, 'your way of asking alms yesterday seemed to me so strange, that I almost commanded you then and there to cease from causing such a public scandal. But I have sent for you to enquire what was your motive in making such a curious vow. When I know the reason I shall be able to judge whether you can be permitted to continue to practise it, for I cannot help thinking that it sets a very bad example to others. Tell me therefore the whole truth, and conceal nothing.'

These words troubled the heart of Baba-Abdalla, who prostrated himself at the feet of the caliph. Then rising, he answered: 'Commander of the Faithful, I crave your pardon humbly, for my persistence in beseeching your highness to do an action which appears on the face of it to be without any meaning. No doubt, in the eyes of men, it has none; but I look on it as a slight expiation for a fearful sin of which I have been guilty, and if your highness will deign to listen to my tale, you will see that no punishment could atone for the crime.'

The Story of the Blind Baba-Abdalla

I was born, Commander of the Faithful, in Bagdad, and was left an orphan while I was yet a very young man, for my parents died within a few days of each other. I had inherited from them a small fortune, which I worked hard night and day to increase, till at last I found myself the owner of eighty camels. These I hired out to travelling merchants, whom I frequently accompanied on their various journeys, and always returned with large profits.

One day I was coming back from Balsora, whither I had taken a supply of goods, intended for India, and halted at noon in a lonely place, which promised rich pasture for my camels. I was resting in the shade under a tree, when a dervish, going on foot towards Balsora, sat down by my side, and I enquired whence he had come and to what place he was going. We soon made friends, and after we had asked each other the usual questions, we produced the food we had with us, and satisfied our hunger. While we were eating, the dervish happened to mention that in a spot only a little way off from where we were sitting, there was hidden a treasure so great that if my eighty camels were loaded till they could carry no more, the hiding place would seem as full as if it had never been touched.

At this news I became almost beside myself with joy and greed, and I flung my arms round the neck of the dervish, exclaiming: 'Good dervish, I see plainly that the riches of this world are nothing to you, therefore of what use is the knowledge of this treasure to you? Alone and on foot, you could carry away a mere handful. But tell me where it is, and I will load my eighty camels with it, and give you one of them as a token of my gratitude.'

Certainly my offer does not sound very magnificent, but it was great to me, for at his words a wave of covetousness had swept over my heart, and I almost felt as if the seventy-nine camels that were left were nothing in comparison.

The dervish saw quite well what was passing in my mind, but he did not show what he thought of my proposal.

'My brother,' he answered quietly, 'you know as well as I do, that you are behaving unjustly. It was open to me to keep my secret, and to reserve the treasure for myself. But the fact that I have told you of its existence shows that I had confidence in you, and that I hoped to earn your gratitude for ever, by making your fortune as well as mine. But before I reveal to you the secret of the treasure, you must swear that, after we have loaded the camels with as much as they can carry, you will give half to me, and let us go our own ways. I think you will see that this is fair, for if you present me with forty camels, I on my side will give you the means of buying a thousand more.'

I could not of course deny that what the dervish said was perfectly reasonable, but, in spite of that, the thought that the dervish would be as rich as I was unbearable to me. Still there was no use in discussing the matter, and I had to accept his conditions or bewail to the end of my life the loss of immense wealth. So I collected my camels and we set out together under the guidance of the dervish. After walking some time, we reached what looked like a valley, but with such a narrow entrance that my camels could only pass one by one. The little valley, or open space, was shut up by two mountains, whose sides were formed of straight cliffs, which no human being could climb.

When we were exactly between these mountains the dervish stopped.

'Make your camels lie down in this open space,' he said, 'so that we can easily load them; then we will go to the treasure.'

I did what I was bid, and rejoined the dervish, whom I found trying to kindle a fire out of some dry wood. As soon as it was alight, he threw on it a handful of perfumes, and pronounced a few words that I did not understand, and immediately a thick column of smoke rose high into the air. He separated the smoke into two columns, and then I saw a rock, which stood like a pillar between the two mountains, slowly open, and a splendid palace appear within.

The dervish separates the smoke and the
palace appears in the rock

But, Commander of the Faithful, the love of gold had taken such possession of my heart, that I could not even stop to examine the riches, but fell upon the first pile of gold within my reach and began to heap it into a sack that I had brought with me.

The dervish likewise set to work, but I soon noticed that he confined himself to collecting precious stones, and I felt I should be wise to follow his example. At length the camels were loaded with as much as they could carry, and nothing remained but to seal up the treasure, and go our ways.

Before, however, this was done, the dervish went up to a great golden vase, beautifully chased, and took from it a small wooden box, which he hid in the bosom of his dress, merely saying that it contained a special kind of ointment. Then he once more kindled the fire, threw on the perfume, and murmured the unknown spell, and the rock closed, and stood whole as before.

The next thing was to divide the camels, and to charge them with the treasure, after which we each took command of our own and marched out of the valley, till we reached the place in the high road where the routes diverge, and then we parted, the dervish going towards Balsora, and I to Bagdad. We embraced each other tenderly, and I poured out my gratitude for the honour he had done me, in singling me out for this great wealth, and having said a hearty farewell we turned our backs, and hastened after our camels.

I had hardly come up with mine when the demon of envy filled my soul. 'What does a dervish want with riches like that?' I said to myself. 'He alone has the secret of the treasure, and can always get as much as he wants,' and I halted my camels by the roadside, and ran back after him.

I was a quick runner, and it did not take me very long to come up with him. 'My brother,' I exclaimed, as soon as I could speak, 'almost at the moment of our leave-taking, a reflection occurred to me, which is perhaps new to you. You are a dervish by profession, and live a very quiet life, only caring to do good, and careless of the things of this world. You do not realise the burden that you lay upon yourself, when you gather into your hands such great wealth, besides the fact that no one, who is not accustomed to camels from his birth, can ever manage the stubborn beasts. If you are wise, you will not encumber yourself with more than thirty, and you will find those trouble enough.'

'You are right,' replied the dervish, who understood me quite well, but did not wish to fight the matter. 'I confess I had not thought about it. Choose any ten you like, and drive them before you.'

I selected ten of the best camels, and we proceeded along the road, to rejoin those I had left behind. I had got what I wanted, but I had found the dervish so easy to deal with, that I rather regretted I had not asked for ten more. I looked back. He had only gone a few paces, and I called after him.

'My brother,' I said, 'I am unwilling to part from you without pointing out what I think you scarcely grasp, that large experience of camel-driving is necessary to anybody who intends to keep together a troop of thirty. In your own interest, I feel sure you would be much happier if you entrusted ten more of them to me, for with my practice it is all one to me if I take two or a hundred.'

As before, the dervish made no difficulties, and I drove off my ten camels in triumph, only leaving him with twenty for his share. I had now sixty, and anyone might have imagined that I should be content.

But, Commander of the Faithful, there is a proverb that says, 'the more one has, the more one wants'. So it was with me. I could not rest as long as one solitary camel remained to the dervish; and returning to him I redoubled my prayers and embraces, and promises of eternal gratitude, till the last twenty were in my hands.

'Make a good use of them, my brother,' said the holy man. 'Remember riches sometimes have wings if we keep them for ourselves, and the poor are at our gates expressly that we may help them.'

My eyes were so blinded by gold, that I paid no heed to his wise counsel, and only looked about for something else to grasp. Suddenly I remembered the little box of ointment that the dervish had hidden, and which most likely contained a treasure more precious than all the rest. Giving him one last embrace, I observed accidentally, 'What are you going to do with that little box of ointment? It seems hardly worth taking with you; you might as well let me have it. And really, a dervish who has given up the world has no need of ointment!'

Oh, if he had only refused my request! But then, supposing he had, I should have got possession of it by force, so great was the madness that had laid hold upon me. However, far from refusing it, the dervish at once held it out, saying gracefully, 'Take it, my friend, and if there is anything else I can do to make you happy you must let me know.'

Directly the box was in my hands I wrenched off the cover. 'As you are so kind,' I said, 'tell me, I pray you, what are the virtues of this ointment?'

'They are most curious and interesting,' replied the dervish. 'If you apply a little of it to your left eye you will behold in an instant all the treasures hidden in the bowels of the earth. But beware lest you touch your right eye with it, or your sight will be destroyed for ever.'

His words excited my curiosity to the highest pitch. 'Make trial on me, I implore you,' I cried, holding out the box to the dervish. 'You will know how to do it better than I! I am burning with impatience to test its charms.'

The dervish took the box I had extended to him, and, bidding me shut my left eye, touched it gently with the ointment. When I opened it again I saw spread out, as it were before me, treasures of every kind and without number. But as all this time I had been obliged to keep my right eye closed, which was very fatiguing, I begged the dervish to apply the ointment to that eye also.

'If you insist upon it I will do it,' answered the dervish, 'but you must remember what I told you just now – that if it touches your right eye you will become blind on the spot.'

Unluckily, in spite of my having proved the truth of the dervish's words in so many instances, I was firmly convinced that he was now keeping concealed from me some hidden and precious virtue of the ointment. So I turned a deaf ear to all he said.

'My brother,' I replied smiling, 'I see you are joking. It is not

The dervish anoints the right eye of Baba Abdalla

natural that the same ointment should have two such exactly opposite effects.'

'It is true all the same,' answered the dervish, 'and it would be well for you if you believed my word.'

But I would not believe, and, dazzled by the greed of avarice, I thought that if one eye could show me riches, the other might teach me how to get possession of them. And I continued to press the dervish to anoint my right eye, but this he resolutely declined to do.

'After having conferred such benefits on you,' said he, 'I am loth indeed to work you such evil. Think what it is to be blind, and do not force me to do what you will repent as long as you live.'

It was of no use. 'My brother,' I said firmly, 'pray say no more, but do what I ask. You have most generously responded to my wishes up to this time, do not spoil my recollection of you for a thing of such little consequence. Let what will happen; I take it on my own head, and will never reproach you.'

'Since you are determined upon it,' he answered with a sigh, 'there is no use talking,' and taking the ointment he laid some on my right eye, which was tight shut. When I tried to open it heavy clouds of darkness floated before me. I was as blind as you see me now!

'Miserable dervish!' I shrieked, 'so it is true after all! Into what a bottomless pit has my lust after gold plunged me. Ah, now that my eyes are closed they are really opened. I know that all my sufferings are caused by myself alone! But, good brother, you, who are so kind and charitable, and know the secrets of such vast learning, have you nothing that will give me back my sight?'

'Unhappy man,' replied the dervish, 'it is not my fault that this has befallen you, but it is a just chastisement. The blindness of your heart has wrought the blindness of your body. Yes, I have secrets; that you have seen in the short time that we have known each other. But I have none that will give you back your sight. You have proved yourself unworthy of the riches that were given you. Now they have passed into my hands, whence they will flow into the hands of others less greedy and ungrateful than you.'

The dervish said no more and left me, speechless with shame and confusion, and so wretched that I stood rooted to the spot, while he collected the eighty camels and proceeded on his way to Balsora. It was in vain that I entreated him not to leave me, but at least to take me within reach of the first passing caravan. He was deaf to my prayers and cries, and I should soon have been dead of hunger and misery if some merchants had not come along the track the following day and kindly brought me back to Bagdad.

From a rich man I had in one moment become a beggar; and up to this time I have lived solely on the alms that have been bestowed on me. But, in order to expiate the sin of avarice, which was my undoing, I oblige each passer-by to give me a blow.

This, Commander of the Faithful, is my story.

When the blind man had ended the caliph addressed him: 'Baba-Abdalla, truly your sin is great, but you have suffered enough. Henceforth repent in private, for I will see that enough money is given you day by day for all your wants.'

At these words Baba-Abdalla flung himself at the caliph's feet, and prayed that honour and happiness might be his portion for ever.

The Story of Sidi-Nouman

The Caliph Haroun-al-Raschid was much pleased with the tale of the blind man and the dervish, and when it was finished he turned to the young man who had ill-treated his horse, and enquired his name also. The young man replied that he was called Sidi-Nouman.

'Sidi-Nouman,' observed the caliph, 'I have seen horses broken all my life long, and have even broken them myself, but I have never seen any horse broken in such a barbarous manner as by you yesterday. Everyone who looked on was indignant, and blamed you loudly. As for myself, I was so angry that I was very nearly disclosing who I was, and putting a stop to it at once. Still, you have not the air of a cruel man, and I would gladly believe that you did not act in this way without some reason. As I am told that it was not the first time, and indeed that every day you are to be seen flogging and spurring your horse, I wish to come to the bottom of the matter. But tell me the whole truth, and conceal nothing.'

Sidi-Nouman changed colour as he heard these words, and his manner grew confused; but he saw plainly that there was no help for it. So he prostrated himself before the throne of the caliph and tried to obey, but the words stuck in his throat, and he remained silent.

The caliph, accustomed though he was to instant obedience, guessed something of what was passing in the young man's mind, and sought to put him at his ease. 'Sidi-Nouman,' he said, 'do not think of me as the caliph, but merely as a friend who would like to hear your story. If there is anything in it that you are afraid may offend me, take courage, for I pardon you beforehand. Speak then openly and without fear, as to one who knows and loves you.'

Reassured by the kindness of the caliph, Sidi-Nouman at length began his tale.

'Commander of the Faithful,' said he, 'dazzled though I am by the lustre of your highness's presence, I will do my best to satisfy your wishes. I am by no means perfect, but I am not naturally cruel, neither do I take pleasure in breaking the law. I admit that the treatment of my horse is calculated to give your Highness a bad opinion of me, and to set an evil example to others; yet I have not chastised it without reason, and I have hopes that I shall be judged more worthy of pity than punishment.'

Commander of the Faithful, I will not trouble to describe my birth; it is not of sufficient distinction to deserve your highness's attention. My ancestors were careful people, and I inherited enough money to enable me to live comfortably, though without show.

Having therefore a modest fortune, the only thing wanting to my happiness was a wife who could return my affection, but this blessing I was not destined to get; for on the very day after my marriage, my bride began to try my patience in every way that was most hard to bear.

Now, seeing that the customs of our land oblige us to marry without ever beholding the person with whom we are to pass our lives, a man has of course no right to complain as long as his wife is not absolutely repulsive, or is not positively deformed. And whatever defects her body may have, pleasant ways and good behaviour will go far to remedy them.

The first time I saw my wife unveiled, when she had been brought to my house with the usual ceremonies, I was enchanted to find that I had not been deceived in regard to the account that had been given me of her beauty. I began my married life in high spirits, and the best hopes of happiness.

The following day a grand dinner was served to us but as my wife did not appear, I ordered a servant to call her. Still she did not come, and I waited impatiently for some time. At last she entered the room, and we took our places at the table, and plates of rice were set before us.

I ate mine, as was natural, with a spoon, but great was my surprise to notice that my wife, instead of doing the same, drew from her pocket a little case, from which she selected a long pin, and by the help of this pin conveyed her rice grain by grain to her mouth.

'Amina,' I exclaimed in astonishment, 'is that the way you eat rice at home? And did you do it because your appetite was so small, or did you wish to count the grains so that you might never eat more than a certain number? If it was from economy, and you are anxious to teach me not to be wasteful, you have no cause for alarm. We shall never ruin ourselves in that way! Our fortune is large enough for all our needs, therefore, dear Amina, do not seek to check yourself, but eat as much as you desire, as I do!'

In reply to my affectionate words, I expected a cheerful answer; yet Amina said nothing at all, but continued to pick her rice as before, only at longer and longer intervals. And, instead of trying the other dishes, all she did was to put every now and then a crumb of bread into her mouth, that would not have made a meal for a sparrow.

I felt provoked by her obstinacy, but to excuse her to myself as far as I could, I suggested that perhaps she had never been used to eat in the company of men, and that her family might have taught her that she ought to behave prudently and discreetly in the presence of her husband. Likewise that she might either have dined already or intend to do so in her own apartments. So I took no further notice, and when I had finished left the room, secretly much vexed at her strange conduct.

The same thing occurred at supper, and all through the next day, whenever we ate together. It was quite clear that no woman could live upon two or three bread-crumbs and a few grains of rice, and I determined to find out how and when she got food. I pretended not to pay attention to anything she did, in the hope that little by little she would get accustomed to me, and become more friendly; but I soon saw that my expectations were quite vain.

One night I was lying with my eyes closed, and to all appearance sound asleep, when Amina arose softly, and dressed herself without making the slightest sound. I could not imagine what she was going to do, and as my curiosity was great I made up my mind to follow her. When she was fully dressed, she stole quietly from the room.

The instant she had let the curtain fall behind her, I flung a garment on my shoulders and a pair of slippers on my feet. Looking

Amina eating the rice

from a lattice which opened into the court, I saw her in the act of passing through the street door, which she carefully left open.

It was bright moonlight, so I easily managed to keep her in sight, till she entered a cemetery not far from the house. There I hid myself under the shadow of the wall, and crouched down cautiously; and hardly was I concealed, when I saw my wife approaching in company with a ghoul – one of those demons which, as your highness is aware, wander about the country making their lairs in deserted buildings and springing out upon unwary travellers whose flesh they eat. If no live being goes their way, they then betake themselves to the cemeteries, and feed upon the dead bodies.

I was nearly struck dumb with horror on seeing my wife with this hideous female ghoul. They passed by me without noticing me, began to dig up a corpse which had been buried that day, and then sat down on the edge of the grave, to enjoy their frightful repast, talking quietly and cheerfully all the while, though I was too far off to hear what they said. When they had finished, they threw back the body into the grave, and heaped back the earth upon it. I made no effort to disturb them, and returned quickly to the house, when I took care to leave the door open, as I had previously found it. Then I got back into bed, and pretended to sleep soundly.

A short time after Amina entered as quietly as she had gone out. She undressed and stole into bed, congratulating herself apparently on the cleverness with which she had managed her expedition.

As may be guessed, after such a scene it was long before I could close my eyes, and at the first sound which called the faithful to prayer, I put on my clothes and went to the mosque. But even prayer did not restore peace to my troubled spirit, and I could not face my wife until I had made up my mind what future course I should pursue in regard to her. I therefore spent the morning roaming about from one garden to another, turning over various plans for compelling my wife to give up her horrible ways; I thought of using violence to make her submit, but felt reluctant to be unkind to her. Besides, I had an instinct that gentle means had the best chance of success; so, a little soothed, I turned towards home, which I reached about the hour of dinner.

As soon as I appeared, Amina ordered dinner to be served, and we sat down together. As usual, she persisted in only picking a few grains of rice, and I resolved to speak to her at once of what lay so heavily on my heart.

'Amina,' I said, as quietly as possible, 'you must have guessed the surprise I felt, when the day after our marriage you declined to eat anything but a few morsels of rice, and altogether behaved in such a manner that most husbands would have been deeply wounded. However I had patience with you, and only tried to tempt your appetite by the choicest dishes I could invent, but all to no purpose. Still, Amina, it seems to me that there be some among them as sweet to the taste as the flesh of a corpse?'

I had no sooner uttered these words than Amina, who instantly understood that I had followed her to the graveyard, was seized with a passion beyond any that I have ever witnessed. Her face became purple, her eyes looked as if they would start from her head, and she positively foamed with rage.

I watched her with terror, wondering what would happen next, but little thinking what would be the end of her fury. She seized a vessel of water that stood at hand, and plunging her hand in it, murmured some words I failed to catch. Then, sprinkling it on my face, she cried madly: 'Wretch, receive the reward of your prying, and become a dog.'

The words were not out of her mouth when, without feeling conscious that any change was passing over me, I suddenly knew that I had ceased to be a man. In the greatness of the shock and surprise – for I had no idea that Amina was a magician – I never dreamed of running away, and stood rooted to the spot, while Amina grasped a stick and began to beat me. Indeed her blows were so heavy, that I only wonder they did not kill me at once. However they succeeded in rousing me from my stupor, and I dashed into the courtyard, followed closely by Amina, who made frantic dives at me, which I was not quick enough to dodge. At last she got tired of pursuing me, or else a new trick entered into her head, which would give me speedy and painful death; she opened the gate leading into the street, intending to crush me as I passed through. Dog though I was, I saw through her design, and stung into presence of mind by the greatness of the danger, I timed my movements so well that I contrived to rush through, and only the tip of my tail received a squeeze as she banged the gate.

I was safe, but my tail hurt me horribly, and I yelped and howled so loud all along the streets, that the other dogs came and attacked me, which made matters no better. In order to avoid them, I took refuge in a cookshop, where tongues and sheep's heads were sold.

At first the owner showed me great kindness, and drove away the other dogs that were still at my heels, while I crept into the darkest corner. But though I was safe for the moment, I was not destined to remain long under his protection, for he was one of those who hold

*She opened the gate, intending to crush
me as I passed through*

all dogs to be unclean, and that all the washing in the world will hardly purify you from their contact. So after my enemies had gone to seek other prey, he tried to lure me from my corner in order to force me into the street. But I refused to come out of my hole, and spent the night in sleep, which I sorely needed, after the pain inflicted on me by Amina.

I have no wish to weary your highness by dwelling on the sad thoughts which accompanied my change of shape, but it may interest you to hear that the next morning my host went out early to do his marketing, and returned laden with the sheep's heads, and tongues and trotters that formed his stock in trade for the day. The smell of meat attracted various hungry dogs in the neighbourhood, and they gathered round the door begging for some bits. I stole out of my corner, and stood with them.

In spite of his objection to dogs, as unclean animals, my protector was a kind-hearted man, and knowing I had eaten nothing since yesterday, he threw me bigger and better bits than those which fell to the share of the other dogs. When I had finished, I tried to go back into the shop, but this he would not allow, and stood so firmly at the entrance with a stout stick, that I was forced to give it up, and seek some other home.

A few paces further on was a baker's shop, which seemed to have a gay and merry man for a master. At that moment he was having his breakfast, and though I gave no signs of hunger, he at once threw me a piece of bread. Before gobbling it up, as most dogs are in the habit of doing, I bowed my head and wagged my tail, in token of thanks, and he understood, and smiled pleasantly. I really did not want the bread at all, but felt it would be ungracious to refuse, so I ate it slowly, in order that he might see that I only did it out of politeness. He understood this also, and seemed quite willing to let me stay in his shop, so I sat down, with my face to the door, to show that I only asked his protection. This he gave me, and indeed encouraged me to come into the house itself, giving me a corner where I might sleep, without being in anybody's way.

The kindness heaped on me by this excellent man was far greater than I could ever have expected. He was always affectionate in his manner of treating me, and I shared his breakfast, dinner and supper, while, on my side, I gave him all the gratitude and attachment to which he had a right.

I sat with my eyes fixed on him, and he never left the house without having me at his heels; and if it ever happened that when he was preparing to go out I was asleep, and did not notice, he would call 'Rufus, Rufus,' for that was the name he gave me.

Some weeks passed in this way, when one day a woman came in to buy bread. In paying for it, she laid down several pieces of money, one of which was bad. The baker perceived this, and declined to take it, demanding another in its place. The woman, for her part, refused to take it back, declaring it was perfectly good, but the baker would have nothing to do with it. 'It is really such a bad imitation,' he exclaimed at last, 'that even my dog would not be taken in. Here Rufus! Rufus!' and hearing his voice, I jumped on to the counter. The baker threw down the money before me, and said, 'Find out if there is a bad coin.' I looked at each in turn, and then laid my paw on the false one, glancing at the same time at my master, so as to point it out.

The baker, who had of course been only in joke, was exceedingly surprised at my cleverness, and the woman, who was at last convinced that the man spoke the truth, produced another piece of money in its place. When she had gone, my master was so pleased that he told all the neighbours what I had done, and made a great deal more of it than there really was.

The neighbours, very naturally, declined to believe his story, and tried me several times with all the bad money they could collect together, but I never failed to stand the test triumphantly.

Soon, the shop was filled from morning till night, with people who on the pretence of buying bread came to see if I was as clever as I was reported to be. The baker drove a roaring trade, and admitted that I was worth my weight in gold to him.

Of course there were plenty who envied him his large custom, and many was the pitfall set for me, so that he never dared to let me out of his sight. One day a woman, who had not been in the shop before, came to ask for bread, like the rest. As usual, I was lying on the counter, and she threw down six coins before me, one of which was false. I detected it at once, and put my paw on it, looking as I did so at the woman. 'Yes,' she said, nodding her head. 'You are quite right, that is the one.' She stood gazing at me attentively for some time, then paid for the bread, and left the shop, making a sign for me to follow her secretly.

Now my thoughts were always running on some means of shaking off the spell laid on me, and noticing the way in which this woman had looked at me, the idea entered my head that perhaps she might have guessed what had happened, and in this I was not deceived. However I let her go on a little way, and merely stood at the door watching her. She turned, and seeing that I was quite still, she again beckoned to me.

The baker all this while was busy with his oven, and had forgotten all about me, so I stole out softly, and ran after the woman.

When we came to her house, which was some distance off, she opened the door and then said to me, 'Come in, come in; you will never be sorry that you followed me.' When I had entered she fastened the door, and took me into a large room, where a beautiful girl was working at a piece of embroidery. 'My daughter,' exclaimed my guide, 'I have brought you the famous dog belonging to the baker which can tell good money from bad. You know that when I first heard of him, I told you I was sure he must be really a man, changed into a dog by magic. Today I went to the baker's, to prove for myself the truth of the story, and persuaded the dog to follow me here. Now what do you say?'

'You are right, mother,' replied the girl, and rising she dipped her hand into a vessel of water. Then sprinkling it over me she said, 'If you were born dog, remain dog; but if you were born man, by virtue of this water resume your proper form.' In one moment the spell was broken. The dog's shape vanished as if it had never been, and it was a man who stood before her.

Overcome with gratitude at my deliverance, I flung myself at her feet, and kissed the hem of her garment. 'How can I thank you for your goodness towards a stranger, and for what you have done? Henceforth I am your slave. Deal with me as you will!'

Then, in order to explain how I came to be changed into a dog, I told her my whole story, and finished with rendering the mother the thanks due to her for the happiness she had brought me.

'Sidi-Nouman,' returned the daughter, 'say no more about the obligation you are under to us. The knowledge that we have been of service to you is ample payment. Let us speak of Amina, your wife, with whom I was acquainted before her marriage. I was aware that she was a magician, and she knew too that I had studied the same art, under the same mistress. We met often going to the same baths, but we did not like each other, and never sought to become friends. As to what concerns you, it is not enough to have broken your spell, she must be punished for her wickedness. Remain for a moment with my mother, I beg,' she added hastily; 'I will return shortly.'

Left alone with the mother, I again expressed the gratitude I felt, to her as well as to her daughter.

'My daughter,' she answered, 'is, as you see, as accomplished a magician as Amina herself, but you would be astonished at the amount of good she does by her knowledge. That is why I have never interfered, otherwise I should have put a stop to it long ago.' As she spoke, her daughter entered with a small bottle in her hand.

'Sidi-Nouman,' she said, 'the books I have just consulted tell me that Amina is not home at present, but she should return at any moment. I have likewise found out by their means, that she pretends before the servants great uneasiness as to your absence. She has circulated a story that, while at dinner with her, you remembered some important business that had to be done at once, and left the house without shutting the door. By this means a dog had strayed in, which she was forced to get rid of by a stick. Go home then without delay, and await Amina's return in your room. When she comes in, go down to meet her, and in her surprise, she will try to run away. Then have this bottle ready, and dash the water it contains over her, saying boldly, "Receive the reward of your crimes." That is all I have to tell you.'

Everything happened exactly as the young magician had fore-told. I had not been in my house many minutes before Amina

Amina is transformed into a horse

returned, and as she approached I stepped in front of her, with the water in my hand. She gave one loud cry, and turned to the door, but she was too late. I had already dashed the water in her face and spoken the magic words. Amina disappeared, and in her place stood the horse you saw me beating yesterday.

This, Commander of the Faithful, is my story, and may I venture to hope that, now you have heard the reason of my conduct, your highness will not think this wicked woman too harshly treated?

'Sidi-Nouman,' replied the caliph, 'your story is indeed a strange one, and there is no excuse to be offered for your wife. But, without condemning your treatment of her, I wish you to reflect how much she must suffer from being changed into an animal, and I hope you will let that punishment be enough. I do not order you to insist upon the young magician finding the means to restore your wife to her human shape, because I know that when once women such as she begin to work evil they never leave off, and I should only bring down on your head a vengeance far worse than the one you have undergone already.'

The Story of Ali Cogia,
Merchant of Bagdad

In the reign of Haroun-al-Raschid, there lived in Bagdad a merchant named Ali Cogia, who, having neither wife nor child, contented himself with the modest profits produced by his trade. He had spent some years quite happily in the house his father had left him, when three nights running he dreamed that an old man had appeared to him, and reproached him for having neglected the duty of a good Mussulman, in delaying so long his pilgrimage to Mecca.

Ali Cogia was much troubled by this dream, as he was unwilling to give up his shop, and lose all his customers. He had shut his eyes for some time to the necessity of performing this pilgrimage, and tried to atone to his conscience by an extra number of good works, but the dream seemed to him a direct warning, and he resolved to put the journey off no longer.

The first thing he did was to sell his furniture and the wares he had in his shop, only reserving to himself such goods as he might trade with on the road. The shop itself he sold also, and easily found a tenant for his private house. The only matter he could not settle satisfactorily was the safe custody of a thousand pieces of gold which he wished to leave behind him.

After some thought, Ali Cogia hit upon a plan which seemed a safe one. He took a large vase, and placing the money in the bottom of it, filled up the rest with olives. After corking the vase tightly down, he carried it to one of his friends, a merchant like himself, and said to him: 'My brother, you have probably heard that I am staffing with a caravan in a few days for Mecca. I have come to ask whether you would do me the favour to keep this vase of olives for me till I come back?'

The merchant replied readily, 'Look, this is the key of my shop:

take it, and put the vase wherever you like. I promise that you shall find it in the same place on your return.'

A few days later, Ali Cogia mounted the camel that he had laden with merchandise, joined the caravan, and arrived in due time at Mecca. Like the other pilgrims he visited the sacred mosque, and after all his religious duties were performed, he set out his goods to the best advantage, hoping to gain some customers among the passers-by.

Very soon two merchants stopped before the pile, and when they had turned it over, one said to the other: 'If this man was wise he would take these things to Cairo, where he would get a much better price than he is likely to do here.'

Ali Cogia heard the words, and lost no time in following the advice. He packed up his wares, and instead of returning to Bagdad, joined a caravan that was going to Cairo. The results of the journey gladdened his heart. He sold off everything almost directly, and bought a stock of Egyptian curiosities, which he intended selling at Damascus; but as the caravan with which he would have to travel would not be starting for another six weeks, he took advantage of the delay to visit the Pyramids, and some of the cities along the banks of the Nile.

Now the attractions of Damascus so fascinated the worthy Ali, that he could hardly tear himself away, but at length he remembered that he had a home in Bagdad, meaning to return by way of Aleppo, and after he had crossed the Euphrates, to follow the course of the Tigris.

But when he reached Mossoul, Ali had made such friends with some Persian merchants, that they persuaded him to accompany them to their native land, and even as far as India, and so it came to pass that seven years had slipped by since he had left Bagdad, and during all that time the friend with whom he had left the vase of olives had never once thought of him or of it. In fact, it was only a month before Ali Cogia's actual return that the affair came into his head at all, owing to his wife's remarking one day, that it was a long time since she had eaten any olives, and would like some.

'That reminds me,' said the husband, 'that before Ali Cogia went to Mecca seven years ago, he left a vase of olives in my care. But really by this time he must be dead, and there is no reason we should not eat the olives if we like. Give me a light, and I will fetch them and see how they taste.'

'My husband,' answered the wife, 'beware, I pray, of your doing anything so base! Supposing seven years have passed without news of Ali Cogia, he need not be dead for all that, and may come back any day. How shameful it would be to have to confess that you had betrayed your trust and broken the seal of the vase! Pay no attention to my idle words, I really have no desire for olives now. And probably after all this while they are no longer good. I have a presentiment that Ali Cogia will return, and what will he think of you? Give it up, I entreat.'

The merchant, however, refused to listen to her advice, sensible though it was. He took a light and a dish and went into his shop.

'If you will be so obstinate,' said his wife, 'I cannot help it; but do not blame me if it turns out ill.'

When the merchant opened the vase he found the topmost olives were rotten, and in order to see if the under ones were in better condition he shook some out into the dish. As they fell out a few of the gold pieces fell out too.

The sight of the money roused all the merchant's greed. He looked into the vase, and saw that all the bottom was filled with gold. He then replaced the olives and returned to his wife.

'My wife,' he said, as he entered the room, 'you were quite right; the olives are rotten, and I have recorked the vase so well that Ali Cogia will never know it has been touched.'

'You would have done better to believe me,' replied the wife. 'I trust that no harm will come of it.'

These words made no more impression on the merchant than the others had done; and he spent the whole night in wondering how he could manage to keep the gold if Ali Cogia should come back and claim his vase. Very early next morning he went out and bought fresh new olives; he then threw away the old ones, took out the gold and hid it, and filled up the vase with the olives he had bought. This done he recorked the vase and put it in the same place where it had been left by Ali Cogia.

The gold pieces fall out of the jar of olives

A month later Ali Cogia re-entered Bagdad, and as his house was still let he went to an inn; and the following day set out to see his friend the merchant, who received him with open arms and many expressions of surprise. After a few moments given to enquiries Ali Cogia begged the merchant to hand him over the vase that he had taken care of for so long.

'Oh certainly,' said he, 'I am only glad I could be of use to you in the matter. Here is the key of my shop; you will find the vase in the place where you put it.'

Ali Cogia fetched his vase and carried it to his room at the inn, where he opened it. He thrust down his hand but could feel no money, but still was persuaded it must be there. So he got some plates and vessels from his travelling kit and emptied out the olives. To no purpose. The gold was not there. The poor man was dumb with horror, then, lifting up his hands, he exclaimed, 'Can my old friend really have committed such a crime?'

In great haste he went back to the house of the merchant. 'My friend,' he cried, 'you will be astonished to see me again, but I can find nowhere in this vase a thousand pieces of gold that I placed in the bottom under the olives. Perhaps you may have taken a loan of them for your business purposes; if that is so you are most welcome. I will only ask you to give me a receipt, and you can pay the money at your leisure.'

The merchant, who had expected something of the sort, had his reply all ready. 'Ali Cogia,' he said, 'when you brought me the vase of olives did I ever touch it? I gave you the key of my shop and you put it yourself where you liked, and did you not find it in exactly the same spot and in the same state? If you placed any gold in it, it must be there still. I know nothing about that; you only told me there were olives. You can believe me or not, but I have not laid a finger on the vase.'

Ali Cogia still tried every means to persuade the merchant to admit the truth. 'I love peace,' he said, 'and shall deeply regret having to resort to harsh measures. Once more, think of your reputation. I shall be in despair if you oblige me to call in the aid of the law.'

'Ali Cogia,' answered the merchant, 'you allow that it was a vase of olives you placed in my charge. You fetched it and removed it yourself, and now you tell me it contained a thousand pieces of gold, and that I must restore them to you! Did you ever say anything about them before? Why, I did not even know that the vase had olives in it! You never showed them to me. I wonder you have not demanded pearls or diamonds. Retire, I pray you, lest a crowd should gather in front of my shop.'

By this time not only the casual passers-by, but also the neighbouring merchants, were standing round, listening to the dispute, and trying every now and then to smooth matters between them. But at the merchant's last words Ali Cogia resolved to lay the cause of the quarrel before them, and told them the whole story. They heard him to the end, and enquired of the merchant what he had to say.

The accused man admitted that he had kept Ali Cogia's vase in his shop; but he denied having touched it, and swore that as to what it contained he only knew what Ali Cogia had told him, and called them all to witness the insult that had been put upon him.

'You have brought it on yourself,' said Ali Cogia, taking him by the arm, 'and as you appeal to the law, the law you shall have! Let us see if you will dare to repeat your story before the Cadi.'

Now as a good Mussulman the merchant was forbidden to refuse this choice of a judge, so he accepted the test, and said to Ali Cogia, 'Very well; I should like nothing better. We shall soon see which of us is in the right.'

So the two men presented themselves before the Cadi, and Ali Cogia again repeated his tale. The Cadi asked what witnesses he had. Ali Cogia replied that he had not taken this precaution, as he had considered the man his friend, and up to that time had always found him honest.

The merchant, on his side, stuck to his story, and offered to swear solemnly that not only had he never stolen the thousand gold pieces, but that he did not even know they were there. The Cadi allowed him to take the oath, and pronounced him innocent.

Ali Cogia, furious at having to suffer such a loss, protested against the verdict, declaring that he would appeal to the Caliph

Haroun-al-Raschid himself. But the Cadi paid no attention to his threats, and was quite satisfied that he had done what was right.

Judgment being given the merchant returned home triumphant, and Ali Cogia went back to his inn to draw up a petition to the caliph. The next morning he placed himself on the road along which the caliph must pass after midday prayer, and stretched out his petition to the officer who walked before the caliph, whose duty it was to collect such things, and on entering the palace to hand them to his master. There Haroun-al-Raschid studied them carefully.

Knowing this custom, Ali Cogia followed the caliph into the public hall of the palace, and waited the result. After some time the officer appeared, and told him that the caliph had read his petition, and had appointed an hour the next morning to give him audience. He then enquired the merchant's address, so that he might be summoned to attend also. That very evening, the caliph, with his grand-vizir Giafar, and Mesrour, chief of the eunuchs, all three disguised, as was their habit, went out to take a stroll through the town.

Going down one street, the caliph's attention was attracted by a noise, and looking through a door which opened into a court he perceived ten or twelve children playing in the moonlight. He hid himself in a dark corner, and watched them.

'Let us play at being the Cadi,' said the brightest and quickest of them all; 'I will be the Cadi. Bring before me Ali Cogia, and the merchant who robbed him of the thousand pieces of gold.'

The boy's words recalled to the caliph the petition he had read that morning, and he waited with interest to see what the children would do.

The proposal was hailed with joy by the other children, who had heard a great deal of talk about the matter, and they quickly settled the part each one was to play. The Cadi took his seat gravely, and an officer introduced first Ali Cogia, the plaintiff, and then the merchant who was the defendant.

Ali Cogia made a low bow, and pleaded his cause point by point; concluding by imploring the Cadi not to inflict on him such a heavy loss.

The Cadi, having heard his case, turned to the merchant, and enquired why he had not repaid Ali Cogia the sum in question.

The false merchant repeated the reasons that the real merchant had given to the Cadi of Bagdad, and also offered to swear that he had told the truth.

'Stop a moment!' said the little Cadi, 'before we come to oaths, I should like to examine the vase with the olives. Ali Cogia,' he added, 'have you got the vase with you?' and finding he had not, the Cadi continued, 'Go and get it, and bring it to me.'

So Ali Cogia disappeared for an instant, and then pretended to lay a vase at the feet of the Cadi, declaring it was his vase, which he had given to the accused for safe custody; and in order to be quite correct, the Cadi asked the merchant if he recognised it as the same vase. By his silence the merchant admitted the fact, and the Cadi then commanded to have the vase opened. Ali Cogia made a movement as if he was taking off the lid, and the little Cadi on his part made a pretence of peering into a vase.

'What beautiful olives!' he said, 'I should like to taste one,' and pretending to put one in his mouth, he added, 'they are really excellent!

'But,' he went on, 'it seems to me odd that olives seven years old should be as good as that! Send for some dealers in olives, and let us hear what they say!'

Two children were presented to him as olive merchants, and the Cadi addressed them. 'Tell me,' he said, 'how long can olives be kept so as to be pleasant eating?'

'My lord,' replied the merchants, 'however much care is taken to preserve them, they never last beyond the third year. They lose both taste and colour, and are only fit to be thrown away.'

'If that is so,' answered the little Cadi, 'examine this vase, and tell me how long the olives have been in it.'

The olive merchants pretended to examine the olives and taste them; then reported to the Cadi that they were fresh and good.

'You are mistaken,' said he, 'Ali Cogia declares he put them in that vase seven years ago.'

'My lord,' returned the olive merchants, 'we can assure you that the olives are those of the present year. And if you consult all the merchants in Bagdad you will not find one to give a contrary opinion.'

The accused merchant opened his mouth as if to protest, but the Cadi gave him no time. 'Be silent,' he said, 'you are a thief. Take him away and hang him.' So the game ended, the children clapping their hands in applause, and leading the criminal away to be hanged.

Haroun-al-Raschid was lost in astonishment at the wisdom of the child, who had given so wise a verdict on the case which he himself was to hear on the morrow. 'Is there any other verdict possible?' he asked the grand-vizir, who was as much impressed as himself. 'I can imagine no better judgment.'

'If the circumstances are really such as we have heard,' replied the grand-vizir, 'it seems to me your highness could only follow the example of this boy, in the method of reasoning, and also in your conclusions.'

'Then take careful note of this house,' said the caliph, 'and bring me the boy tomorrow, so that the affair may be tried by him in my presence. Summon also the Cadi, to learn his duty from the mouth of a child. Bid Ali Cogia bring his vase of olives, and see that two dealers in olives are present.' So saying the caliph returned to the palace.

The next morning early, the grand-vizir went back to the house where they had seen the children playing, and asked for the mistress and her children. Three boys appeared, and the grand-vizir enquired which had represented the Cadi in their game of the previous evening. The eldest and tallest, changing colour, confessed that it was he, and to his mother's great alarm, the grand-vizir said that he had strict orders to bring him into the presence of the caliph.

'Does he want to take my son from me?' cried the poor woman; but the grand-vizir hastened to calm her, by assuring her that she should have the boy again in an hour, and she would be quite satisfied when she knew the reason of the summons. So she dressed the boy in his best clothes, and the two left the house.

When the grand-vizir presented the child to the caliph, he was a little awed and confused, and the caliph proceeded to explain why he had sent for him. 'Approach, my son,' he said kindly. 'I think it was you who judged the case of Ali Cogia and the merchant last night? I overheard you by chance, and was very pleased with the way you conducted it. Today you will see the real Ali Cogia and the real merchant. Seat yourself at once next to me.'

The caliph being seated on his throne with the boy next him, the parties to the suit were ushered in. One by one they prostrated themselves, and touched the carpet at the foot of the throne with their foreheads. When they rose up, the caliph said: 'Now speak. This child will give you justice, and if more should be wanted I will see to it myself.'

Ali Cogia and the merchant pleaded one after the other, but when the merchant offered to swear the same oath that he had taken before the Cadi, he was stopped by the child, who said that before this was done he must first see the vase of olives.

At these words, Ali Cogia presented the vase to the caliph, and uncovered it. The caliph took one of the olives, tasted it, and ordered the expert merchants to do the same. They pronounced the olives good, and fresh that year. The boy informed them that Ali Cogia declared it was seven years since he had placed them in the vase; to which they returned the same answer as the children had done.

The accused merchant saw by this time that his condemnation was certain, and tried to allege something in his defence. The boy had too much sense to order him to be hanged, and looked at the caliph, saying, 'Commander of the Faithful, this is not a game now; it is for your highness to condemn him to death and not for me.'

Then the caliph, convinced that the man was a thief, bade them take him away and hang him, which was done, but not before he had confessed his guilt and the place in which he had hidden Ali Cogia's money. The caliph ordered the Cadi to learn how to deal out justice from the mouth of a child, and sent the boy home, with a purse containing a hundred pieces of gold as a mark of his favour.

The Enchanted Horse

It was the Feast of the New Year, the oldest and most splendid of all the feasts in the kingdom of Persia, and the day had been spent by the king in the city of Schiraz, taking part in the magnificent spectacles prepared by his subjects to do honour to the festival. The sun was setting, and the monarch was about to give his court the signal to retire, when suddenly an Indian appeared before his throne, leading a horse richly harnessed, and looking in every respect exactly like a real one.

'Sire,' said he, prostrating himself as he spoke, 'although I make my appearance so late before your highness, I can confidently assure you that none of the wonders you have seen during the day can be compared to this horse, if you will deign to cast your eyes upon him.'

'I see nothing in it,' replied the king, 'except a clever imitation of a real one; and any skilled workman might do as much.'

'Sire,' returned the Indian, 'it is not of his outward form that I would speak, but of the use that I can make of him. I have only to mount him, and to wish myself in some special place, and no matter how distant it may be, in a very few moments I shall find myself there. It is this, sire, that makes the horse so marvellous, and if your highness will allow me, you can prove it for yourself.'

The King of Persia, who was interested in everything out of the common, and had never before come across a horse with such qualities, bade the Indian mount the animal, and show what he could do. In an instant the man had vaulted on his back, and enquired where the monarch wished to send him.

'Do you see that mountain?' asked the king, pointing to a huge mass that towered into the sky about three leagues from Schiraz; 'go and bring me the leaf of a palm that grows at the foot.'

The words were hardly out of the king's mouth when the Indian turned a screw placed in the horse's neck, close to the saddle, and the animal bounded like lightning up into the air, and was soon beyond the sight even of the sharpest eyes. In a quarter of an hour the Indian was seen returning, bearing in his hand the palm, and, guiding his horse to the foot of the throne, he dismounted, and laid the leaf before the king.

Now the monarch had no sooner proved the astonishing speed of which the horse was capable than he longed to possess it himself, and indeed, so sure was he that the Indian would be quite ready to sell it, that he looked upon it as his own already.

'I never guessed from his mere outside how valuable an animal he was,' he remarked to the Indian, 'and I am grateful to you for having shown me my error,' said he. 'If you will sell it, name your own price.'

'Sire,' replied the Indian, 'I never doubted that a sovereign so wise and accomplished as your highness would do justice to my horse, when he once knew its power; and I even went so far as to think it probable that you might wish to possess it. Greatly as I prize it, I will yield it up to your highness on one condition. The horse was not constructed by me, but it was given me by the inventor, in exchange for my only daughter, who made me take a solemn oath that I would never part with it, except for some object of equal value.'

'Name anything you like,' cried the monarch, interrupting him. 'My kingdom is large, and filled with fair cities. You have only to choose which you would prefer, to become its ruler to the end of your life.'

'Sire,' answered the Indian, to whom the proposal did not seem nearly so generous as it appeared to the king, 'I am most grateful to your highness for your princely offer, and beseech you not to be offended with me if I say that I can only deliver up my horse in exchange for the hand of the princess your daughter.'

A shout of laughter burst from the courtiers as they heard these words, and Prince Firouz Schah, the heir apparent, was filled with anger at the Indian's presumption. The king, however, thought that it would not cost him much to part from the princess in order

*The Indian shows off the enchanted horse before
the King of Persia*

to gain such a delightful toy, and while he was hesitating as to his answer the prince broke in.

'Sire,' he said, 'it is not possible that you can doubt for an instant what reply you should give to such an insolent bargain. Consider what you owe to yourself, and to the blood of your ancestors.'

'My son,' replied the king, 'you speak nobly, but you do not realise either the value of the horse, or the fact that if I reject the proposal of the Indian, he will only make the same to some other monarch, and I should be filled with despair at the thought that anyone but myself should own this Seventh Wonder of the World. Of course I do not say that I shall accept his conditions, and perhaps he may be brought to reason, but meanwhile I should like you to examine the horse, and, with the owner's permission, to make trial of its powers.'

The Indian, who had overheard the king's speech, thought that he saw in it signs of yielding to his proposal, so he joyfully agreed to the monarch's wishes, and came forward to help the prince to mount the horse, and show him how to guide it: but, before he had finished, the young man turned the screw, and was soon out of sight.

They waited some time, expecting that every moment he might be seen returning in the distance, but at length the Indian grew frightened, and prostrating himself before the throne, he said to the king, 'Sire, your highness must have noticed that the prince, in his impatience, did not allow me to tell him what it was necessary to do in order to return to the place from which he started. I implore you not to punish me for what was not my fault, and not to visit on me any misfortune that may occur.'

'But why,' cried the king in a burst of fear and anger, 'why did you not call him back when you saw him disappearing?'

'Sire,' replied the Indian, 'the rapidity of his movements took me so by surprise that he was out of hearing before I recovered my speech. But we must hope that he will perceive and turn a second screw, which will have the effect of bringing the horse back to earth.'

'But supposing he does!' answered the king, 'what is to hinder the horse from descending straight into the sea, or dashing him to pieces on the rocks?'

'Have no fears, your highness,' said the Indian; 'the horse has the gift of passing over seas, and of carrying his rider wherever he wishes to go.'

'Well, your head shall answer for it,' returned the monarch, 'and if in three months he is not safe back with me, or at any rate does not send me news of his safety, your life shall pay the penalty.' So saying, he ordered his guards to seize the Indian and throw him into prison.

Meanwhile, Prince Firouz Schah had gone gaily up into the air, and for the space of an hour continued to ascend higher and higher, till the very mountains were not distinguishable from the plains. Then he began to think it was time to come down, and took for granted that, in order to do this, it was only needful to turn the screw the reverse way; but, to his surprise and horror, he found that, turn as he might, he did not make the smallest impression. He then remembered that he had never waited to ask how he was to get back to earth again, and understood the danger in which he stood. Luckily, he did not lose his head, and set about examining the horse's neck with great care, till at last, to his intense joy, he discovered a tiny little peg, much smaller than the other, close to the right ear. This he turned, and found himself dropping to the earth, though more slowly than he had left it.

It was now dark, and as the prince could see nothing, he was obliged, not without some feeling of disquiet, to allow the horse to direct his own course, and midnight was already passed before Prince Firouz Schah again touched the ground, faint and weary from his long ride, and from the fact that he had eaten nothing since early morning.

The first thing he did on dismounting was to try to find out where he was, and, as far as he could discover in the thick darkness, he found himself on the terraced roof of a huge palace, with a balustrade of marble running round. In one corner of the terrace stood a small door, opening on to a staircase which led down into the palace.

Some people might have hesitated before exploring further, but not so the prince. 'I am doing no harm,' he said, 'and whoever the owner may be, he will not touch me when he sees I am unarmed,' and in dread of making a false step, he went cautiously down the staircase. On a landing, he noticed an open door, beyond which was a faintly lighted hall.

Before entering, the prince paused and listened, but he heard nothing except the sound of men snoring. By the light of a lantern suspended from the roof, he perceived a row of black guards sleeping, each with a naked sword lying by him, and he understood that the hall must form the anteroom to the chamber of some queen or princess.

Standing quite still, Prince Firouz Schah looked about him, till his eyes grew accustomed to the gloom, and he noticed a bright light shining through a curtain in one corner. He then made his way softly towards it, and, drawing aside its folds, passed into a magnificent chamber full of sleeping women, all lying on low couches, except one, who was on a sofa; and this one, he knew, must be the princess.

Gently stealing up to the side of her bed he looked at her, and saw that she was more beautiful than any woman he had ever beheld. But, fascinated though he was, he was well aware of the danger of his position, as one cry of surprise would awake the guards, and cause his certain death.

So sinking quietly on his knees, he took hold of the sleeve of the princess and drew her arm lightly towards him. The princess opened her eyes, and seeing before her a handsome well-dressed man, she remained speechless with astonishment.

This favourable moment was seized by the prince, who bowing low while he knelt, thus addressed her: 'You behold, madame, a prince in distress, son to the King of Persia, who, owing to an adventure so strange that you will scarcely believe it, finds himself here, a suppliant for your protection. But yesterday, I was in my father's court, engaged in the celebration of our most solemn festival; today, I am in an unknown land, in danger of my life.'

Now the princess whose mercy Prince Firouz Schah implored was the eldest daughter of the King of Bengal, who was enjoying rest and change in the palace her father had built her, at a little

Prince Firouz Schah in the chamber of the Princess of Bengal

distance from the capital. She listened kindly to what he had to say, and then answered: 'Prince, be not uneasy; hospitality and humanity are practised as widely in Bengal as they are in Persia. The protection you ask will be given you by all. You have my word for it.' And as the prince was about to thank her for her goodness, she added quickly, 'However great may be my curiosity to learn by what means you have travelled here so speedily, I know that you must be faint for want of food, so I shall give orders to my women to take you to one of my chambers, where you will be provided with supper, and left to repose.'

By this time the princess's attendants were all awake, and listening to the conversation. At a sign from their mistress they rose, dressed themselves hastily, and snatching up some of the tapers which lighted the room, conducted the prince to a large and lofty room, where two of the number prepared his bed, and the rest went down to the kitchen, from which they soon returned with all sorts of dishes. Then, showing him cupboards filled with dresses and linen, they quitted the room.

During their absence the Princess of Bengal, who had been greatly struck by the beauty of the prince, tried in vain to go to sleep again. It was of no use: she felt broad awake, and when her women entered the room, she enquired eagerly if the prince had all he wanted, and what they thought of him.

'Madame,' they replied, 'it is of course impossible for us to tell what impression this young man has made on you. For ourselves, we think you would be fortunate if the king your father should allow you to marry anyone so amiable. Certainly there is no one in the Court of Bengal who can be compared with him.'

These flattering observations were by no means displeasing to the princess, but as she did not wish to betray her own feelings she merely said, 'You are all a set of chatterboxes; go back to bed, and let me sleep.'

When she dressed the following morning, her maids noticed that, contrary to her usual habit, the princess was very particular about her toilette, and insisted on her hair being dressed two or three times over. 'For,' she said to herself, 'if my appearance was not displeasing to the prince when he saw me in the condition I was, how much more will he be struck with me when he beholds me with all my charms.'

Then she placed in her hair the largest and most brilliant diamonds she could find, with a necklace, bracelets and girdle, all of precious stones. And over her shoulders her ladies put a robe of the richest stuff in all the Indies, that no one was allowed to wear except members of the royal family. When she was fully dressed according to her wishes, she sent to know if the Prince of Persia was awake and ready to receive her, as she desired to present herself before him.

When the princess's messenger entered his room, Prince Firouz Schah was in the act of leaving it, to enquire if he might be allowed to pay his homage to her mistress: but on hearing the princess's wishes, he at once gave way. 'Her will is my law,' he said, 'I am only here to obey her orders.'

In a few moments the princess herself appeared, and after the usual compliments had passed between them, the princess sat down on a sofa, and began to explain to the prince her reasons for not giving him an audience in her own apartments. 'Had I done so,' she said, 'we might have been interrupted at any hour by the chief of the eunuchs, who has the right to enter whenever it pleases him, whereas this is forbidden ground. I am all impatience to learn the wonderful accident which has procured the pleasure of your arrival, and that is why I have come to you here, where no one can intrude upon us. Begin then, I entreat you, without delay.'

So the prince began at the beginning, and told all the story of the festival of Nedrouz held yearly in Persia, and of the splendid spectacles celebrated in its honour. But when he came to the enchanted horse, the princess declared that she could never have imagined anything half so surprising. 'Well then,' continued the prince, 'you can easily understand how the king my father, who has a passion for all curious things, was seized with a violent desire to possess this horse, and asked the Indian what sum he would take for it.

'The man's answer was absolutely absurd, as you will agree, when I tell you that it was nothing less than the hand of the princess my sister; but though all the bystanders laughed and mocked, and I was beside myself with rage, I saw to my despair that my father could not make up his mind to treat the insolent proposal as it deserved. I tried to argue with him, but in vain. He only begged me to examine the horse with a view (as I quite understood) of making me more sensible of its value.

'To please my father, I mounted the horse, and, without waiting for any instructions from the Indian, turned the peg as I had seen him do. In an instant I was soaring upwards, much quicker than an arrow could fly, and I felt as if I must be getting so near the sky that I should soon hit my head against it! I could see nothing beneath me, and for some time was so confused that I did not even know in what direction I was travelling. At last, when it was growing dark, I found another screw, and on turning it, the horse began slowly to sink towards the earth. I was forced to trust to chance, and to see what fate had in store, and it was already past midnight when I found myself on the roof of this palace. I crept down the little staircase, and made directly for a light which I perceived through an open door – I peeped cautiously in, and saw, as you will guess, the eunuchs lying asleep on the floor. I knew the risks I ran, but my need was so great that I paid no attention to them, and stole safely past your guards, to the curtain which concealed your doorway.

'The rest, princess, you know; and it only remains for me to thank you for the kindness you have shown me, and to assure you of my gratitude. By the law of nations, I am already your slave, and I have only my heart, that is my own, to offer you. But what am I saying? My own? Alas, madame, it was yours from the first moment I beheld you!'

The air with which he said these words could have left no doubt on the mind of the princess as to the effect of her charms, and the blush which mounted to her face only increased her beauty.

'Prince,' returned she as soon as her confusion permitted her to speak, 'you have given me the greatest pleasure, and I have followed you closely in all your adventures, and though you are positively sitting before me, I even trembled at your danger in the upper regions of the air! Let me say what a debt I owe to the chance that has led you to my house; you could have entered none which would have given you a warmer welcome. As to your being a slave, of course that is merely a joke, and my reception must itself have assured you that you are as free here as at your father's court. As to your heart,' continued she in tones of encouragement, 'I am quite sure that must have been disposed of long ago, to some princess who is well worthy of it, and I could not think of being the cause of your unfaithfulness to her.'

Prince Firouz Schah was about to protest that there was no lady with any prior claims, but he was stopped by the entrance of one of the princess's attendants, who announced that dinner was served, and, after all, neither was sorry for the interruption.

Dinner was laid in a magnificent apartment, and the table was covered with delicious fruits; while during the repast richly dressed girls sang softly and sweetly to stringed instruments. After the prince and princess had finished, they passed into a small room hung with blue and gold, looking out into a garden stocked with flowers and arbutus trees, quite different from any that were to be found in Persia.

'Princess,' observed the young man, 'till now I had always believed that Persia could boast finer palaces and more lovely gardens than any kingdom upon earth. But my eyes have been opened, and I begin to perceive that, wherever there is a great king he will surround himself with buildings worthy of him.'

'Prince,' replied the Princess of Bengal, 'I have no idea what a Persian palace is like, so I am unable to make comparisons. I do not wish to depreciate my own palace, but I can assure you that it is very poor beside that of the king my father, as you will agree when you have been there to greet him, as I hope you will shortly do.'

Now the princess hoped that, by bringing about a meeting between the prince and her father, the king would be so struck with the young man's distinguished air and fine manners, that he would offer him his daughter to wife. But the reply of the Prince of Persia to her suggestion was not quite what she wished.

'Madame,' he said, 'by taking advantage of your proposal to visit the palace of the King of Bengal, I should satisfy not merely my curiosity, but also the sentiments of respect with which I regard him. But, princess, I am persuaded that you will feel with me, that I cannot possibly present myself before so great a sovereign without the attendants suitable to my rank. He would think me an adventurer.'

'If that is all,' she answered, 'you can get as many attendants here as you please. There are plenty of Persian merchants, and as for money, my treasury is always open to you. Take what you please.'

Prince Firouz Schah guessed what prompted so much kindness on the part of the princess, and was much touched by it. Still his passion, which increased every moment, did not make him forget his duty. So he replied without hesitation: 'I do not know, princess, how to express my gratitude for your obliging offer, which I would accept at once if it were not for the recollection of all the uneasiness the king my father must be suffering on my account. I should be unworthy indeed of all the love he showers upon me, if I did not return to him at the first possible moment. For, while I am enjoying the society of the most amiable of all princesses, he is, I am quite convinced, plunged in the deepest grief, having lost all hope of seeing me again. I am sure you will understand my position, and will feel that to remain away one instant longer than is necessary would not only be ungrateful on my part, but perhaps even a crime, for how do I know if my absence may not break his heart?

'But,' continued the prince, 'having obeyed the voice of my con-science, I shall count the moments when, with your gracious permission, I may present myself before the King of Bengal, not as a wanderer, but as a prince, to implore the favour of your hand. My father has always informed me that in my marriage I shall be left quite free, but I am persuaded that I have only to describe your generosity, for my wishes to become his own.'

The Princess of Bengal was too reasonable not to accept the explanation offered by Prince Firouz Schah, but she was much disturbed at his intention of departing at once, for she feared that, no sooner had he left her, than the impression she had made on him would fade away. So she made one more effort to keep him, and after assuring him that she entirely approved of his anxiety to see his father, begged him to give her a day or two more of his company.

In common politeness the prince could hardly refuse this request, and the princess set about inventing every kind of amusement for him, and succeeded so well that two months slipped by almost unnoticed, in balls, spectacles and in hunting, of which, when unattended by danger, the princess was passionately fond. But at last, one day, he declared seriously that he could neglect his duty no longer, and entreated her to put no further obstacles in his way, promising at the same time to return, as soon as he could, with all the magnificence due both to her and to himself.

'Princess,' he added, 'it may be that in your heart you class me with those false lovers whose devotion cannot stand the test of absence. If you do, you wrong me; and were it not for fear of offending you, I would beseech you to come with me, for my life can only be happy when passed with you. As for your reception at the Persian court, it will be as warm as your merits deserve; and as for what concerns the King of Bengal, he must be much more indifferent to your welfare than you have led me to believe if he does not give his consent to our marriage.'

The princess could not find words in which to reply to the arguments of the Prince of Persia, but her silence and her downcast eyes spoke for her, and declared that she had no objection to accompanying him on his travels.

The only difficulty that occurred to her was that Prince Firouz Schah did not know how to manage the horse, and she dreaded lest they might find themselves in the same plight as before. But the prince soothed her fears so successfully, that she soon had no other thought than to arrange for their flight so secretly, that no one in the palace should suspect it.

This was done, and early the following morning, when the whole palace was wrapped in sleep, she stole up on to the roof, where the prince was already awaiting her, with his horse's head towards Persia. He mounted first and helped the princess up behind; then, when she was firmly seated, with her hands holding tightly to his belt, he touched the screw, and the horse began to leave the earth quickly behind him.

He travelled with his accustomed speed, and Prince Firouz Schah guided him so well that in two hours and a half from the time of starting, he saw the capital of Persia lying beneath him. He determined to alight neither in the great square from which he had started, nor in the sultan's palace, but in a country house at a little distance from the town. Here he showed the princess a beautiful suite of rooms, and begged her to rest, while he informed his father of their arrival, and prepared a public reception worthy of her rank. Then he ordered a horse to be saddled, and set out.

All the way through the streets he was welcomed with shouts of joy by the people, who had long lost all hope of seeing him again. On reaching the palace, he found the sultan surrounded by his ministers, all clad in the deepest mourning, and his father almost went out of his mind with surprise and delight at the mere sound of his son's voice. When he had calmed down a little, he begged the prince to relate his adventures.

*The prince and princess arrive at the capital of
Persia on the enchanted horse*

The prince at once seized the opening thus given him, and told the whole story of his treatment by the Princess of Bengal, not even concealing the fact that she had fallen in love with him. 'And, sire,' ended the prince, 'having given my royal word that you would not refuse your consent to our marriage, I persuaded her to return with me on the Indian's horse. I have left her in one of your highness's country houses, where she is waiting anxiously to be assured that I have not promised in vain.'

As he said this the prince was about to throw himself at the feet of the sultan, but his father prevented him, and embracing him again, said eagerly: 'My son, not only do I gladly consent to your marriage with the Princess of Bengal, but I will hasten to pay my respects to her, and to thank her in my own person for the benefits she has conferred on you. I will then bring her back with me, and make all arrangements for the wedding to be celebrated today.'

So the sultan gave orders that the habits of mourning worn by the people should be thrown off and that there should be a concert of drums, trumpets and cymbals. Also that the Indian should be taken from prison, and brought before him.

His commands were obeyed, and the Indian was led into his presence, surrounded by guards. 'I have kept you locked up,' said the sultan, 'so that in case my son was lost, your life should pay the penalty. He has now returned; so take your horse, and begone for ever.'

The Indian hastily quitted the presence of the sultan, and when he was outside, he enquired of the man who had taken him out of prison where the prince had really been all this time, and what he had been doing. They told him the whole story, and how the Princess of Bengal was even then awaiting in the country palace the consent of the sultan, which at once put into the Indian's head a plan of revenge for the treatment he had experienced. Going straight to the country house, he informed the doorkeeper who was left in charge that he had been sent by the sultan and by the Prince of Persia to fetch the princess on the enchanted horse, and to bring her to the palace.

The doorkeeper knew the Indian by sight, and was of course

aware that nearly three months before he had been thrown into prison by the sultan; and seeing him at liberty, the man took for granted that he was speaking the truth, and made no difficulty about leading him before the Princess of Bengal; while on her side, hearing that he had come from the prince, the lady gladly consented to do what he wished.

The Indian, delighted with the success of his scheme, mounted the horse, assisted the princess to mount behind him, and turned the peg at the very moment that the prince was leaving the palace in Schiraz for the country house, followed closely by the sultan and all the court. Knowing this, the Indian deliberately steered the horse right above the city, in order that his revenge for his unjust imprisonment might be all the quicker and sweeter.

When the Sultan of Persia saw the horse and its riders, he stopped short with astonishment and horror, and broke out into oaths and curses, which the Indian heard quite unmoved, knowing that he was perfectly safe from pursuit. But mortified and furious as the sultan was, his feelings were nothing to those of Prince Firouz Schah, when he saw the object of his passionate devotion being borne rapidly away. And while he was struck speechless with grief and remorse at not having guarded her better, she vanished swiftly out of his sight. What was he to do? Should he follow his father into the palace, and there give reins to his despair? Both his love and his courage alike forbade it; and he continued his way to the palace.

The sight of the prince showed the doorkeeper of what folly he had been guilty, and flinging himself at his master's feet, implored his pardon. 'Rise,' said the prince, 'I am the cause of this misfortune, and not you. Go and find me the dress of a dervish, but beware of saying it is for me.'

At a short distance from the country house, a convent of dervishes was situated, and the superior, or scheik, was the doorkeeper's friend. So by means of a false story made up on the spur of the moment, it was easy enough to get hold of a dervish's dress, which the prince at once put on, instead of his own. Disguised like this and concealing about him a box of pearls and diamonds he had intended as a present to the princess, he left the house at nightfall, uncertain where he should go, but firmly resolved not to return without her.

Meanwhile the Indian had turned the horse in such a direction that, before many hours had passed, it had entered a wood close to the capital of the kingdom of Cashmere. Feeling very hungry, and supposing that the princess also might be in want of food, he brought his steed down to the earth, and left the princess in a shady place, on the banks of a clear stream.

At first, when the princess had found herself alone, the idea had occurred to her of trying to escape and hide herself. But as she had eaten scarcely anything since she had left Bengal, she felt she was too weak to venture far, and was obliged to abandon her design. On the return of the Indian with meats of various kinds, she began to eat voraciously, and soon had regained sufficient courage to reply with spirit to his insolent remarks. Goaded by his threats she sprang to her feet, calling loudly for help, and luckily her cries were heard by a troop of horsemen, who rode up to enquire what was the matter.

Now the leader of these horsemen was the Sultan of Cashmere, returning from the chase, and he instantly turned to the Indian to enquire who he was, and whom he had with him. The Indian rudely answered that it was his wife, and there was no occasion for anyone else to interfere between them.

The princess, who, of course, was ignorant of the rank of her deliverer, denied altogether the Indian's story. 'My lord,' she cried, 'whoever you may be, put no faith in this impostor. He is an abominable magician, who has this day torn me from the Prince of Persia, my destined husband, and has brought me here on this enchanted horse.' She would have continued, but her tears choked her, and the Sultan of Cashmere, convinced by her beauty and her distinguished air of the truth of her tale, ordered his followers to cut off the Indian's head, which was done immediately.

But rescued though she was from one peril, it seemed as if she had only fallen into another. The sultan commanded a horse to be given her, and conducted her to his own palace, where he led her to a beautiful apartment, and selected female slaves to wait on her, and eunuchs to be her guard. Then, without allowing her time to thank him for all he had done, he bade her repose, saying she should tell him her adventures on the following day.

The princess fell asleep, flattering herself that she had only to relate her story for the sultan to be touched by compassion, and to restore her to the prince without delay. But a few hours were to undeceive her.

When the King of Cashmere had quitted her presence the evening before, he had resolved that the sun should not set again without the princess becoming his wife, and at daybreak proclamation of his intention was made throughout the town, by the sound of drums, trumpets, cymbals, and other instruments calculated to fill the heart with joy. The Princess of Bengal was early awakened by the noise, but she did not for one moment imagine that it had anything to do with her, till the sultan, arriving as soon as she was dressed to enquire after her health, informed her that the trumpet blasts she heard were part of the solemn marriage ceremonies, for which he begged her to prepare. This unexpected announcement caused the princess such terror that she sank down in a dead faint.

The slaves that were in waiting ran to her aid, and the sultan himself did his best to bring her back to consciousness, but for a long while it was all to no purpose. At length her senses began slowly to come back to her, and then, rather than break faith with the Prince of Persia by consenting to such a marriage, she determined to feign madness. So she began by saying all sorts of absurdities, and using all kinds of strange gestures, while the sultan stood watching her with sorrow and surprise. But as this sudden seizure showed no sign of abating, he left her to her women, ordering them to take the greatest care of her. Still, as the day went on, the malady seemed to become worse, and by night it was almost violent.

Days passed in this manner, till at last the Sultan of Cashmere decided to summon all the doctors of his court to consult together over her sad state. Their answer was that madness is of so many different kinds that it was impossible to give an opinion on the case without seeing the princess, so the sultan gave orders that they were to be introduced into her chamber, one by one, every man according to his rank.

*The Sultan of Cashmere rescues the Princess of Bengal
from the Indian*

This decision had been foreseen by the princess, who knew quite well that if once she allowed the physicians to feel her pulse, the most ignorant of them would discover that she was in perfectly good health, and that her madness was feigned, so as each man approached, she broke out into such violent paroxysms, that not one dared to lay a finger on her. A few, who pretended to be cleverer than the rest, declared that they could diagnose sick people only from sight, ordered her certain potions, which she made no difficulty about taking, as she was persuaded they were all harmless.

When the Sultan of Cashmere saw that the court doctors could do nothing towards curing the princess, he called in those of the city, who fared no better. Then he had recourse to the most celebrated physicians in the other large towns, but finding that the task was beyond their science, he finally sent messengers into the other neighbouring states, with a memorandum containing full particulars of the princess's madness, offering at the same time to pay the expenses of any physician who would come and see for himself, and a handsome reward to the one who should cure her. In answer to this proclamation many foreign professors flocked into Cashmere, but they naturally were not more successful than the rest had been, as the cure depended neither on them nor their skill, but only on the princess herself.

It was during this time that Prince Firouz Schah, wandering sadly and hopelessly from place to place, arrived in a large city of India, where he heard a great deal of talk about the Princess of Bengal who had gone out of her senses, on the very day that she was to have been married to the Sultan of Cashmere. This was quite enough to induce him to take the road to Cashmere, and to enquire at the first inn at which he lodged in the capital the full particulars of the story. When he knew that he had at last found the princess whom he had so long lost, he set about devising a plan for her rescue.

The first thing he did was to procure a doctor's robe, so that his dress, added to the long beard he had allowed to grow on his travels, might unmistakably proclaim his profession. He then lost no time in going to the palace, where he obtained an audience of the chief usher, and while apologising for his boldness in presuming to think that he could cure the princess, where so many others had failed, declared that he had the secret of certain remedies, which had hitherto never failed of their effect.

The chief usher assured him that he was heartily welcome, and that the sultan would receive him with pleasure; and in case of success, he would gain a magnificent reward.

When the Prince of Persia, in the disguise of a physician, was brought before him, the sultan wasted no time in talking, beyond remarking that the mere sight of a doctor threw the princess into transports of rage. He then led the prince up to a room under the roof, which had an opening through which he might observe the princess, without himself being seen.

The prince looked, and beheld the princess reclining on a sofa with tears in her eyes, singing softly to herself a song bewailing her sad destiny, which had deprived her, perhaps for ever, of a being she so tenderly loved. The young man's heart beat fast as he listened, for he needed no further proof that her madness was feigned, and that it was love of him which had caused her to resort to this species of trick. He softly left his hiding-place, and returned to the sultan, to whom he reported that he was sure from certain signs that the princess's malady was not incurable, but that he must see her and speak with her alone.

The sultan made no difficulty in consenting to this, and commanded that he should be ushered in to the princess's apartment. The moment she caught sight of his physician's robe, she sprang from her seat in a fury, and heaped insults upon him. The prince took no notice of her behaviour, and approaching quite close, so that his words might be heard by her alone, he said in a low whisper, 'Look at me, princess, and you will see that I am no doctor, but the Prince of Persia, who has come to set you free.'

At the sound of his voice, the Princess of Bengal suddenly grew calm, and an expression of joy overspread her face, such as only comes when what we wish for most and expect the least suddenly happens to us. For some time she was too enchanted to speak, and Prince Firouz Schah took advantage of her silence to explain to her all that had occurred, his despair at watching her disappear before his very eyes, the oath he had sworn to follow her over the world, and his rapture at finally discovering her in the palace at Cashmere. When he had finished, he begged in his turn that the princess would tell him how she had come there, so that he might the better devise some means of rescuing her from the tyranny of the sultan.

It needed but a few words from the princess to make him acquainted with the whole situation, and how she had been forced to play the part of a mad woman in order to escape from a marriage with the sultan, who had not had sufficient politeness even to ask her consent. If necessary, she added, she had resolved to die sooner than permit herself to be forced into such a union, and break faith with a prince whom she loved.

The prince then enquired if she knew what had become of the enchanted horse since the Indian's death, but the princess could only reply that she had heard nothing about it. Still she did not suppose that the horse could have been forgotten by the sultan, after all she had told him of its value.

To this the prince agreed, and they consulted together over a plan by which she might be able to make her escape and return with him into Persia. And as the first step, she was to dress herself with care, and receive the sultan with civility when he visited her next morning.

The sultan was transported with delight on learning the result of the interview, and his opinion of the doctor's skill was raised still higher when, on the following day, the princess behaved towards him in such a way as to persuade him that her complete cure would not be long delayed. However he contented himself with assuring her how happy he was to see her health so much improved, and exhorted her to make every use of so clever a physician, and to repose entire confidence in him. Then he retired, without awaiting any reply from the princess.

The Prince of Persia left the room at the same time, and asked if he might be allowed humbly to enquire by what means the Princess of Bengal had reached Cashmere, which was so far distant from her father's kingdom, and how she came to be there alone. The sultan thought the question very natural, and told him the same story that the Princess of Bengal had done, adding that he had ordered the enchanted horse to be taken to his treasury as a curiosity, though he was quite ignorant how it could be used.

'Sire,' replied the physician, 'your highness's tale has supplied me with the clue I needed to complete the recovery of the princess. During her voyage hither on an enchanted horse, a portion of its enchantment has by some means been communicated to her person, and it can only be dissipated by certain perfumes of which

I possess the secret. If your highness will deign to consent, and to give the court and the people one of the most astonishing spectacles they have ever witnessed, command the horse to be brought into the big square outside the palace, and leave the rest to me. I promise that in a very few moments, in presence of all the assembled multitude, you shall see the princess as healthy both in mind and body as ever she was in her life. And in order to make the spectacle as impressive as possible, I would suggest that she should be richly dressed and covered with the noblest jewels of the crown.'

The sultan readily agreed to all that the prince proposed, and the following morning he desired that the enchanted horse should be taken from the treasury, and brought into the great square of the palace. Soon the rumour began to spread through the town, that something extraordinary was about to happen, and such a crowd began to collect that the guards had to be called out to keep order, and to make a way for the enchanted horse.

When all was ready, the sultan appeared, and took his place on a platform, surrounded by the chief nobles and officers of his court. When they were seated, the Princess of Bengal was seen leaving the palace, accompanied by the ladies who had been assigned to her by the sultan. She slowly approached the enchanted horse, and with the help of her ladies, she mounted on its back. Directly she was in the saddle, with her feet in the stirrups and the bridle in her hand, the physician placed around the horse some large braziers full of burning coals, into each of which he threw a perfume composed of all sorts of delicious scents. Then he crossed his hands over his breast, and with lowered eyes walked three times round the horse, muttering the while certain words. Soon there arose from the burning braziers a thick smoke which almost concealed both the horse and princess, and this was the moment for which he had been waiting. Springing lightly up behind the lady, he leaned forward and turned the peg, and as the horse darted up into the air, he cried aloud so that his words were heard by all present, 'Sultan of Cashmere, when you wish to marry princesses who have sought your protection, learn first to gain their consent.'

*The Prince of Persia and the Princess of Bengal escape
from the Sultan of Cashmere*

It was in this way that the Prince of Persia rescued the Princess of Bengal, and returned with her to Persia, where they descended this time before the palace of the king himself. The marriage was only delayed just long enough to make the ceremony as brilliant as possible, and, as soon as the rejoicings were over, an ambassador was sent to the King of Bengal, to inform him of what had passed, and to ask his approbation of the alliance between the two countries, which he heartily gave.

The Story of Two Sisters who were Jealous of their Younger Sister

Once upon a time there reigned over Persia a sultan named Kosrouschah, who from his boyhood had been fond of putting on a disguise and seeking adventures in all parts of the city, accompanied by one of his officers, disguised like himself. And no sooner was his father buried and the ceremonies over that marked his accession to the throne, than the young man hastened to throw off his robes of state, and calling to his vizir to make ready likewise, stole out in the simple dress of a private citizen into the less known streets of the capital.

Passing down a lonely street, the sultan heard women's voices in loud discussion; and peeping through a crack in the door, he saw three sisters, sitting on a sofa in a large hall, talking in a very lively and earnest manner. Judging from the few words that reached his ear, they were each explaining what sort of men they wished to marry.

'I ask nothing better,' cried the eldest, 'than to have the sultan's baker for a husband. Think of being able to eat as much as one wanted, of that delicious bread that is baked for his highness alone! Let us see if your wish is as good as mine.'

'I,' replied the second sister, 'should be quite content with the sultan's head cook. What delicate stews I should feast upon! And, as I am persuaded that the sultan's bread is used all through the palace, I should have that into the bargain. You see, my dear sister, my taste is as good as yours.'

It was now the turn of the youngest sister, who was by far the most beautiful of the three, and had, besides, more sense than the other two. 'As for me,' she said, 'I should take a higher flight; and if we are to wish for husbands, nothing less than the sultan himself will do for me.'

The sultan was so much amused by the conversation he had overheard, that he made up his mind to gratify their wishes, and turning to the grand-vizir, he bade him note the house, and on the following morning to bring the ladies into his presence.

The grand-vizir fulfilled his commission, and hardly giving them time to change their dresses, desired the three sisters to follow him to the palace. Here they were presented one by one, and when they had bowed before the sultan, the sovereign abruptly put the question to them: 'Tell me, do you remember what you wished for last night, when you were making merry? Fear nothing, but answer me the truth.'

These words, which were so unexpected, threw the sisters into great confusion, their eyes fell, and the blushes of the youngest did not fail to make an impression on the heart of the sultan. All three remained silent, and he hastened to continue: 'Do not be afraid, I have not the slightest intention of giving you pain, and let me tell you at once, that I know the wishes formed by each one. You,' he said, turning to the youngest, 'who desired to have me for a husband, shall be satisfied this very day. And you,' he added, addressing himself to the other two, 'shall be married at the same moment to my baker and to my chief cook.'

When the sultan had finished speaking the three sisters flung themselves at his feet, and the youngest faltered out, 'Oh, sire, since you know my foolish words, believe, I pray you, that they were only said in joke. I am unworthy of the honour you propose to do me, and I can only ask pardon for my boldness.'

The other sisters also tried to excuse themselves, but the sultan would hear nothing.

'No, no,' he said, 'my mind is made up. Your wishes shall be accomplished.'

So the three weddings were celebrated that same day, but with a great difference. That of the youngest was marked by all the magnificence that was customary at the marriage of the Shah of Persia, while the festivities attending the nuptials of the sultan's baker and his chief cook were only such as were suitable to their conditions.

This, though quite natural, was highly displeasing to the elder sisters, who fell into a passion of jealousy, which in the end caused a great deal of trouble and pain to several people. And the first time that they had the opportunity of speaking to each other, which was not till several days later at a public bath, they did not attempt to disguise their feelings.

'Can you possibly understand what the sultan saw in that little cat,' said one to the other, 'for him to be so fascinated by her?'

'He must be quite blind,' returned the wife of the chief cook. 'As for her looking a little younger than we do, what does that matter? You would have made a far better sultana than she.'

'Oh, I say nothing of myself,' replied the elder, 'and if the sultan had chosen you it would have been all very well; but it really grieves me that he should have selected a wretched little creature like that. However, I will be revenged on her somehow, and I beg you will give me your help in the matter, and to tell me anything that you can think of that is likely to mortify her.'

In order to carry out their wicked scheme the two sisters met constantly to talk over their ideas, though all the while they pretended to be as friendly as ever towards the sultana, who, on her part, invariably treated them with kindness. For a long time no plan occurred to the two plotters that seemed in the least likely to meet with success, but at length the expected birth of an heir gave them the chance for which they had been hoping.

They obtained permission of the sultan to take up their abode in the palace for some weeks, and never left their sister night or day. When at last a little boy, beautiful as the sun, was born, they laid him in his cradle and carried it down to a canal which passed through the grounds of the palace. Then, leaving it to its fate, they informed the sultan that instead of the son he had so fondly desired the sultana had given birth to a puppy. At this dreadful news the sultan was so overcome with rage and grief that it was with great difficulty that the grand-vizir managed to save the sultana from his wrath.

Meanwhile the cradle continued to float peacefully along the canal till, on the outskirts of the royal gardens, it was suddenly

The sisters launch the cradle in the canal

perceived by the intendant, one of the highest and most respected officials in the kingdom.

'Go,' he said to a gardener who was working near, 'and get that cradle out for me.'

The gardener did as he was bid, and soon placed the cradle in the hands of the intendant.

The official was much astonished to see that the cradle, which he had supposed to be empty, contained a baby, which, young though it was, already gave promise of great beauty. Having no children himself, although he had been married some years, it at once occurred to him that here was a child which he could take and bring up as his own. And, bidding the man pick up the cradle and follow him, he turned towards home.

'My wife,' he exclaimed as he entered the room, 'heaven has denied us any children, but here is one that has been sent in their place. Send for a nurse, and I will do what is needful publicly to recognise it as my son.'

The wife accepted the baby with joy, and though the intendant saw quite well that it must have come from the royal palace, he did not think it was his business to enquire further into the mystery.

The following year another prince was born and sent adrift, but happily for the baby, the intendant of the gardens again was walking by the canal, and carried it home as before.

The sultan, naturally enough, was still more furious the second time than the first, but when the same curious accident was repeated in the third year he could control himself no longer, and, to the great joy of the jealous sisters, commanded that the sultana should be executed. But the poor lady was so much beloved at court that not even the dread of sharing her fate could prevent the grand-vizir and the courtiers from throwing themselves at the sultan's feet and imploring him not to inflict so cruel a punishment for what, after all, was not her fault.

'Let her live,' entreated the grand-vizir, 'and banish her from your presence for the rest of her days. That in itself will be punishment enough.'

His first passion spent, the sultan had regained his self-command. 'Let her live then,' he said, 'since you have it so much at heart. But if I grant her life it shall only be on one condition, which shall make her daily pray for death. Let a box be built for her at the door of the principal mosque, and let the window of the box be always open. There she shall sit, in the coarsest clothes, and every Mussulman who enters the mosque shall spit in her face in passing. Anyone that refuses to obey shall be exposed to the same punishment himself. You, vizir, will see that my orders are carried out.'

The grand-vizir saw that it was useless to say more, and, full of triumph, the sisters watched the building of the box, and then listened to the jeers of the people at the helpless sultana sitting inside. But the poor lady bore herself with so much dignity and meekness that it was not long before she had won the sympathy of those that were best among the crowd.

But it is now time to return to the fate of the third baby, this time a princess. Like its brothers, it was found by the intendant of the gardens, and adopted by him and his wife, and all three were brought up with the greatest care and tenderness.

As the children grew older their beauty and air of distinction became more and more marked, and their manners had all the grace and ease that is proper to people of high birth. The princes had been named by their foster-father Bahman and Perviz, after two of the ancient kings of Persia, while the princess was called Parizade, or the child of the genii.

The intendant was careful to bring them up as befitted their real rank, and soon appointed a tutor to teach the young princes how to read and write. And the princess, determined not to be left behind, showed herself so anxious to learn with her brothers, that the intendant consented to her joining in their lessons, and it was not long before she knew as much as they did.

From that time all their studies were done in common. They had the best masters for the fine arts, geography, poetry, history and science, and even for sciences which are learned by few, and every branch seemed so easy to them, that their teachers were astonished at the progress they made. The princess had a passion for music, and could sing and play upon all sorts of instruments; she could also ride and drive as well as her brothers, shoot with a bow and arrow, and throw a javelin with the same skill as they, and sometimes even better.

In order to set off these accomplishments, the intendant resolved that his foster-children should not be pent up any longer in the narrow borders of the palace gardens, where he had always lived, so he bought a splendid country house a few miles from the capital, surrounded by an immense park. This park he filled with wild beasts of various sorts, so that the princes and princess might hunt as much as they pleased.

When everything was ready, the intendant threw himself at the sultan's feet, and after referring to his age and his long services, begged his highness's permission to resign his post. This was granted by the sultan in a few gracious words, and he then enquired what reward he could give to his faithful servant. But the intendant declared that he wished for nothing except the continuance of his highness's favour, and prostrating himself once more, he retired from the sultan's presence.

Five or six months passed away in the pleasures of the country, when death attacked the intendant so suddenly that he had no time to reveal the secret of their birth to his adopted children, and as his wife had long been dead also, it seemed as if the princes and the princess would never know that they had been born to a higher station than the one they filled. Their sorrow for their father was very deep, and they lived quietly on in their new home, without feeling any desire to leave it for court gaieties or intrigues.

One day the princes as usual went out to hunt, but their sister remained alone in her apartments. While they were gone an old Mussulman devotee appeared at the door, and asked leave to enter, as it was the hour of prayer. The princess sent orders at once that the old woman was to be taken to the private oratory in the grounds, and when she had finished her prayers was to be shown the house and gardens, and then to be brought before her.

Although the old woman was very pious, she was not at all indifferent to the magnificence of all around her, which she seemed to understand as well as to admire, and when she had seen it all she was led by the servants before the princess, who was seated in a room which surpassed in splendour all the rest.

'My good woman,' said the princess pointing to a sofa, 'come and sit beside me. I am delighted at the opportunity of speaking for a few moments with so holy a person.' The old woman made some objections to so much honour being done her, but the princess refused to listen, and insisted that her guest should take the best seat, and as she thought she must be tired ordered refreshments.

While the old woman was eating, the princess put several questions to her as to her mode of life, and the pious exercises she practised, and then enquired what she thought of the house now that she had seen it.

'Madam,' replied the pilgrim, 'one must be hard indeed to please to find any fault. It is beautiful, comfortable and well ordered, and it is impossible to imagine anything more lovely than the garden. But since you ask me, I must confess that it lacks three things to make it absolutely perfect.'

'And what can they be?' cried the princess. 'Only tell me, and I will lose no time in getting them.'

'The three things, madam,' replied the old woman, 'are, first, the Talking Bird, whose voice draws all other singing birds to it, to join in chorus. And second, the Singing Tree, where every leaf is a song that is never silent. And lastly the Golden Water, of which it is only needful to pour a single drop into a basin for it to shoot up into a fountain, which will never be exhausted, nor will the basin ever overflow.'

'Oh, how can I thank you,' cried the princess, 'for telling me of such treasures! But add, I pray you, to your goodness by further informing me where I can find them.'

'Madam,' replied the pilgrim, 'I should ill repay the hospitality you have shown me if I refused to answer your question. The three things of which I have spoken are all to be found in one place, on the borders of this kingdom, towards India. Your messenger has only to follow the road that passes by your house, for twenty days, and at the end of that time, he is to ask the first person he meets for the Talking Bird, the Singing Tree, and the Golden Water.' She then rose, and bidding farewell to the princess, went her way.

The old woman had taken her departure so abruptly that the Princess Parizade did not perceive till she was really gone that the directions were hardly clear enough to enable the search to be successful. And she was still thinking of the subject, and how delightful it would be to possess such rarities, when the princes, her brothers, returned from the chase.

'What is the matter, my sister?' asked Prince Bahman; 'why are you so grave? Are you ill? Or has anything happened?'

Princess Parizade did not answer directly, but at length she raised her eyes, and replied that there was nothing wrong.

'But there must be something,' persisted Prince Bahman, 'for you to have changed so much during the short time we have been absent. Hide nothing from us, I beseech you, unless you wish us to believe that the confidence we have always had in one another is now to cease.'

'When I said that it was nothing,' said the princess, moved by his words, 'I meant that it was nothing that affected you, although I admit that it is certainly of some importance to me. Like myself, you have always thought this house that our father built for us was perfect in every respect, but only today I have learned that three things are still lacking to complete it. These are the Talking Bird, the Singing Tree, and the Golden Water.' After explaining the peculiar qualities of each, the princess continued: 'It was a Mussulman devotee who told me all this, and where they might all be found. Perhaps you will think that the house is beautiful enough as it is, and that we can do quite well without them; but in this I cannot agree with you, and I shall never be content until I have got them. So counsel me, I pray, whom to send on the undertaking.'

'My dear sister,' replied Prince Bahman, 'that you should care about the matter is quite enough, even if we took no interest in it ourselves. But we both feel with you, and I claim, as the elder, the right to make the first attempt, if you will tell me where I am to go, and what steps I am to take.'

Prince Perviz at first objected that, being the head of the family, his brother ought not to be allowed to expose himself to danger; but Prince Bahman would hear nothing, and retired to make the needful preparations for his journey.

The next morning Prince Bahman got up very early, and after bidding farewell to his brother and sister, mounted his horse. But just as he was about to touch it with his whip, he was stopped by a cry from the princess.

'Oh, perhaps after all you may never come back; one never can tell what accidents may happen. Give it up, I implore you, for I would a thousand times rather lose the Talking Bird, and the

Singing Tree and the Golden Water, than that you should run into danger.'

'My dear sister,' answered the prince, 'accidents only happen to unlucky people, and I hope that I am not one of them. But as everything is uncertain, I promise you to be very careful. Take this knife,' he continued, handing her one that hung sheathed from his belt, 'and every now and then draw it out and look at it. As long as it keeps bright and clean as it is today, you will know that I am living; but if the blade is spotted with blood, it will be a sign that I am dead, and you shall weep for me.'

So saying, Prince Bahman bade them farewell once more, and started on the high road, well mounted and fully armed. For twenty days he rode straight on, turning neither to the right hand nor to the left, till he found himself drawing near the frontiers of Persia. Seated under a tree by the wayside he noticed a hideous old man, with a long white moustache, and beard that almost fell to his feet. His nails had grown to an enormous length, and on his head he wore a huge hat, which served him for an umbrella.

Prince Bahman, who, remembering the directions of the old woman, had been since sunrise on the look-out for someone, recognised the old man at once to be a dervish. He dismounted from his horse, and bowed low before the holy man, saying by way of greeting, 'My father, may your days be long in the land, and may all your wishes be fulfilled!'

The dervish did his best to reply, but his moustache was so thick that his words were hardly intelligible, and the prince, perceiving what was the matter, took a pair of scissors from his saddle pockets, and requested permission to cut off some of the moustache, as he had a question of great importance to ask the dervish. The dervish made a sign that he might do as he liked, and when a few inches of his hair and beard had been pruned all round the prince assured the holy man that he would hardly believe how much younger he looked. The dervish smiled at his compliments, and thanked him for what he had done.

'Let me,' he said, 'show you my gratitude for making me more comfortable by telling me what I can do for you.'

Prince Bahman prunes the dervish's beard

'Gentle dervish,' replied Prince Bahman, 'I come from far, and I seek the Talking Bird, the Singing Tree, and the Golden Water. I know that they are to be found somewhere in these parts, but I am ignorant of the exact spot. Tell me, I pray you, if you can, so that I may not have travelled on a useless quest.' While he was speaking, the prince observed a change in the countenance of the dervish, who waited for some time before he made reply.

'My lord,' he said at last, 'I do know the road for which you ask, but your kindness and the friendship I have conceived for you make me loth to point it out.'

'But why not?' enquired the prince. 'What danger can there be?'

'The very greatest danger,' answered the dervish. 'Other men, as brave as you, have ridden down this road, and have put me that question. I did my best to turn them also from their purpose, but it was of no use. Not one of them would listen to my words, and not one of them came back. Be warned in time, and seek to go no further.'

'I am grateful to you for your interest in me,' said Prince Bahman, 'and for the advice you have given, though I cannot follow it. But what dangers can there be in the adventure which courage and a good sword cannot meet?'

'And suppose,' answered the dervish, 'that your enemies are invisible, how then?'

'Nothing will make me give it up,' replied the prince, 'and for the last time I ask you to tell me where I am to go.'

When the dervish saw that the prince's mind was made up, he drew a ball from a bag that lay near him, and held it out. 'If it must be so,' he said, with a sigh, 'take this, and when you have mounted your horse throw the ball in front of you. It will roll on till it reaches the foot of a mountain, and when it stops you will stop also. You will then throw the bridle on your horse's neck without any fear of his straying, and will dismount. On each side you will see vast heaps of big black stones, and will hear a multitude of insulting voices, but pay no heed to them, and, above all, beware of ever turning your head. If you do, you will instantly become a black stone like the rest. For those stones are in reality men like yourself, who have been on the same quest, and have failed, as I fear that you may fail also. If you manage to avoid this pitfall, and to reach the top of the mountain, you will find there the Talking Bird in a splendid cage, and you can ask of him where you are to seek the Singing Tree and the Golden Water. That is all I have to say. You know what you have to do, and what to avoid, but if you are wise you will think of it no more, but return whence you have come.'

The prince smilingly shook his head, and thanking the dervish once more, he sprang on his horse and threw the ball before him.

The ball rolled along the road so fast that Prince Bahman had much difficulty in keeping up with it, and it never relaxed its speed till the foot of the mountain was reached. Then it came to a sudden halt, and the prince at once got down and flung the bridle on his horse's neck. He paused for a moment and looked round him at the masses of black stones with which the sides of the mountain were covered, and then began resolutely to ascend. He had hardly gone four steps when he heard the sound of voices around him, although not another creature was in sight.

'Who is this imbecile?' cried some, 'stop him at once.' 'Kill him,' shrieked others, 'Help! robbers! murderers! help! help!' 'Oh, let him alone,' sneered another, and this was the most trying of all, 'he is such a beautiful young man; I am sure the bird and the cage must have been kept for him.'

At first the prince took no heed to all this clamour, but continued to press forward on his way. Unfortunately this conduct, instead of silencing the voices, only seemed to irritate them the more, and they arose with redoubled fury, in front as well as behind. After some time he grew bewildered, his knees began to tremble, and finding himself in the act of falling, he forgot altogether the advice of the dervish. He turned to fly down the mountain, and in one moment became a black stone.

As may be imagined, Prince Perviz and his sister were all this time in the greatest anxiety, and consulted the magic knife, not once but many times a day. Hitherto the blade had remained bright and spotless, but on the fatal hour on which Prince Bahman and his horse were changed into black stones, large drops of blood appeared on the surface. 'Ah! my beloved brother,' cried the princess in horror, throwing the knife from her, 'I shall never see you again, and it is I who have killed you. Fool that I was to listen to the voice of that temptress, who probably was not speaking the truth. What are the Talking Bird and the Singing Tree to me in comparison with you, passionately though I long for them!'

Prince Perviz's grief at his brother's loss was not less than that of Princess Parizade, but he did not waste his time on useless lamentations.

'My sister,' he said, 'why should you think the old woman was deceiving you about these treasures, and what would have been her object in doing so! No, no, our brother must have met his death by some accident, or want of precaution, and tomorrow I will start on the same quest.'

Terrified at the thought that she might lose her only remaining brother, the princess entreated him to give up his project, but he remained firm. Before setting out, however, he gave her a chaplet of a hundred pearls, and said, 'When I am absent, tell this over daily for me. But if you should find that the beads stick, so that they will not slip one after the other, you will know that my brother's fate has befallen me. Still, we must hope for better luck.'

Then he departed, and on the twentieth day of his journey fell in with the dervish on the same spot as Prince Bahman had met him, and began to question him as to the place where the Talking Bird, the Singing Tree and the Golden Water were to be found. As in the case of his brother, the dervish tried to make him give up his project, and even told him that only a few weeks since a young man, bearing a strong resemblance to himself, had passed that way, but had never come back again.

'That, holy dervish,' replied Prince Perviz, 'was my elder brother, who is now dead, though how he died I cannot say.'

'He is changed into a black stone,' answered the dervish, 'like all the rest who have gone on the same errand, and you will become one likewise if you are not more careful in following my directions.' Then he charged the prince, as he valued his life, to take no heed of the clamour of voices that would pursue him up the mountain, and handing him a ball from the bag, which still seemed to be half full, he sent him on his way.

When Prince Perviz reached the foot of the mountain he jumped from his horse, and paused for a moment to recall the instructions the dervish had given him. Then he strode boldly on, but had scarcely gone five or six paces when he was startled by a man's voice that seemed close to his ear, exclaiming: 'Stop, rash fellow, and let me punish your audacity.' This outrage entirely put the dervish's advice out of the prince's head. He drew his sword, and turned to avenge himself, but almost before he had realised that there was nobody there, he and his horse were two black stones.

Not a morning had passed since Prince Perviz had ridden away without Princess Parizade telling her beads, and at night she even hung them round her neck, so that if she woke she could assure herself at once of her brother's safety. She was in the very act of moving them through her fingers at the moment that the prince fell a victim to his impatience, and her heart sank when the first pearl remained fixed in its place. However she had long made up her mind what she would do in such a case, and the following morning the princess, disguised as a man, set out for the mountain.

As she had been accustomed to riding from her childhood, she managed to travel as many miles daily as her brothers had done, and it was, as before, on the twentieth day that she arrived at the place where the dervish was sitting. 'Good dervish,' she said politely, 'will you allow me to rest by you for a few moments, and perhaps you will be so kind as to tell me if you have ever heard of a Talking Bird, a Singing Tree, and some Golden Water that are to be found somewhere near this?'

'Madam,' replied the dervish, 'for in spite of your manly dress your voice betrays you, I shall be proud to serve you in any way I can. But may I ask the purpose of your question?'

'Good dervish,' answered the princess, 'I have heard such glowing descriptions of these three things, that I cannot rest till I possess them.'

'Madam,' said the dervish, 'they are far more beautiful than any description, but you seem ignorant of all the difficulties that stand in your way, or you would hardly have undertaken such an adventure. Give it up, I pray you, and return home, and do not ask me to help you to a cruel death.'

'Holy father,' answered the princess, 'I come from far, and I should be in despair if I turned back without having attained my object. You have spoken of difficulties; tell me, I entreat you, what they are, so that I may know if I can overcome them, or see if they are beyond my strength.'

So the dervish repeated his tale, and dwelt more firmly than before on the clamour of the voices, the horrors of the black stones, which were once living men, and the difficulties of climbing the mountain; and pointed out that the chief means of success was never to look behind till you had the cage in your grasp.

'As far as I can see,' said the princess, 'the first thing is not to mind the tumult of the voices that follow you till you reach the cage, and then never to look behind. As to this, I think I have enough self-control to look straight before me; but as it is quite possible that I might be frightened by the voices, as even the boldest men have been, I will stop up my ears with cotton, so that, let them make as much noise as they like, I shall hear nothing.'

'Madam,' cried the dervish, 'out of all the number who have asked me the way to the mountain, you are the first who has ever suggested such a means of escaping the danger! It is possible that you may succeed, but all the same, the risk is great.'

'Good dervish,' answered the princess, 'I feel in my heart that I shall succeed, and it only remains for me to ask you the way I am to go.'

Then the dervish said that it was useless to say more, and he gave her the ball, which she flung before her.

The first thing the princess did on arriving at the mountain was to stop her ears with cotton, and then, making up her mind which was the best way to go, she began her ascent. In spite of the cotton, some echoes of the voices reached her ears, but not so as to trouble her. Indeed, though they grew louder and more insulting the higher she climbed, the princess only laughed, and said to herself that she certainly would not let a few rough words stand between her and the goal. At last she perceived in the distance the cage and the bird, whose voice joined itself in tones of thunder to those of the rest: 'Return, return! never dare to come near me.'

At the sight of the bird, the princess hastened her steps, and without vexing herself at the noise which by this time had grown deafening, she walked straight up to the cage, and seizing it, she said: 'Now, my bird, I have got you, and I shall take good care that you do not escape.' As she spoke she took the cotton from her ears, for it was needed no longer.

'Brave lady,' answered the bird, 'do not blame me for having joined my voice to those who did their best to preserve my freedom. Although confined in a cage, I was content with my lot, but if I must become a slave, I could not wish for a nobler mistress than one who has shown so much constancy, and from this moment I swear to serve you faithfully. Someday you will put me to the proof, for I know who you are better than you do yourself. Meanwhile, tell me what I can do, and I will obey you.'

'Bird,' replied the princess, who was filled with a joy that seemed strange to herself when she thought that the bird had cost her the lives of both her brothers, 'bird, let me first thank you for your good will, and then let me ask you where the Golden Water is to be found.'

The bird described the place, which was not far distant, and the princess filled a small silver flask that she had brought with her for the purpose. She then returned to the cage, and said: 'Bird, there is still something else, where shall I find the Singing Tree?'

'Behind you, in that wood,' replied the bird, and the princess wandered through the wood, till a sound of the sweetest voices told her she had found what she sought. But the tree was tall and strong, and it was hopeless to think of uprooting it.

'You need not do that,' said the bird, when she had returned to ask counsel. 'Break off a twig, and plant it in your garden, and it will take root, and grow into a magnificent tree.'

When the Princess Parizade held in her hands the three wonders promised her by the old woman, she said to the bird: 'All that is not enough. It was owing to you that my brothers became black stones. I cannot tell them from the mass of others, but you must know, and point them out to me, I beg you, for I wish to carry them away.'

For some reason that the princess could not guess these words seemed to displease the bird, and he did not answer. The princess waited a moment, and then continued in severe tones, 'Have you

The princess climbs over the black stones

forgotten that you yourself said that you are my slave to do my bidding, and also that your life is in my power?'

'No, I have not forgotten,' replied the bird, 'but what you ask is very difficult. However, I will do my best. If you look round,' he went on, 'you will see a pitcher standing near. Take it, and, as you go down the mountain, scatter a little of the water it contains over every black stone and you will soon find your two brothers.'

Princess Parizade took the pitcher, and, carrying with her besides the cage the twig and the flask, returned down the mountain side. At every black stone she stopped and sprinkled it with water, and as the water touched it the stone instantly became a man. When she suddenly saw her brothers before her her delight was mixed with astonishment.

'Why, what are you doing here?' she cried.

'We have been asleep,' they said.

'Yes,' returned the princess, 'but without me your sleep would probably have lasted till the day of judgment. Have you forgotten that you came here in search of the Talking Bird, the Singing Tree, and the Golden Water, and the black stones that were heaped up along the road? Look round and see if there is one left. These gentlemen, and yourselves, and all your horses were changed into these stones, and I have delivered you by sprinkling you with the water from this pitcher. As I could not return home without you, even though I had gained the prizes on which I had set my heart, I forced the Talking Bird to tell me how to break the spell.'

On hearing these words Prince Bahman and Prince Perviz understood all they owed their sister, and the knights who stood by declared themselves her slaves and ready to carry out her wishes. But the princess, while thanking them for their politeness, explained that she wished for no company but that of her brothers, and that the rest were free to go where they would.

So saying the princess mounted her horse, and, declining to allow even Prince Bahman to carry the cage with the Talking Bird, she entrusted him with the branch of the Singing Tree, while Prince Perviz took care of the flask containing the Golden Water.

Then they rode away, followed by the knights and gentlemen, who begged to be permitted to escort them.

It had been the intention of the party to stop and tell their adventures to the dervish, but they found to their sorrow that he was dead, whether from old age, or whether from the feeling that his task was done, they never knew.

As they continued their road their numbers grew daily smaller, for the knights turned off one by one to their own homes, and only the brothers and sister finally drew up at the gate of the palace.

The princess carried the cage straight into the garden, and, as soon as the bird began to sing, nightingales, larks, thrushes, finches, and all sorts of other birds mingled their voices in chorus. The branch she planted in a corner near the house, and in a few days it had grown into a great tree. As for the Golden Water it was poured into a great marble basin specially prepared for it, and it swelled and bubbled and then shot up into the air in a fountain twenty feet high.

The fame of these wonders soon spread abroad, and people came from far and near to see and admire.

After a few days Prince Bahman and Prince Perviz fell back into their ordinary way of life, and passed most of their time hunting. One day it happened that the Sultan of Persia was also hunting in the same direction, and, not wishing to interfere with his sport, the young men, on hearing the noise of the hunt approaching, prepared to retire, but, as luck would have it, they turned into the very path down which the sultan was coming. They threw themselves from their horses and prostrated themselves to the earth, but the sultan was curious to see their faces, and commanded them to rise.

The princes stood up respectfully, but quite at their ease, and the sultan looked at them for a few moments without speaking, then he asked who they were and where they lived.

'Sire,' replied Prince Bahman, 'we are sons of your highness's late intendant of the gardens, and we live in a house that he built a short time before his death, waiting till an occasion should offer itself to serve your highness.'

'You seem fond of hunting,' answered the sultan.

'Sire,' replied Prince Bahman, 'it is our usual exercise, and one that should be neglected by no man who expects to comply with the ancient customs of the kingdom and bear arms.'

The sultan was delighted with this remark, and said at once, 'In that case I shall take great pleasure in watching you. Come, choose what sort of beasts you would like to hunt.'

The princes jumped on their horses and followed the sultan at a little distance. They had not gone very far before they saw a number of wild animals appear at once, and Prince Bahman started to give chase to a lion and Prince Perviz to a bear. Both used their javelins with such skill that, directly they arrived within striking range, the lion and the bear fell, pierced through and through. Then Prince Perviz pursued a lion and Prince Bahman a bear, and in a very few minutes they, too, lay dead. As they were making ready for a third assault the sultan interfered, and, sending one of his officials to summon them, he said smiling, 'If I let you go on, there will soon be no beasts left to hunt. Besides, your courage and manners have so won my heart that I will not have you expose yourselves to further danger. I am convinced that some day or other I shall find you useful as well as agreeable.'

He then gave them a warm invitation to stay with him altogether, but with many thanks for the honour done them, they begged to be excused, and to be suffered to remain at home.

The sultan, who was not accustomed to see his offers rejected, enquired their reasons, and Prince Bahman explained that they did not wish to leave their sister, and were accustomed to do nothing without consulting all three together.

'Ask her advice, then,' replied the sultan, 'and tomorrow come and hunt with me, and give me your answer.'

The two princes returned home, but their adventure made so little impression on them that they quite forgot to speak to their sister on the subject. The next morning when they went to hunt they met the sultan in the same place, and he enquired what advice their sister had given. The young men looked at each other and blushed. At last Prince Bahman said, 'Sire, we must throw ourselves on your highness's mercy. Neither my brother nor myself remembered anything about it.'

'Then be sure you do not forget today,' answered the sultan, 'and bring me back your reply tomorrow.'

When, however, the same thing happened a second time, they feared that the sultan might be angry with them for their carelessness. But he took it in good part, and, drawing three little golden balls from his purse, he held them out to Prince Bahman, saying, 'Put these in your bosom and you will not forget a third time, for when you remove your girdle tonight the noise they will make in falling will remind you of my wishes.'

It all happened as the sultan had foreseen, and the two brothers appeared in their sister's apartments just as she was in the act of stepping into bed, and told their tale.

The Princess Parizade was much disturbed at the news, and did not conceal her feelings. 'Your meeting with the sultan is very honourable to you,' she said, 'and will, I dare say, be of service to you, but it places me in a very awkward position. It is on my account, I know, that you have resisted the sultan's wishes, and I am very grateful to you for it. But kings do not like to have their offers refused, and in time he would bear a grudge against you, which would render me very unhappy. Consult the Talking Bird, who is wise and far-seeing, and let me hear what he says.'

So the bird was sent for and the case laid before him.

'The princes must on no account refuse the sultan's proposal,' said he, 'and they must even invite him to come and see your house.'

'But, bird,' objected the princess, 'you know how dearly we love each other; will not all this spoil our friendship?'

'Not at all,' replied the bird, 'it will make it all the closer.'

'Then the sultan will have to see me,' said the princess.

The bird answered that it was necessary that he should see her, and everything would turn out for the best.

The following morning, when the sultan enquired if they had spoken to their sister and what advice she had given them, Prince Bahman replied that they were ready to agree to his highness's wishes, and that their sister had reproved them for their hesitation about the matter. The sultan received their excuses with great kindness, and told them that he was sure they would be equally faithful to him, and kept them by his side for the rest of the day, to the vexation of the grand-vizir and the rest of the court.

When the procession entered in this order the gates of the capital, the eyes of the people who crowded the streets were fixed on the two young men, strangers to everyone.

'Oh, if only the sultan had had sons like that!' they murmured, 'they look so distinguished and are about the same age that his sons would have been!'

The sultan commanded that splendid apartments should be prepared for the two brothers, and even insisted that they should sit at table with him. During dinner he led the conversation to various scientific subjects, and also to history, of which he was especially fond, but whatever topic they might be discussing he found that the views of the young men were always worth listening to. 'If they were my own sons,' he said to himself, 'they could not be better educated!' and aloud he complimented them on their learning and taste for knowledge.

At the end of the evening the princes once more prostrated themselves before the throne and asked leave to return home; and then, encouraged by the gracious words of farewell uttered by the sultan, Prince Bahman said: 'Sire, may we dare to take the liberty of asking whether you would do us and our sister the honour of resting for a few minutes at our house the first time the hunt passes that way?'

'With the utmost pleasure,' replied the sultan; 'and as I am all impatience to see the sister of such accomplished young men you may expect me the day after tomorrow.'

The princess was of course most anxious to entertain the sultan in a fitting way, but as she had no experience in court customs she ran to the Talking Bird, and begged he would advise her as to what dishes should be served.

'My dear mistress,' replied the bird, 'your cooks are very good and you can safely leave all to them, except that you must be careful to have a dish of cucumbers, stuffed with pearl sauce, served with the first course.'

'Cucumbers stuffed with pearls!' exclaimed the princess. 'Why, bird, who ever heard of such a dish? The sultan will expect a dinner he can eat, and not one he can only admire! Besides, if I were to use all the pearls I possess, they would not be half enough.'

'Mistress,' replied the bird, 'do what I tell you and nothing but good will come of it. And as to the pearls, if you go at dawn tomorrow and dig at the foot of the first tree in the park, on the right hand, you will find as many as you want.'

The princess had faith in the bird, who generally proved to be right, and taking the gardener with her early next morning followed out his directions carefully. After digging for some time they came upon a golden box fastened with little clasps.

These were easily undone, and the box was found to be full of pearls, not very large ones, but well-shaped and of a good colour. So leaving the gardener to fill up the hole he had made under the tree, the princess took up the box and returned to the house.

The two princes had seen her go out, and had wondered what could have made her rise so early. Full of curiosity they got up and dressed, and met their sister as she was returning with the box under her arm.

'What have you been doing?' they asked, 'and did the gardener come to tell you he had found a treasure?'

'On the contrary,' replied the princess, 'it is I who have found one,' and opening the box she showed her astonished brothers the pearls inside. Then, on the way back to the palace, she told them of her consultation with the bird, and the advice it had given her. All three tried to guess the meaning of the singular counsel, but they were forced at last to admit the explanation was beyond them, and they must be content blindly to obey.

The first thing the princess did on entering the palace was to send for the head cook and to order the repast for the sultan. When she had finished she suddenly added, 'Besides the dishes I have mentioned there is one that you must prepare expressly for the sultan, and that no one must touch but yourself. It consists of a stuffed cucumber, and the stuffing is to be made of these pearls.'

The head cook, who had never in all his experience heard of such a dish, stepped back in amazement.

'You think I am mad,' answered the princess, who perceived what was in his mind. 'But I know quite well what I am doing. Go, and do your best, and take the pearls with you.'

The next morning the princes started for the forest, and were soon joined by the sultan. The hunt began and continued till midday, when the heat became so great that they were obliged to leave off. Then, as arranged, they turned their horses' heads towards the palace, and while Prince Bahman remained by the side of the sultan, Prince Perviz rode on to warn his sister of their approach.

The moment his highness entered the courtyard, the princess flung herself at his feet, but he bent and raised her, and gazed at her for some time, struck with her grace and beauty, and also with the indefinable air of courts that seemed to hang round this country girl. 'They are all worthy one of the other,' he said to himself, 'and I am not surprised that they think so much of her opinions. I must know more of them.'

By this time the princess had recovered from the first embarrassment of meeting, and proceeded to make her speech of welcome.

'This is only a simple country house, sire,' she said, 'suitable to people like ourselves, who live a quiet life. It cannot compare with the great city mansions, much less, of course, with the smallest of the sultan's palaces.'

'I cannot quite agree with you,' he replied; 'even the little that I have seen I admire greatly, and I will reserve my judgement until you have shown me the whole.'

The princess then led the way from room to room, and the sultan examined everything carefully. 'Do you call this a simple country house?' he said at last. 'Why, if every country house was like this, the towns would soon be deserted. I am no longer astonished that you do not wish to leave it. Let us go into the gardens, which I am sure are no less beautiful than the rooms.'

A small door opened straight into the garden, and the first object that met the sultan's eyes was the Golden Water.

'What lovely coloured water!' he exclaimed; 'where is the spring,

Parizade shows the Singing Tree to the sultan

and how do you make the fountain rise so high? I do not believe there is anything like it in the world.' He went forward to examine it, and when he had satisfied his curiosity, the princess conducted him towards the Singing Tree.

As they drew near, the sultan was startled by the sound of strange voices, but could see nothing. 'Where have you hidden your musicians?' he asked the princess; 'are they up in the air, or under the earth? Surely the owners of such charming voices ought not to conceal themselves!'

'Sire,' answered the princess, 'the voices all come from the tree which is straight in front of us; and if you will deign to advance a few steps, you will see that they become clearer.'

The sultan did as he was told, and was so wrapped in delight at what he heard that he stood some time in silence.

'Tell me, madam, I pray you,' he said at last, 'how this marvellous tree came into your garden? It must have been brought from a great distance, or else, fond as I am of all curiosities, I could not have missed hearing of it! What is its name?'

'The only name it has, sire,' replied she, 'is the Singing Tree, and it is not a native of this country. Its history is mixed up with those of the Golden Water and the Talking Bird, which you have not yet seen. If your highness wishes I will tell you the whole story, when you have recovered from your fatigue.'

'Indeed, madam,' returned he, 'you show me so many wonders that it is impossible to feel any fatigue. Let us go once more and look at the Golden Water; and I am dying to see the Talking Bird.'

The sultan could hardly tear himself away from the Golden Water, which puzzled him more and more. 'You say,' he observed to the princess, 'that this water does not come from any spring, neither is brought by pipes. All I understand is, that neither it nor the Singing Tree is a native of this country.'

'It is as you say, sire,' answered the princess, 'and if you examine the basin, you will see that it is all in one piece, and therefore the water could not have been brought through it. What is more astonishing is, that I only emptied a small flaskful into the basin, and it increased to the quantity you now see.'

'Well, I will look at it no more today,' said the sultan. 'Take me to the Talking Bird.'

On approaching the house, the sultan noticed a vast quantity of birds, whose voices filled the air, and he enquired why they were so much more numerous here than in any other part of the garden.

'Sire,' answered the princess, 'do you see that cage hanging in one of the windows of the saloon? that is the Talking Bird, whose voice you can hear above them all, even above that of the nightingale. And the birds crowd to this spot, to add their songs to his.'

The sultan stepped through the window, but the bird took no notice, continuing his song as before.

'My slave,' said the princess, 'this is the sultan; make him a pretty speech.'

The bird stopped singing at once, and all the other birds stopped too.

'The sultan is welcome,' he said. 'I wish him long life and all prosperity.'

'I thank you, good bird,' answered the sultan, seating himself before the repast, which was spread at a table near the window, 'and I am enchanted to see in you the sultan and King of the Birds.'

The sultan, noticing that his favourite dish of cucumber was placed before him, proceeded to help himself to it, and was amazed to find that the stuffing was of pearls. 'A novelty, indeed!' cried he, 'but I do not understand the reason of it; one cannot eat pearls!'

'Sire,' replied the bird, before either the princes or the princess could speak, 'surely your highness cannot be so surprised at beholding a cucumber stuffed with pearls, when you believed without any difficulty that the sultana had presented you, instead of children, with a dog, a cat, and a log of wood.'

'I believed it,' answered the sultan, 'because the women attending on her told me so.'

'The women, sire,' said the bird, 'were the sisters of the sultana, who were devoured with jealousy at the honour you had done her, and in order to revenge themselves invented this story. Have them examined, and they will confess their crime. These are your children, who were saved from death by the intendant of your gardens, and brought up by him as if they were his own.'

Like a flash the truth came to the mind of the sultan. 'Bird,' he cried, 'my heart tells me that what you say is true. My children,' he added, 'let me embrace you, and embrace each other, not only as brothers and sister, but as having in you the blood royal of Persia which could flow in no nobler veins.'

When the first moments of emotion were over, the sultan hastened to finish his repast, and then turning to his children he exclaimed: 'Today you have made acquaintance with your father. Tomorrow I will bring you the sultana your mother. Be ready to receive her.'

The sultan then mounted his horse and rode quickly back to the capital. Without an instant's delay he sent for the grand-vizir, and ordered him to seize and question the sultana's sisters that very day. This was done. They were confronted with each other and proved guilty, and were executed in less than an hour.

But the sultan did not wait to hear that his orders had been carried out before going on foot, followed by his whole court, to the door of the great mosque, and drawing the sultana with his own hand out of the narrow prison where she had spent so many years, 'Madam,' he cried, embracing her with tears in his eyes, 'I have come to ask your pardon for the injustice I have done you, and to repair it as far as I may. I have already begun by punishing the authors of this abominable crime, and I hope you will forgive me when I introduce you to our children, who are the most charming and accomplished creatures in the whole world. Come with me, and take back your position and all the honour that is due to you.'

This speech was delivered in the presence of a vast multitude of people, who had gathered from all parts on the first hint of what was happening, and the news was passed from mouth to mouth in a few seconds.

Early next day the sultan and sultana, dressed in robes of state and followed by all the court, set out for the country house of their children. Here the sultan presented them to the sultana one by one, and for some time there was nothing but embraces and tears and tender words. Then they ate of the magnificent dinner which had been prepared for them, and after they were all refreshed they went into the garden, where the sultan pointed out to his wife the Golden Water and the Singing Tree. As to the Talking Bird, she had already made acquaintance with him.

In the evening they rode together back to the capital, the princes on each side of their father, and the princess with her mother. Long before they reached the gates the way was lined with people, and the air filled with shouts of welcome, with which were mingled the songs of the Talking Bird, sitting in its cage on the lap of the princess, and of the birds who followed it.

And in this manner they came back to their father's palace.

TALES FROM KING ARTHUR

Tales from King Arthur

EDITED BY
Andrew Lang

with illustrations by
H. J. FORD

CONTENTS

The Drawing of the Sword

Long, long ago, after Uther Pendragon died, there was no king in Britain, and every knight hoped to seize the crown for himself. The country was like to fare ill when laws were broken on every side, and the corn which was to give the poor bread was trodden underfoot, and there was none to bring the evildoer to justice. Then, when things were at their worst, came forth Merlin the magician, and fast he rode to the place where the Archbishop of Canterbury had his dwelling. And they took counsel together, and agreed that all the lords and gentlemen of Britain should ride to London and meet on Christmas Day, now at hand, in the Great Church. So this was done. And on Christmas morning, as they left the church, they saw in the churchyard a large stone, and on it a bar of steel, and in the steel a naked sword was held, and about it was written in letters of gold, 'Whoso pulleth out this sword is by right of birth king of England.' They marvelled at these words, and called for the Archbishop, and brought him into the place where the stone stood. Then those knights who fain would be king could not hold themselves back, and they tugged at the sword with all their might; but it never stirred. The Archbishop watched them in silence, but when they were faint from pulling he spoke: 'The man is not here who shall lift out that sword, nor do I know where to find him. But this is my counsel – that two knights be chosen, good and true men, to keep guard over the sword.'

Thus it was done. But the lords and gentlemen-at-arms cried out that every man had a right to try to win the sword, and they decided that on New Year's Day a tournament should be held, and any knight who would, might enter the lists.

So on New Year's Day, the knights, as their custom was, went to hear service in the Great Church, and after it was over they met in the field to make ready for the tourney. Among them was a brave knight called Sir Ector, who brought with him Sir Kay, his son, and Arthur, Kay's foster-brother. Now Kay had unbuckled his sword the evening before, and in his haste to be at the tourney had forgotten to put it on again, and he begged Arthur to ride back and fetch it for him. But when Arthur reached the house the door was locked, for the women had gone out to see the tourney, and though Arthur tried his best to get in he could not. Then he rode away in great anger, and said to himself, 'Kay shall not be without a sword this day. I will take that sword in the churchyard, and give it to him'; and he galloped fast till he reached the gate of the church-yard. Here he jumped down and tied his horse tightly to a tree, then, running up to the stone, he seized the handle of the sword, and drew it easily out; afterwards he mounted his horse again, and delivered the sword to Sir Kay.

The moment Sir Kay saw the sword he knew it was not his own, but the sword of the stone, and he sought out his father Sir Ector, and said to him, 'Sir, this is the sword of the stone, therefore I am the rightful king.' Sir Ector made no answer, but signed to Kay and Arthur to follow him, and they all three went back to the church. Leaving their horses outside, they entered the choir, and here Sir Ector took a holy book and bade Sir Kay swear how he came by that sword. 'My brother Arthur gave it to me,' replied Sir Kay. 'How did you come by it?' asked Sir Ector, turning to Arthur. 'Sir,' said Arthur, 'when I rode home for my brother's sword I found no one to deliver it to me, and as I resolved he should not be swordless I thought of the sword in this stone, and I pulled it out.' 'Were any knights present when you did this?' asked Sir Ector. 'No, none,' said Arthur. 'Then it is you,' said Sir Ector, 'who are the rightful king of this land.' 'But why am I the king?' enquired Arthur. 'Because,' answered Sir Ector, 'this is an enchanted sword, and no man could draw it but he who was born a king. Therefore put the sword back into the stone, and let me see you take it out.' 'That is soon done,' said Arthur, replacing the sword, and Sir Ector himself tried to draw it, but he could not. 'Now it is your turn,' he said to Sir Kay, but Sir Kay fared no better than his father, though he tugged with all his might and main. 'Now you, Arthur,' and Arthur

IVRE REX BRITANNIÆ

HOW ARTHVR DREW THE SWORD

pulled it out as easily as if it had been lying in its sheath, and as he did so Sir Ector and Sir Kay sank on their knees before him. 'Why do you, my father and brother, kneel to me?' asked Arthur in surprise. 'Nay, nay, my lord,' answered Sir Ector, 'I was never your father, though till today I did not know who your father really was. You are the son of Uther Pendragon, and you were brought to me when you were born by Merlin himself, who promised that when the time came I should know from whom you sprang. And now it has been revealed to me.' But when Arthur heard that Sir Ector was not his father, he wept bitterly. 'If I am king,' he said at last, 'I ask what you will, and I shall not fail you. For to you, and to my lady and mother, I owe more than to anyone in the world, for she loved me and treated me as her son.'

'Sir,' replied Sir Ector, 'I only ask that you will make your foster-brother, Sir Kay, Seneschal of all your lands.'

'That I will readily,' answered Arthur, 'and while he and I live no other shall fill that office.'

Sir Ector then bade them seek out the Archbishop with him, and they told him all that had happened concerning the sword, which Arthur had left standing in the stone. And on the twelfth day the knights and barons came again, but none could draw it out but Arthur. When they saw this, many of the barons became angry and cried out that they would never own a boy for king whose blood was no better than their own. So it was agreed to wait till Candlemas, when more knights might be there, and meanwhile the same two men who had been chosen before watched the sword night and day; but at Candlemas it was the same thing, and at Easter. And when Pentecost came, the common people who were present, and saw Arthur pull out the sword, cried with one voice that he was their king, and they would kill any man who said differently. Then rich and poor fell on their knees before him, and Arthur took the sword and offered it upon the altar where the Archbishop stood, and the best man that was there made him knight. After that the crown was put on his head, and he swore to his lords and commons that he would be a true king, and would do them justice all the days of his life.

The Questing Beast

But Arthur had many battles to fight and many kings to conquer before he was acknowledged lord of them all, and often he would have failed had he not listened to the wisdom of Merlin, and been helped by his sword Excalibur, which in obedience to Merlin's orders he never drew till things were going ill with him. Later it shall be told how the king got the sword Excalibur, which shone so bright in his enemies' eyes that they fell back, dazzled by the brightness. Many knights came to his standard, and among them Sir Ban, King of Gaul beyond the sea, who was ever his faithful friend. And it was in one of these wars, when King Arthur and King Ban and King Bors went to the rescue of the King of Cameliard, that Arthur saw Guenevere, the king's daughter, whom he afterwards wedded. By and by King Ban and King Bors returned to their own country across the sea, and the king went to Carlion, a town on the river Usk, where a strange dream came to him.

He thought that the land was overrun with gryphons and serpents which burnt and slew his people, and he made war on the monsters, and was sorely wounded, though at last he killed them all. When he awoke the remembrance of his dream was heavy upon him, and to shake it off he summoned his knights to hunt with him, and they rode fast till they reached a forest. Soon they spied a hart before them, which the king claimed as his game, and he spurred his horse and rode after him. But the hart ran fast and the king could not get near it, and the chase lasted so long that the king himself grew heavy and his horse fell dead under him. Then he sat under a tree and rested, till he heard the baying of hounds, and fancied he counted as many as thirty of them. He raised his head to look, and, coming towards him, saw a beast so strange that its like was not to be found throughout his kingdom. It went straight to the well and drank, making as it did so the noise of many hounds baying, and when it had drunk its fill the beast went its way.

While the king was wondering what sort of a beast this could be, a knight rode by, who, seeing a man lying under a tree, stopped and said to him: 'Knight full of thought and sleepy, tell me if a strange beast has passed this way?'

'Yes, truly,' answered Arthur, 'and by now it must be two miles distant. What do you want with it?'

'Oh sir, I have followed that beast from far,' replied he, 'and have ridden my horse to death. If only I could find another I would still go after it.' As he spoke a squire came up leading a fresh horse for the king, and when the knight saw it he prayed that it might be given to him, 'For,' said he, 'I have followed this quest this twelve-month, and either I shall slay him or he will slay me.'

'Sir Knight,' answered the king, 'you have done your part; leave now your quest, and let me follow the beast for the same time that you have done.'

'Ah, fool!' replied the knight, whose name was Pellinore, 'it would be all in vain, for none may slay that beast but I or my next of kin'; and without more words he sprang into the saddle. 'You may take my horse by force,' said the king, 'but I should like to prove first which of us two is the better horseman.'

'Well,' answered the knight, 'when you want me, come to this spring. Here you will always find me,' and, spurring his horse, he galloped away. The king watched him till he was out of sight, then turned to his squire and bade him bring another horse as quickly as he could. While he was waiting for it the wizard Merlin came along in the likeness of a boy, and asked the king why he was so thoughtful.

'I may well be thoughtful,' replied the king, 'for I have seen the most wonderful sight in all the world.'

'That I know well,' said Merlin, 'for I know all your thoughts. But it is folly to let your mind dwell on it, for thinking will mend nothing. I know, too, that Uther Pendragon was your father, and your mother was the Lady Igraine.'

'How can a boy like you know that?' cried Arthur, growing angry; but Merlin only answered, 'I know it better than any man living,'

ARTHVR · AND · THE · QVESTING · BEAST

and passed, returning soon after in the likeness of an old man of fourscore, and sitting down by the well to rest.

'What makes you so sad?' asked he.

'I may well be sad,' replied Arthur, 'there is plenty to make me so. And besides, there was a boy here who told me things that he had no business to know, and among them the names of my father and mother.'

'He told you the truth,' said the old man, 'and if you would have listened he could have told you still more: how that your sister shall have a child who shall destroy you and all your knights.'

'Who are you?' asked Arthur, wondering.

'I am Merlin, and it was I who came to you in the likeness of a boy. I know all things; how that you shall die a noble death, being slain in battle, while my end will be shameful, for I shall be put alive into the earth.'

There was no time to say more, for the man brought up the king's horse and he mounted, and rode fast till he came to Carlion.

The Sword Excalibur

King Arthur had fought a hard battle with the tallest knight in all
the land, and though he struck hard and well, he would have been
slain had not Merlin enchanted the knight and cast him into a deep
sleep, and brought the king to a hermit who had studied the art of
healing, and cured all his wounds in three days. Then Arthur and
Merlin waited no longer, but gave the hermit thanks and departed.

As they rode together Arthur said, 'I have no sword,' but Merlin
bade him be patient and he would soon give him one. In a little
while they came to a large lake, and in the midst of the lake Arthur
beheld an arm rising out of the water, holding up a sword. 'Look!'
said Merlin, 'that is the sword I spoke of.' And the king looked
again, and a maiden stood upon the water. 'That is the Lady of the
Lake,' said Merlin, 'and she is coming to you, and if you ask her
courteously she will give you the sword.' So when the maiden drew
near Arthur saluted her and said, 'Maiden, I pray you tell me whose
sword is that which an arm is holding out of the water? I wish it
were mine, for I have lost my sword.'

'That sword is mine, King Arthur,' answered she, 'and I will give
it to you, if you in return will give me a gift when I ask you.'

'By my faith,' said the king, 'I will give you whatever gift you ask.'
'Well,' said the maiden, 'get into the barge yonder, and row yourself to the sword, and take it and the scabbard with you.' For this
was the sword Excalibur. 'As for my gift, I will ask it in my own
time.' Then King Arthur and Merlin dismounted from their horses
and tied them up safely, and went into the barge, and when they
came to the place where the arm was holding the sword Arthur
took it by the handle, and the arm disappeared. And they brought
the sword back to land. As they rode the king looked lovingly on his
sword, which Merlin saw, and, smiling, said, 'Which do you like
best, the sword or the scabbard?' 'I like the sword,' answered Arthur.
'You are not wise to say that,' replied Merlin, 'for the scabbard is

worth ten of the sword, and as long as it is buckled on you you will lose no blood, however sorely you may be wounded.' So they rode into the town of Carlion, and Arthur's knights gave them a glad welcome, and said it was a joy to serve under a king who risked his life as much as any common man.

The Story of Sir Balin

In those days many kings reigned in the Islands of the Sea, and they constantly waged war upon each other, and on their liege lord, and news came to Arthur that Ryons, King of North Wales, had collected a large host and had ravaged his lands and slain some of his people. When he heard this, Arthur rose in anger, and commanded that all lords, knights, and gentlemen of arms should meet him at Camelot, where he would call a council, and hold a tourney.

From every part the knights flocked to Camelot, and the town was full to overflowing of armed men and their horses. And when they were all assembled, there rode in a damsel, who said she had come with a message from the great Lady Lile of Avelion, and begged that they would bring her before King Arthur. When she was led into his presence she let her mantle of fur slip off her shoulders, and they saw that by her side a richly wrought sword was buckled. The king was silent with wonder at the strange sight, but at last he said, 'Damsel, why do you wear this sword? for swords are not the ornaments of women.' 'Oh, my lord,' answered she, 'I would I could find some knight to rid me of this sword, which weighs me down and causes me much sorrow. But the man who will deliver me of it must be one who is mighty of his hands, and pure in his deeds, without villainy, or treason. If I find a knight such as this, he will draw this sword out of its sheath, and he only. For I have been at the court of King Ryons, and he and his knights tried with all their strength to draw the sword and they could not.'

'Let me see if I can draw it,' said Arthur, 'not because I think myself the best knight, for well I know how far I am outdone by others, but to set them an example that they may follow me.' With that the king took the sword by the sheath and by the girdle, and pulled at it with all his force, but the sword stuck fast. 'Sir,' said the damsel, 'you need not pull half so hard, for he that shall pull it out shall do it with little strength.' 'It is not for me,' answered Arthur, 'and now, my barons, let each man try his fortune.' So most of the Knights of the Round Table there present pulled, one after another, at the sword, but none could stir it from its sheath. 'Alas! alas!' cried the damsel in great grief, 'I thought to find in this court knights that were blameless and true of heart, and now I know not where to look for them.' 'By my faith,' said Arthur, 'there are no better knights in the world than these of mine, but I am sore displeased that they cannot help me in this matter.'

Now at that time there was a poor knight at Arthur's court who had been kept prisoner for a year and a half because he had slain the king's cousin. He was of high birth and his name was Balin, and after he had suffered eighteen months the punishment of his misdeed the barons prayed the king to set him free, which Arthur did willingly. When Balin, standing apart, beheld the knights one by one try the sword, and fail to draw it, his heart beat fast, yet he shrank from taking his turn, for he was meanly dressed, and could not compare with the other barons. But after the damsel had bid farewell to Arthur and his court, and was setting out on her journey homewards, he called to her and said, 'Damsel, I pray you to suffer me to try your sword, as well as these lords, for though I am so poorly clothed, my heart is as high as theirs.' The damsel stopped and looked at him, and answered, 'Sir, it is not needful to put you to such trouble, for where so many have failed it is hardly likely that you will succeed.' 'Ah! fair damsel,' said Balin, 'it is not fine clothes that make good deeds.' 'You speak truly,' replied the damsel, 'therefore do what you can.' Then Balin took the sword by the girdle and sheath, and pulled it out easily, and when he looked at the sword he was greatly pleased with it. The king and the knights were dumb with surprise that it was Balin who had triumphed over them, and many of them envied him and felt anger towards him. 'In truth,' said the damsel, 'this is the best knight that I ever found, but, sir, I pray you give me the sword again.'

'No,' answered Balin, 'I will keep it till it is taken from me by force.' 'It is for your sake, not mine, that I ask for it,' said the

The Damsel Warns Sir Balin.

damsel, 'for with that sword you shall slay the man you love best, and it shall bring about your own ruin.' 'I will take what befalls me,' replied Balin, 'but the sword I will not give up, by the faith of my body.' So the damsel departed in great sorrow. The next day Sir Balin left the court, and, armed with his sword, set forth in search of adventures, which he found in many places where he had not thought to meet with them. In all the fights that he fought, Sir Balin was the victor, and Arthur, and Merlin his friend, knew that there was no knight living of greater deeds, or more worthy of worship. And he was known to all as Sir Balin le Savage, the knight of the two swords.

One day he was riding forth when at the turning of a road he saw a cross, and on it was written in letters of gold, 'Let no knight ride towards this castle.' Sir Balin was still reading the writing when there came towards him an old man with white hair, who said, 'Sir Balin le Savage, this is not the way for you, so turn again and choose some other path.' And so he vanished, and a horn blew loudly, as a horn is blown at the death of a beast. 'That blast,' said Balin, 'is for me, but I am still alive,' and he rode to the castle, where a great company of knights and ladies met him and welcomed him, and made him a feast. Then the lady of the castle said to him, 'Knight with the two swords, you must now fight a knight that guards an island, for it is our law that no man may leave us without he first fight a tourney.'

'That is a bad custom,' said Balin, 'but if I must I am ready; for though my horse is weary my heart is strong.'

'Sir,' said a knight to him, 'your shield does not look whole to me; I will lend you another'; so Balin listened to him and took the shield that was offered, and left his own with his own coat of arms behind him. He rode down to the shore, and led his horse into a boat, which took them across. When he reached the other side, a damsel came to him crying, 'O Knight Balin, why have you left your own shield behind you? Alas! you have put yourself in great danger, for by your shield you should have been known. I grieve over your doom, for there is no man living that can rival you for courage and bold deeds.'

'I repent,' answered Balin, 'ever having come into this country, but for very shame I must go on. Whatever befalls me, either for life or death, I am ready to take it.' Then he examined his armour, and saw that it was whole, and mounted his horse.

As he went along the path he beheld a knight come out of a castle in front, clothed in red, riding a horse with red trappings. When this Red Knight looked on the two swords, he thought for a moment it was Balin, but the shield did not bear Balin's device. So they rode at each other with their spears, and smote each other's shields so hard that both horses and men fell to the ground with the shock, and the knights lay unconscious on the ground for some minutes. But soon they rose up again and began the fight afresh, and they fought till the place was red with their blood, and they had each seven great wounds.

'What knight are you?' asked Balin le Savage, pausing for breath, 'for never before have I found any knight to match me.' 'My name,' said he, 'is Balan, brother to the good Knight Balin.'

'Alas!' cried Balin, 'that I should ever live to see this day,' and he fell back fainting to the ground. At this sight Balan crept on his feet and hands, and pulled off Balin's helmet, so that he might see his face. The fresh air revived Balin, and he awoke and said: 'O Balan, my brother, you have slain me, and I you, and the whole world shall speak ill of us both.'

'Alas,' sighed Balan, 'if I had only known you! I saw your two swords, but from your shield I thought you had been another knight.'

'Woe is me!' said Balin, 'all this was wrought by an unhappy knight in the castle, who caused me to change my shield for his. If I lived, I would destroy that castle that he should not deceive other men.'

'You would have done well,' answered Balan, 'for they have kept me prisoner ever since I slew a knight that guarded this island, and they would have kept you captive too.' Then came the lady of the castle and her companions, and listened as they made their moan. And Balan prayed that she would grant them the grace to lie together, there where they died, and their wish was

The Death of Balin and Balan

given them, and she and those that were with her wept for pity.

So they died; and the lady made a tomb for them, and put Balan's name alone on it, for Balin's name she knew not. But Merlin knew, and next morning he came and wrote it in letters of gold, and he ungirded Balin's sword, and unscrewed the pommel, and put another pommel on it, and bade a knight that stood by handle it, but the knight could not. At that Merlin laughed. 'Why do you laugh?' asked the knight. 'Because,' said Merlin, 'no man shall handle this sword but the best knight in the world, and that is either Sir Lancelot or his son Sir Galahad. With this sword Sir Lancelot shall slay the man he loves best, and Sir Gawaine is his name.' And this was later done, in a fight across the seas.

All this Merlin wrote on the pommel of the sword.

Next he made a bridge of steel to the island, six inches broad, and no man could pass over it that was guilty of any evil deeds. The scabbard of the sword he left on this side of the island, so that Galahad should find it. The sword itself he put in a magic stone, which floated down the stream to Camelot, that is now called Winchester. And the same day Galahad came to the river, having in his hand the scabbard, and he saw the sword and pulled it out of the stone, as is told in another place.

How the Round Table Began

It was told in the story of the Questing Beast that King Arthur married the daughter of Leodegrance, King of Cameliard, but there was not space there to say how it came about. And as the tales of the Round Table are full of this lady, Queen Guenevere, it is well that anybody who reads this book should learn how she became queen.

After King Arthur had fought and conquered many enemies, he said one day to Merlin, whose counsel he took all the days of his life, 'My barons will let me have no rest, but bid me take a wife, and I have answered them that I shall take none, except you advise me.'

'It is well,' replied Merlin, 'that you should take a wife, but is there any woman that you love better than another? 'Yes,' said Arthur, 'I love Guenevere, daughter of Leodegrance, King of Cameliard, in whose house is the Round Table that my father gave him. This maiden is the fairest that I have ever seen, or ever shall see.' 'Sir,' answered Merlin, 'what you say as to her beauty is true, but, if your heart was not set on her, I could find you another as fair, and of more goodness, than she. But if a man's heart is once set it is idle to try to turn him.' Then Merlin asked the king to give him a company of knights and esquires, that he might go to the court of King Leodegrance and tell him that King Arthur desired to wed his daughter, which Arthur did gladly. Therefore Merlin rode forth and made all the haste he could till he came to the Castle of Cameliard, and told King Leodegrance who had sent him and why.

'That is the best news I have ever had,' replied Leodegrance, 'for little did I think that so great and noble a king should seek to marry my daughter. As for lands to endow her with, I would give whatever he chose; but he has lands enough of his own, so I will give him instead something that will please him much more, the Round Table which Uther Pendragon gave me, where a hundred and fifty knights can sit at one time. I myself can call to my side a hundred good knights, but I lack fifty, for the wars have slain many, and some are absent.' And without more words King Leodegrance gave his consent that his daughter should wed King Arthur. And Merlin returned with his knights and esquires, journeying partly by water and partly by land, till they drew near to London.

When King Arthur heard of the coming of Merlin and of the knights with the Round Table he was filled with joy, and said to those that stood about him, 'This news that Merlin has brought me is welcome indeed, for I have long loved this fair lady, and the Round Table is dearer to me than great riches.' Then he ordered that Sir Lancelot should ride to fetch the queen, and that preparations for the marriage and her coronation should be made, which was done. 'Now, Merlin,' said the king, 'go and look about my kingdom and bring fifty of the bravest and most famous knights that can be found throughout the land.' But no more than eight and twenty knights could Merlin find. With these Arthur had to be content, and the Bishop of Canterbury was fetched, and he blessed the seats that were placed by the Round Table, and the knights sat in them. 'Fair sirs,' said Merlin, when the bishop had ended his blessing, 'arise all of you, and pay your homage to the king.' So the knights arose to do his bidding, and in every seat was the name of the knight who had sat on it, written in letters of gold, but two seats were empty. After that young Gawaine came to the king, and prayed him to make him a knight on the day that he should wed Guenevere. 'That I will gladly,' replied the king, 'for you are my sister's son.'

As the king was speaking, a poor man entered the court, bringing with him a youth about eighteen years old, riding on a lean mare, though it was not the custom for gentlemen to ride on mares. 'Where is King Arthur?' asked the man. 'Yonder,' answered the knights. 'Have you business with him?' 'Yes,' said the man, and he went and bowed low before the king: 'I have heard, O King Arthur, flower of knights and kings, that at the time of your marriage you would give any man the gift he should ask for.'

'That is truth,' answered the king, 'as long as I do no wrong to other men or to my kingdom.'

'I thank you for your gracious words,' said the poor man; 'the boon I would ask is that you would make my son a knight.' 'It is a great boon to ask,' answered the king. 'What is your name?'

'Sir, my name is Aries the cowherd.'

'Is it you or your son that has thought of this honour?'

'It is my son who desires it, and not I,' replied the man. 'I have thirteen sons who tend cattle, and work in the fields if I bid them; but this boy will do nothing but shoot and cast darts, or go to watch battles and look on knights, and all day long he beseeches me to bring him to you, that he may be knighted also.'

'What is your name?' said Arthur, turning to the young man.

'Sir, my name is Tor.'

'Where is your sword that I may knight you?' said the king.

'It is here, my lord.'

'Take it out of its sheath,' said the king, 'and require me to make you a knight.' Then Tor jumped off his mare and pulled out his sword, and knelt before the king, praying that he might be made, a knight and a Knight of the Round Table.

'As for a knight, that I will make you,' said Arthur, smiting him in the neck with the sword, 'and if you are worthy of it you shall be a Knight of the Round Table.'

And the next day he made Gawaine knight also.

The Passing of Merlin

Sir Tor proved before long by his gallant deeds that he was worthy to sit in one of the two empty seats of the Round Table. Many of the other knights went out also in search of adventures, and one of them, Sir Pellinore, brought a damsel of the lake to Arthur's court, and when Merlin saw her he fell in love with her, so that he desired to be always in her company. The damsel laughed in secret at Merlin, but made use of him to tell her all she would know, and the wizard had no strength to say her nay, though he knew what would come of it. For he told King Arthur that before long he should be put into the earth alive, for all his cunning. He likewise told the king many things that should befall him, and warned him always to keep the scabbard as well as the sword Excalibur, and foretold that both sword and scabbard should be stolen from him by a woman whom he most trusted. 'You will miss my counsel sorely,' added Merlin, 'and would give all your lands to have me back again.'

'But since you know what will happen,' said the king, 'you may surely guard against it.'

'No,' answered Merlin, 'that will not be.' So he departed from the king, and the maiden followed him whom some call Nimue and others Vivien, and wherever she went Merlin went also.

They journeyed together to many places, both at home and across the seas, and the damsel was wearied of him, and sought by every means to be rid of him, but he would not be shaken off. At last these two wandered back to Cornwall, and one day Merlin showed Vivien a rock under which he said great marvels were hidden. Then Vivien put forth all her powers, and told Merlin how she longed to see the wonders beneath the stone, and, in spite of all his wisdom, Merlin listened to her and crept under the rock to bring forth the strange things that lay there. And when he was under the stone she used the magic he had taught her, and the rock rolled over him, and buried

MERLIN AND VIVIEN

him alive, as he had told King Arthur. But the damsel departed with joy, and thought no more of him: now that she knew all the magic he could teach her.

How Morgan le Fay Tried to Kill King Arthur

King Arthur had a sister called Morgan le Fay, who was skilled in magic of all sorts, and hated her brother because he had slain in battle a knight whom she loved. But to gain her own ends, and to revenge herself upon the king, she kept a smiling face, and let none guess the passion in her heart.

One day Morgan le Fay went to Queen Guenevere, and asked her leave to go into the country. The queen wished her to wait till Arthur returned, but Morgan le Fay said she had had bad news and could not wait. Then the queen let her depart without delay.

Early next morning at break of day Morgan le Fay mounted her horse and rode all day and all night, and at noon next day reached the abbey of nuns where King Arthur had gone to rest, for he had fought a hard battle, and for three nights had slept but little. 'Do not wake him,' said Morgan le Fay, who had come there knowing she would find him, 'I will rouse him myself when I think he has had enough sleep,' for she thought to steal his sword Excalibur from him. The nuns dared not disobey her, so Morgan le Fay went straight into the room where King Arthur was lying fast asleep in his bed, and in his right hand was grasped his sword Excalibur. When she beheld that sight, her heart fell, for she dared not touch the sword, knowing well that if Arthur waked and saw her she was a dead woman. So she took the scabbard, and went away on horseback.

When the king awoke and missed his scabbard, he was angry, and asked who had been there; and the nuns told him that it was his sister, Morgan le Fay, who had gone away with a scabbard under her mantle. 'Alas!' said Arthur, 'you have watched me badly!'

'Sir,' said they, 'we dared not disobey your sister.'

'Saddle the best horse that can be found,' commanded the king,

MORGAN LE FAY CASTS AWAY THE SCABBARD

'and bid Sir Ontzlake take another and come with me.' And they buckled on their armour and rode after Morgan le Fay.

They had not gone far before they met a cowherd, and they stopped to ask if he had seen any lady riding that way. 'Yes,' said the cowherd, 'a lady passed by here, with forty horses behind her, and went into the forest yonder.' Then they galloped hard till Arthur caught sight of Morgan le Fay, who looked back, and, seeing that it was Arthur who gave chase, pushed on faster than before. And when she saw she could not escape him, she rode into a lake that lay in the plain on the edge of the forest, and, crying out, 'Whatever may befall me, my brother shall not have the scabbard,' she threw the scabbard far into the water, and it sank, for it was heavy with gold and jewels. After that she fled into a valley full of great stones, and turned herself and her men and her horses into blocks of marble. Scarcely had she done this when the king rode up, but seeing her nowhere thought some evil must have befallen her in vengeance for her misdeeds. He then sought high and low for the scabbard, but could not find it, so he returned unto the abbey. When Arthur was gone, Morgan le Fay turned herself and her horses and her men back into their former shapes, and said, 'Now, sirs, we may go where we will.' And she departed into the country of Gore, and made her towns and castles stronger than before, for she feared King Arthur greatly.

Meanwhile King Arthur had rested himself at the abbey, and afterwards he rode to Camelot, and was welcomed by his queen and all his knights. And when he told his adventures and how Morgan le Fay sought his death they longed to burn her for her treason.

The next morning there arrived a damsel at the court with a message from Morgan le Fay, saying that she had sent the king her brother a rich mantle for a gift, covered with precious stones, and begged him to receive it and to forgive her in whatever she might have offended him. The king answered little, but the mantle pleased him, and he was about to throw it over his shoulders when the Lady of the Lake stepped forward, and begged that she might speak to him in private.

'What is it?' asked the king. 'Say on here, and fear nothing.'

'Sir,' said the lady, 'do not put on this mantle, or suffer your knights to put it on, till the bringer of it has worn it in your presence.'

'Your words are wise,' answered the king; 'I will do as you counsel me. Damsel, I desire you to put on this mantle that you have brought me, so that I may see it.'

'Sir,' said she, 'it does not become me to wear a king's garment.'

'By my head,' cried Arthur, 'you shall wear it before I put it on my back, or on the back of any of my knights,' and he signed to them to put it on her, and she fell down dead, burnt to ashes by the enchanted mantle. Then the king was filled with anger, more than he was before, that his sister should have dealt so wickedly by him.

What Beaumains Asked of the King

As Pentecost drew near King Arthur commanded that all the Knights of the Round Table should keep the feast at a city called Kin-Kenadon, hard by the sands of Wales, where there was a great castle. Now it was the king's custom that he would eat no food on the day of Pentecost, which we call Whitsunday, until he had heard or seen some great marvel. So on that morning Sir Gawaine was looking from the window a little before noon when he espied three men on horseback, and with them a dwarf on foot, who held their horses when they alighted. Then Sir Gawaine went to the king and said, 'Sir, go to your food, for strange adventures are at hand.' And Arthur called the other kings that were in the castle, and all the Knights of the Round Table that were a hundred and fifty, and they sat down to dine. When they were seated there entered the hall two men well and richly dressed, and upon their shoulders leaned the handsomest young man that ever was seen of any of them, higher than the other two by a cubit. He was wide in the chest and large handed, but his great height seemed to be a burden and a shame to him, therefore it was he leaned on the shoulders of his friends. As soon as Arthur beheld him he made a sign, and without more words all three went up to the high dais, where the king sat. Then the tall young man stood up straight, and said: 'King Arthur, God bless you and all your fair fellowship, and in especial the fellowship of the Round Table. I have come hither to pray you to give me three gifts, which you can grant me honourably, for they will do no hurt to you or to anyone.'

'Ask,' answered Arthur, 'and you shall have your asking.'

'Sir, this is my petition for this feast, for the other two I will ask after. Give me meat and drink for this one twelvemonth.'

'Well,' said the king, 'you shall have meat and drink enough, for that I give to every man, whether friend or foe. But tell me your name!'

'I cannot tell you that,' answered he. 'That is strange,' replied the king, 'but you are the goodliest young man I ever saw,' and, turning to Sir Kay, the steward, charged him to give the young man to eat and drink of the best, and to treat him in all ways as if he were a lord's son. 'There is little need to do that,' answered Sir Kay, 'for if he had come of gentlemen and not of peasants he would have asked of you a horse and armour. But as the birth of a man is so are his requests. And seeing he has no name I will give him one, and it shall be Beaumains, or Fair-hands, and he shall sit in the kitchen and eat broth, and at the end of a year he shall be as fat as any pig that feeds on acorns.' So the young man was left in charge of Sir Kay, that scorned and mocked him.

Sir Lancelot and Sir Gawaine were wroth when they heard what Sir Kay said, and bade him leave off his mocking, for they believed the youth would turn out to be a man of great deeds; but Sir Kay paid no heed to them, and took him down to the great hall, and set him among the boys and lads, where he ate sadly. After he had finished eating both Sir Lancelot and Sir Gawaine bade him come to their room, and would have had him eat and drink there, but he refused, saying he was bound to obey Sir Kay, into whose charge the king had given him. So he was put into the kitchen by Sir Kay, and slept nightly with the kitchen boys. This he bore for a whole year, and was always mild and gentle, and gave hard words to no one. Only, whenever the knights played at tourney he would steal out and watch them. And Sir Lancelot gave him gold to spend, and clothes to wear, and so did Gawaine. Also, if there were any games held whereat he might be, none could throw a bar nor cast a stone as far as he by two good yards.

Thus the year passed by till the feast of Whitsuntide came again, and this time the king held it at Carlion. But King Arthur would eat no meat at Whitsuntide till some adventures were told him, and glad was he when a squire came and said to him, 'Sir, you may go to your food, for here is a damsel with some strange tales.' At this the damsel was led into the hall, and bowed low before the king, and begged he would give her help. 'For whom?' asked the king, 'and what is the adventure?' 'Sir,' answered she, 'my sister is a noble lady of great fame, who is besieged by a tyrant, and may not get out of her castle. And it is because your knights are said to be the noblest in all the world that I came to you for aid.' 'What is your sister's name, and where does she dwell? And who is the man that besieges her, and where does he come from?' 'Sir king,' answered she, 'as for my sister's name, I cannot tell it you now, but she is a lady of great beauty and goodness, and of many lands. As for the tyrant who besieges her, he is called the Red Knight of the Red Lawns.' 'I know nothing of him,' said the king. 'But I know him,' cried Sir Gawaine, 'and he is one of the most dangerous knights in the world. Men say he has the strength of seven, and once when we had crossed swords I hardly escaped from him with my life.' 'Fair damsel,' then said the king, 'there are many knights here who would go gladly to the rescue of your lady, but none of them shall do so with my consent unless you will tell us her name, and the place of her castle.' 'Then I must speak further,' said the damsel. But before she had made answer to the king up came Beaumains, and spoke to Arthur, saying, 'Sir king, I thank you that for this whole year I have lived in your kitchen, and had meat and drink, and now I will ask you for the two gifts that you promised me on this day.' 'Ask them,' answered the king. 'Sir, this shall be my two gifts. First grant me the adventure of this damsel, for it is mine by right.' 'You shall have it,' said the king. 'Then, sir, you shall bid Sir Lancelot du Lake to make me knight, for I will receive knighthood at the hands of no other.' 'All this shall be done,' said the king. 'Fie on you,' cried the damsel, 'will you give me none but a kitchen boy to rescue my lady?' and she went away in a rage, and mounted her horse.

No sooner had she left the hall than a page came to Beaumains and told him that a horse and fair armour had been brought for him, also there had arrived a dwarf carrying all things that a knight needed. And when he was armed there were few men that were handsomer than he, and the court wondered greatly whence these splendid trappings had come. Then Beaumains came into the hall, and took farewell of the king, and Sir Gawaine and Sir Lancelot, and prayed Sir Lancelot that he would follow after him. So he departed, and rode after the damsel. Many looked upon him and marvelled at the strength of his horse, and its golden trappings, and envied Beaumains his shining coat of mail; but they noted that he had neither shield nor spear. 'I will ride after him,' laughed Sir Kay, 'and see if my kitchen boy will own me for his better.' 'Leave him and stay at home,' said Sir Gawaine and Sir Lancelot, but Sir Kay would not listen and sprang upon his horse.

Just as Beaumains came up with the damsel, Sir Kay reached Beaumains, and said, 'Beaumains, do you not know me?'

Beaumains turned and looked at him, and answered, 'Yes, I know you for an ill-mannered knight, therefore beware of me.' At this Sir Kay put his spear in rest and charged him, and Beaumains drew his sword and charged Sir Kay, and dashed aside the spear, and thrust him through the side, till Sir Kay fell down as if he had been dead, and Beaumains took his shield and spear for himself. Then he sprang on his own horse, bidding first his dwarf take Sir Kay's horse, and rode away. All this was seen by Sir Lancelot, who had followed him, and also by the damsel.

In a little while Beaumains stopped, and asked Sir Lancelot if he would tilt with him, and they came together with such a shock that both the horses and their riders fell to the earth and were bruised sorely. Sir Lancelot was the first to rise, and he helped Beaumains from his horse, and Beaumains threw his shield from him, and offered to fight on foot. And they rushed together like wild boars, turning and thrusting and parrying for the space of an hour, and Sir Lancelot marvelled at the young man's strength, and thought he was more like a giant than a knight, and dreading lest he himself should be put to shame, he said: 'Beaumains, do not fight so hard, we have no quarrel that forbids us to leave off.' 'That is true,' answered Beaumains, laying down his arms, 'but it does me good, my lord, to feel your might.' 'Well,' said Sir Lancelot, 'I promise you I had much ado to save myself from you unshamed, therefore have no fear of any other knight.' 'Do you think I could really stand against a proved knight?' asked Beaumains. 'Yes,' said Lancelot, 'if you fight as you have fought today I will be your warrant against anyone.' 'Then I pray you,' cried Beaumains, 'give me the order of knighthood.' 'You must first tell me your name,' replied Lancelot, 'and who are your kindred.' 'You will not betray me if I do?' asked Beaumains. 'No, that I will never do, till it is openly known,' said Lancelot. 'Then, sir, my name is Gareth, and Sir Gawaine is my brother.' 'Ah, sir,' cried Lancelot, 'I am gladder of you than ever I was, for I was sure you came of good blood, and that you did not come to the court for meat and drink only.' And he bade him kneel, and gave him the order of knighthood.

After that Sir Gareth wished to go his own ways, and departed. When he was gone, Sir Lancelot went back to Sir Kay and ordered some men that were by to bear him home on a shield, and in time his wounds were healed; but he was scorned of all men, and especially of Sir Gawaine and Sir Lancelot, who told him it was no good deed to treat any young man so, and no one could tell what his birth might be, or what had brought him to the court.

Then Beaumains rode after the damsel, who stopped when she saw him coming. 'What are you doing here?' said she. 'Your clothes smell of the grease and tallow of the kitchen! Do you think to change my heart towards you because of yonder knight whom you slew? No, truly! I know well who you are, you turner of spits! Go back to King Arthur's kitchen, which is your proper place.' 'Damsel,' replied Beaumains, 'you may say to me what you will, but I shall not quit you whatever you may do, for I have vowed to King Arthur to relieve the lady in the castle, and I shall set her free or die fighting for her.' 'Fie on you, scullion,' answered she. 'You will meet with one who will make you such a welcome that you would give all the broth you ever cooked never to have seen his face.' 'I shall do my best to fight him,' said Beaumains, and held his peace.

Soon they entered the wood, and there came a man lying towards them, galloping with all his might. 'Oh, help! help! lord,' cried he, 'for my master lies in a thicket, bound by six thieves, and I greatly fear they will slay him.' 'Show me the way,' said Sir Beaumains, and they rode together till they reached the place where the knight lay bound. Then Sir Beaumains charged the six thieves, and struck one dead, and another, and another still, and the other three fled, not liking the battle. Sir Beaumains pursued them till they turned at

Faugh Sir! You smell of ye Kitchen

Gareth & Linet

bay, and fought hard for their lives; but in the end Sir Beaumains slew them, and returned to the knight and unbound him. The knight thanked Beaumains heartily for his deliverance, and prayed him to come to his castle, where he would reward him. 'Sir,' said Beaumains, 'I was this day made knight by noble Sir Lancelot, and that is reward enough for anything I may do. Besides, I must follow this damsel.' But when he came near her she reviled him as before, and bade him ride far from her. 'Do you think I set store by what you have done? You will soon see a sight that will make you tell a very different tale.' At this the knight whom Beaumains had rescued rode up to the damsel, and begged that she would rest in his castle that night, as the sun was now setting. The damsel agreed, and the knight ordered a great supper, and gave Sir Beaumains a seat above the seat of the damsel, who rose up in anger. 'Fie! fie! Sir knight,' cried she, 'you are uncourteous to set a mere kitchen page before me; he is not fit to be in the company of high-born people.' Her words struck shame into the knight, and he took Beaumains and set him at a side table, and seated himself before him.

In the early morning Sir Beaumains and the damsel bade farewell to the knight, and rode through the forest till they came to a great river, where stood two knights on the further side, guarding the passage. 'Well, what do you say now?' asked the damsel. 'Will you fight them or turn back?' 'I would not turn if there were six more of them,' answered Sir Beaumains, and he rushed into the water and so did one of the knights. They came together in the middle of the stream, and their spears broke in two with the force of the charge, and they drew their swords, hitting hard at each other. At length Sir Beaumains dealt the other knight such a blow that he fell from his horse, and was drowned in the river. Then Beaumains put his horse at the bank, where the second knight was waiting for him, and they fought long together, till Sir Beaumains clave his helmet in two.

So he left him dead, and rode after the damsel. 'Alas!' she cried, 'that even a kitchen page should have power to destroy two such knights! You think you have done mighty things, but you are wrong! As to the first knight, his horse stumbled, and he was drowned before you ever touched him. And the other you took from behind, and struck him when he was defenceless.' 'Damsel!' answered Beaumains, 'you may say what you will, I care not what it is, so I may deliver this lady.' 'Fie, foul kitchen knave, you shall see knights that will make you lower your crest.' 'I pray you be more civil in your language,' answered Beaumains, 'for it matters not to me what knights they be, I will do battle with them.' 'I am trying to turn you back for your own good,' answered she, 'for if you follow me you are certainly a dead man, as well I know all you have won before has been by luck.' 'Say what you will, damsel,' said he, 'but where you go I will follow you,' and they rode together till eventide, and all the way she chid him and gave him no rest.

At length they reached an open space where there was a black lawn, and on the lawn a black hawthorn, whereon hung a black banner on one side, and a black shield and spear, big and long, on the other. Close by stood a black horse covered with silk, fastened to a black stone. A knight, covered with black armour, sat on the horse, and when she saw him, the damsel bade him ride away, as his horse was not saddled. But the knight drew near and said to her, 'Damsel, have you brought this knight from King Arthur's court to be your champion?' 'No, truly,' answered she, 'this is but a kitchen boy, fed by King Arthur for charity.' 'Then why is he clad in armour?' asked the knight; 'it is a shame that he should even bear you company.' 'I cannot be rid of him,' said she, 'he rides with me against my will. I would that you were able to deliver me from him! Either slay him or frighten him off, for by ill fortune he has this day slain the two knights of the passage.' 'I wonder much,' said the Black Knight, 'that any man who is well born should consent to fight with him.' 'They do not know him,' replied the damsel, 'and they think he must be a famous knight because he rides with me.' 'That may be,' said the Black Knight, 'but he is well made, and looks likely to be a strong man; still I promise you I will just throw him to the ground, and take away his horse and armour, for it would be a shame to me to do more.' When Sir Beaumains heard him talk thus he looked up and said, 'Sir knight, you are lightly disposing of my horse and armour, but I would have you know that

I will pass this lawn, against your will or not, and you will only get my horse and armour if you win them in fair fight. Therefore let me see what you can do.' 'Say you so?' answered the knight, 'now give up the lady at once, for it ill becomes a kitchen page to ride with a lady of high degree.' 'It is a lie,' said Beaumains, 'I am a gentleman born, and my birth is better than yours, as I will prove upon your body.'

With that they drew back their horses so as to charge each other hotly, and for the space of an hour and a half they fought fiercely and well, but in the end a blow from Beaumains threw the knight from his horse, and he swooned and died. Then Beaumains jumped down, and seeing that the knight's horse and armour were better than his own, he took them for himself, and rode after the damsel. While they were thus riding together, and the damsel was chiding him as ever she did, they saw a knight coming towards them dressed all in green. 'Is that my brother the Black Knight who is with you?' asked he of the damsel. 'No, indeed,' she replied, 'this unhappy kitchen knave has slain your brother, to my great sorrow.' 'Alas!' sighed the Green Knight, 'that my brother should die so meanly at the hand of a kitchen knave. Traitor!' he added, turning to Beaumains, 'thou shalt die for slaying my brother, for he was a noble knight, and his name was Sir Percard.' 'I defy you,' said Beaumains, 'for I slew him as a good knight should.'

Then the Green Knight seized a horn which hung from a horn tree, and blew three notes upon it, and two damsels came and armed him, and fastened on him a green shield and a green spear. So the fight began and raged long, first on horseback and then on foot, till both were sore wounded. At last the damsel came and stood beside them, and said, 'My lord the Green Knight, why for very shame do you stand so long fighting a kitchen knave? You ought never to have been made a knight at all!' These scornful words stung the heart of the Green Knight, and he dealt a mighty stroke which cleft asunder the shield of Beaumains. And when Beaumains saw this, he struck a blow upon the knight's helmet which brought him to his knees, and Beaumains leapt on him, and dragged him to the ground. Then the Green Knight cried for

LINET AND THE BLACK KNIGHT

mercy, and offered to yield himself prisoner unto Beaumains. 'It is all in vain,' answered Beaumains, 'unless the damsel prays me for your life,' and therewith he unlaced his helmet as though he would slay him. 'Fie upon thee, false kitchen page!' said the damsel, 'I will never pray to save his life, for I am sure he is in no danger.' 'Suffer me not to die,' entreated the knight, 'when a word may save me!' 'Fair knight,' he went on, turning to Beaumains, 'save my life, and I will forgive you the death of my brother, and will do you service for ever, and will bring thirty of my knights to serve you likewise.' 'It is a shame,' cried the damsel, 'that such a kitchen knave should have you and thirty knights besides.' 'Sir knight,' said Beaumains, 'I care nothing for all this, but if I am to spare your life the damsel must ask for it,' and he stepped forward as if to slay him. 'Let be, foul knave,' then said the damsel, 'do not slay him. If you do, you will repent it.' 'Damsel,' answered Beaumains, 'it is a pleasure to me to obey you, and at your wish I will save his life. Sir knight with the green arms, I release you at the request of this damsel, and I will fulfil all she charges me.'

Then the Green Knight kneeled down, and did him homage with his sword. 'I am sorry,' said the damsel, 'for the wounds you have received, and for your brother's death, for I had great need of you both, and have much dread of passing the forest.' 'Fear nothing,' answered the Green Knight, 'for this evening you shall lodge in my house, and tomorrow I will show you the way through the forest.' And they went with the Green Knight. But the damsel did not mend her ways with Beaumains, and ever more reviled him, till the Green Knight rebuked her, saying Beaumains was the noblest knight that held a spear, and that in the end she would find he had sprung from some great king. And the Green Knight summoned the thirty knights who did him service, and bade them henceforth do service to Beaumains, and keep him from treachery, and when he had need of them they would be ready to obey his orders.

So they bade each other farewell, and Beaumains and the damsel rode forth anew. In like manner did Sir Beaumains overcome the Red Knight, who was the third brother, and the Red Knight cried for mercy, and offered to bring sixty knights to do him service, and

Beaumains spared his life at the request of the damsel, and likewise it so happened to Sir Persant of Inde.

And this time the damsel prayed Beaumains to give up the fight, saying, 'Sir, I wonder who you are and of what kindred you have come. Boldly you speak, and boldly you have done; therefore I pray you to depart and save yourself while you may, for both you and your horse have suffered great fatigues, and I fear we delay too long, for the besieged castle is but seven miles from this place, and all the perils are past save this one only. I dread sorely lest you should get some hurt; yet this Sir Persant of Inde is nothing in might to the knight who has laid siege to my lady.' But Sir Beaumains would not listen to her words, and vowed that by two hours after noon he would have overthrown him, and that it would still be daylight when they reached the castle. 'What sort of a man can you be?' answered the damsel, looking at him in wonder, 'for never did a woman treat a knight as ill and shamefully as I have done you, while you have always been gentle and courteous to me, and no one bears himself like that save he who is of noble blood.' 'Damsel,' replied Beaumains, 'your hard words only drove me to strike the harder, and though I ate in King Arthur's kitchen, perhaps I might have had as much food as I wanted elsewhere. But all I have done was to make proof of my friends, and whether I am a gentleman or not, fair damsel, I have done you gentleman's service, and may perchance do you greater service before we part from each other.' 'Alas, fair Beaumains, forgive me all that I have said and done against you.' 'With all my heart,' he answered, 'and since you are pleased now to speak good words to me, know that I hear them gladly, and there is no knight living but I feel strong enough to meet him.'

So Beaumains conquered Sir Persant of Inde, who brought a hundred knights to be sworn into his service, and the next morning the damsel led him to the castle, where the Red Knight of the Red Lawn held fast the lady. 'Heaven defend you,' cried Sir Persant, when they told him where they were going; 'that is the most perilous knight now living, for he has the strength of seven men. He has done great wrong to that lady, who is one of the fairest in all the world, and it seems to me as if this damsel must be her sister. Is not her name Linet?' 'Yes, sir,' answered she, 'and my lady my sister's name is dame Lyonesse.' 'The Red Knight has drawn out the siege for two years,' said Sir Persant, 'though he might have forced an entrance many a time, but he hoped that Sir Lancelot du Lake or Sir Tristram or Sir Gawaine should come to do battle with him.' 'My Lord Sir Persant of Inde,' said the damsel, 'I bid you knight this gentleman before he fight with the Red Knight.' 'That I will gladly,' replied Sir Persant, 'if it please him to take the order of knighthood from so simple a man as I am.' 'Sir,' answered Beaumains, 'I thank you for your goodwill, but at the beginning of this quest I was made a knight by Sir Lancelot. My name is Sir Gareth of Orkney and Sir Gawaine is my brother, though neither he nor King Arthur, whose sister is my mother, knows of it. I pray you to keep it close also.'

Now word was brought unto the besieged lady by the dwarf that her sister was coming to her with a knight sent by King Arthur. And when the lady heard all that Beaumains had done, and how he had overthrown all who stood in his way, she bade her dwarf take baked venison, and fat capons, and two silver flagons of wine and a gold cup, and put them into the hands of a hermit that dwelt in a hermitage close by. The dwarf did so, and the lady then sent him to greet her sister and Sir Beaumains, and to beg them to eat and drink in the hermit's cell, and rest themselves, which they did. When they drew near the besieged castle Sir Beaumains saw full forty knights, with spurs on their heels and swords in their hands, hanging from the tall trees that stood upon the lawn. 'Fair sir,' said the damsel, 'these knights came hither to rescue my sister, dame Lyonesse; and if you cannot overthrow the Knight of the Red Lawn, you will hang there too.'

'Truly,' answered Beaumains, 'it is a marvel that none of King Arthur's knights has dealt with the Knight of the Red Lawn ere this'; and they rode up to the castle, which had round it high walls and deep ditches, till they came to a great sycamore tree, where hung a horn. And whoso desired to do battle with the Red Knight must blow that horn loudly.

'Sir, I pray you,' said Linet, as Beaumains bent forward to seize it, 'do not blow it till it is full noontide, for during three hours before that the Red Knight's strength so increases that it is as the strength of seven men; but when noon is come, he has the might of one man only.'

'Ah! for shame, damsel, to say such words. I will fight him as he is, or not at all,' and Beaumains blew such a blast that it rang through the castle. And the Red Knight buckled on his armour, and came to where Beaumains stood. So the battle began, and a fierce one it was, and much ado had Beaumains to last out till noon, when the Red Knight's strength began to wane; they rested, and came on again, and in the end the Red Knight yielded to Sir Beaumains, and the lords and barons in the castle did homage to the victor, and begged that the Red Knight's life might be spared on condition they all took service with Beaumains. This was granted to them, and Linet bound up his wounds and put ointment on them, and so she did likewise to Sir Beaumains. But the Red Knight was sent to the court of King Arthur, and told him all that Sir Beaumains had done. And King Arthur and his knights marvelled.

Now Sir Beaumains had looked up at the windows of Castle Perilous before the fight, and had seen the face of the Lady Lyonesse, and had thought it the fairest in all the world. After he had subdued the Red Knight, he hasted into the castle, and the Lady Lyonesse welcomed him, and he told her he had bought her love with the best blood in his body. And she did not say him nay, but put him off for a time. Then the king sent letters to her to bid her, and likewise Sir Gareth, come to his court, and by the counsel of Sir Gareth she prayed the king to let her call a tournament, and to proclaim that the knight who bore himself best should, if he was unwedded, take her and all her lands. But if he had a wife already he should be given a white gyrfalcon, and for his wife a crown of gold, set about with precious stones.

So the Lady Lyonesse did as Sir Gareth had counselled her, and answered King Arthur that where Sir Gareth was she could not tell, but that if the king would call a tourney he might be sure that Sir Gareth would come to it. 'It is well thought of,' said Arthur, and the Lady Lyonesse departed unto Castle Perilous, and summoned all her knights around her, and told them what she had done, and how they were to make ready to fight in the tournament. She began at once to set her castle in order, and to think what she should do with the great array of knights that would ride hither from the furthest parts – from Scotland and Wales and Cornwall – and to lodge fitly the kings, dukes, earls, and barons that should come with Arthur. Queen Guenevere also she awaited, and the Queen of Orkney, Sir Gareth's mother. But Sir Gareth entreated the Lady Lyonesse and those knights that were in the castle with him not to let his name be known, and this they agreed to.

'Sir Gareth,' said dame Lyonesse, 'I will lend you a ring, which I beseech you for the love you bear me to give me back when the tournament is done, for without it I have but little beauty. This ring is like no other ring, it will turn green red, and blue white, and the bearer shall lose no blood, however sore he may be wounded.'

'Truly, my own lady,' answered Sir Gareth, 'this ring will serve me well, and by its help I shall not fear that any man shall know me.' And Sir Gringamore, brother to the Lady Lyonesse, gave him a bay horse, and strong armour, and a sharp sword that had once belonged to his father. On the morning of the fifteenth of August, when the Feast of the Assumption was kept, the king commanded his heralds to blow loudly their trumpets, so that every knight might know that he must enter the lists. It was a noble sight to see them flocking clad in shining armour, each man with his device upon his shield. And the heralds marked who bare them best, and who were overthrown. All marvelled as to who the knight could be whose armour sometimes seemed green, and sometimes white, but no man knew it was Sir Gareth. And whosoever Sir Gareth tilted with was straightway overthrown. 'Of a truth,' cried King Arthur, 'that knight with the many colours is a good knight,' and he called Sir Lancelot and bade him to challenge that knight to combat. But Sir Lancelot said that though the knight had come off victor in every fight, yet his limbs must be weary, for he had fought as a man fights under the eyes of his lady, 'and for this day,' said Sir Lancelot, 'he shall have the honour. Though it lay in my power to put it from him, I would not.'

Then they paused for a while to rest, and afterwards the

The Lady of Lyonesse
sees Sir Gareth

tournament began again more fiercely than before, and Sir Lancelot was set upon by two knights at once. When Sir Gareth saw that, he rode in between them, but no stroke would he deal Sir Lancelot, which Sir Lancelot noted, and guessed that it was the good knight, Sir Gareth. Sir Gareth went hither and thither, smiting anyone that came in his way, and by fortune he met with his brother Sir Gawaine, and knocked off his helmet. Now it happened that while he was fighting a knight dealt Sir Gareth a fierce blow on his helm, and he rode off the field to mend it. Then his dwarf, who had been watching eagerly, cried out to Sir Gareth to leave the ring with him, lest he should lose it while he was drinking, which Sir Gareth did; and when he had drunk and mended his helm he forgot the ring, at which the dwarf was glad, for he knew his name could no longer be hid. And when Sir Gareth returned to the field, his armour shone yellow like gold, and King Arthur marvelled what knight he was, for he saw by his hair that he was the same knight who had worn the many colours. 'Go,' he said to his heralds, 'ride near him and see what manner of knight he is, for none can tell me his name.' So a herald drew close to him, and saw that on his helm was written in golden letters 'This helm belongs to Sir Gareth of Orkney'; and the herald cried out and made proclamation, and the kings and knights pressed to behold him. And when Sir Gareth saw he was discovered, he struck more fiercely than before, and smote down Sir Sagramore, and his brother, Sir Gawaine. 'O brother,' said Sir Gawaine, 'I did not think you would have smitten me!' When Sir Gareth heard him say that he rode out of the press, and cried to his dwarf, 'Boy, you have played me foul, for you have kept my ring. Give it to me now, that I may hide myself,' and he galloped swiftly into the forest, and no one knew where he had gone. 'What shall I do next?' asked he of the dwarf. 'Sir,' answered the dwarf, 'send the Lady Lyonesse back her ring.' 'Your counsel is good,' said Gareth; 'I take it to her, and commend me to her grace, and say I will come when I may, and bid her to be faithful to me, as I am to her.' After that Sir Gareth rode deeper into the forest.

Though Sir Gareth had left the tournament he found that there were as many fights awaiting him as if he had remained there. He overcame all his foes, and sent them and their followers to do homage to King Arthur, but he himself stayed behind. He was standing alone after they had gone, when he beheld an armed knight coming towards him. Sir Gareth sprang on his horse, and without a word the two crashed together like thunder, and strove hard for two hours, till the ground was wet with blood. At that time the damsel Linet came riding by, and saw what was doing, and knew who were the fighters. And she cried, 'Sir Gawaine, Sir Gawaine, leave fighting with your brother Sir Gareth.' Then he threw down his shield and sword, and ran to Sir Gareth, and first took him in his arms and next kneeled down and asked mercy of him.

'Why do you, who were but now so strong and mighty, so suddenly yield to me?' asked Sir Gareth, who had not perceived the damsel. 'O Gareth, I am your brother, and have had much sorrow for your sake.' At this Sir Gareth unlaced his helm and knelt before Sir Gawaine, and they rose and embraced each other. 'Ah, my fair brother,' said Sir Gawaine, 'I ought rightly to do you homage, even if you were not my brother, for in this twelvemonth you have sent King Arthur more knights than any six of the best men of the Round Table.' While he was speaking there came the Lady Linet, and healed the wounds of Sir Gareth and of Sir Gawaine. 'What are you going to do now?' asked she. 'It is time that King Arthur had tidings of you both, and your horses are not fit to bear you.'

'Ride, I pray you,' said Sir Gawaine, 'to my uncle, King Arthur, who is but two miles away, and tell him what adventure has befallen me.' So she mounted her mule, and when she had told her tale to King Arthur, he bade them saddle him a palfrey and invited all the knights and ladies of his court to ride with him. When they reached the place they saw Sir Gareth and Sir Gawaine sitting on the hillside. The king jumped off his horse, and would have greeted them, but he swooned away for gladness, and they ran and comforted him, and also their mother.

The two knights stayed in King Arthur's court for eight days, and rested themselves and grew strong. Then said the king to Linet, 'I wonder that your sister, dame Lyonesse, does not come here to visit me, or more truly to visit my nephew, Sir Gareth, who has worked so hard to win her love.'

'My lord,' answered Linet, 'you must, by your grace, hold her excused, for she does not know that Sir Gareth is here.'

'Go and fetch her, then,' said Arthur.

'That I will do quickly,' replied Linet, and by the next morning she had brought dame Lyonesse, and her brother Sir Gringamore, and forty knights, but among the ladies dame Lyonesse was the fairest, save only Queen Guenevere. They were all welcomed of King Arthur, who turned to his nephew Sir Gareth and asked him whether he would have that lady to his wife.

'My lord,' replied Sir Gareth, 'you know well that I love her above all the ladies in the world.'

'And what say you, fair lady?' asked the king.

'Most noble king,' said dame Lyonesse, 'I would sooner have Sir Gareth as my husband than any king or prince that may be christened, and if I may not have him I promise you I will have none. For he is my first love, and shall be my last. And if you will suffer him to have his will and choice, I dare say he will have me.'

'That is truth,' said Sir Gareth.

'What, nephew,' cried the king, 'sits the wind in that door? Then you shall have all the help that is in my power,' and so said Gareth's mother. And it was fixed that the marriage should be at Michaelmas, at Kin-Kenadon by the seashore, and thus it was proclaimed in all places of the realm. Then Sir Gareth sent his summons to all the knights and ladies that he had won in battle that they should be present, and he gave a rich ring to the Lady Lyonesse, and she gave him one likewise. And before she departed she had from King Arthur a shining golden bee, as a token. After that Sir Gareth set her on her way towards her castle, and returned unto the king. But he would ever be in Sir Lancelot's company, for there was no knight that Sir Gareth loved so well as Sir Lancelot. The days drew fast to Michaelmas, and there came the Lady Lyonesse with her sister Linet and her brother Sir Gringamore to Kin-Kenadon by the sea, and there were they lodged by order of King Arthur. And upon Michaelmas Day the Bishop of Canterbury wedded Sir Gareth and the Lady Lyonesse with great ceremonies, and King Arthur commanded that Sir Gawaine should be joined to the damsel Linet, and Sir Agrawaine to the niece of dame Lyonesse, whose name was Laurel. Then the knights whom Sir Gareth had won in battle came with their followings and did homage to him, and the Green Knight besought him that he might act as chamberlain at the feast, and the Red Knight that he might be his steward. As soon as the feast was ended, they had all manner of minstrelsy and games and a great tournament that lasted three days, but at the prayer of dame Lyonesse the king would not suffer that any man who was wedded should fight at that feast.

The Quest of the Holy Grail

This is a mysterious part of the adventures of King Arthur's knights. We must remember that parts of these stories are very old; they were invented by the heathen Welsh, or by the ancient Britons, from whom the Welsh are descended, and by the old pagan Irish, who spoke Gaelic, a language not very unlike Welsh. Then these ancient stories were translated by French and other foreign writers, and Christian beliefs and chivalrous customs were added in the French romances, and, finally, the French was translated into English about the time of Edward IV by Sir Thomas Malory, who altered as he pleased. The Story of the Holy Grail, in this book, is mostly taken from Malory, but partly from *The High History of the Holy Grail*, translated by Dr Sebastian Evans from an old French book.

What was the Holy Grail? In the stories it is the holy vessel used by our Lord, and brought to Britain by Joseph of Arimathea. But in the older heathen Irish stories there is a mysterious vessel of a magical sort, full of miraculous food, and probably the French writers of the romances confused this with the sacred vessel brought from the Holy Land. On account of the sins of men this relic was made invisible, but now and then it appeared, borne by angels or floating in a heavenly light. The knights, against King Arthur's wish, made a vow to find it, and gave up their duties of redressing wrongs and keeping order, to pursue the beautiful vision. But most of them, for their sins, were unsuccessful, like Sir Lancelot, and the Round Table was scattered and the kingdom was weakened by the neglect of ordinary duties in the search for what could never be gained by mortal men. This appears to be the moral of the story, if it has any moral. But the stories are confused almost like a dream, though it is a beautiful dream.

I   HOW THE KING WENT ON PILGRIMAGE, AND HIS SQUIRE
WAS SLAIN IN A DREAM

Now the king was minded to go on a pilgrimage, and he agreed
with the queen that he would set forth to seek the holy chapel of St
Augustine, which is in the White Forest, and may only be found by
adventure. Much he wished to undertake the quest alone, but this
the queen would not suffer, and to do her pleasure he consented
that a youth, tall and strong of limb, should ride with him as his
squire. Chaus was the youth's name, and he was son to Gwain li
Aoutres. 'Lie within tonight,' commanded the king, 'and take heed
that my horse be saddled at break of day, and my arms ready.' 'At
your pleasure, sir,' answered the youth, whose heart rejoiced because
he was going alone with the king.

As night came on, all the knights quitted the hall, but Chaus the
squire stayed where he was, and would not take off his clothes or
his shoes, lest sleep should fall on him and he might not be ready
when the king called him. So he sat himself down by the great fire,
but in spite of his will sleep fell heavily on him, and he dreamed a
strange dream.

In his dream it seemed that the king had ridden away to the
quest, and had left his squire behind him, which filled the young
man with fear. And in his dream he set the saddle and bridle on his
horse, and fastened his spurs, and girt on his sword, and galloped
out of the castle after the king. He rode on a long space, till he
entered a thick forest, and there before him lay traces of the king's
horse, and he followed till the marks of the hoofs ceased suddenly
at some open ground and he thought that the king had alighted
there. On the right stood a chapel, and about it was a graveyard,
and in the graveyard many coffins, and in his dream it seemed as if
the king had entered the chapel, so the young man entered also.
But no man did he behold save a knight that lay dead upon a bier in
the midst of the chapel, covered with a pall of rich silk, and four
tapers in golden candlesticks were burning round him. The squire

marvelled to see the body lying there so lonely, with no one near it, and likewise that the king was nowhere to be seen. Then he took out one of the tall tapers, and hid the candlestick under his cloak, and rode away until he should find the king.

On his journey through the forest he was stopped by a man black and ill-favoured, holding a large knife in his hand.

'Ho! you that stand there, have you seen King Arthur?' asked the squire.

'No, but I have met you, and I am glad thereof, for you have under your cloak one of the candlesticks of gold that was placed in honour of the knight who lies dead in the chapel. Give it to me, and I will carry it back; and if you do not this of your own will, I will make you.'

'By my faith!' cried the squire, 'I will never yield it to you! Rather will I carry it off and make a present of it to King Arthur.'

'You will pay for it dearly,' answered the man, 'if you yield it not up forthwith.'

To this the squire did not make answer, but dashed forward, thinking to pass him by; but the man thrust at him with his knife, and it entered his body up to the hilt. And when the squire dreamed this, he cried, 'Help! help! for I am a dead man!'

As soon as the king and the queen heard that cry they awoke from their sleep, and the chamberlain said, 'Sir, you must be moving, for it is day'; and the king rose and dressed himself, and put on his shoes. Then the cry came again: 'Fetch me a priest, for I die!' and the king ran at great speed into the hall, while the queen and the chamberlain followed him with torches and candles. 'What aileth you?' asked the king of his squire, and the squire told him of all that he had dreamed. 'Ha,' said the king, 'is it, then, a dream?' 'Yes, sir,' answered the squire, 'but it is a right foul dream for me, for right foully it hath come true,' and he lifted his left arm, and said, 'Sir, look you here! Lo, here is the knife that was struck in my side up to the haft.' After that, he drew forth the candlestick, and showed it to the king. 'Sir, for this candlestick that I present to you was I wounded to the death!' The king took the candlestick in his hands and looked at it, and none so rich had he seen before, and he bade the queen look also. 'Sir,' said the squire again, 'draw not forth the knife out of my body till I be shriven of the priest.' So the king commanded that a priest should be sent for, and when the squire had confessed his sins, the king drew the knife out of the body and the soul departed forthwith. Then the king grieved that the young man had come to his death in such strange wise, and ordered him a fair burial, and desired that the golden candlestick should be sent to the Church of St Paul in London, which at that time was newly built.

After this King Arthur would have none to go with him on his quest, and many strange adventures he achieved before he reached the chapel of St Augustine, which was in the midst of the White Forest. There he alighted from his horse, and sought to enter, but though there was neither door nor bar he might not pass the threshold. But from without he heard wondrous voices singing, and saw a light shining brighter than any that he had seen before, and visions such as he scarcely dared to look upon. And he resolved greatly to amend his sins, and to bring peace and order into his kingdom. So he set forth, strengthened and comforted, and after divers more adventures returned to his court.

2   THE COMING OF THE HOLY GRAIL

It was on the eve of Pentecost that all the Knights of the Round Table met together at Camelot, and a great feast was made ready for them. And as they sat at supper they heard a loud noise, as of the crashing of thunder, and it seemed as if the roof would fall on them. Then, in the midst of the thunder, there entered a sunbeam, brighter by seven times than the brightest day, and its brightness was not of this world. The knights held their peace, but every man looked at his neighbour, and his countenance shone fairer than ever it had done before. As they sat dumb, for their tongues felt as if they could speak nothing, there floated in the hall the Holy Grail, and over it a veil of white samite, so that none might see it nor who bare it. But sweet odours filled the place, and every knight had set before him the food he loved best; and after that the Holy Vessel departed suddenly, they wist not where. When it had gone their tongues were loosened, and the king gave thanks for the wonders that they had been permitted to see. After that he had finished, Sir Gawaine stood up and vowed to depart the next morning in quest of the Holy Grail, and not to return until he had seen it. 'But if after a year and a day I may not speed in my quest,' said he, 'I shall come again, for I shall know that the sight of it is not for me.' And many of the knights there sitting swore a like vow.

But King Arthur, when he heard this, was sore displeased. 'Alas!' cried he unto Sir Gawaine, 'you have undone me by your vow. For through you is broken up the fairest fellowship, and the truest of knighthood, that ever the world saw, and when they have once departed they shall meet no more at the Round Table, for many shall die in the quest. It grieves me sore, for I have loved them as well as my own life.' So he spoke, and paused, and tears came into his eyes. 'Ah, Gawaine, Gawaine! you have set me in great sorrow.'

'Comfort yourself,' said Sir Lancelot, 'for we shall win for our-selves great honour, and much more than if we had died in any other wise, since die we must.' But the king would not be comforted, and the queen and all the court were troubled also for the love which they had to these knights. Then the queen came to Sir Galahad, who was sitting among those knights, though younger he was than any of them, and asked him whence he came, and of what country, and if he was son to Sir Lancelot. And King Arthur did him great honour, and he rested him in his own bed. And next morning the king and queen went into the minster, and the knights followed them, dressed all in armour, save only their shields and their helmets. When the service was finished the king would know how many of the fellowship had sworn to undertake the quest of the Grail, and they were counted, and found to number a hundred and fifty. They bade farewell, and mounted their horses, and rode through the streets of Camelot, and there was weeping of both rich and poor, and the king could not speak for weeping. And at sunrise they all parted company with each other, and every knight took the way he best liked.

3 THE ADVENTURE OF SIR GALAHAD

Now Sir Galahad had as yet no shield, and he rode four days without meeting any adventure, till at last he came to a White Abbey, where he dismounted and asked if he might sleep there that night. The brethren received him with great reverence, and led him to a chamber, where he took off his armour, and then saw that he was in the presence of two knights. 'Sirs,' said Sir Galahad, 'what adventure brought you hither?' 'Sir,' replied they, 'we heard that within this abbey is a shield that no man may hang round his neck without being dead within three days, or some mischief befalling him. And if we fail in the adventure, you shall take it upon you.' 'Sirs,' replied Sir Galahad, 'I agree well thereto, for as yet I have no shield.'

So on the morn they arose and heard mass, and then a monk led them behind an altar where hung a shield white as snow, with a red cross in the middle of it. 'Sirs,' said the monk, 'this shield can be hung round no knight's neck, unless he be the worthiest knight in the world, and therefore I counsel you to be well advised!'

'Well,' answered one of the knights, whose name was King Bagdemagus, 'I know truly that I am not the best knight in the world, but yet shall I try to bear it,' and he bare it out of the abbey. Then he said to Sir Galahad, 'I pray you abide here still, till you know how I shall speed,' and he rode away, taking with him a squire to send tidings back to Sir Galahad.

After King Bagdemagus had ridden two miles he entered a fair valley, and there met him a goodly knight seated on a white horse and clad in white armour. And they came together with their spears, and Sir Bagdemagus was borne from his horse, for the shield covered him not at all. Therewith the strange knight alighted and took the white shield from him, and gave it to the squire, saying, 'Bear this shield to the good knight Sir Galahad that thou hast left in the abbey, and greet him well from me.'

'Sir,' said the squire, 'what is your name?'

'Take thou no heed of my name,' answered the knight, 'for it is not for thee to know, nor for any earthly man.'

'Now, fair sir,' said the squire, 'tell me for what cause this shield may not be borne lest ill befalls him who bears it.'

'Since you have asked me,' answered the knight, 'know that no man shall bear this shield, save Sir Galahad only.'

Then the squire turned to Bagdemagus, and asked him whether he were wounded or not. 'Yes, truly,' said he, 'and I shall hardly escape from death'; and scarcely could he climb on to his horse's back when the squire brought it near him. But the squire led him to a monastery that lay in the valley, and there he was treated of his wounds, and after long lying came back to life. After the squire had given the knight into the care of the monks, he rode back to the abbey, bearing with him the shield. 'Sir Galahad,' said he, alighting before him, 'the knight that wounded Bagdemagus sends you greeting, and bids you bear this shield, which shall bring you many adventures.'

'Now blessed be God and fortune,' answered Sir Galahad, and called for his arms, and mounted his horse, hanging the shield about his neck. Then, followed by the squire, he set out. They rode straight to the hermitage, where they saw the White Knight who had sent the shield to Sir Galahad. The two knights saluted each other courteously, and then the White Knight told Sir Galahad the story of the shield, and how it had been given into his charge. Afterwards they parted, and Sir Galahad and his squire returned unto the abbey whence they came.

The monks made great joy at seeing Sir Galahad again, for they feared he was gone for ever; and as soon as he was alighted from his horse they brought him unto a tomb in the churchyard where there was night and day such a noise that any man who heard it should be driven nigh mad, or else lose his strength. 'Sir,' they said, 'we deem it a fiend.' Sir Galahad drew near, all armed save his helmet, and stood by the tomb. 'Lift up the stone,' said a monk, and Galahad lifted it, and a voice cried, 'Come thou not nigh me, Sir Galahad, for thou shalt make me go again where I have been so long.' But Galahad took no heed of him, and lifted the stone yet higher, and

SIR GALAHAD OPENS THE TOMB

there rushed from the tomb a foul smoke, and in the midst of it leaped out the foulest figure that ever was seen in the likeness of a man. 'Galahad,' said the figure, 'I see about thee so many angels that my power dare not touch thee.' Then Galahad, stooping down, looked into the tomb, and he saw a body all armed lying there, with a sword by his side. 'Fair brother,' said Galahad, 'let us remove this body, for he is not worthy to be in this churchyard, being a false Christian man.'

This being done they all departed and returned unto the monastery, where they lay that night, and the next morning Sir Galahad knighted Melias his squire, as he had promised him aforetime. So Sir Galahad and Sir Melias departed thence, in quest of the Holy Grail, but they soon went their different ways and fell upon different adventures. In his first encounter Sir Melias was sore wounded, and Sir Galahad came to his help, and left him to an old monk who said that he would heal him of his wounds in the space of seven weeks, and that he was thus wounded because he had not come clean to the quest of the Grail, as Sir Galahad had done. Sir Galahad left him there, and rode on till he came to the Castle of Maidens, which he alone might enter who was free from sin. There he chased away the knights who had seized the castle seven years agone, and restored all to the duke's daughter, who owned it of right. Besides this he set free the maidens who were kept in prison, and summoned all those knights in the country round who had held their lands of the duke, bidding them do homage to his daughter. And in the morning one came to him and told him that as the seven knights fled from the Castle of Maidens they fell upon the path of Sir Gawaine, Sir Gareth, and Sir Lewaine, who were seeking Sir Galahad, and they gave battle; and the seven knights were slain by the three knights. 'It is well,' said Galahad, and he took his armour and his horse and rode away.

So when Sir Galahad left the Castle of Maidens he rode till he came to a waste forest, and there he met with Sir Lancelot and Sir Percivale; but they knew him not, for he was now disguised. And they fought together, and the two knights were smitten down out of the saddle. 'God be with thee, thou best knight in the world,' cried a nun who dwelt in a hermitage close by; and she said it in a loud voice, so that Lancelot and Percivale might hear. But Sir Galahad feared that she would make known who he was, so he spurred his horse and struck deep into the forest before Sir Lancelot and Sir Percivale could mount again. They knew not which path he had taken, so Sir Percivale turned back to ask advice of the nun, and Sir Lancelot pressed forward.

4 HOW SIR LANCELOT SAW A VISION, AND REPENTED OF HIS SINS

He halted when he came to a stone cross, which had by it a block of marble, while nigh at hand stood an old chapel. He tied his horse to a tree, and hung his shield on a branch, and looked into the chapel, for the door was waste and broken. And he saw there a fair altar covered with a silken cloth, and a candlestick which had six branches, all of shining silver. A great light streamed from it, and at this sight Sir Lancelot would fain have entered in, but he could not. So he turned back sorrowful and dismayed, and took the saddle and bridle off his horse, and let him pasture where he would, while he himself unlaced his helm, and ungirded his sword, and lay down to sleep upon his shield, at the foot of the cross.

As he lay there, half waking and half sleeping, he saw two white palfreys come by, drawing a litter, wherein lay a sick knight. When they reached the cross they paused, and Sir Lancelot heard the knight say, 'O sweet lord, when shall this sorrow leave me, and when shall the Holy Vessel come by me, through which I shall be blessed? For I have endured long, though my ill deeds were few.' Thus he spoke, and Sir Lancelot heard it, and of a sudden the great candlestick stood before the cross, though no man had brought it. And with it was a table of silver and the Holy Vessel of the Grail, which Lancelot had seen aforetime. Then the knight rose up, and on his hands and knees he approached the Holy Vessel, and prayed, and was made whole of his sickness. After that the Grail went back into the chapel, and the light and the candlestick also, and Sir

Lancelot would fain have followed, but could not, so heavy was the weight of his sins upon him. And the sick knight arose and kissed the cross, and saw Sir Lancelot lying at the foot with his eyes shut. 'I marvel greatly at this sleeping knight,' he said to his squire, 'that he had no power to wake when the Holy Vessel was brought hither.' 'I dare right well say,' answered the squire, 'that he dwelleth in some deadly sin, whereof he was never confessed.' 'By my faith,' said the knight, 'he is unhappy, whoever he is, for he is of the fellowship of the Round Table, which have undertaken the quest of the Grail.' 'Sir,' replied the squire, 'you have all your arms here, save only your sword and your helm. Take therefore those of this strange knight, who has just put them off.' And the knight did as his squire said, and took Sir Lancelot's horse also, for it was better than his own.

After they had gone Sir Lancelot waked up wholly, and thought of what he had seen, wondering if he were in a dream or not. Suddenly a voice spoke to him, and it said, 'Sir Lancelot, more hard than is the stone, more bitter than is the wood, more naked and barren than is the leaf of the fig tree, art thou; therefore go from hence and withdraw thee from this holy place.' When Sir Lancelot heard this, his heart was passing heavy, and he wept, cursing the day when he had been born. But his helm and sword had gone from the spot where he had lain them at the foot of the cross, and his horse was gone also. And he smote himself and cried, 'My sin and my wickedness have done me this dishonour; for when I sought worldly adventures for worldly desires I ever achieved them and had the better in every place, and never was I discomfited in any quarrel, were it right or wrong. And now I take upon me the adventures of holy things, I see and understand that my old sin hinders me, so that I could not name nor speak when the Holy Grail passed by.' Thus he sorrowed till it was day, and he heard the birds sing, and at that he felt comforted. And as his horse was gone also, he departed on foot with a heavy heart.

5 THE ADVENTURE OF SIR PERCIVALE

All this while Sir Percivale had pursued adventures of his own, and came nigh unto losing his life, but he was saved from his enemies by the good knight, Sir Galahad, whom he did not know, although he was seeking him, for Sir Galahad now bore a red shield, and not a white one. And at last the foes fled deep into the forest, and Sir Galahad followed; but Sir Percivale had no horse and was forced to stay behind. Then his eyes were opened, and he knew it was Sir Galahad who had come to his help, and he sat down under a tree and grieved sore.

While he was sitting there a knight passed by riding a black horse, and when he was out of sight a yeoman came pricking after as fast as he might, and, seeing Sir Percivale, asked if he had seen a knight mounted on a black horse. 'Yes, sir, forsooth,' answered Sir Percivale, 'why do you want to know?' 'Ah, sir, that is my steed which he has taken from me, and wherever my lord shall find me, he is sure to slay me.' 'Well,' said Sir Percivale, 'thou seest that I am on foot, but had I a good horse I would soon come up with him.' 'Take my hackney,' said the yeoman, 'and do the best you can, and I shall follow you on foot to watch how you speed.' So Sir Percivale rode as fast as he might, and at last he saw that knight, and he hailed him. The knight turned and set his spear against Sir Percivale, and smote the hackney in the breast, so that he fell dead to the earth, and Sir Percivale fell with him; then the knight rode away. But Sir Percivale was mad with wrath, and cried to the knight to return and fight with him on foot, and the knight answered not and went on his way. When Sir Percivale saw that he would not turn, he threw himself on the ground, and cast away his helm and sword, and bemoaned himself for the most unhappy of all knights; and there he abode the whole day, and, being faint and weary, slept till it was midnight. And at midnight he waked and saw before him a woman, who said to him right fiercely, 'Sir Percivale, what doest thou here?' 'Neither good nor great ill,' answered he. 'If thou wilt promise to do my will when I call upon you,' said she, 'I will lend you my own horse, and he shall bear thee whither thou shalt choose.' This Sir Percivale promised gladly, and the woman went and returned with a black horse, so large and well-apparelled that Sir Percivale marvelled. But he mounted him gladly, and drove in his spurs, and within an hour and less the horse bare him four days' journey hence, and would have borne him into a rough water that roared, had not Sir Percivale pulled at his bridle. The knight stood doubting, for the water made a great noise, and he feared lest his horse could not get through it. Still, wishing greatly to pass over, he made himself ready, and signed the sign of the cross upon his forehead.

At that the fiend which had taken the shape of a horse shook off Sir Percivale and dashed into the water, crying and making great sorrow; and it seemed to him that the water burned. Then Sir Percivale knew that it was not a horse but a fiend, which would have brought him to perdition, and he gave thanks and prayed all that night long. As soon as it was day he looked about him, and saw he was in a wild mountain, girt round with the sea and filled with wild beasts. Then he rose and went into a valley, and there he saw a young serpent bring a young lion by the neck, and after that there passed a great lion, crying and roaring after the serpent, and a fierce battle began between them. Sir Percivale thought to help the lion, as he was the more natural beast of the twain, and he drew his sword and set his shield before him, and gave the serpent a deadly buffet. When the lion saw that, he made him all the cheer that a beast might make a man, and fawned about him like a spaniel, and stroked him with his paws. And about noon the lion took his little whelp, and placed him on his back, and bare him home again, and Sir Percivale, being left alone, prayed till he was comforted. But at eventide the lion returned, and couched down at his feet, and all night long he and the lion slept together.

SIR PERCIVALE SLAYS THE SERPENT

6   AN ADVENTURE OF SIR LANCELOT

As Lancelot went his way through the forest he met with many hermits who dwelled therein, and had adventure with the knight who stole his horse and his helm, and got them back again. And he learned from one of the hermits that Sir Galahad was his son, and that it was he who at the Feast of Pentecost had sat in the Siege Perilous, which it was ordained by Merlin that none should sit in save the best knight in the world. All that night Sir Lancelot abode with the hermit and laid him to rest, a hair shirt always on his body, and it pricked him sorely, but he bore it meekly and suffered the pain. When the day dawned he bade the hermit farewell.

As he rode he came to a fair plain, in which was a great castle set about with tents and pavilions of divers hues. Here were full five hundred knights riding on horseback, and those near the castle were mounted on black horses with black trappings, and they that were without were on white horses and their trappings white. And the two sides fought together, and Sir Lancelot looked on.

At last it seemed to him that the Black Knights nearest the castle fared the worst, so, as he ever took the part of the weaker, he rode to their help and smote many of the White Knights to the earth and did marvellous deeds of arms. But always the White Knights held round Sir Lancelot to tire him out. And as no man may endure for ever, in the end Sir Lancelot waxed so faint of fighting that his arms would not lift themselves to deal a stroke; then they took him, and led him away into the forest and made him alight from his horse and rest, and when he was taken the fellowship of the castle were overcome for want of him. 'Never ere now was I at tournament or jousts but I had the best,' moaned Sir Lancelot to himself, as soon as the knights had left him and he was alone. 'But now am I shamed, and I am persuaded that I am more sinful than ever I was.'

Sorrowfully he rode on till he passed a chapel, where stood a nun, who called to him and asked him his name and what he was seeking. So he told her who he was, and what had befallen him at the tournament, and the vision that had come to him in his sleep. 'Ah, Lancelot,' said she, 'as long as you were a knight of earthly knighthood you were the most wonderful man in the world and the most adventurous. But now, since you are set among knights of heavenly adventures, if you were worsted at that tournament it is no marvel. For the tournament was meant for a sign, and the earthly knights were they who were clothed in black in token of the sins of which they were not yet purged. And the White Knights were they who had chosen the way of holiness, and in them the quest has already begun. Thus you beheld both the sinners and the good men, and when you saw the sinners overcome you went to their help, as they were your fellows in boasting and pride of the world, and all that must be left in that quest. And that caused your misadventure. Now that I have warned you of your vainglory and your pride, beware of everlasting pain, for of all earthly knights I have pity of you, for I know well that among earthly sinful knights you are without peer.'

7 AN ADVENTURE OF SIR GAWAINE

Sir Gawaine rode long without meeting any adventure, and from Pentecost to Michaelmas found none that pleased him. But at Michaelmas he met Sir Ector de Maris and rejoiced greatly.

As they sat talking there appeared before them a hand showing unto the elbow covered with red samite, and holding a great candle that burned right clear; and the hand passed into the chapel and vanished, they know not where. Then they heard a voice which said, 'Knights full of evil faith and poor belief, these two things have failed you, and therefore you may not come to the adventure of the Holy Grail.' And this same told them a holy man to whom they confessed their sins, 'for,' said he, 'you have failed in three things, charity, fasting, and truth, and have been great murderers. But sinful as Sir Lancelot was, since he went into the quest he never slew man, nor shall, till he come into Camelot again. For he has taken upon him to forsake sin. And were he not so unstable, he should be the next to achieve it, after Galahad his son. Yet shall he die a holy man, and in earthly sinful men he has no fellow.'

'Sir,' said Gawaine, 'by your words it seems that our sins will not let us labour in that quest?' 'Truly,' answered the hermit, 'there be a hundred such as you to whom it will bring naught but shame.' So Gawaine departed and followed Sir Ector, who had ridden on before.

8   THE ADVENTURE OF BORS

When Sir Bors left Camelot on his quest he met a holy man riding on an ass, and Sir Bors saluted him. Then the good man knew him to be one of the knights who were in quest of the Holy Grail. 'What are you?' said he, and Sir Bors answered, 'I am a knight that fain would be counselled in the quest of the Grail, for he shall have much earthly worship that brings it to an end.' 'That is true,' said the good man, 'for he will be the best knight in the world, but know well that there shall none attain it but by holiness and by confession of sin.' So they rode together till they came to the hermitage, and the good man led Sir Bors into the chapel, where he made confession of his sins, and they ate bread and drank water together. 'Now,' said the hermit, 'I pray you that you eat none other till you sit at the table where the Holy Grail shall be.' 'Sir,' answered Sir Bors, 'I agree thereto, but how know you that I shall sit there?' 'That know I,' said the holy man, 'but there will be but few of your fellows with you. Also instead of a shirt you shall wear this garment until you have achieved your quest,' and Sir Bors took off his clothes, and put on instead a scarlet coat. Then the good man questioned him, and marvelled to find him pure in life, and he armed him and bade him go. After this Sir Bors rode through many lands, and had many adventures, and was often sore tempted, but remembered the words of the holy man and kept his life clean of wrong. And once he had by mischance almost slain his own brother, but a voice cried, 'Flee, Bors, and touch him not,' and he hearkened and stayed his

HOW SIR BORS WAS SAVED FROM KILLING HIS BROTHER

hand. And there fell between them a fiery cloud, which burned up both their shields, and they two fell to the earth in a great swoon; but when they awakened out of it Bors saw that his brother had no harm. With that the voice spoke to him saying, 'Bors, go hence and bear your brother fellowship no longer; but take your way to the sea, where Sir Percivale abides till you come.' Then Sir Bors prayed his brother to forgive him all he had unknowingly done, and rode straight to the sea. On the shore he found a vessel covered with white samite, and as soon as he stepped in the vessel it set sail so fast it might have been flying, and Sir Bors lay down and slept till it was day. When he waked he saw a knight lying in the midst of the ship, all armed save for his helm, and he knew him for Sir Percivale, and welcomed him with great joy; and they told each other of their adventures and of their temptations, and had great happiness in each other's company. 'We lack nothing but Galahad, the good knight,' Sir Percivale said.

9 AN ADVENTURE OF SIR GALAHAD

Sir Galahad rested one evening at a hermitage. And while he was resting, there came a gentlewoman and asked leave of the hermit to speak with Sir Galahad, and would not be denied, though she was told he was weary and asleep. Then the hermit waked Sir Galahad and bade him rise, as a gentlewoman had great need of him, so Sir Galahad rose and asked her what she wished.

'Galahad,' said she, 'I will that you arm yourself, and mount your horse and follow me, and I will show you the highest adventure that ever any knight saw.' And Sir Galahad bade her go, and he would follow wherever she led. In three days they reached the sea, where they found the ship where Sir Bors and Sir Percivale were lying. And the lady bade him leave his horse behind and said she would leave hers also, but their saddles and bridles they would take on board the ship. This they did, and were received with great joy by the two knights; then the sails were spread, and the ship was driven before the wind at a marvellous pace till they reached the land of

Logris, the entrance to which lies between two great rocks with a whirlpool in the middle.

Their own ship might not get safely through; but they left it and went into another ship that lay there, which had neither man nor woman in it. At the end of the ship was written these words: 'Thou man which shall enter this ship beware thou be in steadfast belief; if thou fail, I shall not help thee.' Then the gentlewoman turned and said, 'Percivale, do you know who I am?' 'No, truly,' answered he. 'I am your sister, and therefore you are the man in the world that I most love. If you are without faith, or have any hidden sin, beware how you enter, else you will perish.' 'Fair sister,' answered he, 'I shall enter therein, for if I am an untrue knight then shall I perish.' So they entered the ship, and it was rich and well adorned, that they all marvelled.

In the midst of it was a fair bed, and Sir Galahad went thereto and found on it a crown of silk, and a sword drawn out of its sheath half a foot and more. The sword was of divers fashions, and the pommel of stone, wrought about with colours, and every colour with its own virtue, and the handle was of the ribs of two beasts. The one was the bone of a serpent, and no hand that handles it shall ever become weary or hurt; and the other is the bone of a fish that swims in Euphrates, and whoso handles it shall not think on joy or sorrow that he has had, but only on that which he beholds before him. And no man shall grip this sword but one that is better than other men. So first Sir Percivale stepped forward and set his hand to the sword, but he might not grasp it. Next Sir Bors tried to seize it, but he also failed. When Sir Galahad beheld the sword, he saw that there was written on it, in letters of blood, that he who tried to draw it should never fail of shame in his body or be wounded to the death. 'By my faith,' said Galahad, 'I would draw this sword out of its sheath, but the offending is so great I shall not lay my hand thereto.' 'Sir,' answered the gentlewoman, 'know that no man can draw this sword save you alone'; and she told him many tales of the knights who had set their hands to it, and of the evil things that had befallen them. And they all begged Sir Galahad to grip the sword, as it was ordained that he should. 'I will grip it,' said Galahad, 'to

give you courage, but it belongs no more to me than it does to you.'
Then he gripped it tight with his fingers, and the gentlewoman girt
him about the middle with the sword, and after that they left that
ship and went into another, which brought them to land, where
they fell upon many strange adventures. And when they had
wrought many great deeds, they departed from each other. But first
Sir Percivale's sister died, being bled to death, so that another lady
might live, and she prayed them to lay her body in a boat and leave
the boat to go as the winds and waves carried it. And so it was done,
and Sir Percivale wrote a letter telling how she had helped them in
all their adventures; and he put it in her right hand, and laid her in a
barge, and covered it with black silk. And the wind arose and drove
it from their sight.

10   SIR LANCELOT MEETS SIR GALAHAD AND
THEY PART FOR EVER

Now we must tell what happened to Sir Lancelot.

When he was come to a water called Mortoise he fell asleep,
awaiting the adventure that should be sent to him, and in his sleep
a voice spoke to him, and bade him rise and take his armour, and
enter the first ship he should find. So he started up and took his
arms and made him ready, and on the strand he found a ship that
was without sail or oar. As soon as he was within the ship, he felt
himself wrapped round with a sweetness such as he had never
known before, as if all that he could desire was fulfilled. And with
this joy and peace about him he fell asleep. When he woke he
found near him a fair bed, with a dead lady lying on it, whom he
knew to be Sir Percivale's sister, and in her hand was the tale of her
adventures, which Sir Lancelot took and read. For a month or
more they dwelt in that ship together, and one day, when it had
drifted near the shore, he heard a sound as of a horse; and when
the steps came nearer he saw that a knight was riding him. At the
sight of the ship the knight alighted and took the saddle and bridle,
and entered the ship. 'You are welcome,' said Lancelot, and the

knight saluted him and said, 'What is your name? for my heart goeth out to you.'

'Truly,' answered he, 'my name is Sir Lancelot du Lake.'

'Sir,' said the new knight, 'you are welcome, for you were the beginner of me in the world.'

'Ah,' cried Sir Lancelot, 'is it you, then, Galahad?'

'Yes, in sooth,' said he, and kneeled down and asked Lancelot's blessing, and then took off his helm and kissed him. And there was great joy between them, and they told each other all that had befallen them since they left King Arthur's court. Then Galahad saw the gentlewoman dead on the bed, and he knew her, and said he held her in great worship, and that she was the best maid in the world, and how it was great pity that she had come to her death. But when Lancelot heard that Galahad had won the marvellous sword he prayed that he might see it, and kissed the pommel and the hilt, and the scabbard. 'In truth,' he said, 'never did I know of adventures so wonderful and strange.' So dwelled Lancelot and Galahad in that ship for half a year, and served God daily and nightly with all their power. And after six months had gone it befell that on a Monday they drifted to the edge of the forest, where they saw a knight with white armour bestriding one horse and holding another all white, by the bridle. And he came to the ship, and saluted the two knights and said, 'Galahad, you have been long enough with your father, therefore leave that ship and start upon this horse, and go on the quest of the Holy Grail.' So Galahad went to his father and kissed him, saying, 'Fair sweet father, I know not if I shall see you more till I have beheld the Holy Grail.' Then they heard a voice which said, 'The one shall never see the other till the day of doom.' 'Now, Galahad,' said Lancelot, 'since we are to bid farewell for ever now, I pray to the great Father to preserve me and you both.'

'Sir,' answered Galahad, 'no prayer availeth so much as yours.'

The next day Sir Lancelot made his way back to Camelot, where he found King Arthur and Guenevere; but many of the Knights of the Round Table were slain and destroyed, more than the half. All the court was passing glad to see Sir Lancelot, and the king asked many tidings of his son Sir Galahad.

11   HOW SIR GALAHAD FOUND THE GRAIL AND DIED
OF THAT FINDING

Sir Galahad rode on till he met Sir Percivale and afterwards Sir Bors, whom they greeted most gladly, and they bare each other company. First they came to the Castle of Carbonek, where dwelled King Pelles, who welcomed them with joy, for he knew by their coming that they had fulfilled the quest of the Grail. They then departed on other adventures, and with the blood out of the Holy Lance Galahad anointed the maimed king and healed him. That same night at midnight a voice bade them arise and quit the castle, which they did, followed by three Knights of Gaul. Then Galahad prayed every one of them that if they reached King Arthur's court, they should salute Sir Lancelot, his father, and those Knights of the Round Table that were present, and with that he left them, and Sir Bors and Sir Percivale with him. For three days they rode till they came to a shore, and found a ship awaiting them. And in the midst of it was the table of silver, and the Holy Grail which was covered with red samite. Then were their hearts right glad, and they made great reverence thereto, and Galahad prayed that at what time he asked, he might depart out of this world. So long he prayed that at length a voice said to him, 'Galahad, thou shalt have thy desire, and when thou askest the death of the body thou shalt have it, and shalt find the life of the Soul.' Percivale likewise heard the voice, and besought Galahad to tell him why he asked such things. And Galahad answered, 'The other day when we saw a part of the adventures of the Holy Grail, I was in such a joy of heart that never did man feel before, and I knew well that when my body is dead my soul shall be in joy of which the other was but a shadow.'

Some time were the three knights in that ship, till at length they saw before them the city of Sarras. Then they took from the ship the table of silver, and Sir Percivale and Sir Bors went first, and Sir Galahad followed after to the gate of the city, where sat an old man that was crooked. At the sight of the old man Sir Galahad called to him to help them carry the table, for it was heavy. 'Truly,' answered the old man, 'it is ten years since I have gone without crutches.' 'Care not for that,' said Galahad, 'but rise up and show your good will.' So he arose and found himself as whole as ever he was, and he ran to the table and held up the side next Galahad. And there was much noise in the city that a cripple was healed by three knights newly entered in. This reached the ears of the king, who sent for the knights and questioned them. And they told him the truth, and of the Holy Grail; but the king listened nothing to all they said, but put them into a deep hole in the prison. Even here they were not without comfort, for a vision of the Holy Grail sustained them. And at the end of a year the king lay sick and felt he should die, and he called the three knights and asked forgiveness of the evil he had done to them, which they gave gladly. Then he died, and the whole city was afraid and knew not what to do, till while they were in counsel a voice came to them and bade them choose the youngest of the three strange knights for their king. And they did so. After Galahad was proclaimed king, he ordered that a coffer of gold and precious stones should be made to encompass the table of silver, and every day he and the two knights would kneel before it and make their prayers.

Now at the year's end, and on the selfsame day that Galahad had been crowned king, he arose up early and came with the two knights to the palace; and he saw a man in the likeness of a bishop, encircled by a great crowd of angels, kneeling before the Holy Vessel. And he called to Galahad and said to him, 'Come forth, thou servant of Christ, and thou shalt see what thou hast much desired to see.' Then Galahad began to tremble right hard, when the flesh first beheld the things of the spirit, and he held up his hands to heaven and said, 'Lord, I thank thee, for now I see that which hath been my desire for many a day. Now, blessed Lord, I would no longer live, if it might please thee.' Then Galahad went to Percivale and kissed him, and commended him to God; and he went to Sir Bors and kissed him, and commended him to God, and said, 'Fair lord, salute m   e to my lord Sir Lancelot, my father, and bid him remember this unstable world.' Therewith he kneeled down before the table and made his prayers, and while he was praying his soul suddenly left the body and was carried by angels up into heaven, which the two knights right well beheld. Also they saw come from heaven a hand, but no body behind it, and it came unto the Vessel, and took it and the spear, and bare them back to heaven. And since then no man has dared to say that he has seen the Holy Grail.

When Percivale and Bors saw Galahad lying dead they made as much sorrow as ever two men did, and the people of the country and of the city were right heavy. And they buried him as befitted their ring. As soon as Galahad was buried, Sir Percivale sought a hermitage outside the city, and put on the dress of a hermit, and Sir Bors was always with him, but kept the dress that he wore at court. When a year and two months had passed Sir Percivale died also, and was buried by the side of Galahad; and Sir Bors left that land, and after long riding came to Camelot. Then was there great joy made of him in the court, for they had held him as dead; and the king ordered great clerks to attend him, and to write down all his adventures with those of Sir Percivale and Sir Galahad. Next, Sir Lancelot told the adventures of the Grail which he had seen, and this likewise was written and placed with the other in almonries at Salisbury. And by and by Sir Bors said to Sir Lancelot, 'Galahad your son saluteth you by me, and after you King Arthur and all the court, and so did Sir Percivale; for I buried them with mine own hands in the City of Sarras. Also, Sir Lancelot, Galahad prayeth you to remember of this uncertain world, as you promised when you were together!' 'That is true,' said Sir Lancelot, 'and I trust his prayer may avail me.' But the prayer but little availed Sir Lancelot, for he fell to his old sins again. And now the knights were few that survived the search for the Grail, and the evil days of Arthur began.

The Fight for the Queen

So the quest of the Holy Grail had been fulfilled, and the few knights that had been left alive returned to the Round Table, and there was great joy in the court. To do them honour the queen made them a dinner; and there were four and twenty knights present, and among them Sir Patrise of Ireland, and Sir Gawaine and his brethren, the king's nephews, which were Sir Agrawaine, Sir Gaheris, Sir Gareth, and Sir Mordred. Now it was the custom of Sir Gawaine daily at dinner and supper to eat all manner of fruit, and especially pears and apples, and this the queen knew, and set fruit of all sorts before him. And there was present at the dinner one Sir Pinel le Savage, who hated Sir Gawaine because he and his brethren had slain Sir Lamorak du Galis, cousin to Sir Pinel; so he put poison into some of the apples, hoping that Sir Gawaine would eat one and die. But by ill fortune it befell that the good knight Sir Patrise took a poisoned apple, and in a few moments he lay dead and stark in his seat. At this sight all the knights leapt to their feet, but said nothing, for they bethought them that Queen Guenevere had made them the dinner, and feared that she had poisoned the fruit.

'My lady, the queen,' said Sir Gawaine, who was the first to speak, 'this fruit was brought for me, for all know how well I love it; therefore, madam, the shame of this ill deed is yours.' The queen stood still, pale and trembling, but kept silence, and next spoke Sir Mador de la Porte.

'This shall not be ended so,' said he, 'for I have lost a noble knight of my blood, and I will be avenged of the person who has wrought this evil.' And he turned to the queen and said, 'Madam, it is you who have brought about the death of my cousin, Sir Patrise!' The knights round listened in silence, for they too thought Sir Mador spake truth. And the queen still said nothing, but fell to weeping bitterly, till King Arthur heard and came to look into the matter. And when they told him of their trouble his heart was heavy within him.

'Fair lords,' said the king at last, 'I grieve for this ill deed; but I cannot meddle therein, or do battle for my wife, for I have to judge justly. Sure I am that this deed is none of hers, therefore many a good knight will stand her champion that she be not burned to death in a wrong quarrel. And, Sir Mador, hold not your head so high, but fix the day of battle, when you shall find a knight to answer you, or else it were great shame to all my court.'

'My gracious lord,' said Sir Mador, 'you must hold me excused. But though you are a king you are also a knight, and must obey the laws of knighthood. Therefore I beseech your forgiveness if I declare that none of the four and twenty knights here present will fight that battle. What say you, my lords?' Then the knights answered that they could not hold the queen guiltless, for as the dinner was made by her either she or her servants must have done this thing.

'Alas!' said the queen, 'no evil was in my heart when I prepared this feast, for never have I done such foul deeds.'

'My lord the king,' cried Sir Mador, 'I require of you, as you are a just king, to fix a day that I may get ready for the fight!'

'Well,' answered the king, 'on the fifteenth day from this come on horseback to the meadow that is by Westminster. And if it happens that there be a knight to fight with you, strike as hard as you will, God will speed the right. But if no knight is there, then must my queen be burned, and a fire shall be made in the meadow.'

'I am answered,' said Sir Mador, and he and the rest of the knights departed.

When the king and queen were left alone he asked her what had brought all this about. 'God help me, that I know not,' said the queen, 'nor how it was done.'

'Where is Sir Lancelot?' said King Arthur, looking round. 'If he were here, he would not grudge to do battle for you.'

'Sir,' replied the queen, 'I know not where he is, but his brother and his kinsmen think he is not in this realm.'

'I grieve for that,' said the king, 'for he would soon stop this

SIR MADOR ACCUSES GUENEVERE

strife. But I counsel you, ask Sir Bors, and he will not refuse you. For well I see that none of the four and twenty knights who were with you at dinner will be your champion, and none will say well of you, but men will speak evil of you at the court.'

'Alas!' sighed the queen, 'I do indeed miss Sir Lancelot, for he would soon ease my heart.'

'What ails you?' asked the king, 'that you cannot keep Sir Lancelot at your side, for well you know that he who Sir Lancelot fights for has the best knight in the world for his champion. Now go your way, and command Sir Bors to do battle with you for Sir Lancelot's sake.' So the queen departed from the king, and sent for Sir Bors into her chamber, and when he came she besought his help.

'Madam,' said he, 'what can I do? for I may not meddle in this matter lest the knights who were at the dinner have me in suspicion, for I was there also. It is now, madam, that you miss Sir Lancelot, whom you have driven away, as he would have done battle for you were you right or wrong, and I wonder how for shame's sake you can ask me, knowing how I love and honour him.'

'Alas,' said the queen, 'I throw myself on your grace,' and she went down on her knees and besought Sir Bors to have mercy on her, 'else I shall have a shameful death, and one I have never deserved.' At that King Arthur came in, and found her kneeling before Sir Bors.

'Madam! you do me great dishonour,' said Sir Bors, raising her up.

'Ah, gentle knight,' cried the king, 'have mercy on my queen, for I am sure that they speak falsely. And I require by the love of Sir Lancelot that you do battle for her instead of him.'

'My lord,' answered Sir Bors, 'you require of me the hardest thing that ever anyone asked of me, for well you know that if I fight for the queen I shall anger all my companions of the Round Table; but I will not say nay, my lord, for Sir Lancelot's sake and for your sake! On that day I will be the queen's champion, unless a better knight is found to do battle for her.'

'Will you promise me this?' asked the king.

'Yes,' answered Sir Bors, 'I will not fail you nor her unless there should come a better knight than I, then he shall have the battle.' Then the king and queen rejoiced greatly, and thanked Sir Bors with all their hearts.

So Sir Bors departed and rode unto Sir Lancelot, who was with the hermit Sir Brasias, and told him of this adventure. 'Ah,' said Sir Lancelot, 'this has befallen as I would have it, and therefore I pray you make ready to do battle, but delay the fight as long as you can that I may appear. For I am sure that Sir Mador is a hot knight, and the longer he waits the more impatient he will be for the combat.'

'Sir,' answered Sir Bors, 'let me deal with him. Doubt not you shall have all your will.' And he rode away, and came again to the court.

It was soon noised about that Sir Bors would be the queen's champion, and many knights were displeased with him; but there were a few who held the queen to be innocent. Sir Bors spoke unto them all, and said, 'It were shameful, my fair lords, if we suffered the most noble queen in the world to be disgraced openly, not only for her sake, but for the king's.' But they answered him: 'As for our lord King Arthur, we love him and honour him as much as you; but as for Queen Guenevere, we love her not, for she is the destroyer of good knights.'

'Fair lords,' said Sir Bors, 'you shall not speak such words, for never yet have I heard that she was the destroyer of good knights. But at all times, as far as I ever knew, she maintained them and gave them many gifts. And therefore it were a shame to us all if we suffered our noble king's wife to be put to death, and I will not suffer it. So much I will say, that the queen is not guilty of Sir Patrise's death; for she owed him no ill will, and bade him and us to the dinner for no evil purpose, which will be proved hereafter. And in any case there was foul dealing among us.'

'We may believe your words,' said some of the knights, but others held that he spoke falsely.

The days passed quickly by until the evening before the battle, when the queen sent for Sir Bors and asked him if he was ready to keep his promise.

'Truly, madam,' answered he, 'I shall not fail you, unless a better

knight than I am come to do battle for you. Then, madam, I am
discharged of my promise.'

'Shall I tell this to my lord Arthur?' said the queen.

'If it pleases you, madam,' answered Sir Bors. So the queen went
to the king, and told him what Sir Bors had said, and the king bade
her to be comforted, as Sir Bors was one of the best Knights of the
Round Table.

The next morning the king and queen, and all manner of knights,
rode into the meadow of Westminster, where the battle was to be;
and the queen was put into the guard of the High Constable, and a
stout iron stake was planted, and a great fire made about it, at which
the queen should be burned if Sir Mador de la Porte won the fight.
For it was the custom in those days that neither fear nor favour, love
nor kinship, should hinder right judgment. Then came Sir Mador de
la Porte, and made oath before the king that the queen had done to
death his cousin Sir Patrise, and he would prove it on her knight's
body, let who would say the contrary. Sir Bors likewise made answer
that Queen Guenevere had done no wrong, and that he would make
good with his two hands. 'Then get you ready,' said Sir Mador. 'Sir
Mador,' answered Sir Bors, 'I know you for a good knight, but I trust
to be able to withstand your malice; and I have promised King Arthur
and my lady the queen that I will do battle for her to the uttermost,
unless there come forth a better knight than I am.'

'Is that all?' asked Sir Mador; 'but you must either fight now or
own that you are beaten.'

'Take your horse,' said Sir Bors, 'for I shall not tarry long,' and
Sir Mador forthwith rode into the field with his shield on his
shoulder, and his spear in his hand, and he went up and down
crying unto King Arthur, 'Bid your champion come forth if he
dare.' At that Sir Bors was ashamed, and took his horse, and rode
to the end of the lists. But from a wood hard by appeared a knight
riding fast on a white horse, bearing a shield full of strange devices.
When he reached Sir Bors he drew rein and said, 'Fair knight, be
not displeased, but this battle must be to a better knight than you.
For I have come a great journey to fight this fight, as I promised
when I spoke with you last, and I thank you heartily for your

goodwill.' So Sir Bors went to King Arthur and told him that a knight had come who wished to do battle for the queen. 'What knight is he?' asked the king.

'That I know not,' said Sir Bors; 'but he made a covenant with me to be here this day, and now I am discharged,' said Sir Bors.

Then the king called to that knight and asked him if he would fight for the queen. 'For that purpose I came hither,' replied he, 'and therefore, Sir King, delay me no longer, for as soon as I have ended this battle I must go hence, as I have many matters elsewhere. And I would have you know that it is a dishonour to all the Knights of the Round Table to let so noble a lady and so courteous a queen as Queen Guenevere be shamed amongst you.'

The knights who were standing round looked at each other at these words, and wondered much what man this was who took the battle upon him, for none knew him save Sir Bors.

'Sir,' said Sir Mador de la Porte unto the king, 'let me know the name of him with whom I have to do.' But the king answered nothing, and made a sign for the fight to begin. They rode to the end of the lists, and couched their spears and rushed together with all their force, and Sir Mador's spear broke in pieces. But the other knight's spear held firm, and he pressed on Sir Mador's horse till it fell backward with a great fall. Sir Mador sprang from his horse, and, placing his shield before him, drew his sword, and bade his foe dismount from his horse also, and do battle with him on foot, which the unknown knight did. For an hour they fought thus, as Sir Mador was a strong man, and had proved himself the victor in many combats. At last the knight smote Sir Mador grovelling to his knees, and the knight stepped forward to have struck him flat upon the ground. Therewith Sir Mador suddenly rose, and smote the knight upon the thigh, so that the blood rain out fiercely. But, when the knight felt himself wounded, and saw his blood, he let Sir Mador rise to his feet, and then he gave him such a buffet on the helm that this time Sir Mador fell his length on the earth, and the knight sprang to him, to unloose his helm. At this Sir Mador prayed for his life, acknowledging that he was overcome, and confessed that the queen's innocence had been proved. 'I will only grant you your life,' said the knight, 'if you will proclaim publicly that you have foully slandered the queen, and that you make no mention, on the tomb of Sir Patrise, that ever Queen Guenevere consented to his murder.' 'All that will I do,' said Sir Mador, and some knights took him up, and carried him away to heal his wounds. And the other knight went straight to the foot of the steps where sat King Arthur, and there the queen had just come, and the king and the queen kissed each other before all the people. When King Arthur saw the knight standing there he stooped down to him and thanked him, and so likewise did the queen; and they prayed him to put off his helmet, and commanded wine to be brought, and when he unlaced his helmet to drink they knew him to be Sir Lancelot du Lake. Then Arthur took the queen's hand and led her to Sir Lancelot and said, 'Sir, I give you the most heartfelt thanks of the great deed you have done this day for me and my queen.'

'My lord,' answered Sir Lancelot, 'you know well that I ought of right ever to fight your battles, and those of my lady the queen. For it was you who gave me the high honour of knighthood, and that same day my lady the queen did me a great service, else I should have been put to shame before all men. Because in my hastiness I lost my sword, and my lady the queen found it and gave it to me when I had sore need of it. And therefore, my lord Arthur, I promised her that day that I would be her knight in right or in wrong.'

'I owe you great thanks,' said the king, 'and some time I hope to repay you.' The queen, beholding Sir Lancelot, wept tears of joy for her deliverance, and felt bowed to the ground with sorrow at the thought of what he had done for her, when she had sent him away with unkind words. Then all the Knights of the Round Table and his kinsmen drew near to him and welcomed him, and there was great mirth in the court.

ARTHUR AND GUENEVERE
KISS BEFORE ALL THE PEOPLE

The Fair Maid of Astolat

Soon after this it befell that the damsel of the lake, called by some Nimue and by others Vivien, wedded Sir Pelleas, and came to the court of King Arthur. And when she heard the talk of the death of Sir Patrise and how the queen had been accused of it, she found out by means of her magic that the tale was false, and told it openly that the queen was innocent and that it was Sir Pinel who had poisoned the apple. Then he fled into his own country, where none might lay hands on him. So Sir Patrise was buried in the Church of Westminster, and on his tomb was written, 'Here lieth Sir Patrise of Ireland, slain by Sir Pinel le Savage, that empoisoned apples to have slain Sir Gawaine, and by misfortune Sir Patrise ate one of those apples and then suddenly he burst.' Also there was put upon the tomb that Queen Guenevere was accused of the death of Sir Patrise by Sir Mador de la Porte, and how Sir Lancelot fought with him and overcame him in battle. All this was written on the tomb.

And daily Sir Mador prayed to have the queen's grace once more, and by means of Sir Lancelot he was forgiven. It was now the middle of the summer, and King Arthur proclaimed that in fifteen days a great tourney should be held at Camelot, which is now called Winchester, and many knights and kings made ready to do themselves honour. But the queen said she would stay behind, for she was sick, and did not care for the noise and bustle of a tourney. 'It grieves me you should say that,' said the king, 'for you will not have seen so noble a company gathered together this seven years past, save at the Whitsuntide when Galahad departed from the court.'

'Truly,' answered the queen, 'the sight will be grand. Nevertheless you must hold me excused, for I cannot be there.'

Sir Lancelot likewise declared that his wounds were not healed and that he could not bear himself in a tourney as he was wont to do. At this the king was wroth, that he might not have either his queen or his best knight with him, and he departed towards Winchester and by the way lodged in a town now called Guildford, but then Astolat. And when the king had set forth, the queen sent for Sir Lancelot, and told him he was to blame for having excused himself from going with the king, who set such store by his company; and Sir Lancelot said he would be ruled by her, and would ride forth next morning on his way to Winchester; 'but I should have you know,' said he, 'that at the tourney I shall be against the king and his knights.'

'You must do as you please,' replied the queen, 'but if you will be ruled by my counsel, you will fight on his side.'

'Madam,' said Sir Lancelot, 'I pray you not to be displeased with me. I will take the adventure as it comes,' and early next morning he rode away till at eventide he reached Astolat. He went through the town till he stopped before the house of an old baron, Sir Bernard of Astolat, and as he dismounted from his horse, the king spied him from the gardens of the castle. 'It is well,' he said smiling to the knights that were beside him, 'I see one man who will play his part in the jousts, and I will undertake that he will do marvels.'

'Who is that?' asked they all. 'You must wait to know that,' replied the king, and went into the castle.

Meantime Sir Lancelot had entered his lodging, and the old baron bade him welcome, but he knew not it was Sir Lancelot. 'Fair sir,' said Sir Lancelot, 'I pray you lend me, if you can, a shield with a device which no man knows, for mine they know well.'

'Sir,' answered Sir Bernard, 'you shall have your wish, for you seem one of the goodliest knights in the world. And, sir, I have two sons, both but lately knighted, Sir Tirre who was wounded on the day of his knighthood, and his shield you shall have. My youngest son, Sir Lavaine, shall ride with you, if you will have his company, to the jousts. For my heart is much drawn to you, and tell me, I beseech you, what name I shall call you by.'

'You must hold me excused as to that, just now,' said Sir Lancelot, 'but if I speed well at the jousts, I will come again and tell you. But let me have Sir Lavaine with me, and lend me, as you have offered, his brother's shield.' 'This shall be done,' replied Sir Bernard.

Besides these two sons, Sir Bernard had a daughter whom every-one called the Fair Maid of Astolat, though her real name was Elaine le Blanc. And when she looked on Sir Lancelot, her love went forth to him and she could never take it back, and in the end it killed her. As soon as her father told her that Sir Lancelot was going to the tourney she besought him to wear her token in the jousts, but he was not willing. 'Fair damsel,' he said, 'if I did that, I should have done more for your love than ever I did for lady or damsel.' But then he remembered that he was to go disguised to the tourney, and because he had before never worn any manner of token of any damsel, he bethought him that, if he should take one of hers, none would know him. So he said to her, 'Fair damsel, I will wear your token on my helmet, if you will show me what it is.'

'Sir,' she answered, 'it is a red sleeve, embroidered in great pearls,' and she brought it to him. 'Never have I done so much for any damsel,' said he, and gave his own shield into her keeping, till he came again. Sir Arthur had waited three days in Astolat for some knights who were long on the road, and when they had arrived they all set forth, and were followed by Sir Lancelot and Sir Lavaine, both with white shields, and Sir Lancelot bore besides the red sleeve that was a token. Now Camelot was filled with a great number of kings and lords and knights, but Sir Lavaine found means to lodge both himself and Sir Lancelot secretly with a rich burgess, and no man knew who they were or whence they came. And there they stayed till the day of the tourney. At earliest dawn the trumpets blew, and King Arthur took his seat upon a high scaffold, so that he might see who had done best; but he would not suffer Sir Gawaine to go from his side, for Sir Gawaine never won the prize when Sir Lancelot was in the field, and as King Arthur knew, Sir Lancelot oftentimes disguised himself.

Then the knights formed into two parties and Sir Lancelot made him ready, and fastened the red sleeve upon his helmet, and he and Sir Lavaine rode into a little wood that lay behind the knights who should fight against those of the Round Table. 'Sir,' said Sir Lancelot, 'yonder is a company of good knights and they hold together as boars that are vexed with dogs.'

ELAINE TIES HER SLEEVE ROVND
SIR LANCELOT'S HELMET

'That is truth,' said Sir Lavaine.

'Now,' said Sir Lancelot, 'if you will help me a little, you shall see King Arthur's side, which is winning, driven back as fast as they came.'

'Spare not, sir,' answered Sir Lavaine, 'for I shall do what I may.' So they rode into the thickest of the press, and smote so hard both with spear and sword that the Knights of the Round Table fell back. 'O mercy!' cried Sir Gawaine, 'what knight is that yonder who does such marvellous deeds?'

'I know well who it is,' said King Arthur, 'but I will not tell you yet.'

'Sir,' answered Sir Gawaine, 'I should say it was Sir Lancelot by the blows he deals and the manner that he rides, but it cannot be he, for this man has a red sleeve upon his helmet, and Sir Lancelot has never borne the token of any lady.'

'Let him be,' said Sir Arthur, 'you will find out his name, and see him do greater deeds yet, before he departs.' And the knights that were fighting against the king's party took heart again, for before they feared they would be beaten. But when Sir Bors saw this, he called unto him the knights that were of kin to Sir Lancelot, and they banded together to make a great charge, and threw Sir Lancelot's horse to the ground, and by misfortune the spear of Sir Bors broke, and its head was left in Sir Lancelot's side. When Sir Lavaine saw that, he unhorsed the King of Scots, and brought his horse to Sir Lancelot, and helped him mount thereon and gave him a spear, with which Sir Lancelot smote Sir Bors to the earth and Sir Ector de Maris, the foster-father of King Arthur, and buffeted sorely the knights that were with them. Afterwards he hurled himself into the thick mêlée of them all, and did the most wonderful deeds that ever were heard of. And Sir Lavaine likewise did well that day, for he smote down full two Knights of the Round Table. 'Mercy,' again cried Sir Gawaine to Arthur, 'I marvel what knight that is with the red sleeve.'

'That you shall know soon,' said King Arthur, and commanded that the trumpets should be blown, and declared that the prize belonged to the knight with the white shield, who bare the red sleeve, for he had unhorsed more than thirty knights. And the kings and lords who were of his party came round him and thanked him for the help he had given them, by which means the honours of the day had been theirs.

'Fair lords,' said Sir Lancelot, 'if I have deserved thanks, I have paid for them sorely, for I shall hardly escape with my life, therefore I pray you let me depart, for my hurt is grievous.' Then he groaned piteously, and galloped from them to a wood's side, followed by Sir Lavaine. 'Oh help me, Sir Lavaine,' said he, 'to get this spear's head out of my side, for it is killing me.' But Sir Lavaine feared to touch it, lest Sir Lancelot should bleed to death. 'I charge you,' said Sir Lancelot, 'if you love me draw out the head,' so Sir Lavaine drew it out. And Sir Lancelot gave a great shriek, and a marvellous grisly groan, and his blood flowed out so fast, that he fell into a swoon. 'Oh what shall I do?' cried Sir Lavaine, and he loosed Sir Lancelot's helm and coat of mail, and turned him so that the wind might blow on him, but for full half an hour he lay as if he had been dead. And at last Sir Lancelot opened his eyes, and said, 'O Lavaine, help me on my horse, for two miles from this place there lives a hermit who once was a Knight of the Round Table, and he can heal my wounds.' Then Sir Lavaine, with much ado, helped him on his horse, and brought him bleeding to the hermit. The hermit looked at him as he rode up, leaning piteously on his saddle-bow, and he thought that he should know him, but could not tell who he was for the paleness of his face, till he saw by a wound on his cheek that it was Sir Lancelot.

'You cannot hide your name from me,' said the hermit, 'for you are the noblest knight in the world, and well I know you to be Sir Lancelot.'

'Since you know me, sir,' said he, 'help me for God's sake, and for death or life put me out of this pain.'

'Fear nothing,' answered the hermit, 'your pain will soon be gone,' and he called his servants to take the armour off the knight, and laid him in bed. After that he dressed the wound, and gave him good wine to drink, and Sir Lancelot slept and awoke free of his pain. So we will leave him to be healed of his wound, under the care of the hermit, and go back to King Arthur.

* * *

Now it was the custom in those days that after a tourney was finished, a great feast should be held at which both parties were assembled, so King Arthur sent to ask the King of Northgalis, where was the knight with the red sleeve, who had fought on his side. 'Bring him before me,' he said, 'that he may have the prize he has won, which is his right.' Then answered the king with the hundred knights, 'we fear the knight must have been sore hurt, and that neither you nor we are ever like to see him again, which is grievous to think of.'

'Alas!' said King Arthur, 'is he then so badly wounded? What is his name?'

'Truly,' said they all, 'we know not his name, nor whence he came, nor whither he went.'

'As for me,' answered King Arthur, 'these tidings are the worst that I have heard these seven years, for I would give all the lands I hold that no harm had befallen this knight.'

'Do you know him?' asked they all.

'Whether I know him or not,' said King Arthur, 'I shall not tell you, but may heaven send me good news of him.'

'Amen,' answered they.

'By my head,' said Sir Gawaine, 'if this good knight is really wounded unto death, it is a great evil for all this land, for he is one of the noblest that ever I saw for handling a sword or spear. And if he may be found, I shall find him, for I am sure he is not far from this town,' so he took his squire with him, and they rode all round Camelot, six or seven miles on every side, but nothing could they hear of him. And he returned heavily to the court of King Arthur.

Two days after the king and all his company set out for London, and by the way, it happened to Sir Gawaine to lodge with Sir Bernard at Astolat. And when he was in his chamber, Sir Bernard and his daughter Elaine came unto Sir Gawaine, to ask him tidings of the court, and who did best in the tourney at Winchester.

'Truly,' said Sir Gawaine, 'there were two knights that bare white shields, but one of them had a red sleeve upon his helm, and he was one of the best knights that ever I saw joust in the field, for I dare say he smote down forty Knights of the Round Table.'

'Now blessed be God,' said the Maid of Astolat, 'that that knight sped so well, for he is the man in the world that I loved first, and he will also be the last that ever I shall love.'

'Fair maid,' asked Sir Gawaine, 'is that knight your love?'

'Certainly he is my love,' said she.

'Then you know his name?' asked Sir Gawaine.

'Nay, truly,' answered the damsel, 'I know neither his name, nor whence he cometh, but I love him for all that.'

'How did you meet him first?' asked Sir Gawaine. At that she told him the whole story, and how her brother went with Sir Lancelot to do him service, and lent him the white shield of her brother Sir Tirre and left his own shield with her. 'Why did he do that?' asked Sir Gawaine.

'For this cause,' said the damsel, 'his shield was too well known among many noble knights.'

'Ah, fair damsel,' said Sir Gawaine, 'I beg of you to let me have a sight of that shield.'

'Sir,' answered she, 'it is in my chamber covered with a case, and if you will come with me, you shall see it.'

'Not so,' said Sir Bernard, and sent his squire for it. And when Sir Gawaine took off the case and beheld the shield, and saw the arms, he knew it to be Sir Lancelot's. 'Ah mercy,' cried he, 'my heart is heavier than ever it was before!'

'Why?' asked Elaine.

'I have great cause,' answered Sir Gawaine. 'Is that knight who owns this shield your love?'

'Yes, truly,' said she; 'I would I were his love.'

'You are right, fair damsel,' replied Gawaine, 'for if you love him, you love the most honourable knight in the world. I have known him for four-and-twenty years, and never did I or any other knight see him wear a token of either lady or damsel at a tournament. Therefore, damsel, he has paid you great honour. But I fear that I may never behold him again upon earth, and that is grievous to think of.'

'Alas!' she said, 'how may this be? Is he slain?'

'I did not say that,' replied Sir Gawaine, 'but he is sorely wounded, and is more likely to be dead than alive. And, maiden, by this shield I know that he is Sir Lancelot.'

'How can this be?' said the Maid of Astolat, 'and what was his hurt?'

'Truly,' answered Sir Gawaine, 'it was the man that loved him best who hurt him so, and I am sure that if that man knew that it was Sir Lancelot whom he had wounded, he would think it was the darkest deed that ever he did.'

'Now, dear father,' said Elaine, 'give me leave to ride and to seek him, for I shall go out of my mind unless I find him and my brother.'

'Do as you will,' answered her father, 'for I am grieved to hear of the hurt of that noble knight.' So the damsel made ready.

On the morn Sir Gawaine came to King Arthur and told him how he had found the shield in the keeping of the Maid of Astolat. 'All that I knew beforehand,' said the king, 'and that was why I would not suffer you to fight at the tourney, for I had espied him when he entered his lodging the night before. But this is the first time that ever I heard of his bearing the token of some lady, and much I marvel at it.'

'By my head,' answered Sir Gawaine, 'the Fair Maiden of Astolat loves him wondrous well. What it all means, or what will be the end, I cannot say, but she has ridden after him to seek him.' So the king and his company came to London, and everyone in the court knew that it was Sir Lancelot who had jousted the best.

And when the tidings came to Sir Bors, his heart grew heavy, and also the hearts of his kinsmen. But when the queen heard that Sir Lancelot bore the red sleeve of the Fair Maid of Astolat, she was nearly mad with wrath, and summoned Sir Bors before her in haste.

'Ah, Sir Bors,' she cried when he was come, 'have the tidings reached you that Sir Lancelot has been a false knight to me?'

'Madam,' answered Sir Bors, 'I pray you say not so, for I cannot hear such language of him.'

'Why, is he not false and a traitor when, after swearing that for right or wrong he would be my knight and mine only, he bore the red sleeve upon his helm at the great jousts at Camelot?'

'Madam,' said Sir Bors, 'I grieve bitterly as to that sleeve-bearing, but I think he did it that none of his kin should know him. For no man before that had seen him bear the token of any lady, be she what she may.'

'Fie on him!' said the queen, 'I myself heard Sir Gawaine tell my lord Arthur of the great love that is between the Fair Maiden of Astolat and him.'

'Madam,' answered Sir Bors, 'I cannot hinder Sir Gawaine from saying what he pleases, but as for Sir Lancelot, I am sure that he loves no one lady or maiden better than another. And therefore I will hasten to seek him wherever he be.'

Meanwhile fair Elaine came to Winchester to find Sir Lancelot, who lay in peril of his life in the hermit's dwelling. And when she was riding hither and thither, not knowing where she should turn, she fell on her brother Sir Lavaine, who was exercising his horse. 'How doth my lord Sir Lancelot?' asked she.

'Who told you, sister, that my lord's name was Sir Lancelot?' answered Sir Lavaine.

'Sir Gawaine, who came to my father's house to rest after the tourney, knew him by his shield,' said she, and they rode on till they reached the hermitage, and Sir Lavaine brought her to Sir Lancelot. And when she saw him so pale, and in such a plight, she fell to the earth in a swoon, but by-and-bye she opened her eyes and said, 'My lord Sir Lancelot, what has brought you to this?' and swooned again. When she came to herself and stood up, Sir Lancelot prayed her to be of good cheer, for if she had come to comfort him she was right welcome, and that his wound would soon heal. 'But I marvel,' said he, 'how you know my name.' Then the maiden told him how Sir Gawaine had been at Astolat and had seen his shield.

'Alas!' sighed Sir Lancelot, 'it grieves me that my name is known, for trouble will come of it.' For he knew full well that Sir Gawaine would tell Queen Guenevere, and that she would be wroth. And Elaine stayed and tended him, and Sir Lancelot begged Sir Lavaine to ride to Winchester and ask if Sir Bors was there, and said that he should know him by token of a wound which Sir Bors had on his forehead. 'For well I am sure,' said Sir Lancelot, 'that Sir Bors will seek me, as he is the same good knight that hurt me.'

Therefore as Sir Lancelot commanded, Sir Lavaine rode to Winchester and enquired if Sir Bors had been seen there, so that when he entered the town Sir Lavaine readily found him. Sir Bors was overjoyed to hear good tidings of Sir Lancelot, and they rode back together to the hermitage. At the sight of Sir Lancelot lying in his bed, pale and thin, Sir Bors's heart gave way, and he wept long without speaking. 'Oh, my lord Sir Lancelot,' he said at last, 'God send you hasty recovery; great is my shame for having wounded you thus, you who are the noblest knight in the world. I wonder that my arm would lift itself against you, and I ask your mercy.'

'Fair cousin,' answered Sir Lancelot, 'such words please me not at all, for it is the fault of my pride which would overcome you all, that I lie here today. We will not speak of it any more, for what is done cannot be undone, but let us find a cure so that I may soon be whole.' Then Sir Bors leaned upon his bed, and told him how the queen was filled with anger against him, because he wore the red sleeve at the jousts.

'I am sorrowful at what you tell me,' replied Sir Lancelot, 'for all I did was to hinder my being known.'

'That I said to excuse you,' answered Sir Bors, 'though it was all in vain. But is this damsel that is so busy about you the Fair Maid of Astolat?'

'She it is, and she will not go from me!'

'Why should she go from you?' asked Sir Bors.

'She is a passing fair damsel, and of gentle breeding, and I would that you could love her, for it is easy to see by her bearing that she loves you entirely.'

'It grieves me to hear that,' said Sir Lancelot.

After this they talked of other things, till in a few days Sir Lancelot's wounds were whole again. When Sir Lancelot felt his strength return, Sir Bors made him ready, and departed for the court of King Arthur, and told them how he had left Sir Lancelot.

And there was on All Hallows a great tournament, and Sir Bors won the prize for the unhorsing of twenty knights, and Sir Gareth did great deeds also, but vanished suddenly from the field, and no man knew where he had gone. After the tourney was over, Sir Bors rode to the hermitage to see Sir Lancelot, whom he found walking on his feet, and on the next morning they bade farewell to the hermit, taking with them Elaine le Blanc. They went first to Astolat, where they were well lodged in the house of Sir Bernard, but when the morrow came, and Sir Lancelot would have departed from them, Elaine called to her father and to her brothers Sir Tirre and Sir Lavaine, and thus she said: 'My lord Sir Lancelot, fair knight, leave me not, I pray you, but have mercy upon me, and suffer me not to die of love of thee.'

'What do you wish me to do?' asked Sir Lancelot.

'I would have you for my husband,' answered she.

'Fair damsel, I thank you,' said Sir Lancelot, 'but truly I shall never have a wife. But in token and thanks of all your good will towards me, gladly will I give a thousand pounds yearly when you set your heart upon some other knight.'

'Of such gifts I will have none,' answered Elaine, 'and I would have you know, Sir Lancelot, that if you refuse to wed me, my good days are done.'

'Fair damsel,' said Sir Lancelot, 'I cannot do the thing that you ask.'

At these words she fell down in a swoon, and her maids bore her to her chamber, where she made bitter sorrow. Sir Lancelot thought it would be well for him to depart before she came to her senses again, and he asked Sir Lavaine what he would do.

'What should I do?' asked Sir Lavaine, 'but follow you if you will have me.'

Then Sir Bernard came and said to Sir Lancelot, 'I see well that my daughter Elaine will die for your sake.'

'I cannot marry her,' answered Sir Lancelot, 'and it grieves me sorely, for she is a good maiden, fair and gentle.'

'Father,' said Sir Lavaine, 'she is as pure and good as Sir Lancelot has said, and she is like me, for since first I saw him I can never leave him.' And after that they bade the old man farewell and came unto Winchester, where the king and all the knights of the Round Table made great joy of him, save only Sir Agrawaine and Sir Mordred. But the queen was angry and would not speak to him, though he tried by all means to make her.

Now when the Fair Maid of Astolat knew he was gone, she would neither eat nor sleep, but cried after Sir Lancelot all the day long. And when she had spent ten days in this manner, she grew so weak that they thought her soul must quit this world, and the priest came to her, and bade her dwell no more on earthly things. She would not listen to him, but cried ever after Sir Lancelot, and how she had loved none other, no, nor ever would, and that her love would be her death. Then she called her father, Sir Bernard, and her brother, Sir Tirre, and begged her brother to write her a letter as she should tell him, and her father that he would have her watched till she was dead. 'And while my body is warm,' said she, 'let this letter be put in my right hand, and my hand bound fast with the letter until I be cold, and let me be dressed in my richest clothes and be lain on a fair bed, and driven in a chariot to the Thames. There let me be put on a barge, and a dumb man with me, to steer the barge, which shall be covered over with black samite. Thus, father, I beseech you, let it be done.' And her father promised her faithfully that so it should be done to her when she was dead. Next day she died, and her body was lain on the bed, and placed in a chariot, and driven to the Thames, where the man awaited her with the barge. When she was put on board, he steered the barge to Westminster and rowed a great while to and fro, before any espied it. At last King Arthur and Queen Guenevere withdrew into a window to speak together, and espied the black barge, and wondered greatly what it meant. The king summoned Sir Kay, and bade him take Sir Brandiles and Sir Agrawaine, and find out who was lying there, and they ran down to the river side, and came and told the king. 'That fair corpse will I see,' returned the king, and he took the queen's hand and led her thither. Then he ordered the barge to be made fast, and he entered it, and the queen likewise, and certain knights with them. And there he saw a fair woman on a rich bed, and her clothing was of cloth of

THE BLACK BARGET

gold, and she lay smiling. While they looked, all being silent, the queen spied a letter in her right hand, and pointed it out to the king, who took it saying, 'Now I am sure this letter will tell us what she was, and why she came hither.' So leaving the barge in charge of a trusty man, they went into the king's chamber, followed by many knights, for the king would have the letter read openly. He then broke the seal himself, and bade a clerk read it, and this was what it said: 'Most noble knight Sir Lancelot, I was your lover, whom men called the Fair Maid of Astolat: therefore unto all ladies I make my moan; yet pray for my soul, and bury me. This is my last request. Pray for my soul, Sir Lancelot, as thou art peerless.'

This was all the letter, and the king and queen and all the knights wept when they heard it.

'Let Sir Lancelot be sent for,' presently said the king, and when Sir Lancelot came the letter was read to him also.

'My lord Arthur,' said he, after he had heard it all, 'I am right grieved at the death of this damsel. God knows I was not, of my own will, guilty of her death, and that I will call on her brother, Sir Lavaine, to witness. She was both fair and good, and much was I beholden to her, but she loved me out of measure.'

'You might have been a little gentle with her,' answered the queen, 'and have found some way to save her life.'

'Madam,' said Sir Lancelot, 'she would have nothing but my

love, and that I could not give her, though I offered her a thousand pounds yearly if she should set her heart on any other knight. For, madam, I love not to be forced to love; love must arise of itself, and not by command.'

'That is truth,' replied the king, 'love is free in himself, and never will be bounden; for where he is bounden he looseth himself. But, Sir Lancelot, be it your care to see that the damsel is buried as is fitting.'

Lancelot and Guenevere

Now we come to the sorrowful tale of Lancelot and Guenevere, and of the death of King Arthur. Already it has been told that King Arthur had wedded Guenevere, the daughter of Leodegrance, King of Cornwall, a damsel who seemed made of all the flowers, so fair was she, and slender, and brilliant to look upon. And the knights in her father's court bowed down before her, and smote their hardest in the jousts where Guenevere was present, but none dared ask her in marriage till Arthur came. Like the rest he saw and loved her, but, unlike them, he was a king, and might lift his eyes even unto Guenevere. The maiden herself scarcely saw or spoke to him, but did her father's bidding in all things, and when he desired her to make everything ready to go clothed as beseemed a princess to King Arthur's court, her heart beat with joy at the sight of rich stuffs and shining jewels. Then one day there rode up to the castle a band of horsemen sent by the king, to bring her to his court, and at the head of them Sir Lancelot du Lake, friend of King Arthur, and winner of all the jousts and tournaments where knights meet to gain honour. Day by day they rode together apart and he told her tales of gallant deeds done for love of beautiful ladies, and they passed under trees gay with the first green of spring, and over hyacinths covering the earth with sheets of blue, till at sunset they drew rein before the silken pavilion, with the banner of Uther Pendragon floating on the top. And Guenevere's heart went out to Lancelot before she knew.

One evening she noted, far across the plain, towers and buildings shining in the sun, and an array of horsemen ride forth to meet her. One stopped before her dazzled eyes, and leaping from his horse bowed low. Arthur had come to welcome her, and do her honour, and to lead her home. But looking up at him, she thought him cold, and, timid and alone, her thoughts turned again to Lancelot. After that the days and years slipped by, and these two were ever nearest the king, and in every time of danger the king cried for Lancelot, and trusted his honour and the queen's to him. Sir Lancelot spoke truly when he told Elaine that he had never worn the badge of lady or maiden, but for all that everyone looked on Sir Lancelot as the queen's knight, who could do no worship to any other woman. The king likewise held Sir Lancelot bound to fight the queen's battles, and if he was absent on adventures of his own, messengers hastened to bring him back, as in the fight with Sir Mador. So things went on for many years, and the king never guessed that the queen loved Lancelot best.

It befell one spring, in the month of May, that Queen Guenevere bethought herself that she would like to go a-maying in the woods and fields that lay round the City of Westminster on both sides of the river. To this intent she called her own especial knights, and bade them be ready the next morning clothed all in green, whether of silk or cloth, 'and,' said she, 'I shall bring with me ten ladies, and every knight shall have a lady behind him, and be followed by a squire and two yeomen, and I will that you shall all be well horsed.' Thus it was done, and the ten knights, arrayed in fresh green, the emblem of the spring, rode with the queen and her ladies in the early dawn, and smelt the sweet of the year, and gathered flowers which they stuck in their girdles and doublets. The queen was as happy and light of heart as the youngest maiden, but she had promised to be with the king at the hour of ten, and gave the signal for departure unwillingly. The knights were mounting their horses, when suddenly out of a wood on the other side rode Sir Meliagraunce, who for many years had loved the queen, and had sought an occasion to carry her off, but found none so fair as this. Out of the forest he rode, with two score men in armour, and a hundred archers behind him, and bade the queen and her followers stay where they were, or they would fare badly. 'Traitor,' cried the queen, 'what evil deed would you do? You are a king's son and a Knight of the Round Table, yet you seek to shame the man who gave you knighthood. But I tell you that you may bring dishonour on yourself, but you will bring none on me, for rather would I cut my throat in twain.'

'As for your threats, madam, I pay them no heed,' returned Sir Meliagraunce; 'I have loved you many a year, and never could I get you at such an advantage as I do now, and therefore I will take you as I find you.' Then all the knights spoke together saying, 'Sir Meliagraunce, bethink yourself that in attacking men who are unarmed you put not only our lives in peril but your own honour. Rather than allow the queen to be shamed we will each one fight to the death, and if we did aught else we should dishonour our knighthood for ever.'

'Fight as well as you can,' answered Sir Meliagraunce, 'and keep the queen if you may.' So the Knights of the Round Table drew their swords, and the men of Sir Meliagraunce ran at them with spears; but the knights stood fast, and clove the spears in two before they touched them. Then both sides fought with swords, and Sir Kay and five other knights were felled to the ground with wounds all over their bodies. The other four fought long, and slew forty of the men and archers of Sir Meliagraunce; but in the end they too were overcome. When the queen saw that she cried out for pity and sorrow, 'Sir Meliagraunce, spare my noble knights and I will go with you quietly on this condition, that their lives be saved, and that wherever you may carry me they shall follow. For I give you warning that I would rather slay myself than go with you without my knights, whose duty it is to guard me.'

'Madam,' replied Sir Meliagraunce, 'for your sake they shall be led with you into my own castle, if you will consent to ride with me.' So the queen prayed the four knights to fight no more, and she and they would not part, and to this, though their hearts were heavy, they agreed.

The fight being ended the wounded knights were placed on horseback, some sitting, some lying across the saddle, according as they were hurt, and Sir Meliagraunce forbade anyone to leave the castle (which had been a gift to him from King Arthur), for sore he dreaded the vengeance of Sir Lancelot if this thing should reach his ears. But the queen knew well what was passing in his mind, and she called a little page who served her in her chamber and desired him to take her ring and hasten with all speed to Sir Lancelot, 'and pray him, if he loves me, to rescue me. Spare not your horse, neither for water nor for land.' And the boy bided his time, then mounted his horse, and rode away as fast as he might. Sir Meliagraunce spied him as he flew, and knew whither he went, and who had sent him; and he commanded his best archers to ride after him and shoot him ere he reached Sir Lancelot. But the boy escaped their arrows, and vanished from their sight. Then Sir Meliagraunce said to the queen, 'You seek to betray me, madam; but Sir Lancelot shall not so lightly come at you.' And he bade his men follow him to the castle in haste, and left an ambush of thirty archers in the road, charging them that if a knight mounted on a white horse came along that way they were to slay the horse but to leave the man alone, as he was hard to overcome. After Sir Meliagraunce had given these orders his company galloped fast to the castle; but the queen would listen to nothing that he said, demanding always that her knights and ladies should be lodged with her, and Sir Meliagraunce was forced to let her have her will.

Guenevere Sends her Page
to Lancelot for Help

The castle of Sir Meliagraunce was distant seven miles from Westminster, so it did not take long for the boy to find Sir Lancelot, and to give him the queen's ring and her message. 'I am shamed for ever,' said Sir Lancelot, 'unless I can rescue that noble lady,' and while he put on his armour, he called to the boy to tell him the whole adventure. When he was armed and mounted, he begged the page to warn Sir Lavaine where he had gone, and for what cause. 'And pray him, as he loves me, that he follow me to the castle of Sir Meliagraunce, for if I am a living man, he will find me there.'

Sir Lancelot put his horse into the water at Westminster, and he swam straight over to Lambeth, and soon after he landed he found traces of the fight. He rode along the track till he came to the wood, where the archers were lying waiting for him, and when they saw him, they bade him on peril of his life to go no further along that path.

'Why should I, who am a Knight of the Round Table, turn out of any path that pleases me?' asked Sir Lancelot.

'Either you will leave this path or your horse will be slain,' answered the archers.

'You may slay my horse if you will,' said Sir Lancelot, 'but when my horse is slain I shall fight you on foot, and so would I do, if there were five hundred more of you.' With that they smote the horse with their arrows, but Sir Lancelot jumped off, and ran into the wood, and they could not catch him. He went on some way, but the ground was rough, and his armour was heavy, and sore he dreaded the treason of Sir Meliagraunce. His heart was near to fail him, when there passed by a cart with two carters that came to fetch wood. 'Tell me, carter,' asked Sir Lancelot, 'what will you take to suffer me to go in your cart till we are within two miles of the castle of Sir Meliagraunce?'

'I cannot take you at all,' answered the carter, 'for I am come to fetch wood for my lord Sir Meliagraunce.'

'It is with him that I would speak.'

'You shall not go with me,' said the carter, but hardly had he uttered the words when Sir Lancelot leapt up into the cart, and gave him such a buffet that he fell dead on the ground. At this sight the other carter cried that he would take the knight where he would if he would only spare his life. 'Then I charge you,' said Sir Lancelot, 'that you bring me to the castle gate.' So the carter drove at a great gallop, and Sir Lancelot's horse, who had espied his master, followed the cart, though more than fifty arrows were standing in his body. In an hour and a half they reached the castle gate, and were seen of Guenevere and her ladies, who were standing in a window. 'Look, madam,' cried one of her ladies, 'in that cart yonder is a goodly armed knight. I suppose he is going to his hanging.'

'Where?' asked the queen, and as she spoke she espied that it was Sir Lancelot, and that his horse was following riderless. 'Well is he that has a trusty friend,' said she, 'for a noble knight is hard pressed when he rides in a cart,' and she rebuked the lady who had declared he was going to his hanging. 'It was foul talking, to liken the noblest knight in the world to one going to a shameful death.' By this Sir Lancelot had come to the gate of the castle, and he got down and called till the castle rang with his voice. 'Where is that false traitor Sir Meliagraunce, Knight of the Round Table? Come forth, you and your company, for I, Sir Lancelot du Lake, am here to do battle with you.' Then he burst the gate open wide, and smote the porter who tried to hold it against him. When Sir Meliagraunce heard Sir Lancelot's voice, he ran into Queen Guenevere's chamber, and fell on his knees before her: 'Mercy, madam, mercy! I throw myself upon your grace.'

'What ails you now?' said she; 'of a truth I might well expect some good knight to avenge me, though my lord Arthur knew not of your work.'

'Madam, I will make such amends as you yourself may desire,' pleaded Sir Meliagraunce, 'and I trust wholly to your grace.'

'What would you have me do?' asked the queen.

Guenevere sends her page to Lancelot for help

'Rule in this castle as if it were your own, and give Sir Lancelot cheer till tomorrow, and then you shall all return to Westminster.'

'You say well,' answered the queen. 'Peace is ever better than war, and I take no pleasure in fighting.' So she went down with her ladies to Sir Lancelot, who still stood full of rage in the inner court, calling as before, 'Traitor knight, come forth!'

'Sir Lancelot,' asked the queen, 'what is the cause of all this wrath?'

'Madam,' replied Sir Lancelot, 'does such a question come from you? Methinks your wrath should be greater than mine, for all the hurt and the dishonour have fallen upon you. My own hurt is but little, but the shame is worse than any hurt.'

'You say truly,' replied the queen, 'but you must come in with me peaceably, as all is put into my hand, and the knight repents bitterly of his adventure.'

'Madam,' said Sir Lancelot, 'since you have made agreement with him, it is not my part to say nay, although Sir Meliagraunce has borne himself both shamefully and cowardly towards me. But had I known you would have pardoned him so soon, I should not have made such haste to come to you.'

'Why do you say that?' asked the queen; 'do you repent yourself of your good deeds? I only made peace with him to have done with all this noise of slanderous talk, and for the sake of my knights.'

'Madam,' answered Sir Lancelot, 'you understand full well that I was never glad of slander nor noise, but there is neither king, queen nor knight alive, save yourself, madam, and my lord Arthur, that should hinder me from giving Sir Meliagraunce a cold heart before I departed hence.'

'That I know well,' said the queen, 'but what would you have more? Everything shall be ordered as you will.'

'Madam,' replied Sir Lancelot, 'as long as you are pleased, that is all I care for,' so the queen led Sir Lancelot into her chamber, and commanded him to take off his armour, and then took him to where her ten knights were lying sore wounded. And their souls leapt with joy when they saw him, and he told them how falsely Sir Meliagraunce had dealt with him, and had set archers to slay his

THE ARCHERS THREATEN LANCELOT

horse, so that he was fain to place himself in a cart. Thus they complained each to the other, and would have avenged themselves on Sir Meliagraunce but for the peace made by the queen. And in the evening came Sir Lavaine, riding in great haste, and Sir Lancelot was glad that he was come.

Now Sir Lancelot was right when he feared to trust Sir Meliagraunce, for that knight only sought to work ill both to him and to the queen, for all his fair words. And first he began to speak evil of the queen to Sir Lancelot, who dared him to prove his foul words, and it was settled between them that a combat should take place in eight days in the field near Westminster. 'And now,' said Sir Meliagraunce, 'since it is decided that we must fight together, I beseech you, as you are a noble knight, do me no treason nor villainy in the meantime.'

'Any knight will bear me witness,' answered Sir Lancelot, 'that never have I broken faith with any man, nor borne fellowship with those that have done so.' 'Then let us go to dinner,' said Sir Meliagraunce, 'and afterwards you may all ride to Westminster. Meanwhile would it please you to see the inside of this castle?' 'That I will gladly,' said Sir Lancelot, and they went from chamber to chamber, till they reached the floor of the castle, and as he went Sir Lancelot trod on a trap, and the board rolled, and he fell down in a cave which was filled with straw, and Sir Meliagraunce departed and no man knew where Sir Lancelot might be. The queen bethought herself that he was wont to disappear suddenly, and as Sir Meliagraunce had first removed Sir Lavaine's horse from the place where it had been tethered, the knights agreed with her. So time passed till dinner had been eaten, and then Sir Lavaine demanded litters for the wounded knights, that they might be carried to Westminster with as little hurt as might be. And the queen and her ladies followed. When they arrived, the knights told of their adventure, and how Sir Meliagraunce had accused the queen of treason, and how he and Sir Lancelot were to fight for her good name in eight days.

'Sir Meliagraunce has taken a great deal upon him,' said the king, 'but where is Sir Lancelot?'

'Sir,' answered they all, 'we know not, but we think he has ridden

GUENEVERE SENDS HER PAGE TO LANCELOT

to some adventure.' 'Well, leave him alone,' said the king. 'He will be here when the day comes, unless some treason has befallen him.'

All this while Sir Lancelot was lying in great pain within the cave, and he would have died for lack of food had not one of the ladies in the castle found out the place where he was held captive, and brought him meat and drink, and hoped that he might be brought to love her. But he would not. 'Sir Lancelot,' said she, 'you are not wise, for without my help you will never get out of this prison, and if you do not appear on the day of battle, your lady, Queen Guenevere, will be burnt in default.' 'If I am not there,' replied Sir Lancelot, 'the king and the queen and all men of worship will know that I am either dead or in prison. And sure I am that there is some good knight who loves me or is of my kin, that will take my quarrel in hand, therefore you cannot frighten me by such words as these. If there was not another woman in the world, I could give you no different answer.' 'Then you will be shamed openly,' replied the lady, and left the dungeon. But on the day that the battle was to be fought she came again, and said, 'Sir Lancelot, if you will only kiss me once, I will deliver you, and give you the best horse in Sir Meliagraunce's stable.' 'Yes, I will kiss you,' answered Sir Lancelot, 'since I may do that honourably; but if I thought it were any shame to kiss you, I would not do it, whatever the cost.' So he kissed her, and she brought him his armour, and led him to a stable where twelve noble horses stood, and bade him choose the best. He chose a white courser, and bade the keepers put on the best saddle they had, and with his spear in his hand and his sword by his side, he rode away, thanking the lady for all she had done for him, which some day he would try to repay.

As the hours passed on and Sir Lancelot did not come, Sir Meliagraunce called ever on King Arthur to burn the queen, or else bring forth Sir Lancelot, for he deemed full well that he had Sir Lancelot safe in his dungeon. The king and queen were sore distressed that Sir Lancelot was missing, and knew not where to look for him, and what to do. Then stepped forth Sir Lavaine and said, 'My lord Arthur, you know well that some ill-fortune has happened to Sir Lancelot, and if he is not dead, he is either sick or in prison.

Therefore I beseech you, let me do battle instead of my lord and master for my lady the queen.'

'I thank you heartily, gentle knight,' answered Arthur, 'for I am sure that Sir Meliagraunce accuses the queen falsely, and there is not one of the ten knights who would not fight for her were it not for his wounds. So do your best, for it is plain that some evil has been wrought on Sir Lancelot.' Sir Lavaine was filled with joy when the king gave him leave to do battle with Sir Meliagraunce, and rode swiftly to his place at the end of the lists. And just as the heralds were about to cry 'Lesses les aler!' Sir Lancelot dashed into the middle on his white horse. 'Hold and abide!' commanded the king, and Sir Lancelot rode up before him, and told before them all how Sir Meliagraunce had treated him. When the king and queen and all the lords heard Sir Lancelot's tale, their hearts stirred within them with anger, and the queen took her seat by the king, in great trust of her champion. Sir Lancelot and Sir Meliagraunce prepared themselves for battle, and took their spears, and came together as thunder, and Sir Lancelot bore Sir Meliagraunce right over his horse. Then Sir Lancelot jumped down, and they fought on foot, till in the end Sir Meliagraunce was smitten to the ground by a blow on his head from his enemy. 'Most noble knight, save my life,' cried he, 'for I yield myself unto you, and put myself into the king's hands and yours.' Sir Lancelot did not know what to answer, for he longed above anything in the world to have revenge upon him; so he looked at the queen to see whether she would give him any sign of what she would have done. The queen wagged her head in answer, and Sir Lancelot knew by that token that she would have him dead, and he understood, and bade Sir Meliagraunce get up, and continue the fight. 'Nay,' said Sir Meliagraunce, 'I will never rise till you accept my surrender.' 'Listen,' answered Sir Lancelot. 'I will leave my head and left side bare, and my left arm shall be bound behind me, and in this guise I will fight with you.' At this Sir Meliagraunce started to his feet, and cried, 'My lord Arthur, take heed to this offer, for I will take it, therefore let him be bound and unarmed as he has said.' So the knights disarmed Sir Lancelot, first his head and then his side, and his left hand was bound behind his back, in such a manner that he could not use his shield, and full many a knight and lady marvelled that Sir Lancelot would risk himself so. And Sir Meliagraunce lifted his sword on high and would have smitten Sir Lancelot on his bare head, had he not leapt lightly to one side, and, before Sir Meliagraunce could right himself, Sir Lancelot had struck him so hard upon his helmet that his skull split in two, and there was nothing left to do but to carry his dead body from the field. And because the Knights of the Round Table begged to have him honourably buried, the king agreed thereto, and on his tomb mention was made of how he came by his death, and who slew him. After this Sir Lancelot was more cherished by the king and queen than ever he was before.

Among the many knights at Arthur's court who owned kings for their fathers were Sir Mordred and Sir Agrawaine, who had for brothers Sir Gawaine, Sir Gaheris, and Sir Gareth. And their mother was Queen of Orkney, sister to King Arthur. Now Sir Agrawaine and Sir Mordred had evil natures, and loved both to invent slanders and to repeat them. And at this time they were full of envy of the noble deeds Sir Lancelot had done, and how men called him the bravest Knight of the Round Table, and said that he was the friend of the king, and the sworn defender of the queen. So they cast about how they might ruin him, and found the way by putting jealous thoughts into the mind of Arthur.

As was told in the tale of the marriage of Arthur, Queen Guenevere's heart had gone out to Lancelot, on the journey to the court, and ever she loved to have him with her. This was known well to Sir Mordred, who watched eagerly for a chance to work her ill.

It came one day when Arthur proclaimed a hunt, and Sir Mordred guessed that Sir Lancelot, who did not love hunting, would stay behind, and would spend the time holding talk with the queen. Therefore he went to the king and began to speak evil of the queen and Sir Lancelot. At first King Arthur would listen to nothing, but slowly his jealousy burned within him, and he let the ill words that accused the queen of loving Sir Lancelot the best, sink into his mind, and told Sir Mordred and Sir Agrawaine that they might do their worst, and he would not meddle with them. But they let so many of their fellowship into the secret of their foul plot, that at last it came to the ears of Sir Bors, who begged Sir Lancelot not to go near the queen that day, or harm would come of it. But Sir Lancelot answered that the queen had sent for him, and that she was his liege lady, and never would he hold back when she summoned him to her presence. Therefore Sir Bors went heavily away. By ill fortune, Sir Lancelot only wore his sword under his great mantle, and scarcely had he passed inside the door when Sir Agrawaine and Sir Mordred, and twelve other Knights of the Round Table, all armed and ready for battle, cried loudly upon Sir Lancelot, that all the court might hear.

'Madam,' said Sir Lancelot, 'is there any armour within your chamber that I might cover my body withal, for if I was armed as they are I would soon crush them?'

'Alas!' replied the queen, 'I have neither sword nor spear nor armour, and how can you resist them? You will be slain and I shall be burnt. If you could only escape their hands, I know you would deliver me from danger.'

'It is grievous,' said Sir Lancelot, 'that I who was never conquered in all my life should be slain for lack of armour.'

'Traitor knight,' cried Sir Mordred again, 'come out and fight us, for you are so sore beset that you cannot escape us.'

'Oh, mercy,' cried Sir Lancelot, 'I may not suffer longer this shame and noise! For better were death at once than to endure this pain.' Then he took the queen in his arms and kissed her, and said, 'Most noble Christian queen, I beseech you, as you have ever been my special good lady, and I at all times your true poor knight, and as I never failed you in right or in wrong, since the first day that King Arthur made me knight, that you will pray for my soul, if I be here slain. For I am well assured that Sir Bors, my nephew, and Sir Lavaine and many more, will rescue you from the fire, and therefore, mine own lady, comfort yourself whatever happens to me, and go with Sir Bors, my nephew, and you shall live like a queen on my lands.'

'Nay, Lancelot,' said the queen, 'I will never live after your days, but if you are slain I will take my death as meekly as ever did any Christian queen.'

'Well, madam,' answered Lancelot, 'since it is so I shall sell my life as dear as I may, and a thousandfold I am more heavy for you than for myself.'

Therewith Sir Lancelot wrapped his mantle thickly round his arm, and stood beside the door, which the knights without were trying to break in by aid of a stout wooden form.

'Fair lords,' said Sir Lancelot, 'leave this noise, and I will open the door, and you may do with me what you will.'

'Open it then,' answered they, 'for well you know you cannot escape us, and we will save your life and bring you before King Arthur.' So Sir Lancelot opened the door and held it with his left hand, so that but one man could come in at once. Then came forward a strong knight, Sir Colgrevance of Gore, who struck fiercely at Lancelot with his sword. But Sir Lancelot stepped on one side, that the blow fell harmless, and with his arm he gave Sir Colgrevance a buffet on the head so that he fell dead. And Sir Lancelot drew him into the chamber, and barred the door.

Hastily he unbuckled the dead knight's armour, and the queen and her ladies put it on him, Sir Agrawaine and Sir Mordred ever calling to him the while, 'Traitor knight, come out of that chamber!' But Sir Lancelot cried to them all to go away and he would appear next morning before the king, and they should accuse him of what they would, and he would answer them, and prove his words in battle. 'Fie on you, traitor,' said Sir Agrawaine, 'we have you in our power, to save or to slay, for King Arthur will listen to our words, and will believe what we tell him.'

'As you like,' answered Sir Lancelot, 'look to yourself,' and he flung open the chamber door, and strode in amongst them and killed Sir Agrawaine with his first blow, and in a few minutes the bodies of the other twelve knights lay on the ground beside his, for no man ever withstood that buffet of Sir Lancelot's. He wounded Sir Mordred also, so that he fled away with all his might. When the clamour of the battle was still, Sir Lancelot turned back to the queen and said, 'Alas, madam, they will make King Arthur my foe, and yours also, but if you will come with me to my castle, I will save you from all dangers.'

'I will not go with you now,' answered the queen, 'but if you see tomorrow that they will burn me to death, then you may deliver me as you shall think best.'

'While I live I will deliver you,' said Sir Lancelot, and he left her and went back to his lodging. When Sir Bors, who was awaiting him, saw Sir Lancelot, he was gladder than he ever had been in his whole life before. 'Mercy!' cried Sir Lancelot, 'why, you are all armed!'

'Sir,' answered Sir Bors, 'after you had left us I and your friends and your kinsmen were so troubled that we felt some great strife was at hand, and that perchance some trap had been laid for you. So we put on armour that we might help you whatever need you were in.' 'Fair nephew,' said Lancelot, 'but now I have been more hardly beset than ever I was in my life, and yet I escaped,' and he told them all that had happened. 'I pray you, my fellows, that you will be of good courage and stand by me in my need, for war is come to us all.'

'Sir,' answered Sir Bors, 'all is welcome that God sends us, and we have had much good with you and much fame, so now we will take the bad as we have taken the good.' And so said they all.

'I thank you for your comfort in my great distress,' replied Sir Lancelot, 'and you, fair nephew, haste to the knights which be in this place, and find who is with me and who is against me, for I would know my friends from my foes.'

'Sir,' said Sir Bors, 'before seven of the clock in the morning you shall know.'

By seven o'clock, as Sir Bors had promised, many noble knights stood before Sir Lancelot, and were sworn to his cause. 'My lords,' said he, 'you know well that since I came into this country I have given faithful service unto my lord King Arthur and unto my lady Queen Guenevere. Last evening my lady, the queen, sent for me to speak to her, and certain knights that were lying in wait for me cried, "Treason", and much ado I had to escape their blows. But I slew twelve of them, and Sir Agrawaine, who is Sir Gawaine's brother; and for this cause I am sure of mortal war, as these knights were ordered by King Arthur to betray me, and therefore the queen will be judged to the fire, and I may not suffer that she should be burnt for my sake.'

And Sir Bors answered Sir Lancelot that it was truly his part to rescue the queen, as he had done so often before, and that if she was burned the shame would be his. Then they all took counsel together how the thing might best be done, and Sir Bors deemed it wise to carry her off to the Castle of Joyous Gard, and counselled that she should be kept there, a prisoner, till the king's anger was past and he would be willing to welcome her back again. To this the other knights agreed, and by the advice of Sir Lancelot they hid themselves in a wood close by the town till they saw what King Arthur would do.

Meanwhile Sir Mordred, who had managed to escape the sword of Sir Lancelot, rode, wounded and bleeding, unto King Arthur, and told the king all that had passed, and how, of the fourteen knights, he only was left alive. The king grieved sore at his tale, which Sir Mordred had made to sound as ill as was possible; for, in spite of all, Arthur loved Sir Lancelot. 'It is a bitter blow,' he said, 'that Sir Lancelot must be against me, and the fellowship of the Round Table is broken for ever, as many a noble knight will go with him. And as I am the judge, the queen will have to die, as she is the cause of the death of these thirteen knights.'

'My lord Arthur,' said Sir Gawaine, 'be not overhasty; listen not to the foul tongue of Sir Mordred, who laid this trap for Sir Lancelot, that we all know to be the queen's own knight, who has done battle for her when none else would. As for Sir Lancelot, he will prove the right on the body of any knight living that shall accuse him of wrong – either him, or my lady Guenevere.'

'That I believe well,' said King Arthur, 'for he trusts so much in his own might that he fears no man; and never more shall he fight for the queen, for she must suffer death by the law. Put on, therefore, your best armour, and go with your brothers, Sir Gaheris and Sir Gareth, and bring the queen to the fire, there to have her judgment and suffer her death.'

'Nay, my lord, that I will never do,' cried Sir Gawaine; 'my heart will never serve me to see her die, and I will never stand by and see so noble a lady brought to a shameful end.'

'Then,' said the king, 'let your brothers, Sir Gaheris and Sir Gareth, be there.'

'My lord,' replied Sir Gawaine, 'I know well how loth they will be, but they are young and unable to say you nay.'

At this Sir Gaheris and Sir Gareth spoke to King Arthur: 'Sir, if you command us we will obey, but it will be sore against our will. And if we go we shall be dressed as men of peace, and wear no armour.'

'Make yourselves ready, then,' answered the king, 'for I would delay no longer in giving judgment.'

'Alas!' cried Sir Gawaine, 'that I should have lived to see this day'; and he turned and wept bitterly, and went into his chamber.

So the queen was led outside the gates, and her rich dress was taken off, while her lords and ladies wrung their hands in grief, and few men wore armour, for in that day it was held that the presence of mail-clad knights made death more shameful. Now among those present was one sent by Sir Lancelot, and when he saw the queen's dress unclasped, and the priest step forth to listen to her confession, he rode to warn Sir Lancelot that the hour had come. And suddenly there was heard a sound as of rushing horses, and Sir Lancelot dashed up to the fire, and all the knights that stood around were slain, for few men wore armour. Sir Lancelot looked not where he struck, and Sir Gaheris and Sir Gareth were found in the thickest of the throng. At last he reached the queen, and, throwing a mantle over her, he caught her on to his saddle and rode away with her. Right thankful was the queen at being snatched from the fire, and her heart was grateful to Sir Lancelot, who took her to his Castle of Joyous Gard, and many noble knights and kings had fellowship with them.

After King Arthur had given judgment for the queen to die he went back into his palace of Westminster, where men came and told him how Sir Lancelot had delivered her, and of the death of his knights, and in especial of Sir Gaheris and Sir Gareth, and he swooned away from sorrow. 'Alas!' he cried, when he recovered from his swoon, 'alas! that a crown was ever on my head, for in these two days I have lost forty knights and the fellowship of Sir Lancelot and his kinsmen, and never more will they be of my company. But I charge you that none tell Sir Gawaine of the death

LANCELOT COMES OVT OF GVENEVERE'S ROOM

of his brothers, for I am sure that when he hears of Sir Gareth he will go out of his mind. Oh, why did Sir Lancelot slay them? for Sir Gareth loved Sir Lancelot more than any other man.'

'That is true,' answered some of the knights, 'but Sir Lancelot saw not whom he smote, and therefore were they slain.'

'The death of those two,' said Arthur, 'will cause the greatest mortal war that ever was. I am sure that when Sir Gawaine knows Sir Gareth is slain he will never suffer me to rest till I have destroyed Sir Lancelot and all his kin, or till they have destroyed me. My heart was never so heavy as it is now, and far more grievous to me is the loss of my good knights than of my queen; for queens I might have in plenty, but no man had ever such a company of knights, and it hurts me sore that Sir Lancelot and I should be at war. It is the ill will borne by Sir Agrawaine and Sir Mordred to Sir Lancelot that has caused all this sorrow.' Then one came to Sir Gawaine and told him that Sir Lancelot had borne off the queen, and that twenty-four knights had been slain in the combat. 'I knew well he would deliver her,' said Sir Gawaine, 'and in that, he has but acted as a knight should and as I would have done myself. But where are my brethren? I marvel they have not been to seek me.'

'Truly,' said the man, 'Sir Gaheris and Sir Gareth are slain.'

'Heaven forbid any such thing,' returned Sir Gawaine. 'I would not for all the world that that had happened, especially to my brother, Sir Gareth.'

'He is slain,' said the man, 'and it is grievous news.'

'Who slew him?' asked Sir Gawaine.

'Sir Lancelot slew them both,' answered the man.

'He cannot have slain Sir Gareth,' replied Sir Gawaine, 'for my brother Gareth loved him better than me and all his brethren, and King Arthur too. And had Sir Lancelot desired my brother to go with him, he would have turned his back on us all. Therefore I can never believe that Sir Lancelot slew my brother.'

'Sir, it is in everyone's mouth,' said the man. At this Sir Gawaine fell back in a swoon and lay long as if he were dead. Then he ran to the king crying, 'O King Arthur, mine uncle, my good brother Sir Gareth is slain, and Sir Gaheris also,' and the king wept with him.

At length Sir Gawaine said, 'Sir, I will go and see my brother Sir Gareth.'

'You cannot do that,' returned the king, 'for I have caused him to be buried with Sir Gaheris, as I knew well that the sight would cause you overmuch sorrow.'

'How came he, Sir Lancelot, to slay Sir Gareth?' asked Sir Gawaine; 'mine own good lord, I pray you tell me, for neither Sir Gareth nor Sir Gaheris bore arms against him.'

'It is said,' answered the king, 'that Sir Lancelot slew them in the thickest of the press and knew them not. Therefore let us think upon a plan to avenge their deaths.'

'My king, my lord and mine uncle,' said Sir Gawaine, 'I swear to you by my knighthood that from this day I will never rest until Sir Lancelot or I be slain. And I will go to the world's end till I find him.'

'You need not seek him so far,' answered the king, 'for I am told that Sir Lancelot will await me and you in the Castle of Joyous Gard, and many people are flocking to him. But call your friends together, and I will call mine,' and the king ordered letters to be sent throughout all England summoning his knights and vassals to the siege of Joyous Gard. The Castle of Joyous Gard was strong, and after fifteen weeks had passed no breach had been made in its walls. And one day, at the time of harvest, Sir Lancelot came forth on a truce, and the king and Sir Gawaine challenged him to do battle.

'Nay,' answered Sir Lancelot, 'with yourself I will never strive, and I grieve sorely that I have slain your knights. But I was forced to it, for the saving of my life and that of my lady the queen. And except yourself, my lord, and Sir Gawaine, there is no man that shall call me traitor but he shall pay for it with his body. As to Queen Guenevere, oft times, my lord, you have consented in the heat of your passion that she should be burnt and destroyed, and it fell to me to do battle for her, and her enemies confessed their untruth, and acknowledged her innocent. And at such times, my lord Arthur, you loved me and thanked me when I saved your queen from the fire, and promised ever to be my good lord, for I have fought for her many times in other quarrels than my own. Therefore, my gracious lord, take your queen back into your grace again.'

To these words of Sir Lancelot's King Arthur answered nothing, but in his heart he would fain have made peace with Sir Lancelot, but Sir Gawaine would not let him. He reproached Sir Lancelot bitterly for the deaths of his brothers and kinsmen, and called Sir Lancelot a craven and other ill names that he would not fight with King Arthur. So at the last Sir Lancelot's patience and courtesy failed him, and he told them that the next morning he would give them battle.

The heart of Sir Gawaine leaped with joy when he heard these words of Sir Lancelot, and he summoned all his friends and his kinsfolk, and bade them watch well Sir Lancelot, and to slay him if a chance offered. But he knew not that Sir Lancelot had bidden the knights of his following in no wise to touch King Arthur or Sir Gawaine. And when the dawn broke a great host marched out of the Castle of Joyous Gard, with Sir Lancelot at the head, and Sir Bors and Sir Lionel commanding on either side. All that day they fought, and sometimes one army seemed to be gaining, and sometimes the other. Many times King Arthur drew near Sir Lancelot, and would have slain him, and Sir Lancelot suffered him, and would not strike again. But the king was unhorsed by Sir Bors, and would have been slain but for Sir Lancelot, who stayed his hand. 'My lord Arthur,' he said, 'for God's love stop this strife. I cannot strike you, so you will gain no fame by it, though your friends never cease from trying to slay me. My lord, remember what I have done in many places and how evil is now my reward.' Then when King Arthur was on his horse again he looked on Sir Lancelot, and tears burst from his eyes, thinking of the great courtesy that was in Sir Lancelot more than in any other man. He sighed to himself, saying softly, 'Alas! that ever this war began,' and rode away, while the battle ended for that time and the dead were buried.

But Sir Gawaine would not suffer the king to make peace, and they fought on, now in one place, and now in another, till the Pope heard of the strife and sent a noble clerk, the Bishop of Rochester, to charge the king to make peace with Sir Lancelot, and to take back unto him his queen, the Lady Guenevere. Now the king, as has been said, would fain have followed the Pope's counsel and have accorded with Sir Lancelot, but Sir Gawaine would not suffer him. However, as to the queen Sir Gawaine said nothing; and King Arthur gave audience to the bishop, and swore on his great seal that he would take back the queen as the Pope desired, and that if Sir Lancelot brought her he should come safe and go safe. So the bishop rode to Joyous Gard and showed Sir Lancelot what the Pope had written and King Arthur had answered, and told him of the perils which would befall him if he withheld the queen. 'It was never in my thought,' answered Sir Lancelot, 'to withhold the queen from King Arthur, but as she would have been dead for my sake it was my part to save her life, and to keep her from danger till better times came. And I thank God that the Pope has made peace, and I shall be a thousand times gladder to bring her back than I was to take her away. Therefore ride to the king, and say that in eight days I myself will bring the Lady Guenevere unto him.' So the bishop departed, and came to the king at Carlisle and told him what Sir Lancelot had answered, and tears burst from the king's eyes once more.

A goodly host of a hundred knights rode eight days later from the Castle of Joyous Gard; every knight was clothed in green velvet, and held in his hand a branch of olive, and bestrode a horse with trappings down to his heels. And behind the queen were four and twenty gentlewomen clad in green likewise, while twelve esquires attended on Sir Lancelot. He and the queen wore dresses of white and gold tissue, and their horses were clothed in housings of the same, set with precious stones and pearls; and no man had ever gazed on such a noble pair, as they rode from Joyous Gard to Carlisle. When they reached the castle, Sir Lancelot sprang from his horse and helped the queen from hers, and led her to where King Arthur sat, with Sir Gawaine and many lords around him. He kneeled down, and the queen kneeled with him, and many knights wept as though it had been their own kin. But Arthur sat still and said nothing.

At that Sir Lancelot rose, and the queen likewise, and, looking straight at the king, he spoke: 'Most noble king, I have brought to you my lady the queen, as right requires; and time hath been, my lord Arthur, that you have been greatly pleased with me when I did battle for my lady your queen. And full well you know that she has been put to great wrong ere this, and it seems to me I had more cause to deliver her from this fire, seeing she would have been burnt for my sake.'

'Well, well, Sir Lancelot,' said the king, 'I have given you no cause to do to me as you have done, for I have held you dearer than any of my knights.' But Sir Gawaine would not suffer the king to listen to anything Sir Lancelot said, and told him roughly that while one of them lived peace could never be made, and desired on behalf of the king that in fifteen days he should be gone out of the country. And still King Arthur said nothing, but suffered Sir Gawaine to talk as he would; and Sir Lancelot took farewell of him and of the queen, and rode, grieving sorely, out of the court, and sailed to his lands beyond the sea.

Though the queen was returned again, and Sir Lancelot was beyond the sea, the hate of Sir Gawaine towards him was in no way set at rest, but he raised a great host and persuaded the king to follow him. And after many sieges and long fighting Sir Gawaine did battle with Sir Lancelot once more, and was worsted, and Sir Lancelot might have slain him, but would not. While he lay wounded tidings came to King Arthur from England that caused the king to give up his war with Sir Lancelot and return in all haste to his own country.

The End of it All

Now when King Arthur left England to fight with Sir Lancelot he ordered his nephew Sir Mordred to govern the land, which that false knight did gladly. And as soon as he thought he might safely do so he caused some letters to be written saying that King Arthur had been slain in battle, and he had himself crowned king at Canterbury, where he made a great feast which lasted fifteen days. After it was over, he went to Winchester and summoned Queen Guenevere, and told her that on a certain day he would wed her and that she should make herself ready. Queen Guenevere's soul grew cold and heavy as she heard these words of Sir Mordred's, for she hated him with all her might, as he hated her; but she dared show nothing, and answered softly that she would do his bidding, only she desired that first she might go to London to buy all manner of things for her wedding. Sir Mordred trusted her because of her fair speech, and let her go. Then the queen rode to London with all speed, and went straight to the Tower, which she filled in haste with food, and called her men-at-arms round her. When Sir Mordred knew how she had beguiled him he was wroth out of measure, and besieged the Tower, and assaulted it many times with battering rams and great engines, but could prevail nothing, for the queen would never, for fair speech nor for foul, give herself into his hands again.

The Bishop of Canterbury hastened unto Sir Mordred, and rebuked him for wishing to marry his uncle's wife.

'Leave such desires,' said the bishop, 'or else I shall curse you with bell, book, and candle. Also, you noise abroad that my lord Arthur is slain, and that is not so, and therefore you will make ill work in the land.' At this Sir Mordred waxed very wroth, and would have killed the bishop had he not fled to Glastonbury, where he became a hermit, and lived in poverty and prayed all day long for the realm, for he knew that a fierce war was at hand. Soon word came to Sir Mordred that King Arthur was hurrying home across the seas, to be avenged on his nephew, who had proved traitor. Wherefore Sir Mordred sent letters to all the people throughout the kingdom, and many followed after him, for he had cunningly sown among them that with him was great joy and softness of life, while King Arthur would bring war and strife with him. So Sir Mordred drew with a great host to Dover, and waited for the king. Before King Arthur and his men could land from the boats and ships that had brought them over the sea Sir Mordred set upon them, and there was heavy slaughter. But in the end he and his men were driven back, and he fled, and his people with him. After the fight was over the king ordered the dead to be buried; and there came a man and told him that he had found Sir Gawaine lying in a boat, and that he was sore wounded. And the king went to him, and made moan over him: 'You were ever the man in the world that I loved most,' said he; 'you and Sir Lancelot.' 'Mine uncle King Arthur,' answered Sir Gawaine, 'my death day has come, and all through my own fault. Had Sir Lancelot been with you as he used to be this unhappy war had never begun, and of that I am the cause, for I would not accord with him. And therefore, I pray you, give me paper, pen, and ink that I may write to him.' So paper and ink were brought, and Sir Gawaine was held up by King Arthur, and a letter was writ wherein Sir Gawaine confessed that he was dying of an old wound given him by Sir Lancelot in the siege of one of the cities across the sea, and thus was fulfilled the prophecy of Merlin. 'Of a more noble man might I not be slain,' said he. 'Also, Sir Lancelot, make no tarrying, but come in haste to King Arthur, for sore bested is he with my brother Sir Mordred, who has taken the crown, and would have wedded my lady Queen Guenevere had she not sought safety in the Tower of London. Pray for my soul, I beseech you, and visit my tomb.' And after writing this letter, at the hour of noon, Sir Gawaine gave up his spirit, and was buried by the king in the chapel within Dover Castle. Then was it told King Arthur that Sir Mordred had pitched a new field upon Barham Down, and the next morning the king rode hither to him, and there was a fierce battle between them, and many on both sides were slain. But at the last King Arthur's party stood best, and Sir Mordred and his men fled to Canterbury.

After the knights which were dead had been buried, and those that were wounded tended with healing salves, King Arthur drew westwards towards Salisbury, and many of Sir Mordred's men followed after him, but they that loved Sir Lancelot went unto Sir Mordred. And a day was fixed between the king and Sir Mordred that they should meet upon a down near Salisbury, and give battle once more. But the night before the battle Sir Gawaine appeared unto the king in a vision and warned him not to fight next day, which was Trinity Sunday, as he would be slain and many of his knights also; but to make a truce for a month, and at the end of that time Sir Lancelot would arrive, and would slay Sir Mordred, and all his knights with him. As soon as he awoke the king called the bishops and the wisest men of his army, and told them of his vision, and took counsel what should be done. And it was agreed that the king should send an embassage of two knights and two bishops unto Sir Mordred, and offer him as much goods and lands as they thought best if he would engage to make a treaty for a month with King Arthur.

So they departed, and came to Sir Mordred, where he had a grim host of a hundred thousand men. For a long time he would not suffer himself to be entreated, but at the last he agreed to have Cornwall and Kent in King Arthur's days, and after all England. Furthermore, it was decided that King Arthur and Sir Mordred should meet in the plain between their hosts, each with fourteen persons. 'I am glad of this,' said King Arthur, when he heard what had been done; but he warned his men that if they were to see a sword drawn they were to come on swiftly and slay that traitor, Sir Mordred, 'for I in no wise trust him'. And in like wise spake Sir Mordred unto his host. Then they two met, and agreed on the truce, and wine was fetched and they drank, and all was well. But while they were drinking an adder crept out of a bush, and stung one of the fourteen knights on his foot, and he drew his sword to slay the adder, not thinking of anything but his pain. And when the men of both armies beheld that drawn sword, they blew trumpets and horns and shouted grimly, and made them ready for battle. So King Arthur leaped on his horse, and Sir Mordred on his, and they went back to their own armies, and thus began the fight, and never was there seen one more doleful in any Christian land. For all day long there was rushing and riding, spearing and striking, and many a grim word was there spoken, and many a deadly stroke given. And at the end full a hundred thousand dead men lay upon the down, and King Arthur had but two knights left living, Sir Lucan and his brother, Sir Bedivere. 'Alas! that I should have lived to see this day,' cried the king, 'for now I am come to mine end; but would to God that I knew where were that traitor Sir Mordred that hath caused all this mischief.' Then suddenly he saw Sir Mordred leaning on his sword among a great heap of dead men.

'Give me my spear,' said King Arthur unto Sir Lucan.

'Sir, let him be,' answered Sir Lucan. 'Remember your dream, and leave off by this. For, blessed be God, you have won the field, and we three be alive, and of the others none is alive save Sir Mordred himself. If you leave off now, the day of destiny is past.'

'Tide me death, tide me life,' said the king, 'he shall not escape my hands, for a better chance I shall never have,' and he took his spear in both hands and ran towards Sir Mordred, crying 'Traitor! now is your death day come,' and smote him under the shield, so that the spear went through his body. And when Sir Mordred felt he had his death wound, he raised himself up and struck King Arthur such a blow that the sword clave his helmet, and then fell stark dead on the earth again. When Sir Lucan and Sir Bedivere saw that sight they carried the king to a little chapel, but they hoped not to leave him there long, for Sir Lucan had noted that many people were stealing out to rob the slain of the ornaments on their armour. And those that were not dead already they slew.

'Would that I could quit this place to go to some large town,' said the king, when he had heard this, 'but I cannot stand, my head works so. Ah, Lancelot, sorely have I missed thee.' At that Sir Lucan and Sir Bedivere tried to lift him, but Sir Lucan had been grievously wounded in the fight, and the blood burst forth again as he lifted Arthur, and he died and fell at the feet of the king.

'Alas!' said the king, 'he has died for my sake, and he had more need of help than I. But he would not complain, his heart was so set to help me. And I should sorrow yet more if I were still to live long, but my time flieth fast. Therefore, Sir Bedivere, cease moaning and weeping, and take Excalibur, my good sword, and go with it to yonder water side, and when thou comest there, I charge thee, throw my sword in that water, and come again and tell me what thou hast seen.'

'My lord,' answered Sir Bedivere, 'your commandment shall be done,' and he departed. But when he looked at that noble sword, and beheld the jewels and gold that covered the pommel and hilt, he said to himself, 'If I throw this rich sword into the water no good will come of it, but only harm and loss'; so he hid Excalibur under a tree, and returned unto the king and told him his bidding was done. 'What did you see there?' asked the king.

'Sir,' answered Sir Bedivere, 'I saw nothing but the winds and waves.'

'You have not dealt truly with me,' said the king. 'Go back, and do my command; spare not, but throw it in.' But again Sir Bedivere's heart failed him, and he hid the sword, and returned to tell the king he had seen nothing but the wan water.

'Ah, traitor!' cried King Arthur, 'this is twice you have betrayed me. If you do not now fulfil my bidding, with mine own hands will I slay you, for you would gladly see me dead for the sake of my sword.' Then Sir Bedivere was shamed at having disobeyed the king, and drew forth the sword from its hiding place, and carried it to the water side, and with a mighty swing threw it far into the water. And as it flew through the air, an arm and hand lifted itself out of the water, and caught the hilt, and brandished the sword thrice, and vanished with it beneath the water. So Sir Bedivere came again unto the king, and told him what he saw.

'Alas!' said the king, 'help me hence, for I have tarried overlong,' and Sir Bedivere took him on his back, and bare him to the water side. And when they stood by the bank, a little barge containing many fair ladies and a queen, all in black hoods, drew near, and they wept and shrieked when they beheld King Arthur.

'Now put me into the barge,' said the king, and Sir Bedivere laid him softly down, and the ladies made great mourning and the barge rowed from the land.

'Ah, my lord Arthur!' cried Sir Bedivere, 'what shall become of me now you go from me, and I am left here alone with my enemies?'

'Comfort yourself,' replied the king, 'and do as well as you may, for I go unto the valley of Avilion, to be healed of my grievous wound. And if you never more hear of me, pray for my soul.'

But Sir Bedivere watched the barge till it was beyond his sight, then he rode all night till he came to a hermitage.

Now when Queen Guenevere heard of the battle, and how that King Arthur was slain and Sir Mordred and all their knights, she stole away, and five ladies with her, and rode to Amesbury; and there she put on clothes of black and white, and became a nun, and did great penance, and many alms deeds, and people marvelled at her and at her godly life. And ever she wept and moaned over the years that were past, and for King Arthur.

As soon as the messenger whom the king had sent with Sir Gawaine's letter reached Sir Lancelot, and he learned that Sir Mordred had taken for himself the crown of England, he rose up in wrath, and, calling Sir Bors, bid him collect their host, that they should pass at once over the sea to avenge themselves on that false knight. A fair wind blew them to Dover, and there Sir Lancelot asked tidings of King Arthur. Then the people told him that the king was slain, and Sir Mordred, and a hundred thousand men besides, and that the king had buried Sir Gawaine in the chapel at Dover Castle. 'Fair sirs,' said Sir Lancelot, 'show me that tomb'; and they showed it to him, and Sir Lancelot kneeled before it, and wept and prayed, and this he did for two days. And on the third morning he summoned before him all the great lords and leaders of his host, and said to them, 'Fair lords, I thank you all for coming here with me, but we come too late, and that will be bitter grief to me as long as I shall live. But since it is so, I will myself ride and seek my lady Guenevere in the west country, where they say she has gone, and tarry you here, I entreat you, for fifteen days, and if I should not return take your ships and depart into your own country.'

THE LAST BATTLE

H.J.FORD

Sir Mordred

Sir Bors strove to reason with him that the quest was fruitless, and that in the west country he would find few friends; but his words availed nothing. For seven days Sir Lancelot rode, and at last he came to a nunnery, where Queen Guenevere was looking out from her lattice, and was aware of his presence as he walked in the cloister. And when she saw him she swooned, and her ladies and gentlewomen tended her. When she was recovered, she spoke to them and said, 'You will marvel, fair ladies, why I should swoon. It was caused by the sight of yonder knight who stands there, and I pray you bring him to me.' As soon as Sir Lancelot was brought she said to her ladies, 'Through me and this man has this war been wrought, for which I repent me night and day. Therefore, Sir Lancelot, I require and pray you never to see my face again, but go back to your own land, and govern it and protect it; and take to yourself a wife, and pray that my soul may be made clean of its ill doing.'

'Nay, madam,' answered Sir Lancelot, 'that shall I never do; but the same life that you have taken upon you, will I take upon me likewise.'

'If you will do so,' said the queen, 'it is well; but I may never believe but that you will turn to the world again.'

'Well, madam,' answered he, 'you speak as it pleases you, but you never knew me false to my promise, and I will forsake the world as you have done. For if in the quest of the Sangreal I had forsaken its vanities with all my heart and will, I had passed all knights in the quest, except Sir Galahad my son. And therefore, lady, since you have taken you to perfection, I must do so also, and if I may find a hermit that will receive me I will pray and do penance while my life lasts. Wherefore, madam, I beseech you to kiss me once again.'

'No,' said the queen, 'that I may not do,' and Sir Lancelot took his horse and departed in great sorrow. All that day and the next night he rode through the forest till he beheld a hermitage and a chapel between two cliffs, and heard a little bell ring to mass. And he that sang mass was the Bishop of Canterbury, and Sir Bedivere was with him. After mass Sir Bedivere told Sir Lancelot how King Arthur had thrown away his sword and had sailed to the valley of

EXCALIBVR RETURNS TO THE MERE

Avilion, and Sir Lancelot's heart almost burst for grief. Then he kneeled down and besought the bishop that he might be his brother. 'That I will, gladly,' said the bishop, and put a robe upon him.

After the fifteen days were ended, and still Sir Lancelot did not return, Sir Bors made the great host go back across the sea, while he and some of Sir Lancelot's kin set forth to seek all over England till they found Sir Lancelot. They rode different ways, and by fortune Sir Bors came one day to the chapel where Sir Lancelot was. And he prayed that he might stay and be one of their fellowship, and in six months six other knights were joined to them, and their horses went where they would, for the knights spent their lives in fasting and prayer, and kept no riches for themselves.

In this wise six years passed, and one night a vision came to Sir Lancelot in his sleep charging him to hasten unto Amesbury. 'By the time that thou come there,' said the vision, 'thou shalt find Queen Guenevere dead; therefore take thy fellows with thee and fetch her corpse, and bury it by the side of her husband, the noble King Arthur.'

Then Sir Lancelot rose up and told the hermit, and the hermit ordered him to make ready and to do all as the vision had commanded. And Sir Lancelot and seven of the other knights went on foot from Glastonbury to Amesbury, and it took them two days to compass the distance, for it was far and they were weak with fasting. When they reached the nunnery Queen Guenevere had been dead but half an hour, and she had first summoned her ladies to her, and told them that Sir Lancelot had been a priest for near a twelvemonth. 'And hither he cometh as fast as he may,' she said, 'to fetch my corpse, and beside my lord King Arthur he shall bury me. And I beseech Almighty God that I may never have power to see Sir Lancelot with my bodily eyes.' 'Thus,' said the ladies, 'she prayed for two days till she was dead.' Then Sir Lancelot looked upon her face and sighed, but wept little, and next day he sang mass. After that the queen was laid on a bier drawn by horses, and a hundred torches were carried round her, and Sir Lancelot and his fellows walked behind her singing holy chants, and at times one would come forward and throw incense on the dead. So they came to Glastonbury, and the Bishop of Canterbury sang a Requiem Mass over the queen, and she was wrapped in cloth, and placed first in a web of lead, and then in a coffin of marble, and when she was put into the earth Sir Lancelot swooned away.

'You are to blame,' said the hermit, when he awaked from his swoon, 'you ought not make such manner of sorrow.'

'Truly,' answered Sir Lancelot, 'I trust I do not displease God, but when I remember her beauty, and her nobleness, and that of the king, and when I saw his corpse and her corpse lie together, my heart would not bear up my body. And I remembered, too, that it was through me and my pride that they both came to their end.'

From that day Sir Lancelot ate so little food that he dwindled away, and for the most part was found kneeling by the tomb of King Arthur and Queen Guenevere. None could comfort him, and after six weeks he was too weak to rise from his bed. Then he sent for the hermit and to his fellows, and asked in a weary voice that they would give him the last rites of the Church; and begged that when he was dead his body might be taken to Joyous Gard, which some say is Alnwick and others Bamborough. That night the hermit had a vision that he saw Sir Lancelot being carried up to heaven by the angels, and he waked Sir Bors and bade him go and see if anything ailed Sir Lancelot. So Sir Bors went and Sir Lancelot lay on his bed, stark dead, and he smiled as he lay there. Then was there great weeping and wringing of hands, more than had been made for any man; but they placed him on the horse bier that had carried Queen Guenevere, and lit a hundred torches, and in fifteen days they reached Joyous Gard. There his body was laid in the choir, with his face uncovered, and many prayers were said over him. And there, in the midst of their praying, came Sir Ector de Maris, who for seven years had sought Sir Lancelot through all the land.

'Ah, Lancelot,' he said, when he stood looking beside his dead body, 'thou wert head of all Christian knights. Thou wert the courtliest knight that ever drew sword, and the faithfulest friend that ever bestrode a horse. Thou wert the goodliest knight that ever man has seen, and the truest lover that ever loved a woman.'

TALES OF TROY AND GREECE

Tales of Troy and Greece

Andrew Lang

with illustrations by
H. J. FORD

CONTENTS

ULYSSES THE SACKER OF CITIES

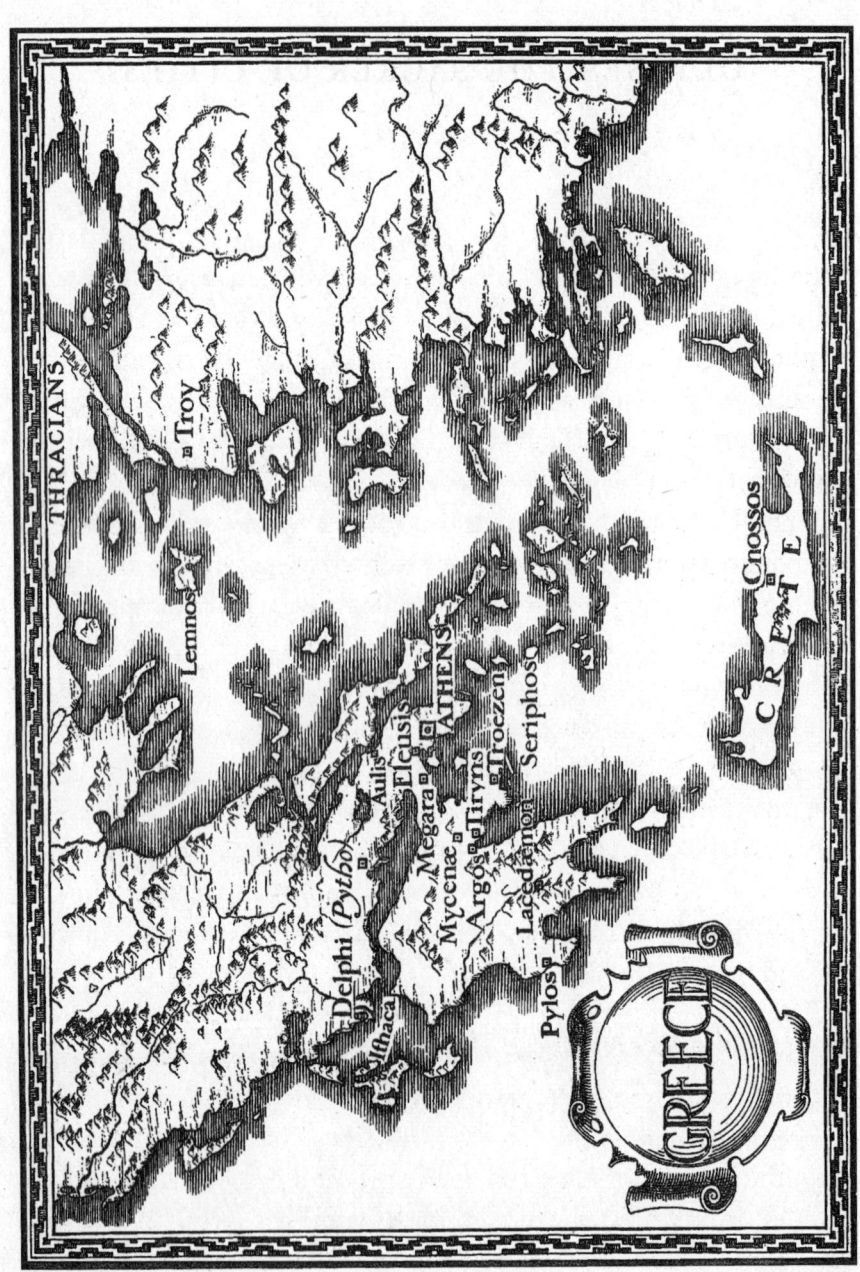

THRACIANS

Troy

Lemnos

Delphi (Pytho)

Aulis

Eleusis

Megara

Mycenæ

Argos

Tiryns

ATHENS

Trœzen

Seriphos

Lacedæmon

Pylos

Ithaca

Cnossos

CRETE

GREECE

CHAPTER ONE

The Boyhood and Parents of Ulysses

Long ago, in a little island called Ithaca, on the west coast of Greece, there lived a king named Laertes. His kingdom was small and mountainous. People used to say that Ithaca 'lay like a shield upon the sea', which sounds as if it were a flat country. But in those times shields were very large, and rose at the middle into two peaks with a hollow between them, so that Ithaca, seen far off in the sea, with her two chief mountain peaks, and a cloven valley between them, looked exactly like a shield. The country was so rough that men kept no horses, for, at that time, people drove, standing up in little light chariots with two horses; they never rode, and there was no cavalry in battle: men fought from chariots. When Ulysses, the son of Laertes, King of Ithaca grew up, he never fought from a chariot, for he had none, but always on foot.

If there were no horses in Ithaca, there was plenty of cattle. The father of Ulysses had flocks of sheep, and herds of swine, and wild goats, deer, and hares lived in the hills and in the plains. The sea was full of fish of many sorts, which men caught with nets, and with rod and line and hook.

Thus Ithaca was a good island to live in. The summer was long, and there was hardly any winter; only a few cold weeks, and then the swallows came back, and the plains were like a garden, all covered with wild flowers – violets, lilies, narcissus, and roses. With the blue sky and the blue sea, the island was beautiful. White temples stood on the shores; and the Nymphs, a sort of fairies, had their little shrines built of stone, with wild rose-bushes hanging over them.

Other islands lay within sight, crowned with mountains, stretching away, one behind the other, into the sunset. Ulysses in the course of his life saw many rich countries, and great cities of men, but, wherever he was, his heart was always in the little isle of Ithaca, where he had learned how to row, and how to sail a boat, and how to shoot with bow and arrow, and to hunt boars and stags, and manage his hounds.

The mother of Ulysses was called Anticleia: she was the daughter of King Autolycus, who lived near Parnassus, a mountain on the mainland. This King Autolycus was the most cunning of men. He was a master thief, and could steal a man's pillow from under his head, but he does not seem to have been thought worse of for this. The Greeks had a god of thieves, named Hermes, whom Autolycus worshipped, and people thought more good of his cunning tricks than harm of his dishonesty. Perhaps these tricks of his were only practised for amusement; however that may be, Ulysses became as artful as his grandfather; he was both the bravest and the most cunning of men, but Ulysses never stole things, except once, as we shall hear, from the enemy in time of war. He showed his cunning in stratagems of war, and in many strange escapes from giants and man-eaters.

Soon after Ulysses was born, his grandfather came to see his mother and father in Ithaca. He was sitting at supper when the nurse of Ulysses, whose name was Eurycleia, brought in the baby, and set him on the knees of Autolycus, saying, 'Find a name for your grandson, for he is a child of many prayers.'

'I am very angry with many men and women in the world,' said Autolycus, 'so let the child's name be "A Man of Wrath",' which, in Greek, was Odysseus. So the child was called Odysseus by his own people, but the name was changed into Ulysses, and we shall call him Ulysses.

We do not know much about Ulysses when he was a little boy, except that he used to run about the garden with his father, asking questions, and begging that he might have fruit trees 'for his very own'. He was a great pet, for his parents had no other son, so his father gave him thirteen pear trees, and forty fig trees, and promised him fifty rows of vines, all covered with grapes, which he

*Ulysses, when a youth, fights the wild boar
and gets his wound in his thigh*

could eat when he liked, without asking leave of the gardener. So he was not tempted to steal fruit, like his grandfather.

When Autolycus gave Ulysses his name, he said that he must come to stay with him, when he was a big boy, and he would get splendid presents. Ulysses was told about this, so, when he was a tall lad, he crossed the sea and drove in his chariot to the old man's house on Mount Parnassus. Everybody welcomed him, and next day his uncles and cousins and he went out to hunt a fierce wild boar, early in the morning. Probably Ulysses took his own dog, named Argos, the best of hounds, of which we shall hear again, long afterwards, for the dog lived to be very old. Soon the hounds came on the scent of a wild boar, and after them the men went, with spears in their hands, and Ulysses ran foremost, for he was already the swiftest runner in Greece.

He came on a great boar lying in a tangled thicket of boughs and bracken, a dark place where the sun never shone, nor could the rain pierce through. Then the noise of the men's shouts and the barking of the dogs awakened the boar, and up he sprang, bristling all over his back, and with fire shining from his eyes. In rushed Ulysses first of all, with his spear raised to strike, but the boar was too quick for him, and ran in, and drove his sharp tusk sideways, ripping up the thigh of Ulysses. But the boar's tusk missed the bone, and Ulysses sent his sharp spear into the beast's right shoulder, and the spear went clean through, and the boar fell dead, with a loud cry. The uncles of Ulysses bound up his wound carefully, and sang a magical song over it, as the French soldiers wanted to do to Joan of Arc when the arrow pierced her shoulder at the siege of Orleans. Then the blood ceased to flow, and soon Ulysses was quite healed of his wound. They thought that he would be a good warrior, and gave him splendid presents, and when he went home again he told all that had happened to his father and mother, and his nurse, Eurycleia. But there was always a long white mark or scar above his left knee, and about that scar we shall hear again, many years afterwards.

CHAPTER TWO

How People Lived in the Time of Ulysses

When Ulysses was a young man he wished to marry a princess of his own rank. Now there were at that time many kings in Greece, and you must be told how they lived. Each king had his own little kingdom, with his chief town, walled with huge walls of enormous stone. Many of these walls are still standing, though the grass has grown over the ruins of most of them, and in later years, men believed that those walls must have been built by giants, the stones are so enormous. Each king had nobles under him, rich men, and all had their palaces, each with its courtyard, and its long hall, where the fire burned in the midst, and the king and queen sat beside it on high thrones, between the four chief carved pillars that held up the roof. The thrones were made of cedar wood and ivory, inlaid with gold, and there were many other chairs and small tables for guests, and the walls and doors were covered with bronze plates, and gold and silver, and sheets of blue glass. Sometimes they were painted with pictures of bull hunts, and a few of these pictures may still be seen. At night torches were lit, and placed in the hands of golden figures of boys, but all the smoke of fire and torches escaped by a hole in the roof, and made the ceiling black. On the walls hung swords and spears and helmets and shields, which needed to be often cleaned from the stains of the smoke. The minstrel or poet sat beside the king and queen, and, after supper he struck his harp, and sang stories of old wars. At night the king and queen slept in their own place, and the women in their own rooms; the princesses had their chambers upstairs, and the young princes had each his room built separate in the courtyard.

There were bath rooms with polished baths, where guests were taken when they arrived dirty from a journey. The guests lay at night on beds in the portico, for the climate was warm. There were plenty of servants, who were usually slaves taken in war, but they were very kindly treated, and were friendly with their masters. No coined money was used; people paid for things in cattle, or in weighed pieces of gold. Rich men had plenty of gold cups, and gold-hilted swords, and bracelets, and brooches. The kings were the leaders in war and judges in peace, and did sacrifices to the gods, killing cattle and swine and sheep, on which they afterwards dined.

They dressed in a simple way, in a long smock of linen or silk, which fell almost to the feet, but was tucked up into a belt round the waist, and worn longer or shorter, as they happened to choose. Where it needed fastening at the throat, golden brooches were used, beautifully made, with safety pins. This garment was much like the plaid that the Highlanders used to wear, with its belt and brooches. Over it the Greeks wore great cloaks of woollen cloth when the weather was cold, but these they did not use in battle. They fastened their breastplates, in war, over their smocks, and had other armour covering the lower parts of the body, and leg armour called 'greaves'; while the great shield which guarded the whole body from throat to ankles was carried by a broad belt slung round the neck. The sword was worn in another belt, crossing the shield belt. They had light shoes in peace, and higher and heavier boots in war, or for walking across country.

The women wore the smock, with more brooches and jewels than the men; and had head coverings, with veils, and mantles over all, and necklaces of gold and amber, earrings, and bracelets of gold or of bronze. The colours of their dresses were various, chiefly white and purple; and, when in mourning, they wore very dark blue, not black. All the armour, and the sword blades and spear-heads were made, not of steel or iron, but of bronze, a mixture of copper and tin. The shields were made of several thicknesses of leather, with a plating of bronze above; tools, such as axes and ploughshares, were either of iron or bronze; and so were the blades of knives and daggers.

To us the houses and way of living would have seemed very

splendid, and also, in some ways, rather rough. The palace floors, at least in the house of Ulysses, were littered with bones and feet of the oxen slain for food, but this happened when Ulysses had been long from home. The floor of the hall in the house of Ulysses was not boarded with planks, or paved with stone: it was made of clay; for he was a poor king of small islands. The cooking was coarse: a pig or sheep was killed, roasted and eaten immediately. We never hear of boiling meat, and though people probably ate fish, we do not hear of their doing so, except when no meat could be procured. Still some people must have liked them; for in the pictures that were painted or cut in precious stones in these times we see the half-naked fisherman walking home, carrying large fish.

The people were wonderful workers of gold and bronze. Hundreds of their golden jewels have been found in their graves, but probably these were made and buried two or three centuries before the time of Ulysses. The dagger blades had pictures of fights with lions, and of flowers, inlaid on them, in gold of various colours, and in silver; nothing so beautiful is made now. There are figures of men hunting bulls on some of the gold cups, and these are wonderfully lifelike. The vases and pots of earthenware were painted in charming patterns: in short, it was a splendid world to live in.

The people believed in many gods, male and female, under the chief god, Zeus. The gods were thought to be taller than men, and immortal, and to live in much the same way as men did, eating, drinking, and sleeping in glorious palaces. Though they were supposed to reward good men, and to punish people who broke their oaths and were unkind to strangers, there were many stories told in which the gods were fickle, cruel, selfish, and set very bad examples to men. How far these stories were believed is not sure; it is certain that 'all men felt a need of the gods', and thought that they were pleased by good actions and displeased by evil. Yet, when a man felt that his behaviour had been bad, he often threw the blame on the gods, and said that they had misled him, which really meant no more than that 'he could not help it'.

There was a curious custom by which the princes bought wives from the fathers of the princesses, giving cattle and gold, and bronze and iron, but sometimes a prince got a wife as the reward for some very brave action. A man would not give his daughter to a wooer whom she did not love, even if he offered the highest price, at least this must have been the general rule, for husbands and wives were very fond of each other, and of their children, and husbands always allowed their wives to rule the house, and give their advice on everything. It was thought a very wicked thing for a woman to like another man better than her husband, and there were few such wives, but among them was the most beautiful woman who ever lived.

CHAPTER THREE

The Wooing of Helen of the Fair Hands

This was the way in which people lived when Ulysses was young, and wished to be married. The worst thing in the way of life was that the greatest and most beautiful princesses might be taken prisoners, and carried off as slaves to the towns of the men who had killed their fathers and husbands. Now at that time one lady was far the fairest in the world: namely, Helen, daughter of King Tyndarus. Every young prince heard of her and desired to marry her; so her father invited them all to his palace, and entertained them, and found out what they would give. Among the rest Ulysses went, but his father had a little kingdom, a rough island, with others near it, and Ulysses had not a good chance. He was not tall; though very strong and active, he was a short man with broad shoulders, but his face was handsome, and, like all the princes, he wore long yellow hair, clustering like a hyacinth flower. His manner was rather hesitating, and he seemed to speak very slowly at first, though afterwards his words came freely. He was good at everything a man can do; he could plough, and build houses, and make ships, and he was the best archer in Greece, except one, and could bend the great bow of a dead king, Eurytus, which no other man could string. But he had no horses, and had no great train of followers; and, in short, neither Helen nor her father thought of choosing Ulysses for her husband out of so many tall, handsome young princes, glittering with gold ornaments. Still, Helen was very kind to Ulysses, and there was great friendship between them, which was fortunate for her in the end.

Tyndarus first made all the princes take an oath that they would stand by the prince whom he chose, and would fight for him in all his quarrels. Then he named for her husband Menelaus, King of Lacedaemon. He was a very brave man, but not one of the strongest; he was not such a fighter as the gigantic Aias, the tallest and strongest of men; or as Diomede, the friend of Ulysses; or as his own brother, Agamemnon, the king of the rich city of Mycenae, who was chief over all other princes, and general of the whole army in war. The great lions carved in stone that seemed to guard his city are still standing above the gate through which Agamemnon used to drive his chariot.

The man who proved to be the best fighter of all, Achilles, was not among the lovers of Helen, for he was still a boy, and his mother, Thetis of the silver feet, a goddess of the sea, had sent him to be brought up as a girl, among the daughters of Lycomedes of Scyros, in an island far away. Thetis did this because Achilles was her only child, and there was a prophecy that, if he went to the wars, he would win the greatest glory, but die very young, and never see his mother again. She thought that if war broke out he would not be found hiding in girl's dress, among girls, far away.

So at last, after thinking over the matter for long, Tyndarus gave fair Helen to Menelaus, the rich King of Lacedaemon; and her twin sister Clytaemnestra, who was also very beautiful, was given to King Agamemnon, the chief over all the princes. They all lived very happily together at first, but not for long.

In the meantime King Tyndarus spoke to his brother Icarius, who had a daughter named Penelope. She also was very pretty, but not nearly so beautiful as her cousin, fair Helen, and we know that Penelope was not very fond of her cousin. Icarius, admiring the strength and wisdom of Ulysses, gave him his daughter Penelope to be his wife, and Ulysses loved her very dearly; no man and wife were ever dearer to each other. They went away together to rocky Ithaca, and perhaps Penelope was not sorry that a wide sea lay between her home and that of Helen; for Helen was not only the fairest woman that ever lived in the world, but she was so kind and gracious and charming that no man could see her without loving her. When she was only a child, the famous prince Theseus, who was famous in Greek Story, carried her away to his own city of Athens, meaning to marry her when she grew up, and even at that time, there was a war for her sake, for her brothers followed Theseus with an army, and fought him, and brought her home.

She had fairy gifts; for instance, she had a great red jewel, called 'the Star', and when she wore it red drops seemed to fall from it and vanished before they touched and stained her white breast – so white that people called her the 'Daughter of the Swan'. She could speak in the very voice of any man or woman, so folk also named her Echo, and it was believed that she could neither grow old nor die, but would at last pass away to the Elysian plain and the world's end, where life is easiest for men. No snow comes thither, nor great storm, nor any rain; but always the river of Ocean that rings round the whole earth sends forth the west wind to blow cool on the people of King Rhadamanthus of the fair hair. These were some of the stories that men told of fair Helen, but Ulysses was never sorry that he had not the fortune to marry her, so fond he was of her cousin, his wife, Penelope, who was very wise and good.

When Ulysses brought his wife home they lived, as the custom was, in the palace of his father, King Laertes, but Ulysses, with his own hands, built a chamber for Penelope and himself. There grew a great olive tree in the inner court of the palace, and its stem was as large as one of the tall carved pillars of the hall. Round about this tree Ulysses built the chamber, and finished it with close-set stones, and roofed it over, and made close-fastening doors. Then he cut off all the branches of the olive tree, and smoothed the trunk, and shaped it into the bedpost, and made the bedstead beautiful with inlaid work of gold and silver and ivory. There was no such bed in Greece, and no man could move it from its place, and this bed comes again into the story, at the very end.

Now time went by, and Ulysses and Penelope had one son called Telemachus; and Eurycleia, who had been his father's nurse, took care of him. They were all very happy, and lived in peace in rocky Ithaca, and Ulysses looked after his lands, and flocks, and herds, and went hunting with his dog Argos, the swiftest of hounds.

CHAPTER FOUR

The Stealing of Helen

This happy time did not last long, and Telemachus was still a baby, when war arose, so great and mighty and marvellous as had never been known in the world. Far across the sea that lies on the east of Greece, there dwelt the rich King Priam. His town was called Troy, or Ilios, and it stood on a hill near the seashore, where are the straits of Hellespont, between Europe and Asia; it was a great city surrounded by strong walls, and its ruins are still standing. The kings could make merchants who passed through the straits pay toll to them, and they had allies in Thrace, a part of Europe opposite Troy, and Priam was chief of all princes on his side of the sea, as Agamemnon was chief king in Greece. Priam had many beautiful things; he had a vine made of gold, with golden leaves and clusters, and he had the swiftest horses, and many strong and brave sons; the strongest and bravest was named Hector, and the youngest and most beautiful was named Paris.

There was a prophecy that Priam's wife would give birth to a burning torch, so, when Paris was born, Priam sent a servant to carry the baby into a wild wood on Mount Ida, and leave him to die or be eaten by wolves and wild cats. The servant left the child, but a shepherd found him, and brought him up as his own son. The boy became as beautiful, for a boy, as Helen was for a girl, and was the best runner, and hunter, and archer among the country people. He was loved by the beautiful Oenone, a nymph – that is, a kind of fairy – who dwelt in a cave among the woods of Ida. The Greeks and Trojans believed in these days that such fair nymphs haunted all beautiful woodland places, and the mountains, and wells, and had crystal palaces, like mermaids, beneath the waves of the sea. These fairies were not mischievous, but gentle and kind. Sometimes they married mortal men, and Oenone was the bride of Paris, and hoped to keep him for her own all the days of his life.

It was believed that she had the magical power of healing wounded men, however sorely they were hurt. Paris and Oenone lived most happily together in the forest; but one day, when the servants of Priam had driven off a beautiful bull that was in the herd of Paris, he left the hills to seek it, and came into the town of Troy. His mother, Hecuba, saw him, and looking at him closely, perceived that he wore a ring which she had tied round her baby's neck when he was taken away from her soon after his birth. Then Hecuba, beholding him so beautiful, and knowing him to be her son, wept for joy, and they all forgot the prophecy that he would be a burning torch of fire, and Priam gave him a house like those of his brothers, the Trojan princes.

The fame of beautiful Helen reached Troy, and Paris quite forgot unhappy Oenone, and must needs go to see Helen for himself. Perhaps he meant to try to win her for his wife, before her marriage. But sailing was little understood in these times, and the water was wide, and men were often driven for years out of their course, to Egypt, and Africa, and far away into the unknown seas, where fairies lived in enchanted islands, and cannibals dwelt in caves of the hills.

Paris came much too late to have a chance of marrying Helen; however, he was determined to see her, and he made his way to her palace beneath the mountain Taygetus, beside the clear swift river Eurotas. The servants came out of the hall when they heard the sound of wheels and horses' feet, and some of them took the horses to the stables, and tilted the chariots against the gateway, while others led Paris into the hall, which shone like the sun with gold and silver. Then Paris and his companions were led to the baths, where they were bathed, and clad in new clothes, mantles of white, and robes of purple, and next they were brought before King Menelaus, and he welcomed them kindly, and meat was set before them, and wine in cups of gold. While they were talking, Helen came forth from her fragrant chamber, like a goddess, her maidens following her, and carrying for her an ivory distaff with violet-coloured wool, which she span as she sat, and heard Paris tell how far he had travelled to see her who was so famous for her beauty even in countries far away.

Then Paris knew that he had never seen, and never could see, a lady so lovely and gracious as Helen as she sat and span, while the red drops fell and vanished from the ruby called the Star; and Helen knew that among all the princes in the world there was none so beautiful as Paris. Now some say that Paris, by art magic, put on the appearance of Menelaus, and asked Helen to come sailing with him, and that she, thinking he was her husband, followed him, and he carried her across the wide waters of Troy, away from her lord and her one beautiful little daughter, the child Hermione. And others say that the gods carried Helen herself off to Egypt, and that they made in her likeness a beautiful ghost, out of flowers and sunset clouds, whom Paris bore to Troy, and this they did to cause war between Greeks and Trojans. Another story is that Helen and her bower maiden and her jewels were seized by force, when Menelaus was out hunting. It is only certain that Paris and Helen did cross the seas together, and that Menelaus and little Hermione were left alone in the melancholy palace beside the Eurotas. Penelope, we know for certain, made no excuses for her beautiful cousin, but hated her as the cause of her own sorrows and of the deaths of thousands of men in war, for all the Greek princes were bound by their oath to fight for Menelaus against anyone who injured him and stole his wife away. But Helen was very unhappy in Troy, and blamed herself as bitterly as all the other women blamed her, and most of all Oenone, who had been the love of Paris. The men were much more kind to Helen, and were determined to fight to the death rather than lose the sight of her beauty among them.

The news of the dishonour done to Menelaus and to all the princes of Greece ran through the country like fire through a forest. East and west and south and north went the news: to kings in their castles on the hills, and beside the rivers and on cliffs above the sea. The cry came to ancient Nestor of the white beard at Pylos, Nestor who had reigned over two generations of men, who had fought against the wild folk of the hills, and remembered the strong

The stealing of Helen

Heracles, and Eurytus of the black bow that sang before the day of battle.

The cry came to black-bearded Agamemnon, in his strong town called 'golden Mycenae', because it was so rich; it came to the people in Thisbe, where the wild doves haunt; and it came to rocky Pytho, where is the sacred temple of Apollo and the maid who prophesies. It came to Aias, the tallest and strongest of men, in his little isle of Salamis; and to Diomede of the loud war-cry, the bravest of warriors, who held Argos and Tiryns of the black walls of huge stones, that are still standing. The summons came to the western islands and to Ulysses in Ithaca, and even far south to the great island of Crete of the hundred cities, where Idomeneus ruled in Cnossos; Idomeneus, whose ruined palace may still be seen with the throne of the king, and pictures painted on the walls, and the king's own draughtboard of gold and silver, and hundreds of tablets of clay, on which are written the lists of royal treasures. Far north went the news to Pelasgian Argos, and Hellas, where the people of Peleus dwelt, the Myrmidons; but Peleus was too old to fight, and his boy, Achilles, dwelt far away, in the island of Scyros, dressed as a girl, among the daughters of King Lycomedes. To many another town and to a hundred islands went the bitter news of approaching war, for all princes knew that their honour and their oaths compelled them to gather their spearmen, and bowmen, and slingers from the fields and the fishing, and to make ready their ships, and meet King Agamemnon in the harbour of Aulis, and cross the wide sea to besiege Troy town.

Now the story is told that Ulysses was very unwilling to leave his island and his wife Penelope, and little Telemachus; while Penelope had no wish that he should pass into danger, and into the sight of Helen of the fair hands. So it is said that when two of the princes came to summon Ulysses, he pretended to be mad, and went ploughing the sea sand with oxen, and sowing the sand with salt. Then the prince Palamedes took the baby Telemachus from the arms of his nurse, Eurycleia, and laid him in the line of the furrow, where the ploughshare would strike him and kill him. But Ulysses turned the plough aside, and they cried that he was not mad, but sane, and he must keep his oath, and join the fleet at Aulis, a long voyage for him to sail, round the stormy southern Cape of Maleia.

Whether this tale be true or not, Ulysses did go, leading twelve black ships, with high beaks painted red at prow and stern. The ships had oars, and the warriors manned the oars, to row when there was no wind. There was a small raised deck at each end of the ships; on these decks men stood to fight with sword and spear when there was a battle at sea. Each ship had but one mast, with a broad lugger sail, and for anchors they had only heavy stones attached to cables. They generally landed at night, and slept on the shore of one of the many islands, when they could, for they greatly feared to sail out of sight of land.

The fleet consisted of more than a thousand ships, each with fifty warriors, so the army was of more than fifty thousand men. Agamemnon had a hundred ships, Diomede had eighty, Nestor had ninety, the Cretans with Idomeneus, had eighty, Menelaus had sixty; but Aias and Ulysses, who lived in small islands, had only twelve ships apiece. Yet Aias was so brave and strong, and Ulysses so brave and wise, that they were ranked among the greatest chiefs and advisers of Agamemnon, with Menelaus, Diomede, Idomeneus, Nestor, Menestheus of Athens, and two or three others. These chiefs were called the Council, and gave advice to Agamemnon, who was commander-in-chief. He was a brave fighter, but so anxious and fearful of losing the lives of his soldiers that Ulysses and Diomede were often obliged to speak to him very severely. Agamemnon was also very insolent and greedy, though, when anybody stood up to him, he was ready to apologise, for fear the injured chief should renounce his service and take away his soldiers.

Nestor was much respected because he remained brave, though he was too old to be very useful in battle. He generally tried to make peace when the princes quarrelled with Agamemnon. He loved to tell long stories about his great deeds when he was young, and he wished the chiefs to fight in old-fashioned ways.

For instance, in his time the Greeks had fought in clan regiments, and the princely men had never dismounted in battle, but had fought in squadrons of chariots, but now the owners of chariots fought on

foot, each man for himself, while his squire kept the chariot near him
to escape on if he had to retreat. Nestor wished to go back to the
good old way of chariot charges against the crowds of foot soldiers of
the enemy. In short, he was a fine example of the old-fashioned
soldier.

Aias, though so very tall, strong, and brave, was rather stupid. He
seldom spoke, but he was always ready to fight, and the last to
retreat. Menelaus was weak of body, but as brave as the best, or
more brave, for he had a keen sense of honour, and would attempt
what he had not the strength to do. Diomede and Ulysses were
great friends, and always fought side by side, when they could, and
helped each other in the most dangerous adventures.

These were the chiefs who led the great Greek armada from the
harbour of Aulis. A long time had passed, after the flight of Helen,
before the large fleet could be collected, and more time went by in
the attempt to cross the sea to Troy. There were tempests that
scattered the ships, so they were driven back to Aulis to refit; and
they fought, as they went out again, with the peoples of unfriendly
islands, and besieged their towns. What they wanted most of all
was to have Achilles with them, for he was the leader of fifty ships
and 2,500 men, and he had magical armour made, men said, for his
father, by Hephaestus, the god of armour-making and smithy work.

At last the fleet came to the Isle of Scyros, where they suspected
that Achilles was concealed. King Lycomedes received the chiefs
kindly, and they saw all his beautiful daughters dancing and playing
at ball, but Achilles was still so young and slim and so beautiful that
they did not know him among the others. There was a prophecy
that they could not take Troy without him, and yet they could not
find him out. Then Ulysses had a plan. He blackened his eyebrows
and beard and put on the dress of a Phoenician merchant. The
Phoenicians were a people who lived near the Jews, and were of the
same race, and spoke much the same language, but, unlike the Jews,
who, at that time were farmers in Palestine, tilling the ground,
and keeping flocks and herds, the Phoenicians were the greatest of
traders and sailors, and stealers of slaves. They carried cargoes of
beautiful cloths, and embroideries, and jewels of gold, and necklaces

of amber, and sold these everywhere about the shores of Greece and the islands.

Ulysses then dressed himself like a Phoenician pedlar, with his pack on his back: he only took a stick in his hand, his long hair was turned up, and hidden under a red sailor's cap, and in this figure he came, stooping beneath his pack, into the courtyard of King Lycomedes. The girls heard that a pedlar had come, and out they all ran, Achilles with the rest to watch the pedlar undo his pack. Each chose what she liked best: one took a wreath of gold; another a necklace of gold and amber; another earrings; a fourth a set of brooches, another a dress of embroidered scarlet cloth; another a veil; another a pair of bracelets; but at the bottom of the pack lay a great sword of bronze, the hilt studded with golden nails. Achilles seized the sword. 'This is for me!' he said, and drew the sword from the gilded sheath, and made it whistle round his head.

'You are Achilles, Peleus' son!' said Ulysses; 'and you are to be the chief warrior of the Achaeans,' for the Greeks then called themselves Achaeans. Achilles was only too glad to hear these words, for he was quite tired of living among maidens. Ulysses led him into the hall where the chiefs were sitting at their wine, and Achilles was blushing like any girl.

'Here is the Queen of the Amazons,' said Ulysses – for the Amazons were a race of warlike maidens – 'or rather here is Achilles, Peleus' son, with sword in hand.' Then they all took his hand, and welcomed him, and he was clothed in man's dress, with the sword by his side, and presently they sent him back with ten ships to his home. There his mother, Thetis, of the silver feet, the goddess of the sea, wept over him, saying, 'My child, thou hast the choice of a long and happy and peaceful life here with me, or of a brief time of war and undying renown. Never shall I see thee again in Argos if thy choice is for war.' But Achilles chose to die young, and to be famous as long as the world stands. So his father gave him fifty ships, with Patroclus, who was older than he, to be his friend, and with an old man, Phoenix, to advise him; and his mother gave him the glorious armour that the god had made for his father, and the heavy ashen spear that none but he could wield, and he sailed to join the host of the Achaeans, who all praised and thanked Ulysses that had found for them such a prince. For Achilles was the fiercest fighter of them all, and the swiftest-footed man, and the most courteous prince, and the gentlest with women and children, but he was proud and high of heart, and when he was angered his anger was terrible.

The Trojans would have had no chance against the Greeks if only the men of the city of Troy had fought to keep Helen of the fair hands. But they had allies, who spoke different languages, and came to fight for them both from Europe and from Asia. On the Trojan as well as on the Greek side were people called Pelasgians, who seem to have lived on both shores of the sea. There were Thracians, too, who dwelt much further north than Achilles, in Europe and beside the strait of Hellespont, where the narrow sea runs like a river. There were warriors of Lycia, led by Sarpedon and Glaucus; there were Carians, who spoke in a strange tongue; there were Mysians and men from Alybe, which was called 'the birthplace of silver', and many other peoples sent their armies, so that the war was between Eastern Europe, on one side, and Western Asia Minor on the other. The people of Egypt took no part in the war: the Greeks and Islesmen used to come down in their ships and attack the Egyptians as the Danes used to invade England. You may see the warriors from the islands, with their horned helmets, in old Egyptian pictures.

The commander-in-chief, as we say now, of the Trojans was Hector, the son of Priam. He was thought a match for any one of the Greeks, and was brave and good. His brothers also were leaders, but Paris preferred to fight from a distance with bow and arrows. He and Pandarus, who dwelt on the slopes of Mount Ida, were the best archers in the Trojan army. The princes usually fought with heavy spears, which they threw at each other, and with swords, leaving archery to the common soldiers who had no armour of bronze. But Teucer, Meriones, and Ulysses were the best archers of the Achaeans. People called Dardanians were led by Aeneas, who was said to be the son of the most beautiful of the goddesses. These, with Sarpedon and Glaucus, were the most famous of the men who fought for Troy.

Troy was a strong town on a hill. Mount Ida lay behind it, and in front was a plain sloping to the sea shore. Through this plain ran two beautiful clear rivers, and there were scattered here and there what you would have taken for steep knolls, but they were really mounds piled up over the ashes of warriors who had died long ago. On these mounds sentinels used to stand and look across the water to give warning if the Greek fleet drew near, for the Trojans had heard that it was on its way. At last the fleet came in view, and the sea was black with ships, the oarsmen pulling with all their might for the honour of being the first to land. The race was won by the ship of the prince Protesilaus, who was first of all to leap on shore, but as he leaped he was struck to the heart by an arrow from the bow of Paris. This must have seemed a good omen to the Trojans, and to the Greeks evil, but we do not hear that the landing was resisted in great force, any more than that of Norman William was, when he invaded England.

The Greeks drew up all their ships on shore, and the men camped in huts built in front of the ships. There was thus a long row of huts with the ships behind them, and in these huts the Greeks lived all through the ten years that the siege of Troy lasted. In these days they do not seem to have understood how to conduct a siege. You would have expected the Greeks to build towers and dig trenches all round Troy, and from the towers watch the roads, so that provisions might not be brought in from the country. This is called 'investing' a town, but the Greeks never invested Troy. Perhaps they had not men enough; at all events the place remained open, and cattle could always be driven in to feed the warriors and the women and children.

Moreover, the Greeks for long never seem to have tried to break down one of the gates, nor to scale the walls, which were very high, with ladders. On the other hand, the Trojans and allies never ventured to drive the Greeks into the sea; they commonly remained within the walls or skirmished just beneath them. The older men insisted on this way of fighting, in spite of Hector, who always wished to attack and storm the camp of the Greeks. Neither side had machines for throwing heavy stones, such as the

Romans used later, and the most that the Greeks did was to follow Achilles and capture small neighbouring cities, and take the women for slaves, and drive the cattle. They got provisions and wine from the Phoenicians, who came in ships, and made much profit out of the war.

It was not till the tenth year that the war began in real earnest, and scarcely any of the chief leaders had fallen. Fever came upon the Greeks, and all day the camp was black with smoke, and all night shone with fire from the great piles of burning wood, on which the Greeks burned their dead, whose bones they then buried under hillocks of earth. Many of these hillocks are still standing on the plain of Troy. When the plague had raged for ten days, Achilles called an assembly of the whole army, to try to find out why the gods were angry. They thought that the beautiful god Apollo (who took the Trojan side) was shooting invisible arrows at them from his silver bow, though fevers in armies are usually caused by dirt and drinking bad water. The great heat of the sun, too, may have helped to cause the disease; but we must tell the story as the Greeks told it themselves. So Achilles spoke in the assembly, and proposed to ask some prophet why Apollo was angry. The chief prophet was Calchas. He rose and said that he would declare the truth if Achilles would promise to protect him from the anger of any prince whom the truth might offend.

Achilles knew well whom Calchas meant. Ten days before, a priest of Apollo had come to the camp and offered ransom for his daughter Chryseis, a beautiful girl, whom Achilles had taken prisoner, with many others, when he captured a small town. Chryseis had been given as a slave to Agamemnon, who always got the best of the plunder because he was chief king, whether he had taken part in the fighting or not. As a rule he did not. To Achilles had been given another girl, Briseis, of whom he was very fond. Now when Achilles had promised to protect Calchas, the prophet spoke out, and boldly said, what all men knew already, that Apollo caused the plague because Agamemnon would not return Chryseis, and had insulted her father, the priest of the god.

On hearing this, Agamemnon was very angry. He said that he

would send Chryseis home, but that he would take Briseis away from Achilles. Then Achilles was drawing his great sword from the sheath to kill Agamemnon, but even in his anger he knew that this was wrong, so he merely called Agamemnon a greedy coward, 'with face of dog and heart of deer', and he swore that he and his men would fight no more against the Trojans. Old Nestor tried to make peace, and swords were not drawn, but Briseis was taken away from Achilles, and Ulysses put Chryseis on board of his ship and sailed away with her to her father's town, and gave her up to her father. Then her father prayed to Apollo that the plague might cease, and it did cease – when the Greeks had cleansed their camp, and purified themselves and cast their filth into the sea.

We know how fierce and brave Achilles was, and we may wonder that he did not challenge Agamemnon to fight a duel. But the Greeks never fought duels, and Agamemnon was believed to be chief king by right divine. Achilles went alone to the sea shore when his dear Briseis was led away, and he wept, and called to his mother, the silver-footed lady of the waters. Then she arose from the grey sea, like a mist, and sat down beside her son, and stroked his hair with her hand, and he told her all his sorrows. So she said that she would go up to the dwelling of the gods, and pray Zeus, the chief of them all, to make the Trojans win a great battle, so that Agamemnon should feel his need of Achilles, and make amends for his insolence, and do him honour.

Thetis kept her promise, and Zeus gave his word that the Trojans should defeat the Greeks. That night Zeus sent a deceitful dream to Agamemnon. The dream took the shape of old Nestor, and said that Zeus would give him victory that day. While he was still asleep, Agamemnon was full of hope that he would instantly take Troy, but, when he woke, he seems not to have been nearly so confident, for in place of putting on his armour, and bidding the Greeks arm themselves, he merely dressed in his robe and mantle, took his sceptre, and went and told the chiefs about his dream. They did not feel much encouraged, so he said that he would try the temper of the army. He would call them together, and propose to return to Greece; but, if the soldiers took him at his word, the other chiefs were to stop them. This was a foolish plan, for the soldiers were wearying for beautiful Greece, and their homes, and wives and children. Therefore, when Agamemnon did as he had said, the whole army rose, like the sea under the west wind, and, with a shout, they rushed to the ships, while the dust blew in clouds from under their feet. Then they began to launch their ships, and it seems that the princes were carried away in the rush, and were as eager as the rest to go home.

But Ulysses only stood in sorrow and anger beside his ship, and never put hand to it, for he felt how disgraceful it was to run away. At last he threw down his mantle, which his herald Eurybates of Ithaca, a round-shouldered, brown, curly-haired man, picked up, and he ran to find Agamemnon, and took his sceptre, a gold-studded staff, like a marshal's baton, and he gently told the chiefs whom he met that they were doing a shameful thing; but he drove the common soldiers back to the place of meeting with the sceptre. They all returned, puzzled and chattering, but one lame, bandy-legged, bald, round-shouldered, impudent fellow, named Thersites, jumped up and made an insolent speech, insulting the princes, and advising the army to run away. Then Ulysses took him and beat him till the blood came, and he sat down, wiping away his tears, and looking so foolish that the whole army laughed at him, and cheered Ulysses when he and Nestor bade them arm and fight. Agamemnon still believed a good deal in his dream, and prayed that he might take Troy that very day, and kill Hector. Thus Ulysses alone saved the army from a cowardly retreat; but for him the ships would have been launched in an hour. But the Greeks armed and advanced in full force, all except Achilles and his friend Patroclus with their two or three thousand men. The Trojans also took heart, knowing that Achilles would not fight, and the armies approached each other. Paris himself, with two spears and a bow, and without armour, walked into the space between the hosts, and challenged any Greek prince to single combat. Menelaus, whose wife Paris had carried away, was as glad as a hungry lion when he finds a stag or a goat, and leaped in armour from his chariot, but Paris turned and slunk away, like a man when he meets a great serpent on a narrow path in the hills. Then Hector rebuked Paris for his cowardice, and Paris was ashamed and offered to end the war by fighting Menelaus. If he himself fell, the Trojans must give up Helen and all her jewels; if Menelaus fell, the Greeks were to return without fair Helen. The Greeks accepted this plan, and both sides disarmed themselves to look on at the fight in comfort, and they meant to take the most solemn oaths to keep peace till the combat was lost and won, and the quarrel settled. Hector sent into Troy for two lambs, which were to be sacrificed when the oaths were taken.

In the meantime Helen of the fair hands was at home working at a great purple tapestry on which she embroidered the battles of the Greeks and Trojans. It was just like the tapestry at Bayeux on which Norman ladies embroidered the battles in the Norman Conquest of England. Helen was very fond of embroidering, like poor Mary, Queen of Scots, when a prisoner in Loch Leven Castle. Probably the work kept both Helen and Mary from thinking of their past lives and their sorrows.

When Helen heard that her husband was to fight Paris, she wept, and threw a shining veil over her head, and with her two bower maidens went to the roof of the gate tower, where King Priam was sitting with the old Trojan chiefs. They saw her and said that it was small blame to fight for so beautiful a lady, and Priam called her 'dear child', and said, 'I do not blame you, I blame the gods who brought about this war.' But Helen said that she wished she had died before she left her little daughter and her husband, and her home: 'Alas! shameless me!' Then she told Priam the names of the chief Greek warriors, and of Ulysses, who was shorter by a head than Agamemnon, but broader in chest and shoulders. She wondered that she could not see her own two brothers, Castor and Polydeuces, and thought that they kept aloof in shame for her sin; but the green grass covered their graves, for they had both died in battle, far away in Lacedaemon, their own country.

Then the lambs were sacrificed, and the oaths were taken, and Paris put on his brother's armour, helmet, breastplate, shield, and leg-armour. Lots were drawn to decide whether Paris or Menelaus should throw his spear first, and, as Paris won, he threw his spear, but the point was blunted against the shield of Menelaus. But when

*Helen points out the chief heroes in the
Greek host to Priam*

Menelaus threw his spear it went clean through the shield of Paris, and through the side of his breastplate, but only grazed his robe. Menelaus drew his sword, and rushed in, and smote at the crest of the helmet of Paris, but his bronze blade broke into four pieces. Menelaus caught Paris by the horsehair crest of his helmet, and dragged him towards the Greeks, but the chin-strap broke, and Menelaus turning round threw the helmet into the ranks of the Greeks. But when Menelaus looked again for Paris, with a spear in his hand, he could see him nowhere! The Greeks believed that the beautiful goddess Aphrodite, whom the Romans called Venus, hid him in a thick cloud of darkness and carried him to his own house, where Helen of the fair hands found him and said to him, 'Would that thou hadst perished, conquered by that great warrior who was my lord! Go forth again and challenge him to fight thee face to face.' But Paris had no more desire to fight, and the goddess threatened Helen, and compelled her to remain with him in Troy, coward as he had proved himself. Yet on other days Paris fought well; it seems that he was afraid of Menelaus because, in his heart, he was ashamed of himself.

Meanwhile Menelaus was seeking for Paris everywhere, and the Trojans, who hated him, would have shown his hiding place. But they knew not where he was, and the Greeks claimed the victory, and thought that, as Paris had the worst of the fight, Helen would be restored to them, and they would all sail home.

CHAPTER FIVE

Trojan Victories

The war might now have ended, but an evil and foolish thought came to Pandarus, a prince of Ida, who fought for the Trojans. He chose to shoot an arrow at Menelaus, contrary to the sworn vows of peace, and the arrow pierced the breastplate of Menelaus through the place where the clasped plates meet, and drew his blood. Then Agamemnon, who loved his brother dearly, began to lament, saying that if he died, the army would all go home and Trojans would dance on the grave of Menelaus. 'Do not alarm all our army,' said Menelaus, 'the arrow has done me little harm'; and so it proved, for the surgeon easily drew the arrow out of the wound.

Then Agamemnon hastened here and there, bidding the Greeks arm and attack the Trojans, who would certainly be defeated, for they had broken the oaths of peace. But with his usual insolence he chose to accuse Ulysses and Diomede of cowardice, though Diomede was as brave as any man, and Ulysses had just prevented the whole army from launching their ships and going home. Ulysses answered him with spirit, but Diomede said nothing at the moment; later he spoke his mind. He leaped from his chariot, and all the chiefs leaped down and advanced in line, the chariots following them, while the spearmen and bowmen followed the chariots. The Trojan army advanced, all shouting in their different languages, but the Greeks came on silently. Then the two front lines clashed, shield against shield, and the noise was like the roaring of many flooded torrents among the hills. When a man fell he who had slain him tried to strip off his armour, and his friends fought over his body to save the dead from this dishonour.

Ulysses fought above a wounded friend, and drove his spear through head and helmet of a Trojan prince, and everywhere men were falling beneath spears and arrows and heavy stones which the warriors threw. Here Menelaus speared the man who built the ships with which Paris had sailed to Greece; and the dust rose like a cloud, and a mist went up from the fighting men, while Diomede stormed across the plain like a river in flood, leaving dead bodies behind him as the river leaves boughs of trees and grass to mark its course. Pandarus wounded Diomede with an arrow, but Diomede slew him, and the Trojans were being driven in flight, when Sarpedon and Hector turned and hurled themselves on the Greeks; and even Diomede shuddered when Hector came on, and charged at Ulysses, who was slaying Trojans as he went, and the battle swayed this way and that, and the arrows fell like rain.

But Hector was sent into the city to bid the women pray to the goddess Athene for help, and he went to the house of Paris, whom Helen was imploring to go and fight like a man, saying: 'Would that the winds had wafted me away, and the tides drowned me, shameless that I am, before these things came to pass!'

Then Hector went to see his dear wife, Andromache, whose father had been slain by Achilles early in the siege, and he found her and her nurse carrying her little boy, Hector's son, and like a star upon her bosom lay his beautiful and shining golden head. Now, while Helen urged Paris to go into the fight, Andromache prayed Hector to stay with her in the town, and fight no more lest he should be slain and leave her a widow, and the boy an orphan, with none to protect him. The army, she said, should come back within the walls, where they had so long been safe, not fight in the open plain. But Hector answered that he would never shrink from battle, 'yet I know this in my heart, the day shall come for holy Troy to be laid low, and Priam and the people of Priam. But this and my own death do not trouble me so much as the thought of you, when you shall be carried as a slave to Greece, to spin at another woman's bidding, and bear water from a Grecian well. May the heaped up earth of my tomb cover me ere I hear thy cries and the tale of thy captivity.'

Then Hector stretched out his hands to his little boy, but the child was afraid when he saw the great glittering helmet of his father and the nodding horsehair crest. So Hector laid his helmet on the ground and dandled the child in his arms, and tried to comfort his wife, and said goodbye for the last time, for he never came back to Troy alive. He went on his way back to the battle, and Paris went with him, in glorious armour, and soon they were slaying the princes of the Greeks.

The battle raged till nightfall, and in the night the Greeks and Trojans burned their dead; and the Greeks made a trench and wall round their camp, which they needed for safety now that the Trojans came from their town and fought in the open plain.

Next day the Trojans were so successful that they did not retreat behind their walls at night, but lit great fires on the plain: a thousand fires, with fifty men taking supper round each of them, and drinking their wine to the music of flutes. But the Greeks were much discouraged, and Agamemnon called the whole army together, and proposed that they should launch their ships in the night and sail away home. Then Diomede stood up, and said: 'You called me a coward lately. You are the coward! Sail away if you are afraid to remain here, but all the rest of us will fight till we take Troy town.'

Then all shouted in praise of Diomede, and Nestor advised them to send five hundred young men, under his own son, Thrasymedes, to watch the Trojans, and guard the new wall and the ditch, in case the Trojans attacked them in the darkness. Next Nestor counselled Agamemnon to send Ulysses and Aias to Achilles, and promise to give back Briseis, and rich presents of gold, and beg pardon for his insolence. If Achilles would be friends again with Agamemnon, and fight as he used to fight, the Trojans would soon be driven back into the town.

Agamemnon was very ready to beg pardon, for he feared that the whole army would be defeated, and cut off from their ships, and killed or kept as slaves. So Ulysses and Aias and the old tutor of Achilles, Phoenix, went to Achilles and argued with him, praying him to accept the rich presents, and help the Greeks. But Achilles answered that he did not believe a word that Agamemnon said; Agamemnon had always hated him, and always would hate him.

No; he would not cease to be angry, he would sail away next day with all his men, and he advised the rest to come with him. 'Why be so fierce?' said tall Aias, who seldom spoke. 'Why make so much trouble about one girl? We offer you seven girls, and plenty of other gifts.'

Then Achilles said that he would not sail away next day, but he would not fight till the Trojans tried to burn his own ships, and there he thought that Hector would find work enough to do. This was the most that Achilles would promise, and all the Greeks were silent when Ulysses delivered his message. But Diomede arose and said that, with or without Achilles, fight they must; and all men, heavy at heart, went to sleep in their huts or in the open air at their doors.

Agamemnon was much too anxious to sleep. He saw the glow of the thousand fires of the Trojans in the dark, and heard their merry flutes, and he groaned and pulled out his long hair by handfuls. When he was tired of crying and groaning and tearing his hair, he thought that he would go for advice to old Nestor. He threw a lion skin, the coverlet of his bed, over his shoulder, took his spear, went out and met Menelaus – for he, too, could not sleep – and Menelaus proposed to send a spy among the Trojans, if any man were brave enough to go, for the Trojan camp was all alight with fires, and the adventure was dangerous. Therefore the two wakened Nestor and the other chiefs, who came just as they were, wrapped in the fur coverlets of their beds, without any armour. First they visited the five hundred young men set to watch the wall, and then they crossed the ditch and sat down outside and considered what might be done. 'Will nobody go as a spy among the Trojans?' said Nestor; he meant would none of the young men go. Diomede said that he would take the risk if any other man would share it with him, and, if he might choose a companion, he would take Ulysses.

'Come, then, let us be going,' said Ulysses, 'for the night is late, and the dawn is near.' As these two chiefs had no armour on, they borrowed shields and leather caps from the young men of the guard, for leather would not shine as bronze helmets shine in the firelight. The cap lent to Ulysses was strengthened outside with rows of boars' tusks. Many of these tusks, shaped for this purpose, have been found, with swords and armour, in a tomb in Mycenae, the town of Agamemnon. This cap which was lent to Ulysses had once been stolen by his grandfather, Autolycus, who was a Master Thief, and he gave it as a present to a friend, and so, through several hands, it had come to young Meriones of Crete, one of the five hundred guards, who now lent it to Ulysses. So the two princes set forth in the dark, so dark it was that though they heard a heron cry, they could not see it as it flew away.

While Ulysses and Diomede stole through the night silently, like two wolves among the bodies of dead men, the Trojan leaders met and considered what they ought to do. They did not know whether the Greeks had set sentinels and outposts, as usual, to give warning if the enemy were approaching; or whether they were too weary to keep a good watch; or whether perhaps they were getting ready their ships to sail homewards in the dawn. So Hector offered a reward to any man who would creep through the night and spy on the Greeks; he said he would give the spy the two best horses in the Greek camp.

Now among the Trojans there was a young man named Dolon, the son of a rich father, and he was the only boy in a family of five sisters. He was ugly, but a very swift runner, and he cared for horses more than for anything else in the world. Dolon arose and said, 'If you will swear to give me the horses and chariot of Achilles, son of Peleus, I will steal to the hut of Agamemnon and listen and find out whether the Greeks mean to fight or flee.' Hector swore to give these horses, which were the best in the world, to Dolon, so he took his bow and threw a grey wolf's hide over his shoulders, and ran towards the ships of the Greeks.

Now Ulysses saw Dolon as he came, and said to Diomede, 'Let us suffer him to pass us, and then do you keep driving him with your spear towards the ships, and away from Troy.' So Ulysses and Diomede lay down among the dead men who had fallen in the battle, and Dolon ran on past them towards the Greeks. Then they rose and chased him as two greyhounds course a hare, and, when Dolon was near the sentinels, Diomede cried 'Stand, or I will slay you with my spear!' and he threw his spear just over Dolon's shoulder. So Dolon stood still, green with fear, and with his teeth chattering. When the two came up, he cried, and said that his father was a rich man, who would pay much gold, and bronze, and iron for his ransom.

Ulysses said, 'Take heart, and put death out of your mind, and tell us what you are doing here.' Dolon said that Hector had promised him the horses of Achilles if he would go and spy on the Greeks. 'You set your hopes high,' said Ulysses, 'for the horses of Achilles are not earthly steeds, but divine; a gift of the gods, and Achilles alone can drive them. But, tell me, do the Trojans keep good watch, and where is Hector with his horses?' for Ulysses thought that it would be a great adventure to drive away the horses of Hector.

'Hector is with the chiefs, holding council at the tomb of Ilus,' said Dolon; 'but no regular guard is set. The people of Troy, indeed, are round their watch fires, for they have to think of the safety of their wives and children; but the allies from far lands keep no watch, for their wives and children are safe at home.' Then he told where all the different peoples who fought for Priam had their stations; but, said he, 'if you want to steal horses, the best are those of Rhesus, King of the Thracians, who has only joined us tonight. He and his men are asleep at the furthest end of the line, and his horses are the best and greatest that ever I saw: tall, white as snow, and swift as the wind, and his chariot is adorned with gold and silver, and golden is his armour. Now take me prisoner to the ships, or bind me and leave me here while you go and try whether I have told you truth or lies.'

'No,' said Diomede, 'if I spare your life you may come spying again,' and he drew his sword and smote off the head of Dolon. They hid his cap and bow and spear where they could find them easily, and marked the spot, and went through the night to the dark camp of King Rhesus, who had no watch fire and no guards. Then Diomede silently stabbed each sleeping man to the heart, and Ulysses seized the dead by the feet and threw them aside lest they should frighten the horses, which had never been in battle, and would shy if they were led over the bodies of dead men. Last of all Diomede killed King Rhesus, and Ulysses led forth his horses, beating them with his bow, for he had forgotten to take the whip from the chariot. Then Ulysses and Diomede leaped on the backs of the horses, as they had not time to bring away the chariot, and they galloped to the ships, stopping to pick up the spear, and bow, and cap of Dolon. They rode to the princes, who welcomed them, and all laughed for glee when they saw the white horses and heard that King Rhesus was dead, for they guessed that all his army would now go home to Thrace. This they must have done, for we never hear of them in the battles that followed, so Ulysses and Diomede deprived the Trojans of thousands of men. The other princes went to bed in good spirits, but Ulysses and Diomede took a swim in the sea, and then went into hot baths, and so to breakfast, for rosy-fingered Dawn was coming up the sky.

CHAPTER SIX

Battle at the Ships

With dawn Agamemnon awoke, and fear had gone out of his heart. He put on his armour, and arrayed the chiefs on foot in front of their chariots, and behind them came the spearmen, with the bowmen and slingers on the wings of the army. Then a great black cloud spread over the sky, and red was the rain that fell from it. The Trojans gathered on a height in the plain, and Hector, shining in armour, went here and there, in front and rear, like a star that now gleams forth and now is hidden in a cloud.

The armies rushed on each other and hewed each other down, as reapers cut their way through a field of tall corn. Neither side gave ground, though the helmets of the bravest Trojans might be seen deep in the ranks of the Greeks; and the swords of the bravest Greeks rose and fell in the ranks of the Trojans, and all the while the arrows showered like rain. But at noonday, when the weary woodman rests from cutting trees, and takes his dinner in the quiet hills, the Greeks of the first line made a charge, Agamemnon running in front of them, and he speared two Trojans, and took their breastplates, which he laid in his chariot, and then he speared one brother of Hector and struck another down with his sword, and killed two more who vainly asked to be made prisoners of war. Footmen slew footmen, and chariot men slew chariot men, and they broke into the Trojan line as fire falls on a forest in a windy day, leaping and roaring and racing through the trees. Many an empty chariot did the horses hurry madly through the field, for the charioteers were lying dead, with the greedy vultures hovering above them, flapping their wide wings. Still Agamemnon followed and slew the hindmost Trojans, but the rest fled till they came to the gates, and the oak tree that grew outside the gates, and there they stopped.

But Hector held his hands from fighting, for in the meantime he was making his men face the enemy and form up in line and take breath, and was encouraging them, for they had retreated from the wall of the Greeks across the whole plain, past the hill that was the tomb of Ilus, a king of old, and past the place of the wild fig tree. Much ado had Hector to rally the Trojans, but he knew that when men do turn again they are hard to beat. So it proved, for when the Trojans had rallied and formed in line, Agamemnon slew a Thracian chief who had come to fight for Troy before King Rhesus came. But the eldest brother of the slain man smote Agamemnon through the arm with his spear, and, though Agamemnon slew him in turn, his wound bled much and he was in great pain, so he leaped into his chariot and was driven back to the ships.

Then Hector gave the word to charge, as a huntsman cries on his hounds against a lion, and he rushed forward at the head of the Trojan line, slaying as he went. Nine chiefs of the Greeks he slew, and fell upon the spearmen and scattered them, as the spray of the waves is scattered by the wandering wind.

Now the ranks of the Greeks were broken, and they would have been driven among their ships and killed without mercy, had not Ulysses and Diomede stood firm in the centre, and slain four Trojan leaders. The Greeks began to come back and face their enemies in line of battle again, though Hector, who had been fighting on the Trojan right, rushed against them. But Diomede took good aim with his spear at the helmet of Hector, and struck it fairly. The spear-point did not go through the helmet, but Hector was stunned and fell; and, when he came to himself, he leaped into his chariot, and his squire drove him against the Pylians and Cretans, under Nestor and Idomeneus, who were on the left wing of the Greek army. Then Diomede fought on till Paris, who stood beside the pillar on the hillock that was the tomb of old King Ilus, sent an arrow clean through his foot. Ulysses went and stood in front of Diomede, who sat down, and Ulysses drew the arrow from his foot, and Diomede stepped into his chariot and was driven back to the ships.

Ulysses was now the only Greek chief that still fought in the centre. The Greeks all fled, and he was alone in the crowd of

Trojans, who rushed on him as hounds and hunters press round a wild boar that stands at bay in a wood. 'They are cowards that flee from the fight,' said Ulysses to himself; 'but I will stand here, one man against a multitude.' He covered the front of his body with his great shield, that hung by a belt round his neck, and he smote four Trojans and wounded a fifth. But the brother of the wounded man drove a spear through the shield and breastplate of Ulysses, and tore clean through his side. Then Ulysses turned on this Trojan, and he fled, and Ulysses sent a spear through his shoulder and out at his breast, and he died. Ulysses dragged from his own side the spear that had wounded him, and called thrice with a great voice to the other Greeks, and Menelaus and Aias rushed to rescue him, for many Trojans were round him, like jackals round a wounded stag that a man has struck with an arrow. But Aias ran and covered the wounded Ulysses with his huge shield till he could climb into the chariot of Menelaus, who drove him back to the ships.

Meanwhile, Hector was slaying the Greeks on the left of their battle, and Paris struck the Greek surgeon, Machaon, with an arrow; and Idomeneus bade Nestor put Machaon in his chariot and drive him to Nestor's hut, where his wound might be tended. Meanwhile, Hector sped to the centre of the line, where Aias was slaying the Trojans; but Eurypylus, a Greek chief, was wounded by an arrow from the bow of Paris, and his friends guarded him with their shields and spears.

Thus the best of the Greeks were wounded and out of the battle, save Aias, and the spearmen were in flight. Meanwhile Achilles was standing by the stern of his ship watching the defeat of the Greeks, but when he saw Machaon being carried past, sorely wounded, in the chariot of Nestor, he bade his friend Patroclus, whom he loved better than all the rest, to go and ask how Machaon did. He was sitting drinking wine with Nestor when Patroclus came, and Nestor told Patroclus how many of the chiefs were wounded, and though Patroclus was in a hurry Nestor began a very long story about his own great deeds of war, done when he was a young man. At last he bade Patroclus tell Achilles that, if he would not fight himself, he should at least send out his men under Patroclus, who should wear the splendid armour of Achilles. Then the Trojans would think that Achilles himself had returned to the battle, and they would be afraid, for none of them dared to meet Achilles hand to hand.

So Patroclus ran off to Achilles; but, on his way, he met the wounded Eurypylus, and he took him to his hut and cut the arrow out of his thigh with a knife, and washed the wound with warm water, and rubbed over it a bitter root to take the pain away. Thus he waited for some time with Eurypylus, but the advice of Nestor was in the end to cause the death of Patroclus. The battle now raged more fiercely, while Agamemnon and Diomede and Ulysses could only limp about leaning on their spears; and again Agamemnon wished to moor the ships near shore, and embark in the night and run away. But Ulysses was very angry with him, and said: 'You should lead some other inglorious army, not us, who will fight on till every soul of us perish, rather than flee like cowards! Be silent, lest the soldiers hear you speaking of flight, such words as no man should utter. I wholly scorn your counsel, for the Greeks will lose heart if, in the midst of battle, you bid them launch the ships.'

Agamemnon was ashamed, and, by Diomede's advice, the wounded kings went down to the verge of the war to encourage the others, though they were themselves unable to fight. They rallied the Greeks, and Aias led them and struck Hector full in the breast with a great rock, so that his friends carried him out of the battle to the river side, where they poured water over him, but he lay fainting on the ground, the black blood gushing up from his mouth. While Hector lay there, and all men thought that he would die, Aias and Idomeneus were driving back the Trojans, and it seemed that, even without Achilles and his men, the Greeks were able to hold their own against the Trojans. But the battle was never lost while Hector lived. People in those days believed in 'omens': they thought that the appearance of birds on the right or left hand meant good or bad luck. Once during the battle a Trojan showed Hector an unlucky bird, and wanted him to retreat into the town. But Hector said, 'One omen is the best: to fight for our own country.' While Hector lay between death and life the Greeks were winning, for the Trojans had no other great chief to lead them. But Hector awoke from his faint, and leaped to his feet and ran here and there, encouraging the men of Troy. Then the most of the Greeks fled when they saw him; but Aias and Idomeneus, and the rest of the bravest, formed in a square between the Trojans and the ships, and down on them came Hector and Aeneas and Paris, throwing their spears, and slaying on every hand. The Greeks turned and ran, and the Trojans would have stopped to strip the armour from the slain men, but Hector cried: 'Haste to the ships and leave the spoils of war. I will slay any man who lags behind!'

On this, all the Trojans drove their chariots down into the ditch that guarded the ships of the Greeks, as when a great wave sweeps at sea over the side of a vessel; and the Greeks were on the ship decks, thrusting with very long spears, used in sea fights, and the Trojans were boarding the ships, and striking with swords and axes. Hector had a lighted torch and tried to set fire to the ship of Aias; but Aias kept him back with the long spear, and slew a Trojan, whose lighted torch fell from his hand. And Aias kept shouting: 'Come on, and drive away Hector; it is not to a dance that he is calling his men, but to battle.'

The dead fell in heaps, and the living ran over them to mount the heaps of slain and climb the ships. Hector rushed forward like a sea wave against a great steep rock, but like the rock stood the Greeks; still the Trojans charged past the beaks of the foremost ships, while Aias, thrusting with a spear more than twenty feet long, leaped from deck to deck like a man that drives four horses abreast, and leaps from the back of one to the back of another. Hector seized with his hand the stern of the ship of Protesilaus, the prince whom Paris shot when he leaped ashore on the day when the Greeks first landed; and Hector kept calling: 'Bring fire!' and even Aias, in this strange sea fight on land, left the decks and went below, thrusting with his spear through the portholes. Twelve men lay dead who had brought fire against the ship which Aias guarded.

CHAPTER SEVEN

The Slaying and Avenging of Patroclus

At this moment, when torches were blazing round the ships, and all seemed lost, Patroclus came out of the hut of Eurypylus, whose wound he had been tending, and he saw that the Greeks were in great danger, and ran weeping to Achilles. 'Why do you weep,' said Achilles, 'like a little girl that runs by her mother's side, and plucks at her gown and looks at her with tears in her eyes, till her mother takes her up in her arms? Is there bad news from home that your father is dead, or mine; or are you sorry that the Greeks are getting what they deserve for their folly?' Then Patroclus told Achilles how Ulysses and many other princes were wounded and could not fight, and begged to be allowed to put on Achilles' armour and lead his men, who were all fresh and unwearied, into the battle, for a charge of two thousand fresh warriors might turn the fortune of the day.

Then Achilles was sorry that he had sworn not to fight himself till Hector brought fire to his own ships. He would lend Patroclus his armour, and his horses, and his men; but Patroclus must only drive the Trojans from the ships, and not pursue them. At this moment Aias was weary, so many spears smote his armour, and he could hardly hold up his great shield, and Hector cut off his spearhead with the sword; the bronze head fell ringing on the ground, and Aias brandished only the pointless shaft. So he shrank back and fire blazed all over his ship; and Achilles saw it, and smote his thigh, and bade Patroclus make haste. Patroclus armed himself in the shining armour of Achilles, which all Trojans feared, and leaped into the chariot where Automedon, the squire, had harnessed Xanthus and Balius, two horses that were the children, men said, of the West Wind, and a led horse was harnessed beside them in the side traces.

Meanwhile the two thousand men of Achilles, who were called Myrmidons, had met in armour, five companies of four hundred apiece, under five chiefs of noble names. Forth they came, as eager as a pack of wolves that have eaten a great red deer and run to slake their thirst with the dark water of a well in the hills.

So all in close array, helmet touching helmet and shield touching shield, like a moving wall of shining bronze, the men of Achilles charged, and Patroclus in the chariot led the way. Down they came at full speed on the flank of the Trojans, who saw the leader, and knew the bright armour and the horses of the terrible Achilles, and thought that he had returned to the war. Then each Trojan looked round to see by what way he could escape, and when men do that in battle they soon run by the way they have chosen. Patroclus rushed to the ship of Protesilaus, and slew the leader of the Trojans there, and drove them out, and quenched the fire; while they of Troy drew back from the ships, and Aias and the other unwounded Greek princes leaped among them, smiting with sword and spear. Well did Hector know that the break in the battle had come again; but even so he stood, and did what he might, while the Trojans were driven back in disorder across the ditch, where the poles of many chariots were broken and the horses fled loose across the plain.

The horses of Achilles cleared the ditch, and Patroclus drove them between the Trojans and the wall of their own town, slaying many men, and, chief of all, Sarpedon, king of the Lycians; and round the body of Sarpedon the Trojans rallied under Hector, and the fight swayed this way and that, and there was such a noise of spears and swords smiting shields and helmets as when many woodcutters fell trees in a glen of the hills. At last the Trojans gave way, and the Greeks stripped the armour from the body of brave Sarpedon; but men say that sleep and death, like two winged angels, bore his body away to his own country. Now Patroclus forgot how Achilles had told him not to pursue the Trojans across the plain, but to return when he had driven them from the ships. On he raced, slaying as he went, even till he reached the foot of the wall of Troy. Thrice he tried to climb it, but thrice he fell back.

Hector was in his chariot in the gateway, and he bade his squire lash his horses into the war, and struck at no other man, great or small, but drove straight against Patroclus, who stood and threw a heavy stone at Hector; which missed him, but killed his charioteer. Then Patroclus leaped on the charioteer to strip his armour, but Hector stood over the body, grasping it by the head, while Patroclus dragged at the feet, and spears and arrows flew in clouds around the fallen man. At last, towards sunset, the Greeks drew him out of the war, and Patroclus thrice charged into the thick of the Trojans. But the helmet of Achilles was loosened in the fight, and fell from the head of Patroclus, and he was wounded from behind, and Hector, in front, drove his spear clean through his body. With his last breath Patroclus prophesied: 'Death stands near thee, Hector, at the hands of noble Achilles.' But Automedon was driving back the swift horses, carrying to Achilles the news that his dearest friend was slain.

After Ulysses was wounded, early in this great battle, he was not able to fight for several days, and, as the story is about Ulysses, we must tell quite shortly how Achilles returned to the war to take vengeance for Patroclus, and how he slew Hector. When Patroclus fell, Hector seized the armour which the gods had given to Peleus, and Peleus to his son Achilles, while Achilles had lent it to Patroclus that he might terrify the Trojans. Retiring out of reach of spears, Hector took off his own armour and put on that of Achilles, and Greeks and Trojans fought for the dead body of Patroclus. Then Zeus, the chief of the gods, looked down and said that Hector should never come home out of the battle to his wife, Andromache. But Hector returned into the fight around the dead Patroclus, and here all the best men fought, and even Automedon, who had been driving the chariot of Patroclus. Now when the Trojans seemed to have the better of the fight, the Greeks sent Antilochus, a son of old Nestor, to tell Achilles that his friend was slain, and Antilochus ran, and Aias and his brother protected the Greeks who were trying to carry the body of Patroclus back to the ships.

Swiftly Antilochus came running to Achilles, saying: 'Fallen is Patroclus, and they are fighting round his naked body, for Hector has his armour.' Then Achilles said never a word, but fell on the floor of his hut, and threw black ashes on his yellow hair, till

Antilochus seized his hands, fearing that he would cut his own throat with his dagger, for very sorrow. His mother, Thetis, arose from the sea to comfort him, but he said that he desired to die if he could not slay Hector, who had slain his friend. Then Thetis told him that he could not fight without armour, and now he had none; but she would go to the god of armour-making and bring from him such a shield and helmet and breastplate as had never been seen by men.

Meanwhile the fight raged round the dead body of Patroclus, which was defiled with blood and dust, near the ships, and was being dragged this way and that, and torn and wounded. Achilles could not bear this sight, yet his mother had warned him not to enter without armour the battle where stones and arrows and spears were flying like hail; and he was so tall and broad that he could put on the arms of no other man. So he went down to the ditch as he was, unarmed, and as he stood high above it, against the red sunset, fire seemed to flow from his golden hair like the beacon blaze that soars into the dark sky when an island town is attacked at night, and men light beacons that their neighbours may see them and come to their help from other isles. There Achilles stood in a splendour of fire, and he shouted aloud, as clear as a clarion rings when men fall on to attack a besieged city wall. Thrice Achilles shouted mightily, and thrice the horses of the Trojans shuddered for fear and turned back from the onslaught – and thrice the men of Troy were confounded and shaken with terror. Then the Greeks drew the body of Patroclus out of the dust and the arrows, and laid him on a bier, and Achilles followed, weeping, for he had sent his friend with chariot and horses to the war; but home again he welcomed him never more. Then the sun set and it was night.

Now one of the Trojans wished Hector to retire within the walls of Troy, for certainly Achilles would tomorrow be foremost in the war. But Hector said, 'Have ye not had your fill of being shut up behind walls? Let Achilles fight; I will meet him in the open field.' The Trojans cheered, and they camped in the plain, while in the hut of Achilles women washed the dead body of Patroclus, and Achilles swore that he would slay Hector.

In the dawn came Thetis, bearing to Achilles the new splendid armour that the god had made for him. Then Achilles put on that armour, and roused his men; but Ulysses, who knew all the rules of honour, would not let him fight till peace had been made, with a sacrifice and other ceremonies, between him and Agamemnon, and till Agamemnon had given him all the presents which Achilles had before refused. Achilles did not want them; he wanted only to fight, but Ulysses made him obey, and do what was usual. Then the gifts were brought, and Agamemnon stood up, and said that he was sorry for his insolence, and the men took breakfast, but Achilles would neither eat nor drink. He mounted his chariot, but the horse Xanthus bowed his head till his long mane touched the ground, and, being a fairy horse, the child of the West Wind, he spoke (or so men said), and these were his words: 'We shall bear thee swiftly and speedily, but thou shalt be slain in fight, and thy dying day is near at hand.' 'Well I know it,' said Achilles, 'but I will not cease from fighting till I have given the Trojans their fill of war.'

So all that day he chased and slew the Trojans. He drove them into the river, and, though the river came down in a red flood, he crossed, and slew them on the plain. The plain caught fire, the bushes and long dry grass blazed round him, but he fought his way through the fire, and drove the Trojans to their walls. The gates were thrown open, and the Trojans rushed through like frightened fawns, and then they climbed to the battlements, and looked down in safety, while the whole Greek army advanced in line under their shields.

But Hector stood still, alone, in front of the gate, and old Priam, who saw Achilles rushing on, shining like a star in his new armour, called with tears to Hector, 'Come within the gate! This man has slain many of my sons, and if he slays thee whom have I to help me in my old age?' His mother also called to Hector, but he stood firm, waiting for Achilles. Now the story says that he was afraid, and ran thrice in full armour round Troy, with Achilles in pursuit. But this cannot be true, for no mortal men could run thrice, in heavy armour, with great shields that clanked against their ankles, round the town of Troy: moreover Hector was the bravest of men, and all the Trojan women were looking down at him from the walls.

We cannot believe that he ran away, and the story goes on to tell that he asked Achilles to make an agreement with him. The conqueror in the fight should give back the body of the fallen to be buried by his friends, but should keep his armour. But Achilles said that he could make no agreement with Hector, and threw his spear, which flew over Hector's shoulder. Then Hector threw his spear, but it could not pierce the shield which the god had made for Achilles. Hector had no other spear, and Achilles had one, so Hector cried, 'Let me not die without honour!' and drew his sword, and rushed at Achilles, who sprang to meet him, but before Hector could come within a sword-stroke Achilles had sent his spear clean through the neck of Hector. He fell in the dust and Achilles said, 'Dogs and birds shall tear your flesh unburied.' With his dying breath Hector prayed him to take gold from Priam, and give back his body to be burned in Troy. But Achilles said, 'Hound! would that I could bring myself to carve and eat thy raw flesh, but dogs shall devour it, even if thy father offered me thy weight in gold.' With his last words Hector prophesied and said, 'Remember me in the day when Paris shall slay thee in the Scaean gate.' Then his brave soul went to the land of the Dead, which the Greeks called Hades. To that land Ulysses sailed while he was still a living man, as the story tells later.

Then Achilles did a dreadful deed; he slit the feet of dead Hector from heel to ankle, and thrust thongs through, and bound him by the thongs to his chariot and trailed the body in the dust. All the women of Troy who were on the walls raised a shriek, and Hector's wife, Andromache, heard the sound. She had been in an inner room of her house, weaving a purple web, and embroidering flowers on it, and she was calling her bower maidens to make ready a bath for Hector when he should come back tired from battle. But when she heard the cry from the wall she trembled, and the shuttle with which she was weaving fell from her hands. 'Surely I heard the cry of my husband's mother,' she said, and she bade two of her maidens come with her to see why the people lamented.

She ran swiftly, and reached the battlements, and thence she saw her dear husband's body being whirled through the dust towards the ships, behind the chariot of Achilles. Then night came over her eyes and she fainted. But when she returned to herself she cried out that now none would defend her little boy, and other children would push him away from feasts, saying, 'Out with you; no father of thine is at our table,' and his father, Hector, would lie naked at the ships, unclad, unburned, unlamented. To be unburned and unburied was thought the greatest of misfortunes, because the dead man unburned could not go into the House of Hades, god of the Dead, but must always wander, alone and comfortless, in the dark borderland between the dead and the living.

CHAPTER EIGHT

The Cruelty of Achilles, and
the Ransoming of Hector

When Achilles was asleep that night the ghost of Patroclus came, saying, 'Why dost thou not burn and bury me? for the other shadows of dead men suffer me not to come near them, and lonely I wander along the dark dwelling of Hades.' Then Achilles awoke, and he sent men to cut down trees, and make a huge pile of faggots and logs. On this they laid Patroclus, covered with white linen, and then they slew many cattle, and Achilles cut the throats of twelve Trojan prisoners of war, meaning to burn them with Patroclus to do him honour. This was a deed of shame, for Achilles was mad with sorrow and anger for the death of his friend. Then they drenched with wine the great pile of wood, which was thirty yards long and broad, and set fire to it, and the fire blazed all through the night and died down in the morning. They put the white bones of Patroclus in a golden casket, and laid it in the hut of Achilles, who said that, when he died, they must burn his body, and mix the ashes with the ashes of his friend, and build over it a chamber of stone, and cover the chamber with a great hill of earth, and set a pillar of stone above it. This is one of the hills on the plain of Troy, but the pillar has fallen from the tomb, long ago.

Then, as the custom was, Achilles held games – chariot races, foot races, boxing, wrestling, and archery – in honour of Patroclus. Ulysses won the prize for the foot race, and for the wrestling, so now his wound must have been healed.

But Achilles still kept trailing Hector's dead body each day round the hill that had been raised for the tomb of Patroclus, till the gods in heaven were angry, and bade Thetis tell her son that he must give back the dead body to Priam, and take ransom for it, and they sent a messenger to Priam to bid him redeem the body of his son. It was terrible for Priam to have to go and humble himself before Achilles, whose hands had been red with the blood of his sons, but he did not disobey the gods. He opened his chests, and took out twenty-four beautiful embroidered changes of raiment; and he weighed out ten heavy bars, or talents, of gold, and chose a beautiful golden cup, and he called nine of his sons, Paris, and Helenus, and Deiphobus, and the rest, saying, 'Go, ye bad sons, my shame; would that Hector lived and all of you were dead!' for sorrow made him angry; 'go, and get ready for me a wain, and lay on it these treasures.' So they harnessed mules to the wain, and placed in it the treasures, and, after praying, Priam drove through the night to the hut of Achilles. In he went, when no man looked for him, and kneeled to Achilles, and kissed his terrible death-dealing hands. 'Have pity on me, and fear the gods, and give me back my dead son,' he said, 'and remember thine own father. Have pity on me, who have endured to do what no man born has ever done before, to kiss the hands that slew my sons.'

Then Achilles remembered his own father, far away, who now was old and weak: and he wept, and Priam wept with him, and then Achilles raised Priam from his knees and spoke kindly to him, admiring how beautiful he still was in his old age, and Priam him-self wondered at the beauty of Achilles. And Achilles thought how Priam had long been rich and happy, like his own father, Peleus, and now old age and weakness and sorrow were laid upon both of them, for Achilles knew that his own day of death was at hand, even at the doors. So Achilles bade the women make ready the body of Hector for burial, and they clothed him in a white mantle that Priam had brought, and laid him in the wain; and supper was made ready, and Priam and Achilles ate and drank together, and the women spread a bed for Priam, who would not stay long, but stole away back to Troy while Achilles was asleep.

All the women came out to meet him, and to lament for Hector. They carried the body into the house of Andromache and laid it on a bed, and the women gathered around, and each in turn sang her song over the great dead warrior. His mother bewailed him, and his wife, and Helen of the fair hands, clad in dark mourning raiment, lifted up her white arms, and said: 'Hector, of all my brethren in Troy thou wert the dearest, since Paris brought me hither. Would that ere that day I had died! For this is now the twentieth year since I came, and in all these twenty years never heard I a word from thee that was bitter and unkind; others might upbraid me, thy sisters or thy mother, for thy father was good to me as if he had been my own; but then thou wouldst restrain them that spoke evil by the courtesy of thy heart and thy gentle words. Ah! woe for thee, and woe for me, whom all men shudder at, for there is now none in wide Troyland to be my friend like thee, my brother and my friend!'

So Helen lamented, but now was done all that men might do; a great pile of wood was raised, and Hector was burned, and his ashes were placed in a golden urn, in a dark chamber of stone, within a hollow hill.

CHAPTER NINE

How Ulysses Stole the Luck of Troy

After Hector was buried, the siege went on slowly, as it had done during the first nine years of the war. The Greeks did not know at that time how to besiege a city, as we saw, by way of digging trenches and building towers, and battering the walls with machines that threw heavy stones. The Trojans had lost courage, and dared not go into the open plain, and they were waiting for the coming up of new armies of allies – the Amazons, who were girl warriors from far away, and an Eastern people called the Khita, whose king was Memnon, the son of the bright dawn.

Now everyone knew that, in the temple of the goddess Pallas Athene, in Troy, was a sacred image, which fell from heaven, called the Palladium, and this very ancient image was the Luck of Troy. While it remained safe in the temple people believed that Troy could never be taken, but as it was in a guarded temple in the middle of the town, and was watched by priestesses day and night, it seemed impossible that the Greeks should ever enter the city secretly and steal the Luck away.

As Ulysses was the grandson of Autolycus, the master thief, he often wished that the old man was with the Greeks, for if there was a thing to steal Autolycus could steal it. But by this time Autolycus was dead, and so Ulysses could only puzzle over the way to steal the Luck of Troy, and wonder how his grandfather would have set about it. He prayed for help secretly to Hermes, the god of thieves, when he sacrificed goats to him, and at last he had a plan.

There was a story that Anius, the King of the Isle of Delos, had three daughters, named Oeno, Spermo, and Elais, and that Oeno could turn water into wine, while Spermo could turn stones into bread, and Elais could change mud into olive oil. Those fairy gifts, people said, were given to the maidens by the wine god, Dionysus, and by the goddess of corn, Demeter. Now corn, and wine, and oil were sorely needed by the Greeks, who were tired of paying much gold and bronze to the Phoenician merchants for their supplies. Ulysses therefore went to Agamemnon one day, and asked leave to take his ship and voyage to Delos, to bring, if he could, the three maidens to the camp, if indeed they could do these miracles. As no fighting was going on, Agamemnon gave Ulysses leave to depart, so he went on board his ship, with a crew of fifty men of Ithaca, and away they sailed, promising to return in a month.

Two or three days after that, a dirty old beggar man began to be seen in the Greek camp. He had crawled in late one evening, dressed in a dirty smock and a very dirty old cloak, full of holes, and stained with smoke. Over everything he wore the skin of a stag, with half the hair worn off, and he carried a staff, and a filthy tattered wallet, to put food in, which swung from his neck by a cord. He came crouching and smiling up to the door of the hut of Diomede, and sat down just within the doorway, where beggars still sit in the East. Diomede saw him, and sent him a loaf and two handfuls of flesh, which the beggar laid on his wallet, between his feet, and he made his supper greedily, gnawing a bone like a dog.

After supper Diomede asked him who he was and whence he came, and he told a long story about how he had been a Cretan pirate, and had been taken prisoner by the Egyptians when he was robbing there, and how he had worked for many years in their stone quarries, where the sun had burned him brown, and had escaped by hiding among the great stones, carried down the Nile in a raft, for building a temple on the seashore. The raft arrived at night, and the beggar said that he stole out from it in the dark and found a Phoenician ship in the harbour, and the Phoenicians took him on board, meaning to sell him somewhere as a slave. But a tempest came on and wrecked the ship off the Isle of Tenedos, which is near Troy, and the beggar alone escaped to the island on a plank of the ship. From Tenedos he had come to Troy in a fisher's boat, hoping to make himself useful in the camp, and earn enough to keep body and soul together till he could find a ship sailing to Crete.

He made his story rather amusing, describing the strange ways of the Egyptians; how they worshipped cats and bulls, and did everything in just the opposite of the Greek way of doing things. So Diomede let him have a rug and blankets to sleep on in the portico of the hut, and next day the old wretch went begging about the camp and talking with the soldiers. Now he was a most impudent and annoying old vagabond, and was always in quarrels. If there was a disagreeable story about the father or grandfather of any of the princes, he knew it and told it, so that he got a blow from the baton of Agamemnon, and Aias gave him a kick, and Idomeneus drubbed him with the butt of his spear for a tale about his grandmother, and everybody hated him and called him a nuisance. He was forever jeering at Ulysses, who was far away, and telling tales about Autolycus, and at last he stole a gold cup, a very large cup, with two handles, and a dove sitting on each handle, from the hut of Nestor. The old chief was fond of this cup, which he had brought from home, and, when it was found in the beggar's dirty wallet, everybody cried that he must be driven out of the camp and well whipped. So Nestor's son, young Thrasymedes, with other young men, laughing and shouting, pushed and dragged the beggar close up to the Scaean gate of Troy, where Thrasymedes called with a loud voice, 'O Trojans, we are sick of this shameless beggar. First we shall whip him well, and if he comes back we shall put out his eyes and cut off his hands and feet, and give him to the dogs to eat. He may go to you, if he likes; if not, he must wander till he dies of hunger.'

The young men of Troy heard this and laughed, and a crowd gathered on the wall to see the beggar punished. So Thrasymedes whipped him with his bowstring till he was tired, and they did not leave off beating the beggar till he ceased howling and fell, all bleeding, and lay still. Then Thrasymedes gave him a parting kick, and went away with his friends. The beggar lay quiet for some time, then he began to stir, and sat up, wiping the tears from his eyes, and shouting curses and bad words after the Greeks, praying that they might be speared in the back, and eaten by dogs.

At last he tried to stand up, but fell down again, and began to crawl on hands and knees towards the Scaean gate. There he sat down, within the two side walls of the gate, where he cried and lamented. Now Helen of the fair hands came down from the gate tower, being sorry to see any man treated so much worse than a beast, and she spoke to the beggar and asked him why he had been used in this cruel way?

At first he only moaned, and rubbed his sore sides, but at last he said that he was an unhappy man, who had been shipwrecked, and was begging his way home, and that the Greeks suspected him of being a spy sent out by the Trojans. But he had been in Lacedae-mon, her own country, he said, and could tell her about her father, if she were, as he supposed, the beautiful Helen, and about her brothers, Castor and Polydeuces, and her little daughter, Hermione.

'But perhaps,' he said, 'you are no mortal woman, but some goddess who favours the Trojans, and if indeed you are a goddess then I liken you to Aphrodite, for beauty, and stature, and shape-liness.' Then Helen wept; for many a year had passed since she had heard any word of her father, and daughter, and her brothers, who were dead, though she knew it not. So she stretched out her white hand, and raised the beggar, who was kneeling at her feet, and bade him follow her to her own house, within the palace garden of King Priam.

Helen walked forward, with a bower maiden at either side, and the beggar crawling after her. When she had entered her house, Paris was not there, so she ordered the bath to be filled with warm water, and new clothes to be brought, and she herself washed the old beggar and anointed him with oil. This appears very strange to us, for though Saint Elizabeth of Hungary used to wash and clothe beggars, we are surprised that Helen should do so, who was not a saint. But long afterwards she herself told the son of Ulysses, Telemachus, that she had washed his father when he came into Troy disguised as a beggar who had been sorely beaten.

You must have guessed that the beggar was Ulysses, who had not gone to Delos in his ship, but stolen back in a boat, and appeared disguised among the Greeks. He did all this to make sure that nobody could recognise him, and he behaved so as to deserve a whipping that he might not be suspected as a Greek spy by the Trojans, but rather be pitied by them. Certainly he deserved his name of 'the much-enduring Ulysses'.

Meanwhile he sat in his bath and Helen washed his feet. But when she had done, and had anointed his wounds with olive oil, and when she had clothed him in a white tunic and a purple mantle, then she opened her lips to cry out with amazement, for she knew Ulysses; but he laid his finger on her lips, saying 'Hush!' Then she remembered how great danger he was in, for the Trojans, if they found him, would put him to some cruel death, and she sat down, trembling and weeping, while he watched her.

'Oh thou strange one,' she said, 'how enduring is thy heart and how cunning beyond measure! How hast thou borne to be thus beaten and disgraced, and to come within the walls of Troy? Well it is for thee that Paris, my lord, is far from home, having gone to guide Penthesilea, the queen of the warrior maids whom men call Amazons, who is on her way to help the Trojans.'

Then Ulysses smiled, and Helen saw that she had said a word which she ought not to have spoken, and had revealed the secret hope of the Trojans. Then she wept, and said, 'Oh cruel and cunning! You have made me betray the people with whom I live, though woe is me that ever I left my own people, and my husband dear, and my child! And now if you escape alive out of Troy, you will tell the Greeks, and they will lie in ambush by night for the Amazons on the way to Troy and will slay them all. If you and I were not friends long ago, I would tell the Trojans that you are here, and they would give your body to the dogs to eat, and fix your head on the palisade above the wall. Woe is me that ever I was born.'

Ulysses answered, 'Lady, as you have said, we two are friends from of old, and your friend I will be till the last, when the Greeks break into Troy, and slay the men, and carry the women captives. If I live till that hour no man shall harm you, but safely and in honour you shall come to your palace in Lacedaemon of the rifted hills. Moreover, I swear to you a great oath, by Zeus above, and by Them that under earth punish the souls of men who swear falsely, that I shall tell no man the thing which you have spoken.'

So when he had sworn and done that oath, Helen was comforted and dried her tears. Then she told him how unhappy she was, and how she had lost her last comfort when Hector died. 'Always am I wretched,' she said, 'save when sweet sleep falls on me. Now the wife of Thon, King of Egypt, gave me this gift when we were in Egypt, on our way to Troy, namely, a drug that brings sleep even to the most unhappy, and it is pressed from the poppy heads of the garland of the god of sleep.' Then she showed him strange phials of gold, full of this drug: phials wrought by the Egyptians, and covered with magic spells and shapes of beasts and flowers. 'One of these I will give you,' she said, 'that even from Troy town you may not go without a gift in memory of the hands of Helen.' So Ulysses took the phial of gold, and was glad in his heart, and Helen set before him meat and wine. When he had eaten and drunk, and his strength had come back to him, he said: 'Now I must dress me again in my old rags, and take my wallet, and my staff, and go forth, and beg through Troy town. For here I must abide for some days as a beggar man, lest if I now escape from your house in the night the Trojans may think that you have told me the secrets of their counsel, which I am carrying to the Greeks, and may be angry with you.' So he clothed himself again as a beggar, and took his staff, and hid the phial of gold with the Egyptian drug in his rags, and in his wallet also he put the new clothes that Helen had given him, and a sword, and he took farewell, saying, 'Be of good heart, for the end of your sorrows is at hand. But if you see me among the beggars in the street, or by the well, take no heed of me, only I will salute you as a beggar who has been kindly treated by a queen.'

So they parted, and Ulysses went out, and when it was day he was with the beggars in the streets, but by night he commonly slept near the fire of a smithy forge, as is the way of beggars. So for some days he begged, saying that he was gathering food to eat while he walked to some town far away that was at peace, where he might find work to do. He was not impudent now, and did not go to rich men's houses or tell evil tales, or laugh, but he was much in the temples, praying to the gods, and above all in the temple of

Pallas Athene. The Trojans thought that he was a pious man for a beggar.

Now there was a custom in these times that men and women who were sick or in distress, should sleep at night on the floors of the temples. They did this hoping that the god would send them a dream to show them how their diseases might be cured, or how they might find what they had lost, or might escape from their distresses.

Ulysses slept in more than one temple, and once in that of Pallas Athene, and the priests and priestesses were kind to him, and gave him food in the morning when the gates of the temple were opened.

In the temple of Pallas Athene, where the Luck of Troy lay always on her altar, the custom was that priestesses kept watch, each for two hours, all through the night, and soldiers kept guard within call. So one night Ulysses slept there, on the floor, with other distressed people, seeking for dreams from the gods. He lay still all through the night till the turn of the last priestess came to watch. The priestess used to walk up and down with bare feet among the dreaming people, having a torch in her hand, and muttering hymns to the goddess. Then Ulysses, when her back was turned, slipped the gold phial out of his rags, and let it lie on the polished floor beside him. When the priestess came back again, the light from her torch fell on the glittering phial, and she stooped and picked it up, and looked at it curiously. There came from it a sweet fragrance, and she opened it, and tasted the drug. It seemed to her the sweetest thing that ever she had tasted, and she took more and more, and then closed the phial and laid it down, and went along murmuring her hymn.

But soon a great drowsiness came over her, and she sat down on the step of the altar, and fell sound asleep, and the torch sunk in her hand, and went out, and all was dark. Then Ulysses put the phial in his wallet, and crept very cautiously to the altar, in the dark, and stole the Luck of Troy. It was only a small black mass of what is now called meteoric iron, which sometimes comes down with meteorites from the sky, but it was shaped like a shield, and the people thought it an image of the warlike shielded goddess, fallen from heaven.

Such sacred shields, made of glass and ivory, are found deep in the earth in the ruined cities of Ulysses' time. Swiftly Ulysses hid the Luck in his rags and left in its place on the altar a copy of the Luck, which he had made of blackened clay. Then he stole back to the place where he had lain, and remained there till dawn appeared, and the sleepers who sought for dreams awoke, and the temple gates were opened, and Ulysses walked out with the rest of them.

He stole down a lane, where as yet no people were stirring, and crept along, leaning on his staff, till he came to the eastern gate, at the back of the city, which the Greeks never attacked, for they had never drawn their army in a circle round the town. There Ulysses explained to the sentinels that he had gathered food enough to last for a long journey to some other town, and opened his bag, which seemed full of bread and broken meat. The soldiers said he was a lucky beggar, and let him out. He walked slowly along the waggon road by which wood was brought into Troy from the forests on Mount Ida, and when he found that nobody was within sight he slipped into the forest, and stole into a dark thicket, hiding beneath the tangled boughs. Here he lay and slept till evening, and then took the new clothes which Helen had given him out of his wallet, and put them on, and threw the belt of the sword over his shoulder, and hid the Luck of Troy in his bosom. He washed himself clean in a mountain brook, and now all who saw him must have known that he was no beggar, but Ulysses of Ithaca, Laertes' son.

So he walked cautiously down the side of the brook which ran between high banks deep in trees, and followed it till it reached the river Xanthus, on the left of the Greek lines. Here he found Greek sentinels set to guard the camp, who cried aloud in joy and surprise, for his ship had not yet returned from Delos, and they could not guess how Ulysses had come back alone across the sea. So two of the sentinels guarded Ulysses to the hut of Agamemnon, where he and Achilles and all the chiefs were sitting at a feast. They all leaped up, but when Ulysses took the Luck of Troy from within his mantle, they cried that this was the bravest deed that had been done in the war, and they sacrificed ten oxen to Zeus.

'So you were the old beggar,' said young Thrasymedes.

'Yes,' said Ulysses, 'and when next you beat a beggar, Thrasymedes, do not strike so hard and so long.'

That night all the Greeks were full of hope, for now they had the Luck of Troy, but the Trojans were in despair, and guessed that the beggar was the thief, and that Ulysses had been the beggar. The priestess, Theano, could tell them nothing; they found her, with the extinguished torch drooping in her hand, asleep, as she sat on the step of the altar, and she never woke again.

CHAPTER TEN

The Battles with the Amazons and Memnon – the Death of Achilles

Ulysses thought much and often of Helen, without whose kindness he could not have saved the Greeks by stealing the Luck of Troy. He saw that, though she remained as beautiful as when the princes all sought her hand, she was most unhappy, knowing herself to be the cause of so much misery, and fearing what the future might bring. Ulysses told nobody about the secret which she had let fall, the coming of the Amazons.

The Amazons were a race of warlike maids, who lived far away on the banks of the river Thermodon. They had fought against Troy in former times, and one of the great hill-graves on the plain of Troy covered the ashes of an Amazon, swift-footed Myrine. People believed that they were the daughters of the god of war, and they were reckoned equal in battle to the bravest men. Their young queen, Penthesilea, had two reasons for coming to fight at Troy: one was her ambition to win renown, and the other her sleepless sorrow for having accidentally killed her sister, Hippolyte, when hunting. The spear which she threw at a stag struck Hippolyte and slew her, and Penthesilea cared no longer for her own life, and desired to fall gloriously in battle. So Penthesilea and her body-guard of twelve Amazons set forth from the wide streams of Thermodon, and rode into Troy. The story says that they did not drive in chariots, like all the Greek and Trojan chiefs, but rode horses, which must have been the manner of their country.

Penthesilea was the tallest and most beautiful of the Amazons, and shone among her twelve maidens like the moon among the stars, or the bright Dawn among the Hours which follow her chariot wheels. The Trojans rejoiced when they beheld her, for she looked both terrible and beautiful, with a frown on her brow, and fair shining eyes, and a blush on her cheeks. To the Trojans she came like Iris, the Rainbow, after a storm, and they gathered round her cheering, and throwing flowers and kissing her stirrup, as the people of Orleans welcomed Joan of Arc when she came to deliver them. Even Priam was glad, as is a man long blind, when he has been healed, and again looks upon the light of the sun. Priam held a great feast, and gave to Penthesilea many beautiful gifts: cups of gold, and embroideries, and a sword with a hilt of silver, and she vowed that she would slay Achilles. But when Andromache, the wife of Hector, heard her she said within herself, 'Ah, unhappy girl, what is this boast of thine! Thou hast not the strength to fight the unconquerable son of Peleus, for if Hector could not slay him, what chance hast thou? But the piled-up earth covers Hector!'

In the morning Penthesilea sprang up from sleep and put on her glorious armour, with spear in hand, and sword at side, and bow and quiver hung behind her back, and her great shield covering her side from neck to stirrup, and mounted her horse, and galloped to the plain. Beside her charged the twelve maidens of her bodyguard, and all the company of Hector's brothers and kinsfolk. These headed the Trojan lines, and they rushed towards the ships of the Greeks.

Then the Greeks asked each other, 'Who is this that leads the Trojans as Hector led them, surely some god rides in the van of the charioteers!' Ulysses could have told them who the new leader of the Trojans was, but it seems that he had not the heart to fight against women, for his name is not mentioned in this day's battle. So the two lines clashed, and the plain of Troy ran red with blood, for Penthesilea slew Molios, and Persinoos, and Eilissos, and Antiphates, and Lernos high of heart, and Hippalmos of the loud war-cry, and Haemonides, and strong Elasippus, while her maidens Derinoe and Clonie slew each a chief of the Greeks. But Clonie fell beneath the spear of Podarkes, whose hand Penthesilea cut off with the sword, while Idomeneus speared the Amazon Bremousa, and Meriones of Crete slew Evadre, and Diomede killed Alcibie and Derimacheia in close fight with the sword, so the company of the Twelve were thinned, the bodyguard of Penthesilea.

The Trojans and Greeks kept slaying each other, but Penthesilea avenged her maidens, driving the ranks of Greece as a lioness drives the cattle on the hills, for they could not stand before her. Then she shouted, 'Dogs! today shall you pay for the sorrows of Priam! Where is Diomede, where is Achilles, where is Aias, that, men say, are your bravest? Will none of them stand before my spear?' Then she charged again, at the head of the Household of Priam, brothers and kinsmen of Hector, and where they came the Greeks fell like yellow leaves before the wind of autumn. The white horse that Penthesilea rode, a gift from the wife of the North Wind, flashed like lightning through a dark cloud among the companies of the Greeks, and the chariots that followed the charge of the Amazon rocked as they swept over the bodies of the slain. Then the old Trojans, watching from the walls, cried: 'This is no mortal maiden but a goddess, and today she will burn the ships of the Greeks, and they will all perish in Troyland, and see Greece never more again.'

Now it so was that Aias and Achilles had not heard the din and the cry of war, for both had gone to weep over the great new grave of Patroclus. Penthesilea and the Trojans had driven back the Greeks within their ditch, and they were hiding here and there among the ships, and torches were blazing in men's hands to burn the ships, as in the day of the valour of Hector: when Aias heard the din of battle, and called to Achilles to make speed towards the ships.

So they ran swiftly to their huts, and armed themselves, and Aias fell smiting and slaying upon the Trojans, but Achilles slew five of the bodyguard of Penthesilea. She, beholding her maidens fallen, rode straight against Aias and Achilles, like a dove defying two falcons, and cast her spear, but it fell back blunted from the glorious shield that the god had made for the son of Peleus. Then she threw another spear at Aias, crying, 'I am the daughter of the god of war,' but his armour kept out the spear, and he and Achilles laughed aloud. Aias paid no more heed to the Amazon, but rushed against the Trojan men; while Achilles raised the heavy spear that none but he could throw, and drove it down through breastplate and breast of Penthesilea, yet still her hand grasped her sword-hilt. But, ere she could draw her sword, Achilles speared her horse, and horse and rider fell, and died in their fall.

There lay fair Penthesilea in the dust, like a tall poplar tree that the wind has overthrown, and her helmet fell, and the Greeks who gathered round marvelled to see her lie so beautiful in death, like Artemis, the goddess of the woods, when she sleeps alone, weary with hunting on the hills. Then the heart of Achilles was pierced with pity and sorrow, thinking how she might have been his wife in his own country, had he spared her, but he was never to see pleasant Phthia, his native land, again. So Achilles stood and wept over Penthesilea dead.

Now the Greeks, in pity and sorrow, held their hands, and did not pursue the Trojans who had fled, nor did they strip the armour from Penthesilea and her twelve maidens, but laid the bodies on biers, and sent them back in peace to Priam. Then the Trojans burned Penthesilea in the midst of her dead maidens, on a great pile of dry wood, and placed their ashes in a golden casket, and buried them all in the great hill-grave of Laomedon, an ancient King of Troy, while the Greeks with lamentation buried them whom the Amazon had slain.

The old men of Troy and the chiefs now held a council, and Priam said that they must not yet despair, for, if they had lost many of their bravest warriors, many of the Greeks had also fallen. Their best plan was to fight only with arrows from the walls and towers, till King Memnon came to their rescue with a great army of Aethiopes. Now Memnon was the son of the bright Dawn, a beautiful goddess who had loved and married a mortal man, Tithonus. She had asked Zeus, the chief of the gods, to make her lover immortal, and her prayer was granted. Tithonus could not die, but he began to grow grey, and then white-haired, with a long white beard, and very weak, till nothing of him seemed to be left but his voice, always feebly chattering like the grasshoppers on a summer day.

Memnon was the most beautiful of men, except Paris and Achilles, and his home was in a country that borders on the land of sunrising. There he was reared by the lily maidens called Hesperides, till he came to his full strength, and commanded the whole army of the

Achilles pities Penthesilea after slaying her

Aethiopes. For their arrival Priam wished to wait, but Polydamas advised that the Trojans should give back Helen to the Greeks, with jewels twice as valuable as those which she had brought from the house of Menelaus. Then Paris was very angry, and said that Polydamas was a coward, for it was little to Paris that Troy should be taken and burned in a month if for a month he could keep Helen of the fair hands.

At length Memnon came, leading a great army of men who had nothing white about them but the teeth, so fiercely the sun burned on them in their own country. The Trojans had all the more hopes of Memnon because, on his long journey from the land of sun-rising, and the river Oceanus that girdles the round world, he had been obliged to cross the country of the Solymi. Now the Solymi were the fiercest of men and rose up against Memnon, but he and his army fought them for a whole day, and defeated them, and drove them to the hills. When Memnon came, Priam gave him a great cup of gold, full of wine to the brim, and Memnon drank the wine at one draught. But he did not make great boasts of what he could do, like poor Penthesilea, 'For,' said he, 'whether I am a good man at arms will be known in battle, where the strength of men is tried. So now let us turn to sleep, for to wake and drink wine all through the night is an ill beginning of war.'

Then Priam praised his wisdom, and all men betook them to bed, but the bright Dawn rose unwillingly next day, to throw light on the battle where her son was to risk his life. Then Memnon led out the dark clouds of his men into the plain, and the Greeks foreboded evil when they saw so great a new army of fresh and unwearied warriors, but Achilles, leading them in his shining armour, gave them courage. Memnon fell upon the left wing of the Greeks, and on the men of Nestor, and first he slew Ereuthus, and then attacked Nestor's young son, Antilochus, who, now that Patroclus had fallen, was the dearest friend of Achilles. On him Memnon leaped, like a lion on a kid, but Antilochus lifted a huge stone from the plain, a pillar that had been set on the tomb of some great warrior long ago, and the stone smote full on the helmet of Memnon, who reeled beneath the stroke. But Memnon seized his heavy spear, and drove it through shield and corselet of Antilochus, even into his heart, and he fell and died beneath his father's eyes. Then Nestor in great sorrow and anger strode across the body of Antilochus and called to his other son, Thrasymedes, 'Come and drive afar this man that has slain thy brother, for if fear be in thy heart thou art no son of mine, nor of the race of Periclymenus, who stood up in battle even against the strong man Heracles!'

But Memnon was too strong for Thrasymedes, and drove him off, while old Nestor himself charged sword in hand, though Memnon bade him begone, for he was not minded to strike so aged a man, and Nestor drew back, for he was weak with age. Then Memnon and his army charged the Greeks, slaying and stripping the dead. But Nestor had mounted his chariot and driven to Achilles, weeping, and imploring him to come swiftly and save the body of Antilochus, and he sped to meet Memnon, who lifted a great stone, the landmark of a field, and drove it against the shield of the son of Peleus. But Achilles was not shaken by the blow; he ran forward, and wounded Memnon over the rim of his shield. Yet wounded as he was Memnon fought on and struck his spear through the arm of Achilles, for the Greeks fought with no sleeves of bronze to protect their arms.

Then Achilles drew his great sword, and flew on Memnon, and with sword-strokes they lashed at each other on shield and helmet, and the long horsehair crests of the helmets were shorn off, and flew down the wind, and their shields rang terribly beneath the sword-strokes. They thrust at each other's throats between shield and visor of the helmet, they smote at knee, and thrust at breast, and the armour rang about their bodies, and the dust from beneath their feet rose up in a cloud around them, like mist round the falls of a great river in flood. So they fought, neither of them yielding a step, till Achilles made so rapid a thrust that Memnon could not parry it, and the bronze sword passed clean through his body beneath the breastbone, and he fell, and his armour clashed as he fell.

Then Achilles, wounded as he was and weak from loss of blood, did not stay to strip the golden armour of Memnon, but shouted his war-cry, and pressed on, for he hoped to enter the gate of Troy with the fleeing Trojans, and all the Greeks followed after him. So they pursued, slaying as they went, and the Scaean gate was choked with the crowd of men, pursuing and pursued. In that hour would the Greeks have entered Troy, and burned the city, and taken the women captive, but Paris stood on the tower above the gate, and in his mind was anger for the death of his brother Hector. He tried the string of his bow, and found it frayed, for all day he had showered his arrows on the Greeks; so he chose a new bowstring, and fitted it, and strung the bow, and chose an arrow from his quiver, and aimed at the ankle of Achilles, where it was bare beneath the greave, or leg-guard of metal, that the god had fashioned for him. Through the ankle flew the arrow, and Achilles wheeled round, weak as he was, and stumbled, and fell, and the armour that the god had wrought was defiled with dust and blood.

Then Achilles rose again, and cried: 'What coward has smitten me with a secret arrow from afar? Let him stand forth and meet me with sword and spear!' So speaking he seized the shaft with his strong hands and tore it out of the wound, and much blood gushed, and darkness came over his eyes. Yet he staggered forward, striking blindly, and smote Orythaon, a dear friend of Hector, through the helmet, and others he smote, but now his force failed him, and he leaned on his spear, and cried his war-cry, and said, 'Cowards of Troy, ye shall not all escape my spear, dying as I am.' But as he spoke he fell, and all his armour rang around him, yet the Trojans stood apart and watched; and as hunters watch a dying lion not daring to go nigh him, so the Trojans stood in fear till Achilles drew his latest breath. Then from the wall the Trojan women raised a great cry of joy over him who had slain the noble Hector: and thus was fulfilled the prophecy of Hector, that Achilles should fall in the Scaean gateway, by the hand of Paris.

Then the best of the Trojans rushed forth from the gate to seize the body of Achilles, and his glorious armour, but the Greeks were as eager to carry the body to the ships that it might have due burial. Round the dead Achilles men fought long and sore, and both sides were mixed, Greeks and Trojans, so that men dared not shoot arrows from the walls of Troy lest they should kill their own friends. Paris, and Aeneas, and Glaucus, who had been the friend of Sarpedon, led the Trojans, and Aias and Ulysses led the Greeks, for we are not told that Agamemnon was fighting in this great battle of the war. Now as angry wild bees flock round a man who is taking their honeycombs, so the Trojans gathered round Aias, striving to stab him, but he set his great shield in front, and smote and slew all that came within reach of his spear. Ulysses, too, struck down many, and though a spear was thrown and pierced his leg near the knee he stood firm, protecting the body of Achilles. At last Ulysses caught the body of Achilles by the hands, and heaved it upon his back, and so limped towards the ships, but Aias and the men of Aias followed, turning round if ever the Trojans ventured to come near, and charging into the midst of them. Thus very slowly they bore the dead Achilles across the plain, through the bodies of the fallen and the blood, till they met Nestor in his chariot and placed Achilles therein, and swiftly Nestor drove to the ships.

There the women, weeping, washed Achilles' comely body, and laid him on a bier with a great white mantle over him, and all the women lamented and sang dirges, and the first was Briseis, who loved Achilles better than her own country, and her father, and her brothers whom he had slain in war. The Greek princes, too, stood round the body, weeping and cutting off their long locks of yellow hair, a token of grief and an offering to the dead.

Men say that forth from the sea came Thetis of the silver feet, the mother of Achilles, with her ladies, the deathless maidens of the waters. They rose up from their glassy chambers below the sea, moving on, many and beautiful, like the waves on a summer day, and their sweet song echoed along the shores, and fear came upon the Greeks. Then they would have fled, but Nestor cried: 'Hold, flee not, young lords of the Achaeans! Lo, she that comes from the sea is his mother, with the deathless maidens of the waters, to look on the face of her dead son.' Then the sea nymphs stood around the dead Achilles and clothed him in the garments of the gods, fragrant raiment, and all the nine muses, one to the other replying with sweet voices, began their lament.

Next the Greeks made a great pile of dry wood, and laid Achilles on it, and set fire to it, till the flames had consumed his body except the white ashes. These they placed in a great golden cup and mingled with them the ashes of Patroclus, and above all they built a tomb like a hill, high on a headland above the sea, that men for all time may see it as they go sailing by, and may remember Achilles. Next they held in his honour foot races and chariot races, and other games, and Thetis gave splendid prizes. Last of all, when the games were ended, Thetis placed before the chiefs the glorious armour that the god had made for her son on the night after the slaying of Patroclus by Hector. 'Let these arms be the prize of the best of the Greeks,' she said, 'and of him that saved the body of Achilles out of the hands of the Trojans.'

Then stood up on one side Aias and on the other Ulysses, for these two had rescued the body, and neither thought himself a worse warrior than the other. Both were the bravest of the brave, and if Aias was the taller and stronger, and upheld the fight at the ships on the day of the valour of Hector, Ulysses had alone withstood the Trojans, and refused to retreat even when wounded, and his courage and cunning had won for the Greeks the Luck of Troy. Therefore old Nestor arose and said: 'This is a luckless day, when the best of the Greeks are rivals for such a prize. He who is not the winner will be heavy at heart, and will not stand firm by us in battle, as of old, and hence will come great loss to the Greeks. Who can be a just judge in this question, for some men will love Aias better, and some will prefer Ulysses, and thus will arise disputes among ourselves. Lo! have we not here among us many Trojan prisoners, waiting till their friends pay their ransom in cattle and gold and bronze and iron? These hate all the Greeks alike, and will favour neither Aias nor Ulysses. Let them be the judges, and decide who is the best of the Greeks, and the man who has done most harm to the Trojans.'

Agamemnon said that Nestor had spoken wisely. The Trojans were then made to sit as judges in the midst of the Assembly, and Aias and Ulysses spoke, and told the stories of their own great deeds, of which we have heard already, but Aias spoke roughly and discourteously, calling Ulysses a coward and a weakling. 'Perhaps the Trojans know,' said Ulysses quietly, 'whether they think that I deserve what Aias has said about me, that I am a coward; and perhaps Aias may remember that he did not find me so weak when we wrestled for a prize at the funeral of Patroclus.'

Then the Trojans all with one voice said that Ulysses was the best man among the Greeks, and the most feared by them, both for his courage and his skill in stratagems of war. On this, the blood of Aias flew into his face, and he stood silent and unmoving, and could not speak a word, till his friends came round him and led him away to his hut, and there he sat down and would not eat or drink, and the night fell.

Long he sat, musing in his mind, and then rose and put on all his armour, and seized a sword that Hector had given him one day when they two fought in a gentle passage of arms, and took courteous farewell of each other, and Aias had given Hector a broad sword-belt, wrought with gold. This sword, Hector's gift, Aias took, and went towards the hut of Ulysses, meaning to carve him limb from limb, for madness had come upon him in his great grief. Rushing through the night to slay Ulysses he fell upon the flock of sheep that the Greeks kept for their meat. And up and down among them he went, smiting blindly till the dawn came, and, lo! his senses returned to him, and he saw that he had not smitten Ulysses, but stood in a pool of blood among the sheep that he had slain. He could not endure the disgrace of his madness, and he fixed the sword, Hector's gift, with its hilt firmly in the ground, and went back a little way, and ran and fell upon the sword, which pierced his heart, and so died the great Aias, choosing death before a dishonoured life.

CHAPTER ELEVEN

Ulysses Sails to Seek the Son of Achilles – the Valour of Eurypylus

When the Greeks found Aias lying dead, slain by his own hand, they made great lament, and above all the brother of Aias, and his wife Tecmessa bewailed him, and the shores of the sea rang with their sorrow. But of all no man was more grieved than Ulysses, and he stood up and said: 'Would that the sons of the Trojans had never awarded to me the arms of Achilles, for far rather would I have given them to Aias than that this loss should have befallen the whole army of the Greeks. Let no man blame me, or be angry with me, for I have not sought for wealth, to enrich myself, but for honour only, and to win a name that will be remembered among men in times to come.' Then they made a great fire of wood, and burned the body of Aias, lamenting him as they had sorrowed for Achilles.

Now it seemed that though the Greeks had won the Luck of Troy and had defeated the Amazons and the army of Memnon, they were no nearer taking Troy than ever. They had slain Hector, indeed, and many other Trojans, but they had lost the great Achilles, and Aias, and Patroclus, and Antilochus, with the princes whom Penthesilea and Memnon slew, and the bands of the dead chiefs were weary of fighting, and eager to go home. The chiefs met in council, and Menelaus arose and said that his heart was wasted with sorrow for the death of so many brave men who had sailed to Troy for his sake. 'Would that death had come upon me before I gathered this host,' he said, 'but come, let the rest of us launch our swift ships, and return each to our own country.'

He spoke thus to try the Greeks, and see of what courage they were, for his desire was still to burn Troy town and to slay Paris with his own hand. Then up rose Diomede, and swore that never would the Greeks turn cowards. No! he bade them sharpen their swords, and make ready for battle. The prophet Calchas, too, arose and reminded the Greeks how he had always foretold that they would take Troy in the tenth year of the siege, and how the tenth year had come, and victory was almost in their hands. Next Ulysses stood up and said that, though Achilles was dead, and there was no prince to lead his men, yet a son had been born to Achilles, while he was in the isle of Scyros, and that son he would bring to fill his father's place.

'Surely he will come, and for a token I will carry to him those unhappy arms of the great Achilles. Unworthy am I to wear them, and they bring back to my mind our sorrow for Aias. But his son will wear them, in the front of the spearmen of Greece and in the thickest ranks of Troy shall the helmet of Achilles shine, as it was wont to do, for always he fought among the foremost.' Thus Ulysses spoke, and he and Diomede, with fifty oarsmen, went on board a swift ship, and sitting all in order on the benches they smote the grey sea into foam, and Ulysses held the helm and steered them towards the isle of Scyros.

Now the Trojans had rest from war for a while, and Priam, with a heavy heart, bade men take his chief treasure, the great golden vine, with leaves and clusters of gold, and carry it to the mother of Eurypylus, the king of the people who dwell where the wide marsh-lands of the river Cayster clang with the cries of the cranes and herons and wild swans. For the mother of Eurypylus had sworn that never would she let her son go to the war unless Priam sent her the vine of gold, a gift of the gods to an ancient King of Troy.

With a heavy heart, then, Priam sent the golden vine, but Eurypylus was glad when he saw it, and bade all his men arm, and harness the horses to the chariots, and glad were the Trojans when the long line of the new army wound along the road and into the town. Then Paris welcomed Eurypylus who was his nephew, son of his sister Astyoche, a daughter of Priam; but the grandfather of Eurypylus was the famous Heracles, the strongest man who ever lived on earth. So Paris brought Eurypylus to his house, where Helen sat working at her embroideries with her four bower maidens, and Eurypylus marvelled when he saw her, she was so beautiful. But the Khita, the people of Eurypylus, feasted in the open air among the Trojans, by the light of great fires burning, and to the music of pipes and flutes. The Greeks saw the fires, and heard the merry music, and they watched all night lest the Trojans should attack the ships before the dawn. But in the dawn Eurypylus rose from sleep and put on his armour, and hung from his neck by the belt the great shield on which were fashioned, in gold of many colours and in silver, the Twelve Adventures of Heracles, his grandfather; strange deeds that he did, fighting with monsters and giants and with the Hound of Hades, who guards the dwellings of the dead. Then Eurypylus led on his whole army, and with the brothers of Hector he charged against the Greeks, who were led by Agamemnon.

In that battle Eurypylus first smote Nireus, who was the most beautiful of the Greeks now that Achilles had fallen. There lay Nireus, like an apple tree, all covered with blossoms red and white, that the wind has overthrown in a rich man's orchard. Then Eurypylus would have stripped off his armour, but Machaon rushed in, Machaon who had been wounded and taken to the tent of Nestor, on the day of the Valour of Hector, when he brought fire against the ships. Machaon drove his spear through the left shoulder of Eurypylus, but Eurypylus struck at his shoulder with his sword, and the blood flowed; nevertheless, Machaon stooped, and grasped a great stone, and sent it against the helmet of Eurypylus. He was shaken, but he did not fall, he drove his spear through breastplate and breast of Machaon, who fell and died. With his last breath he said, 'Thou, too, shalt fall,' but Eurypylus made answer, 'So let it be! Men cannot live for ever, and such is the fortune of war.'

Thus the battle rang, and shone, and shifted, till few of the Greeks kept steadfast, except those with Menelaus and Agamemnon, for Diomede and Ulysses were far away upon the sea, bringing from Scyros the son of Achilles. But Teucer slew Polydamas, who had warned Hector to come within the walls of Troy; and Menelaus wounded Deiphobus, the bravest of the sons of Priam who were still in arms, for many had fallen; and Agamemnon slew certain spearmen of the Trojans. Round Eurypylus fought Paris, and

Aeneas, who wounded Teucer with a great stone, breaking in his helmet, but he drove back in his chariot to the ships. Menelaus and Agamemnon stood alone and fought in the crowd of Trojans, like two wild boars that a circle of hunters surrounds with spears, so fiercely they stood at bay. There they would both have fallen, but Idomeneus, and Meriones of Crete, and Thrasymedes, Nestor's son, ran to their rescue, and fiercer grew the fighting. Eurypylus desired to slay Agamemnon and Menelaus, and end the war, but, as the spears of the Scots encompassed King James at Flodden Field till he ran forward, and fell within a lance's length of the English general, so the men of Crete and Pylos guarded the two princes with their spears.

There Paris was wounded in the thigh with a spear, and he retreated a little way, and showered his arrows among the Greeks; and Idomeneus lifted and hurled a great stone at Eurypylus which struck his spear out of his hand, and he went back to find it, and Menelaus and Agamemnon had a breathing space in the battle. But soon Eurypylus returned, crying on his men, and they drove back foot by foot the ring of spears round Agamemnon, and Aeneas and Paris slew men of Crete and of Mycenae till the Greeks were pushed to the ditch round the camp; and then great stones and spears and arrows rained down on the Trojans and the people of Eurypylus from the battlements and towers of the Grecian wall. Now night fell, and Eurypylus knew that he could not win the wall in the dark, so he withdrew his men, and they built great fires, and camped upon the plain.

The case of the Greeks was now like that of the Trojans after the death of Hector. They buried Machaon and the other chiefs who had fallen, and they remained within their ditch and their wall, for they dared not come out into the open plain. They knew not whether Ulysses and Diomede had come safely to Scyros, or whether their ship had been wrecked or driven into unknown seas. So they sent a herald to Eurypylus, asking for a truce, that they might gather their dead and burn them, and the Trojans and Khita also buried their dead.

Meanwhile the swift ship of Ulysses had swept through the sea to

Scyros, and to the palace of King Lycomedes. There they found Neoptolemus, the son of Achilles, in the court before the doors. He was as tall as his father, and very like him in face and shape, and he was practising the throwing of the spear at a mark. Right glad were Ulysses and Diomede to behold him, and Ulysses told Neoptolemus who they were, and why they came, and implored him to take pity on the Greeks and help them.

'My friend is Diomede, Prince of Argos,' said Ulysses, 'and I am Ulysses of Ithaca. Come with us, and we Greeks will give you countless gifts, and I myself will present you with the armour of your father, such as it is not lawful for any other mortal man to wear, seeing that it is golden, and wrought by the hands of a god. Moreover, when we have taken Troy, and gone home, Menelaus will give you his daughter, the beautiful Hermione, to be your wife, with gold in great plenty.'

Then Neoptolemus answered: 'It is enough that the Greeks need my sword. Tomorrow we shall sail for Troy.' He led them into the palace to dine, and there they found his mother, beautiful Deidamia, in mourning raiment, and she wept when she heard that they had come to take her son away. But Neoptolemus comforted her, promising to return safely with the spoils of Troy, 'or, even if I fall,' he said, 'it will be after doing deeds worthy of my father's name.' So next day they sailed, leaving Deidamia mournful, like a swallow whose nest a serpent has found, and has killed her young ones; even so she wailed, and went up and down in the house. But the ship ran swiftly on her way, cleaving the dark waves till Ulysses showed Neoptolemus the far-off snowy crest of Mount Ida; and Tenedos, the island near Troy; and they passed the plain where the tomb of Achilles stands, but Ulysses did not tell the son that it was his father's tomb.

Now all this time the Greeks, shut up within their wall and fighting from their towers, were looking back across the sea, eager to spy the ship of Ulysses, like men wrecked on a desert island, who keep watch every day for a sail afar off, hoping that the seamen will touch at their isle and have pity upon them, and carry them home, so the Greeks kept watch for the ship bearing Neoptolemus.

Diomede, too, had been watching the shore, and when they came in sight of the ships of the Greeks, he saw that they were being besieged by the Trojans, and that all the Greek army was penned up within the wall, and was fighting from the towers. Then he cried aloud to Ulysses and Neoptolemus, 'Make haste, friends, let us arm before we land, for some great evil has fallen upon the Greeks. The Trojans are attacking our wall, and soon they will burn our ships, and for us there will be no return.'

Then all the men on the ship of Ulysses armed themselves, and Neoptolemus, in the splendid armour of his father, was the first to leap ashore. The Greeks could not come from the wall to welcome him, for they were fighting hard and hand-to-hand with Eurypylus and his men. But they glanced back over their shoulders and it seemed to them that they saw Achilles himself, spear and sword in hand, rushing to help them. They raised a great battle-cry, and, when Neoptolemus reached the battlements, he and Ulysses, and Diomede leaped down to the plain, the Greeks following them, and they all charged at once on the men of Eurypylus, with levelled spears, and drove them from the wall.

Then the Trojans trembled, for they knew the shields of Diomede and Ulysses, and they thought that the tall chief in the armour of Achilles was Achilles himself, come back from the land of the dead to take vengeance for Antilochus. The Trojans fled, and gathered round Eurypylus, as in a thunderstorm little children, afraid of the lightning and the noise, run and cluster round their father, and hide their faces on his knees.

But Neoptolemus was spearing the Trojans, as a man who carries at night a beacon of fire in his boat on the sea spears the fishes that flock around, drawn by the blaze of the flame. Cruelly he avenged his father's death on many a Trojan, and the men whom Achilles had led followed Achilles' son, slaying to right and left, and smiting the Trojans, as they ran, between the shoulders with the spear. Thus they fought and followed while daylight lasted, but when night fell, they led Neoptolemus to his father's hut, where the women washed him in the bath, and then he was taken to feast with Agamemnon and Menelaus and the princes. They all welcomed him, and gave him glorious gifts, swords with silver hilts, and cups of gold and silver, and they were glad, for they had driven the Trojans from their wall, and hoped that tomorrow they would slay Eurypylus, and take Troy town.

But their hope was not to be fulfilled, for though next day Eurypylus met Neoptolemus in the battle, and was slain by him, when the Greeks chased the Trojans into their city so great a storm of lightning and thunder and rain fell upon them that they retreated again to their camp. They believed that Zeus, the chief of the gods, was angry with them, and the days went by, and Troy still stood unconquered.

CHAPTER TWELVE

The Slaying of Paris

When the Greeks were disheartened, as they often were, they consulted Calchas the prophet. He usually found that they must do something, or send for somebody, and in doing so they diverted their minds from their many misfortunes. Now, as the Trojans were fighting more bravely than before, under Deiphobus, a brother of Hector, the Greeks went to Calchas for advice, and he told them that they must send Ulysses and Diomede to bring Philoctetes the bowman from the isle of Lemnos. This was an unhappy deserted island, in which the married women, some years before, had murdered all their husbands, out of jealousy, in a single night. The Greeks had landed in Lemnos, on their way to Troy, and there Philoctetes had shot an arrow at a great water dragon which lived in a well within a cave in the lonely hills. But when he entered the cave the dragon bit him, and, though he killed it at last, its poisonous teeth wounded his foot. The wound never healed, but dripped with venom, and Philoctetes, in terrible pain, kept all the camp awake at night by his cries.

The Greeks were sorry for him, but he was not a pleasant companion, shrieking as he did, and exuding poison wherever he came. So they left him on the lonely island, and did not know whether he was alive or dead. Calchas ought to have told the Greeks not to desert Philoctetes at the time, if he was so important that Troy, as the prophet now said, could not be taken without him. But now, as he must give some advice, Calchas said that Philoctetes must be brought back, so Ulysses and Diomede went to bring him. They sailed to Lemnos; a melancholy place they found it, with no smoke rising from the ruinous houses along the shore. As they were landing they learned that Philoctetes was not dead, for his dismal old cries of pain, *otototoi, ai, ai; pheu, pheu; otototoi*, came echoing from a cave on the beach. To this cave the princes went, and found a terrible-looking man, with long, dirty, dry hair and beard; he was worn to a skeleton, with hollow eyes, and lay moaning in a mass of the feathers of sea birds. His great bow and his arrows lay ready to his hand: with these he used to shoot the sea birds, which were all that he had to eat, and their feathers littered all the floor of his cave, and they were none the better for the poison that dripped from his wounded foot.

When this horrible creature saw Ulysses and Diomede coming near, he seized his bow and fitted a poisonous arrow to the string, for he hated the Greeks, because they had left him in the desert isle. But the princes held up their hands in sign of peace, and cried out that they had come to do him kindness, so he laid down his bow, and they came in and sat on the rocks, and promised that his wound should be healed, for the Greeks were very much ashamed of having deserted him. It was difficult to resist Ulysses when he wished to persuade anyone, and at last Philoctetes consented to sail with them to Troy. The oarsmen carried him down to the ship on a litter, and there his dreadful wound was washed with warm water, and oil was poured into it, and it was bound up with soft linen, so that his pain grew less fierce, and they gave him a good supper and wine enough, which he had not tasted for many years.

Next morning they sailed, and had a fair west wind, so that they soon landed among the Greeks and carried Philoctetes on shore. Here Podaleirius, the brother of Machaon, being a physician, did all that could be done to heal the wound, and the pain left Philoctetes. He was taken to the hut of Agamemnon, who welcomed him, and said that the Greeks repented of their cruelty. They gave him seven female slaves to take care of him, and twenty swift horses, and twelve great vessels of bronze, and told him that he was always to live with the greatest chiefs and feed at their table. So he was bathed, and his hair was cut and combed and anointed with oil, and soon he was eager and ready to fight, and to use his great bow and poisoned arrows on the Trojans. The use of poisoned arrow-tips was thought unfair, but Philoctetes had no scruples.

Now in the next battle Paris was shooting down the Greeks with his arrows, when Philoctetes saw him, and cried: 'Dog, you are proud of your archery and of the arrow that slew the great Achilles. But, behold, I am a better bowman than you, by far, and the bow in my hands was borne by the strong man Heracles!' So he cried and drew the bowstring to his breast and the poisoned arrowhead to the bow, and the bowstring rang, and the arrow flew, and did but graze the hand of Paris. Then the bitter pain of the poison came upon him, and the Trojans carried him into their city, where the physicians tended him all night. But he never slept, and lay tossing in agony till dawn, when he said: 'There is but one hope. Take me to Oenone, the nymph of Mount Ida!'

Then his friends laid Paris on a litter, and bore him up the steep path to Mount Ida. Often had he climbed it swiftly, when he was young, and went to see the nymph who loved him; but for many a day he had not trod the path where he was now carried in great pain and fear, for the poison turned his blood to fire. Little hope he had, for he knew how cruelly he had deserted Oenone, and he saw that all the birds which were disturbed in the wood flew away to the left hand, an omen of evil.

At last the bearers reached the cave where the nymph Oenone lived, and they smelled the sweet fragrance of the cedar fire that burned on the floor of the cave, and they heard the nymph singing a melancholy song. Then Paris called to her in the voice which she had once loved to hear, and she grew very pale, and rose up, saying to herself, 'The day has come for which I have prayed. He is sore hurt, and has come to bid me heal his wound.' So she came and stood in the doorway of the dark cave, white against the darkness, and the bearers laid Paris on the litter at the feet of Oenone, and he stretched forth his hands to touch her knees, as was the manner of suppliants. But she drew back and gathered her robe about her, that he might not touch it with his hands.

Then he said: 'Lady, despise me not, and hate me not, for my pain is more than I can bear. Truly it was by no will of mine that I left you lonely here, for the Fates that no man may escape led me to Helen. Would that I had died in your arms before I saw her face! But now I beseech you in the name of the gods, and for the memory of our love, that you will have pity on me and heal my hurt, and not refuse your grace and let me die here at your feet.'

Then Oenone answered scornfully: 'Why have you come here to me? Surely for years you have not come this way, where the path was once worn with your feet. But long ago you left me lonely and lamenting, for the love of Helen of the fair hands. Surely she is much more beautiful than the love of your youth, and far more able to help you, for men say that she can never know old age and death. Go home to Helen and let her take away your pain.'

Thus Oenone spoke, and went within the cave, where she threw herself down among the ashes of the hearth and sobbed for anger and sorrow. In a little while she rose and went to the door of the cave, thinking that Paris had not been borne away back to Troy, but she found him not; for his bearers had carried him by another path, till he died beneath the boughs of the oak trees. Then his bearers carried him swiftly down to Troy, where his mother bewailed him, and Helen sang over him as she had sung over Hector, remembering many things, and fearing to think of what her own end might be. But the Trojans hastily built a great pile of dry wood, and thereon laid the body of Paris and set fire to it, and the flame went up through the darkness, for now night had fallen.

But Oenone was roaming in the dark woods, crying and calling after Paris, like a lioness whose cubs the hunters have carried away. The moon rose to give her light, and the flame of the funeral fire shone against the sky, and then Oenone knew that Paris had died – beautiful Paris – and that the Trojans were burning his body on the plain at the foot of Mount Ida. Then she cried that now Paris was all her own, and that Helen had no more hold on him: 'And though when he was living he left me, in death we shall not be divided,' she said, and she sped down the hill, and through the thickets where the wood nymphs were wailing for Paris, and she reached the plain, and, covering her head with her veil like a bride, she rushed through the throng of Trojans. She leaped upon the burning pile of wood, she clasped the body of Paris in her arms, and the flame of fire consumed the bridegroom and the bride, and their ashes mingled. No man could divide them any more, and the ashes were placed in a

Paris comes back to Oenone

golden cup, within a chamber of stone, and the earth was mounded above them. On that grave the wood nymphs planted two rose trees, and their branches met and plaited together.

This was the end of Paris and Oenone.

CHAPTER THIRTEEN

How Ulysses Invented the Device
of the Horse of Tree

After Paris died, Helen was not given back to Menelaus. We are often told that only fear of the anger of Paris had prevented the Trojans from surrendering Helen and making peace. Now Paris could not terrify them, yet for all that the men of the town would not part with Helen, whether because she was so beautiful, or because they thought it dishonourable to yield her to the Greeks, who might put her to a cruel death. So Helen was taken by Deiphobus, the brother of Paris, to live in his own house, and Deiphobus was at this time the best warrior and the chief captain of the men of Troy.

Meanwhile, the Greeks made an assault against the Trojan walls and fought long and hardily; but, being safe behind the battlements, and shooting through loopholes, the Trojans drove them back with loss of many of their men. It was in vain that Philoctetes shot his poisoned arrows; they fell back from the stone walls, or stuck in the palisades of wood above the walls, and the Greeks who tried to climb over were speared, or crushed with heavy stones. When night fell, they retreated to the ships and held a council, and, as usual, they asked the advice of the prophet Calchas. It was the business of Calchas to go about looking at birds, and taking omens from what he saw them doing, a way of prophesying which the Romans also used, and some savages do the same to this day. Calchas said that yesterday he had seen a hawk pursuing a dove, which hid herself in a hole in a rocky cliff. For a long while the hawk tried to find the hole, and follow the dove into it, but he could not reach her. So he flew away for a short distance and hid himself; then the dove fluttered out into the sunlight, and the hawk swooped on her and killed her.

The Greeks, said Calchas, ought to learn a lesson from the

hawk, and take Troy by cunning, as by force they could do nothing. Then Ulysses stood up and described a trick which it is not easy to understand. The Greeks, he said, ought to make an enormous hollow horse of wood, and place the bravest men in the horse. Then all the rest of the Greeks should embark in their ships and sail to the Isle of Tenedos, and lie hidden behind the island. The Trojans would then come out of the city, like the dove out of her hole in the rock, and would wander about the Greek camp, and wonder why the great horse of tree had been made, and why it had been left behind. Lest they should set fire to the horse, when they would soon have found out the warriors hidden in it, a cunning Greek, whom the Trojans did not know by sight, should be left in the camp or near it. He would tell the Trojans that the Greeks had given up all hope and gone home, and he was to say that they feared the goddess Pallas was angry with them, because they had stolen her image that fell from heaven, and was called the Luck of Troy. To soothe Pallas and prevent her from sending great storms against the ships, the Trojans (so the man was to say) had built this wooden horse as an offering to the goddess. The Trojans, believing this story, would drag the horse into Troy, and, in the night, the princes would come out, set fire to the city, and open the gates to the army, which would return from Tenedos as soon as darkness came on.

The prophet was much pleased with the plan of Ulysses, and, as two birds happened to fly away on the right hand, he declared that the stratagem would certainly be lucky. Neoptolemus, on the other hand, voted for taking Troy, without any trick, by sheer hard fighting. Ulysses replied that if Achilles could not do that, it could not be done at all, and that Epeius, a famous carpenter, had better set about making the horse at once.

Next day half the army, with axes in their hands, were sent to cut down trees on Mount Ida, and thousands of planks were cut from the trees by Epeius and his workmen, and in three days he had finished the horse. Ulysses then asked the best of the Greeks to come forward and go inside the machine; while one, whom the Trojans did not know by sight, should volunteer to stay behind in the camp and deceive the Trojans. Then a young man called Sinon stood up and said that he would risk himself and take the chance that the Trojans might disbelieve him, and burn him alive. Certainly, none of the Greeks did anything more courageous, yet Sinon had not been considered brave.

Had he fought in the front ranks, the Trojans would have known him; but there were many brave fighters who would not have dared to do what Sinon undertook.

Then old Nestor was the first that volunteered to go into the horse; but Neoptolemus said that, brave as he was, he was too old, and that he must depart with the army to Tenedos. Neoptolemus himself would go into the horse, for he would rather die than turn his back on Troy. So Neoptolemus armed himself and climbed into the horse, as did Menelaus, Ulysses, Diomede, Thrasymedes (Nestor's son), Idomeneus, Philoctetes, Meriones, and all the best men except Agamemnon, while Epeius himself entered last of all. Agamemnon was not allowed by the other Greeks to share their adventure, as he was to command the army when they returned from Tenedos. They meanwhile launched their ships and sailed away.

But first Menelaus had led Ulysses apart, and told him that if they took Troy (and now they must either take it or die at the hands of the Trojans), he would owe to Ulysses the glory. When they came back to Greece, he wished to give Ulysses one of his own cities, that they might always be near each other. Ulysses smiled and shook his head; he could not leave Ithaca, his own rough island kingdom. 'But if we both live through the night that is coming,' he said, 'I may ask you for one gift, and giving it will make you none the poorer.' Then Menelaus swore by the splendour of Zeus that Ulysses could ask him for no gift that he would not gladly give; so they embraced, and both armed themselves and went up into the horse. With them were all the chiefs except Nestor, whom they would not allow to come, and Agamemnon, who, as chief general, had to command the army. They swathed themselves and their arms in soft silks, that they might not ring and clash, when the Trojans, if they were so foolish, dragged the horse up into their town, and there they sat in the dark waiting. Meanwhile, the army burned their huts and launched their ships, and with oars and sails made their way to the back of the isle of Tenedos.

CHAPTER FOURTEEN

The End of Troy and the Saving of Helen

From the walls the Trojans saw the black smoke go up thick into the sky, and the whole fleet of the Greeks sailing out to sea. Never were men so glad, and they armed themselves for fear of an ambush, and went cautiously, sending forth scouts in front of them, down to the seashore. Here they found the huts burned down and the camp deserted, and some of the scouts also caught Sinon, who had hid himself in a place where he was likely to be found. They rushed on him with fierce cries, and bound his hands with a rope, and kicked and dragged him along to the place where Priam and the princes were wondering at the great horse of tree. Sinon looked round upon them, while some were saying that he ought to be tortured with fire to make him tell all the truth about the horse. The chiefs in the horse must have trembled for fear lest torture should wring the truth out of Sinon, for then the Trojans would simply burn the machine and them within it.

But Sinon said: 'Miserable man that I am, whom the Greeks hate and the Trojans are eager to slay!' When the Trojans heard that the Greeks hated him, they were curious, and asked who he was, and how he came to be there. 'I will tell you all, oh king!' he answered Priam. 'I was a friend and squire of an unhappy chief, Palamedes, whom the wicked Ulysses hated and slew secretly one day, when he found him alone, fishing in the sea. I was angry, and in my folly I did not hide my anger, and my words came to the ears of Ulysses. From that hour he sought occasion to slay me. Then Calchas – ' here he stopped, saying: 'But why tell a long tale? If you hate all Greeks alike, then slay me; this is what Agamemnon and Ulysses desire; Menelaus would thank you for my head.'

The Trojans were now more curious than before. They bade

him go on, and he said that the Greeks had consulted an Oracle, which advised them to sacrifice one of their army to appease the anger of the gods and gain a fair wind homewards. 'But who was to be sacrificed? They asked Calchas, who for fifteen days refused to speak. At last, being bribed by Ulysses, he pointed to me, Sinon, and said that I must be the victim. I was bound and kept in prison, while they built their great horse as a present for Pallas Athene the goddess. They made it so large that you Trojans might never be able to drag it into your city; while, if you destroyed it, the goddess might turn her anger against you. And now they have gone home to bring back the image that fell from heaven, which they had sent to Greece, and to restore it to the Temple of Pallas Athene, when they have taken your town, for the goddess is angry with them for that theft of Ulysses.'

The Trojans were foolish enough to believe the story of Sinon, and they pitied him and unbound his hands. Then they tied ropes to the wooden horse, and laid rollers in front of it, like men launching a ship, and they all took turns to drag the horse up to the Scaean gate. Children and women put their hands to the ropes and hauled, and with shouts and dances, and hymns they toiled, till about night-fall the horse stood in the courtyard of the inmost castle.

Then all the people of Troy began to dance, and drink, and sing. Such sentinels as were set at the gates got as drunk as all the rest, who danced about the city till after midnight, and then they went to their homes and slept heavily.

Meanwhile the Greek ships were returning from behind Tenedos as fast as the oarsmen could row them.

One Trojan did not drink or sleep; this was Deiphobus, at whose house Helen was now living. He bade her come with them, for he knew that she was able to speak in the very voice of all men and women whom she had ever seen, and he armed a few of his friends and went with them to the citadel. Then he stood beside the horse, holding Helen's hand, and whispered to her that she must call each of the chiefs in the voice of his wife. She was obliged to obey, and she called Menelaus in her own voice, and Diomede in the voice of his wife, and Ulysses in the very voice of Penelope. Then Menelaus and Diomede were eager to answer, but Ulysses grasped their hands and whispered the word 'Echo!' Then they remembered that this was a name of Helen, because she could speak in all voices, and they were silent; but Anticlus was still eager to answer, till Ulysses held his strong hand over his mouth. There was only silence, and Deiphobus led Helen back to his house. When they had gone away Epeius opened the side of the horse, and all the chiefs let themselves down softly to the ground. Some rushed to the gate, to open it, and they killed the sleeping sentinels and let in the Greeks. Others sped with torches to burn the houses of the Trojan princes, and terrible was the slaughter of men, unarmed and half awake, and loud were the cries of the women. But Ulysses had slipped away at the first, none knew where. Neoptolemus ran to the palace of Priam, who was sitting at the altar in his courtyard, praying vainly to the gods, for Neoptolemus slew the old man cruelly, and his white hair was dabbled in his blood. All through the city was fighting and slaying; but Menelaus went to the house of Deiphobus, knowing that Helen was there.

In the doorway he found Deiphobus lying dead in all his armour, a spear standing in his breast. There were footprints marked in blood, leading through the portico and into the hall. There Menelaus went, and found Ulysses leaning, wounded, against one of the central pillars of the great chamber, the firelight shining on his armour.

'Why hast thou slain Deiphobus and robbed me of my revenge?' said Menelaus. 'You swore to give me a gift,' said Ulysses, 'and will you keep your oath?' 'Ask what you will,' said Menelaus; 'it is yours and my oath cannot be broken.' 'I ask the life of Helen of the fair hands,' said Ulysses; 'this is my own life-price that I pay back to her, for she saved my life when I took the Luck of Troy, and I swore that hers should be saved.'

Then Helen stole, glimmering in white robes, from a recess in the dark hall, and fell at the feet of Menelaus; her golden hair lay in the dust of the hearth, and her hands moved to touch his knees. His drawn sword fell from the hands of Menelaus, and pity and love came into his heart, and he raised her from the dust and her white arms were round his neck, and they both wept. That night Menelaus

*Menelaus refains from killing Helen at the
intercession of Ulysses*

fought no more, but they tended the wound of Ulysses, for the sword of Deiphobus had bitten through his helmet.

When dawn came Troy lay in ashes, and the women were being driven with spear shafts to the ships, and the men were left unburied, a prey to dogs and all manner of birds. Thus the grey city fell, that had lorded it for many centuries. All the gold and silver and rich embroideries, and ivory and amber, the horses and chariots, were divided among the army; all but a treasure of silver and gold, hidden in a chest within a hollow of the wall, and this treasure was found, not very many years ago, by men digging deep on the hill where Troy once stood. The women, too, were given to the princes, and Neoptolemus took Andromache to his home in Argos, to draw water from the well and to be the slave of a master, and Agamemnon carried beautiful Cassandra, the daughter of Priam, to his palace in Mycenae, where they were both slain in one night. Only Helen was led with honour to the ship of Menelaus.

THE WANDERINGS OF ULYSSES

CHAPTER ONE

The Slaying of Agamemnon and the Sorrows of Ulysses

The Greeks left Troy a mass of smouldering ashes; the marks of fire are still to be seen in the ruins on the hill which is now called Hissarlik. The Greeks had many troubles on their way home, and years passed before some of the chiefs reached their own cities. As for Agamemnon, while he was at Troy his wife, Clytemnestra, the sister of Helen, had fallen in love with a young man named Aegisthus, who wished to be king, so he married Clytemnestra, just as if Agamemnon had been dead. Meanwhile Agamemnon was sailing home with his share of the wealth of Troy, and many a storm drove him out of his course. At last he reached the harbour, about seven miles from his city of Mycenae, and he kissed the earth when he landed, thinking that all his troubles were over, and that he would find his son and daughter, Orestes and Electra, grown up, and his wife happy because of his return.

But Aegisthus had set, a year before, a watchman on a high tower, to come with the news as soon as Agamemnon landed, and the watchman ran to Mycenae with the good news. Aegisthus placed twenty armed men in a hidden place in the great hall, and then he shouted for his chariots and horses, and drove down to meet Agamemnon, and welcome him, and carry him to his own palace. Then he gave a great feast, and when men had drunk much wine, the armed men, who had been hiding behind curtains, rushed out, with sword and spear, and fell on Agamemnon and his company. Though taken by surprise they drew their swords, and fought so well for their lives that none were left alive, not one, neither of the company of Agamemnon nor of the company of Aegisthus; they were all slain in the hall except Aegisthus, who had hidden himself when the fray began. The bodies lay round the great mixing bowl of wine, and about the tables, and the floor ran with blood. Before Agamemnon died he saw Clytemnestra herself stab Cassandra, the daughter of Priam, whom he had brought from Troy.

In the town of Agamemnon, Mycenae, deep down in the earth, have been found five graves, with bones of men and women, and these bones were all covered with beautiful ornaments of gold, hundreds of them, and swords and daggers inlaid with gold, and golden cups, and a sceptre of gold and crystal, and two gold breast-plates. There were also golden masks that had been made to cover the faces of the dead kings, and who knows but that one of these masks may show us the features of the famous Agamemnon?

Ulysses, of course, knew nothing about these murders at the time, for he was being borne by the winds into undiscovered seas. But later he heard all the story from the ghost of a dead prophet, in the Land of the Dead, and he determined to be very cautious if ever he reached his own island, for who knew what the young men might do, that had grown up since he sailed to Troy?

Of the other Greeks Nestor soon and safely arrived at his town of Pylos, but Menelaus and Helen were borne by the winds to Egypt and other strange countries, and the ship of the brother of Ajax was wrecked on a rock, and there he was drowned, and Calchas the prophet died on land, on his way across Greece.

When Ulysses left Troy the wind carried him to the coast of Thrace, where the people were allies of the Trojans. It was a king of the Thracians that Diomedes killed when he and Ulysses stole into the camp of the Trojans in the night, and drove away the white horses of the king, as swift as the winds. Ismarus was the name of the Thracian town where Ulysses landed, and his men took it and plundered it, yet Ulysses allowed no one to harm the priest of Apollo, Maron, but protected him and his wife and child, in their house within the holy grove of the god. Maron was grateful, and gave Ulysses twelve talents, or little wedges, of gold, and a great bowl of silver, and twelve large clay jars, as big as barrels, full of the best and strongest wine. It was so strong that men put into the mixing bowl but one measure of wine to twenty measures of water.

These presents Ulysses stored up in his ship, and lucky for him it was that he was kind to Maron.

Meanwhile his men, instead of leaving the town with their plunder, sat eating and drinking till dawn. By that time the people of the town had warned their neighbours in the country farms, who all came down in full armour, and attacked the men of Ulysses. In this fight he lost seventy-two men, six from each of his twelve ships, and it was only by hard fighting that the others were able to get on board their ships and sail away.

A great storm arose and beat upon the ships, and it seems that Ulysses and his men were driven into Fairyland, where they remained for ten years. We have heard that King Arthur and Thomas the Rhymer were carried into Fairyland, but what adventures they met with there we do not know. About Ulysses we have the stories which are now to be told. For ten days his ships ran due south, and, on the tenth, they reached the land of the Lotus Eaters, who eat food of flowers. They went on shore and drew water, and three men were sent to try to find the people of that country, who were a quiet, friendly people, and gave the fruit of the lotus to the strange sailors. Now whoever tastes of that fruit has no mind ever to go home, but to sit between the setting sun and the rising moon, dreaming happy dreams, and forgetting the world. The three men ate the lotus, and sat down to dream, but Ulysses went after them, and drove them to the ships, and bound their hands and feet, and threw them on board, and sailed away. Then he with his ships reached the coast of the land of the Cyclopes, which means the round-eyed men, men with only one eye apiece, set in the middle of their foreheads. They lived not in houses, but in caves among the hills, and they had no king and no laws, and did not plough or sow, but wheat and vines grew wild, and they kept great flocks of sheep.

There was a beautiful wild desert island lying across the opening of a bay; the isle was full of wild goats, and made a bar against the waves, so that ships could lie behind it safely, run up on the beach, for there was no tide in that sea. There Ulysses ran up his ships, and the men passed the time in hunting wild goats, and feasting on fresh meat and the wine of Maron, the priest of Apollo. Next day Ulysses left all the ships and men there, except his own ship, and his own crew, and went to see what kind of people lived on the mainland, for as yet none had been seen. He found a large cave close to the sea, with laurels growing on the rocky roof, and a wall of rough stones built round a court in front. Ulysses left all his men but twelve with the ship; filled a goat skin with the strong wine of Maron, put some corn flour in a sack, and went up to the cave. Nobody was there, but there were all the things that are usually in a dairy, baskets full of cheese, pails and bowls full of milk and whey, and kids and lambs were playing in their folds.

All seemed very quiet and pleasant. The men wanted to take as much cheese as they could carry back to the ship, but Ulysses wished to see the owner of the cave. His men, making themselves at home, lit a fire, and toasted and ate the cheeses, far within the cave. Then a shadow thrown by the setting sun fell across the opening of the cave, and a monstrous man entered, and threw down a dry trunk of a tree that he carried for firewood. Next he drove in the ewes of his flock, leaving the rams in the yard, and he picked up a huge flat stone, and set it so as to make a shut door to the cave, for twenty-four yoke of horses could not have dragged away that stone. Lastly the man milked his ewes, and put the milk in pails to drink at supper. All this while Ulysses and his men sat quiet and in great fear, for they were shut up in a cave with a one-eyed giant, whose cheese they had been eating.

Then the giant, when he had lit the fire, happened to see the men, and asked them who they were. Ulysses said that they were Greeks, who had taken Troy, and were wandering lost on the seas, and he asked the man to be kind to them in the name of their chief god, Zeus.

'We Cyclopes,' said the giant, 'do not care for Zeus or the gods, for we think that we are better men than they. Where is your ship?' Ulysses answered that it had been wrecked on the coast, to which the man made no answer, but snatched up two of the twelve, knocked out their brains on the floor, tore the bodies limb from limb, roasted them at his fire, ate them, and, after drinking many pailfuls of milk, lay down and fell asleep. Now Ulysses had a mind to drive his sword-point into the giant's liver, and he felt for the place with his hand. But he remembered that, even if he killed the giant, he could not move the huge stone that was the door of the cave, so he and his men would die of hunger, when they had eaten all the cheeses.

In the morning the giant ate two more men for breakfast, drove out his ewes, and set the great stone in the doorway again, as lightly as a man would put a quiverlid on a quiver of arrows. Then away he went, driving his flock to graze on the green hills.

Ulysses did not give way to despair. The giant had left his stick in the cave: it was as large as the mast of a great ship. From this Ulysses cut a portion six feet long, and his men cut and rubbed as if they were making a spear shaft: Ulysses then sharpened it to a point, and hardened the point in the fire. It was a thick rounded bar of wood, and the men cast lots to choose four, who should twist the bar in the giant's eye when he fell asleep at night. Back he came at sunset, and drove his flocks into the cave, rams and all. Then he put up his stone door, milked his ewes, and killed two men and cooked them.

Ulysses meanwhile had filled one of the wooden ivy bowls full of the strong wine of Maron, without putting a drop of water into it. This bowl he offered to the giant, who had never heard of wine. He drank one bowl after another, and when he was merry he said that he would make Ulysses a present. 'What is your name?' he asked. 'My name is *Nobody*,' said Ulysses. 'Then I shall eat the others first and Nobody last,' said the giant. 'That shall be your gift.' Then he fell asleep.

Ulysses took his bar of wood, and made the point red-hot in the fire. Next his four men rammed it into the giant's one eye, and held it down, while Ulysses twirled it round, and the eye hissed like red-hot iron when men dip it into cold water, which is the strength of iron. The Cyclops roared and leaped to his feet, and shouted for help to the other giants who lived in the neighbouring caves. 'Who is troubling you, Polyphemus?' they answered. 'Why do you wake us out of our sleep?' The giant answered, 'Nobody is killing me by his cunning, not at all in fair fight.' 'Then if nobody is harming you nobody can help you,' shouted a giant. 'If you are ill pray to your father, Poseidon, who is the god of the sea.' So the giants all went back to bed, and Ulysses laughed low to see how his cunning had deceived them. Then the giant went and took down his door and sat in the doorway, stretching out his arms, so as to catch his prisoners as they went out.

But Ulysses had a plan. He fastened sets of three rams together with twisted withies, and bound a man to each ram in the middle, so that the blind giant's hands would only feel the two outside rams. The biggest and strongest ram Ulysses seized, and held on by his hands and feet to its fleece, under its belly, and then all the sheep went out through the doorway, and the giant felt them, but did not know that they were carrying out the men. 'Dear ram!' he said to the biggest, which carried Ulysses, 'you do not come out first, as usual, but last, as if you were slow with sorrow for your master, whose eye Nobody has blinded!'

Then all the rams went out into the open country, and Ulysses unfastened his men, and drove the sheep down to his ship and so on board. His crew wept when they heard of the death of six of their friends, but Ulysses made them row out to sea. When he was just so far away from the cave as to be within hearing distance he shouted at the Cyclops and mocked him. Then that giant broke off the rocky peak of a great hill and threw it in the direction of the sound. The rock fell in front of the ship, and raised a wave that drove it back to shore, but Ulysses punted it off with a long pole, and his men rowed out again, far out. Ulysses again shouted to the giant, 'If anyone asks who blinded you, say that it was Ulysses, Laertes' son, of Ithaca, the stormer of cities.'

Then the giant prayed to the sea god, his father, that Ulysses might never come home, or if he did, that he might come late and lonely, with loss of all his men, and find sorrow in his house. Then the giant heaved and threw another rock, but it fell at the stern of the ship, and the wave drove the ship further out to sea, to the shore of the island. There Ulysses and his men landed, and killed some of the giant's sheep, and took supper, and drank wine.

But the sea god heard the prayer of his son the blind giant.

Ulysses and his men sailed on, in what direction and for how long we do not know, till they saw far off an island that shone in the sea. When they came nearer they found that it had a steep cliff of bronze, with a palace on the top. Here lived Aeolus, the King of the Winds, with his six sons and six daughters. He received Ulysses kindly on his island, and entertained him for a whole month. Then he gave him a leather bag, in which he had bound the ways of all the noisy winds. This bag was fastened with a silver cord, and Aeolus left no wind out except the West Wind, which would blow Ulysses straight home to Ithaca. Where he was we cannot guess, except that he was to the west of his own island.

So they sailed for nine days and nights towards the east, and Ulysses always held the helm and steered, but on the tenth day he fell asleep. Then his men said to each other, 'What treasure is it that he keeps in the leather bag, a present from King Aeolus? No doubt the bag is full of gold and silver, while we have only empty hands.' So they opened the bag when they were so near Ithaca that they could see people lighting fires on the shore. Then out rushed all the winds, and carried the ship into unknown seas, and when Ulysses woke he was so miserable that he had a mind to drown himself. But he was of an enduring heart, and he lay still, and the ship came back to the isle of Aeolus, who cried, 'Away with you! You are the most luckless of living men: you must be hated by the gods.'

Thus Aeolus drove them away, and they sailed for seven days and nights, till they saw land, and came to a harbour with a narrow entrance, and with tall steep rocks on either side. The other eleven ships sailed into the haven, but Ulysses did not venture in; he fastened his ship to a rock at the outer end of the harbour. The place must have been very far north, for, as it was summer, the sun had hardly set till dawn began again, as it does in Norway and Iceland, where there are many such narrow harbours within walls of rock. These places are called *fiords*. Ulysses sent three men to spy out the country, and at a well outside the town they met a damsel drawing water; she was the child of the king of the people, the Laestrygonians. The damsel led them to her father's house; he was a giant and seized one of the men of Ulysses, meaning to kill and eat him. The two other men fled to the ships, but the Laestrygonians ran along the tops of the cliffs and threw down great rocks, sinking the vessels and killing the sailors. When Ulysses saw this he drew his sword and cut the cable that fastened his ship to the rock outside the harbour, and his crew rowed for dear life and so escaped, weeping for the death of their friends. Thus the prayer of the blind Cyclops was being fulfilled, for now out of twelve ships Ulysses had but one left.

CHAPTER TWO

The Enchantress Circe, the Land of the Dead and the Sirens

On they sailed till they came to an island, and there they landed. What the place was they did not know, but it was called Aeaea, and here lived Circe, the enchantress, sister of the wizard king Aeetes, who was the lord of the fleece of gold, that Jason won from him by help of the king's daughter, Medea. For two days Ulysses and his men lay on land beside their ship, which they anchored in a bay of the island. On the third morning Ulysses took his sword and spear, and climbed to the top of a high hill, whence he saw the smoke rising out of the wood where Circe had her palace. He thought of going to the house, but it seemed better to return to his men and send some of them to spy out the place. Since the adventure of the Cyclops Ulysses did not care to risk himself among unknown people, and for all that he knew there might be man-eating giants on the island. So he went back, and, as he came to the bank of the river, he found a great red deer drinking under the shadow of the green boughs. He speared the stag, and, tying his feet together, slung the body from his neck, and so, leaning on his spear, he came to his fellows. Glad they were to see fresh venison, which they cooked, and so dined with plenty of wine.

Next morning Ulysses divided his men into two companies, Eurylochus led one company and he himself the other. Then they put two marked pieces of wood, one for Eurylochus, one for Ulysses, in a helmet, to decide who should go to the house in the wood. They shook the helmet, and the lot of Eurylochus leaped out, and, weeping for fear, he led his twenty-two men away into the forest. Ulysses and the other twenty-two waited, and, when Eurylochus came back alone, he was weeping, and unable to speak for sorrow. At last he told his story: they had come to the beautiful house of Circe, within the wood, and tame wolves and lions were walking about in front of the house. They wagged their tails, and jumped up, like friendly dogs, round the men of Ulysses, who stood in the gateway and heard Circe singing in a sweet voice, as she went up and down before the loom at which she was weaving. Then one of the men of Ulysses called to her, and she came out, a beautiful lady in white robes covered with jewels of gold. She opened the doors and bade them come in, but Eurylochus hid himself and watched, and saw Circe and her maidens mix honey and wine for the men, and bid them sit down on chairs at tables, but, when they had drunk of her cup, she touched them with her wand. Then they were all changed into swine, and Circe drove them out and shut them up in the sties.

When Ulysses heard that he slung his sword-belt round his shoulders, seized his bow, and bade Eurylochus come back with him to the house of Circe; but Eurylochus was afraid. Alone went Ulysses through the woods, and in a dell he met a most beautiful young man, who took his hand and said, 'Unhappy one! how shalt thou free thy friends from so great an enchantress?' Then the young man plucked a plant from the ground; the flower was as white as milk, but the root was black: it is a plant that men may not dig up, but to the gods all things are easy, and the young man was the cunning god Hermes, whom Autolycus, the grandfather of Ulysses, used to worship. 'Take this herb of grace,' he said, 'and when Circe has made thee drink of the cup of her enchantments the herb will so work that they shall have no power over thee. Then draw thy sword, and rush at her, and make her swear that she will not harm thee with her magic.'

Then Hermes departed, and Ulysses went to the house of Circe, and she asked him to enter, and seated him on a chair, and gave him the enchanted cup to drink, and then smote him with her wand and bade him go to the sties of the swine. But Ulysses drew his sword, and Circe, with a great cry, fell at his feet, saying, 'Who art thou on whom the cup has no power? Truly thou art Ulysses of Ithaca, for the god Hermes has told me that he should come to my island on his way from Troy. Come now, fear not; let us be friends!'

Circe sends the swine, the companions of
Ulysses, to the sties

Then the maidens of Circe came to them, fairy damsels of the wells and woods and rivers. They threw covers of purple silk over the chairs, and on the silver tables they placed golden baskets, and mixed wine in a silver bowl, and heated water, and bathed Ulysses in a polished bath, and clothed him in new raiment, and led him to the table and bade him eat and drink. But he sat silent, neither eating nor drinking, in sorrow for his company, till Circe called them out from the sties and disenchanted them. Glad they were to see Ulysses, and they embraced him, and wept for joy.

So they went back to their friends at the ship, and told them how Circe would have them all to live with her; but Eurylochus tried to frighten them, saying that she would change them into wolves and lions. Ulysses drew his sword to cut off the head of Eurylochus for his cowardice, but the others prayed that he might be left alone to guard the ship. So Ulysses left him; but Eurylochus had not the courage to be alone, and slunk behind them to the house of Circe. There she welcomed them all, and gave them a feast, and there they dwelt for a whole year, and then they wearied for their wives and children, and longed to return to Ithaca. They did not guess by what a strange path they must sail.

When Ulysses was alone with Circe at night he told her that his men were homesick, and would fain go to Ithaca. Then Circe said, 'There is no way but this: you must sail to the last shore of the stream of the river Oceanus, that girdles round the world. There is the Land of the Dead, and the House of Hades and Persephone, the king and queen of the ghosts. There you must call up the ghost of the blind prophet, Tiresias of Thebes, for he alone has knowledge of your way, and the other spirits sweep round shadowlike.'

Then Ulysses thought that his heart would break, for how should he, a living man, go down to the awful dwellings of the dead? But Circe told him the strange things that he must do, and she gave him a black ram and a black ewe, and next day Ulysses called his men together. All followed him to the ship, except one, Elpenor. He had been sleeping, for the sake of the cool air, on the flat roof of the house, and, when suddenly wakened, he missed his foothold on the tall ladder, and fell to the ground and broke his neck. They left him unburned and unburied, and, weeping, they followed Ulysses, as follow they must, to see the homes of the ghosts and the house of Hades. Very sorrowfully they all went on board, taking with them the black ram and the black ewe, and they set the sails, and the wind bore them at its will.

Now in midday they sailed out of the sunlight into darkness, for they had come to the land of the Cimmerian men, which the sun never sees, but all is dark cloud and mist. There they ran the ship ashore, and took out the two black sheep, and walked along the dark banks of the river Oceanus to a place of which Circe had told Ulysses. There the two rivers of the dead meet, where a rock divides the two dark roaring streams. There they dug a trench and poured out mead, and wine, and water, and prayed to the ghosts, and then they cut the throat of the black ewe, and the grey ghosts gathered to smell the blood. Pale spectres came, spirits of brides who died long ago, and youths unwed, and old unhappy men; and many phantoms were there of men who fell in battle, with shadowy spears in their hands, and battered armour. Then Ulysses sacrificed the black ram to the ghost of the prophet Tiresias, and sat down with his sword in his hand, that no spirit before Tiresias might taste the blood in the trench.

First the spirit of Elpenor came, and begged Ulysses to burn his body, for till his body was burned he was not allowed to mingle with the other souls of dead men. So Ulysses promised to burn and bury him when he went back to Circe's island. Then came the shadow of the mother of Ulysses, who had died when he was at Troy, but, for all his grief, he would not allow the shadow to come near the blood till Tiresias had tasted it. At length came the spirit of the blind prophet, and he prayed Ulysses to sheathe his sword and let him drink the blood of the black sheep.

When he had tasted it he said that the sea god was angry because of the blinding of his son, the Cyclops, and would make his voyaging vain. But if the men of Ulysses were wise, and did not slay and eat the sacred cattle of the sun god, in the isle called Thrinacia, they might all win home. If they were unwise, and if Ulysses did come home, lonely and late he would arrive, on the ship of strangers, and he would find proud men wasting his goods and seeking to wed his wife, Penelope. Even if Ulysses alone could kill these men his troubles would not be ended. He must wander over the land, as he had wandered over the waters, carrying an oar on his shoulder, till he came to men who had never heard of the sea or of boats. When one of these men, not knowing what an oar was, came and told him that he carried a fan for winnowing corn, then Ulysses must fix the oar in the ground, and offer a sacrifice to the sea god, and go home, where he would at last live in peace. Ulysses said, 'So be it!' and asked how he could have speech with the ghosts. Tiresias told him how this might be done, and then his mother told him how she died of sorrow for him, and Ulysses tried to embrace and kiss her, but his arms only clasped the empty air.

Then came up the beautiful spirits of many dead, unhappy ladies of old times, and then came the souls of Agamemnon, and of Achilles, and of Ajax. Achilles was glad when he heard how bravely his young son had fought at Troy, but he said it was better to be the servant of a poor farmer on earth than to rule over all the ghosts of the dead in the still grey land where the sun never shone, and no flowers grew but the mournful asphodel. Many other spirits of Greeks slain at Troy came and asked for news about their friends, but Ajax stood apart and silent, still in anger because the arms of Achilles had been given to Ulysses. In vain Ulysses told him that the Greeks had mourned as much for him as for Achilles; he passed silently away into the House of Hades. At last the legions of the innumerable dead, all that have died since the world began, flocked, and filled the air with their low wailing cries, and fear fell on Ulysses, and he went back along that sad last shore of the world's end to his ship, and sailed again out of the darkness into the sunlight, and to the isle of Circe. There they burned the body of Elpenor, and piled a mound over it, and on the mound set the oar of the dead man, and so went to the palace of Circe.

Ulysses told Circe all his adventures, and then she warned him of dangers yet to come, and showed him how he might escape them. He listened, and remembered all that she spoke, and these two said goodbye for ever. Circe wandered away alone into the woods, and

Ulysses and his men set sail and crossed the unknown seas. Presently the wind fell, and the sea was calm, and they saw a beautiful island from which came the sound of sweet singing. Ulysses knew who the singers were, for Circe had told him that they were the Sirens, a kind of beautiful Mermaids, deadly to men. Among the flowers they sit and sing, but the flowers hide the bones of men who have listened and landed on the island, and died of that strange music, which carries the soul away.

Ulysses now took a great cake of bees' wax and cut it up into small pieces, which he bade his men soften and place in their ears, that they might not hear that singing. But, as he desired to hear it and yet live, he bade the sailors bind him tightly to the mast with ropes, and they must not unbind him, however much he might implore them to set him free. When all this was done the men sat down on the benches, all orderly, and smote the grey sea with their oars, and the ship rushed along through the clear still water, and came opposite the island.

Then the sweet singing of the Sirens was borne over the sea,

> 'Hither, come hither, renowned Ulysses,
> Great glory of the Achaean name.
> Here stay thy ship, that thou mayest listen to our song.
> Never has any man driven his ship past our island
> Till he has heard our voices, sweet as the honeycomb;
> Gladly he has heard, and wiser has he gone on his way.
> Hither, come hither, for we know all things,
> All that the Greeks wrought and endured in Troyland,
> All that shall hereafter be upon the fruitful earth.'

Thus they sang, offering Ulysses all knowledge and wisdom, which they knew that he loved more than anything in the world. To other men, no doubt, they would have offered other pleasures. Ulysses desired to listen, and he nodded to his men to loosen his bonds. But Perimedes and Eurylochus arose, and laid on him yet stronger bonds, and the ship was driven past that island, till the song of the Sirens faded away, and then the men set Ulysses free and took the wax out of their ears.

CHAPTER THREE

The Whirlpool, the Sea Monster and the Cattle of the Sun

They had not sailed far when they heard the sea roaring, and saw a great wave, over which hung a thick shining cloud of spray. They had drifted to a place where the sea narrowed between two high black rocks; under the rock on the left was a boiling whirlpool in which no ship could live; the opposite rock showed nothing dangerous, but Ulysses had been warned by Circe that here too lay great peril. We may ask, Why did Ulysses pass through the narrows between these two rocks? why did he not steer on the outer side of one or the other? The reason seems to have been that, on the outer side of these cliffs, were the tall reefs which men called the Rocks Wandering. Between them the sea water leaped in high columns of white foam, and the rocks themselves rushed together, grinding and clashing, while fire flew out of the crevices and crests as from a volcano.

Circe had told Ulysses about the Rocks Wandering, which do not even allow flocks of doves to pass through them; even one of the doves is always caught and crushed, and no ship of men escapes that tries to pass that way, and the bodies of the sailors and the planks of the ships are confusedly tossed by the waves of the sea and the storms of ruinous fire. Of all ships that ever sailed the sea, only *Argo*, the ship of Jason, has escaped the Rocks Wandering, as you may read in the story of the Fleece of Gold. For these reasons Ulysses was forced to steer between the rock of the whirlpool and the rock which seemed harmless. In the narrows between these two cliffs the sea ran like a rushing river, and the men, in fear, ceased to hold the oars, and down the stream the oars splashed in confusion. But Ulysses, whom Circe had told of this new danger, bade them grasp the oars again and row hard. He told the man at the helm to steer under the great rocky cliff, on the right, and to keep clear of the whirlpool and the cloud of spray on the left. Well he knew the danger of the rock on the left, for within it was a deep cave, where a monster named Scylla lived, yelping with a shrill voice out of her six hideous heads. Each head hung down from a long, thin, scaly neck, and in each mouth were three rows of greedy teeth, and twelve long feelers, with claws at the ends of them, dropped down, ready to catch at men. There in her cave Scylla sits, fishing with her feelers for dolphins and other great fish, and for men, if any men sail by that way. Against this deadly thing none may fight, for she cannot be slain with the spear.

All this Ulysses knew, for Circe had warned him. But he also knew that on the other side of the strait, where the sea spray for ever flew high above the rock, was a whirlpool, called Charybdis, which would swallow up his ship if it came within the current, while Scylla could only catch some of his men. For this reason he bade the helmsman to steer close to the rock of Scylla, and he did not tell the sailors that she lurked there with her body hidden in her deep cave. He himself put on his armour, and took two spears, and went and stood in the raised half-deck at the front of the ship, thinking that, at least, he would have a stroke at Scylla. Then they rowed down the swift sea stream, while the wave of the whirlpool now rose up, till the spray hid the top of the rock, and now fell, and bubbled with black sand. They were watching the whirlpool, when out from the hole in the cliff sprang the six heads of Scylla, and up into the air went six of Ulysses' men, each calling to him, as they were swept within her hole in the rock, where she devoured them. 'This was the most pitiful thing,' Ulysses said, 'that my eyes have seen, of all my sorrows in searching out the paths of the sea.'

The ship swept through the roaring narrows between the rock of Scylla and the whirlpool of Charybdis, into the open sea, and the men, weary and heavy of heart, bent over their oars, and longed for rest.

Now a place of rest seemed near at hand, for in front of the ship lay a beautiful island, and the men could hear the bleating of sheep and the lowing of cows as they were being herded into their stalls. But Ulysses remembered that, in the Land of the Dead, the ghost of the blind prophet had warned him of one thing. If his men killed and ate the cattle of the sun, in the sacred island of Thrinacia, they would all perish. So Ulysses told his crew of this prophecy, and bade them row past the island. Eurylochus was angry and said that the men were tired, and could row no further, but must land, and take supper, and sleep comfortably on shore. On hearing Eurylochus, the whole crew shouted and said that they would go no further that night, and Ulysses had no power to compel them. He could only make them swear not to touch the cattle of the sun god, which they promised readily enough, and so went ashore, took supper, and slept.

In the night a great storm arose: the clouds and driving mist blinded the face of the sea and sky, and for a whole month the wild south wind hurled the waves on the coast, and no ship of these times could venture out in the tempest. Meanwhile the crew ate up all the stores in the ship, and finished the wine, so that they were driven to catch sea birds and fishes, of which they took but few, the sea being so rough upon the rocks. Ulysses went up into the island alone, to pray to the gods, and when he had prayed he found a sheltered place, and there he fell asleep.

Eurylochus took the occasion, while Ulysses was away, to bid the crew seize and slay the sacred cattle of the sun god, which no man might touch, and this they did, so that, when Ulysses wakened, and came near the ship, he smelled the roast meat, and knew what had been done. He rebuked the men, but, as the cattle were dead, they kept eating them for six days; and then the storm ceased, the wind fell, the sun shone, and they set the sails, and away they went. But this evil deed was punished, for when they were out of sight of land, a great thunder cloud overshadowed them, the wind broke the mast, which crushed the head of the helmsman, the lightning struck the ship in the centre; she reeled, the men fell overboard, and the heads of the crew floated a moment, like cormorants, above the waves.

But Ulysses had kept hold of a rope, and, when the vessel righted, he walked the deck till a wave stripped off all the tackling, and

The adventure with Scylla

loosened the sides from the keel. Ulysses had only time to lash the broken mast with a rope to the keel, and sit on this raft with his feet in the water, while the South Wind rose again furiously, and drove the raft back till it came under the rock where was the whirlpool of Charybdis. Here Ulysses would have been drowned, but he caught at the root of a fig tree that grew on the rock, and there he hung, clinging with his toes to the crumbling stones till the whirlpool boiled up again, and up came the timbers. Down on the timbers Ulysses dropped, and so sat rowing with his hands, and the wind drifted him at last to a shelving beach of an island.

Here dwelt a kind of fairy, called Calypso, who found Ulysses nearly dead on the beach, and was kind to him, and kept him in her cave, where he lived for seven long years, always desiring to leave the beautiful fairy and return to Ithaca and his wife Penelope. But no ship of men ever came near that isle, which is the central place of all the seas, and he had no ship, and no men to sail and row. Calypso was very kind, and very beautiful, being the daughter of the wizard Atlas, who holds the two pillars that keep earth and sea asunder. But Ulysses was longing to see if it were but the smoke going up from the houses of rocky Ithaca, and he had a desire to die.

CHAPTER FOUR

How Telemachus Went to Seek his Father

When Ulysses had lived nearly seven years in the island of Calypso, his son Telemachus, whom he had left in Ithaca as a little child, went forth to seek for his father. In Ithaca he and his mother, Penelope, had long been very unhappy. As Ulysses did not come home after the war, and as nothing was heard about him from the day when the Greeks sailed from Troy, it was supposed that he must be dead. But Telemachus was still but a boy of twelve years old, and the father of Ulysses, Laertes, was very old, and had gone to a farm in the country, where he did nothing but take care of his garden. There was thus no king in Ithaca, and the boys, who had been about ten years old when Ulysses went to Troy, were now grown up, and, as their fathers had gone to the war, they did just as they pleased. Twelve of them wanted to marry Penelope, and they, with about a hundred others as wild as themselves, from the neighbouring islands, by way of paying court to Penelope ate and drank all day at her house. They killed the cattle, sheep and swine; they drank the wine, and amused themselves with Penelope's maidens, of whom she had many. Nobody could stop them; they would never go away, they said, till Penelope chose one of them to be her husband, and king of the island, though Telemachus was the rightful prince.

Penelope at last promised that she would choose one of them when she had finished a great shroud of linen, to be the death shroud of old Laertes when he died. All day she wove it, but at night, when her wooers had gone (for they did not sleep in her house), she unwove it again. But one of her maidens told this to the wooers, so she had to finish the shroud, and now they pressed her more than ever to make her choice. But she kept hoping that

Ulysses was still alive, and would return, though, if he did, how was he to turn so many strong young men out of his house?

The goddess of wisdom, Athene, had always favoured Ulysses, and now she spoke up among the gods, where they sat, as men say, in their holy heaven. Not by winds is it shaken, nor wet with rain, nor does the snow come thither, but clear air is spread about it cloudless, and the white light floats over it. Athene told how good, wise, and brave Ulysses was, and how he was kept in the isle of Calypso, while men ruined his wealth and wooed his wife. She said that she would herself go to Ithaca, and make Telemachus appeal to all the people of the country, showing how evilly he was treated, and then sail abroad to seek news of his father. So Athene spoke, and flashed down from Olympus to Ithaca, where she took the shape of a mortal man, Mentes, a chief of the Taphians. In front of the doors she found the proud wooers playing at draughts and other games while supper was being made ready. When Telemachus, who was standing apart, saw the stranger, he went to him, and led him into the house, and treated him kindly, while the wooers ate and drank, and laughed noisily.

Then Telemachus told Athene (or, as he supposed, the stranger), how evilly he was used, while his father's white bones might be wasting on an unknown shore or rolling in the billows of the salt sea. Athene said, or Mentes said, that he himself was an old friend of Ulysses, and had touched at Ithaca on his way to Cyprus to buy copper. 'But Ulysses,' he said, 'is not dead; he will certainly come home, and that speedily. You are so like him, you must be his son.' Telemachus replied that he was, and Mentes was full of anger, seeing how the wooers insulted him, and told him first to complain to an assembly of all the people, and then to take a ship, and go seeking news of Ulysses.

Then Athene departed, and next day Telemachus called an assembly, and spoke to the people, but though they were sorry for him they could not help him. One old man, however, a prophet, said that Ulysses would certainly come home, but the wooers only threatened and insulted him. In the evening Athene came again, in the appearance of Mentor, not the same man as Mentes, but an

Ithacan, and a friend of Ulysses. She encouraged Telemachus to take a ship, with twenty oarsmen, and he told the wooers that he was going to see Menelaus and Nestor, and ask tidings of his father. They only mocked him, but he made all things ready for his voyage without telling his mother. It was old Eurycleia, who had been his nurse and his father's nurse, that brought him wine and food for his journey; and at night, when the sea wind wakens in summer, he and Mentor went on board, and all night they sailed, and at noon next day they reached Pylos on the sea sands, the city of Nestor the Old.

Nestor received them gladly, and so did his sons, Pisistratus and Thrasymedes, who fought at Troy, and next day, when Mentor had gone, Pisistratus and Telemachus drove together, up hill and down dale, a two days' journey, to Lacedaemon, lying beneath Mount Taygetus on the bank of the clear river Eurotas.

Not one of the Greeks had seen Ulysses since the day when they all sailed from Troy, yet Menelaus, in a strange way, was able to tell Telemachus that his father still lived, and was with Calypso on a lonely island, the centre of all the seas. We shall see how Menelaus knew this. When Telemachus and Pisistratus came, he was giving a feast, and called them to his table. It would not have been courteous to ask them who they were till they had been bathed and clothed in fresh raiment, and had eaten and drunk. After dinner, Menelaus saw how much Telemachus admired his house, and the flashing of light from the walls, which were covered with bronze panels, and from the cups of gold, and the amber and ivory and silver. Such things Telemachus had never seen in Ithaca. Noticing his surprise, Menelaus said that he had brought many rich things from Troy, after eight years wandering to Cyprus, and Phoenicia, and Egypt, and even to Libya, on the north coast of Africa. Yet he said that, though he was rich and fortunate, he was unhappy when he remembered the brave men who had died for his sake at Troy. But above all he was miserable for the loss of the best of them all, Ulysses, who was so long unheard of, and none knew whether, at that hour, he was alive or dead. At these words Telemachus hid his face in his purple mantle and shed tears, so that Menelaus guessed who he was, but he said nothing.

Then came into the hall, from her own fragrant chamber, Helen of the fair hands, as beautiful as ever she had been, her bower maidens carrying her golden distaff, with which she span, and a silver basket to hold her wool, for the white hands of Helen were never idle.

Helen knew Telemachus by his likeness to his father, Ulysses, and when she said this to Menelaus, Pisistratus overheard her, and told how Telemachus had come to them seeking for news of his father. Menelaus was much moved in his heart, and Helen no less, when they saw the son of Ulysses, who had been the most trusty of all their friends. They could not help shedding tears, for Pisistratus remembered his dear brother Antilochus, whom Memnon slew in battle at Troy, Memnon the son of the bright Dawn. But Helen wished to comfort them, and she brought a drug of magical virtue, which Polydamna, the wife of Thon, King of Egypt had given to her. This drug lulls all pain and anger, and brings forgetfulness of every sorrow, and Helen poured it from a golden vial into the mixing bowl of gold, and they drank the wine and were comforted.

Then Helen told Telemachus what great deeds Ulysses did at Troy, and how he crept into the town disguised as a beggar, and came to her house, when he stole the Luck of Troy. Menelaus told how Ulysses kept him and the other princes quiet in the horse of tree, when Deiphobus made Helen call to them all in the very voices of their own wives, and to Telemachus it was great joy to hear of his father's courage and wisdom.

Next day Telemachus showed to Menelaus how hardly he and his mother were treated by the proud wooers, and Menelaus prayed that Ulysses might come back to Ithaca, and slay the wooers every one. 'But as to what you ask me,' he said, 'I will tell you all that I have heard about your father. In my wanderings after I sailed from Troy the storm winds kept me for three weeks in the island called Pharos, a day's voyage from the mouth of the river Aegyptus' (which is the old name of the Nile). 'We were almost starving, for our food was done, and my crew went round the shores, fishing with hook and line. Now in that isle lives a goddess, the daughter of Proteus, the Old Man of the Sea. She advised me that if I could but catch her father when he came out of the sea to sleep on the shore he would tell me everything that I needed to know. At noonday he was used to come out, with all his flock of seals round him, and to sleep among them on the sands. If I could seize him, she said, he would turn into all manner of shapes in my hands: beasts, and serpents, and burning fire; but at last he would appear in his own shape, and answer all my questions.

'So the goddess spoke, and she dug hiding-places in the sands for me and three of my men, and covered us with the skins of seals. At noonday the Old Man came out with his seals, and counted them, beginning with us, and then he lay down and fell asleep. Then we leaped up and rushed at him and gripped him fast. He turned into the shapes of a lion, and of a leopard, of a snake, and a huge boar; then he was running water, and next he was a tall, blossoming tree. But we held him firmly, and at last he took his own shape, and told me that I should never have a fair wind till I had sailed back into the river Aegyptus and sacrificed there to the gods in heaven. Then I asked him for news about my brother, Agamemnon, and he told me how my brother was slain in his own hall, and how Ajax was drowned in the sea. Lastly, he told me about Ulysses: how he was kept on a lonely island by the fairy Calypso, and was unhappy, and had no ship and no crew to escape and win home.'

This was all that Menelaus could tell Telemachus, who stayed with Menelaus for a month. All that time the wooers lay in wait for him, with a ship, in a narrow strait which they thought he must sail through on his way back to Ithaca. In that strait they meant to catch him and kill him.

CHAPTER FIVE

How Ulysses Escaped from the
Island of Calypso

Now the day after Menelaus told Telemachus that Ulysses was still
a living man, the gods sent Hermes to Calypso. So Hermes bound
on his feet his fair golden sandals, that wax not old, and bear him,
alike over wet sea and dry land, as swift as the wind. Along the crests
of the waves he flew, like the cormorant that chases fishes through
the sea deeps, with his plumage wet in the sea brine. He reached
the island, and went up to the cave of Calypso, wherein dwelt the
nymph of the braided tresses, and he found her within. And on
the hearth there was a great fire burning, and from afar, through the
isle, was smelt the fragrance of cleft cedar blazing, and of sandal
wood. And the nymph within was singing with a sweet voice as she
fared to and fro before the loom, and wove with a shuttle of gold.
All round about the cave there was a wood blossoming, alder and
poplar and sweet-smelling cypress. Therein roosted birds long of
wing – owls and falcons and chattering sea-crows, which have their
business in the waters. And lo! there, about the hollow cave, trailed
a gadding garden vine, all rich with clusters. And fountains, four set
orderly, were running with clear water hard by one another, turned
each to his own course. Around soft meadows bloomed of violets
and parsley; yea, even a deathless god who came thither might
wonder at the sight and be glad at heart.

There the messenger, the slayer of Argos, stood and wondered.
Now when he had gazed at all with wonder, he went into the wide
cave; nor did Calypso, that fair goddess, fail to know him when she
saw him face to face; for the gods use not to be strange one to
another, not though one have his habitation far away. But he found
not Ulysses, the great-hearted, within the cave, who sat weeping on

the shore even as aforetime, straining his soul with tears and groans and griefs, and as he wept he looked wistfully over the unharvested deep. And Calypso, that fair goddess, questioned Hermes, when she had made him sit on a bright shining star: 'Wherefore, I pray thee, Hermes of the golden wand, hast thou come hither, worshipful and welcome, whereas as of old thou wert not wont to visit me? Tell me all thy thought; my heart is set on fulfilling it, if fulfil it I may, and if it hath been fulfilled in the counsel of fate. But now follow me further, that I may set before thee the entertainment of strangers.'

Therewith the goddess spread a table with ambrosia and set it by him, and mixed the ruddy nectar. So the messenger, the slayer of Argos, did eat and drink. Now after he had supped and comforted his soul with food, at the last he answered, and spake to her on this wise: 'Thou makest question of me on my coming, a goddess of a god, and I will tell thee this my saying truly, at thy command. 'Twas Zeus that bade me come hither, by no will of mine; nay, who of his free will would speed over such a wondrous space of sea whereby is no city of mortals that do sacrifice to the gods. He saith that thou hast with thee a man most wretched beyond his fellows, beyond those men that round the city of Priam for nine years fought, and in the tenth year sacked the city and departed homeward. Yet on the way they sinned against Athene, and she raised upon them an evil blast and long waves of the sea. Then all the rest of his good company was lost, but it came to pass that the wind bare and the wave brought him hither. And now Zeus biddeth thee send him hence with what speed thou mayest, for it is not ordained that he die away from his friends, but rather it is his fate to look on them even yet, and to come to his high-roofed home and his own country.'

So spake he, and Calypso, that fair goddess, shuddered and spake unto him: 'Hard are ye gods and jealous exceeding, who ever grudge goddesses openly to mate with men. Him I saved as he went all alone bestriding the keel of a bark, for that Zeus had crushed and cleft his swift ship with a white bolt in the midst of the wine-dark deep. There all the rest of his good company was lost, but it came to pass that the wind bare and the wave brought him hither. And him have I loved and cherished, and I said that I would make him to know not death and age for ever. But I will give him no despatch, not I, for I have no ships by me with oars, nor company to bear him on his way over the broad back of the sea. Yet will I be forward to put this in his mind, and will hide nought, that all unharmed he may come to his own country.'

Then the messenger, the slayer of Argos, answered her: 'Yea, speed him now upon his path and have regard unto the wrath of Zeus, lest haply he be angered and bear hard on thee hereafter.'

Therewith the great slayer of Argos departed, but the lady nymph went on her way to the great-hearted Ulysses, when she had heard the message of Zeus. And there she found him sitting on the shore, and his eyes were never dry of tears, and his sweet life was ebbing away as he mourned for his return. In the daytime he would sit on the rocks and on the beach, straining his soul with tears and groans and griefs, and through his tears he would look wistfully over the unharvested deep. So, standing near him, that fair goddess spake to him: 'Hapless man, sorrow no more I pray thee in this isle, nor let thy good life waste away, for even now will I send thee hence with all my heart. Nay, arise and cut long beams, and fashion a wide raft with the axe, and lay deckings high thereupon, that it may bear thee over the misty deep. And I will place therein bread and water, and red wine to thy heart's desire, to keep hunger far away. And I will put raiment upon thee, and send a fair gale, that so thou mayest come all unharmed to thine own country, if indeed it be the good pleasure of the gods who hold wide heaven, who are stronger than I am both to will and to do.'

Then Ulysses was glad and sad: glad that the gods took thought for him, and sad to think of crossing alone the wide unsailed seas. Calypso said to him: 'So it is indeed thy wish to get thee home to thine own dear country even in this hour? Good fortune go with thee even so! Yet didst thou know in thine heart what thou art ordained to suffer, or ever thou reach thine own country, here, even here, thou wouldst abide with me and keep this house, and wouldst never taste of death, though thou longest to see thy wife, for whom thou hast ever a desire day by day. Not, in sooth, that I avow me to be less noble than she in form or fashion, for it is in no

Calypso takes pity on Ulysses

wise meet that mortal women should match them with immortals in shape and comeliness.'

And Ulysses of many counsels answered, and spake unto her: 'Be not wroth with me, goddess and queen. Myself I know it well, how wise Penelope is meaner to look upon than thou in comeliness and stature. But she is mortal, and thou knowest not age nor death. Yet, even so, I wish and long day by day to fare homeward and see the day of my returning. Yea, and if some god shall wreck me in the wine-dark deep, even so I will endure, with a heart within me patient of affliction. For already have I suffered full much, and much have I toiled in perils of waves and war; let this be added to the tale of those.'

Next day Calypso brought to Ulysses carpenters' tools, and he felled trees, and made a great raft, and a mast, and sails out of canvas. In five days he had finished his raft and launched it, and Calypso placed in it skins full of wine and water, and flour and many pleasant things to eat, and so they kissed for that last time and took farewell, he going alone on the wide sea, and she turning lonely to her own home. He might have lived for ever with the beautiful fairy, but he chose to live and die, if he could, with his wife Penelope.

CHAPTER SIX

How Ulysses was Wrecked, yet Reached Phaeacia

As long as the fair wind blew Ulysses sat and steered his raft, never seeing land or any ship of men. He kept his eye at night on the Great Bear, holding it always on his left hand, as Calypso taught him. Seventeen days he sailed, and on the eighteenth day he saw the shadowy mountain peaks of an island called Phaeacia. But now the sea god saw him, and remembered how Ulysses had blinded his son the Cyclops. In anger he raised a terrible storm: great clouds covered the sky, and all the winds met. Ulysses wished that he had died when the Trojans gathered round him as he defended the dead body of Achilles. For, had he died then, he would have been burned and buried by his friends, but if he were now drowned his ghost would always wander alone on the fringes of the Land of the Dead, like the ghost of Elpenor.

As he thought thus, the winds broke the mast of his raft, and the sail and yardarm fell into the sea, and the waves dragged him deep down. At last he rose to the surface and swam after his raft, and climbed on to it, and sat there, while the winds tossed the raft about like a feather. The sea goddess, Ino, saw him and pitied him, and rose from the water as a seagull rises after it has dived. She spoke to him, and threw her bright veil to him, saying, 'Wind this round your breast, and throw off your clothes. Leap from the raft and swim, and, when you reach land, cast the veil back into the sea, and turn away your head.'

Ulysses caught the veil, and wound it about his breast, but he determined not to leave the raft while the timbers held together. Even as he thought thus, the timbers were driven asunder by the waves, and he seized a plank, and sat astride it as a man rides a horse. Then the winds fell, all but the north wind, which drifted Ulysses on for two days and nights. On the third day all was calm, and the land was very near, and Ulysses began to swim towards it, through a terrible surf, which crashed and foamed on sheer rocks, where all his bones would be broken. Thrice he clasped a rock, and thrice the back wash of the wave dragged him out to sea. Then he swam outside of the breakers, along the line of land, looking for a safe place, and at last he came to the mouth of the river. Here all was smooth, with a shelving beach, and his feet touched bottom. He staggered out of the water and swooned away as soon as he was on dry land. When he came to himself he unbound the veil of Ino, and cast it into the sea, and fell back, quite spent, among the reeds of the river, naked and starving. He crept between two thick olive trees that grew close together and made a shelter against the wind, and he covered himself all over thickly with fallen dry leaves, till he grew warm again and fell into a deep sleep.

While Ulysses slept, alone and naked in an unknown land, a dream came to beautiful Nausicaa, the daughter of the king of that country, which is called Phaeacia. The dream was in the shape of a girl who was a friend of Nausicaa, and it said: 'Nausicaa, how has your mother such a careless daughter? There are many beautiful garments in the house that need to be washed, against your wedding day, when, as is the custom, you must give mantles and tunics to the guests. Let us go a-washing to the river tomorrow, taking a car to carry the raiment.'

When Nausicaa wakened next day she remembered the dream, and went to her father, and asked him to lend her a car to carry the clothes. She said nothing about her marriage day, for though many young princes were in love with her, she was in love with none of them. Still, the clothes must be washed, and her father lent her a waggon with a high frame, and mules to drive. The clothes were piled in the car, and food was packed in a basket, every sort of dainty thing, and Nausicaa took the reins and drove slowly while many girls followed her, her friends of her own age. They came to a deep clear pool, that overflowed into shallow paved runs of water, and there they washed the clothes, and trod them down in the runlets. Next they laid them out to dry in the sun and wind on the pebbles, and then they took their meal of cakes and other good things.

When they had eaten they threw down their veils and began to play at ball, at a game like rounders. Nausicaa threw the ball at a girl who was running, but missed her, and the ball fell into the deep swift river. All the girls screamed and laughed, and the noise they made wakened Ulysses where he lay in the little wood. 'Where am I?' he said to himself; 'is this a country of fierce and savage men? A sound of girls at play rings round me. Can they be fairies of the hill tops and the rivers, and the water meadows?' As he had no clothes, and the voices seemed to be voices of women, Ulysses broke a great leafy bough which hid all his body, but his feet were bare, his face was wild with weariness, and cold, and hunger, and his hair and beard were matted and rough with the salt water.

The girls, when they saw such a face peering over the leaves of the bough, screamed, and ran this way and that along the beach. But Nausicaa, as became the daughter of the king, stood erect and unafraid, and as Ulysses dared not go near and kneel to her, he spoke from a distance and said: 'I pray thee, O queen, whether thou art a goddess or a mortal! If indeed thou art a goddess of them that keep the wide heaven, to Artemis, then, the daughter of great Zeus, I mainly liken thee for beauty and stature and shapeliness. But if thou art one of the daughters of men who dwell on earth, thrice blessed are thy father and thy lady mother, and thrice blessed thy brethren. Surely their souls ever glow with gladness for thy sake each time they see thee entering the dance, so fair a flower of maidens. But he is of heart the most blessed beyond all other who shall prevail with gifts of wooing, and lead thee to his home. Never have mine eyes beheld such a one among mortals, neither man nor woman; great awe comes upon me as I look on thee. Yet in Delos once I saw as goodly a thing: a young sapling of a palm tree springing by the altar of Apollo. For thither, too, I went, and much people with me, on that path where my sore troubles were to be. Yea! and when I looked thereupon, long time I marvelled in spirit – for never grew there yet so goodly a shoot from ground – even in such wise as I wonder at thee, lady, and am astonished and do greatly fear to touch thy knees, though grievous sorrow is upon me.

'Yesterday, on the twentieth day, I escaped from the wine-dark deep, but all that time continually the wave bare me, and the vehement winds drave from the isle Ogygia. And now some god has cast me on this shore that here too, methinks, some evil may betide me; for I think not that trouble will cease; the gods ere that time will yet bring many a thing to pass. But, queen, have pity on me, for, after many trials and sore, to thee first of all am I come, and of the other folk, who hold this city and land, I know no man. Nay, show me the town; give me an old garment to cast about me, if thou hadst, when thou camest here, any wrap for the linen. And may the gods grant thee all thy heart's desire: a husband and a home, and a mind at one with his may they give – a good gift, for there is nothing mightier and nobler than when man and wife are of one heart and mind in a house, a grief to their foes, and to their friends great joy, but their own hearts know it best.'

Then Nausicaa of the white arms answered him, and said: 'Stranger, as thou seemest no evil man nor foolish – and it is Olympian Zeus himself that giveth weal to men, to the good and to the evil, to each one as he will, and this thy lot doubtless is of him, and so thou must in anywise endure it – now, since thou hast come to our city and our land, thou shalt not lack raiment nor aught else that is the due of a hapless suppliant when he has met them who can befriend him. And I will show thee the town, and name the name of the people. The Phaeacians hold this city and land, and I am the daughter of Alcinous, great of heart, on whom all the might and force of the Phaeacians depend.'

Thus she spake, and called to her maidens of the fair tresses: 'Halt, my maidens, whither flee ye at the sight of a man? Ye surely do not take him for an enemy? That mortal breathes not, and never will be born, who shall come with war to the land of the Phaeacians, for they are very dear to the gods. Far apart we live in the wash of the waves, the outermost of men, and no other mortals are conversant with us. Nay, but this man is some helpless one come hither in his wanderings, whom now we must kindly entreat, for all strangers and beggars are from Zeus, and a little gift is dear. So, my maidens, give the stranger meat and drink, and bathe him in the river, where there is a shelter from the winds.'

So she spake, but they halted and called each to the other, and they brought Ulysses to the sheltered place, and made him sit down, as Nausicaa bade them, the daughter of Alcinous, high of heart. Beside him they laid a mantle and a doublet for raiment, and gave him soft olive oil in the golden cruse, and bade him wash in the streams of the river. Then goodly Ulysses spake among the maidens, saying: 'I pray you stand thus apart while I myself wash the brine from my shoulders, and anoint me with olive oil, for truly oil is long a stranger to my skin. But in your sight I will not bathe, for I am ashamed to make me naked in the company of fair-tressed maidens.'

Then they went apart and told all to their lady. But with the river water the goodly Ulysses washed from his skin the salt scurf that covered his back and broad shoulders, and from his head he wiped the crusted brine of the barren sea. But when he had washed his whole body, and anointed him with olive oil, and had clad himself in the raiment that the unwedded maiden gave him, then Athene, the daughter of Zeus, made him greater and more mighty to behold, and from his head caused deep curling locks to flow, like the hyacinth flower. And, as when some skilful man overlays gold upon silver – one that Hephaestus and Pallas Athene have taught all manner of craft, and full of grace is his handiwork – even so did Athene shed grace about his head and shoulders.

Then to the shore of the sea went Ulysses apart, and sat down, glowing in beauty and grace, and the princess marvelled at him, and spake among her fair-tressed maidens, saying: 'Listen, my white-armed maidens, and I will say somewhat. Not without the will of all the gods who hold Olympus has this man come among the godlike Phaeacians. Erewhile he seemed to me uncomely, but now he is like the gods that keep the wide heaven. Would that such a one might be called my husband, dwelling here, and that it might please him here to abide! But come, my maidens, give the stranger meat and drink.'

Thus she spake, and they gave ready ear and hearkened, and set beside Ulysses meat and drink, and the steadfast goodly Ulysses did eat and drink eagerly, for it was long since he had tasted food.

Now Nausicaa of the white arms had another thought. She folded the raiment and stored it in the goodly wain, and yoked the mules, strong of hoof, and herself climbed into the car. Then she called on Ulysses, and spake and hailed him: 'Up now, stranger, and rouse thee to go to the city, that I may convey thee to the house of my wise father, where, I promise thee, thou shalt get knowledge of all the noblest of the Phaeacians. But do thou even as I tell thee, and thou seemest a discreet man enough. So long as we are passing along the fields and farms of men, do thou fare quickly with the maidens behind the mules and the chariot, and I will lead the way. But when we set foot within the city, whereby goes a high wall with towers, and there is a fair haven on either side of the town, and narrow is the entrance, and curved ships are drawn up on either hand of the mole, thou shalt find a fair grove of Athene, a poplar grove, near the road, and a spring wells forth therein, and a meadow lies all around.

'There is my father's land, and his fruitful close, within the sound of a man's shout from the city. Sit thee down there and wait until such time as we may have come into the city, and reached the house of my father. But when thou deemest that we are got to the palace, then go up to the city of the Phaeacians, and ask for the house of my father, Alcinous, high of heart. It is easily known, and a young child could be thy guide, for nowise like it are builded the houses of the Phaeacians, so goodly is the palace of the hero Alcinous. But when thou art within the shadow of the halls and the court, pass quickly through the great chamber till thou comest to my mother, who sits at the hearth in the light of the fire, weaving yarn of sea-purple stain, a wonder to behold. Her chair is leaned against a pillar, and her maidens sit behind her. And there my father's throne leans close to hers, wherein he sits and drinks his wine, like an immortal. Pass thou by him, and cast thy hands about my mother's knees that thou mayest see quickly and with joy the day of thy returning, even if thou art from a very far country. If but her heart be kindly disposed towards thee, then is there hope that thou shalt see thy friends, and come to thy well-builded house, and to thine own country.'

She spake and smote the mules with the shining whip, and quickly they left behind them the streams of the river; and well they trotted and well they paced, and she took heed to drive in such wise that the maidens and Ulysses might follow on foot, and cunningly she plied the lash. Then the sun set, and they came to the famous grove, the sacred place of Athene; so there the goodly Ulysses sat him down. Then straightway he prayed to the daughter of mighty Zeus: 'Listen to me, child of Zeus, lord of the aegis, unwearied maiden; hear me even now, since before thou heardest not when I was smitten on the sea, when the renowned earth-shaker smote me. Grant me to come to the Phaeacians as one dear and worthy of pity.'

So he spake in prayer, and Pallas Athene heard him; but she did not yet appear to him face to face, for she had regard unto her father's brother, who furiously raged against the godlike Ulysses till he should come to his own country.

While Nausicaa and her maidens went home, Ulysses waited near the temple till they should have arrived, and then he rose and walked to the city, wondering at the harbour, full of ships, and at the strength of the walls. The goddess Athene met him, disguised as a mortal girl, and told him again how the name of the king was Alcinous, and his wife's name was Arete: she was wise and kind, and had great power in the city. The goddess caused Ulysses to pass unseen among the people till he reached the palace, which shone with bronze facings to the walls, while within the hall were golden hounds and golden statues of young men holding torches burning to give light to those who sat at supper. The gardens were very beautiful, full of fruit trees, and watered by streams that flowed from two fountains. Ulysses stood and wondered at the beauty of the gardens, and then walked, unseen, through the hall, and knelt at the feet of Queen Arete, and implored her to send him in a ship to his own country.

A table was brought to him, and food and wine were set before him, and Alcinous, as his guests were going home, spoke out and said that the stranger was to be entertained, whoever he might be, and sent safely on his way. The guests departed, and Arete, looking at Ulysses, saw that the clothes he wore were possessions of her house, and asked him who he was, and how he got the raiment? Then he told her how he had been shipwrecked, and how Nausicaa had given him food, and garments out of those which she had been washing. Then Arete said that Nausicaa should have brought Ulysses straight to her house; but Ulysses answered: 'Chide not, I pray you, the blameless damsel,' and explained that he himself was shy, and afraid that Nausicaa's parents might not like to see her coming with an unknown stranger. King Alcinous answered that he was not jealous and suspicious. To a stranger so noble as Ulysses he would very gladly see his daughter married, and would give him a house and plenty of everything. But if the stranger desired to go to his own country, then a ship should be made ready for him. Thus courteous was Alcinous, for he readily saw that Ulysses, who had not yet told his name, was of noble birth, strong and wise. Then all went to bed, and Ulysses had a soft bed and a warm, with blankets of purple.

Next day Alcinous sent two-and-fifty young men to prepare a ship, and they moored her in readiness out in the shore water; but the chiefs dined with Alcinous, and the minstrel sang about the Trojan war, and so stirred the heart of Ulysses, that he held his mantle before his face and wept. When Alcinous saw that, he proposed that they should go and amuse themselves with sports in the open air; races, wrestling, and boxing. The son of Alcinous asked Ulysses if he would care to take part in the games, but Ulysses answered that he was too heavy at heart. To this a young man, Euryalus, said that Ulysses was probably a captain of a merchant ship, a tradesman, not a sportsman.

At this Ulysses was ill pleased, and replied that while he was young and happy, he was well skilled in all sports, but now he was heavy and weak with war and wandering. Still, he would show what he could do. Then he seized a heavy weight, much heavier than any that the Phaeacians used in putting the stone. He whirled it up, and hurled it far – far beyond the furthest mark that the Phaeacians had reached when putting a lighter weight. Then he challenged any man to run a race with him or box with him, or shoot at a mark with him. Only his speed in running did he doubt, for his limbs were stiffened by the sea. Perhaps Alcinous saw that it would go ill with any man who matched himself against the stranger, so he sent for the harper, who sang a merry song, and then he made the young men dance and play ball, and bade the elder men go and bring rich presents of gold and garments for the wanderer. Alcinous himself gave a beautiful coffer and chest, and a great golden cup, and Arete tied up all the gifts in the coffer, while the damsels took Ulysses to the bath, and bathed him and anointed him with oil.

As he left the bath he met Nausicaa, standing at the entrance of the hall. She bade him goodbye, rather sadly, saying: 'Farewell, and do not soon forget me in your own country, for to me you owe the ransom of your life.' 'May god grant to me to see my own country, lady,' he answered, 'for there I will think of you with worship, as I think of the blessed gods, all my days, for to you, lady, I owe my very life.' These were the last words they spoke to each other, for Nausicaa did not sit at meat in the hall with the great company of men. When they had taken supper, the blind harper sang again a song about the deeds of Ulysses at Troy, and again Ulysses wept, so that Alcinous asked him: 'Hast thou lost a dear friend or a kinsman in the great war?' Then Ulysses spoke out: 'I am Ulysses, Laertes' son, of whom all men have heard tell.' While they sat amazed, he began, and told them the whole story of his adventures, from the day when he left Troy till he arrived at Calypso's island; he had already told them how he was shipwrecked on his way thence to Phaeacia.

All that wonderful story he told to their pleasure, and Euryalus made amends for his rude words at the games, and gave Ulysses a beautiful sword of bronze, with an ivory hilt set with studs of gold. Many other gifts were given to him, and were carried and stored on board the ship which had been made ready, and then Ulysses spoke goodbye to the queen, saying: 'Be happy, oh queen, till old age and death come to you, as they come to all. Be joyful in your house with your children and your people, and Alcinous the King.' Then he

departed, and lay down on sheets and cloaks in the raised deck of
the ship, and soundly he slept while the fifty oars divided the waters
of the sea, and drove the ship to Ithaca.

How Ulysses Came to his own Country, and for Safety Disguised himself as an Old Beggar Man

When Ulysses awoke, he found himself alone, wrapped in the linen sheet and the bright coverlet, and he knew not where he was. The Phaeacians had carried him from the ship as he slept, and put him on shore, and placed all the rich gifts that had been given him under a tree, and then had sailed away. There was a morning mist that hid the land, and Ulysses did not know the haven of his own island, Ithaca, and the rock whence sprang a fountain of the water fairies that men call Naiads. He thought that the Phaeacians had set him in a strange country, so he counted all his goods, and then walked up and down sadly by the seashore. Here he met a young man, delicately clad, like a king's son, with a double mantle, such as kings wear, folded round his shoulders, and a spear in his hand. 'Tell me pray,' said Ulysses, 'what land is this, and what men dwell here?'

The young man said: 'Truly, stranger, you know little, or you come from far away. This isle is Ithaca, and the name of it is known even in Troyland.'

Ulysses was glad, indeed, to learn that he was at home at last; but how the young men who had grown up since he went away would treat him, all alone as he was, he could not tell. So he did not let out that he was Ulysses the King, but said that he was a Cretan. The stranger would wonder why a Cretan had come alone to Ithaca, with great riches, and yet did not know that he was there. So he pretended that, in Crete, a son of Idomeneus had tried to rob him of all the spoil he took at Troy, and that he had killed this prince, and packed his wealth and fled on board a ship of the Phoenicians, who promised to land him at Pylos. But the wind had borne them out of their way, and they had all landed and slept on shore, here; but the Phoenicians had left him asleep and gone off in the dawn.

On this the young man laughed, and suddenly appeared as the great goddess, Pallas Athene. 'How clever you are,' she said; 'yet you did not know me, who helped you in Troyland. But much trouble lies before you, and you must not let man or woman know who you really are, your enemies are so many and powerful.'

'You never helped me in my dangers on the sea,' said Ulysses, 'and now do you make mock of me, or is this really mine own country?'

'I had no mind,' said the goddess, 'to quarrel with my brother the sea god, who had a feud against you for the blinding of his son, the Cyclops. But come, you shall see this is really Ithaca,' and she scattered the white mist, and Ulysses saw and knew the pleasant cave of the Naiads, and the forests on the side of the mountain called Neriton. So he knelt down and kissed the dear earth of his own country, and prayed to the Naiads of the cave. Then the goddess helped him to hide all his gold, and bronze, and other presents in a secret place in the cavern; and she taught him how, being lonely as he was, he might destroy the proud wooers of his wife, who would certainly desire to take his life.

The goddess began by disguising Ulysses, so that his skin seemed wrinkled, and his hair thin, and his eyes dull, and she gave him dirty old wraps for clothes, and over all a great bald skin of a stag, like that which he wore when he stole into Troy disguised as a beggar. She gave him a staff, too, and a wallet to hold scraps of broken food. There was not a man or a woman that knew Ulysses in this disguise. Next, the goddess bade him go across the island to his own swine-herd, who remained faithful to him, and to stay there among the swine till she brought home Telemachus, who was visiting Helen and Menelaus in Lacedaemon. She fled away to Lacedaemon, and Ulysses climbed the hills that lay between the cavern and the farm where the swineherd lived.

When Ulysses reached the farmhouse, the swineherd, Eumaeus, was sitting alone in front of his door, making himself a pair of brogues out of the skin of an ox. He was a very honest man, and, though he was a slave, he was the son of a prince in his own country. When he was a little child some Phoenicians came in their ship to his father's house and made friends with his nurse, who was a Phoenician woman. One of them, who made love to her, asked her who she was, and she said that her father was a rich man in Sidon, but that pirates had carried her away and sold her to her master. The Phoenicians promised to bring her back to Sidon, and she fled to their ship, carrying with her the child whom she nursed, little Eumaeus; she also stole three cups of gold. The woman died at sea, and the pirates sold the boy to Laertes, the father of Ulysses, who treated him kindly. Eumaeus was fond of the family which he served, and he hated the proud wooers for their insolence.

When Ulysses came near his house the four great dogs rushed out and barked at him; they would have bitten, too, but Eumaeus ran up and threw stones at them, and no farm dog can face a shower of stones. He took Ulysses into his house, gave him food and wine, and told him all about the greed and pride of the wooers. Ulysses said that the master of Eumaeus would certainly come home, and told a long story about himself. He was a Cretan, he said, and had fought at Troy, and later had been shipwrecked, but reached a country called Thesprotia, where he learned that Ulysses was alive, and was soon to leave Thesprotia and return to Ithaca.

Eumaeus did not believe this tale, and supposed that the beggar man only meant to say what he would like to hear. However, he gave Ulysses a good dinner of his own pork, and Ulysses amused him and his fellow slaves with stories about the Siege of Troy, till it was bedtime.

In the meantime Athene had gone to Lacedaemon to the house of Menelaus, where Telemachus was lying awake. She told him that Penelope, his mother, meant to marry one of the wooers, and advised him to sail home at once, avoiding the strait between Ithaca and another isle, where his enemies were lying in wait to kill him. When he reached Ithaca he must send his oarsmen to the town, but himself walk alone across the island to see the swineherd. In the morning Telemachus and his friend, Pisistratus, said goodbye to

Menelaus and Helen, who wished to make him presents, and so went to their treasure house. Now when they came to the place where the treasures were stored, then Atrides took a double cup, and bade his son, Megapenthes, to bear a mixing-bowl of silver. And Helen stood by the coffers, wherein were her robes of curious needlework which she herself had wrought. So Helen, the fair lady, lifted one and brought it out – the widest and most beautifully embroidered of all – and it shone like a star, and lay far beneath the rest.

Then they went back through the house till they came to Telemachus; and Menelaus, of the fair hair, spake to him, saying: 'Telemachus, may Zeus the thunderer, and the lord of Hera, in very truth bring about thy return according to the desire of thy heart. And of the gifts, such as are treasures stored in my house, I will give thee the goodliest and greatest of price. I will give thee a mixing-bowl beautifully wrought; it is all of silver, and the lips thereof are finished with gold, the work of Hephaestus; and the hero Phaedimus, the king of the Sidonians, gave it to me when his house sheltered me, on my coming thither. This cup I would give to thee.'

Therewith the hero Atrides set the double cup in his hands. And the strong Megapenthes bare the shining silver bowl and set it before him. And Helen came up, beautiful Helen, with the robe in her hands, and spake and hailed him: 'Lo! I, too, give thee this gift, dear child, a memorial of the hands of Helen, against the day of thy desire, even of thy bridal, for thy bride to wear it. But, meanwhile, let it lie by thy dear mother in her chamber. And may joy go with thee to thy well-builded house and thine own country.'

Just when Telemachus was leaving her palace door, an eagle stooped from the sky and flew away with a great white goose that was feeding on the grass, and the farm servants rushed out shouting, but the eagle passed away to the right hand, across the horses of Pisistratus.

Then Helen explained the meaning of this omen. 'Hear me, and I will prophesy as the immortals put it into my heart, and as I deem it will be accomplished. Even as yonder eagle came down from the hill, the place of his birth and kin, and snatched away the goose that was fostered in the house, even so shall Ulysses return home after much trial and long wanderings and take vengeance; yea! or even now is he at home and sowing the seeds of evil for all the wooers.' We are told no more about Helen of the fair hands, except that she and Menelaus never died, but were carried by the gods to the beautiful Elysian plain, a happy place where war and trouble never came, nor old age, nor death. After that she was worshipped in her own country as if she had been a goddess, kind, gentle, and beautiful.

Telemachus thanked Helen for prophesying good luck, and he drove to the city of Nestor, on the sea, but was afraid to go near the old king, who would have kept him and entertained him, while he must sail at once for Ithaca. He went to his own ship in the harbour, and, while his crew made ready to sail, there came a man running hard, and in great fear of the avenger of blood. This was a second-sighted man, called Theoclymenus, and he implored Telemachus to take him to Ithaca, for he had slain a man in his own country, who had killed one of his brothers, and now the brothers and cousins of that man were pursuing him to take his life. Telemachus made him welcome, and so sailed north to Ithaca, wondering whether he should be able to slip past the wooers, who were lying in wait to kill him. Happily the ship of Telemachus passed them unseen in the night, and arrived at Ithaca. He sent his crew to the town, and was just starting to walk across the island to the swineherd's house, when the second-sighted man asked what *he* should do. Telemachus told Piraeus, one of his friends, to take the man home and be kind to him, which he gladly promised to do, and then he set off to seek the swineherd.

The swineherd, with Ulysses, had just lit a fire to cook breakfast, when they saw the farm dogs frolicking round a young man who was walking towards the house. The dogs welcomed him, for he was no stranger, but Telemachus. Up leaped the swineherd in delight, and the bowl in which he was mixing wine and water fell from his hands. He had been unhappy for fear the wooers who lay in wait for Telemachus should kill him, and he ran and embraced the young man as gladly as a father welcomes a son who has long been in a far country. Telemachus, too, was anxious to hear whether his mother had married one of the wooers, and glad to know that she still bore her troubles patiently.

When Telemachus stepped into the swineherd's house Ulysses arose from his seat, but Telemachus bade the old beggar man sit down again, and a pile of brushwood with a fleece thrown over it was brought for himself. They breakfasted on what was ready, cold pork, wheaten bread, and wine in cups of ivy wood, and Eumaeus told Telemachus that the old beggar gave himself out as a wanderer from Crete. Telemachus answered that he could not take strangers into his mother's house, for he was unable to protect them against the violence of the wooers, but he would give the wanderer clothes and shoes and a sword, and he might stay at the farm. He sent the swineherd to tell his mother, Penelope, that he had returned in safety, and Eumaeus started on his journey to the town.

At this moment the farm dogs, which had been taking their share of the breakfast, began to whine, and bristle up, and slunk with their tails between their legs to the inmost corner of the room. Telemachus could not think why they were afraid, or of what, but Ulysses saw the goddess Athene, who appeared to him alone, and the dogs knew that something strange and terrible was coming to the door. Ulysses went out, and Athene bade him tell Telemachus who he really was, now that they were alone, and she touched Ulysses with her golden wand, and made him appear like himself, and his clothes like a king's raiment.

Telemachus, who neither saw nor heard Athene, wondered greatly, and thought the beggar man must be some god, wandering in disguise. But Ulysses said, 'No god am I, but thine own father,' and they embraced each other and wept for joy.

At last Ulysses told Telemachus how he had come home in a ship of the Phaeacians, and how his treasure was hidden in the cave of the Naiads, and asked him how many the wooers were, and how they might drive them from the house. Telemachus replied that the wooers were one hundred and eight, and that Medon, a servant of his own, took part with them, there was also the minstrel of the house, whom they compelled to sing at their feasts. They were all strong young men, each with his sword at his side, but they had with them no shields, helmets, and breastplates. Ulysses said that, with the help of the goddess, he hoped to get the better of them, many as they were. Telemachus must go to the house, and Ulysses would come next day, in the disguise of an old beggar. However ill the wooers might use him, Telemachus must take no notice, beyond saying that they ought to behave better. Ulysses, when he saw a good chance, would give Telemachus a sign to take away the shields, helmets, and weapons that hung on the walls of the great hall, and to hide them in a secret place. If the wooers missed them, he must say – first, that the smoke of the fire was spoiling them; and, again, that they were better out of the reach of the wooers, in case they quarrelled over their wine. Telemachus must keep two swords, two spears, and two shields for himself and Ulysses to use, if they saw a chance, and he must let neither man nor woman know that the old beggar man was his father.

While they were talking, one of the crew of Telemachus and the swineherd went to Penelope and told her how her son had landed. On hearing this the wooers held a council as to how they should behave to him: Antinous was for killing him, but Amphinomus and Eurymachus were for waiting, and seeing what would happen. Before Eumaeus came back from his errand to Penelope, Athene changed Ulysses into the dirty old beggar again.

CHAPTER EIGHT

Ulysses Comes Disguised as a Beggar to his own Palace

Next morning Telemachus went home, and comforted his mother, and told her how he had been with Nestor and Menelaus, and seen her cousin, Helen of the fair hands, but this did not seem to interest Penelope, who thought that her beautiful cousin was the cause of all her misfortunes. Then Theoclymenus, the second-sighted man whom Telemachus brought from Pylos, prophesied to Penelope that Ulysses was now in Ithaca, taking thought how he might kill the wooers, who were then practising spear-throwing at a mark, while some of them were killing swine and a cow for breakfast.

Meanwhile Ulysses, in disguise, and the swineherd were coming near the town, and there they met the goatherd, Melanthius, who was a friend of the wooers, and an insolent and violent slave. He insulted the old beggar, and advised him not to come near the house of Ulysses, and kicked him off the road. Then Ulysses was tempted to slay him with his hands, but he controlled himself lest he should be discovered, and he and Eumaeus walked slowly to the palace. As they lingered outside the court, lo! a hound raised up his head and pricked his ears, even where he lay: Argos, the hound of Ulysses, of the hardy heart, which of old himself had bred. Now in time past the young men used to lead the hound against wild goats and deer and hares; but, as then, he lay despised (his master being afar) in the deep dung of mules and kine, whereof an ample bed was spread before the doors till the slaves of Ulysses should carry it away to dung therewith his wide demesne. There lay the dog Argos, full of vermin. Yet even now, when he was aware of Ulysses standing by, he wagged his tail and dropped both his ears, but nearer to his master he had not now the strength to draw. But Ulysses looked aside and wiped away a tear that he easily hid from Eumaeus, and straightway he asked him, saying: 'Eumaeus, verily this is a great marvel: this hound lying here in the dung. Truly he is goodly of growth, but I know not certainly if he have speed with this beauty, or if he be comely only, like men's trencher dogs that their lords keep for the pleasure of the eye.'

Then answered the swineherd Eumaeus: 'In very truth this is the dog of a man that has died in a far land. If he were what once he was in limb and in the feats of the chase, when Ulysses left him to go to Troy, soon wouldst thou marvel at the sight of his swiftness and his strength. There was no beast that could flee from him in the deep places of the wood when he was in pursuit; for even on a track he was the keenest hound. But now he is holden in an evil case, and his lord hath perished far from his own country, and the careless women take no charge of him.'

Therewith he passed within the fair-lying house, and went straight to the hall, to the company of the proud wooers. But upon Argos came death even in the hour that he beheld Ulysses again, in the twentieth year.

Thus the good dog knew Ulysses, though Penelope did not know him when she saw him, and tears came into Ulysses' eyes as he stood above the body of the hound that loved him well. Eumaeus went into the house, but Ulysses sat down where it was the custom for beggars to sit, on the wooden threshold outside the door of the hall. Telemachus saw him, from his high seat under the pillars on each side of the fire, in the middle of the room, and bade Eumaeus carry a loaf and a piece of pork to the beggar, who laid them in his wallet between his feet, and ate. Then he thought he would try if there were one courteous man among the wooers, and he entered the hall and began to beg among them. Some gave him crusts and bones, but Antinous caught up a footstool and struck him hard on the shoulder. 'May death come upon Antinous before his wedding day!' said Ulysses, and even the other wooers rebuked him for striking a beggar.

Penelope heard of this, and told Eumaeus to bring the beggar to her; she thought he might have news of her husband. But Ulysses

made Eumaeus say that he had been struck once in the hall, and
would not come to her till after sunset, when the wooers left the
house. Then Eumaeus went to his own farmhouse, after telling
Telemachus that he would come next day, driving swine for the
wooers to eat.

Ulysses was the new beggar in Ithaca: he soon found that he had
a rival, an old familiar beggar, named Irus. This man came up to
the palace, and was angry when he saw a newcomer sitting in the
doorway, 'Get up,' he said, 'I ought to drag you away by the foot:
begone before we quarrel!' 'There is room enough for both of us,'
said Ulysses, 'do not anger me.' Irus challenged him to fight, and
the wooers thought this good sport, and they made a ring, and
promised that the winner should be beggar-in-chief, and have the
post to himself. Ulysses asked the wooers to give him fair play, and
not to interfere, and then he stripped his shoulders, and kilted up
his rags, showing strong arms and legs. As for Irus he began to
tremble, but Antinous forced him to fight, and the two put up their
hands. Irus struck at the shoulder of Ulysses, who hit him with his
right fist beneath the ear, and he fell, the blood gushing from his
mouth, and his heels drumming in the ground, and Ulysses dragged
him from the doorway and propped him against the wall of the
court, while the wooers laughed. Then Ulysses spoke gravely to
Amphinomus, telling him that it would be wise in him to go home,
for that if Ulysses came back it might not be so easy to escape his
hands.

After sunset Ulysses spoke so fiercely to the maidens of Penelope,
who insulted him, that they ran to their own rooms, but Eurymachus
threw a footstool at him. He slipped out of the way, and the stool hit
the cupbearer and knocked him down, and all was disorder in the
hall. The wooers themselves were weary of the noise and disorder,
and went home to the houses in the town where they slept. Then
Telemachus and Ulysses, being left alone, hid the shields and
helmets and spears that hung on the walls of the hall in an armoury
within the house, and when this was done Telemachus went to
sleep in his own chamber, in the courtyard, and Ulysses waited till
Penelope should come into the hall.

Ulysses sat in the dusky hall, where the wood in the braziers that gave light had burned low, and waited to see the face of his wife, for whom he had left beautiful Calypso. The maidens of Penelope came trooping, laughing, and cleared away the food and the cups, and put faggots in the braziers. They were all giddy girls, in love with the handsome wooers, and one of them, Melantho, bade Ulysses go away, and sleep at the blacksmith's forge, lest he should be beaten with a torch. Penelope heard Melantho, whom she had herself brought up, and she rebuked her, and ordered a chair to be brought for Ulysses. When he was seated, she asked him who he was, and he praised her beauty, for she was still very fair, but did not answer her question. She insisted that he should tell her who he was, and he said that he was a Cretan prince, the younger brother of Idomeneus, and that he did not go to fight in Troyland. In Crete he stayed, and met Ulysses, who stopped there on his way to Troy, and he entertained Ulysses for a fortnight. Penelope wept when she heard that the stranger had seen her husband, but, as false stories were often told to her by strangers who came to Ithaca, she asked how Ulysses was dressed, and what manner of men were with him.

The beggar said that Ulysses wore a double mantle of purple, clasped with a gold brooch fastened by two safety pins (for these were used at that time), and on the face of the brooch was a figure of a hound holding a struggling fawn in his forepaws. (Many such brooches have been found in the graves in Greece.) Beneath his mantle Ulysses wore a shining smock, smooth and glittering like the skin of an onion. Probably it was made of silk: women greatly admired it. With him was a squire named Eurybates, a brown, round-shouldered man.

On hearing all this Penelope wept again and said that she herself had given Ulysses the brooch and the garments. She now knew that the beggar had really met Ulysses, and he went on to tell her that, in his wanderings, he had heard how Ulysses was still alive, though he had lost all his company, and that he had gone to Dodona in the west of Greece to ask for advice from the oak tree of Zeus, the whispering oak tree, as to how he should come home, openly or secretly. Certainly, he said, Ulysses would return that year.

Penelope was still unable to believe in such good news, but she bade Eurycleia, the old nurse, wash the feet of the beggar in warm water, so a foot bath was brought. Ulysses turned his face away from the firelight, for the nurse said that he was very like her master. As she washed his legs she noticed the long scar of the wound made by the boar, when he hunted with his cousins, long ago, before he was married. The nurse knew him now, and spoke to him in a whisper, calling him by his name. But he caught her throat with his hand, and asked why she would cause his death, for the wooers would slay him if they knew who he was. Eurycleia called him her child, and promised that she would be silent, and then she went to fetch more hot water, for she had let his foot fall into the bath and upset it when she found the scar.

When she had washed him, Penelope told the beggar that she could no longer refuse to marry one of the wooers. Ulysses had left a great bow in the house, the old bow of King Eurytus, that few could bend, and he had left twelve iron axes, made with a round opening in the blade of each. Axes of this shape have been found at Lacedaemon, where Helen lived, so we know what the axes of Ulysses were like. When he was at home he used to set twelve of them in a straight line, and shoot an arrow through the twelve holes in the blades. Penelope therefore intended, next day, to bring the bow and the axes to the wooers, and to marry any one of them who could string the bow, and shoot an arrow through the twelve axes.

'I think,' said the beggar, 'that Ulysses will be here before any of the wooers have bent his bow.' Then Penelope went to her upper chamber, and Ulysses slept in an outer gallery of the house on piled-up sheepskins.

There Ulysses lay, thinking how he might destroy all the wooers, and the goddess Athene came and comforted him, and, in the morning, he rose and made his prayer to Zeus, asking for signs of his favour. There came, first a peal of thunder, and then the voice of a woman, weak and old, who was grinding corn to make bread for the wooers. All the other women of the mill had done their work and were asleep, but she was feeble and the round upper stone of the quern, that she rolled on the corn above the under stone, was too heavy for her.

She prayed, and said, 'Father Zeus, king of gods and men, loudly hast thou thundered. Grant to me my prayer, unhappy as I am. May this be the last day of the feasting of the wooers in the hall of Ulysses: they have loosened my knees with cruel labour in grinding barley for them: may they now sup their last!' Hearing this prayer Ulysses was glad, for he thought it a lucky sign. Soon the servants were at work, and Eumaeus came with swine, and was as courteous to the beggar as Melanthius, who brought some goats, was insolent. The cowherd, called Philoetius, also arrived; he hated the wooers, and spoke friendly to the beggar. Last appeared the wooers, and went in to their meal, while Telemachus bade the beggar sit on a seat just within the hall, and told the servants to give him as good a share of the food as any of them received. One wooer, Ctesippus, said: 'His fair share this beggar man has had, as is right, but I will give him a present over and above it!' Then he picked up the foot of an ox, and threw it with all his might at Ulysses, who merely moved aside, and the ox-foot struck the wall.

Telemachus rebuked him, and the wooers began to laugh wildly and to weep, they knew not why, but Theoclymenus, the second-sighted man, knew that they were all fey men, that is, doomed to die, for such men are gay without reason. 'Unhappy that you are,' cried Theoclymenus, 'what is coming upon you? I see shrouds covering you about your knees and about your faces, and tears are on your cheeks, and the walls and the pillars of the roof are dripping blood, and in the porch and the court are your fetches, shadows of yourselves, hurrying hellward, and the sun is darkened.'

On this all the wooers laughed, and advised him to go out of doors, where he would see that the sun was shining. 'My eyes and ears serve me well,' said the second-sighted man, 'but out I will go, seeking no more of your company, for death is coming on every man of you.' Then he arose and went to the house of Piraeus, the friend of Telemachus. The wooers laughed all the louder, as fey men do, and told Telemachus that he was unlucky in his guests: one a beggar, the other a madman. But Telemachus kept watching his father while the wooers were cooking a meal that they did not live to enjoy.

Through the crowd of them came Penelope, holding in her hand the great bow of Eurytus, and a quiver full of arrows, while her maidens followed, carrying the chest in which lay the twelve iron axes. She stood up, stately and scornful, among the wooers, and told them that, as marry she must, she would take the man who could string the bow and shoot the arrow through the axes. Telemachus said that he would make the first trial, and that, if he succeeded, he would not allow any man of the wooers to take his mother away with him from her own house. Then thrice he tried to string the bow, and the fourth time he would have strung it, but Ulysses made a sign to him, and he put it down. 'I am too weak,' he said, 'let a stronger man achieve this adventure.' So they tried each in turn, beginning with the man who sat next the great mixing-bowl of wine, and so each rising in his turn.

First their prophet tried, Leiodes the Seer, who sat next the bowl, but his white hands were too weak, and he prophesied, saying that the bow would be the death of all of them. Then Antinous bade the goatherd light a fire, and bring grease to heat the bow, and make it more supple. They warmed and greased the bow, and one after another tried to bend it. Eumaeus and the cowherd went out into the court, and Ulysses followed them. 'Whose side would you two take,' he asked, 'if Ulysses came home? Would you fight for him or for the wooers?' 'For Ulysses!' they both cried, 'and would that he was come indeed!' 'He is come, and I am he!' said Ulysses. Then he promised to give them lands of their own if he was victorious, and he showed them the scar on his thigh that the boar dealt with his white tusk, long ago. The two men kissed him and shed tears of joy, and Ulysses said that he would go back first into the hall, and that they were to follow him. He would ask to be allowed to try to bend the bow, and Eumaeus, whatever the wooers said, must place it in his hands, and then see that the women were locked up in their own separate hall. Philoetius was to fasten the door leading from the courtyard into the road. Ulysses then went back to his seat in the hall, near the door, and his servants followed.

Eurymachus was trying in vain to bend the bow, and Antinous proposed to put off the trial till next day, and then sacrifice to the god Apollo, and make fresh efforts. They began to drink, but Ulysses asked to be allowed to try if he could string the bow. They told him that wine had made him impudent, and threatened to put him in a ship and send him to King Echetus, an ogre, who would cut him to pieces. But Penelope said that the beggar must try his strength; not that she would marry him, if he succeeded. She would only give him new clothes, a sword, and a spear, and send him wherever he wanted to go. Telemachus cried out that the bow was his own; he would make a present of it to the beggar if he chose; and he bade his mother join her maidens, and work at her weaving. She was amazed to hear her son speak like the master of the house, and she went upstairs with her maidens to her own room.

Eumaeus was carrying the bow to Ulysses, when the wooers made such an uproar that he laid it down, in fear for his life. But Telemachus threatened to punish him if he did not obey his master, so he placed the bow in the hands of Ulysses, and then went and told Eurycleia to lock the women servants up in their own separate hall. Philoetius slipped into the courtyard, and made the gates fast with a strong rope, and then came back, and watched Ulysses, who was turning the bow this way and that, to see if the horns were still sound, for horns were then used in bow making. The wooers were mocking him, but suddenly he bent and strung the great bow as easily as a harper fastens a new string to his harp. He tried the string, and it twanged like the note of a swallow. He took up an arrow that lay on the table (the others were in the quiver beside him), he fitted it to the string, and from the chair where he sat he shot it through all the twelve axe-heads. 'Your guest has done you no dishonour, Telemachus,' he said, 'but surely it is time to eat,' and he nodded. Telemachus drew his sword, took a spear in his left hand, and stood up beside Ulysses.

CHAPTER NINE

The Slaying of the Wooers

Ulysses let all his rags fall down, and with one leap he reached the high threshold, the door being behind him, and he dropped the arrows from the quiver at his feet. 'Now,' he said, 'I will strike another mark that no man yet has stricken!' He aimed the arrow at Antinous, who was drinking out of a golden cup. The arrow passed clean through the throat of Antinous; he fell, the cup rang on the ground, and the wooers leaped up, looking round the walls for shields and spears, but the walls were bare.

'Thou shalt die, and vultures shall devour thee,' they shouted, thinking the beggar had let the arrow fly by mischance.

'Dogs!' he answered, 'ye said that never should I come home from Troy; ye wasted my goods, and insulted my wife, and had no fear of the gods, but now the day of death has come upon you! Fight or flee, if you may, but some shall not escape!'

'Draw your blades!' cried Eurymachus to the others; 'draw your blades, and hold up the tables as shields against this man's arrows. Have at him, and drive him from the doorway.' He drew his own sword, and leaped on Ulysses with a cry, but the swift arrow pierced his breast, and he fell and died. Then Amphinomus rushed towards Ulysses, but Telemachus sent his spear from behind through his shoulders. He could not draw forth the spear, but he ran to his father, and said, 'Let me bring shields, spears, and helmets from the inner chamber, for us, and for the swineherd and cowherd.' 'Go!' said Ulysses, and Telemachus ran through a narrow doorway, down a gallery to the secret chamber, and brought four shields, four helmets, and eight spears, and the men armed themselves, while Ulysses kept shooting down the wooers. When his arrows were spent he armed himself, protected by the other three. But the

Ulysses shoots the first arrow at the wooers

goatherd, Melanthius, knew a way of reaching the armoury, and he climbed up, and brought twelve helmets, spears, and shields to the wooers.

Ulysses thought that one of the women was showering down the weapons into the hall, but the swineherd and cowherd went to the armoury, through the doorway, as Telemachus had gone, and there they caught Melanthius, and bound him like a bundle, with a rope, and, throwing the rope over a rafter, dragged him up, and fastened him there, and left him swinging. Then they ran back to Ulysses, four men keeping the doorway against all the wooers that were not yet slain. But the goddess Athene appeared to Ulysses, in the form of Mentor, and gave him courage. He needed it, for the wooers, having spears, threw them in volleys, six at a time, at the four. They missed, but the spears of the four slew each his man. Again the wooers threw, and dealt two or three slight wounds, but the spears of the four were winged with death. They charged, striking with spear and sword, into the crowd, who lost heart, and flew here and there, crying for mercy and falling at every blow. Ulysses slew the prophet, Leiodes, but Phemius, the minstrel, he spared, for he had done no wrong, and Medon, a slave, crept out from beneath an ox hide, where he had been lying, and asked Telemachus to pity him, and Ulysses sent him and the minstrel into the courtyard, where they sat trembling. All the rest of the wooers lay dead in heaps, like heaps of fish on the seashore, when they have been netted, and drawn to land.

Then Ulysses sent Telemachus to bring Eurycleia, who, when she came and saw the wooers dead, raised a scream of joy, but Ulysses said 'it is an unholy thing to boast over dead men'. He bade Telemachus and the servants carry the corpses into the courtyard, and he made the women wash and clean the hall, and the seats, and tables, and the pillars. When all was clean, they took Melanthius and slew him, and then they washed themselves, and the maidens who were faithful to Penelope came out of their rooms, with torches in their hands, for it was now night, and they kissed Ulysses with tears of joy. These were not young women, for Ulysses remembered all of them.

Meanwhile old Eurycleia ran to tell Penelope all the good news:

up the stairs to her chamber she ran, tripping, and falling, and rising, and laughing for joy. In she came and awakened Penelope, saying: 'Come and see what you have long desired: Ulysses in his own house, and all the wicked wooers slain by the sword.' 'Surely you are mad, dear nurse,' said Penelope, 'to waken me with such a wild story. Never have I slept so sound since Ulysses went to that ill Ilios, never to be named. Angry would I have been with any of the girls that wakened me with such a silly story; but you are old: go back to the women's working room.' The good nurse answered: 'Indeed, I tell you no silly tale. Indeed he is in the hall; he is that poor guest whom all men struck and insulted, but Telemachus knew his father.'

Then Penelope leaped up gladly, and kissed the nurse, but yet she was not sure that her husband had come, she feared that it might be some god disguised as a man, or some evil man pretending to be Ulysses. 'Surely Ulysses has met his death far away,' she said, and though Eurycleia vowed that she herself had seen the scar dealt by the boar, long ago, she would not be convinced. 'None the less,' she said, 'let us go and see my son, and the wooers lying dead, and the man who slew them.' So they went down the stairs and along a gallery on the ground floor that led into the courtyard, and so entered the door of the hall, and crossed the high stone threshold on which Ulysses stood when he shot down Antinous. Penelope went up to the hearth and sat opposite Ulysses, who was leaning against one of the four tall pillars that supported the roof; there she sat and gazed at him, still wearing his rags, and still not cleansed from the blood of battle. She did not know him, and was silent, though Telemachus called her hard of belief and cold of heart.

'My child,' she said, 'I am bewildered, and can hardly speak, but if this man is Ulysses, he knows things unknown to any except him and me.' Then Ulysses bade Telemachus go to the baths and wash, and put on fresh garments, and bade the maidens bring the minstrel to play music, while they danced in the hall. In the town the friends and kinsfolk of the wooers did not know that they were dead, and when they heard the music they would not guess that anything strange had happened. It was necessary that nobody should know, for, if the kinsfolk of the dead men learned the truth, they would seek to take revenge, and might burn down the house. Indeed, Ulysses was still in great danger, for the law was that the brothers and cousins of slain men must slay their slayers, and the dead were many, and had many clansmen.

Now Eurynome bathed Ulysses himself, and anointed him with oil, and clad him in new raiment, so that he looked like himself again, full of strength and beauty. He sat down on his own high seat beside the fire, and said: 'Lady, you are the fairest and most cruel queen alive. No other woman would harden her heart against her husband, come home through many dangers after so many years. Nurse,' he cried to Eurycleia, 'strew me a bed to lie alone, for her heart is hard as iron.'

Now Penelope put him to a trial. 'Eurycleia,' she said, 'strew a bed for him outside the bridal chamber that he built for himself, and bring the good bedstead out of that room for him.'

'How can any man bring out that bedstead?' said Ulysses, 'did I not make it with my own hands, with a standing tree for the bed-post? No man could move that bed unless he first cut down the tree trunk.'

Then at last Penelope ran to Ulysses and threw her arms round his neck, kissing him, and said: 'Do not be angry, for always I have feared that some strange man of cunning would come and deceive me, pretending to be my lord. But now you have told me the secret of the bed, which no mortal has ever seen or knows but you and I, and my maiden whom I brought from my own home, and who kept the doors of our chamber.' Then they embraced, and it seemed as if her white arms would never quite leave their hold on his neck.

Ulysses told her many things, all the story of his wanderings, and how he must wander again, on land, not on the sea, till he came to the country of men who had never seen salt. 'The gods will defend you and bring you home to your rest in the end,' said Penelope, and then they went to their own chamber, and Eurynome went before them with lighted torches in her hands, for the gods had brought them to the haven where they would be.

CHAPTER TEN

The End

With the coming of the golden dawn Ulysses awoke, for he had still much to do. He and Telemachus and the cowherd and Eumaeus put on full armour, and took swords and spears, and walked to the farm where old Laertes, the father of Ulysses, lived among his servants and worked in his garden. Ulysses sent the others into the farmhouse to bid the old housekeeper get breakfast ready, and he went alone to the vines, being sure that his father was at work among them.

There the old man was, in his rough gardening clothes, with leather gloves on, and patched leather leggings, digging hard. His servants had gone to gather loose stones to make a rough stone dyke, and he was all alone. He never looked up till Ulysses went to him, and asked him whose slave he was, and who owned the garden. He said that he was a stranger in Ithaca, but that he had once met the king of the island, who declared that one Laertes was his father.

Laertes was amazed at seeing a warrior all in mail come into his garden, but said that he was the father of Ulysses, who had long been unheard of and unseen. 'And who are you?' he asked. 'Where is your own country?' Ulysses said that he came from Sicily, and that he had met Ulysses five years ago, and hoped that by this time he had come home.

Then the old man sat down and wept, and cast dust on his head, for Ulysses had not arrived from Sicily in five long years; certainly he must be dead. Ulysses could not bear to see his father weep, and told him that he was himself, come home at last, and that he had killed all the wooers.

But Laertes asked him to prove that he really was Ulysses, so he showed the scar on his leg, and, looking round the garden, he said: 'Come, I will show you the very trees that you gave me when I was a little boy running about after you, and asking you for one thing or another, as children do. These thirteen pear trees are my very own; you gave them to me, and mine are these fifty rows of vines, and these forty fig trees.'

Then Laertes was fainting for joy, but Ulysses caught him in his arms and comforted him. But, when he came to himself, he sighed, and said: 'How shall we meet the feud of all the kin of the slain men in Ithaca and the other islands?' 'Be of good courage, father,' said Ulysses. 'And now let us go to the farmhouse and breakfast with Telemachus.'

So Laertes first went to the baths, and then put on fresh raiment, and Ulysses wondered to see him look so straight and strong. 'Would I were as strong as when I took the castle of Nericus, long ago,' said the old man, 'and would that I had been in the fight against the wooers!' Then all the old man's servants came in, over-joyed at the return of Ulysses, and they breakfasted merrily together.

By this time all the people in the town knew that the wooers had been slain, and they crowded to the house of Ulysses in great sorrow, and gathered their dead and buried them, and then met in the market place. The father of Antinous, Eupeithes, spoke, and said that they would all be dishonoured if they did not slay Ulysses before he could escape to Nestor's house in Pylos. It was in vain that an old prophet told them that the young men had deserved their death. The most of the men ran home and put on armour, and Eupeithes led them towards the farm of Laertes, all in shining mail. But the gods in heaven had a care for Ulysses, and sent Athene to make peace between him and his subjects.

She did not come too soon, for the avengers were drawing near the farmhouse, which had a garrison of only twelve men: Ulysses, Laertes, Telemachus, the swineherd, the cowherd, and servants of Laertes. They all armed themselves, and not choosing to defend the house, they went boldly out to meet their enemies. They encouraged each other, and Laertes prayed to Athene, and then threw his spear at Eupeithes. The spear passed clean through helmet and through head, and Eupeithes fell with a crash, and his armour rattled as he fell. But now Athene appeared, and cried: 'Hold your hands, ye men of Ithaca, that no more blood may be shed, and peace may be made.' The foes of Ulysses, hearing the terrible voice of the goddess, turned and fled, and Ulysses uttered his war-cry, and was rushing among them, when a thunderbolt fell at his feet, and Athene bade him stop, lest he should anger Zeus, the Lord of Thunder. Gladly he obeyed, and peace was made with oaths and with sacrifice, peace in Ithaca and the islands.

Here ends the story of Ulysses, Laertes' son, for we do not know anything about his adventures when he went to seek a land of men who never heard of the sea, nor eat meat savoured with salt.

THE FLEECE OF GOLD

CHAPTER ONE

The Children of the Cloud

Whole Troy still stood fast, and before King Priam was born, there was a king called Athamas, who reigned in a country beside the Grecian sea. Athamas was a young man, and was unmarried; because none of the princesses who then lived seemed to him beautiful enough to be his wife. One day he left his palace and climbed high up into a mountain, following the course of a little river. He came to a place where a great black rock stood on one side of the river, jutting into the stream. Round the rock the water flowed deep and dark. Yet, through the noise of the river, the king thought he heard laughter and voices like the voices of girls. So he climbed very quietly up the back of the rock, and, looking over the edge, there he saw three beautiful maidens bathing in a pool, and splashing each other with the water. Their long yellow hair covered them like cloaks and floated behind them on the pool. One of them was even more beautiful than the others, and as soon as he saw her the king fell in love with her, and said to himself, 'This is the wife for me.'

As he thought this, his arm touched a stone, which slipped from the top of the rock where he lay, and went leaping, faster and faster as it fell, till it dropped with a splash into the pool below. Then the three maidens heard it, and were frightened, thinking someone was near. So they rushed out of the pool to the grassy bank where their clothes lay, lovely soft clothes, white and grey, and rosy-coloured, all shining with pearl drops, and diamonds like dew.

In a moment they had dressed, and then it was as if they had wings, for they rose gently from the ground, and floated softly up and up the windings of the brook. Here and there among the green tops of the mountain-ash trees the king could just see the white robes shining and disappearing, and shining again, till they rose far off like a mist, and so up and up into the sky, and at last he only followed them with his eyes, as they floated like clouds among the other clouds across the blue. All day he watched them, and at sunset he saw them sink, golden and rose-coloured and purple, and go down into the dark with the setting sun.

The king went home to his palace, but he was very unhappy, and nothing gave him any pleasure. All day he roamed about among the hills, and looked for the beautiful girls, but he never found them, and all night he dreamed about them, till he grew thin and pale and was like to die.

Now, the way with sick men then was that they made a pilgrimage to the temple of a god, and in the temple they offered sacrifices. Then they hoped that the god would appear to them in a dream, or send them a true dream at least, and tell them how they might be made well again. So the king drove in his chariot a long way, to the town where this temple was. When he reached it, he found it a strange place. The priests were dressed in dogs' skins, with the heads of the dogs drawn down over their faces, and there were live dogs running all about the shrines, for they were the favourite beasts of the god, whose name was Asclepius. There was an image of him, with a dog crouched at his feet, and in his hand he held a serpent, and fed it from a bowl.

The king sacrificed before the god, and when night fell he was taken into the temple, and there were many beds strewn on the floor and many people lying on them, both rich and poor, hoping that the god would appear to them in a dream, and tell them how they might be healed. There the king lay, like the rest, and for long he could not close his eyes. At length he slept, and he dreamed a dream. But it was not the god of the temple that he saw in his dream; he saw a beautiful lady, she seemed to float above him in a chariot drawn by doves, and all about her was a crowd of chattering sparrows, and he knew that she was Aphrodite, the queen of love. She was more beautiful than any woman in the world, and she smiled as she looked at the king, and said, 'Oh, King Athamas, you are sick for love! Now this you must do: go home and on the first

*King Athamas steals Nephele's clothes so
that she cannot float away with her sisters*

night of the new moon, climb the hills to that place where you saw the three maidens. In the dawn they will come again to the river, and bathe in the pool. Then do you creep out of the wood, and steal the clothes of her you love, and she will not be able to fly away with the rest, and she will be your wife.'

Then she smiled again, and her doves bore her away, and the king woke, and remembered the dream, and thanked the lady in his heart, for he knew that she was a goddess, the queen of love.

Then he drove home, and did all that he had been told to do. On the first night of the new moon, when she shines like a thin gold thread in the sky, he left his palace, and climbed up through the hills, and hid in the wood by the edge of the pool. When the dawn began to shine silvery, he heard voices, and saw the three girls come floating through the trees, and alight on the river bank, and undress, and run into the water. There they bathed, and splashed each other with the water, laughing in their play. Then he stole to the grassy bank, and seized the clothes of the most beautiful of the three; and they heard him move, and rushed out to their clothes. Two of them were clad in a moment, and floated away up the glen, but the third crouched sobbing and weeping under the thick cloak of her yellow hair. Then she prayed the king to give her back her soft grey and rose-coloured raiment, but he would not till she had promised to be his wife. And he told her how long he had loved her, and how the goddess had sent him to be her husband, and at last she promised, and took his hand, and in her shining robes went down the hill with him to the palace. But he felt as if he walked on the air, and she scarcely seemed to touch the ground with her feet. She told him that her name was Nephele, which meant 'a cloud', in their language, and that she was one of the Cloud Fairies who bring the rain, and live on the hilltops, and in the high lakes, and water springs, and in the sky.

So they were married, and lived very happily, and had two children, a boy called Phrixus, and a daughter named Helle. The two children had a beautiful pet, a Ram with a fleece all of gold, which was given them by the young god called Hermes, a beautiful god, with wings on his shoon – for these were the very Shoon of

Swiftness, that he lent afterwards to the boy, Perseus, who slew the Gorgon, and took her head. This Ram the children used to play with, and they would ride on his back, and roll about with him on the flowery meadows.

They would all have been happy, but for one thing. When there were clouds in the sky, and when there was rain, then their mother, Nephele, was always with them; but when the summer days were hot and cloudless, then she went away, they did not know where. The long dry days made her grow pale and thin, and, at last, she would vanish altogether, and never come again, till the sky grew soft and grey with rain.

King Athamas grew weary of this, for often his wife would be long away. Besides there was a very beautiful girl called Ino, a dark girl, who had come in a ship of Phoenician merchantmen, and had stayed in the city of the king when her friends sailed from Greece. The king saw her, and often she would be at the palace, playing with the children when their mother had disappeared with the Clouds, her sisters.

This Ino was a witch, and one day she put a drug into the king's wine, and when he had drunk it, he quite forgot Nephele, his wife, and fell in love with Ino. At last he married her, and they had two children, a boy and a girl, and Ino wore the crown, and was queen, and gave orders that Nephele should never be allowed to enter the palace any more. So Phrixus and Helle never saw their mother, and they were dressed in ragged old skins of deer, and were ill fed, and were set to do hard work in the house, while the children of Ino wore gold crowns in their hair, and were dressed in fine raiment, and had the best of everything.

One day when Phrixus and Helle were in the field, herding the sheep (for now they were treated like peasant children, and had to work for their bread), they met an old woman, all wrinkled, and poorly clothed, and they took pity on her, and brought her home with them. Queen Ino saw her, and as she wanted a nurse for her own children, she took her in to be the nurse, and the old woman had charge of the children, and lived in the house, and she was kind to Phrixus and Helle. But neither of them knew that she was their own mother, Nephele, who had disguised herself as an old woman and a servant, that she might be with her children.

Phrixus and Helle grew strong and tall, and more beautiful than Ino's children, so she hated them, and determined, at last, to kill them. They all slept at night in one room, but Ino's children had gold crowns in their hair, and beautiful coverlets on their beds. One night, Phrixus was half-awake, and he heard the old nurse come, in the dark, and put something on his head, and on his sister's, and change their coverlets. But he was so drowsy that he half thought it was a dream, and he lay and fell asleep. In the dead of night, the wicked stepmother, Ino, crept into the room with a dagger in her hand, and she stole up to the bed of Phrixus, and felt his hair, and his coverlet. Then she went softly to the bed of Helle, and felt her coverlet, and her hair with the gold crown on it. So she supposed these to be her own children, and she kissed them in the dark, and went to the beds of the other two children. She felt their heads, and they had no crowns on, so she killed them, supposing that they were Phrixus and Helle. Then she crept downstairs and went back to bed.

In the morning, there lay the stepmother Ino's children cold and dead, and nobody knew who had killed them. Only the wicked queen knew, and she, of course, would not tell of herself, but if she hated Phrixus and Helle before, now she hated them a hundred times worse than ever. But the old nurse was gone; nobody ever saw her there again, and everybody but the queen thought that *she* had killed the two children. Everywhere the king sought for her, to burn her alive, but he never found her, for she had gone back to her sisters, the Clouds.

And the Clouds were gone, too! For six long months, from winter to harvest time, the rain never fell. The country was burned up, the trees grew black and dry, there was no water in the streams, the corn turned yellow and died before it was come into the ear. The people were starving, the cattle and sheep were perishing, for there was no grass. And every day the sun rose hot and red, and went blazing through the sky without a cloud.

Here the wicked stepmother, Ino, saw her chance. The king sent messengers to Pytho, to consult the prophetess, and to find out what should be done to bring back the clouds and the rain. Then Ino took the messengers, before they set out on their journey, and gave them gold, and threatened also to kill them, if they did not bring the message she wished from the prophetess. Now this message was that Phrixus and Helle must be burned as a sacrifice to the gods.

So the messengers went, and came back dressed in mourning. And when they were brought before the king, at first they would tell him nothing. But he commanded them to speak, and then they told him, not the real message from the prophetess, but what Ino had bidden them to say: that Phrixus and Helle must be offered as a sacrifice to appease the gods.

The king was very sorrowful at this news, but he could not disobey the gods. So poor Phrixus and Helle were wreathed with flowers, as sheep used to be when they were led to be sacrificed, and they were taken to the altar, all the people following and weeping, and the Golden Ram went between them, as they walked to the temple. Then they came within sight of the sea, which lay beneath the cliff where the temple stood, all glittering in the sun, and the happy white sea-birds flying over it.

Here the Ram stopped, and suddenly he spoke to Phrixus, for the god gave him utterance, and said: 'Lay hold of my horn, and get on my back, and let Helle climb up behind you, and I will carry you far away.'

Then Phrixus took hold of the Ram's horn, and Helle mounted behind him, and grasped the golden fleece, and suddenly the Ram rose in the air, and flew above the people's heads, far away over the sea.

Far away to the eastward he flew, and deep below them they saw the sea, and the islands, and the white towers and temples, and the fields, and ships. Eastward always he went, towards the rising sun, and Helle grew dizzy and weary. At last a deep sleep came over her, and she let go her hold of the Fleece, and fell from the Ram's back, down and down, into the narrow seas, that run between Europe and Asia, and there she was drowned. And that strait is called Helle's Ford, or Hellespont, to this day.

But Phrixus and the Ram flew on up the narrow seas, and over the great sea which the Greeks called the Euxine and we call the Black Sea, till they reached a country named Colchis. There the Ram alighted, so tired and weary that he died, and Phrixus had his beautiful Golden Fleece stripped off, and hung on an oak tree in a dark wood. And there it was guarded by a monstrous Dragon, so that nobody dared to go near it. And Phrixus married the king's daughter, and lived long, till he died also, and a king called Aeetes, the brother of the enchantress, Circe, ruled that country. Of all the things he had, the rarest was the Golden Fleece, and it became a proverb that nobody could take that Fleece away, nor deceive the Dragon who guarded it.

CHAPTER TWO

The Search for the Fleece

Some years after the Golden Ram died in Colchis, far across the sea, a certain king reigned in Iolcos in Greece, and his name was Pelias. He was not the rightful king, for he had turned his step-brother, King Aeson, from the throne, and taken it for himself. Now, Aeson had a son, a boy called Jason, and he sent him far away from Pelias, up into the mountains. In these hills there was a great cave, and in that cave lived Chiron the Wise, who, the story says, was half a horse. He had the head and breast of a man, but a horse's body and legs. He was famed for knowing more about everything than anyone else in all Greece. He knew about the stars, and the plants of earth, which were good for medicine and which were poisonous. He was the best archer with the bow, and the best player of the harp; he could sing songs and tell stories of old times, for he was the last of a people, half horse and half man, who had dwelt in ancient days on the hills. Therefore the kings in Greece sent their sons to him to be taught shooting, singing, and telling the truth, and that was all the teaching they had then, except that they learned to hunt, fish, and fight, and throw spears, and toss the hammer and the stone. There Jason lived with Chiron and the boys in the cave, and many of the boys became famous.

There was Orpheus who played the harp so sweetly that wild beasts followed his minstrelsy, and even the trees danced after him, and settled where he stopped playing. There was Mopsus who could understand what the birds say to each other; and there was Butes, the handsomest of men; and Tiphys, the best steersman of a ship; and Castor, with his brother Polydeuces, the boxer. Heracles, too, the strongest man in the whole world, was there; and Lynceus, whom they called Keen-Eye, because he could see so far, and could see even the dead men in their graves under the earth. There was Ephemus, so swift and light-footed that he could run upon the grey sea and never wet his feet; and there were Calais and Zetes, the two sons of the North Wind, with golden wings upon their feet. There also was Peleus, who later married Thetis of the silver feet, goddess of the sea foam, and was the father of Achilles. Many others were there whose names it would take too long to tell. They all grew up together in the hills good friends, healthy, and brave, and strong. And they all went out to their own homes at last; but Jason had no home to go to, for his uncle, Pelias, had taken it, and his father was a wanderer.

So at last he wearied of being alone, and he said goodbye to his teacher, and went down through the hills towards Iolcos, his father's old home, where his wicked uncle Pelias was reigning. As he went, he came to a great, flooded river, running red from bank to bank, rolling the round boulders along. And there on the bank was an old woman sitting.

'Cannot you cross, mother?' said Jason; and she said she could not, but must wait until the flood fell, for there was no bridge.

'I'll carry you across,' said Jason, 'if you will let me carry you.'

So she thanked him, and said it was a kind deed, for she was longing to reach the cottage where her little grandson lay sick.

Then he knelt down, and she climbed upon his back, and he used his spear for a staff, and stepped into the river. It was deeper than he thought, and stronger, but at last he staggered out on the farther bank, far below where he went in. And then he set the old woman down.

'Bless you, my lad, for a strong man and a brave!' she said, 'and my blessing go with you to the world's end.'

Then he looked and she was gone he did not know where, for she was the greatest of the goddesses, Hera, the wife of Zeus, who had taken the shape of an old woman, to try Jason, whether he was kind and strong, or rude and churlish. From this day her grace went with him, and she helped him in all dangers.

Then Jason went down limping to the city, for he had lost one shoe in the flood. And when he reached the town he went straight up to the palace, and through the court, and into the open door, and up the hall, where the king was sitting at his table among his men. There Jason stood, leaning on his spear.

When the king saw him he turned white with terror. For he had been told by the prophetess of Pytho that a man with only one shoe would come someday and take away his kingdom. And here was the half-shod man of whom the prophecy had spoken.

But Pelias still remembered to be courteous, and he bade his men lead the stranger to the baths, and there the attendants bathed him, pouring hot water over him. And they anointed his head with oil, and clothed him in new raiment, and brought him back to the hall, and set him down at a table beside the king, and gave him meat and drink.

When he had eaten and was refreshed, the king said: 'Now it is time to ask the stranger who he is, and who his parents are, and whence he comes to Iolcos?'

And Jason answered, 'I am Jason, son of the rightful king, Aeson, and I am come to take back my kingdom.'

The king grew pale again, but he was cunning, and he leaped up and embraced the lad, and made much of him, and caused a gold circlet to be twisted in his hair. Then he said he was old, and weary of judging the people. 'And weary work it is,' he said, 'and no joy therewith shall any king have. For there is a curse on the country, that shall not be taken away till the Fleece of Gold is brought home, from the land of the world's end. The ghost of Phrixus stands by my bedside every night, wailing, and will not be comforted, till the Fleece is brought home again.'

When Jason heard that he cried, 'I shall take the curse away, for by the splendour of Lady Hera's brow, I shall bring the Fleece of Gold from the land of the world's end before I sit on the throne of my father.'

Now this was the very thing that the king wished, for he thought that if once Jason went after the Fleece, certainly he would never come back living to Iolcos. So he said that it could never be done, for the land was far away across the sea, so far that the birds could not come and go in one year, so great a sea was that and perilous.

Also, there was a dragon that guarded the Fleece of Gold, and no man could face it and live.

But the idea of fighting a dragon was itself a temptation to Jason, and he made a great vow by the water of Styx, an oath the very gods feared to break, that certainly he would bring home that Fleece to Iolcos. And he sent out messengers all over Greece, to all his old friends, who were with him in the Centaur's cave, and bade them come and help him, for that there was a dragon to kill, and that there would be fighting. And they all came, driving in their chariots down dales and across hills: Heracles, the strong man, with the bow that none other could bend; and Orpheus with his harp, and Castor and Polydeuces, and Zetes and Calais of the golden wings, and Tiphys, the steersman, and young Hylas, still a boy, and as fair as a girl, who always went with Heracles the strong.

These came, and many more, and they set shipbuilders to work, and oaks were felled for beams, and ashes for oars, and spears were made, and arrows feathered, and swords sharpened. But in the prow of the ship they placed a bough of an oak tree from the forest of Zeus in Dodona where the trees can speak, and that bough spoke, and prophesied things to come. They called the ship *Argo*, and they launched her, and put bread, and meat, and wine on board, and hung their shields outside the bulwarks. Then they said goodbye to their friends, went aboard, sat down at the oars, set sail, and so away eastward to Colchis, in the land of the world's end.

All day they rowed, and at night they beached the ship, as was then the custom, for they did not sail at night, and they went on shore, and took supper, and slept, and next day to the sea again. And old Chiron, the man-horse, saw the swift ship from his mountain heights, and ran down to the beach; there he stood with the waves of the grey sea breaking over his feet, waving with his mighty hands, and wishing his boys a safe return. And his wife stood beside him, holding in her arms the little son of one of the ship's company, Achilles, the son of Peleus of the spear, and of Thetis the goddess of the sea foam.

So they rowed ever eastward, and ere long they came to a strange isle where dwelt men with six hands apiece, unruly giants. And these giants lay in wait for them on cliffs above the river's mouth where the ship was moored, and before the dawn they rolled down great rocks on the crew. But Heracles drew his huge bow, the bow for which he slew Eurytus, king of Oechalia, and wherever a giant showed hand or shoulder above the cliff, he pinned him through with an arrow, till all were slain. After that they still held eastward, passing many islands, and towns of men, till they reached Mysia, and the Asian shore. Here they landed, with bad luck. For while they were cutting reeds and grass to strew their beds on the sands, young Hylas, beautiful Hylas, went off with a pitcher in his hand to draw water. He came to a beautiful spring, a deep, clear, green pool, and there the water-fairies lived, whom men called Nereids. There were Eunis, and Nycheia with her April eyes, and when they saw the beautiful Hylas, they longed to have him always with them, to live in the crystal caves beneath the water, for they had never seen anyone so beautiful. As he stooped with his pitcher and dipped it into the stream, they caught him softly in their arms, and drew him down below, and no man ever saw him any more, but he dwelt with the water-fairies.

But Heracles the strong, who loved him like a younger brother, wandered all over the country crying '*Hylas! Hylas!*' and the boy's voice answered so faintly from below the stream that Heracles never heard him. So he roamed alone in the forests, and the rest of the crew thought he was lost.

Then the sons of the North Wind were angry, and bade them set sail without him, and sail they did, leaving the strong man behind. Long afterwards, when the fleece was won, Heracles met the sons of the North Wind, and slew them with his arrows. And he buried them, and set a great stone on each grave, and one of these is ever stirred, and shakes when the North Wind blows. There they lie, and their golden wings are at rest.

Still they sped on, with a west wind blowing, and they came to a country whose king was strong, and thought himself the best boxer then living, so he came down to the ship and challenged anyone of that crew; and Polydeuces, the boxer, took up the challenge. All the rest, and the people of the country, made a ring, and Polydeuces and huge King Amycus stepped into the midst, and put up their hands. First they moved round each other cautiously, watching for a chance, and then, as the sun shone forth in the giant's face, Polydeuces leaped in and struck him between the eyes with his left hand, and, strong as he was, the giant staggered and fell. Then his friends picked him up, and sponged his face with water, and all the crew of *Argo* shouted with joy. He was soon on his feet again, and rushed at Polydeuces, hitting out so hard that he would have killed him if the blow had gone home. But Polydeuces just moved his head a little on one side, and the blow went by, and, as the giant slipped, Polydeuces planted one in his mouth and another beneath his ear, and was away before the giant could recover.

There they stood, breathing heavily, and glaring at each other, till the giant made another rush, but Polydeuces avoided him, and struck him several blows quickly in the eyes, and now the giant was almost blind. Then Polydeuces at once ended the combat by a right-hand blow on the temple. The giant fell, and lay as if he were dead. When he came to himself again, he had no heart to go on, for his knees shook, and he could hardly see. So Polydeuces made him swear never to challenge strangers again as long as he lived, and then the crew of *Argo* crowned Polydeuces with a wreath of poplar leaves, and they took supper, and Orpheus sang to them, and they slept, and next day they came to the country of the unhappiest of kings.

His name was Phineus, and he was a prophet; but, when he came to meet Jason and his company, he seemed more like the ghost of a beggar than a crowned king. For he was blind, and very old, and he wandered like a dream, leaning on a staff, and feeling the wall with his hand. His limbs all trembled, he was but a thing of skin and bone, and foul and filthy to see. At last he reached the doorway of the house where Jason was, and sat down, with his purple cloak fallen round him, and he held up his skinny hands, and welcomed Jason, for, being a prophet, he knew that now he should be delivered from his wretchedness.

He lived, or rather lingered, in all this misery because he had offended the gods, and had told men what things were to happen in the future beyond what the gods desired that men should know. So they blinded him, and they sent against him hideous monsters with wings and crooked claws, called Harpies, which fell upon him at his meat, and carried it away before he could put it to his mouth. Sometimes they flew off with all the meat; sometimes they left a little, that he might not quite starve, and die, and be at peace, but might live in misery. Yet what they left was made so foul, and of such evil savour, that even a starving man could scarcely take it within his lips. Thus this king was the most miserable of all men living.

He welcomed the heroes, and, above all, Zetes and Calais, the sons of the North Wind, for they, he knew, would help him. And they all went into his wretched, naked hall, and sat down at the tables, and the servants brought meat and drink and placed it before them, the latest and last supper of the Harpies. Then down on the meat swooped the Harpies, like lightning or wind, with clanging brazen wings, and iron claws, and the smell of a battlefield where men lie dead; down they swooped, and flew shrieking away with the food. But the two sons of the North Wind drew their short swords, and rose in the air on their golden wings, and followed where the Harpies fled, over many a sea and many a land, till they came to a distant isle, and there they slew the Harpies with their swords. And that isle was called 'Turn Again', for there the sons of the North Wind turned, and it was late in the night when they came back to the hall of Phineus, and to their companions.

Here Phineus was telling Jason and his company how they might win their way to Colchis and the world's end, and the wood of the Fleece of Gold. 'First,' he said, 'you shall come in your ship to the Rocks Wandering, for these rocks wander like living things in the sea, and no ship has ever sailed between them. They open, like a great mouth, to let ships pass, and when she is between their lips they clash again, and crush her in their iron jaws. By this way even winged things may never pass; nay, not even the doves that bear ambrosia to Father Zeus, the lord of Olympus, but the rocks ever catch one even of these. So, when you come near them, you must let loose a dove from the ship, and let her go before you to try the way. And if she flies safely between the rocks from one sea to the other sea, then row with all your might when the rocks open again. But if the rocks close on the bird, then return, and do not try the adventure. But, if you win safely through, then hold right on to the mouth of the river Phasis, and there you shall see the towers of Aeetes, the king, and the grove of the Fleece of Gold. And then do as well as you may.'

So they thanked him, and the next morning they set sail, till they came to a place where the Rocks Wandering wallowed in the water, and all was foam; but when the rocks leaped apart the stream ran swift, and the waves roared beneath the rocks, and the wet cliffs bellowed. Then Euphemus took the dove in his hands, and set her free, and she flew straight at the pass where the rocks met, and sped right through, and the rocks gnashed like gnashing teeth, but they caught only a feather from her tail.

Then slowly the rocks opened again, like a wild beast's mouth that opens, and Tiphys, the helmsman, shouted, 'Row on, hard all!' and he held the ship straight for the pass. Then the oars bent like bows in the hands of men, and the good ship leaped at the stroke. Three strokes they pulled, and at each the ship leaped, and now they were within the black jaws of the rocks, the water boiling round them, and so dark it was that overhead they could see the stars, but the oarsmen could not see the daylight behind them, and the steersman could not see the daylight in front. Then the great tide rushed in between the rocks like a rushing river, and lifted the ship as if it were lifted by a hand, and through the strait she passed like a bird, and the rocks clashed, and only broke the carved wood of the ship's stern. And the ship reeled into the seething sea beyond, and all the men of Jason bowed their heads over their oars, half-dead with the fierce rowing.

Then they set all sail, and the ship sped merrily on, past the shores of the inner sea, past bays and towns, and river mouths, and round green hills, the tombs of men slain long ago. And, behold, on the top of one mound stood a tall man, clad in rusty armour, and with a broken sword in his hand, and on his head a helmet with a blood-red crest. Thrice he waved his hand, and thrice he shouted aloud, and was no more seen, for this was the ghost of Sthenelus, Actaeon's son, whom an arrow had slain there long since, and he had come forth from his tomb to see men of his own blood, and to greet Jason and his company. So they anchored there, and slew sheep in sacrifice, and poured blood and wine on the grave of Sthenelus. There Orpheus left a harp, placing it in the bough of a tree, that the wind might sing in the chords, and make music to Sthenelus below the earth.

Then they sailed on, and at evening they saw above their heads the snowy crests of Mount Caucasus, flushed in the sunset; and high in the air they saw, as it were, a black speck that grew greater and greater, and fluttered black wings, and then fell sheer down like a stone. Then they heard a dreadful cry from a valley of the mountain, for there Prometheus was fastened to the rock, and the eagles fed upon him, because he stole fire from the gods, and gave it to men. All the heroes shuddered when they heard his cry; but not long after Heracles came that way, and he slew the eagle with his bow, and set Prometheus free.

But at nightfall they came into the wide mouth of the river Phasis, that flows through the land of the world's end, and they saw the lights burning in the palace of Aeetes the king. So now they were come to the last stage of their journey, and there they slept, and dreamed of the Fleece of Gold.

The Winning of the Fleece

Next morning the heroes awoke, and left the ship moored in the river's mouth, hidden by tall reeds, for they took down the mast, lest it should be seen. Then they walked towards the city of Colchis, and they passed through a strange and horrible wood. Dead men, bound together with cords, were hanging from the branches, for the Colchis people buried women, but hung dead men from the branches of trees. Then they came to the palace, where King Aeetes lived, with his young son Absyrtus, and his daughter Chalciope, who had been the wife of Phrixus, and his younger daughter, Medea, who was a witch, and the priestess of Brimo, a dreadful goddess. Now Chalciope came out and welcomed Jason, for she knew the heroes were of her dear husband's country. And beautiful Medea, the dark witch-girl, came forth and saw Jason, and as soon as she saw him she loved him more than her father and her brother and all her father's house. For his bearing was gallant, and his armour golden, and long yellow hair fell over his shoulders, and over the leopard skin that he wore above his armour. Medea turned white and then red, and cast down her eyes, but Chalciope took the heroes to the baths, and gave them food, and they were brought to Aeetes, who asked them why they came, and they told him that they desired the Fleece of Gold, and he was very angry, and told them that only to a better man than himself would he give up that Fleece. If any wished to prove himself worthy of it he must tame two bulls which breathed flame from their nostrils, and must plough four acres with these bulls, and next he must sow the field with the teeth of a dragon, and these teeth when sown would immediately grow up into armed men. Jason said that, as it must be, he would try this adventure, but he went sadly enough back to the ship and did not notice how kindly Medea was looking after him as he went.

Now, in the dead of night, Medea could not sleep, because she was so sorry for the stranger, and she knew that she could help him by her magic. But she remembered how her father would burn her for a witch if she helped Jason, and a great shame, too, came on her that she should prefer a stranger to her own people. So she arose in the dark, and stole just as she was to her sister's room, a white figure roaming like a ghost in the palace. At her sister's door she turned back in shame, saying, 'No, I will never do it,' and she went back again to her chamber, and came again, and knew not what to do; but at last she returned to her own bower, and threw herself on her bed, and wept. Her sister heard her weeping, and came to her and they cried together, but softly, that no one might hear them. For Chalciope was as eager to help the Greeks for love of Phrixus, her dead husband, as Medea was for the love of Jason.

At last Medea promised to carry to the temple of the goddess of whom she was a priestess, a drug that would tame the bulls which dwelt in the field of that temple. But still she wept and wished that she were dead, and had a mind to slay herself; yet, all the time, she was longing for the dawn, that she might go and see Jason, and give him the drug, and see his face once more, if she was never to see him again. So, at dawn she bound up her hair, and bathed her face, and took the drug, which was pressed from a flower. That flower first blossomed when the eagle shed the blood of Prometheus on the earth. The virtue of the juice of the flower was this, that if a man anointed himself with it, he could not that day be wounded by swords, and fire could not burn him. So she placed it in a vial beneath her girdle, and she went with other girls, her friends, to the temple of the goddess. Now Jason had been warned by Chalciope to meet her there, and he was coming with Mopsus who knew the speech of birds. But Mopsus heard a crow that sat on a poplar tree speaking to another crow, saying: 'Here comes a silly prophet, and sillier than a goose. He is walking with a young man to meet a maid, and does not know that, while he is there to hear, the maid will not say a word that is in her heart. Go away, foolish prophet; it is not you she cares for.'

Then Mopsus smiled, and stopped where he was; but Jason went on, where Medea was pretending to play with the girls, her companions. When she saw Jason she felt as if she could neither go forward, nor go back, and she was very pale. But Jason told her not to be afraid, and asked her to help him, but for long she could not answer him; however, at the last, she gave him the drug, and taught him how to use it. 'So shall you carry the Fleece to Iolcos, far away, but what is it to me where you go when you have gone from here? Still remember the name of me, Medea, as I shall remember you. And may there come to me some voice, or some bird bearing the message, whenever you have quite forgotten me.'

But Jason answered, 'Lady, let the winds blow what voice they will, and what that bird will, let him bring. But no wind or bird shall ever bear the news that I have forgotten you, if you will cross the sea with me, and be my wife.'

Then she was glad, and yet she was afraid, at the thought of that dark voyage, with a stranger, from her father's home and her own. So they parted, Jason to the ship, and Medea to the palace. But in the morning Jason anointed himself and his armour with the drug, and all the heroes struck at him with spears and swords, but the swords would not bite on him nor on his armour. He felt so strong and light that he leaped in the air with joy, and the sun shone on his glittering shield. Now they all went up together to the field where the bulls were breathing flame. There already was Aeetes, with Medea, and all the Colchians had come to see Jason die. A plough had been brought to which he was to harness the bulls. Then he walked up to them, and they blew fire at him that flamed all round him, but the magic drug protected him. He took a horn of one bull in his right hand, and a horn of the other in his left, and dashed their heads together so mightily that they fell.

When they rose, all trembling, he yoked them to the plough, and drove them with his spear, till all the field was ploughed in straight ridges and furrows. Then he dipped his helmet in the river, and drank water, for he was weary; and next he sowed the dragon's teeth on the right and left. Then you might see spear-points, and sword-points, and crests of helmets break up from the soil like shoots of corn, and presently the earth was shaken like sea waves, as armed men leaped out of the furrows, all furious for battle, and all rushed to slay Jason. But he, as Medea had told him to do, caught up a great rock, and threw it among them, and he who was struck by the rock said to his neighbour, 'You struck me; take that!' and ran his spear through that man's breast, but before he could draw it out another man had cleft his helmet with a stroke, and so it went: an hour of striking and shouting, while the sparks of fire sprang up from helmet and breastplate and shield. The furrows ran red with blood, and wounded men crawled on hands and knees to strike or stab those that were yet standing and fighting. So axes and sword and spear flashed and fell, till now all the men were down but one, taller and stronger than the rest. Round him he looked, and saw only Jason standing there, and he staggered towards him, bleeding, and lifting his great axe above his head. But Jason only stepped aside from the blow which would have cloven him to the waist, the last blow of the Men of the Dragon's Teeth, for he who struck fell, and there he lay and died.

Then Jason went to the king, where he sat looking darkly on, and said, 'O King, the field is ploughed, the seed is sown, the harvest is reaped. Give me now the Fleece of Gold, and let me be gone.' But the king said, 'Enough is done. Tomorrow is a new day. Tomorrow shall you win the Fleece.'

Then he looked sidewise at Medea, and she knew that he suspected her, and she was afraid.

Aeetes went and sat brooding over his wine with the captains of his people; and his mood was bitter, both for loss of the Fleece, and because Jason had won it not by his own prowess, but by the magic aid of Medea. As for Medea herself, it was the king's purpose to put her to a cruel death, and this she needed not her witchery to know, and a fire was in her eyes, and terrible sounds were ringing in her ears, and it seemed she had but two choices: to drink poison and die, or to flee with the heroes in the ship *Argo*. But at last flight seemed better than death. So she hid all her engines of witchcraft in the folds of her gown, and she kissed her bed where she would never sleep again, and the posts or the door, and she caressed the very walls with her hand in that last farewell. And she cut a long lock of her yellow hair, and left it in the room, a keepsake to her mother dear, in memory of her maiden days. 'Goodbye, my mother,' she said, 'this long lock I leave thee in place of me; goodbye, a long goodbye, to me who am going on a long journey; goodbye, my sister Chalciope, goodbye! dear house, goodbye!'

Then she stole from the house, and the bolted doors leaped open at their own accord at the swift spell Medea murmured. With her bare feet she ran down the grassy paths, and the daisies looked black against the white feet of Medea. So she sped to the temple of the goddess, and the moon overhead looked down on her. Many a time had she darkened the moon's face with her magic song, and now the Lady Moon gazed white upon her, and said, 'I am not, then, the only one that wanders in the night for love, as I love Endymion the sleeper, who sleeps on the crest of the Latmian hill, and beholds me in his dreams. Many a time hast thou darkened my face with thy songs, and made night black with thy sorceries, and now thou too art in love! So go thy way, and bid thy heart endure, for a sore fate is before thee!'

But Medea hastened on till she came to the high river bank, and saw the heroes, merry at their wine in the light of a blazing fire. Thrice she called aloud, and they heard her, and came to her, and she said, 'Save me, my friends, for all is known, and my death is sure. And I will give you the Fleece of Gold for the price of my life.'

Then Jason swore that she should be his wife, and more dear to him than all the world. So she went aboard their boat, and swiftly they rowed up stream to the dark wood where the dragon who never sleeps lay guarding the Fleece of Gold. There she landed, and Jason, and Orpheus with his harp, and through the wood they went, but that old serpent saw them coming, and hissed so loud that women wakened in Colchis town, and children cried to their mothers. But Orpheus struck softly on his harp, and he sang a hymn to Sleep, bidding him come and cast a slumber on the dragon's wakeful eyes. This was the song he sang:

'Sleep! King of gods and men!
Come to my call again,
Swift over field and fen,
    Mountain and deep:
Come, bid the waves be still;
Sleep, streams on height and hill;
Beasts, birds, and snakes, thy will
    Conquereth, Sleep!
Come on thy golden wings,
Come ere the swallow sings,
Lulling all living things,
    Fly they or creep!
Come with thy leaden wand,
Come with thy kindly hand,
Soothing on sea or land
    Mortals that weep.
Come from the cloudy west,
Soft over brain and breast,
Bidding the Dragon rest,
    Come to me, Sleep!'

This was Orpheus's song, and he sang so sweetly that the bright, small eyes of the dragon closed, and all his hard coils softened and uncurled. Then Jason set his foot on the dragon's neck and hewed off his head, and lifted down the Golden Fleece from the sacred oak tree, and it shone like a golden cloud at dawn. He waited not to wonder at it, but he and Medea and Orpheus hurried through the wet wood paths to the ship, and threw it on board, cast a cloak over it, and bade the heroes sit down to the oars, half of them, but the others to take their shields and stand each beside the oarsmen, to guard them from the arrows of the Colchians. Then he cut the stern cables with his sword, and softly they rowed, under the bank, down the dark river to the sea. But the hissing of the dragon had already awakened the Colchians, and lights were flitting by the palace windows, and Aeetes was driving in his chariot with all his men down to the banks of the river. Then their arrows fell like hail about the ship, but they rebounded from the shields of the heroes, and the swift ship sped over the bar, and leaped as she felt the first waves of the salt sea.

And now the Fleece was won. But it was weary work bringing it home to Greece, and Medea and Jason did a deed which angered the gods. They slew her brother Absyrtus, who followed after them with a fleet, and cut him limb from limb, and when Aeetes came with his ships, and saw the dead limbs, he stopped, and went home, for his heart was broken. The gods would not let the Greeks return by the way they had come, but by strange ways where never another ship has sailed. Up the Ister (the Danube) they rowed, through countries of savage men, till the *Argo* could go no farther, by reason of the narrowness of the stream. Then they hauled her overland, where no man knows, but they launched her on the Elbe at last, and out into a sea where never sail had been seen. Then they were driven wandering out into Ocean, and to a fairy, far-off isle where Lady Circe dwelt. Circe was the sister of King Aeetes, both were children of the sun god, and Medea hoped that Circe would be kind to her, as she could not have heard of the slaying of Absyrtus. Medea and Jason went up through the woods of the isle to the house of Circe, and had no fear of the lions and wolves and bears that guarded the house. These knew that Medea was an enchantress, and they fawned on her and Jason and let them pass. But in the house they found Circe clad in dark mourning raiment, and all her long black hair fell wet and dripping to her feet, for she had seen visions of terror and sin, and therefore she had purified herself in salt water of the sea. The walls of her chamber, in the night, had shone as with fire, and dripped as with blood, and a voice of wailing had broken forth, and the spirit of dead Absyrtus had cried in her ears.

When Medea and Jason entered her hall, Circe bade them sit down, and called her bower maidens, fairies of woods and waters, to strew a table with a cloth of gold, and set on it food and wine. But Jason and Medea ran to the hearth, the sacred place of the house to which men that have done murder flee, and there they are safe, when they come in their flight to the house of a stranger. They cast ashes from the hearth on their heads, and Circe knew that they

How the serpent that guarded the Golden
Fleece was slain

had slain Absyrtus. Yet she was of Medea's near kindred, and she respected the law of the hearth. Therefore she did the rite of purification, as was the custom, cleansing blood with blood, and she burned in the fire a cake of honey, and meal, and oil, to appease the Furies who revenge the deaths of kinsmen by the hands of kinsmen.

When all was done, Jason and Medea rose from their knees, and sat down on chairs in the hall, and Medea told Circe all her tale, except the slaying of Absyrtus.

'More and worse than you tell me you have done,' said Circe, 'but you are my brother's daughter.'

Then she advised them of all the dangers of their way home to Greece, how they must shun the Sirens, and Scylla and Charybdis, and she sent a messenger, Iris, the goddess of the Rainbow, to bid Thetis help them through the perils of the sea, and bring them safe to Phaeacia, where the Phaeacians would send them home.

'But you shall never be happy, nor know one good year in all your lives,' said Circe, and she bade them farewell.

They went by the way that Ulysses went on a later day; they passed through many perils, and came to Iolcos, where Pelias was old, and made Jason reign in his stead.

But Jason and Medea loved each other no longer, and many stories, all different from each other, are told concerning evil deeds that they wrought, and certainly they left each other, and Jason took another wife, and Medea went to Athens. Here she lived in the palace of Aegeus, an unhappy king who had been untrue to his own true love, and therefore the gods took from him courage and strength. But about Medea at Athens the story is told in the next tale, the tale of Theseus, Aegeus's son.

THESEUS

CHAPTER ONE

The Wedding of Aethra

Long before Ulysses was born, there lived in Athens a young king, strong, brave, and beautiful, named Aegeus. Athens, which later became so great and famous, was then but a little town, perched on the top of a cliff which rises out of the plain, two or three miles from the sea. No doubt the place was chosen so as to be safe against pirates, who then used to roam all about the seas, plundering merchant ships, robbing cities, and carrying away men, women, and children, to sell as slaves. The Athenians had then no fleet with which to put the pirates down, and possessed not so much land as would make a large estate in England: other little free towns held the rest of the surrounding country.

King Aegeus was young, and desired to take a wife, indeed a wife had been found for him. But he wanted to be certain, if he could, that he was to have sons to succeed him: so many misfortunes happen to kings who have no children. But how was he to find out whether he should have children or not? At that time, and always in Greece before it was converted to Christianity, there were temples of the gods in various places, at which it was supposed that men might receive answers to their questions. These temples were called oracles, or places where oracles were given, and the most famous of them was the temple of Apollo at Pytho, or Delphi, far to the north-west of Athens. Here was a deep ravine of a steep mountain, where the god Apollo was said to have shot a monstrous dragon with his arrows. He then ordered that a temple should be built here, and in this temple a maiden, being inspired by the god, gave her prophecies. The people who came to consult her made the richest presents to the priests, and the temple was full of cups and bowls of gold and silver, and held more wealth in its chambers than the treasure houses of the richest kings.

Aegeus determined to go to Delphi to ask his question: would he have sons to come after him? He did not tell his people where he was going; he left the kingdom to be governed by his brother Pallas, and he set out secretly at night, taking no servant. He did not wear royal dress, and he drove his own chariot, carrying for his offering only a small cup of silver, for he did not wish it to be known that he was a king, and told the priests that he was a follower of Peleus, King of Phthia. In answer to his question, the maiden sang two lines of verse, for she always prophesied in verse. Her reply was difficult to understand, as oracles often were, for the maiden seldom spoke out clearly, but in a kind of riddle that might be understood in more ways than one; so that, whatever happened, she could not be proved to have made a mistake.

Aegeus was quite puzzled by the answer he got. He did not return to Athens, but went to consult the prince of Troezen, named Pittheus, who was thought the wisest man then living. Pittheus did not know who Aegeus was, but saw that he seemed of noble birth, tall and handsome, so he received him very kindly, and kept him in his house for some time, entertaining him with feasts, dances, and hunting parties. Now Pittheus had a very lovely daughter, named Aethra. She and Aegeus fell in love with each other, so deeply that they desired to be married. It was the custom that the bridegroom should pay a price, a number of cattle, to the father of the bride, and Aegeus, of course, had no cattle to give. But it was also the custom, if the lover did some very brave and useful action, to reward him with the hand of his lady, and Aegeus had his opportunity. A fleet of pirates landed at Troezen and attacked the town, but Aegeus fought so bravely and led the men of Pittheus so well, that he not only slew the pirate chief, and defeated his men, but also captured some of his ships, which were full of plunder, gold, and bronze, and iron, and slaves. With this wealth Aegeus paid the bride price, as it was called, for Aethra, and they were married. Pittheus thought himself a lucky man, for he had no son, and here was a son-in-law who could protect his little kingdom, and wear the crown when he himself was dead.

Though Pittheus was believed to be very wise, in this matter he was very foolish. He never knew who Aegeus really was, that is the King of Athens, nor did poor Aethra know. In a short time Aegeus wearied of beautiful Aethra, who continued to love him dearly. He was anxious also to return to his kingdom, for he heard that his brother Pallas and his many sons were governing badly; and he feared that Pallas might keep the crown for himself, so he began to speak mysteriously to Aethra, talking about a long and dangerous journey which he was obliged to make, for secret reasons, and from which he might never return alive. Aethra wept bitterly, and sometimes thought, as people did in these days, that the beautiful stranger might be no man, but a god, and that he might return to Olympus, the home of the gods, and forget her; for the gods never tarried long with the mortal women who loved them.

At last Aegeus took Aethra to a lonely glen in the woods, where, beside a little mountain stream, lay a great moss-grown boulder that an earthquake, long ago, had shaken from the rocky cliff above. 'The time is coming,' said Aegeus, 'when you and I must part, and only the gods can tell when we shall meet again! It may be that you will bear a child, and, if he be a boy, when he has come to his strength you must lead him to this great stone, and let no man or woman be there but you two only. You must then bid him roll away the stone, and, if he has no strength to raise it, so must it be. But if he can roll it away, then let him take such things as he finds there, and let him consider them well, and do what the gods put into his heart.'

Thus Aegeus spoke, and on the dawn of the third night after this day, when Aethra awoke from sleep, she did not find him by her side. She arose, and ran through the house, calling his name, but there came no answer, and from that time Aegeus was never seen again in Troezen, and people marvelled, thinking that he, who came whence no man knew, and was so brave and beautiful, must be one of the immortal gods. 'Who but a god,' they said, 'would leave for no cause a bride, the flower of Greece for beauty, young, and loving; and a kingdom to which he was not born? Truly he must be Apollo of the silver bow, or Hermes of the golden wand.'

So they spoke among each other, and honoured Aethra greatly, but she pined and drooped with sorrow, like a tall lily flower, that the frost has touched in a rich man's garden.

CHAPTER TWO

The Boyhood of Theseus

Time went by, and Aethra had a baby, a son. This was her only comfort, and she thought that she saw in him a likeness to his father, whose true name she did not know. Certainly he was a very beautiful baby, well formed and strong, and, as soon as he could walk he was apt to quarrel with other children of his own age, and fight with them in a harmless way. He never was an amiable child, though he was always gentle to his mother. From the first he was afraid of nothing, and when he was about four or five he used to frighten his mother by wandering from home, with his little bow and arrows, and staying by himself in the woods. However, he always found his own way back again, sometimes with a bird or a snake that he had shot, and once dragging the body of a fawn that was nearly as heavy as himself. Thus his mother, from his early boyhood, had many fears for him, that he might be killed by some fierce wild boar in the woods, for he would certainly shoot at what- ever beast he met; or that he might kill some other boy in a quarrel, when he would be obliged to leave the country. The other boys, however, soon learned not to quarrel with Theseus (so Aethra had named her son), for he was quick of temper, and heavy of hand, and, as for the wild beasts, he was cool as well as eager, and seemed to have an untaught knowledge of how to deal with them.

Aethra was therefore very proud of her son, and began to hope that when he was older he would be able to roll away the great stone in the glen. She told him nothing about it when he was little, but, in her walks with him in the woods or on the seashore, she would ask him to try his force in lifting large stones. When he succeeded she kissed and praised him, and told him stories of the famous strong man, Heracles, whose name was well known through all Greece. Theseus could not bear to be beaten at lifting any weight, and, if he failed, he would rise early and try again in the morning, for many men, as soon as they rise from bed, can lift weights which are too heavy for them later in the day.

When Theseus was seven years old, Aethra found for him a tutor, named Connidas, who taught him the arts of netting beasts and hunting, and how to manage the dogs, and how to drive a chariot, and wield sword and shield, and to throw the spear. Other things Connidas taught him which were known to few men in Greece, for Connidas came from the great rich island of Crete. He had killed a man there in a quarrel, and fled to Troezen to escape the revenge of the man's brothers and cousins. In Crete many people could read and write, which in Greece, perhaps none could do, and Connidas taught Theseus this learning.

When he was fifteen years old, Theseus went, as was the custom of young princes, to the temple of Delphi, not to ask questions, but to cut his long hair, and sacrifice it to the god, Apollo. He cut the forelock of his hair, so that no enemy, in battle, might take hold of it, for Theseus intended to fight at close quarters, hand to hand, in war, not to shoot arrows and throw spears from a distance. By this time he thought himself a man, and was always asking where his father was, while Aethra told him how her husband had left her soon after their marriage, and that she had never heard of him since, but that some day Theseus might find out all about him for himself, which no other person would ever be able to do.

Aethra did not wish to tell Theseus too soon the secret of the great stone, which hid she knew not what. She saw that he would leave her and go to seek his father, if he was able to raise the stone and find out the secret, and she could not bear to lose him, now that day by day he grew more like his father, her lost lover. Besides, she wanted him not to try to raise the stone till he came to his strength. But when he was in his nineteenth year, he told her that he would now go all over Greece and the whole world seeking for his father. She saw that he meant what he said, and one day she led him alone to the glen where the great stone lay, and sat down with him there, now talking, and now silent as if she were listening to the pleasant song of the burn that fell from a height into a clear deep pool. Really she was listening to make sure that no hunter and no lovers were near them in the wood, but she only heard the songs of the water and the birds, no voices, or cry of hounds, or fallen twig cracking under a footstep.

At last, when she was quite certain that nobody was near, she whispered, and told Theseus how her husband, before he disappeared, had taken her to this place, and shown her the great moss-grown boulder, and said that, when his son could lift that stone away, he would find certain tokens, and that he must then do what the gods put into his heart. Theseus listened eagerly, and said, 'If my father lifted that stone, and placed under it certain tokens, I also can lift it, perhaps not yet, but some day I shall be as strong a man as my father.' Then he set himself to move the stone, gradually putting out all his force, but it seemed rooted in the earth, though he tried it now on one side and now on another. At last he flung himself at his mother's feet, with his head in the grass, and lay without speaking. His breath came hard and quick, and his hands were bleeding. Aethra laid her hand on his long hair, and was silent. 'I shall not lose my boy this year,' she thought.

They were long in that lonely place, but at last Theseus rose, and kissed his mother, and stretched his arms. 'Not today!' he said, but his mother thought in her heart, 'Not for many a day, I hope!' Then they walked home to the house of Pittheus, saying little, and when they had taken supper, Theseus said that he would go to bed and dream of better fortune. So he arose, and went to his own chamber, which was built apart in the court of the palace, and soon Aethra too went to sleep, not unhappy, for her boy, she thought, would not leave her for a long time.

But in the night Theseus arose, and put on his shoes, and his smock, and a great double mantle. He girt on his sword of bronze, and went into the housekeeper's chamber, where he took a small skin of wine, and some food. These he placed in a wallet which he slung round his neck by a cord, and lastly he stole out of the court, and walked to the lonely glen, and to the pool in the burn near which the great stone lay. Here he folded his purple mantle of fine wool round him, and lay down to sleep in the grass, with his sword lying near his hand.

When he awoke the clear blue morning light was round him, and all the birds were singing their song to the dawn. Theseus arose, threw off his mantle and smock, and plunged into the cold pool of the burn, and then he drank a little of the wine, and ate of the bread and cold meat, and set himself to move the stone. At the first effort, into which he put all his strength, the stone stirred. With the second he felt it rise a little way from the ground, and then he lifted with all the might in his heart and body, and rolled the stone clean over.

Beneath it there was nothing but the fresh turned soil, but in a hollow of the foot of the rock, which now lay uppermost, there was a wrapping of purple woollen cloth, that covered something. Theseus tore out the packet, unwrapped the cloth, and found within it a wrapping of white linen. This wrapping was in many folds, which he undid, and at last he found a pair of shoon, such as kings wear, adorned with gold, and also the most beautiful sword that he had ever seen. The handle was of clear rock crystal, and through the crystal you could see gold, inlaid with pictures of a lion hunt done in different shades of gold and silver. The sheath was of leather, with patterns in gold nails, and the blade was of bronze, a beautiful pattern ran down the centre to the point, the blade was straight, and double-edged, supple, sharp, and strong. Never had Theseus seen so beautiful a sword, nor one so well balanced in his hand.

He saw that this was a king's sword; and he thought that it had not been wrought in Greece, for in Greece was no swordsmith that could do such work. Examining it very carefully he found characters engraved beneath the hilt, not letters such as the Greeks used in later times, but such Cretan signs as Connidas had taught him to read, for many a weary hour, when he would like to have been following the deer in the forest.

Theseus pored over these signs till he read:

Icmalius me made. Of Aegeus of Athens am I.

Now he knew the secret. His father was Aegeus, the King of Athens. Theseus had heard of him and knew that he yet lived, a

Theseus tries to lift the stone

sad life full of trouble. For Aegeus had no child by his Athenian wife, and the fifty sons of his brother, Pallas (who were called the Pallantidae), despised him, and feasted all day in his hall, recklessly and fiercely, robbing the people, and Aegeus had no power in his own kingdom.

'Methinks that my father has need of me!' said Theseus to himself. Then he wrapped up the sword and shoon in the linen and the cloth of wool, and walked home in the early morning to the palace of Pittheus.

When Theseus came to the palace, he went straight to the upper chamber of his mother, where she was spinning wool with a distaff of ivory. When he laid before her the sword and the shoon, the distaff fell from her hand, and she hid her head in a fold of her robe. Theseus kissed her hands and comforted her, and she dried her eyes, and praised him for his strength. 'These are the sword and the shoon of your father,' she said, 'but truly the gods have taken away his strength and courage. For all men say that Aegeus of Athens is not master in his own house; his brother's sons rule him, and with them Medea, the witch woman, that once was the wife of Jason.'

'The more he needs his son!' said Theseus. 'Mother, I must go to help him, and be the heir of his kingdom, where you shall be with me always, and rule the people of Cecrops that fasten the locks of their hair with grasshoppers of gold.'

'So may it be, my child,' said Aethra, 'if the gods go with you to protect you. But you will sail to Athens in a ship with fifty oarsmen, for the ways by land are long, and steep, and dangerous, beset by cruel giants and monstrous men.'

'Nay, mother,' said Theseus, 'by land must I go, for I would not be known in Athens, till I see how matters fall out; and I would destroy these giants and robbers, and give peace to the people, and win glory among men. This very night I shall set forth.'

He had a sore and sad parting from his mother, but under cloud of night he went on his way, girt with the sword of Aegeus, his father, and carrying in his wallet the shoon with ornaments of gold.

Adventures of Theseus

Theseus walked through the night, and slept for most of the next day at a shepherd's hut. The shepherd was kind to him, and bade him beware of one called the Maceman, who guarded a narrow path with a sheer cliff above, and a sheer precipice below. 'No man born may deal with the Maceman,' said the shepherd, 'for his great club is of iron, that cannot be broken, and his strength is as the strength of ten men, though his legs have no force to bear his body. Men say that he is the son of the lame god, Hephaestus, who forged his iron mace; there is not the like of it in the world.'

'Shall I fear a lame man?' said Theseus, 'and is it not easy, even if he be so terrible a fighter, for me to pass him in the darkness, for I walk by night?'

The shepherd shook his head. 'Few men have passed Periphetes the Maceman,' said he, 'and wiser are they who trust to swift ships than to the upland path.'

'You speak kindly, father,' said Theseus, 'but I am minded to make the upland paths safe for all men.'

So they parted, and Theseus walked through the sunset and the dusk, always on a rising path, and the further he went the harder it was to see the way, for the path was overgrown with grass, and the shadows were deepening. Night fell, and Theseus hardly dared to go further, for on his left hand was a wall of rock, and on his right hand a cliff sinking sheer and steep to the sea. But now he saw a light in front of him, a red light flickering, as from a great fire, and he could not be content till he knew why that fire was lighted. So he went on, slowly and warily, till he came in full view of the fire which covered the whole of a little platform of rock; on one side the blaze shone up the wall of cliff on his left hand, on the other was the steep fall to the sea. In front of this fire was a great black bulk; Theseus knew not what it might be. He walked forward till he saw that the black bulk was that of a monstrous man, who sat with his back to the fire. The man nodded his heavy head, thick with red unshorn hair, and Theseus went up close to him.

'Ho, sir,' he cried, 'this is my road, and on my road I must pass!'

The seated man opened his eyes sleepily.

'Not without my leave,' he said, 'for I keep this way, I and my club of iron.'

'Get up and begone!' said Theseus.

'That were hard for me to do,' said the monstrous man, 'for my legs will not bear the weight of my body, but my arms are strong enough.'

'That is to be seen!' said Theseus, and he drew his sword, and leaped within the guard of the iron club that the monster, seated as he was, swung lightly to this side and that, covering the whole width of the path. The Maceman swung the club at Theseus, but Theseus sprang aside, and in a moment, before the monster could recover his stroke, drove through his throat the sword of Aegeus, and he fell back dead.

'He shall have his rights of fire, that his shadow may not wander outside the House of Hades,' said Theseus to himself, and he toppled the body of the Maceman into his own great fire. Then he went back some way, and wrapping himself in his mantle, he slept till the sun was high in heaven, while the fire had sunk into its embers, and Theseus lightly sprang over them, carrying with him the Maceman's iron club. The path now led downwards, and a burn that ran through a green forest kept him company on the way, and brought him to pleasant farms and houses of men

They marvelled to see him, a young man, carrying the club of the Maceman. 'Did you find him asleep?' they asked, and Theseus smiled and said, 'No, I found him awake. But now he sleeps an iron sleep, from which he will never waken, and his body had due burning in his own watch-fire.' Then the men and women praised Theseus, and wove for him a crown of leaves and flowers, and sacrificed sheep to the gods in heaven, and on the meat they dined, rejoicing that now they could go to Troezen by the hill path, for they did not love ships and the sea.

When they had eaten and drunk, and poured out the last cup of wine on the ground, in honour of Hermes, the god of luck, the country people asked Theseus where he was going. He said that he was going to walk to Athens, and at this the people looked sad. 'No man may walk across the neck of land where Ephyre is built,' they said, 'because above it Sinis the Pine-Bender has his castle, and watches the way.'

'And who is Sinis, and why does he bend pine trees?' asked Theseus.

'He is the strongest of men, and when he catches a traveller, he binds him hand and foot, and sets him between two pine trees. Then he bends them down till they meet, and fastens the traveller to the boughs of each tree, and lets them spring apart, so that the man is riven asunder.'

'Two can play at that game,' said Theseus, smiling, and he bade farewell to the kind country people, shouldered the iron club of Periphetes, and went singing on his way. The path led him over moors, and past farmhouses, and at last rose towards the crest of the hill whence he would see the place where two seas would have met, had they not been sundered by the neck of land which is now called the Isthmus of Corinth. Here the path was very narrow, with thick forests of pine trees on each hand, and 'here', thought Theseus to himself, 'I am likely to meet the Pine-Bender.'

Soon he knew that he was right, for he saw the ghastly remains of dead men that the pine trees bore like horrible fruit, and presently the air was darkened overhead by the waving of vultures and ravens that prey upon the dead. 'I shall fight the better in the shade,' said Theseus, and he loosened the blade of the sword in its sheath, and raised the club of Periphetes aloft in his hand.

Well it was for him that he raised the iron club, for, just as he lifted it, there flew out from the thicket something long, and slim, and black, that fluttered above his head for a moment, and then a loop at the end of it fell round the head of Theseus, and was drawn tight with a sudden jerk. But the loop fell also above and round the club, which Theseus held firm, pushing away the loop, and so pushed it off that it did not grip his neck. Drawing with his left hand his bronze dagger, he cut through the leather lasso with one stroke, and bounded into the bushes from which it had flown. Here he found a huge man, clad in the skin of a lion, with its head fitting to his own like a mask. The man lifted a club made of the trunk of a young pine tree, with a sharp-edged stone fastened into the head of it like an axe-head. But, as the monster raised his long weapon it struck on a strong branch of a tree above him, and was entangled in the boughs, so that Theseus had time to thrust the head of the iron club full in his face, with all his force, and the savage fell with a crash like a falling oak among the bracken. He was one of the last of an ancient race of savage men, who dwelt in Greece before the Greeks, and he fought as they had fought, with weapons of wood and stone.

Theseus dropped with his knees on the breast of the pine-bender, and grasped his hairy throat with both his hands, not to strangle him, but to hold him sure and firm till he came to himself again. When at last the monster opened his eyes, Theseus gripped his throat the harder, and spoke, 'Pine-Bender, for thee shall pines be bent. But I am a man and not a monster, and thou shalt die a clean death before thy body is torn in twain to be the last feast of thy vultures.' Then, squeezing the throat of the wretch with his left hand, he drew the sword of Aegeus, and drove it into the heart of Sinis the Pine-Bender, and he gave a cry like a bull's, and his soul fled from him. Then Theseus bound the body of the savage with his own leather cord, and, bending down the tops of two pine trees, he did to the corpse as Sinis had been wont to do to living men.

Lastly he cleaned the sword-blade carefully, wiping it with grass and bracken, and thrusting it to the hilt through the soft fresh ground under the trees, and so went on his way till he came to a little stream that ran towards the sea from the crest of the hill above the town of Ephyre, which is now called Corinth. But as he cleansed himself in the clear water, he heard a rustle in the boughs of the wood, and running with sword drawn to the place whence the sound seemed to come, he heard the whisper of a woman.

Then he saw a strange sight. A tall and very beautiful girl was kneeling in a thicket, in a patch of asparagus thorn, and was weeping, and praying, in a low voice, and in a childlike innocent manner, to the thorns, begging them to shelter and defend her.

Theseus wondered at her, and, sheathing his sword, came softly up to her, and bade her have no fear. Then she threw her arms about his knees, and raised her face, all wet with tears, and bade him take pity upon her, for she had done no harm.

'Who are you, maiden? You are safe with me,' said Theseus. 'Do you dread the Pine-Bender?'

'Alas, sir,' answered the girl, 'I am his daughter, Perigyne, and his blood is on your hands.'

'Yet I do not war with women,' said Theseus, 'though that has been done which was decreed by the gods. If you follow with me, you shall be kindly used, and marry, if you will, a man of a good house, being so beautiful as you are.'

When she heard this, the maiden rose to her feet, and would have put her hand in his. 'Not yet,' said Theseus, kindly, 'till water has clean washed away that which is between thee and me. But wherefore, maiden, being in fear as you were, did you not call to the gods in heaven to keep you, but to the asparagus thorns that cannot hear or help?'

'My father, sir,' she said, 'knew no gods, but he came of the race of the asparagus thorns, and to them I cried in my need.'

Theseus marvelled at these words, and said, 'From this day you shall pray to Zeus, the Lord of Thunder, and to the other gods.' Then he went forth from the wood, with the maiden following, and wholly cleansed himself in the brook that ran by the way.

So they passed down to the rich city of Ephyre, where the king received him gladly, when he heard of the slaying of the Maceman, Periphetes, and of Sinis the Pine-Bender. The queen, too, had pity on Perigyne, so beautiful she was, and kept her in her own palace. Afterwards Perigyne married a prince, Deiones, son of Eurytus, King of Oechalia, whom the strong man Heracles slew for the sake of his bow, the very bow with which Ulysses, many years afterwards, destroyed the wooers in his halls. The sons of Perigyne and

Deiones later crossed the seas to Asia, and settled in a land called Caria, and they never burned or harmed the asparagus thorn to which Perigyne had prayed in the thicket.

Greece was so lawless in these days that all the road from Troezen northward to Athens was beset by violent and lawless men. They loved cruelty even more than robbery, and each of them had carefully thought out his particular style of being cruel. The cities were small, and at war with each other, or at war among themselves, one family fighting against another for the crown. Thus there was no chance of collecting an army to destroy the monstrous men of the roads, which it would have been easy enough for a small body of archers to have done. Later Theseus brought all into great order, but now, being but one man, he went seeking adventures.

On the border of a small country called Megara, whose people were much despised in Greece, he found a chance of advancing himself, and gaining glory. He was walking in the middle of the day along a narrow path at the crest of a cliff above the sea, when he saw the flickering of a great fire in the blue air, and steam going up from a bronze cauldron of water that was set on the fire. On one side of the fire was a foot-bath of glittering bronze. Hard by was built a bower of green branches, very cool on that hot day, and from the door of the bower stretched a great thick hairy pair of naked legs.

Theseus guessed, from what he had been told, that the owner of the legs was Sciron the Kicker. He was a fierce outlaw who was called the Kicker because he made all travellers wash his feet, and, as they were doing so, kicked them over the cliff. Some say that at the foot of the cliff dwelt an enormous tortoise, which ate the dead and dying when they fell near his lair, but as tortoises do not eat flesh, generally, this may be a mistake. Theseus was determined not to take any insolence from Sciron, so he shouted: 'Slave, take these dirty legs of yours out of the way of a prince.'

'Prince!' answered Sciron, 'if my legs are dirty, the gods are kind who have sent you to wash them for me.'

Then he got up, lazily, laughing and showing his ugly teeth, and stood in front of his bath with his heavy wooden club in his hand. He whirled it round his head insultingly, but Theseus was quicker than he, and again, as when he slew the Pine-Bender, he did not strike, for striking is slow compared to thrusting, but like a flash he lunged forward and drove the thick end of his iron club into the breast of Sciron. He staggered, and, as he reeled, Theseus dealt him a blow across the thigh, and he fell. Theseus seized the club which dropped from the hand of Sciron, and threw it over the cliff; it seemed long before the sound came up from the rocks on which it struck. 'A deep drop into a stony way, Sciron,' said Theseus, 'now wash my feet! Stand up, and turn your back to me, and be ready when I tell you.' Sciron rose, slowly and sulkily, and stood as Theseus bade him do.

Now Theseus was not wearing light shoes or sandals, like the golden sandals of Aegeus, which he carried in his wallet. He was wearing thick boots, with bronze nails in the soles, and the upper leathers were laced high up his legs, for the Greeks wore such boots when they took long walks on mountain roads. As soon as Theseus had trained Sciron to stand in the proper position, he bade him stoop to undo the lacings of his boots. As Sciron stooped, Theseus gave him one tremendous kick, that lifted him over the edge of the cliff, and there was an end of Sciron.

Theseus left the marches of Megara, and walked singing on his way, above the sea, for his heart was light, and he was finding adventures to his heart's desire. Being so young and well trained, his foot and hand, in a combat, moved as swift as lightning, and his enemies were older than he, and, though very strong, were heavy with full feeding, and slow to move. Now it is speed that wins in a fight, whether between armies or single men, if strength and courage go with it.

At last the road led Theseus down from the heights to a great fertile plain, called the Thriasian plain, not far from Athens. There, near the sea, stands the famous old city of Eleusis. When Hades, the god of the dead, carried away beautiful Persephone, the daughter of Demeter, the goddess of corn and all manner of grain, to his dark palace beside the stream of Ocean, it was to Eleusis that Demeter wandered. She was clad in mourning robes, and she sat down on a stone by the way, like a weary old woman. Now the three daughters of the king who then reigned in Eleusis came by, on the way to the well, to fetch water, and when they saw the old woman they set down their vessels and came round her, asking what they could do for her, who was so tired and poor. They said that they had a baby brother at home, who was the favourite of them all, and that he needed a nurse. Demeter was pleased with their kindness, and they left their vessels for water beside her, and ran home to their mother. Their long golden hair danced on their shoulders as they ran, and they came, out of breath, to their mother the queen, and asked her to take the old woman to be their brother's nurse. The queen was kind, too, and the old woman lived in their house, till Zeus, the chief god, made the god of the Dead send back Persephone, to be with her mother through spring, and summer, and early autumn, but in winter she must live with her husband in the dark palace beside the river of Ocean.

Then Demeter was glad, and she caused the grain to grow abundantly for the people of Eleusis, and taught them ceremonies, and a kind of play in which all the story of her sorrows and joy was acted. It was also taught that the souls of men do not die with the death of their bodies, any more than the seed of corn dies when it is buried in the dark earth, but that they live again in a world more happy and beautiful than ours. These ceremonies were called the Mysteries of Eleusis, and were famous in all the world.

Theseus might have expected to find Eleusis a holy city, peaceful and quiet. But he had heard, as he travelled, that in Eleusis was a strong bully, named Cercyon; he was one of the rough Highlanders of Arcadia, who lived in the hills of the centre of Southern Greece, which is called Peloponnesus. He is said to have taken the kingship, and driven out the descendants of the king whose daughters were kind to Demeter. The strong man used to force all strangers to wrestle with him, and, when he threw them, for he had never been thrown, he broke their backs.

Knowing this, and being himself fond of wrestling, Theseus walked straight to the door of the king's house, though the men in the town warned him, and the women looked at him with sad eyes. He found the gate of the courtyard open, with the altar of Zeus the high god smoking in the middle of it, and at the threshold two servants welcomed him, and took him to the polished bath, and women washed him, and anointed him with oil, and clothed him in fresh raiment, as was the manner in kings' houses. Then they led him into the hall, and he walked straight up to the high seats between the four pillars beside the hearth, in the middle of the hall.

There Cercyon sat, eating and drinking, surrounded by a score of his clan, great, broad, red-haired men, but he himself was the broadest and the most brawny. He welcomed Theseus, and caused a table to be brought, with meat, and bread, and wine, and when Theseus had put away his hunger, began to ask him who he was and whence he came. Theseus told him that he had walked from Troezen, and was on his way to the court of King Peleus (the father of Achilles), in the north, for he did not want the news of his coming to go before him to Athens.

'You walked from Troezen?' said Cercyon. 'Did you meet or hear of the man who killed the Maceman and slew the Pine-Bender, and kicked Sciron into the sea?'

'I walk fast, but news flies faster,' said Theseus.

'The news came through my second-sighted man,' said Cercyon, 'there he is, in the corner,' and Cercyon threw the leg bone of an ox at his prophet, who just managed to leap out of the way. 'He seems to have foreseen that the bone was coming at him,' said Cercyon, and all his friends laughed loud. 'He told us this morning that a stranger was coming, he who had killed the three watchers of the way. From your legs and shoulders, and the iron club that you carry, methinks you are that stranger?'

Theseus smiled, and nodded upwards, which the Greeks did when they meant 'Yes!'

'Praise be to all the gods!' said Cercyon. 'It is long since a good man came my way. Do they practise wrestling at Troezen?'

'Now and then,' said Theseus.

'Then you will try a fall with me? There is a smooth space strewn with sand in the courtyard.'

Theseus answered that he had come hoping that the king would graciously honour him by trying a fall. Then all the wild guests shouted, and out they all went and made a circle round the wrestling-place, while Theseus and Cercyon threw down their clothes and were anointed with oil over their bodies. To it they went, each straining forward and feeling for a grip, till they were locked, and then they swayed this way and that, their feet stamping the ground; and now one would yield a little, now the other, while the rough guests shouted, encouraging each of them. At last they rested and breathed, and now the men began to bet; seven oxen to three was laid on Cercyon, and taken in several places. Back to the wrestle they went, and Theseus found this by far the hardest of his adventures, for Cercyon was heavier than he, and as strong, but not so active. So Theseus for long did little but resist the awful strain of the arms of Cercyon, till, at last, for a moment Cercyon weakened. Then Theseus slipped his hip under the hip of Cercyon, and heaved him across and up, and threw him on the ground. He lighted in such a way that his neck broke, and there he lay dead.

'Was it fairly done?' said Theseus.

'It was fairly done!' cried the highlanders of Arcadia; and then they raised such a wail for the dead that Theseus deemed it wise to put on his clothes and walk out of the court; and, leaping into a chariot that stood empty by the gate, for the servant in the chariot feared the club of iron, he drove away at full speed.

Though Cercyon was a cruel man and a wild, Theseus was sorry for him in his heart.

The groom in the chariot tried to leap out, but Theseus gripped him tight. 'Do not hurry, my friend,' said Theseus, 'for I have need of you. I am not stealing the chariot and horses, and you shall drive them back after we reach Athens.'

'But, my lord,' said the groom, 'you will never reach Athens.'

'Why not?' asked Theseus.

'Because of the man Procrustes, who dwells in a strong castle among the hills on the way. He is the maimer of all mortals, and has at his command a company of archers and spearmen, pirates from the islands. He meets every traveller, and speaks to him courteously, praying him to be his guest, and if any refuses the archers leap out of ambush and seize and bind him. With them no one man can contend. He has a bed which he says is a thing magical, for it is of the same length as the tallest or the shortest man who sleeps in it, so that all are fitted. Now the manner of it is this – there is an engine with ropes at the head of the bed, and a saw is fitted at the bed foot. If a man is too short, the ropes are fastened to his hands, and are strained till he is drawn to the full length of the bed. If he is too long the saw shortens him. Such a monster is Procrustes.

'Verily, my lord, King Cercyon was tomorrow to lead an army against him, and the king had a new device, as you may see, by which two great shields are slung along the side of this chariot, to ward off the arrows of the men of Procrustes.'

'Then you and I will wear the shields when we come near the place where Procrustes meets travellers by the way, and I think that tonight his own bed will be too long for him,' said Theseus.

To this the groom made no answer, but his body trembled.

Theseus drove swiftly on till the road began to climb the lowest spur of Mount Parnes, and then he drew rein, and put on one of the great shields that covered all his body and legs, and he bade the groom do the like. Then he drove slowly, watching the bushes and underwood beside the way. Soon he saw the smoke going up from the roof of a great castle high in the woods beside the road; and on the road there was a man waiting. Theseus, as he drove towards him, saw the glitter of armour in the underwood, and the setting sun shone red on a spear-point above the leaves. 'Here is our man,' he said to the groom, and pulled up his horses beside the stranger. He loosened his sword in the sheath, and leaped out of the chariot, holding the reins in his left hand, and bowed courteously to the man, who was tall, weak-looking, and old, with grey hair and a clean-shaven face, the colour of ivory. He was clad like a king, in garments of dark silk, with gold bracelets, and gold rings that clasped the leather gaiters on his legs, and he smiled and smiled, and rubbed his hands, while he looked to right and left, and not at Theseus.

'I am fortunate, fair sir,' said he to Theseus, 'for I love to entertain strangers, with whom goes the favour and protection of Zeus. Surely strangers are dear to all men, and holy! You, too, are not unlucky, for the night is falling, and the ways will be dark and dangerous. You will sup and sleep with me, and tonight I can give you a bed that is well spoken of, for its nature is such that it fits all men, the short and the tall, and you are of the tallest.'

'Tonight, fair sir,' quoth Theseus, 'your own bed will be full long for you.' And, drawing the sword of Aegeus, he cut sheer through the neck of Procrustes at one blow, and the head of the man flew one way, and his body fell another way.

Then with a swing of his hand Theseus turned his shield from his front to his back, and leaped into the chariot. He lashed the horses forward with a cry, while the groom also turned his own shield from front to back; and the arrows of the bowmen of Procrustes rattled on the bronze shields as the chariot flew along, or struck the sides and the seat of it. One arrow grazed the flank of a horse, and the pair broke into a wild gallop, while the yells of the bowmen grew faint in the distance. At last the horses slackened in their pace as they climbed a hill, and from the crest of it Theseus saw the lights in the city of Aphidnae.

'Now, my friend,' he said to the groom, 'the way is clear to Athens, and on your homeward road with the horses and the chariot you shall travel well guarded. By the splendour of Lady Athene's brow, I will burn that raven's nest of Procrustes!'

So they slept that night on safe beds at the house of the sons of Phytalus, who bore rule in Aphidnae. Here they were kindly welcomed, and the sons of Phytalus rejoiced when they heard how Theseus had made safe the ways, and slain the beasts that guarded them. 'We are your men,' they said, 'we and all our people, and our spears will encircle you when you make yourself King of Athens, and of all the cities in the Attic land.'

CHAPTER FOUR

Theseus Finds his Father

Next day Theseus said farewell to the sons of Phytalus, and drove slowly through the pleasant green woods that overhung the clear river Cephisus. He halted to rest his horses in a glen, and saw a very beautiful young man walking in a meadow on the other side of the river. In his hand he bore a white flower, and the root of it was black; in the other hand he carried a golden wand, and his upper lip was just beginning to darken, he was of the age when youth is most gracious. He came towards Theseus, and crossed the stream where it broke deep, and swift, and white, above a long pool, and it seemed to Theseus that his golden shoon did not touch the water.

'Come, speak with me apart,' the young man said; and Theseus threw the reins to the groom, and went aside with the youth, watching him narrowly, for he knew not what strange dangers might beset him on the way.

'Whither art thou going, unhappy one,' said the youth, 'thou that knowest not the land? Behold, the sons of Pallas rule in Athens, fiercely and disorderly. Thy father is of no force, and in the house with him is a fair witch woman from a far country. Her name is Medea, the daughter of Aeetes, the brother of Circe the Sorceress. She wedded the famous Jason, and won for him the Fleece of Gold, and slew her own brother Absyrtus. Other evils she wrought, and now she dwells with Aegeus, who fears and loves her greatly. Take thou this herb of grace, and if Medea offers you a cup of wine, drop this herb in the cup, and so you shall escape death. Behold, I am Hermes of the golden wand.'

Then he gave to Theseus the flower, and passed into the wood, and Theseus saw him no more; so then Theseus knelt down, and prayed, and thanked the gods. The flower he placed in the breast of his garment, and, returning to his chariot, he took the reins, and drove to Athens, and up the steep narrow way to the crest of the rock where the temple of Athene stood and the palace of King Aegeus.

Theseus drove through to the courtyard, and left his chariot at the gate. In the court young men were throwing spears at a mark, while others sat at the house door, playing draughts, and shouting and betting. They were heavy, lumpish, red-faced young men, all rather like each other. They looked up and stared, but said nothing. Theseus knew that they were his cousins, the sons of Pallas, but as they said nothing to him he walked through them, iron club on shoulder, as if he did not see them, and as one tall fellow stood in his way, the tall fellow spun round from a thrust of his shoulder. At the hall door Theseus stopped and shouted, and at his cry two or three servants came to him.

'Look to my horses and man,' said Theseus; 'I come to see your master.' And in he went, straight up to the high chairs beside the fire in the centre. The room was empty, but in a high seat sat, fallen forward and half-asleep, a man in whose grey hair was a circlet of gold and a golden grasshopper. Theseus knew that it was his father, grey and still, like the fallen fire on the hearth. As the king did not look up, Theseus touched his shoulder, and then knelt down, and put his arms round the knees of the king. The king aroused himself with a start. 'Who? What want you?' he said, and rubbed his red, bloodshot eyes.

'A suppliant from Troezen am I, who come to your knees, oh, king, and bring you gifts.'

'From Troezen!' said the king sleepily, as if he were trying to remember something.

'From Aethra, your wife, your son brings your sword and your shoon,' said Theseus; and he laid the sword and the shoon at his father's feet.

The king rose to his feet with a great cry. 'You have come at last,' he cried, 'and the gods have forgiven me and heard my prayers. But gird on the sword, and hide the shoon, and speak not the name of "wife", for there is one that hears.'

'One that has heard,' said a sweet silvery voice, and from behind a pillar came a woman, dark and pale, but very beautiful, clothed in a rich Eastern robe that shone and shifted from colour to colour. Lightly she threw her white arms round the neck of Theseus, lightly she kissed his cheeks, and a strange sweet fragrance hung about her. Then, holding him apart, with her hands on his shoulders, she laughed, and half-turning to Aegeus, who had fallen back into his chair, she said: 'My lord, did you think that you could hide anything from me?' Then she fixed her great eyes on the eyes of Theseus. 'We are friends?' she said, in her silvery voice.

'Lady, I love you even as you love my father, King Aegeus,' said Theseus.

'Even so much?' said the lady Medea. 'Then we must both drink to him in wine.' She glided to the great golden mixing-cup of wine that stood on a table behind Aegeus, and with her back to Theseus she ladled wine into a cup of strange coloured glass. 'Pledge me and the king,' she said, bringing the cup to Theseus. He took it, and from his breast he drew the flower of black root and white blossom that Hermes had given him, and laid it in the wine. Then the wine bubbled and hissed, and the cup burst and broke, and the wine fell on the floor, staining it as with blood.

Medea laughed lightly. 'Now we are friends indeed, for the gods befriend you,' she said, 'and I swear by the Water of Styx that your friends are my friends, and your foes are my foes, always, to the end. The gods are with you; and by the great oath of the gods I swear, which cannot be broken; for I come of the kin of the gods who live for ever.'

Now the father of the father of Medea was the sun god.

Theseus took both her hands. 'I also swear,' he said, 'by the splendour of Zeus, that your friends shall be my friends, and that your foes shall be my foes, always, to the end.'

Then Medea sat by the feet of Aegeus and drew down his head to her shoulder, while Theseus took hold of his hand, and the king wept for joy. For the son he loved, and the woman whom he loved and feared, were friends, and they two were stronger than the sons of Pallas.

While they sat thus, one of the sons of Pallas – the Pallantidae they were called – slouched into the hall to see if dinner was ready.

He stared, and slouched out again, and said to his brothers: 'The old man is sitting in the embraces of the foreign woman, and of the big stranger with the iron club!' Then they all came together, and growled out their threats and fears, kicking at the stones in the courtyard, and quarrelling as to what it was best for them to do.

Meanwhile, in the hall, the servants began to spread the tables with meat and drink, and Theseus was taken to the bath, and clothed in new raiment.

While Theseus was at the bath Medea told Aegeus what he ought to do. So when Theseus came back into the hall, where the sons of Pallas were eating and drinking noisily, Aegeus stood up, and called to Theseus to sit down at his right hand. He added, in a loud voice, looking all round the hall: 'This is my son, Theseus, the slayer of monsters, and his is the power in the house!'

The sons of Pallas grew pale with fear and anger, but not one dared to make an insolent answer. They knew that they were hated by the people of Athens, except some young men of their own sort, and they did not dare to do anything against the man who had slain Periphetes and Sinis, and Cercyon and Sciron, and, in the midst of his paid soldiers, had struck off the head of Procrustes. Silent all through dinner sat the sons of Pallas, and, when they had eaten, they walked out silently, and went to a lonely place, where they could make their plans without being overheard.

Theseus went with Medea into her fragrant chamber, and they spake a few words together. Then Medea took a silver bowl, filled it with water, and, drawing her dark silken mantle over her head, she sat gazing into the bowl. When she had gazed silently for a long time she said: 'Some of them are going towards Sphettus, where their father dwells, to summon his men in arms, and some are going to Gargettus on the other side of the city, to lie in ambush, and cut us off when they of Sphettus assail us. They will attack the palace just before the dawn. Now I will go through the town, and secretly call the trusty men to arm and come to defend the palace, telling them that the son of Aegeus, the man who cleared the ways, is with us. And do you take your chariot, and drive speedily to the sons of Phytalus, and bring all their spears, chariot men and foot men, and place them in ambush around the village of Gargettus, where one band of the Pallantidae will lie tonight till dawn. The rest you know.'

Theseus nodded and smiled. He drove at full speed to Aphidnae, where the sons of Phytalus armed their men, and by midnight they lay hidden in the woods round the village of Gargettus. When the stars had gone onward, and the second of the three watches of the night was nearly past, they set bands of men to guard every way from the little town, and Theseus with another band rushed in, and slew the men of the sons of Pallas around their fires, some of them awake, but most of them asleep. Those who escaped were taken by the bands who watched the ways, and when the sky was now clear at the earliest dawn, Theseus led his companions to the palace of Aegeus, where they fell furiously upon the rear of the men from Sphettus, who were besieging the palace of Aegeus.

The Sphettus company had broken in the gate of the court, and were trying to burn the house, while arrows flew thick from the bows of the trusty men of Athens on the palace roof. The Pallantids had set no sentinels, for they thought to take Theseus in the palace, and there to burn him, and win the kingdom for themselves. Then silently and suddenly the friends of Theseus stole into the courtyard, and, leaving some to guard the gate, they drew up in line, and charged the confused crowd of the Pallantids. Their spears flew thick among the enemy, and then they charged with the sword, while the crowd, in terror, ran this way and that way, being cut down at the gate, and dragged from the walls, when they tried to climb them. The daylight found the Pallantidae and their men lying dead in the courtyard, all the sort of them.

Then Theseus with the sons of Phytalus and their company marched through the town, proclaiming that the rightful prince was come, and that the robbers and oppressors were fallen, and all honest men rejoiced. They burned the dead, and buried their ashes and bones, and for the rest of that day they feasted in the hall of Aegeus. Next day Theseus led his friends back to Aphidnae, and on the next day they attacked and stormed the castle of Procrustes, and slew the pirates, and Theseus divided all the rich plunder among the sons of Phytalus and their company, but the evil bed they burned to ashes.

CHAPTER FIVE

Heralds Come for Tribute

The days and weeks went by, and Theseus reigned with his father in peace. The chief men came to Athens from the little towns in the country, and begged Theseus to be their lord, and they would be his men, and he would lead their people if any enemy came up against them. They would even pay tribute to be used for buying better arms, and making strong walls, and providing ships, for then the people of Athens had no navy. Theseus received them courteously, and promised all that they asked, for he did not know that soon he himself would be sent away as part of the tribute which the Athenians paid every nine years to King Minos of Crete.

Though everything seemed to be peaceful and happy through the winter, yet Theseus felt that all was not well. When he went into the houses of the town's people, where all had been merry and proud of his visits, he saw melancholy, silent mothers, and he missed the young people, lads and maidens. Many of them were said to have gone to visit friends in faraway parts of Greece. The elder folk, and the young people who were left, used to stand watching the sea all day, as if they expected something strange to come upon them from the sea, and Aegeus sat sorrowful over the fire, speaking little, and he seemed to be in fear.

Theseus was disturbed in his mind, and he did not choose to put questions to Aegeus or to the townsfolk. He and Medea were great friends, and one day when they were alone in her chamber, where a fragrant fire of cedar wood burned, he told her what he had noticed. Medea sighed, and said: 'The curse of the sons of Pallas is coming upon the people of Athens – such a curse and so terrible that not even you, Prince Theseus, can deal with it. The enemy is not one man or one monster only, but the greatest and most powerful king in the world.'

'Tell me all,' said Theseus, 'for though I am but one man, yet the ever-living gods protect and help me.'

'The story of the curse is long,' said Medea. 'When your father Aegeus was young, after he returned to Athens from Troezen, he decreed that games should be held every five years, contests in running, boxing, wrestling, foot races, and chariot races. Not only the people of Athens, but strangers were allowed to take part in the games, and among the strangers came Androgeos, the eldest son of great Minos, King of Knossos, in the isle of Crete of the Hundred Cities, far away in the southern sea. Minos is the wisest of men, and the most high god, even Zeus, is his counsellor, and speaks to him face to face. He is the richest of men, and his ships are without number, so that he rules all the islands, and makes war, when he will, even against the King of Egypt. The son of Minos it was who came to the sports with three fair ships, and he was the strongest and swiftest of men. He won the foot race, and the prizes for boxing and wrestling, and for shooting with the bow, and throwing the spear, and hurling the heavy weight, and he easily overcame the strongest of the sons of Pallas.

'Then, being unjust men and dishonourable, they slew him at a feast in the hall of Aegeus, their own guest in the king's house they slew, a thing hateful to the gods above all other evil deeds. His ships fled in the night, bearing the news to King Minos, and, a year after that day, the sea was black with his countless ships. His men landed, and they were so many, all glittering in armour of bronze, that none dared to meet them in battle. King Aegeus and all the elder men of the city went humbly to meet Minos, clad in mourning, and bearing in their hands boughs of trees, wreathed with wool, to show that they came praying for mercy. "Mercy ye shall have when ye have given up to me the men who slew my son," said Minos. But Aegeus could not give up the sons of Pallas, for long ago they had fled in disguise, and were lurking here and there, in all the uttermost parts of Greece, in the huts of peasants. Such mercy, then, the Athenians got as Minos was pleased to give. He did not burn the city, and slay the men, and carry the women captives. But he made Aegeus and the chief men swear that every nine years they would choose by lot seven of the strongest youths, and seven of the fairest maidens, and give them to his men, to carry away to Crete. Every nine years he sends a ship with dark sails, to bear away the captives, and this is the ninth year, and the day of the coming of the ship is at hand. Can you resist King Minos?'

'His ship we could burn, and his men we could slay,' said Theseus; and his hand closed on the hilt of his sword.

'That may well be,' said Medea, 'but in a year Minos would come with his fleet and his army, and burn the city; and the other cities of Greece, fearing him and not loving us, would give us no aid.'

'Then,' said Theseus, 'we must even pay the tribute for this last time; but in nine years, if I live, and the gods help me, I shall have a fleet, and Minos must fight for his tribute. For in nine years Athens will be queen of all the cities round about, and strong in men and ships. Yet, tell me, how does Minos treat the captives from Athens, kindly or unkindly?'

'None has ever come back to tell the tale,' said Medea, 'but the sailors of Minos say that he places the captives in a strange prison called the Labyrinth. It is full of dark winding ways, cut in the solid rock, and therein the captives are lost and perish of hunger, or live till they meet a Thing called the Minotaur. This monster has the body of a strong man, and a man's legs and arms, but his head is the head of a bull, and his teeth are the teeth of a lion, and no man may deal with him. Those whom he meets he tosses, and gores, and devours. Whence this evil beast came I know, but the truth of it may not be spoken. It is not lawful for King Minos to slay the Horror, which to him is great shame and grief; neither may he help any man to slay it. Therefore, in his anger against the Athenians he swore that, once in every nine years, he would give fourteen of the Athenian men and maidens to the Thing, and that none of them should bear sword or spear, dagger or axe, or any other weapon. Yet, if one of the men, or all of them together, could slay the monster, Minos made oath that Athens should be free of him and his tribute.'

Theseus laughed and stood up. 'Soon,' he said, 'shall King Minos be free from the Horror, and Athens shall be free from the tribute, if, indeed, the gods be with me. For me need no lot be cast; gladly I will go to Crete of my free will.'

'I needed not to be a prophetess, to know that you would speak thus,' said Medea. 'But one thing even I can do. Take this phial, and bear it in your breast, and, when you face the Minotaur, do as I shall tell you.' Then she whispered some words to Theseus, and he marked them carefully.

He went forth from Medea's bower; he walked to the crest of the hill upon which Athens is built, and there he saw all the people gathered, weeping, and looking towards the sea. Swiftly a ship with black sails was being rowed towards the shore, and her sides shone with the bronze shields of her crew, that were hung on the bulwarks.

'My friends,' cried Theseus, 'I know that ship, and wherefore she comes, and with her I shall sail to Crete and slay the Minotaur. Did I not slay Sinis and Sciron, Cercyon and Procrustes, and Periphetes? Let there be no drawing of lots. Where are seven men and seven maidens who will come with me, and meet these Cretans when they land, and sail back with them, and see this famous Crete, for the love of Theseus?'

Then there stepped forth seven young men of the best of Athens, tall, and strong, and fair, the ancestors of them who smote, a thousand years afterwards, the Persians at Marathon and in the strait of Salamis. 'We will live or die with you, Prince Theseus,' they said.

Next, one by one, came out of the throng, blushing, but with heads erect and firm steps, the seven maidens whom the seven young men loved. They, too, were tall, and beautiful, and stately, like the stone maidens called Caryatides who bear up the roofs of temples.

'We will live and die with you, Prince Theseus, and with our lovers,' they cried; and all the people gave such a cheer that King Aegeus heard it, and came from his palace, leaning on his staff, and Medea walked beside him.

'Why do you raise a glad cry, my children?' said Aegeus. 'Is not that the Ship of Death, and must we not cast lots for the tribute to King Minos?'

'Sir,' said Theseus, 'we rejoice because we go as free folk, of our own will, these men and maidens and I, to take such fortune as the gods may give us, and to do as well as we may. Nay, delay us not, for from this hour shall Athens be free, without master or lord among Cretan men.'

'But, my son, who shall defend me, who shall guide me, when I have lost thee, the light of mine eyes, and the strength of my arm?' whimpered Aegeus.

'Is the king weeping alone, while the fathers and mothers of my companions have dry eyes?' said Theseus. 'The gods will be your helpers, and the lady who is my friend, and who devised the slaying of the sons of Pallas. Hers was the mind, if the hand was my own, that wrought their ruin. Let her be your counsellor, for no other is so wise. But that ship is near the shore, and we must go.'

Then Theseus embraced Aegeus, and Medea kissed him, and the young men and maidens kissed their fathers and mothers, and said farewell. With Theseus at their head they marched down the hill, two by two; but Medea sent after them chariots laden with changes of raiment, and food, and skins of wine, and all things of which they had need. They were to sail in their own hired ship, for such was the custom, and the ship was ready with her oarsmen. But Theseus and the Seven, by the law of Minos, might carry no swords or other weapons of war. The ship had a black sail, but Aegeus gave to the captain a sail dyed scarlet with the juice of the scarlet oak, and bade him hoist it if he was bringing back Theseus safe, but, if not, to return under the black sail.

The captain, and the outlook man, and the crew, and the ship came all from the isle of Salamis, for as yet the Athenians had no vessels fit for long voyages – only fishing-boats. As Theseus and his company marched along they met the herald of King Minos, bearing a sacred staff, for heralds were holy, and to slay a herald was a deadly sin. He stopped when he met Theseus, and wondered at his beauty and strength. 'My lord,' said he, 'wherefore come you with the Fourteen? Know you to what end they are sailing?'

'That I know not, nor you, nor any man, but they and I are going to one end, such as the gods may give us,' answered Theseus. 'Speak with me no more, I pray you, and go no nearer Athens, for there men's hearts are high today, and they carry swords.'

The voice and the eyes of Theseus daunted the herald, and he with his men turned and followed behind, humbly, as if they were captives and Theseus were conqueror.

CHAPTER SIX

Theseus in Crete

After many days' sailing, now through the straits under the beautiful peaks of the mountains that crowned the islands, and now across the wide sea far from sight of land, they beheld the crest of Mount Ida of Crete, and ran into the harbour, where a hundred ships lay at anchor, and a great crowd was gathered. Theseus marvelled at the ships, so many and so strong, and at the harbour with its huge walls, while he and his company landed. A hundred of the guardsmen of Minos, with large shields, and breastplates made of ribs of bronze, and helmets of bronze with horns on them, were drawn up on the pier. They surrounded the little company of Athenians, and they all marched to the town of Knossos, and the palace of the king.

If Theseus marvelled at the harbour he wondered yet more at the town. It was so great that it seemed endless, and round it went a high wall, and at every forty yards was a square tower with small square windows high up. These towers were exactly like those which you may see among the hills and beside the burns in the Border country, the south of Scotland and the north of England; towers built when England and Scotland were at war. But when they had passed through the gateway in the chief tower, the town seemed more wonderful than the walls, for in all things it was quite unlike the cities of Greece. The street, paved with flat paving stones, wound between houses like our own, with a ground floor (in this there were no windows) and with two or three stories above, in which there were windows, with sashes, and with so many panes to each window, the panes were coloured red. Each window opened on a balcony, and the balconies were crowded with ladies in gay dresses like those which are now worn. Under their hats their hair fell in long plaits over their shoulders: they had very fine white blouses, short jackets, embroidered in bright coloured silk, and skirts with flounces. Laughing merrily they looked down at the little troop of prisoners, chatting, and some saying they were sorry for the Athenian girls. Others, seeing Theseus marching first, a head taller than the tallest guardsman, threw flowers that fell at his feet, and cried, 'Go on, brave prince!' for they could not believe that he was one of the prisoners.

The crowd in the street being great, the march was stopped under a house taller than the rest; in the balcony one lady alone was seated, the others stood round her as if they were her handmaidens. This lady was most richly dressed, young, and very beautiful and stately, and was, indeed, the king's daughter, Ariadne. She looked grave and full of pity, and, as Theseus happened to glance upwards, their eyes met, and remained fixed on each other. Theseus, who had never thought much about girls before, grew pale, for he had never seen so beautiful a maiden: Ariadne also turned pale, and then blushed and looked away, but her eyes glanced down again at Theseus, and he saw it, and a strange feeling came into his heart.

The guards cleared the crowd, and they all marched on till they came to the palace walls and gate, which were more beautiful even than the walls of the town. But the greatest wonder of all was the palace, standing in a wide park, and itself far greater than such towns as Theseus had seen, Troezen, or Aphidnae, or Athens. There was a multitude of roofs of various heights, endless roofs, endless windows, terraces, and gardens: no king's palace of our times is nearly so great and strong. There were fountains and flowers and sweet-smelling trees in blossom, and, when the Athenians were led within the palace, they felt lost among the winding passages and halls.

The walls of them were painted with pictures of flying fishes, above a clear white sea, in which fish of many kinds were swimming, with the spray and bubbles flying from their tails, as the sea flows apart from the rudder of a ship. There were pictures of bull fights, men and girls teasing the bull, and throwing somersaults over him, and one bull had just tossed a girl high in the air. Ladies were painted in balconies, looking on, just such ladies as had watched

Theseus and his company; and young men bearing tall cool vases full of wine were painted on other walls; and others were decorated with figures of bulls and stags, in hard plaster, fashioned marvellously, and standing out from the walls 'in relief', as it is called. Other walls, again, were painted with patterns of leaves and flowers.

The rooms were full of the richest furniture, chairs inlaid with ivory, gold, and silver, chests inlaid with painted porcelain in little squares, each square containing a separate bright coloured picture. There were glorious carpets, and in some passages stood rows of vases, each of them large enough to hold a man, like the pots in the story of Ali Baba and the Forty Thieves in the Arabian Nights. There were tablets of stone brought from Egypt, with images carved of gods and kings, and strange Egyptian writing, and there were cups of gold and silver – indeed, I could not tell you half the beautiful and wonderful things in the palace of Minos. We know that this is true, for the things themselves, all of them, or pictures of them, have been brought to light, dug out from under ground; and, after years of digging, there is still plenty of this wonderful palace to be explored.

The Athenians were dazzled, and felt lost and giddy with passing through so many rooms and passages, before they were led into the great hall named the Throne Room, where Minos was sitting in his gilded throne that is still standing. Around him stood his chiefs and princes, gloriously clothed in silken robes with jewels of gold; they left a lane between their ranks, and down this lane was led Theseus at the head of his little company. Minos, a dark-faced man, with touches of white in his hair and long beard, sat with his elbow on his knee, and his chin in his hand, and he fixed his eyes on the eyes of Theseus. Theseus bowed and then stood erect, with his eyes on the eyes of Minos.

'You are fifteen in number,' said Minos at last, 'my law claims fourteen.'

'I came of my own will,' answered Theseus, 'and of their own will came my company. No lots were cast.'

'Wherefore?' asked Minos.

'The people of Athens have a mind to be free, O king.'

'There is a way,' said Minos. 'Slay the Minotaur and you are free from my tribute.'

'I am minded to slay him,' said Theseus, and, as he spoke, there was a stir in the throng of chiefs, and priests, and princes, and Ariadne glided through them, and stood a little behind her father's throne, at one side. Theseus bowed low, and again stood erect, with his eyes on the face of Ariadne.

'You speak like a king's son that has not known misfortune,' said Minos.

'I have known misfortune, and my name is Theseus, Aegeus' son,' said Theseus.

'This is a new thing. When I saw King Aegeus he had no son, but he had many nephews.'

'No son that he wotted of,' said Theseus, 'but now he has no nephews, and one son.'

'Is it so?' asked Minos, 'then you have avenged me on the slayers of my own son, fair sir, for it was your sword, was it not, that delivered Aegeus from the sons of Pallas?'

'My sword and the swords of my friends, of whom seven stand before you.'

'I will learn if this be true,' said Minos.

'True!' cried Theseus, and his hand flew to the place where his sword-hilt should have been, but he had no sword.

King Minos smiled. 'You are young,' he said; 'I will learn more of these matters. Lead these men and maidens to their own chambers in the palace,' he cried to his guard. 'Let each have a separate chamber, and all things that are fitting for princes. Tomorrow I will take counsel.'

Theseus was gazing at Ariadne. She stood behind her father, and she put up her right hand as if to straighten her veil, but, as she raised her hand, she swiftly made the motion of lifting a cup to the lips; and then she laid on her lips the fingers of her left hand, closing them fast. Theseus saw the token, and he bowed, as did all his company, to Minos and to the princess, and they were led upstairs and along galleries, each to a chamber more rich and beautiful than they had seen before in their dreams. Then each was taken to a

bath, they were washed and clothed in new garments, and brought
back to their chambers, where meat was put before them, and wine
in cups of gold. At the door of each chamber were stationed two
guards, but four guards were set at the door of Theseus. At nightfall
more food was brought, and, for Theseus, much red wine, in a great
vessel adorned with ropes and knobs of gold.

Theseus ate well, but he drank none, and, when he had finished,
he opened the door of his chamber, and carried out all the wine and
the cup. 'I am one,' he said, 'who drinks water, and loves not the
smell of wine in his chamber.'

The guards thanked him, and soon he heard them very merry
over the king's best wine, next he did not hear them at all, next – he
heard them snoring!

Theseus opened the door gently and silently: the guards lay asleep
across and beside the threshold. Something bright caught his eye, he
looked up, a lamp was moving along the dark corridor, a lamp in the
hand of a woman clad in a black robe; the light fell on her white
silent feet, and on the feet of another woman who followed her.

Theseus softly slipped back into his chamber. The light, though
shaded by the girl's hand, showed in the crevice between the door
and the doorpost. Softly entered Ariadne, followed by an old woman
that had been her nurse. 'You guessed the token?' she whispered. 'In
the wine was a sleepy drug.'

Theseus, who was kneeling to her, nodded.

'I can show you the way to flee, and I bring you a sword.'

'I thank you, lady, for the sword, and I pray you to show me the
way – to the Minotaur.'

Ariadne grew pale, and her hand flew to her heart.

'I pray you make haste. Flee I will not, nor, if the king have
mercy on us, will I leave Crete till I have met the Minotaur: for he
has shed the blood of my people.'

Ariadne loved Theseus, and knew well in her heart that he loved
her. But she was brave, and she made no more ado; she beckoned to
him, and stepped across the sleeping guardsmen that lay beside the
threshold. Theseus held up his hand, and she stopped, while he took
two swords from the men of the guard. One was long, with a strong

straight narrow blade tapering to a very sharp point; the other sword was short and straight, with keen cutting double edges. Theseus slung them round his neck by their belts, and Ariadne walked down the corridor, Theseus following her, and the old nurse following him. He had taken the swords from the sleeping men lest, if Ariadne gave him one, it might be found out that she had helped him, and she knew this in her heart, for neither of them spoke a word.

Swiftly and silently they went, through galleries and corridors that turned and wound about, till Ariadne came to the door of her own chamber. Here she held up her hand, and Theseus stopped, till she came forth again, thrusting something into the bosom of her gown. Again she led the way, down a broad staircase between great pillars, into a hall, whence she turned, and passed down a narrower stair, and then through many passages, till she came into the open air, and they crossed rough ground to a cave in a hill. In the back of the cave was a door plated with bronze which she opened with a key. Here she stopped and took out of the bosom of her gown a coil of fine strong thread.

'Take this,' she said, 'and enter by that door, and first of all make fast the end of the coil to a stone, and so walk through the labyrinth, and, when you would come back, the coil shall be your guide. Take this key also, to open the door, and lock it from within. If you return place the key in a cleft in the wall within the outer door of the palace.'

She stopped and looked at Theseus with melancholy eyes, and he threw his arms about her, and they kissed and embraced as lovers do who are parting and know not if they may ever meet again.

At last she sighed and said, 'The dawn is near – farewell; the gods be with you. I give you the watchword of the night, that you may pass the sentinels if you come forth alive,' and she told him the word. Then she opened the door and gave him the key, and the old nurse gave him the lamp which she carried, and some food to take with him.

CHAPTER SEVEN

The Slaying of the Minotaur

Theseus first fastened one end of his coil of string to a pointed rock, and then began to look about him. The labyrinth was dark, and he slowly walked, holding the string, down the broadest path, from which others turned off to right or left. He counted his steps, and he had taken near three thousand steps when he saw the pale sky showing in a small circle cut in the rocky roof, above his head, and he saw the fading stars. Sheer walls of rock went up on either hand of him, a roof of rock was above him, but in the roof was this one open place, across which were heavy bars. Soon the daylight would come.

Theseus set the lamp down on a rock behind a corner, and he waited, thinking, at a place where a narrow dark path turned at right angles to the left. Looking carefully round he saw a heap of bones, not human bones, but skulls of oxen and sheep, hoofs of oxen, and shank bones. 'This,' he thought, 'must be the place where the food of the Minotaur is let down to him from above. They have not Athenian youths and maidens to give him every day! Beside his feeding place I will wait.' Saying this to himself, he rose and went round the corner of the dark narrow path cut in the rock to the left. He made his own breakfast, from the food that Ariadne had given him, and it occurred to his mind that probably the Minotaur might also be thinking of breakfast time.

He sat still, and from afar away within he heard a faint sound, like the end of the echo of a roar, and he stood up, drew his long sword, and listened keenly. The sound came nearer and louder, a strange sound, not deep like the roar of a bull, but more shrill and thin. Theseus laughed silently. A monster with the head and tongue of a bull, but with the chest of a man, could roar no better than that!

The sounds came nearer and louder, but still with the thin sharp tone in them. Theseus now took from his bosom the phial of gold that Medea had given him in Athens when she told him about the Minotaur. He removed the stopper, and held his thumb over the mouth of the phial, and grasped his long sword with his left hand, after fastening the clue of thread to his belt.

The roars of the hungry Minotaur came nearer and nearer; now his feet could be heard padding along the echoing floor of the labyrinth. Theseus moved to the shadowy corner of the narrow path, where it opened into the broad light passage, and he crouched there; his heart was beating quickly. On came the Minotaur, up leaped Theseus, and dashed the contents of the open phial in the eyes of the monster; a white dust flew out, and Theseus leaped back into his hiding-place. The Minotaur uttered strange shrieks of pain; he rubbed his eyes with his monstrous hands; he raised his head up towards the sky, bellowing and confused; he stood tossing his head up and down; he turned round and round about, feeling with his hands for the wall. He was quite blind. Theseus drew his short sword, crept up, on naked feet, behind the monster, and cut through the back sinews of his legs at the knees. Down fell the Minotaur, with a crash and a roar, biting at the rocky floor with his lion's teeth, and waving his hands, and clutching at the empty air. Theseus waited for his chance, when the clutching hands rested, and then, thrice he drove the long sharp blade of bronze through the heart of the Minotaur. The body leaped, and lay still.

Theseus kneeled down, and thanked all the gods, and promised rich sacrifices, and a new temple to Pallas Athene, the Guardian of Athens. When he had finished his prayer, he drew the short sword, and hacked off the head of the Minotaur. He sheathed both his swords, took the head in his hand, and followed the string back out of the daylit place, to the rock where he had left his lamp. With the lamp and the guidance of the string he easily found his way to the door, which he unlocked. He noticed that the thick bronze plates of the door were dinted and scarred by the points of the horns of the Minotaur, trying to force his way out.

He went out into the fresh early morning; all the birds were singing merrily, and merry was the heart of Theseus. He locked the door, and crossed to the palace, which he entered, putting the key in the place which Ariadne had shown him. She was there, with fear and joy in her eyes. 'Touch me not,' said Theseus, 'for I am foul with the blood of the Minotaur.' She brought him to the baths on the ground floor, and swiftly fled up a secret stair. In the bathroom Theseus made himself clean, and clad himself in fresh raiment which was lying ready for him. When he was clean and clad he tied a rope of byblus round the horns of the head of the Minotaur, and went round the back of the palace, trailing the head behind him, till he came to a sentinel. 'I would see King Minos,' he said, 'I have the password, *Androgeos!*'

The sentinel, pale and wondering, let him pass, and so he went through the guards, and reached the great door of the palace, and there the servants wrapped the bleeding head in cloth, that it might not stain the floors. Theseus bade them lead him to King Minos, who was seated on his throne, judging the four guardsmen, that had been found asleep.

When Theseus entered, followed by the serving men with their burden, the king never stirred on his throne, but turned his grey eyes on Theseus. 'My lord,' said Theseus, 'that which was to be done is done.' The servants laid their burden at the feet of King Minos, and removed the top fold of the covering.

The king turned to the captain of his guard. 'A week in the cells for each of these four men,' said he, and the four guards, who had expected to die by a cruel death, were led away. 'Let that head and the body also be burned to ashes and thrown into the sea, far from the shore,' said Minos, and his servants silently covered the head of the Minotaur, and bore it from the throne room.

Then, at last, Minos rose from his throne, and took the hand of Theseus, and said, 'Sir, I thank you, and I give you back your company safe and free; and I am no more in hatred with your people. Let there be peace between me and them. But will you not abide with us awhile, and be our guests?'

Theseus was glad enough, and he and his company tarried in the palace, and were kindly treated. Minos showed Theseus all the

How Theseus slew the Minotaur

splendour and greatness of his kingdom and his ships, and great armouries, full of all manner of weapons: the names and numbers of them are yet known, for they are written on tablets of clay, that were found in the storehouse of the king. Later, in the twilight, Theseus and Ariadne would walk together in the fragrant gardens where the nightingales sang, and Minos knew it, and was glad. He thought that nowhere in the world could he find such a husband for his daughter, and he deemed it wise to have the alliance of so great a king as Theseus promised to be. But, loving his daughter, he kept Theseus with him long, till the prince was ashamed of his delay, knowing that his father, King Aegeus, and all the people of his country, were looking for him anxiously.

Therefore he told what was in his heart to Minos, who sighed, and said, 'I knew what is in your heart, and I cannot say you nay. I give to you my daughter as gladly as a father may.' Then they spoke of things of state, and made firm alliance between Knossos and Athens while they both lived; and the wedding was done with great splendour, and, at last, Theseus and Ariadne and all their company went aboard, and sailed from Crete. One misfortune they had: the captain of their ship died of a sickness while they were in Crete, but Minos gave them the best of his captains. Yet by reason of storms and tempests they had a long and terrible voyage, driven out of their course into strange seas. When at length they found their bearings, a grievous sickness fell on beautiful Ariadne. Day by day she was weaker, till Theseus, with a breaking heart, stayed the ship at an isle but two days' sail from Athens. There Ariadne was carried ashore, and laid in a bed in the house of the king of that island, and the physicians and the wise women did for her what they could. But she died with her hands in the hands of Theseus, and his lips on her lips. In that isle she was buried, and Theseus went on board his ship, and drew his cloak over his head, and so lay for two days, never moving nor speaking, and tasting neither meat nor drink. No man dared to speak to him, but when the vessel stopped in the harbour of Athens, he arose, and stared about him.

The shore was dark with people all dressed in mourning raiment, and the herald of the city came with the news that Aegeus the King was dead. For the Cretan captain did not know that he was to hoist the scarlet sail if Theseus came home in triumph, and Aegeus, as he watched the waters, had descried the dark sail from afar off, and, in his grief, had thrown himself down from the cliff, and was drowned. This was the end of the voyaging of Theseus.

Theseus wished to die, and be with Ariadne, in the land of Queen Persephone. But he was a strong man, and he lived to be the greatest of the Kings of Athens, for all the other towns came in, and were his subjects, and he ruled them well. His first care was to build a great fleet in secret harbours far from towns and the ways of men, for, though he and Minos were friends while they both lived, when Minos died the new Cretan king might oppress Athens.

Minos died, at last, and his son picked a quarrel with Theseus, who refused to give up a man that had fled to Athens because the new king desired to slay him, and news came to Theseus that a great navy was being made ready in Crete to attack him. Then he sent heralds to the king of a fierce people, called the Dorians, who were moving through the countries to the north-west of Greece, seizing lands, settling on them, and marching forward again in a few years. They were wild, strong, and brave, and they are said to have had swords of iron, which were better than the bronze weapons of the Greeks. The heralds of Theseus said to them, 'Come to our king, and he will take you across the sea, and show you plunder enough. But you shall swear not to harm his kingdom.'

This pleased the Dorians well, and the ships of Theseus brought them round to Athens, where Theseus joined them with many of his own men, and they did the oath. They sailed swiftly to Crete, where, as they arrived in the dark, the Cretan captains thought that they were part of their own navy, coming in to join them in the attack on Athens; for that Theseus had a navy the Cretans knew not; he had built it so secretly. In the night he marched his men to Knossos, and took the garrison by surprise, and burned the palace, and plundered it. Even now we can see that the palace has been partly burned, and hurriedly robbed by some sudden enemy.

The Dorians stayed in Crete, and were there in the time of

Ulysses, holding part of the island, while the true Cretans held the greater part of it. But Theseus returned to Athens, and married Hippolyte, Queen of the Amazons. The story of their wedding festival is told in Shakespeare's play, *A Midsummer Night's Dream*. And Theseus had many new adventures, and many troubles, but he left Athens rich and strong, and in no more danger from the kings of Crete. Though the Dorians, after the time of Ulysses, swept all over the rest of Greece, and seized Mycenae and Lacedaemon, the towns of Agamemnon and Menelaus, they were true to their oath to Theseus, and left Athens to the Athenians.

PERSEUS

CHAPTER ONE

The Prison of Danae

Many years before the Siege of Troy there lived in Greece two princes who were brothers and deadly enemies. Each of them wished to be king both of Argos (where Diomedes ruled in the time of the Trojan War), and of Tiryns. After long wars one of the brothers, Proetus, took Tiryns, and built the great walls of huge stones, and the palace, while the other brother, Acrisius, took Argos, and he married Eurydice, a princess of the Royal House of Lacedaemon, where Menelaus and Helen were king and queen in later times.

Acrisius had one daughter, Danae, who became the most beautiful woman in Greece, but he had no son. This made him very unhappy, for he thought that, when he grew old, the sons of his brother Proetus would attack him, and take his lands and city, if he had no son to lead his army. His best plan would have been to find some brave young prince, like Theseus, and give Danae to him for his wife, and their sons would be leaders of the men of Argos. But Acrisius preferred to go to the prophetic maiden of the temple of Apollo at Delphi (or Pytho, as it was then called), and ask what chance he had of being the father of a son.

The maiden seldom had good news to give any man; but at least this time it was easy to understand what she said. She went down into the deep cavern below the temple floor, where it was said that a strange mist or steam flowed up out of the earth, and made her fall into a strange sleep, in which she could walk and speak, but knew not what she was singing, for she sang her prophecies. At last she came back, very pale, with her laurel wreath twisted awry, and her eyes open, but seeing nothing. She sang that Acrisius would never have a son; but that his daughter would bear a son, who would kill him.

Acrisius mounted his chariot, sad and sorry, and was driven homewards. On the way he never spoke a word, but was thinking how he might escape from the prophecy, and baffle the will of Zeus, the chief of the gods. He did not know that Zeus himself had looked down upon Danae and fallen in love with her, nor did Danae know.

The only sure way to avoid the prophecy was to kill Danae, and Acrisius thought of doing this; but he loved her too much; and he was afraid that his people would rise against him, if he slew his daughter, the pride of their hearts. Still another fear was upon Acrisius, which will be explained later in the story. He could think of nothing better than to build a house all of bronze, in the court of his palace, a house sunk deep in the earth, but with part of the roof open to the sky, as was the way in all houses then; the light came in from above, and the smoke of the fire went out in the same way. This chamber Acrisius built, and in it he shut up poor Danae with the woman that had been her nurse. They saw nothing, hills or plains or sea, men or trees, they only saw the sun at midday, and the sky, and the free birds flitting across it. There Danae lay, and was weary and sad, and she could not guess why her father thus imprisoned her. He used to visit her often and seemed kind and sorry for her, but he would never listen when she implored him to sell her for a slave into a far country, so that, at least, she might see the world in which she lived.

Now on a day a mysterious thing happened; the old poet Pindar, who lived long after, in the time of the war between the Greeks and the King of Persia, says that a living stream of gold flowed down from the sky and filled the chamber of Danae. Some time after this Danae bore a baby, a son, the strongest and most beautiful of children. She and her nurse kept it secret, and the child was brought up in an inner chamber of the house of bronze. It was difficult to prevent so lively a child from making a noise in his play, and one day, when Acrisius was with Danae, the boy, now three or four years old, escaped from his nurse, and ran from her room, laughing and shouting. Acrisius rushed out, and saw the nurse catch the child, and throw her mantle over him. Acrisius seized the boy, who stood firm on his little legs, with his head high, frowning at his grandfather, and gazing in anger out of his large blue eyes. Acrisius saw that this child would be dangerous when he became a man, and in great anger he bade his guards take the nurse out, and strangle her with a rope, while Danae knelt weeping at his feet.

When they were alone he said to Danae: 'Who is the father of this child?' but she, with her boy on her arm, slipped past Acrisius, and out of the open door, and up the staircase, into the open air. She ran to the altar of Zeus, which was built in the court, and threw her arms round it, thinking that there no man dared to touch her. 'I cry to Zeus that is throned in the highest, the Lord of Thunder,' she said: 'for he and no other is the father of my boy, even Perseus.' The sky was bright and blue without a cloud, and Danae cried in vain. There came no flash of lightning nor roll of thunder.

'Is it even so?' said Acrisius, 'then let Zeus guard his own.' He bade his men drag Danae from the altar; and lock her again in the house of bronze; while he had a great strong chest made. In that chest he had the cruelty to place Danae and her boy, and he sent them out to sea in a ship, the sailors having orders to let the chest down into the waters when they were far from shore. They dared not disobey, but they put food and a skin of wine, and two skins of water in the chest, and lowered it into the sea, which was perfectly calm and still. It was their hope that some ship would come sailing by, perhaps a ship of Phoenician merchantmen, who would certainly save Danae and the child, if only that they might sell them for slaves.

King Acrisius himself was not ignorant that this might happen and that his grandson might live to be the cause of his death. But the Greeks believed that if any man killed one of his own kinsfolk, he would be pursued and driven mad by the Furies called the Erinyes, terrible winged women with cruel claws. These winged women drove Orestes, the son of Agamemnon, fleeing like a madman through the world, because he slew his own mother, Clytemnestra, to avenge his father, whom she and Aegisthus had slain. Nothing was so much dreaded as these Furies, and therefore Acrisius did not dare to slay his daughter and his grandson, Perseus, but only put them in the way of being drowned. He heard no more of them, and hoped that both of their bodies were rolling in the waves, or that their bones lay bleaching on some unknown shore. But he could not be certain – indeed, he soon knew better – and as long as he lived, he lived in fear that Perseus had escaped, and would come and slay him, as the prophetess had said in her song.

The chest floated on the still waters, and the sea birds swooped down to look at it, and passed by, with one waft of their wings. The sun set, and Danae watched the stars, the Bear and Orion with his belt, and wrapped her boy up warm, and he slept sound, for he never knew fear, in his mother's arms. The Dawn came in her golden throne, and Danae saw around her the blue sharp crests of the mountains of the islands that lay scattered like water lilies on the seas of Greece. If only the current would drift her to an island, she thought, and prayed in her heart to the gods of good help, Pallas Athene, and Hermes of the golden wand. Soon she began to hope that the chest was drawing near an island. She turned her head in the opposite direction for a long while, and then looked forward again. She was much nearer the island, and could see the smoke going up from cottages among the trees. But she drifted on and drifted past the end of the isle, and on with the current, and so all day.

A weary day she had, for the boy was full of play, and was like to capsize the chest. She gave him some wine and water, and presently he fell asleep, and Danae watched the sea and the distant isles till night came again. It was dark, with no moon, and the darker because the chest floated into the shadow of a mountain, and the current drew it near the shore. But Danae dared not hope again; men would not be abroad, she thought, in the night. As she lay thus helpless, she saw a light moving on the sea, and she cried as loud as she could cry. Then the light stopped, and a man's shout came to her over the water, and the light moved swiftly towards her. It came from a brazier set on a pole in a boat, and now Danae could see the bright sparks that shone in the drops from the oars, for the boat was being rowed towards her, as fast as two strong men could pull.

Being weak from the heat of the sun that had beaten on her for two days, and tired out with hopes and fears, Danae fainted, and knew nothing till she felt cold water on her face. Then she opened

her eyes, and saw kind eyes looking at her own, and the brown face
of a bearded man, in the light of the blaze that fishermen carry in
their boats at night, for the fish come to wonder at it, and the
fishermen spear them. There were many dead fish in the boat, into
which Danae and the child had been lifted, and a man with a fish
spear in his hand was stooping over her.

Then Danae knew that she and her boy were saved, and she lay,
unable to speak, till the oarsmen had pulled their boat to a little
pier of stone. There the man with the fish spear lifted her up lightly
and softly set her on her feet on land, and a boatman handed to him
the boy, who was awake, and was crying for food.

'You are safe, lady!' said the man with the spear, 'and I have
taken fairer fish than ever swam the sea. I am called Dictys; my
brother, Polydectes, is king of this island, and my wife is waiting
for me at home, where she will make you welcome, and the boy
thrice welcome, for the gods have taken our only son.'

He asked no questions of Danae; it was reckoned ill manners to
put questions to strangers and guests, but he lighted two torches at
the fire in the boat, and bade his two men walk in front, to show
the way, while he supported Danae, and carried the child on his
shoulder. They had not far to go, for Dictys, who loved fishing of
all things, had his house near the shore. Soon they saw the light
shining up from the opening in the roof of the hall; and the wife of
Dictys came running out, crying: 'Good sport?' when she heard
their voices and footsteps.

'Rare sport,' shouted Dictys cheerily, and he led in Danae, and
gave the child into the arms of his wife. Then they were taken to
the warm baths, and dressed in fresh raiment. Food was set before
them, and presently Danae and Perseus slept on soft beds, with
coverlets of scarlet wool.

Dictys and his wife never asked Danae any questions about how
and why she came floating on the sea through the night. News was
carried quickly enough from the mainland to the islands by fishers
in their boats and merchantmen, and pedlars. Dictys heard how the
King of Argos had launched his daughter and her son on the sea,
hoping that both would be drowned. All the people knew in the

island, which was called Seriphos, and they hated the cruelty of Acrisius, and many believed that Perseus was the son of Zeus.

If the news from Argos reached Seriphos, we may guess that the news from Seriphos reached Argos, and that Acrisius heard how a woman as beautiful as a goddess, with a boy of the race of the gods, had drifted to the shore of the little isle. Acrisius knew, and fear grew about his heart, fear that was sharper as the years went on, while Perseus was coming to his manhood. Acrisius often thought of ways by which he might have his grandson slain; but none of them seemed safe. By the time when Perseus was fifteen, Acrisius dared not go out of doors, except among the spears of his armed guards, and he was so eaten up by fear that it would have been happier for him if he had never been born.

CHAPTER TWO

The Vow of Perseus

It was fortunate for Perseus that Dictys treated him and taught him like his own son, and checked him if he was fierce and quarrelsome, as so strong a boy was apt to be. He was trained in all the exercises of young men, the use of spear and sword, shield and bow; and in running, leaping, hunting, rowing, and the art of sailing a boat. There were no books in Seriphos, nobody could read or write; but Perseus was told the stories of old times, and of old warriors who slew monsters by sea and land. Most of the monsters had been killed, as Perseus was sorry to hear, for he desired to try his own luck with them when he came to be a man. But the most terrible of all, the Gorgons, who were hated by men and gods, lived still, in an island near the Land of the Dead; but the way to that island was unknown. These Gorgons were two sisters, and a third woman; the two were hideous to look on, with hair and wings and claws of bronze, and with teeth like the white tusks of swine. Swinish they were, ugly and loathsome, feeding fearfully on the bodies of unburied men. But the third Gorgon was beautiful save for the living serpents that coiled in her hair. She alone of the three Gorgons was mortal, and could be slain, but who could slay her? So terrible were her eyes that men who had gone up against her were changed into pillars of stone.

This was one of the stories that Perseus heard when he was a boy; and there was a proverb that this or that hard task was 'as difficult to do as to slay the Gorgon'. Perseus, then, ever since he was a little boy, was wondering how he could slay the Gorgon and become as famous as the strong man Heracles, or the good knight Bellerophon, who slew the Chimaera. Perseus was always thinking of such famous men as these, and especially loved the story of Bellerophon, which is this: In the city of Ephyre, now called Corinth, was a king named

Glaucus, who had a son, Bellerophon. He was brought up far from
home, in Argos, by King Proetus (the great-uncle of Perseus), who
was his foster-father, and loved him well. Proetus was an old man,
but his wife, Anteia, was young and beautiful, and Bellerophon also
was beautiful and young, and, by little and little, Anteia fell in love
with him, and could not be happy without him, but no such love was
in Bellerophon's heart for her, who was his foster-mother. At last
Anteia, forgetting all shame, told Bellerophon that she loved him,
and hated her husband, and she asked him to fly with her to the
seashore, where she had a ship lying ready, and they two would sail
to some island far away, and be happy together.

Bellerophon knew not what to say; he could not wrong King
Proetus, his foster-father. He stood speechless, his face was red
with shame, but the face of Anteia grew white with rage.

'Dastard!' she said, 'thou shalt not live long in Argos to boast of
my love and your own virtue!' She ran from him, straight to King
Proetus, and flung herself at his feet. 'What shall be done, oh king,'
she cried, 'to the man who speaks words of love dishonourable to
the Queen of Argos?'

'By the splendour of Zeus,' cried Proetus, 'if he were my own
foster-son he shall die!'

'Thou hast named him!' said Anteia, and she ran to her own
upper chamber, and locked the door, and flung herself on the bed,
weeping for rage as if her heart would break. Proetus followed
her, but she would not unlock her door, only he heard her bitter
weeping, and he went apart, alone, and took thought how he should
be revenged on Bellerophon. He had no desire to slay him openly,
for then the King of Ephyre would make war against him. He could
not bring him to trial before the judges, for there was no witness
against him except Anteia; and he did not desire to make his subjects
talk about the queen, for it was the glory of a woman, in those days,
not to be spoken of in the conversation of men.

Therefore Proetus, for a day or two, seemed to favour Bellerophon more kindly than ever. Next he called him into his chamber,
alone, and said that it was well for young men to see the world, to
cross the sea and visit foreign cities, and win renown. The eyes of

Bellerophon brightened at these words, not only because he desired to travel, but because he was miserable in Argos, where he saw every day the angry eyes of Anteia. Then Proetus said that the King of Lycia, in Asia far across the sea, was his father-in-law, and his great friend. To him he would send Bellerophon, and Proetus gave him a folded tablet, in which he had written many deadly signs. Bellerophon took the folded tablet, not looking, of course, at what was written in it, and away he sailed to Lycia. The king of that country received him well, and on the tenth day after his arrival asked him if he brought any token from King Proetus.

Bellerophon gave him the tablet, which he opened and read. The writing said that Bellerophon must die. Now at that time Lycia was haunted by a monster of no human birth; her front was the front of a lion, in the middle of her body she was a goat, she tapered away to a strong swift serpent, and she breathed flame from her nostrils. The King of Lycia, wishing to get rid of Bellerophon, had but to name this curse to his guest, who vowed that he would meet her if he might find her. So he was led to the cavern where she dwelt, and there he watched for her all night till the day dawned.

He was cunning as well as brave, and men asked him why he took with him no weapon but his sword, and two spears with heavy heads, not of bronze, but of soft lead. Bellerophon told his companions that he had his own way of fighting, and bade them go home, and leave him alone, while his charioteer stood by the horses and chariot in a hollow way, out of sight. Bellerophon himself watched, lying on his face, hidden behind a rock in the mouth of the cavern. The moment that the rising sun touched with a red ray the dark mouth of the cave, forth came the Chimaera, and, setting her forepaws on the rock, looked over the valley. The moment that she opened her mouth, breathing flame, Bellerophon plunged his leaden spears deep down her throat, and sprang aside. On came the Chimaera, her serpent tail lashing the stones, but Bellerophon ever kept on the further side of a great tall rock. The Chimaera ceased to pursue him, she rolled on the earth, uttering screams of pain, for the lead was melting in the fire that was within her, and at last the molten lead burned through her, and she died. Bellerophon hacked off her head, and several feet of her tail, stowed them in his chariot, and drove back to the palace of the King of Lycia, while the people followed him with songs of praise.

The king set him three other terrible tasks, but he achieved each of the adventures gloriously, and the king gave him his daughter to be his bride, and half of all the honours of his kingdom. This is the story of Bellerophon (there were other ways of telling it), and Perseus was determined to do as great deeds as he. But Perseus was still a boy, and he did not know, and no man could tell him, the way to the island of the Gorgons.

When Perseus was about sixteen years old, the King of Seriphos, Polydectes, saw Danae, fell in love with her, and wanted to take her into his palace, but he did not want Perseus. He was a bad and cruel man, but Perseus was so much beloved by the people that he dared not kill him openly. He therefore made friends with the lad, and watched him carefully to see how he could take advantage of him. The king saw that he was of a rash, daring and haughty spirit, though Dictys had taught him to keep himself well in hand, and that he was eager to win glory. The king fell on this plan: he gave a great feast on his birthday, and invited all the chief men and the richest on the island; Perseus, too, he asked to the banquet. As the custom was, all the guests brought gifts, the best that they had, cattle, women-slaves, golden cups, wedges of gold, great vessels of bronze, and other splendid things, and the king met the guests at the door of his hall, and thanked them graciously.

Last came Perseus: he had no gift to give, for he had nothing of his own. The others began to sneer at him, saying, 'Here is a birthday guest without a birthday gift!' 'How should No Man's son have a present fit for a king.' 'This lad is lazy, tied to his mother; he should long ago have taken service with the captain of a merchant ship.' 'He might at least watch the town's cows on the town's fields,' said another. Thus they insulted Perseus, and the king, watching him with a cruel smile, saw his face grow red, and his blue eyes blaze, as he turned from one to another of the mockers, who pointed their fingers at him and jeered.

At last Perseus spoke: 'Ye farmers and fishers, ye ship-captains and slave dealers of a little isle, I shall bring to your master such a present as none of you dare to seek. Farewell. Ye shall see me once again and no more. I go to slay the Gorgon, and bring such a gift as no king possesses – the Head of the Gorgon.'

They laughed and hooted, but Perseus turned away, his hand on his sword-hilt, and left them to their festival, while the king rejoiced in his heart. Perseus dared not see his mother again, but he spoke to Dictys, saying that he knew himself now to be of an age when he must seek his fortune in other lands; and he bade Dictys guard his mother from wrong, as well as he might. Dictys promised that he would find a way of protecting Danae, and he gave Perseus three weighed wedges of gold (which were called 'talents', and served as money), and lent him a ship, to take him to the mainland of Greece, there to seek his fortune.

In the dawn Perseus secretly sailed away, landed at Malea, and thence walked and wandered everywhere, seeking to learn the way to the island of the Gorgons. He was poorly clad, and he slept at night by the fires of smithies, where beggars and wanderers lay: listening to the stories they told, and asking old people, when he met them, if they knew anyone who knew the way to the island of the Gorgons. They all shook their heads. 'Yet I should be near knowing,' said one old man, 'if that isle be close to the Land of the Dead, for I am on its borders. Yet I know nothing. Perchance the dead may know; or the maid that prophesies at Pytho, or the Selloi, the priests with unwashen feet, who sleep on the ground below the sacred oaks of Zeus in the grove of Dodona far away.'

Perseus could learn no more than this, and he wandered on and on. He went to the cave that leads down to the Land of the Dead, where the ghosts answer questions in their thin voices, like the twittering of bats. But the ghosts could not tell him what he desired to know. He went to Pytho, where the maid, in her song, bade him seek the land of men who eat acorns instead of the yellow grain of Demeter, the goddess of harvest. Thence he wandered to Epirus, and to the Selloi who dwell in the oak forest of Zeus, and live on the flour ground from acorns. One of them lay on the ground in the wood, with his head covered up in his mantle, and listened to what the wind says, when it whispers to the forest leaves. The leaves said, 'We bid the young man be of good hope, for the gods are with him.'

This answer did not tell Perseus where the isle of the Gorgons lay, but the words put hope in his heart, weary and footsore as he was. He ate of the bread made of the acorns, and of the flesh of the swine that the Selloi gave him, and he went alone, and, far in the forest, he laid his head down on the broad mossy root of an old oak tree. He did not sleep, but watched the stars through the boughs, and he heard the cries of the night-wandering beasts in the woodland.

'If the gods be with me, I shall yet do well,' he said, and, as he spoke, he saw a white clear light moving through the darkness. That clear white light shone from a golden lamp in the hand of a tall and beautiful woman, clad in armour, and wearing, hung by a belt from her neck, a great shield of polished bronze. With her there came a young man, with winged shoon of gold on his feet, and belted with a strange short curved sword: in his hand was a golden wand, with wings on it, and with golden serpents twisted round it.

Perseus knew that these beautiful folk were the goddess Athene, and Hermes, who brings all fortunate things. He fell upon his face before them, but Athene spoke in a sweet grave voice, saying, 'Arise, Perseus, and speak to us face to face, for we are of your kindred, we also are children of Zeus, the Father of gods and men.'

Then Perseus arose and looked straight into their eyes.

'We have watched you long, Perseus, to learn whether you have the heart of a hero, that can achieve great adventures; or whether you are an idle dreaming boy. We have seen that your heart is steadfast, and that you have sought through hunger, and long travels to know the way wherein you must find death or win glory. That way is not to be found without the help of the gods. First you must seek the Three Grey Women, who dwell beyond the land that lies at the back of the North Wind. They will tell you the road to the three Nymphs of the West, who live in an island of the sea that never knew a sail; for it is beyond the pillars that Heracles set up when he wearied in his journey to the Well of the World's End, and turned again. You must go to these nymphs, where never foot of man has trod, and they will show you the measure of the way to the Isle of the Gorgons. If you see the faces of the Gorgons, you will be turned to stone. Yet you have vowed to bring the head of the youngest of the three, she who was not born a Gorgon but became one of them by reason of her own wickedness. If you slay her, you must not see even her dead head, but wrap it round in this goat-skin which hangs beside my shield; see not the head yourself, and let none see it but your enemies.'

'This is a great adventure,' said Perseus, 'to slay a woman whom I may not look upon, lest I be changed into stone.'

'I give you my polished shield,' said Athene. 'Let it never grow dim, if you would live and see the sunlight.' She took off her shield from her neck, with the goatskin cover of the shield, and hung them round the neck of Perseus. He knelt and thanked her for her grace, and, looking up through a clear space between the forest boughs, he said, 'I see the Bear, the stars of the North that are the guide of sailors. I shall walk towards them even now, by your will, for my heart burns to find the Three Grey Women, and learn the way.'

Hermes smiled, and said, 'An old man and white-bearded would you be, ere you measured out that way on foot! Here, take my winged sandals, and bind them about your feet. They know all the paths of the air, and they will bring you to the Three Grey Women. Belt yourself, too, with my sword, for this sword needs no second stroke, but will cleave through that you set it to smite.'

So Perseus bound on the Shoes of Swiftness, and the Sword of Sharpness, the name of it was Herpe; and when he rose from binding on the shoon, he was alone. The gods had departed. He drew the sword, and cut at an oak tree trunk, and the blade went clean through it, while the tree fell with a crash like thunder. Then Perseus rose through the clear space in the wood, and flew under the stars, towards the constellation of the Bear. North of Greece he flew, above the Thracian mountains, and the Danube (which was then called the Ister) lay beneath him like a long thread of silver. The air grew cold as he crossed lands then unknown to the Greeks, lands where wild men dwelt, clad in the skins of beasts, and using axe-heads and spear-heads made of sharpened stones. He passed to the land at the back of the North Wind, a sunny warm land, where the people sacrifice wild asses to the god Apollo. Beyond this he came to a burning desert of sand, but far away he saw trees that love the water, poplars and willows, and thither he flew.

He came to a lake among the trees, and round and round the lake were flying three huge grey swans, with the heads of women, and their long grey hair flowed down below their bodies, and floated on the wind. They sang to each other as they flew, in a voice like the cry of the swan. They had but one eye among them, and but one tooth, which they passed to each other in turn, for they had arms and hands under their wings. Perseus dropped down in his flight, and watched them. When one was passing the eye to the other, none of them could see him, so he waited for his chance and took it, and seized the eye.

'Where is our eye? Have *you* got it?' said the grey woman from whose hand Perseus took it. 'I have it not.'

'I have it not!' cried each of the others, and they all wailed like swans.

'I have it,' said Perseus, and hearing his voice they all flew to the sound of it but he easily kept out of their way. 'The eye will I keep,' said Perseus, 'till you tell me what none knows but you, the way to the Isle of the Gorgons.'

'We know it not,' cried the poor grey women. 'None knows it but the Nymphs of the Isle of the West: give us our eye!'

'Then tell me the way to the Nymphs of the Isle of the West,' said Perseus.

'Turn your back, and hold your course past the Isle of Albion, with the white cliffs, and so keep with the land on your left hand, and the unsailed sea on your right hand, till you mark the Pillars of Heracles on your left, then take your course west by south, and a curse on you! Give us our eye!'

Perseus gave them their eye, and she who took it flew at him, but he laughed, and rose high above them and flew as he was told. Over many and many a league of sea and land he went, till he turned to his right from the Pillars of Heracles (at Gibraltar), and sailed along, west by south, through warm air, over the lonely endless Atlantic waters. At last he saw a great blue mountain, with snow feathering its crests, in a far-off island, and on that island he alighted. It was a country of beautiful flowers, and pine forests high on the hill, but below the pines all was like a garden, and in that garden was a tree bearing apples of gold, and round the tree were dancing three fair maidens, clothed in green, and white, and red.

'These must be the Nymphs of the Isle of the West,' said Perseus, and he floated down into the garden, and drew near them.

As soon as they saw him they left off dancing, and catching each other by the hands they ran to Perseus laughing, and crying, 'Hermes, our playfellow Hermes has come!' The arms of all of them went round Perseus at once, with much laughing and kissing. 'Why have you brought a great shield, Hermes?' they cried, 'here there is no unfriendly god or man to fight against you.'

Perseus saw that they had mistaken him for the god whose sword and winged shoon he wore, but he did not dislike the mistake of the merry maidens.

'I am not Hermes,' he said, 'but a mortal man, to whom the god has graciously lent his sword and shoon and the shield was lent to me by Pallas Athene. My name is Perseus.'

The girls leaped back from him, blushing and looking shy. The eldest girl answered, 'We are the daughters of Hesperus, the god of the evening star. I am Aegle, this is my sister Erytheia, and this is Hesperia. We are the keepers of this island, which is the garden of the gods, and they often visit us; our cousins, Dionysus, the young god of wine and mirth, and Hermes of the golden wand come often; and bright Apollo, and his sister Artemis the huntress. But a mortal man we have never seen, and wherefore have the gods sent you hither?'

'The two gods sent me, maidens, to ask you the way to the Isle of the Gorgons, that I may slay Medusa of the snaky hair, whom gods and men detest.'

'Alas!' answered the nymphs, 'how shall you slay her, even if we knew the way to that island, which we know not?'

Perseus sighed: he had gone so far, and endured so much, and had come to the Nymphs of the Isle of the West, and even they could not tell how to reach the Gorgons' island.

'Do not fear,' said the girl, 'for if we know not the way we know one that knows it: Atlas is his name – the giant of the mountain. He dwells on the highest peak of the snow-crested hill, and it is he who holds up the heavens, and keeps heaven and earth asunder. He looks over all the world, and over the wide western sea: him we must ask to answer your question. Take off your shield, which is so heavy, and sit down with us among the flowers, and let us think how you may slay the Gorgon.'

Perseus gladly unslung his heavy shield, and sat down among the white and purple wind flowers. Aegle, too, sat down; but young Erytheia held the shield upright, while beautiful Hesperia admired herself, laughing, in the polished surface.

Perseus smiled as he watched them, and a plan came into his mind. In all his wanderings he had been trying hard to think how, if he found the Gorgon, he might cut off her head, without seeing the face which turned men into stone. Now his puzzle was ended. He could hold up the shield above the Gorgon, and see the reflection of her face, as in a mirror, just as now he saw the fair reflected face of Hesperia. He turned to Aegle, who sat silently beside him: 'Maiden,' he said, 'I have found out the secret that has perplexed me long, how I may strike at the Gorgon without seeing her face that turns men to stone. I will hang above her in the air, and see her face reflected in the mirror of the shield, and so know where to strike.' The two other girls had left the shield on the grass, and they clapped their hands when Perseus said this, but Aegle still looked grave.

'It is much that you should have found this cunning plan; but the Gorgons will see you, and two of them are deathless and cannot be slain, even with the sword Herpe. These Gorgons have wings almost as swift as the winged shoon of Hermes, and they have claws of bronze that cannot be broken.'

Hesperia clapped her hands. 'Yet I know a way,' she said, 'so that this friend of ours may approach the Gorgons, yet not be seen

Perseus in the garden of the Hesperides

by them. You must be told,' she said, turning to Perseus, 'that we three sisters were of the company of the fairy queen, Persephone, daughter of Demeter, the goddess of the harvest. We were gathering flowers with her, in the plain of Enna, in a spring morning, when there sprang up a new flower, fragrant and beautiful, the white narcissus. No sooner had Persephone plucked that flower than the earth opened beside her, and up came the chariot and horses of Hades, the king of the dead, who caught Persephone into his chariot, and bore her down with him to the House of Hades. We wept and were in great fear, but Zeus granted to Persephone to return to earth with the first snowdrop, and remain with her mother, Demeter, till the last rose had faded. Now I was the favourite of Persephone, and she carried me with her to see her husband, who is kind to me for her sake, and can refuse me nothing, and he has what will serve your turn. To him I will go, for often I go to see my playmate, when it is winter in your world: it is always summer in our isle. To him I will go, and return again, when I will so work that you may be seen of none, neither by god, or man, or monster. Meanwhile my sisters will take care of you, and tomorrow they will lead you to the mountain top, to speak with the giant.'

'It is well spoken,' said tall, grave Aegle, and she led Perseus to their house, and gave him food and wine, and at night he slept full of hope, in a chamber in the courtyard.

Next morning, early, Perseus and Aegle and Erytheia floated up to the crest of the mountain, for Hesperia had departed in the night, to visit Queen Persephone. Perseus took a hand of each of the Nymphs, and they had no weary climbing; they all soared up together, so great was the power of the winged shoon of Hermes. They found the good giant Atlas, kneeling on a black rock above the snow, holding up the vault of heaven with either hand. When Aegle had spoken to him, he bade his girls go apart, and said to Perseus, 'Yonder, far away to the west, you see an island with a mountain that rises to a flat top, like a table. There dwell the Gorgons.'

Perseus thanked him eagerly, but Atlas sighed and said, 'Mine is a weary life. Here have I knelt and done my task, since the giants fought against the gods, and were defeated. Then, for my punishment, I was set here by Zeus to keep sky and earth asunder. But he told me that after hundreds of years I should have rest, and be changed to a stone. Now I see that the day of rest appointed is come, for you shall show me the head of the Gorgon when you have slain her, and my body shall be stone, but my spirit shall be with the ever living gods.'

Perseus pitied Atlas; he bowed to the will of Zeus, and to the prayer of the giant, and gave his promise. Then he floated to Aegle and Erytheia, and they all three floated down again to the garden of the golden apples. Here as they walked on the soft grass, and watched the wind toss the white and red and purple bells of the wind flowers, they heard a low laughter close to them, the laughter of Hesperia, but her they saw not. 'Where are you, Hesperia, where are you hiding?' cried Aegle, wondering, for the wide lawn was open, without bush or tree where the girl might be lurking.

'Find me if you can,' cried the voice of Hesperia, close beside them, and handfuls of flowers were lightly tossed to them, yet they saw none who threw them. 'This place is surely enchanted,' thought Perseus, and the voice of Hesperia answered: 'Come follow, follow me. I will run before you to the house, and show you my secret.'

Then they all saw the flowers bending, and the grass waving, as if a light-footed girl were running through it, and they followed to the house the path in the trodden grass. At the door, Hesperia met them: 'You could not see me,' she said, 'nor will the Gorgons see Perseus. Look, on that table lies the Helmet of Hades, which mortal men call the Cap of Darkness. While I wore it you could not see me, nay, a deathless god cannot see the wearer of that helmet.' She took up a dark cap of hard leather, that lay on a table in the hall, and raised it to her head, and when she had put it on, she was invisible. She took it off, and placed it on the brows of Perseus. 'We cannot see you, Perseus,' cried all the girls. 'Look at yourself in your shining shield: can you see yourself?'

Perseus turned to the shield, which he had hung on a golden nail in the wall. He saw only the polished bronze, and the faces of the girls who were looking over his shoulder. He took off the

Helmet of Hades and gave a great sigh. 'Kind are the gods,' he said. 'Methinks that I shall indeed keep my vow, and bring to Polydectes the Gorgon's head.'

They were merry that night, and Perseus told them his story, how he was the son of Zeus, and the girls called him 'cousin Perseus'. 'We love you very much, and we could make you immortal, without old age and death,' said Hesperia. 'You might live with us here for ever – it is lonely, sometimes, for three maidens in the garden of the gods. But you must keep your vow, and punish your enemies, and cherish your mother, and do not forget your cousins three, when you have married the lady of your heart's desire, and are King of Argos.'

The tears stood in the eyes of Perseus. 'Cousins dear,' he said, 'never shall I forget you, not even in the House of Hades. You will come thither now and again, Hesperia? But I love no woman.'

'I think you will not long be without a lady and a love, Perseus,' said Erytheia; 'but the night is late, and tomorrow you have much to do.'

So they parted, and next morning they bade Perseus be of good hope. He burnished and polished the shield, and covered it with the goat's skin, he put on the Shoes of Swiftness, and belted himself with the Sword of Sharpness, and placed on his head the Cap of Darkness. Then he soared high in the air, till he saw the Gorgons' Isle, and the table-shaped mountain, a speck in the western sea.

The way was long, but the shoes were swift, and, far aloft, in the heat of the noonday, Perseus looked down on the top of the table-mountain. There he could dimly see three bulks of strange shape-less shape, with monstrous limbs that never stirred, and he knew that the Gorgons were sleeping their midday sleep. Then he held the shield so that the shapes were reflected in its polished face, and very slowly he floated down, and down, till he was within striking distance. There they lay, two of them uglier than sin, breathing loud in their sleep like drunken men. But the face of her who lay between the others was as quiet as the face of a sleeping child; and as beautiful as the face of the goddess of Love, with long dark eyelashes veiling the eyes, and red lips half-open. Nothing stirred but the serpents in the hair of beautiful Medusa; they were never still, but coiled and twisted, and Perseus loathed them as he watched them in the mirror. They coiled and uncoiled, and left bare her ivory neck, and then Perseus drew the sword Herpe, and struck once.

In the mirror he saw the fallen head, and he seized it by the hair, and wrapped it in the goatskin, and put the goatskin in his wallet. Then he towered high in the air, and, looking down, he saw the two sister Gorgons turning in their sleep; they woke, and saw their sister dead. They seemed to speak to each other; they looked this way and that, into the bright empty air, for Perseus in the Cap of Darkness they could not see. They rose on their mighty wings, hunting low, and high, and with casts behind their island and in front of it, but Perseus was flying faster than ever he flew before, stooping and rising to hide his scent. He dived into the deep sea, and flew under water as long as he could hold his breath, and then rose and fled swiftly forward. The Gorgons were puzzled by each double he had made, and, at the place where he dived they lost the scent, and from far away Perseus heard their loud yelps, but soon these faded in the distance. He often looked over his shoulder as he flew straight towards the far-off blue hill of the giant Atlas, but the sky was empty behind him, and the Gorgons he never saw again. The mountain turned from blue to clear grey and red and gold, with pencilled rifts and glens, and soon Perseus stood beside the giant Atlas. 'You are welcome and blessed,' said the giant. 'Show me the head that I may be at rest.'

Then Perseus took the bundle from the wallet, and carefully unbound the goatskin, and held up the head, looking away from it, and the giant was a great grey stone. Down sailed Perseus, and stood in the garden of the gods, and laid the Cap of Darkness on the grass. The three Nymphs who were sitting there, weaving garlands of flowers, leaped up, and came round him, and kissed him, and crowned him with the flowery chaplets. That night he rested with them, and in the morning they kissed and said farewell.

'Do not forget us,' said Aegle, 'nor be too sorry for our loneliness. Today Hermes has been with us, and tomorrow he comes again with Dionysus, the god of the vine, and all his merry company.

Hermes left a message for you, that you are to fly eastward, and south, to the place where your wings shall guide you, and there, he said, you shall find your happiness. When that is won, you shall turn north and west, to your own country. We say, all three of us, that our love is with you always, and we shall hear of your gladness, for Hermes will tell us; then we too shall be glad. Farewell!'

So the three maidens embraced him with kind faces and smiling eyes, and Perseus, too, smiled as well as he might, but in his eastward way he often looked back, and was sad when he could no longer see the kindly hill above the garden of the gods.

CHAPTER THREE

Perseus and Andromeda

Perseus flew where the wings bore him, over great mountains, and over a wilderness of sand. Below his feet the wind woke the sand storms, and beneath him he saw nothing but a soft floor of yellow grey, and when that cleared he saw islands of green trees round some well in the waste, and long trains of camels, and brown men riding swift horses, at which he wondered; for the Greeks in his time drove in chariots, and did not ride. The red sun behind him fell, and all the land was purple, but, in a moment, as it seemed, the stars rushed out, and he sped along in the starlight till the sky was grey again, and rosy, and full of fiery colours, green and gold and ruby and amethyst. Then the sun rose, and Perseus looked down on a green land, through which was flowing north a great river, and he guessed that it was the river Aegyptus, which we now call the Nile. Beneath him was a town, with many white houses in groves of palm trees, and with great temples of the gods, built of red stone. The Shoes of Swiftness stopped above the wide market-place, and there Perseus hung poised, till he saw a multitude of men pour out of the door of a temple.

At their head walked the king, who was like a Greek, and he led a maiden as white as snow wreathed with flowers and circlets of wool, like the oxen in Greece, when men sacrifice them to the gods. Behind the king and the maid came a throng of brown men, first priests and magicians and players on harps, and women shaking metal rattles that made a wild mournful noise, while the multitude lamented.

Slowly, while Perseus watched, they passed down to the shore of the great river, so wide a river as Perseus had never seen. They went to a steep red rock, like a wall, above the river; at its foot was a flat shelf of rock – the water just washed over it. Here they stopped, and the king kissed and embraced the white maiden. They bound her by chains of bronze to rings of bronze in the rock; they sang a strange hymn; and then marched back to the town, throwing their mantles over their heads. There the maiden stood, or rather hung forward supported by the chains. Perseus floated down, and, the nearer he came, the more beautiful seemed the white maid, with her soft dark hair falling to her white feet. Softly he floated down, till his feet were on the ledge of rock. She did not hear him coming, and when he gently touched her she gave a cry, and turned on him her large dark eyes, wild and dry, without a tear. 'Is it a god?' she said, clasping her hands.

'No god, but a mortal man am I, Perseus the slayer of the Gorgon. What do you here? What cruel men have bound you?'

'I am Andromeda, the daughter of Cepheus, king of a strange people. The lot fell on me, of all the maidens in the city, to be offered to the monster fish that walks on feet, who is their god. Once a year they give to him a maiden.'

Perseus thereon drew the sword Herpe, and cut the chains of bronze that bound the girl as if they had been ropes of flax, and she fell at his feet, covering her eyes with her hands. Then Perseus saw the long reeds on the further shore of the river waving and stirring and crashing, and from them came a monstrous fish walking on feet, and slid into the water. His long sharp black head showed above the stream as he swam, and the water behind him showed like the water in the wake of a ship.

'Be still and hide your eyes!' whispered Perseus to the maiden.

He took the goatskin from his wallet, and held up the Gorgon's head, with the back of it turned towards him, and he waited till the long black head was lifted from the river's edge, and the forefeet of that fish were on the wet ledge of rock. Then he held the head before the eyes of the monster, and from the head downward it slowly stiffened. The head and forefeet and shoulders were of stone before the tail had ceased to lash the water. Then the tail stiffened into a long jagged sharp stone, and Perseus, wrapping up the head in the goatskin, placed it in his wallet. He turned his back

The rescue of Andromeda

to Andromeda, while he did this lest by mischance her eyes should open and see the head of the Gorgon. But her eyes were closed, and Perseus found that she had fainted, from fear of the monster, and from the great heat of the sun. Perseus put the palms of his hands together like a cup, and stooping to the stream he brought water, and threw it over the face and neck of Andromeda, wondering at her beauty. Her eyes opened at last, and she tried to rise to her feet, but she dropped on her knees, and clung with her fingers to the rock. Seeing her so faint and weak Perseus raised her in his arms, with her beautiful head pillowed on his shoulder, where she fell asleep like a tired child. Then he rose in the air and floated over the sheer wall of red stone above the river, and flew slowly towards the town.

There were no sentinels at the gate; the long street was empty, for all the people were in their houses, praying and weeping. But a little girl stole out of a house near the gate. She was too young to understand why her father and mother and elder brothers were so sad, and would not take any notice of her. She thought she would go out and play in the street, and when she looked up from her play, she saw Perseus bearing the king's daughter in his arms. The child stared, and then ran into her house, crying aloud, for she could hardly speak, and pulled so hard at her mother's gown that her mother rose and followed her to the house door. The mother gave a joyful cry, her husband and her children ran forth, and they, too, shouted aloud for pleasure. Their cries reached the ears of people in other houses, and presently all the folk, as glad as they had been sorrowful, were following Perseus to the palace of the king. Perseus walked through the empty court, and stood at the door of the hall, where the servants came to him, both men and women, and with tears of joy the women bore Andromeda to the chamber of her mother, Queen Cassiopeia.

Who can tell how happy were the king and queen, and how gladly they welcomed Perseus! They made a feast for him, and they sent oxen and sheep to all the people, and wine, that all might rejoice and make merry. Andromeda, too, came, pale but smiling, into the hall, and sat down beside her mother's high seat, listening while Perseus told the whole story of his adventures. Now Perseus could scarcely keep his eyes from Andromeda's face while he spoke, and she stole glances at him. When their eyes met, the colour came into her face again, which glowed like ivory that a Carian woman has lightly tinged with rose colour, making an ornament for some rich king. Perseus remembered the message of Hermes, which Aegle had given him, that if he flew to the east and south he would find his happiness. He knew that he had found it, if this maiden would be his wife, and he ended his tale by repeating the message of Hermes.

'The gods speak only truth,' he said, 'and to have made you all happy is the greatest happiness to Perseus of Argos.' Yet he hoped in his heart to see a yet happier day, when the rites of marriage should be done between Andromeda and him, and the young men and maidens should sing the wedding song before their door.

Andromeda was of one mind with him, and, as Perseus must needs go home, her parents believed that she could not live without him who had saved her from such a cruel death. So with heavy hearts they made the marriage feast, and with many tears Andromeda and her father and mother said farewell. Perseus and his bride sailed down the great river Aegyptus in the king's own boat; and at every town they were received with feasts, and songs, and dances. They saw all the wonderful things of Egypt, palaces and pyramids and temples and tombs of kings, and at last they found a ship of the Cretans in the mouth of the Nile. This they hired, for they carried with them great riches, gold, and myrrh, and ivory, gifts of the princes of Egypt.

CHAPTER FOUR

How Perseus Avenged Danae

With a steady south wind behind them they sailed to Seriphos, and landed, and brought their wealth ashore, and went to the house of Dictys. They found him lonely and sorrowful, for his wife had died, and his brother, King Polydectes, had taken Danae, and set her to grind corn in his house, among his slave women. When Perseus heard that word, he asked, 'Where is King Polydectes?'

'It is his birthday, and he holds his feast among the princes,' said Dictys.

'Then bring me,' said Perseus, 'the worst of old clothes that any servant of your house can borrow from a beggar man, if there be a beggar man in the town.' Such a man there was – he came limping through the door of the courtyard, and up to the threshold of the house, where he sat whining, and asking for alms. They gave him food and wine, and Perseus cried, 'New clothes for old, father, I will give you, and new shoes for old.' The beggar could not believe his ears, but he was taken to the baths, and washed, and new clothes were given to him, while Perseus clad himself in the beggar's rags, and Dictys took charge of the winged shoon of Hermes and the sword Herpe, and the burnished shield of Athene. Then Perseus cast dust and wood ashes on his hair, till it looked foul and grey, and placed the goatskin covering and the Gorgon's head in his wallet, and with the beggar's staff in his hand he limped to the palace of Polydectes. On the threshold he sat down, like a beggar, and Polydectes saw him and cried to his servants, 'Bring in that man; is it not the day of my feast? Surely all are welcome.' Perseus was led in, looking humbly at the ground, and was brought before the king.

'What news, thou beggar man?' said the king.

'Such news as was to be looked for,' whined Perseus. 'Behold, I am he who brought no present to the king's feast, seven long years agone, and now I come back, tired and hungry, to ask his grace.'

'By the splendour of Zeus,' cried Polydectes, 'it is none but the beggar brat who bragged that he would fetch me such a treasure as lies in no king's chamber! The beggar brat is a beggar man; how time and travel have tamed him! Ho, one of you, run and fetch his mother who is grinding at the mill, that she may welcome her son.'

A servant ran from the hall, and the chiefs of Seriphos mocked at Perseus. 'This is he who called us farmers and dealers in slaves. Verily he would not fetch the price of an old cow in the slave market.' Then they threw at him crusts of bread, and bones of swine, but he stood silent.

Then Danae was led in, clad in vile raiment, but looking like a queen, and the king cried, 'Go forward, woman: look at that beggar man; dost thou know thy son?' She walked on, her head high, and Perseus whispered, 'Mother, stand thou beside me, and speak no word!'

'My mother knows me not, or despises me,' said Perseus, 'yet, poor as I am, I do not come empty-handed. In my wallet is a gift, brought from very far away, for my lord the king.'

He swung his wallet round in front of him; he took off the covering of goatskin, and he held the Gorgon's head on high, by the hair, facing the king and the chiefs. In one moment they were all grey stones, all along the hall, and the chairs whereon they sat crashed under the weight of them, and they rolled on the hard clay floor. Perseus wrapped the head in the goatskin, and shut it in the wallet carefully, and cried, 'Mother, look round, and see thy son and thine own revenge.'

Then Danae knew her son, by the sound of his voice, if not by her eyesight, and she wept for joy. So they two went to the house of Dictys, and Perseus was cleansed, and clad in rich raiment, and Danae, too, was apparelled like a free woman, and embraced Andromeda with great joy.

Perseus made the good Dictys king of Seriphos; and he placed the winged shoes in the temple of Hermes, with the sword Herpe, and the Gorgon's head, in its goatskin cover; but the polished shield he laid on the altar in the temple of Athene. Then he bade all who served in the temples come forth, both young and old, and he locked the doors, and he and Dictys watched all night, with the armed Cretans, the crew of his ship, that none might enter. Next day Perseus alone went into the temple of Athene. It was as it had been, but the Gorgon's head and the polished shield were gone, and the winged shoon and the sword Herpe had vanished from the temple of Hermes.

With Danae and Andromeda Perseus sailed to Greece, where he learned that the sons of King Proetus had driven King Acrisius out of Argos, and that he had fled to Phthia in the north, where the ancestor of the great Achilles was king. Thither Perseus went, to see his grandfather, and he found the young men holding games and sports in front of the palace. Perseus thought that his grand-father might love him better if he showed his strength in the games, which were open to strangers, so he entered and won the race, and the prize for leaping, and then came the throwing of the disc of bronze. Perseus threw a great cast, far beyond the rest, but the disc swerved, and fell among the crowd. Then Perseus was afraid, and ran like the wind to the place where the disc fell. There lay an old man, smitten sorely by the disc, and men said that he had killed King Acrisius.

Thus the word of the prophetess and the will of Fate were fulfilled. Perseus went weeping to the King of Phthia, and told him all the truth, and the king, who knew, as all Greece knew, how Acrisius had tried to drown his daughter and her child, believed the tale, and said that Perseus was guiltless. He and Danae and Andromeda dwelt for a year in Phthia, with the king, and then Perseus, with an army of Pelasgians and Myrmidons, marched south to Argos, and took the city, and drove out his cousins, the sons of Proetus. There in Argos, Perseus, with his mother and beautiful Andromeda, dwelt long and happily, and he left the kingdom to his son when he died.